"The discovery of Mrs Thomas's skull after all these years was incredible enough in itself. For it to be found when and where it was beggars belief.

Kate Webster, guilty of the grisliest murder in the blood-soaked history of Victorian crime, and William Marwood, the well-mannered 'gentleman executioner' who must hang her: two people who should never have met, and never have loved. In a unique blend of fact, fiction, speculation and analysis, Matt Fullerty has taken the historical true crime novel into unexplored territory where the question for the reader is not Who dunnit? but What if...?

1879. In the hard times of Charles Dickens's England, who can blame a woman for seeking a little amusement? But when the entertainment is as brutal as the times, her love of the macabre draws Kate ever closer to the world of the hangman. From the respectability of wealthy suburbia, through the criminal lowlife of the London streets, a relentless nationwide pursuit by officers of England's modernised police force finally brings Kate back to where she belongs—into the waiting arms of William Marwood."

Pamela Pattison, author of *Collars and Cuffs*

Winner

The Bookhabit Novel Award 2008

For *The Knight of New Orleans*

"Matt Fullerty's excellent novel transports us back to a different age. He takes us into the murky world of murderess Kate Webster and her nemesis, public executioner William Marwood. We tread the dirty streets of Olde London Town and feast on the evocative atmosphere of Mr Fullerty's entertaining prose. We visit the grim edifice of the notorious Newgate Gaol, we travel to the far-off sleepy rural market town of Horncastle, long-time home of hangman Marwood, and we tread the streets of the leafy suburb of Richmond.

Mr Fullerty weaves a wondrous picture of life in a bygone age at the same time utilising real life characters and a most horrifying crime. It is an evocative re-creation of characters who are brought to life instead of being mere names adhering to a factual script in the stark annals of criminal history. This is a factual crime, a classic in the annals of British criminal history, subjected to the refreshing freedom of fictional treatment. It will transport you to an age long ago consigned to the pages of history."

Stewart Evans, author of *Executioner, the Chronicles of James Berry, Victorian Hangman*

"A well researched blend of fact and fiction. *The Murderess and the Hangman* paints a vivid and lively picture that is full of Victorian atmosphere. The characters are bought to life in this fascinating and enlightening tale!"

Sara Marshall, Great, Great, Great Grandniece of William Marwood

Second Round, Amazon Breakthrough Novel Award 2010

For *The Knight of New Orleans*

Novels by Matt Fullerty

www.mattfullerty.com

www.parkgateoriginals.com
www.dionysusbooks.com

THE KNIGHT OF NEW ORLEANS
THE PRIDE AND THE SORROW OF PAUL MORPHY

Paul Morphy, the world's greatest chess player,
devastates opponents in New York, Paris and
London, but what about the girl he left behind?

AMERICAN CON ARTIST

The infamous story of U.S. illegal immigrant
Elmyr de Hory, art forger, criminal, painter, conman...
and innocent man?

To the Fullerty, Hutchings, and Willers families—

For Katharine—

Map of London, 1843

3 ¼ inches to a mile

Credit: B. R. Davis & Old House Books

www.themurderessandthehangman.com

THE MURDERESS AND THE HANGMAN

www.mattfullerty.com

William Marwood, Hangman for London and Middlesex

Unchallenged on the scaffold December 1874–September 1883

"The jury agrees with the judge, but the judge agrees with me, for mine is a higher calling."

Photograph by Stewart Evans

1. A hanging drop in the late 19th century was usually between 4 and 10 feet depending on the weight of the prisoner (including clothes).

2. From 1886 to 1892, the length of drop was calculated to provide a final 'striking force' of approximately 1,260 ft/lbs. which combined with the positioning of the eyelet caused fracture / dislocation of the neck, usually at the 2nd and 3rd or 3rd and 4th cervical vertebrae. This is the classic 'hangman's fracture'.

3. Between 1892 and 1913, a shorter length of drop was used, presumably to avoid the decapitation and near decapitations that occurred using the old table.

4. After 1913, other factors were also taken into account and the drop was calculated to give a final 'striking force' of around 1,000 ft/lbs. The Home Office issued a rule restricting all drops to between 5 feet and 8 feet 6 inches.

5. From around 1939 it became customary to add a further nine inches to the drop calculated from the 1913 table.

6. The 1913 table is still used in Singapore and probably Malaysia and may have been adopted by other countries which use the British method, e.g. Australia, Canada, the Caribbean nations and Egypt. Pakistan, India and Bangladesh use the measured 'long drop' but it is not known whether they use the British drop tables.

Guide to history of British hanging

Credit: www.capitalpunishmentuk.org

Kate Webster.
From a contemporary print.

Catherine Lawler, alias Kate Webster, as Mrs Julia Thomas.

"The hangman told me so. I knew him personally."

Every dog has its day.

THE MURDERESS AND THE HANGMAN

A Novel of Criminal Minds

by

Matt Fullerty

Dionysus Books / Parkgate Press

Publishers Online!

For updates and more resources, visit
Dionysus Books and Parkgate Press online at

www.dionysusbooks.com
www.parkgatepress.com

Page layout and cover design by Parkgate Originals

ISBN-13: 978-1-937056-11-7

Library of Congress Control Number: 2012939709
Library of Congress Subject Headings:

Biographical fiction
Biography as a literary form--Fiction
Crime--Fiction
Epistolary fiction
Fiction
Historical fiction
London (England)--Fiction
Murder--Fiction
Psychological fiction
Trials (Murder)--Fiction

First Edition (UK) November 2012
[Parkgate Press: Dionysus Books reference number: 013]

"Man stands amazed to see his deformity
In any other creature but himself."

John Webster, *The Duchess of Malfi* (1613)

"Like beer and tea, sprouts and plum duff, hanging suited England."

Howard Engel, *Lord High Executioner* (1997)

Cast of Characters

The protagonist and antagonist (in no particular order)

Kate Webster, murderess, thief, liar, loving mother

William Marwood, state hangman, gentleman executioner, man of science, loving father

The family bonds (the close blood)

Ellen Marwood, William's wife

Aldous Marwood, William's son

Daniel Webster, Kate's son

Billy Thomas, Mrs Julia Thomas's son

The guilty and the innocent (in no particular order)

Jonathan Clatter, schoolmaster

Nathan Crane, loving dupe

Henry Porter, landlord of *The Rising Sun*

Robert Porter, Henry's younger son

Mrs Ann Porter, wife of Henry Porter

Mrs Sarah Crease, caretaker of Daniel Webster

Dr Adams, examiner of the body

Mrs Beryl Ives, neighbour at Mayfield Gardens

The law (the old bill)

Detective Gil Sequin, police detective

Assistant Detective Nimrod Jones, 'muscle'

The victim (the old lady)

Mrs Julia Thomas, church-goer, Kate's landlady

The trial (the pleasure of the state)

Sir Justice Denman, trial judge

Mr Warner Sleigh, defence

Harry B. Poland, prosecutor

Sir Hardinge Gifford, K.C., consultant

Father McEnrey and Jean Baptiste Dupris, Catholic priests

Characters in this book are composites of reality and fantasy. Many names have been changed, more real in their changed form than they were in historical accounts, newspaper archives and *Old Bailey* transcripts. All the places exist but are now much changed.

This much is perhaps true: no written account can capture the reality of a real person in a real place, their heart beating a little faster for one reason or another. Such moments are for life alone.

Contents

Part One
Toe the Line

Part Two
The Road to Tyburn

Part Three
Steady, Steady, This Won't Hurt a Bit

Part One
Toe the Line

"The cradle rocks above an abyss, and common sense tells us that our existence is but a brief crack of light between two eternities of darkness."

Vladimir Nabokov, *Speak, Memory* (1947)

Preface

Today is my 35th birthday, which in some quarters makes me half dead (assuming, somewhat pessimistically, that I will only make the twentieth century's layman's average of three score years and ten). Moments ago I mentioned this fact (of my birthday, not imminent death) to a good friend and he said "and you were half dead already, so does that mean you're a quarter alive?" Given such friendly support, I am in an in contemplative mood as I consider the strangeness of words, even before I committed them in this 'non-fiction novel' to print, posterity and ultimately, obscurity.

The Murderess and the Hangman has strange origins. According to the old adage, art imitates life. In other words, however transformed, life is always the chronological origin of art, the unmoved mover of creativity. But in this instance, art *preceded* life too. The novel's events were buried in the past, I dug them up, and the story came to life from beyond the grave, a living breathing ghost with its own free will. My reaction was "What on earth?"

On Friday 22nd October 2010, an extraordinary event occurred: the surprise discovery of a 131-year-old female skull in the garden of naturalist Sir David Attenborough in Richmond, south London. I first heard of this event in New York while visiting a friend who happened to live above a chess shop in Greenwich Village, close to Washington Square Park where the chess players hang out. But chess was soon forgotten, as very memorably, I read an email one

Sunday morning, a little worse for wear after our night out in Alphabet City, to learn that Paul Bentley, a *Daily Mail* reporter, wanted me to contact him as soon as possible. I would appear to be the expert on the human skull just dug up in London. What? In the words of Mr Bentley: "…sounds ridiculous, but the Met police have just confirmed it to me…. I see you've written a book based on the murder story—so you seem the ideal person to speak to about this."

And here I reach the kernel of why *The Murderess and the Hangman* has such strange origins. The reason is that I completed writing it *before* the skull came out of the ground. I'd spent a year of my life composing this long narrative about Kate Webster and William Marwood, and now the victim of her murderous crime, Mrs Julia Thomas, was coincidentally dug up in London when a famous naturalist and broadcaster just happened to be renovating his garden.

It was strange enough that the skull was dug up 131 years later, only months after I wrote the novel, but to have it dug up by Sir David Attenborough, who constantly investigates (and explains to the rest of us) the puzzling mortal dance of survival and stark natural beauty exhibited by countless creatures across the globe, was doubly strange.

I took the opportunity and wrote to Sir David, and he very kindly took time to sign a short note returned to me expressing his uncertainty over his desire to be involved with anything related to the skull, which he declared was an obstacle—understandably—to his current garden renovations. I saw no irony in this, only the sober scientific side of his relations to the natural world, and the professionalism of his bothering to reply to me at all. Fortunately, responding to Paul Bentley of the *Daily Mail*, I was able to write a follow-up article profiling Kate Webster for the *Mail* (published on 26th October 2010); subsequently I was asked to comment by Matt Blake, Crime Correspondent for *The Independent*, further adding to the peculiarity of being considered an expert in something I had thoroughly researched, but essentially for fictional purposes.

The story then got even stranger. Next, I received a phone call from Acting Detective Inspector (ADI) David Bolton of Richmond police, who was heading the digging operation. Detective Bolton inquired about my knowledge of the crime, which I confessed was based on historical research, and he informed me there would be a coroner's inquest to identify the skull's identity through soil sampling and carbon dating. ADI Bolton proved to be as interested in the original story as I was, but he also revealed, in a willing moment, that the crime was also being investigated as a possible *more recent* murder from the 1970s, which would make it an ongoing, present-day murder investigation. Again, I was amused, thrilled, if not a little wary, to get further involved in this odd situation—people now giving me all kinds of advice over 'the story' and 'new facts' as they were emerging or being circulated, and that I should 'be careful'. Suffice to say, the inquest into the skull's identity was resolved on 6th July 2011, and the skull was determined to in fact belong to Mrs Thomas.

Then on 6th July 2011, I was lucky enough to be interviewed by BBC Radio London 94.9 to discuss the skull's surprise discovery and possible meaning (the audio is accessible from www.mattfullerty.com). The presenter, Eddie Nestor of evening 'Drivetime', asked me a few questions in a serious but amusingly jaunty manner to entertain the homebound rush-hour commuters, focusing on the disturbing aspects of the story. Seeing my chance, I flooded the airwaves with the macabre details of the murder, to which he responded "Bit gruesome, isn't it?" I had to admit, it was a bit gruesome.

This radio moment was topped, in a sense, though, when television became interested. On 19th January 2011, I received an email from a Sydney-based Australian production company, Beyond Productions, makers of the popular Discovery Channel TV programme *Deadly Women*. Would I be interested in being interviewed? Here the twist was a female killer being the central attraction, a story macabre enough for combined US, the UK and Australian markets. How could I resist? I didn't.

Instead, and a little lightheaded, I found myself heading to New York's Greenwich Village for an on-camera interview, a Q & A conducted by a friendly Australian every-bloke about the grisly nature of Kate Webster's crime. Eventually the need for ratings-drama kicked in, though, and I was quizzed about the nature of her personality, motivations, and propensity for inhumanity. I cracked a little, and remember delivering the line: "When you look at what she actually did, how could you not say that's *evil?*" This conservative judgement, fulfilling my role as resident British-American expert, was what they wanted. For some reason, I've always resisted in conversation labelling any individual evil or a monster, and yet Kate

Webster's actual crimes were clearly themselves evil and monstrous. But too late, the comment was on celluloid, and the copyright was signed over. The episode 'Breaking Point' aired on 9th September 2011 to an audience of millions of hungry American eyes, perhaps with nightmares to follow (the episode is very bloody). Of course, there was still no book to profit from all this.

Subsequently, I was asked to interview with Al Arabiya, the premier Arabic Language 24-hours news television channel in the Middle East. Headquartered in Dubai but with a London office, Al Arabiya broadcasts worldwide with viewing figures estimated at more than 60 million households, and is the first ever independent Arabic satellite television. They too wanted a piece of Kate Webster, and while *The Murderess and the Hangman* does not have an Arab-related focus, it is about a female killer and I guess that fascination is universal, a lovely modern way to break down social, cultural and religious values.

The Murderess and the Hangman has strange origins, but probably no more peculiar than the beginnings of my first novel *The Knight of New Orleans*. That book (published in September 2011) was a novel about the art, ambition, sanity and insanity of chess, chess players and large families. It was inspired by the life of a great American chess player, Paul Morphy, the world's greatest and most forgotten player—only chess players have really heard of him—since Morphy lived in a time before the first organised world chess championship (he was crowned unofficial American champion in New York in 1857). Moreover, Paul Morphy was the most talented and near-unbeatable player not just in America, but in Europe following an incredible and devastating series of victories he achieved in Paris and London in 1858. This 'career' alone is strange enough, but his at once aggressive and elegant talent was even more peculiar. Morphy played chess *fast*, throwing his pieces out in an attacking fashion. He looked to control the space with power, using the cumulative pressure of all his pieces, in a style overwhelming to opponents, filled with threat, feint and risk. Curiously, he seemed to arrive fully formed on the chess stage, somewhat mythically knowing the moves—the best moves—simply by watching his father's and uncle's Sunday chess games from an early age.

Speed was important to the Creoles of New Orleans, but so were social values, expectations of success and the importance of position, prestige and clannish breeding, but not to young Morphy. His story is emblematic of a boy fleeing the overwhelmingly expectations of his high-powered family, generations of lawyers, judges and aristocrats, living the high life on Royal Street in the French Quarter. Life was a party, not a game, and he was expected to play his part socially and professionally; but Morphy rebelled, delaying his career as an attorney, a life pre-arranged since birth with prep school and private university, to embark on a mad adventure to Europe's capital cities of sin, London and Paris, by way of New York City and Havana, Cuba.

Off the parental-and-sibling leash (Morphy had two sisters), the ingénue challenged the grandmasters of the Old World—the French, English and Germans, all great rivals before the Soviet chess dominance of the twentieth century). In 1858, 'the boy from the crescent city' would beat all comers, professors and professionals alike, aged only twenty-one. Morphy's bouts even included memory and blindfolded chess that astonished the public back in America too. The world placed fame at his feet; he was praised for months by monarchs including Queen Victoria, Russian princes, even Emperor Napoleon III…that is until he returned to New Orleans where the devastation of the American Civil War was looming. Back on home soil, Morphy's mind seemed to turn inside out, reshaped by infinite imaginings provoked by 'the royal game', creating a mind beset by fear of family betrayal, self-deception, paranoia and horror.

The story is strange, given Morphy's youth, the singularity of his purpose and its devastating consequences. But what about the origins of writing the story? *The Knight of New Orleans* had strange origins too, not only as a 'non-fiction novel' inspired like *The Murderess and the Hangman* by the life of a real, historical person, and an equally forgotten story, but because I decided on the novel I wished to write, before willing it into life, only after I went to see Morphy's grave—in the middle of a boys' road trip Spring Break-style holiday to the American South, driving from Washington, D.C. to Louisiana with four British school friends. If that were not unusual enough as context, to combine Bourbon Street with a literary pilgrimage, Hurricane cocktails with the pre-Katrina nightlight of May 2005

(Hurricane Katrina hit in late August 2005), Paul Morphy's life story was an inspirational, if dark refuge suited to a city famous for its voodoo as much as its faded Southern manners, its licentiousness as much as its Catholic beliefs, its corruption and Red Light district as much as its welcoming spirit of resilience and steamboat charm. Overall, the story of Paul Morphy's turbulent life *was* New Orleans in its ambition and sadness, its rise and fall, its magnificence and mystery that preceded a romantic and harrowing decline, its creative and destructive power a reflection of the Mississippi herself.

The Morphy family woes gripped me more than I expected. I was as a young writer aged twenty-six, a Briton who had moved to America in 2003, but I was still searching for a subject that could encompass all the elements I wanted to include in a biographical-historical novel. I found the answer in the story of Morphy's great, troubled and enigmatic genius, but I actually decided to write the book after visiting his final resting-place in St. Louis Cemetery No. 1, just north of the French Quarter, off Basin Street. I remember the day was blazing hot, almost too hot to walk across Rampart Street onto the old, wide boulevards away from the elegant, small buildings of the Quarter. The cemetery has tall white-stone walls, but I could see the ceremonial crosses, spires and stone angels jutting into the sky. I entered and walked randomly down on of the main paths. There it was.

I stood by Morphy's above-ground tomb, one of those large stone edifices escaping the corrupting waters of the Mississippi that would wash cemetery bones to the surface in previous decades, and feeling in the presence of a rich family's rich history, I decided I could and would now write the story. In a way, I finally realised, as respectfully as I could, that Morphy was dead and I was alive, and that his story is only remembered by chess players (and overshadowed by Bobby Fisher in the twentieth century).

For some intangible reason I still cannot place, beyond a love for the French Quarter and chess, his European origins (Morphy was from a Spanish-French Creole family) and the fact that he played chess fast, reigned supreme at a young age, and then dissolved into trauma and madness, I only realised I wanted to write the book when I was standing by his family tomb with the word MORPHY inscribed on the face of white stone. There is no mention of his chess games at all.

That was in 2005. It took me eight months to write the novel, two more to edit, and three years of wrestling with two agents, one in New York and one in London, before it was eventually published in September 2011.

These are all very strange events, and I remain immersed in the story behind *The Murderess and the Hangman* as a critic, journalist, amazed bystander and fiction writer. And yet it has all happened, a publicity trail *in reverse*, encompassing national newspapers, London radio and global television. Even now, I am amazed that the discovery of Julia Thomas's skull *followed* my own unknowing decision to choose this story, of countless, to dramatise. Like with *The Knight of New Orleans*, beneath surface facts lay a story like a buried fossil I needed to dig up and dust off, reimagine, yet embellish, and enjoy presenting to a chess-playing or murder-obsessed world.

For which is stranger, being inspired by an above-ground tomb to write the story of a dead man, or writing the story of a dead women only to be surprised by the unexpected re-earthing of her victim's skull, I cannot say. But both are true. If fiction is the retelling of the lie that history bends into a narrative shape, what follows is the retelling of a lie that sounds and operates like the truth. It frightens and charms with equal measure, or so I hope.

My next novel, due for release in January 2013, is *American Con Artist*, the story of Hungarian-American painter and world-famous forger, conman and illegal US immigrant, Elmyr de Hory. A genius striving for originality trapped inside the body of a man who could paint glorious Matisse and Picasso forgery-originals (new 'undiscovered' art as opposed to copies of existing works), Elmyr presented many faces to the world, his mirror and his canvas, but who was he really? How was he caught? And for how long did he dupe the art world? Today his paintings are still discovered each year inside famous public private collections, so his serious joke, the worst and best kind, lives on, although he passed away in 1976, three days before I was born.

I am also researching the story of a present-day convict, James Hogue, a talented American athlete, Princeton phony, self-invented refashioner of his own identity, and currently serving a 10-year sentence for bicycle theft and fraud, amongst other crimes. His nephew, a Professor of Biology specialising in the study of spiders and beetles, wrote to me on 16th December 2010 saying he does occasional Google searches his uncle, and is interested in the novel. As yet, I haven't written a full chapter and yet Hogue's story—my first inspired by a person still living—is quite literally more than alive. The novel is a thematic sequel to *American Con Artist* and is provisionally titled *American Scholar Athlete*.

Following these two books, I have every intention of writing a science fiction novel, working title *The Necklace*. Creating a future world, I will find it harder to create a historical-biographical story—and yet, if this future occurs across the galaxy, in a younger part of space, its future would occur during the Earth's past. In other words, perhaps I can find a way of writing a science fiction novel in the future that is also a historical novel. Now I just need to discover the skull of an extra-terrestrial, on Earth or otherwise, that points to a race of chess-playing aliens, and my literary oeuvre will be complete.

For now, though, I must go and celebrate my half-death, or half-life birthday, whatever is most ambiguous—for that, akin to *The Knight of New Orleans*'s celebration of fused genius and madness, is the ultimate spirit of *The Murderess and the Hangman*. I hope you enjoy its display of homicidal mayhem, hangings, desperation, redemption and salvation. As Mr Rudyard Kipling cautioned, remember to 'keep your head'. If you let them, the crowd will hang you for fun and say you deserved it. Kate Webster perhaps did deserve her fate. But who deserves to be the hangman tying the rope?

Matt Fullerty
Washington, D.C.
14th December 2011

Table of Drops

William Marwood's 'drop table' for the 'long drop': the necessary weight v drop distance to ensure a clean break.

1892 table	
Weight of prisoner (in pounds)	Drop (in feet & inches)
105 & under	8' 0"
110	7' 10"
115	7' 3"
120	7' 0"
125	6' 9"
130	6' 5"
135	6' 2"
140	6' 0"
145	5' 9"
150	5' 7"
155	5' 5"
160	5' 3"
165	5' 1"
170	4' 11"
175	4' 9"
180	4' 8"
185	4' 7"
190	4' 5"
195	4' 4"
200 & over	4' 2"

THE MURDERESS AND THE HANGMAN

Prologue
The Prison Sleeps
25th March 1879, Tuesday

In the dark of a past sunken world William Marwood stands with his hand on a prison wall. He is fifty-nine years old and thinking about retirement. All around him the blind, narrow, crooked streets of London spiral from his feet into blackness as though Newgate were the centre of an unseen world. He looks up at old pigeons clustered on a rough ledge, demented and cramped as the prison herself. For a while Marwood is still—he feels the cold stone under his skin, awakening memories of the last four weeks, of policemen, lawyers, politicians and a girl he met in Covent Garden. He waits for the feeling of regret, of mournfulness, a sensation that will come tomorrow perhaps. But the feeling does not come. The night could prove eternal; the dawn may never arrive. From where will peace come? Tomorrow at nine o'clock, when it is all over? Then, perhaps, he can return home a contented man.

At hand height, an open grate catches his eye with a wooden box hanging from a rough rope—the alms box—and now and then, even at this hour, a soft voice whispers "remember the prisoners, have gentleness in thy heart." He ignores the voice of the stone ledge. As a spectator he is not a hard man, yet any pain he does not witness or feel himself he cannot understand. It is that simple. He passes below the Newgate Great Tower, his fingers dragging the prison wall, the cold teasing his blood with no reaction. She is inside there, he knows, somewhere behind these walls her last hours are draining away. Tomorrow she will be no more.

From the fame of Tyburn to the pillory of Charing Cross, eastwards to Execution Dock gibbets where pirates are strung to rot by the Navy to Coldbath Fields and Bedlam in the north—all London is consumed by prisons. Fleet Street itself is a veritable sewer of clinks: Newgate, Ludgate, the Fleet and Bridewell then over the Thames to the Surrey prison at Horsemonger Lane to 'the gibbet on the hill' and the grey morning exposing the hulk of prison transportation ships. Close by, mutineers and murderous seaman are strung up together at Execution Dock, the crowd favourites hung in Surrey prison, on Kennington common or Horsemonger Lane Gaol roof for the discerning paying public. But the centre is Newgate, the old matriarch of footpads and pickpockets, the home of thieves and murderers, grave-robbers, rich debtors and any criminal-unfortunate thrown down for good: keep them at the centre of the city, make them part of the crowd, feed them through the hole in the wall and march them across the courtyard to their deaths. Disturbing in its brutality, the mother keeps all her children at the heart of London justice. For next to Newgate stands the Central Criminal Court or affectionately for Londoners, the bloody Old Bailey, just a stone's throw from the prison—if there were windows to permit such disturbances. Instead, Newgate lives in the shadow of its sibling, two arms of the law never touching but side by side.

Between them now stands William Marwood, searching for his feelings. Inside is his captive bird Kate Webster alias Catherine Lawler, his *raison d'être*, his victim. Here between righteous justice and deathly vengeance amid six million lives of an Empire's capital, Marwood stands in the dead of night touching the cold prison and waiting for any sign, not of escape or repentance or forgiveness—it is too late for that—but an emotion within his chest, a measuring of his soul. He waits, searches for his sadness or a reason to flee and never come back, but nothing passes over his heart except the dead silence of a moonless Tuesday night, the quietest time of the month.

Within hours Kate will walk through the prison yard, past the kitchens, to the outdoor scaffold and over graves of the dead. Without ceremony or celebration, she will be executed in the open air on Wednesday morning at nine o' clock. The prisoners will light torch-paper in their cells, fling the rolls between the bars to unravel and burn before hitting the ground. Fellow condemned inmates will see her, hear the words of the Common Prayer, and wait for the bell to toll. In the prison yard only feet away, the prison chaplain will bow but not shed a tear. He will sip a sherry to steady his nerves and avert his eyes from the newly commissioned 'long drop' that will break Kate's neck.

Even now, as Marwood ponders Newgate's insides and takes the air, she crouches in her cell. She is awake, unseen, forgotten, and unrepentant. Already Kate can hear tomorrow, the mourning bells of nearby St Sepulchre's church, and she laughs as only Kate can, at the trick of her imagination. But right now in the garden of good and evil, suspended between one day and the next, between one uncertain life and the uncertain hope of the next, she can only live this present—the church bell sounds of her days ending and beginning. Her last day is no different than her first. The relief of execution, she believes, will be a blessing in a life of indignity and struggle.

Marwood knows nothing of this but as he touches the wall outside, Kate is kneeling, and she too is thinking of him for a moment, of one of his hanging stories. It casts a smirk on her face, despite all. She remembers that in decades gone by, and not too long ago, the condemned would dress merrily for the final occasion in wedding suits and gaudy colours, hats thrown to the crowd, flowers in their buttonholes. One glorious moment of public love was theirs, their true and defiant plights not diminished to notoriety or the passion of the rowdy mob. The people knew who their heroes were, that life was precarious and painful, and no one would stop them celebrating the dance of death. The images bubble in Kate's mind, now that she is beyond resignation and seeking to embrace her fate. "Marwood," she whispers, reciting the old joke. "If Pa killed Ma, who'll kill Pa? Mar-wood, of course."

She remembers how he told her of those Tyburn days, how the crowd always supports the dying hero's bravado. She remembers his reciting how the drink and holiday atmosphere carried the victim down Holborn to the Triple Tree. The hanging was worse, he told her, but the glory was far greater in those days before executions were moved inside prisons—out of sight. Kate smirks at the warning. But then she remembers how the condemned had their gallows voices ready and their 'Last Dying Speeches' would hit the streets and become famous. Unfortunately she has not written a line.

The stone is cold on Kate's knees, not because she is praying but because there is no bench, the assumption being sleep will not come on the last night. Rightly so: sleep is impossible. Instead Kate remembers last Sunday in the chapel, when black coffins were displayed to terrify all those gathered in the condemned pew, and when her name was drawn from a hat, literally, for Queen Victoria's pleasure—just a few days away. Now that time has passed.

Kate, true to form, smiles at the thought of these childish attempts to frighten her: she is scared but only for the rope, not for the theatricals. She will embrace the performance as much as the next accused and she will die as she's lived these last weeks, in the costume of an imagined self, playing a role. Only at the last second will she step to the line, only when the hangman asks.

Outside, Marwood is passing by Newgate's tiny entrance, an iron door three feet from the ground. He stares at it momentarily and shuffles on. Along the Old Bailey the street gaslights expand and shrink his shadow as he walks under each lamp. The hangman, he tells himself, has stayed too long and must now retire. A strange mood overtakes him at last. He feels all the sadness for Kate's plight lift from him, and in that moment he makes the decision that she must be hung. Then he begins the slow walk back to Dorset Square and his lodgings in Gloucester Place. He mouths the following lines, a faint note on his breath:

"As clever Tom Clinch, while the rabble was bawling,
    Rode stately through Holborn, to die in his calling;
        He stopped at the George for a bottle of sack,
        And promised to pay for it when he came back."

He smiles—all will be well. To further quiet his soul, Marwood whispers how hangmen are 'closest to the thin red line', how their perception is keenest of life's homage to death. But hangmen too need to go home. So he glances briefly up at the spire of the Old Bailey where the stone maiden on the roof is weighing justice in her hands. At the corner his shadow disappears as the streetlights dim, the mystery and the majesty of the law is sucked into a cloud overhead. His ordinary coat with its tails and side-pockets flaps in the wind. His usual cravat is black, but tonight he supports a low felt hat, which as he once tipped low for the ladies in the market place, he now tips it for the graceful lady on the spire and for the prison behind, its inmates comatose except for one.

Again, he mouths the words of a hanging ballad, changing his processor's name—the butcher Calcraft—to his own:

> "My name it is Marwood by every one known
> And a sad life is mine to you I now own,
> For I hang people up and I cut people down,
> Before all the rebel of great London town.
>
> For my old friend Cheshire he learned me the trick,
> And I dine in the clouds tonight with Old Nick,
> For the people on earth do use me so bad,
> That with tears I could drown for I feel so sad."

As Marwood departs, morning is still hours away and he should get a good five hours rest. At the corner, he tosses a penny in the jar of a sleeping boy with the face of a future angel. He fails to notice the sores covering the child's cheeks, where he lies like a broken puppet in a chestnut cart, curled in a doorway behind *The Virginia and Maryland Coffee House*. The boy opens one eye, checking on the dawn when he needs to sweep the streets. For that moment Marwood is relieved by the night. The boy rolls his jutting shoulder. No more than eight years old, he smiles inside his dream as the hangman walks away under the lamps.

Chapter 1
A School for Pickpockets
14th February 1879, Friday

Her keen grey eyes, darker because of her thick eyelashes, look up and down the street before she puts her foot outside. There she stands, blanket in hand, before the morning rush of Bow Street where it bears onto Covent Garden, watching all London surging to the fruit and vegetable market covering the Piazza. Two weeks later she will be arrested but for now Kate Webster is free to wander the streets, to turn her back on the Bow Street roundhouse, the police runners and all the 'big houses' of London town, to "make a clean slate of it."

Kate tosses the prison blanket on the gutter. The wooden door is bolted behind her and the hand of the policemen releases her then disappears back. The prison world is half forgotten—she is free. Kate strains her neck to gloomy skies already threatening a rainstorm to add to the night's drizzle, and allows the pale moonlight to open her eyes. She yawns and bends to tie her shoes, rough cobbled boots with leather laces that have seen her through many a scrape. The rest of her clothes: black stockings pulled to the knee, a grey apron that hangs low, and a grooved tartan belt for no reason other than she swopped it with a young woman last night for ready tobacco. Above her waist, wide with strength more than weight, Kate supports two tops—an incongruous blue blouse under a white shirt—the blue colour hinting at friendliness within an otherwise plain and coarse garb. Overall, Kate gives the appearance of a vaudeville dancer on bad times, dangling a fool's gold earring. Her twin collars double up against the cold. She tests the wind with her finger, turns towards the market where favourable opportunities are blowing.

For an hour, Kate crosses half of west central London in search of her son. She leaves the theatres of Bow Street and Drury Lane, the Theatre Royal itself looking crumpled and worn, and turns into the flower market corner of the Piazza. Only twelve hours ago she was arrested here for common vagrancy and 'insulting an officer', the usual wording for causing too much noise in the street; she'd been spending a merry evening at the *Pig and Whistle* trying to hustle free lodgings from the drunkest man. On finally seeing Kate under the streetlamp, her chosen man had turned on her and the ensuing argument attracted the night constable. Hence her sojourn in the Bow Street 'roundhouse' and a stony corner for the night—a blanket too, more than she would find on the street. But as Kate would tell you she is no prostitute, just a woman trying to make her way in the world who no more trusts men "than the flick of a nail."

The market reeks with flowers all tightly packed into wooden display-carts, their wheels pinned with blooms. Wire mesh encircles each bouquet, protecting it from the loose hands of Artful Dodgers. Picking her way along the stalls, the clamour of voices cautioning her to keep her distance, Kate turns in the direction of the slum of Seven Dials. But she changes her mind on noticing the lodging houses, Turkish baths and brothels all around Covent Garden, the 'Great Square of Venus'. What the market men and the polite shoppers of London fail to see in the daytime, Kate knows only too well from the night. Here is life in all its economic exchange, body and mind, but she is no Turkish brothel girl and "would not sink so low." Walking past the mock façades of Elizabethan buildings doubling as houses of pleasure, Kate decides she has unfinished business concerning the theft of a necklace the day before. As she changes direction, the odour of flowers becomes the crude smell of unwashed bodies on Bedford Street among shops selling the new invention of soap, a fearful novelty because of its newness. Reminding herself to look presentable and to escape the sweet stink, Kate takes a lozenge from one of her many inside pockets under her shawl: she does not fear lozenges to sweeten the breath but eats so few that the effect is negligible. Body perfumes generally make her feel sick, so Kate relies on a healthy odour of alcohol, the trusted currency of the street. Turning away from the queasiness that is the mixture of brothels and soap sellers, she weaves on to the Strand avoiding the fog of early morning carriages and hustles the long walk to Pickett Corner, past Temple Bar and Ludgate Hill to Blackfriars Bridge. She pauses under the bridge, a known spot for children selling tobacco, ducks her head into a brown mist, and is instantly recognised.

"Why, Miss Webster," says a ten-year-old mite. "You came back, ma'am." He pushes his thumbs along the pockets of a silver waistcoat as though impersonating the Mayor of London.

"Enough," says Kate. "I smoked all me last 'uns last night, never you mind. So I'm 'ere for a few more, jus' to get o' Blackkies."

"Cold mornin' n' all," says the child.

Kate eyes him narrowly then winks. "Ain't you got the sales pitch! What you got?" A table of brightly coloured pipes is presented before her. "I got the pipe kid, the 'nuff's my only stuff, if you catch m' drift."

"I surely do, Miss Webster, I surely do."

A sneeze from behind exposes more faces along a corrugated barrier before the river. A little girl is cradling what appears to be a doll, but as Kate peers through the gloom, her eyes adjusting, the baby again sneezes, and Kate leaps back.

"You want to get *that* turned in," she says, but the boy refuses to explain the baby's origin. He dishes the black tobacco on scales from his pocket and pretends to weigh. Addicted to snuff himself, he counts "four-three-two" while oily soot crawls from his nostril. Kate ignores all until he hands over the wiry substance. She looks over the black sludge of the riverbank where detritus of the night has gathered ready to be picked clean, the discarded treasures of hundreds of night boats that will keep the children busy. The sale is made. Kate delivers two bars of soap she acquired in prison and they shake on it.

"Take care o' that babby."

"He's ours now. Don't tell no-one, as they'll take 'im away."

"I know that," Kate says and leaves it at that, but clambering to the austere lights of the grassy bank she turns, and imitates a proud city accent: "You know tobacco may be a charm against worry, and make you sleep like a baby. But babbies can't take it. So keep the stuff for yourselves, you hear?" She pauses. "You know the song, how the 'old gangs smoked, the Roaring Boys and the Bonaventoes choked', well that's for me and you, not for the young 'uns." Puzzled by her tone, the children decide to salute her instead, their blackened faces reflected off the river. Kate turns away and is gone.

Soon she is south of the river, and is reminded of the East End's overpowering stench of fish, old wood and decaying bricks. She turns to the timber wharfs at Holland Street and cuts under an abandoned aqueduct in a route she knows well, past Bleeding Heart Alley to a forgotten little square that prepares meals for the men of the timber yard. It is past six o' clock. Here she waits, on sunken land behind Commercial Road and London's three vast timber plots, while greasy cooks are sweating to rival those of Fowle Street and Stinking Alley by mixing vast iron vats of pea soup. As Kate arrives, they strap seconds-old bread to little wheel-carts ready for the wharf and London's wider belly. The Thames is dark on the other side of Commercial Street, but wooden sparks from the machine-ovens fly up and give the false impression of falling snow.

Kate shuffles to a baker's stall with a sign overhead announcing 'Mrs Crease's Good Pies'. She has come to pick up her boy Daniel, safeguarded by that crusty old woman. Usually he is in her bakery's back room, gluing crushed matchboxes for re-sale, an occupation whose profits they share. A woman minces forward.

"Your husband with you, Miss Lawler?"

"The boy got none, and he ain't my husband."

"I was wonderin' if he wants t'shave? John Sweeney is back upstairs."

"The boy's only seven."

"But Mr Sweeney…"

"There ain't no mister, now let's be 'avin' Danny along, and we'll be off. Plus the week's takings."

A fat woman in a flatiron apron, Mrs Crease sinks into the dark glow of her bakery and reappears holding the boy's hand. Daniel stands there dutifully, his red hair curled over his forehead, a blank expression on his face. He is thin and pale. Mrs Crease holds his shoulder tightly, displeased at this extra 'minding' job. Squirming a little, Daniel is motionless when he sees his mother.

"That's your mama's boy," says Mrs Crease, "why not say 'hello'?"

She releases him and Daniel hovers in the bakery's entrance under the sign, darkness at his back, but takes no steps. Gently Kate kneels before her son and takes his hand, interpreting the expression in his eyes as another week of harsh treatment. "Give me the money. Looks like you o'erworked 'im."

"He's lazy." Mrs Crease is ready. "And then can't sleep at night. Dun't do what ya's told." Daniel holds up his wrist and shows a mark, fresh that morning and still red. Kate shows no reaction but touches the bruise, whispers how it will itch, and Daniel almost smiles.

"Just you pay what's owed, and I won't tell the yardmen in Bleeding Heart Alley."

Mrs Crease opens her apron and tips a coin into her own hand. She explains how the watchmen who patrol the lumber yards are paid by the Bow Street Runners to act as local vigilantes in the vicinity of her business. Her bakery could catch fire, if she "gets on the wrong side of the law."

"And the rest o' it," Kate says ignoring the usual excuses, and soon enough from Crease's garters more coins appear. The atmosphere relaxes. The exchange is complete and the two women, seemingly at odds, now hug each other. Money has been made and together they have lost little. Mrs Crease twists Daniel's ear before he leaves. "Same time next week, I can do Tuesday to Friday?"

"I'll be back sooner," Kate says, "unless I get work in Covent Garden."

"Ha, what you gonna be, a flower girl?"

"Theatre usher." They laugh at the joke, a mystery to the boy. Kate turns to the ovens of the bakery. "If I can find a dress."

"Well," Mrs Crease replies, "I'll be here slaving, if you need me."

Kate waves her exit, and leads Daniel further south. Mother and son march at a clip. They head back over Blackfriars Road to Bear Lane, enter Southwark in the direction of London Bridge, then cross again, drifting down Sugar Key Walk to mud banks of the City. The neighbourhood resembles the one they've just left, except for the twin fingers of Tower Bridge rising and glimpses of St Paul's Cathedral through morning smoke dispersing in cold air. Kate wraps her shawl tighter, senses Daniel shivering.

"Almost," she says. "Just be thankful we're in the City. There's worse pickings down south."

"South o' the river," the boy says. Kate eyes him shrewdly,

tapping him on the head.

Eventually they arrive at their destination, a tavern under Southwark Bridge—the musty alehouse *The Cat and Salutation*. All around Bell Wharf is deserted except for a handful of wooden shacks, old boxes and weeds. *The Cat and Salutation*, the name eerily jovial for bleak surroundings, rises up before them, a two-storey brick building solid-seeming in a street fighting the river and losing. Wheezing lightly as though sleeping, visible either side of the isolated beer-shop, the mighty Thames laps its brickwork, undercutting the foundations so that the pub's top storey is wider than the lower and the tide is slowly claiming the ground floor. The whole structure is leaning. Outside a dog stares at broken bottles in the street, sniffs desolately and trots away looking over its shoulder at Kate and Daniel. Beyond the edge of Bell Wharf, the ground rises to a narrow passageway, the light of Vintner's Court glinting beyond with the promise of escape.

"To malt and hops!" Kate calls on seeing the pub. Arms linked tight, they descend the muddy bank, treading on jutting stones trying to be steps. She hurries into the saloon, swinging Daniel by his arm. The heavy oak door is held ajar by a thick leather strap, threatening to slap the wall and alert the barman to new clientele—an old-style customer doorbell. Kate twists her boy ahead so the strap cannot catch her, and sits on a stool before the zinc-topped counter. Sawdust settles back on the wooden floor, the room returning to gloom as their eyes adjust. Before long, a tall and wiry man appears behind the horseshoe bar, polishing a glass in one hand.

"Welcome to my humble abode!" he gestures to the wooden benches, the spittoons hooked to barrels behind the bar, the coloured bottles more like medicine than liquor.

"You're Jonathan Clatter?"

"I am." He peers through the gloom, still twisting the glass.

"Sarah Crease sent me here with the boy." She twirls Daniel into view and immediately the owner comes to life from his slumbering daze. He leaves the horseshoe by a side door, appearing under a kerosene lamp. Abruptly he closes the tavern's heavy purple curtains, his face hidden with intrigue.

"You brought him for the school?"

"I did."

"Wonderful." An Englishman of the upper classes but disbarred from the Bar after alcoholic disgrace, Jonathan Clatter has discovered his *métier* is serving booze. Cornered by the substance is the only way he can stay sober, watching the ill effects of what he calls "the merry killer" in his own tavern. The barman's grey eyebrows twitch at the new arrivals, his toes encased in soft black pumps pressed together. His excitement is inexpressible—when he smiles his lips trouble his cheeks, his hands walk along on the bar and his oversized fingers stack together like branches of a deformed tree. He looks down on Daniel.

"You can leave him with me. The expenses are all sorted through that woman Crease."

"As is everythin' else."

"He'll get looked after, Mrs…"

"Lawler," Kate says—using her real name as a pseudonym now that she goes by Miss Webster. "Miss Catherine Lawler and this is Daniel."

"He'll be fed three times a day, and only sent out once in the afternoon, and then only to Cannon Street, until he gets fixed with the game, you see."

"I see."

"The older boys will show him the ropes. It's all a bit rough, I won't tell no lie, but he'll soon settle in. Just like a school."

"Right," Kate says and her black eyebrows fold over her eyes. For some reason she can't decide if Clatter is a genuine shady dealer with a friendly edge, or the reverse, not so much a crook with a heart as a gentleman on hard times who has turned to petty theft. Separating her feelings, she touches Daniel's shoulder and kneels to his height.

"I'm sorry," Kate says and puts her arm around his shoulder for her own benefit. "I don't want to leave you."

"But then don't, mama. Why are you…?"

"I…please don't ask questions, Danny. We mus' make our ways in th' world, you know. It ain't no party out there, not this ol' city. The world is what it is, tha's one thing you'll learn. She's what she is."

He frowns holding his arms out straight, and the plaintive expression on his face, freckled and innocent, is too much for her.

"I shouldn't, I can't…" she begins, but something in her reaction steels the boy, and he senses he has to impress.

"It's okay, mama." He takes her face to his chest, a gesture that causes her a brief moment of sobbing, some humiliation. Kate gets a grip and repays him with a shake. "Now you go, Danny, there's no other way."

"I know, mama, there's no need…" He trembles but her expression is tight as a fist and steadies him. With peculiar logic, she raises her hand to slap him but refrains and then confused, pushes him to the bar. Jonathan Clatter is already there with the two drinks, a consolation for each. He instructs them to drink "for fortitude" and watches as the boy has a nip of house-beer and Kate is offered a shot of the emerald witch, absinthe.

"What is it?" she asks innocently.

"Now, now, Miss Lawler, let's not pretend," says Clatter. "This 'ere's the green fairy, the opalescent muse, or bottled madness to me and you. The essence of life."

Kate feigns surprise and resists a grimace as she tips it back. "One more for the road—not you," she says to Daniel. "You're a big boy, n' we can't have you legless before you've graduated from Mr Clatter's fine school."

Clatter prepares another two shots. He places a spoon flat on a tulip-shaped glass and balancing a sugar cube on top. "This is what the greatest minds of London drink," he says, opening a narrow-spouted spigot on a tabletop fountain; he allows the trickle of water to melt the sugar into the clear liquid below.

"Were they great minds after?" Kate asks, watching the green liquid filter through, eyes glowing.

"You have to use old-fashioned glass fountains," Clatter says. "Check out the elegant metal pedestals I bought recently," he adds, while behind this fraudulent teacher-gentleman-crook, plaster is peeling the dank walls and last night's stale beer clouds the glasses he produces. He pours Kate a double "for the road."

"To drink without the ability to get drunk, that's my talent," Kate jokes, while Daniel is almost forgotten on his bar stool.

"Such is the delightful madness of the goblin!" the barman whispers.

The day is now easier on Kate's naturally fraught temperament. Not especially one to remain lighthearted, rather a stern character prone to fits of melancholy and temper, she allows the absinthe to suffuse her brain with a vaporous delight. Its sudden waves roll one upon another, like storm clouds brooding and waiting to soak the lighter clouds of memory with nothing but oblivion.

Fortunately she stops. Clatter wouldn't try to con her, she considers, otherwise he's picked the wrong adversary.

After the drink Kate is led into the back room by the schoolmaster-barman, treading gingerly. They pass through a low-slung room of bunk beds with boys sleeping haphazardly, two to a bed, some on rugs. Three of the corners are filled with tiny bodies wrapped together, frazzled hair and mouths hanging open. The relief of sleep is palpable on their eyelids.

"Such heavy sleepers," Clatter says, "young lads!"

"What time is bedtime?" asks Daniel. By way of an answer Clatter kicks objects from the floor, old pieces of wire, toy trucks, knitting needles, rags, discarded kettle tops and empty bottles of beer. Then he repeats his trick of previous introductions. He parts a curtain and reveals the back area, a triangular partition separating his own lodgings from a third room, the one he claims for "a special boy" who has worked hard.

"This will be Daniel's room for the first week. Better he's separated from the boys—you know how they can be. This way, Miss Lawler, he grows used to his surroundings and he'll learn to compete like the others for the prize of winning the room back!"

All this is said in front of Daniel, and after her three shots of absinthe Kate receives the news with mild comprehension. "Your room," she says.

"For a week," Clatter says, "but a grand way to start his *sojourn*, as the Europeans say." Rolling his fingers he turns Kate back to the partition door, the boys stirring from slumber, groaning, kicking and going back to sleep. "We should talk of charges…" He places his hands on the boy's shoulder, Kate doing the same. Daniel is caught between them like a piece of property.

"Now now, Clatter-er, don't get your hopes high. I know Sarah Crease paid you up front."

"She did that." He smiles maliciously, lips cutting high into the cheeks like a serious clown. "For two weeks only. After that I'll keep him one week, but if you don't show…"

"What then?"

"Well…" Clatter now directs Daniel to the third room, out of earshot. He pulls a wide curtain which has the ability to cover all the three rooms so Daniel at least has privacy—or imprisonment—for a moment. "This ain't no Oliver Twist get-up, Lawler," he begins. "We *are* famous as a school for pickpockets, I'll give you that. But we're moral too—all is merit-based, like an academy. We're Clatter's Double Dozen—as one group sleeps, another works!"

"I thought they don't go out at night?"

"Listen—" he ignores her question, "—we only target my old friends of the City, the ones who did us wrong! I was a broker, yer know, and they forced mi' hand and made m' look like a criminal. I will not be known as a criminal! I am a gentleman bartender, and that's the end of the deal. Miss Lawler, the end of my story!"

"I'll be here in a fortnight," Kate says. "Just to see you ain't thrown 'im on the street." She steps forward and raises a grubby finger to Clatter's chin and prods him. "Start 'im slowly, Clatter-er, "that's all I'll say. Start 'im slowly 'cos he's green as they come, but he's my boy. And I love him. No doubts about that—I'd cut and swing for that boy, make no mistake."

"He's in safe hands here."

"So watch your p's and q's."

"I do nothing else, Miss Lawler, nothing else."

With that Clatter draws back the curtain revealing Daniel standing in the same spot, clearly aware of the whole conversation. His reaction is sidelined, though, as a minor brouhaha from the adjacent room reveals a boy in black shorts and an overlarge white shirt: he is banging the bottom of a soup pan with a stick, grinning with one tooth. On seeing Kate and Daniel he runs away knowing he'll be in trouble, before the boys all rouse and line up for inspection.

"I'll be leaving you then," Kate says, timing her exit, but once more Clatter swirls the curtain to reveal a passageway outside. He turns to the line of boys and commands they "prepare breakfast on the double!" Then he ushers Kate—both ducking heads—through a passage of dark-red bricks into a scrubby little yard, bound in a square by iron railings. An incongruous white bench known as 'Clatter's Reading Bench' is jammed up against *The Cat and Salutation*'s back door. From here Kate can see Bell Wharf in one direction and the Thames in the other, either the barman's getaway in a tight spot. Clatter sits on his Reading Bench really used for spying and apes sadness, as mother leads son to the grilled gate to say their goodbyes.

Kate makes hers quick. She circles the railings, their high spikes arcing craftily back to entrap the boys.

"Mama," says Daniel, chasing her along the railings. "Wait!"

Kate approaches him, the grilles separating them. She can see Clatter in the background striking up a pipe, sucking it meditatively from the corner of his mouth. What a villain, she thinks, his lank hair in grey-matted folds on his collarbone where it sticks to his shirt. Between the teacher and the mother stretches a long taut washing line, six feet high over the rugged yard grass.

"Pockets and purses," Clatter calls from his seat. "Just rich folks' discarded hankies."

Kate nods falsely and turns back to her boy. Her eyes are glistening and she tries to wipe them but her cloth is too rough.

"See those 'hawkes bells', I don't know what he'll call 'em?" She points at the line. "Pigeon scarin' bells maybe!"

"Yes, I know mama, I guessed it. We's a thieves' shop, that's what. I got it figured up here," and little Daniel taps the side of his head. "I's to be trained to rob and kill."

"Not to kill," Kate snaps. "Not that." They stare at the washing line and hear the voice of the teacher.

"If a child can nab a coin from the line without triggering the bell," Clatter says, "well then, he's a judicious Nypper. There's more pea soup for those special ones. We conduct a competition on Sundays and the winner gets the top bunk."

Kate scowls at him and walks briefly to the middle of the yard. She sways over Clatter, and spits at his feet. "I don't trust you one inch with my boy. But I'll be back, soon enough, to save him from…your filthy claw." Clatter rolls his fingers in mocking menace at her anger, and chews on his pipe.

"Look, I can blow the smoke from my ears."

"Like they did to you in the City," Kate says. "These kids aren't safe, but you touch one hair on my Daniel's head and I'll cut *your* head off, see." She tips her neck back, and bizarrely, winks and giggles. "Don't think me wrong, Mr Clatter, I'll do it." For a moment he is silent. "You'd teach 'em to steal from under the rope that'd hang 'em if you could, at ol' Tyburn."

"Tyburn is Marble Arch, missy, those days are gone."

"Do they still hang kids, Mr Clatter? Do they? Tell me that!" Kate raises her fist and scratches her head, and laughs again. "Thanks for the absinthe." She bows and Clatter frowns, uncertain of her shifting moods.

"You're welcome," he says, the colour slowly returning to

his neck.

"I'll tell you this much," she says. "If Londoners catch 'em, they don't turn 'em in. They just drag 'em to the nearest well or fountain and duck 'em half drowned."

"That won't happen to your boy."

"On your life, it'd bettn' not."

Clatter stands up and hands her a small phial of absinthe. "One more for the long drop." She glares at him but takes the gift.

Then Kate walks back to her son. Despite all the talk of safety she doesn't know how to soothe the boy, whose tears have not stopped. She talks through the railings about going to see a fairground, or a hanging, whatever he prefers in the weeks to come.

"I'll be the same," Daniel says. "I won't change here. I don't want to see no hanging!"

"Sometimes a hanging's all they've got on a holiday," Kate says. She lifts his chin where the salt is beginning to crust. "It's a joke, Daniel, you're too young for a hanging."

The boy frowns, and grips his mother's arm. "Don't leave me, not now."

Once again she bends down. He is sad, but tries to look happy.

"Be good for your mother. This is a good place, a learnin' school for the street. He'll teach you more than 'istory and numbers." She taps her chest. "I was never so lucky to see such a school."

Reaching out, she touches the bruise on his face, and thinks of his father the merchant sailor, now long gone. "Oh Daniel, I'll come back for you. Ten days, you'll see. "And she covers the bruise with her shawl so he won't get bullied. "Cover it up," she says. "Find some tape and cover your face a bit."

Then she is gone, scrambling up the embankment to Southwark Bridge, forcing herself not to look back. At the bridge she crosses the black dirt road just as the sun hits the river, and illuminates the whole of London. She opens the absinthe phial and tips it to the back of her throat, letting the 'divine fire' trickle on her tongue to burn away the pain. Instead of a soothing though, a brooding desperate anger is stirred, then soaked away in the calm lotus drowsiness of the green liquid. She lets the sun—with a foreign pleasure—stir her eyelids and hide her feelings, then she crosses the bridge.

Back on the north side, destination unknown, Kate tosses away the empty container. She watches it fall into the water and disappear with a tiny bubble. A crooked smile crosses her lips. "Gone, gone," she whispers. "Gone for good—for better days to come." In her mind the absinthe is deepening effect. She twirls in the morning light, bumping into people who brush her back, just another lost stray of the city, no one's pride, no one's sorrow. Inside she hears sonorous chamber music, vast and echoing. Tripping on half delirious and drunk, fake happy for her lungful of freedom, the music carries her through the smell and rush of waking London. Kate can feel the fullness of her mind, the beating of her heart. Her mind is hollow, her heart cold without her boy—Daniel, the only one she has left.

After a minute, Kate realises the sounds are distortions of St Paul's Cathedral. The grand bell is clanking eight in the morning: time for the men to return to their city drudgery, for women of leisure to head to matins, for old people to stoke the fires of their memories. Time for the Clatter boys to awake too, for those small boys initiated into a league of urchins to begin their day, to venture out into the city's sunshine and capture a little of London life, to cut a few purses before nightfall.

Chapter 2
The Shoemaker of Horncastle
14th February 1879, Friday

That same day, William Marwood Esquire is home in Horncastle, Lincolnshire, a country village on the eastern shoulder of England, a far cry from London's metropolis. He sits in *The Portland Arms*, his local pub on the corner of Church Lane, drinking a single stout. Staring into the middle distance, he is relaxing after a day in his cobbler's shop. At nine o' clock the new steel clock behind the bar chimes the hour and Marwood will walk the cobbled street sixty yards back to his shop, his wife and son.

The bar atmosphere is more subdued than normal; for several weeks now William Marwood Esquire has been the talk of the village—as usual—but rarely showed his face. This evening he sits in an alcove both with a panoramic view of the bar rack, with its hanging bottles of spirits and beer mugs, and the entrance where the farmers, locals and traders mingle. Marwood is busy rolling his fingers over a letter, his black eyes sunk into his cheeks, a whisper of a smile cut into the smoothly shaven chin with its single dimple at the centre. Drawn by the prospect of free travel and new adventure, he has almost decided to accept the letter's proposal, a commission from the Sheriff of London and Middlesex to take up a new post in the city: hangman for the South. It is the promise he has been waiting for, working for, practicing his trade for, and now it has come. But ever a cautious man, Marwood sits folding the paper in his long careful fingers, peering into the dark mist of his settling pint. He waits; he looks up at the faces lining the bar, the farmers all trussed up in hardy coats, the blacksmith, the church chaplain in his faded dog collar, their eyes flickering at the well-known stranger.

"You remember the Phoenix Park murders?"

"As if it were yesterday."

The individuals waddle over and sit chummily facing Marwood. Both are burly men, one losing his hair but sprouting a beard like a manic vegetable growth, the other clean shaven but more suspicious-looking with thatches of red hair clamped to his ears. Marwood recognises the ironmonger and butcher of Horncastle, the Tooley brothers who know all the local talk, and fearless of no-one. They draw bar stools together in solidarity and self-amused intimidation.

"So Willy, my boy," says Fred the butcher.

"Mr Marwood, head of the headless," laughs Iain the ironmonger.

"You came back to us!"

Marwood looks up over his pint, pretending he isn't worried. "I couldn't leave you for long," he says, reaching for his pint.

"The village wouldn't have you gone long."

"No, no, we can't be doin' all the law n' order."

The brothers laugh and slap palms, long hair shaking and teetering on their stools.

"Steady," Marwood says, summoning the nerve. "I wouldn't want you to drop."

"A hit!" cries Fred, the more learned of the Tooleys, "a palpable hit!"

But Iain recognises the challenge and decides to make his move. He leans on the table, elbow high. Then he takes Marwood's pint, lifts it, threatens to pour it over him, and drinks it down in four large gulps. All three regard the froth bubbling up Iain's chin and slipping back down the glass. He coughs a little, showing no embarrassment, and Marwood is wise enough not to smile.

"Now listen here, we know you've been to Kilmainham Gaol, and took care of them boys."

"The Queen's enemies, you mean."

"If you believe in the Queen," Fred, the bigger brother with the beard, chimes in.

Marwood glances up. "I'm not sure this crowd would appreciate your anti-royalist speech."

"This crowd don't know its arse from its elbow," Fred says. "You aren't in the home counties here, ma' boy."

"I've lived in Horncastle all my life," Marwood replies, determined not to lean back.

"Well, we ain't *all* Queen's men here, boyo, and there's plenty like us. Now you listen again, hangman, and listen good. I'll count 'em out once. Brady, Kelly, Curley, Fagen and Caffrey. You took care of 'em all. Dublin Castle."

"That was months ago."

"Well, you keep a low profile, and here's a public place."

"You can come to my shop anytime."

"We don't need shoes, we just need the laces to hang you by."

"That's a threat, Iain. You step too far out of line…" but Marwood isn't able to finish the sentence. Fred fixes his hand on Marwood's, and takes up the pepper pot and sprinkles it over his fingers.

"It could be you next," Iain continues, his red hair bouncing up and down. "That's all we're saying. Like they do in the southern United States."

"You know what lynching is?"

"I do, Fred," Marwood replies. "But this is England. We operate according to justice."

"It ain't no machine," Iain replies, letting go of the pepper and shoving it back in Marwood's face. The butcher then proceeds to talk while Marwood coughs, and the men all stand up. "I told you their names, and their deaths 're on your conscience."

"I am a servant of the Crown," Marwood replies. "Ask any man in here." He looks over his shoulder, but the Tooley brothers are being ignored by the rest of the pub. "The remainder of the gang were imprisoned in Downpatrick Gaol. They have their lives."

"I heard the story," Fred says. "You went to Ireland dressed as a clergyman with that assistant of yours, Bartholomew Binns."

"You'll never find him," Marwood says. "He's long gone."

"Yes, back down south, where they all go."

Marwood thinks of the letter in his pocket. A quiet unboastful man, the locals will soon regard his move to London with mixed pride and shame. He is one of theirs, but leaving them, and they have mixed feelings about what he did in Ireland.

"I'm still supported here for the Dublin hangings," Marwood says. "Even by the Irish ex-pats. That's the difference."

At these words, the brothers step back, and hook their thumbs in their belts.

"We're Anglo-Irish, and as Protestants we have as much right to be here as you do there. So chew that, Marwood, and chew carefully. We came back because we didn't like the way Catholic Irish were ruled over, so call us sympathisers if you like. There's plenty of us left in England."

Marwood now stands. "Those boys were responsible for killing Thomas Henry Burke, permanent Under-secretary and Lord Cavendish the Chief Secretary of State for Ireland. They called them the Invincibles…"

Iain takes this moment to spit at Marwood's feet and the whole pub goes quiet.

"You hanged 'em," and they were ordinary men facing up to the government," Fred says. "You should be ashamed."

"I'm ashamed of nothing," Marwood says and weighs his words. "Those men were a mob, and they went from brawling that night to stumbling on Lord Cavendish in Phoenix Park, and beating him to death with sticks and broken glass. Call that heroic?"

"I call that fine rebellion," Iain says, puffing up his chest.

"I saw to them on the scaffold and I would do it again. I'll stick to my shoes and you stick to your trades."

Marwood stands defiant, and despite his narrow frame he is taller than expected. The moment hangs uncomfortably in the air, and his adversaries begin to smirk. The Tooley brothers point at him silently and announce to the pub: "He'll get his in the end, he'll get his. Don't be too proud of your local hero."

"That's just it," Fred echoes, "you don't stick enough to your trade."

"The people *don't* love me for it, be sure of that," Marwood says, sitting back down. "It depends which trade you're talking about."

"We can see that," Iain laughs and together they leave the pub, the door closing behind them with a defiant click. The cold country air ruffles the pub before calm descends once more.

Marwood sits for a minute, somewhat bewildered, then walks

to the bar and orders a fresh pint. He sits between the old men of Horncastle, farmers and schoolteachers, clergy and retired labourers too tired to wish for anything beyond conversation and comfort, and he is not shunned. Known as a raconteur, Marwood has always been welcome in pubs, most of all in his local.

"So, no one will stand up for me when the time comes." I am the outsider in a small place, he thinks, the outsider among outsiders.

They look at him, as ever weighing the ups and downs of shielding a professional with duel trades of opposite social purpose. No one replies, but Marwood is patted on the back by landlord Fortinbras Truman, a childhood friend now sporting a pot belly and brown apron he's worn for decades.

"You stood up to them well," Truman says.

Marwood looks up and nods, his black eyebrows raised for amusement then dropping over the hooded supports of his soft eyes.

"How's your plan going to solve the national debt by more hangings?" asks Albert Watkins, a local dairy farmer.

"It isn't," Marwood replies.

"You gonna pick it up?"

"Nope," the hangman replies. "I'm gonna let it lie." Ponderously he drinks his pint and stares at the old steel clock, built for the railway line that never quite made it to Horncastle, and watches the second hand click round. "Toe the line, that's what I should have said. Toe the line."

"Like you were about to hang him? He wouldn't have liked that."

Marwood looks up at Truman. "No, he wouldn't, and it might make him think we'd meet on the scaffold one fine day."

"Any of us could meet there one day," Watkins says.

They laugh, a circle of old camaraderie.

"True, true. Well, that's me," Marwood says as the clock ticks nine. "Save my pint for whoever's here last."

"That'll be me, then," Truman replies.

"Goodnight then."

Marwood takes his hat from behind the door and slips into the night, a tall shapeless fellow, slim from head to toe. He glances down to the High Street to ensure his friends have gone. Then he turns his back on *The Portland Arms* and looks from the pale full moon to the Methodist Church opposite, its ribbed arches in stained glass shadowing the grass. Like a schoolboy making good time, Marwood walks the links of raised stones, thinking of his 'split trapdoor' invention he has yet to try out, or the myriad Da Vinci anatomy drawings he's been copying into his notebook. But somehow he cannot piece together, despite untold effort, an overall proof of the best hanging technique. As these thoughts skim the surface of his mind, he reaches his house and pauses under the small but important sign, carved in trim bronze:

William Marwood, Esq
Crown Officer & Public Executioner
Church Lane, Horncastle, Lincolnshire
For hire, for the public good

No mention is made of his daytime craft. The locals all know Marwood as the mender of shoes, so the sign is part vanity, part confirmation of his residence for the traveller or occasional employee. An average neck-width, the sign announces a humble cottage and the last of a row of thatched terraces; but unlike the other dwellings the front entrance is on Church Lane and looks out at the Wesleyan Methodist church graveyard. A sense of privacy is preserved, consolidated by the churchyard opposite snaking away to the river via the small plot of gravestones: here Marwood savours these few seconds of private walk at the end of the day.

The front of the house is far different from the backyard, where the garden exits onto Foundry Lane and opens into fields stretching the mind all the way to the North Sea. The garden is hidden from the street and naturally this is where Marwood conducts his experiments, where noise will not travel and people cannot see. He pauses and thinks. Rarely is he accosted for his fame unless cornered inside a pub somewhere or held up by those bullying or brave enough. On the contrary, unlike his predecessor—a showy man who bungled most of his hangings called William Calcraft—Marwood is never followed home by gangs of shouting boys. As his private notepaper announces, he is a 'gentleman executioner' who keeps body and soul separate from the public. As he is fond of saying, "I am solemn, like a shadow."

Marwood scratches the sign with his nail and wonders (as he does every day) why he does what he does? The question cannot be addressed so late. All he knows is that his cottage is two storeys of which his workshop is the ground floor. Upstairs is for living, downstairs for experimenting with the boundaries of life. Down there he makes both shoes—so people can travel—and ropes that keep people quite still.

Once inside, he descends a few stone steps and looks from the window and sees *The Portland Arms*, a cloud over its chimney. Looking left he sees the heads of the gravestones, raised over the road, meditating. Nor are there any windows in neighbouring houses from which to spy on his musings. He is quite alone. February is a quiet time in Horncastle, north of the West and Wildmore Fens. Horncastle is known for horses, for its canal and the frequently of flooding from the River Bain.

The horse-fair of last August is long over, and the winter has erased memories of the clear, mild weather of spring, so that sleep and forgetfulness seem the only way to survive the cold. Marwood stokes the iron-grated fire behind the steps, and clears last night's fallen branches from the chimney. He snaps some kindling and lights the remaining paper fire-lights, presses them and watches as a small flame burns. Slowly the room glows into life.

Before the fire can climb too high Marwood is busy at work. Since cooking the evening meal of roast duck with carrots with his wife, marking the Valentine's Day when they met thirty-one years ago, Marwood has not quite completed the next day's orders. As he works, he thinks of all the good times since he married Ellen Andrews of Northallerton, Yorkshire. Still affectionate to his wife, he smiles at the prospect of the warm bed waiting for him although she will be most likely asleep. He transfers this latent desire into his workshop, into the solid iron last, using proper thread, linen and hemp combined, and leather of various types for uppers, soles, heels. For the next hour he indulges the love he has for work and leaves his wife to dream on the anniversary of their meeting.

Marwood has a new pair of shoes to make for Fortinbras Truman, his old friend and faithful barman. As he works, the shoemaker often thinks of the people in his life. First he takes the barge cement, dips it in the alcohol he left out, rolls it in beeswax, and waits. The thread soaks and he stares into the liquid, thinking how nicely Truman prepared his pint and a half of stout just as he entered the pub at a quarter of eight. Then he takes the hammer and pincers, scours the edge off a single razor blade, and places the five shoe nails in his mouth. The butt-stitching will require an edge-flesh for the shoes Truman likes to wear, or else a grain stitch if the leather is too tough.

True to his methodical nature, Marwood prepares the curved awl, soaks the thread skein in the beeswax, now melted, and again waits. As he smooths the wax through the heat of his fingers—globs falling onto the long wooden table—he thinks of his wife, sleeping Ellen. He wonders how much gin she's consumed tonight while he was at the pub, the drinking of the cheap sloe-gin their only shared vice, their mutual chastisement. Setting the candle aside a moment he takes a seat in his old raised work-chair high on makeshift stilts like a scarecrow's throne while his mind drifts to his son, Aldous, and whether he will cope alone—with his mother?—with the bullies of Horncastle? What will become of the Marwoods if he takes the job in London? How will they survive?

"I must teach Aldous how to stitch," he whispers while the flame, a blue-and-orange reflection around his face, creates a kaleidoscope. He continues to work silently, threading both pieces of leather and wiggling together the fibres. In creating the diagonal angle Marwood finds himself a little sleepy with the effect of his stout and the fire. His focus is slipping. The flame softens as he threads hole after hole until the thread suddenly buckles and unwinds. He applies more beeswax, straightens and re-twists, but the thread keeps hitting the join and won't pass.

As ever he solves the problem by re-imagining the shoe as a man's head, and for a few seconds he is no longer a cobbler, but preparing a hanging. He points the awl towards the joint as though it were the ear of the prisoner, tightening the leather as though it were the large knotted rope around the victim's neck, the washer rolling free on a metal ring. Not yet does Marwood see he has made the first step towards a surer way of hanging, and a safer way, in that it will prevent either strangulation or decapitation. This metal 'X' secure against the prisoner's neck will ensure all—a steady fall, a close grip, a sudden death. But for now he playfully mends the shoe with the dexterity he applies to the scaffold. He does not see the improvement, the invention.

Instead he grows sleepy. Tightening the last threads on the shoe, his fingers roll the awl automatically and once again Marwood is thinking of people he knows. Only this time, since the shoe-mending reminds him of darker experiments, a face slowly moulds out of the split beeswax. He is looking into the past, before he was born. Taken from his reading of the *Newgate Calendars*, there is Mary Blandy now, convicted over a hundred years ago at Oxford Assizes for the murder of her father at Henley. The record of Newgate executions is so striking, Marwood feels her presence, the disappearance of her father, the accusation, the witch-hunt, the hanging. As though it were happening now in the basement, he sees Mary's heart-shaped face dissolve into a supplicating plea in the molten wax, her mouth half open, her prayer choking to horror. Tightening the shoes, working in a vaguely puzzled way, he remembers the rest of the case. Could she be guilty of poisoning her father, adding arsenic to his wineglass but claiming the drug was a 'love philtre' to make him kind to her lover? So that her father would let a certain Captain Cranstoun marry her? Did anyone believe her?

Marwood stitches up the last shoe, quite aware that Cranstoun abandons her to her fate. But as a stout Methodist, Marwood is a modern man, a believer in free will, and as such he is conservative on the subject of 'just desserts:' in his eyes, Mary Blandy chose her future when she chose her lover over her father. As though to confirm his belief, the shoemaker tightens the last leather noose, then lays aside to dry Fortinbras Truman's completed leather walking shoes. But the haunting of Mary Blandy is not quite finished. Her pained face is melting in the leftover beeswax, a ghost of an ugly past. Marwood is a practical man, though, and he destroys the image by wiping the redness from below his eyes, using the base of the candle, down his thin black eyebrows. He takes a deep breath.

It is then that he sees her, a woman hanging in a black crepe dress, her arms and legs tied with black paduasoy ribbons, her whole dress extremely neat. What upsets Marwood is the way she dies, not the fact she is executed. Second by second, as though he were executioner, he sees the rope circle her neck without care. It touches her face, giving her cheeks a dreadful and unwarranted shiver. Then with her own fingers, a poignant detail, she moves it to one side. Mary is holding a rose, and for all of Oxford in Port Meadow, high on the hill she is strung between two trunks on the 'fatal tree', a beam between two fruit trees. Marwood shakes gently, his hands wavering around the table. He can see nothing but Mary Blandy's face, her shame and horror, the quivering of her limbs as they tighten the rope. For her fear of pain before death itself he feels for her, but cannot explain his empathy to himself. After climbing four rungs of the ladder, she whispers: "Gentleman, do not hang me high, for the sake of decency." They do not tie her dress, and the wind blows. The sight is disgraceful, Marwood thinks, the scene warped and the memory false, but justice is done in Oxford town.

Marwood shivers in the warmth of his worktop, his scarecrow throne rocking, his own black frock coat hung on a peg below the window. Fixed by the daydream, though, he is elsewhere, his gold watch-chain bouncing on his executioner's waistcoat. He was executing Mary Blandy in his mind, according to English justice and God's law, and no one dares complain. Laughing now, his black hood falls off and reveals a mane of silver hair swirling in the wind, transforming him into a devilish wizard. But looking closely, the dreaming Marwood sees a flash of suffering in his *doppelgänger's* eye that causes the reverie to break.

Standing in the doorway is Marwood's son Aldous, staring at the long wooden table, its shoes and twisted pieces of leather.

"Good evening, father." He moves to Marwood's elbow and slides a cigar into a miniature guillotine. "There you go."

Marwood smiles. "Thank you. I was just having a bad dream."

"The shoes raining from the sky?" the twelve-year-old asks.

"No, not this time," Marwood says. "Not tonight." He turns to face the boy. "Aldous, you know I'm 'grooming' you, so to speak, to take over the family business?"

"Yes, so we can move house…"

"Well, first it means I'll be away for a while. On business…"

Aldous knows his father is a hangman but they pretend otherwise for mutual comfort if not amusement. "Father, you already keep the shoes of dead men and repair them for sale."

"I know, like Sweeney Todd's victims ended up in the pies, right?"

They smile.

"But why do you have to leave, then?"

"It won't be for long. A few weeks. You must take care of your mother, Aldous." He touches the boy's arm. "And you must stop her drinking." He looks stern.

"Yes, father, I'll try."

Aldous is bigger than most boys his age, but clumsy and lacks his father's wiry shape. He is a country boy and could not survive in the city, and despite this timidity—too shy for the rough and tumble of the open fields—Marwood fails to give him the attention he deserves. Tonight is different, though, and Marwood knows a fresh path is leading him. So he allows the boy to sit on a raised stool nearby. Together they watch the fire die. Later Aldous beckons to the chess set in the corner.

"That's only for the talented," he says. "I'm too tired." So the chessboard stays under dusty leather. Instead, Marwood takes a cloth on the table edge and slowly peels it back, revealing a phrenological plaster cast. The object is exposed as a bald head with large eyes, white all over, and Aldous wobbles on his stool in surprise.

"The head of an executed criminal," says Marwood. "Not the real head. An organic replica, made of pigskin."

"Who is he?" the boy says, wincing, but curious nonetheless. With a flutter of his fingers, Marwood tells his son of "Courvoisier, the Swiss valet. He murdered his employer, a gentleman called Lord William Russell in 1840. But that's not the best bit…" Aldous levels his head with Courvoisier's cranium, trying to discern a flicker of life. The eyes stare obliquely at back, the skin white as chalk; no pupils remain. "Forty thousand people turned out for the hanging. And over a million and a half broadsides were sold for a penny each. Made a dozen Londoners rich!"

"A pretty penny," Aldous says, and stretches out his hand.

"No, don't touch," the hangman says, and restrains his son. "That's only for the sick. If you touch him when you're not ill, you might get sick yourself." The boy drinks in every word. "It was before my time, and certainly before yours. He was a foreigner anyway, never found his place."

"Why did he do it?"

"No one knows for sure," Marwood muses. "He blamed crime books himself—'penny bloods'—for his murders. Too many thrillers back in those days. That's why I stick to the science books!"

Aldous stares into the eyes of the long dead killer, and feels almost hypnotised. Before long Aldous is half asleep and curled in a chair, head in the crook of his arm. Meanwhile Marwood tidies the table, pats Courvoisier on his bald head and covers him up.

"Time passes," he says to the dying fire, then before long, he takes Aldous gently in his arms. He blows out the candle. At the stone steps, he turns briefly. Only a little dust falls from the back of his wizard's chair.

Listening to his son's breathing, Marwood steps outside to smoke a cigarette, stares across at the graveyard. The moon is up, a hollow scythe, smiling, with no stars to accompany her silent melancholy. Marwood feels the same. He takes a step into the street, kicks at some gravel, and crosses to the nearest tomb, where he places his hand and feels the cold stone.

"Life is short," he whispers, taps his pipe of the headstone. Then he turns on his heel and returns to his front door. He wipes the dew from the metal plaque announcing his job as executioner—a small sign, no more prominent than any on Church Lane for the midwife, the butcher, the undertaker. Nowhere does it say he is the cobbler.

Marwood pushes the door open, proud to have a secret profession so publicly known and a public job so secret. Even he no longer knows which is more prominent in his psyche, his quiet narcissism or his sacrifices to public service. "Only time will tell." With a firm shove and twist, as though practicing both his crafts at the same time, he closes the door.

Chapter 3
Richmond, A Nice Place to Live
16th February 1879, Sunday

The fruit and vegetable vendors are unloading their carts as Kate pays for a cheap boarding house for an extended two nights. After a long rest, she leaves Covent Garden just before dawn. Between a cloudy sunrise and pale-sinking moon, day follows night in sleepy harmony. The theatres in nearby Drury Lane are all silent from the Theatre Royal to Bow Street. No policeman haunts the early morning streets. All the newspapers and suspicious litter of the night has gone, washed into makeshift gutters to Trafalgar Square.

Gingerly, in new clothes clean from the prison wash-room and bent on fresh employment, Kate follows the slum route to Seven Dials, past the flower market and beyond the Piazza. Her white petticoat and purple frock flutter about her legs, distracting her. She is not used to ladylike clothes. Known for seedy lodging houses, she weaves up alleyways between the Turkish baths and brothels—the Great Square of Venus—and leaves central London. At the corner of Chandos Street and the Strand she pays a boy a penny to take her down to the Thames. From there she can walk alone.

At eleven o'clock, the winter sun still muffled in cloud, Kate Webster knocks on the door of Mrs Julia Martha Thomas at No. 2 Mayfield Gardens, off Park Road, Richmond. She has arranged the meeting but is early and Mrs Thomas is just going to church.

"Yes?" the older lady says, opening the door a jar. "Can I

help you?"

Unknowingly Kate stands on the brink of her future, stares into the void of the hallway. She spies a grandfather clock lining the wall, and next to it, a small crumpled woman edging seventy, hard skin under her ears.

Mrs Thomas peers into the daylight, cheeks sagging, hair tied up in a comical bun. Her expression is shrewd, focused on the surprise visitor, and not unfriendly but not welcoming either.

Kate looks back, surprised.

"'ello," she says, suddenly lost for words. "I've come about the job. I'm new in the city and I saw your note in the *London Illustrated*." She touches a hand to her hat, drawing attention to its mock finery, its yellow sash tied neatly under her chin in the new fashion of seventeenth century. Somehow the gesture works and she attempts a smile, fearing it must be crooked, but her melancholy expression is sufficient to relax Mrs Thomas, who opens the door, then closes it. The quiet expanse of a secluded street, flowerbeds along the hedgerows, is cut away.

"Well, you better come in then. Mind the carpet."

They move into the living room. Kate looks around at the gentility. She is in a curious mood and Mrs Thomas seems stern, but something in Kate is drawn to the older woman's firmness, to its promise of direction. They stand either side of a rug displaying a giant red rose; behind Kate a newly fitted double-glazed window looks out on the lawn. An upright piano dozes in the corner of the room. All is perfect, except the white curtain is caught under the piano lid, the victim of a playful crocodile.

"You said you were in service?"

"I was, both here and in Ireland. I'm from Killane near Wexford."

"Irish," Mrs Thomas says and tuts audibly. "I once hired a Catholic girl like you from Cork. She turned out a 'bad'un' as they say—ran away with the silver plate." She gestures to the mantelpiece where a wooden case holds cheap silverware. "So I had to move her out!"

"Well, you won't need to worry with me," Kate says. "I've been in Lord Rochester's house in Dublin, and I can send references from his Farthing House. They are late in coming."

"How long have you been in the city?"

"Well, almost a year, after six months in Liverpool."

"Liverpool is no place to be."

Kate nods, uncertain how to proceed, until Mrs Thomas ignores her and strides over to the window with a surprising burst of energy. "I must be going, anyway," she says and lifts an umbrella from a stand in the corner and gestures to the street. "The gang is waiting for me." Outside a small collection of elderly women is gathered at the end of the garden. "Paradise calls—St Barnabus—and I cannot miss another service. I've not been well recently, you see. This dreadful cold!"

"Yes, of course." Kate's eyes, filmy with staged weakness, alight on Mrs Thomas and she sees that the old woman's sternness is not an intolerable air. "I would like to work here," she says and waits.

"Well, if you can send those references you can start right away. And if all works out next week, there won't be a problem."

"I used to lodge with the Mitchell family too in Teddington. But I left because they suffered hard times."

"Hard times?"

"Their child died, a little girl."

Mrs Thomas peers at Kate and twirls her umbrella like a walking stick to the door. "Hmm...I have a daughter...She lives in Camden Town." Mrs Thomas's face changes as though connecting the two families, and her sympathy for the non-existent Teddingtons clinches the job. "Can you provide a reference from them?"

"Well, I wouldn't like to bother them."

"No matter," says Mrs Thomas and turns at the door. "The Irish connection will do. Now follow me, young lady. I must be going. You can come back tomorrow, after four o' clock when my Rummy friends will have gone. Rummy the card game, that is! Do you play?"

"I used to, Mrs Thomas."

"Mighty fine game! And your name is?"

"Catherine, ma'am. Catherine Lawler."

"Well, tomorrow at five, good show. I can show you your room then." Together the two ladies exit the premises. "Fly ahead, fly ahead," Mrs Thomas pronounces, her hair bob still attached, and follows her new maid up the garden path. Kate nods to the three women at the gate, each pruned in the face in her own way. They smile graciously in open judgement and pretend to gesture to the weather. Mrs Thomas says nothing more, except to greet her friends, and Kate is left standing in the street.

"Looks like she bought new clothes," one of the women whispers, trying not to be quiet.

"And has cleaned herself somewhere…"

Kate decides not to watch but, picking up her dress in amusement, begins the gentle incline of Park Road to the High Street. She glances over the manicured gardens through the lace-curtained windows of Richmond. A face appears here or there in disapproval; immediately Kate turns away. But the first flush of her success is upon her. The wear and tear of the last few days, the release from the Roundhouse, the looking after Daniel…all is ebbing away!

In a matter of hours she has acquired fine clothes, a school for her boy, and a job. Could this be a new start? She even has the whole day stretching ahead with nothing to do, and in a polite neighbourhood. What better thing to do than have a little drink? *"Yes? Can I help?"* Kate mimics her newfound self, chuckling. *"Oh, hard times, you say? I've seen some hard times, dearie."* She pulls away the bonnet to feel the cold air. *"I bet you have!"*

Over the crown of Kew Hill, Kate turns towards Richmond Bridge. Now the day is stronger, the sun has cleared away the hump of night clouds: Kate gently turns her knuckles in her eyes and looks along the High Street—all is quiet on a Sunday morning. Cut off from London and its own private plot of heaven, Richmond enjoys much of the feel of a village. By squinting Kate instinctively can tell the Richmond village hall and *petite* Norman tower churches dotting the High Street; the market pubs are closer to the bridge. Deciding on a compromise she quietly doubles back on herself, sensing the finer establishments might intersect. Following the bend she is not wrong and soon strays upon a delicate-looking tea-drinking suburban pub, *The White Conduite House*, half restaurant half traveller's house.

At the door Kate takes a seat at a private round table, the bar an earshot away, though no one is around. Immediately she announces she is Mrs Jacobs of 11 Worcester Place, Kew Gardens.

"Put it on my tab, young sir." A lad of no more than twelve, the serving boy does so. "I'm new—where is known for good scones?" Kate asks, enjoying the ridiculousness of her costume and repartee.

"Cuper's Gardens," the boy says, "does a good cuppa."

"Cup of tea," Kate corrects. "Cup of tea."

"That's right ma'am. You be wanting owt else?"

"Anything else, my man. Will I be wanting anything else?"

"That'z wot I sez." He stares at Kate dumb-looking. "You know Kew 'cos that's where you're from? That tea garden inside the garden of Kew Gardens."

She leans in. "How about a decent liquor place?"

"Begnigge Wells has got 'em best. You can bet on bridge with orange brandy, aniseed, citron."

"Barbadoes water?"

"They got that too."

Kate nods sagely. "Just bring me a double brandy and we'll call it a morning. And a cheap Spanish cigar too, if you would."

"A cigar."

"You heard me, lad."

An hour later, she tops it with a pint of Genuine Stunning, best ale of the South.

"To keep the cold out," the boy says, wiping the spillage on his blue apron, and reminding her for a moment of Daniel. Her eyes gain their transparent watery look and then roll back to steady.

"Yes," she muses, "and to put the hell fire in." She winks at him as she leaves.

Kate smokes the cigar walking up to Richmond Bridge, knowing she's got the better of the village during church services.

"Tea, with three cups, and six slices of bread and butter, a shilling," she whispers softly, reading the signs and puffing on her cigar. Passing three workmen constructing a fence on the corner of the High Street and Pine Grove, their wagon loafing on the grassy curb, Kate ignores the wolf-whistle, the first she has experienced in a long while, and blows the smoke over her shoulder. She cannot help but blush—men never the last thing on her mind—but does not turn. The feeling of being 'half cut' on a Sunday morning in Richmond will not leave her for a while, least of all because she has to be back at 2 Mayfield Gardens in the morning.

Next she's tempted to go for lunch, spying *The Mountaineer's Arms* up ahead. A cloth signboard unfurling the brick wall displays all the treats for Sunday lunch. In a formal dining-house, the salmon n' shrimp sauce is a half-rice special, not to mention rump-steak puddings and warm pigeon-pie.

"I should do this just once," Kate says. "If I still had any ill-gotten gains, I'd eat in fine style!" Peering through the window, neck staining and hot breath on the glass, she sees a communal long table dining being set up, all the silverware glinting, the maids milling round in sky blue pinafores. No one is there yet—and Kate imagines them taking their places just like the *Café Savoy*, their faces disgusting like pigs, bottle-noses and pimpled cheeks all signs of the debauchery that passes for good living away from the grime of London.

For once, though, Kate resists. Mrs Thomas might be heading here and burst her good fortune. Stumbling from the window and gathering his wits, Kate heads back across Richmond Bridge. She looks down at the river and thinks of all the silver in Mrs Thomas's house. One day she will partake of a seat at the *Cafe Royal*, the *Criterion Restaurant*, or the *Pond Gaiety Restaurant*, and *The Mountaineer's Arms* has only whetted her appetite. Next to the Gaiety Theatre luncheon room in the Strand, the *Pond Gaiety* is the one to aspire to. Kate will park her Hansom cab in the entrance, men in top hats will escort her to the dining hall where Jamaica rum and Madeira port will be mixed as a light welcome for her, the *entrée* dishes will sizzle in the pan placed before her, still on fire, and the whole circular ceiling will dazzle with ostentatious design, stained glass windows mixing—somewhat irreligiously—with carnivorous hunting scenes dripping blood and beauty from the walls.

The reverie must end. Water bubbling in her mind, Kate stares at the Thames, the face of Mrs Thomas her employer staring formally back at her in devout reproach. A single diamond jewel sparkles from Mrs Thomas's arm and Kate tries to recall if she definitely saw it there.

Eventually she is huffing up Kennington Lane and over Vauxhall Bridge. Needing to rest she buys a baked potato from a street stall and spies Green Park where she can finally lie down. Lowering her expectations, she plods along, her clothes more rumpled, her lemon bonnet dusty. She dreams of *Gatti's Hole* at Charing Cross because they play music. She knows *Gatti's* is an all-male old-fashioned chop-house, but something about the smell every time she passes drives her to unwarranted acts. So much temptation in God's own world, she thinks. Kate is tired now and another day trudging the city streets has left her 'ready for the knackers' yard'. Weaving down where the Chelsea Road becomes the King's Road and eventually the Queen's Road, she rounds the Palace Garden stables and slumps into Green Park, barely making it to the base of Constitution Hill.

Here Kate takes to a bench and instead of politely resting, she drags herself behind a bush and lies down full-length hoping the Bow Street runners will take pity on her, if they find her. Another night in the Roundhouse would be unbearable. She sits very still, and can't help but laugh. Already she knows what has to be done—that old woman has to go. The revelation washes over her in little alcoholic waves of joy.

Eureka! She giggles, and lays the yellow sash from her hat neatly on the ground beside her. "Can't damage that!" she whispers. "Got to be good for a disguise!"

The last words on her lips are "Daniel" before she falls into a day-time sleep, fully five o'clock in the afternoon-evening, only waking when it is darker and colder still.

Chapter 4
A Man of Science, Her Majesty's Public Servant
16th February 1879, Sunday

That same morning William Marwood is up early, walking his garden and looking out over Foundry Street. After the morning service at Wesleyan Methodist Church, he is tending his garden, jabbing at the tomatoes with a rake, making sure his leeks are hardy enough to withstand the frost. The grass is wet. After dragging the rake deeply through the soil in the flowerbed under the house, just to loosen it, he starts to wheeze. He feels drained and settles on a bench, looks at his plum tree.

Ellen comes out of the house with Nero their Scottish terrier and releases him. His wife places a hand on Marwood's shoulder and he looks up and smiles.

"I'll be going to London soon."

"Tomorrow?"

"This evening, I expect. Charles Peace's trial is over and, well, the decision is final. There's a job to be done." Nero is scampering and the hangman watches as a blossom falls from the plum tree and drifts sideways onto the lawn. Another follows and is chased back and forth by the dog, exhilarated and confused by the tiny pink bud.

Ellen smiles, a tad lop-sided. A small woman with reddish hair to her shoulders, she is quiet and yet carries herself with dignity and resilience hard to witness on the surface. She is freckled, her skin fair, and she steps nimbly—as he watches her circle the lawn—like a creature of the forest, a fawn moving through an imagined landscape. For Marwood she is a second wife, his first, Jessey, having died in childbirth with Aldous. Elusive, but not lacking in opinion, Ellen allows Marwood time to work on his private projects, his anatomical diagrams and government tax reform schemes. She is little surprised, though, when he begins a new career as a travelling executioner—and he immediately tries to improve on the mechanisms.

Ellen stands over him now and reads a Mr Motion's article from the local newspaper, *The Horncastle Tribune*:

> There is something intangible in Marwood's character, ladies and gentleman. For all his workmanlike concern, he disappears into the ether, arguably more chilling than William Calcraft, the great bungler and botcher. Where Calcraft was rotund and steadied his belly with wine before a hanging, Marwood hangs 'em sober. Pale and narrow like the Grim Reaper, his dark coat stretching from throat to ankle and a felt cap hiding his receding hairline, Marwood is often found prostrate on the lawn in his front garden, pondering the weights and pulleys of the world, before disappearing into his dungeon room to make calculations...

As she reads, Marwood gazes indifferently at his upturned hands, the coarse fingers, the fine-trimmed nails. He grimaces, not enjoying his whole history being laid bare for 'all and sundry':

> He was born in 1818—lucky double figures—in the village of Goulceby to William and Elizabeth Marwood, the fifth of ten children. His father was a shoe-maker—but William Marwood was first an apprentice miller before following in his footsteps. It is believed this formative alternative career, working the grinding wheel in Red's Windmill on the Lincoln Road, Sleaford, first drew Marwood's mind in the direction of weights used to hang a man as easily as dropping a bag of corn through a trapdoor.

Marwood cannot help himself and scoffs a little. His wife leans closer and her voice is hushed:

But Marwood 'the middling child' is not content to while away the years shoeing the good folk of nearby Horncastle from his workshop in Church Street, to which he repaired (notable pun) aged twenty-six. He is an amateur, solitary student of anatomy—a great fan of Leonardo Da Vinci. He also wishes to publicise his Pythagorean solution to the country's escalating foreign debts. But as hangman, could he truly be an antidote to widespread theft and murder? Clearly, Mr Marwood himself believes his noose brings a 'cure-all', and this self-aggrandisement, the *Tribune* would suggest, originates in his committed Methodism—though by all accounts he is partial to Turkish cigarettes and drinking gin.

Primarily, the key to Marwood is that he cannot brook indolence. Hence a favourite, oft-repeated saying of the Hangman of Horncastle is: "Where there is guilt, there is bad sleeping. It would be better for those I execute if they preferred industry to idleness." Marwood claims that he sleeps soundly, since he lives a blameless life. "Detesting idleness, I pass my vacant time working in my shoe-shop near the church, day after day, until such time as I am required elsewhere."

Most curious is how Marwood was appointed hangman seemingly from nowhere: the public records suggest a determined, self-made man. Believing in his destiny as a do-gooder, he frequently pestered Albert Corsair, the governor of Lincoln Gaol, to permit his 'hanging show' of innovative techniques. The gaol rented him an underused gallows, pressed into theatrical service. Within days, Marwood performed a full dress rehearsal at the county fair, with his wife Ellen acting the part of mistrusted criminal (rightfully to be executed). This occurred almost four years before Mr Calcraft 'stepped off' into retirement. As we reported at the time, this 'sideshow hanging' seems to have entertained and impressed the gaol officials, markedly the governor, securing ambitious Mr Marwood's reputation when 'the bungler' Calcraft was finally dropped in 1874.

It is said in the alehouses of Lincolnshire that

William Marwood has strangely powerful hands, thin fingers, it's true. But whatever he touches they say is comforted by his touch, as though he has the death-touch. All those who fall under his spell are escorted calmly into the next life. At least in the seconds before the drop!

The words linger. Ellen senses his change in mood, though, and repairs indoors with: "Only for your amusement, William. They have to write something." The wife is gone and the boy appears at his father's shoulder.

"I brought you a rope."

The father snaps it straight. "It's like Isaac Newton, you see, the greater the fall, the harder the force to straighten the rope. Like so!" Marwood claps his hands together and the boy's startled expression makes him sway in the breeze. "I learned that one afternoon, you know, sitting right here looking at the Holy Trinity Church. Suddenly I sensed a shadow in the sky, and looking up, a fine bird of prey—a kestrel—landed right opposite on a gravestone. The bird immediately looked around, and called, and I felt that a signal was being transmitted, so complicated was the low, screeching sound. What do you think happened?"

"I don't know, father."

"Well, after a few seconds a second kestrel appeared and then a third. Their grey wings, Aldous, brushed low under this very plum tree where I was sitting, just as you see me. They hovered perfectly and I could see something in their claws, and not a shrew or a field mouse or anything like that—but crabs from the shore!—they flew from the ocean, son, with crabs upside down in their feet."

The boy appears faintly sick, but cannot turn his head away.

"It's an act of nature, son. They drop these crabs to break them on the road, to get inside their shells. But you know which ones were successful? Only those that knew the trick…"

"The trick?"

Marwood leans forward, and a glint escapes under the pale skin of his eyelid.

"Height," he says. "The ones who knew the right height—not too high, not too low—just enough to crack the shell. Too high and the crab would smash and scatter, too low and the shell splits, yes, but the kestrel would never get inside—to the meat."

"Oh, stop telling the boy horror tales," Ellen says, appearing at the foot of the tree with a tray of water. As she crouches she hands Marwood one glass and Aldous the other, the boy looking over at the gravestone and the missing bird, the water shaking in his hand. Aldous imagines the kestrel sitting there, picking at the inside of the crab's head and its legs waving in the air. "I don't like birds of prey."

Ellen frowns and taps Marwood on the top of the head. "William, you'll put him off working, and the last thing you want is a lazy son."

Marwood smiles and pats the boy on *his* crown. "Aldous will have a clean profession one day, a doctor or a vicar maybe, or a district magistrate. Certainly not a cobbler or a travelling businessman like me."

"There you go again with your euphemisms."

"Euphe-what?"

"You're a travelling showman," she says. "Those bootstraps you brought home from Coventry have all sold out, see."

"Well, all the more reason to go on the road!"

Marwood now struggles to his feet, breaking the boy out of his reverie of kestrels and crabs. Ellen watches as her husband leads Aldous back into the house, ducking for the stone doorway and disappearing into the dim basement. For a second she feels the wind blow her fine blond hair, a few strands touching her mouth which she blows out, surprised. Collecting the trays and drinking water, Ellen peers at the gravestones herself, tries to connect with what Marwood must feel so strongly. She shivers and heads inside, preferring to hide under *petit bourgeois* village life. Is she the wife of a shoemaker, a good man, or someone else entirely? She cannot even say the word.

Her husband re-emerges into the grassy back garden followed by his son, both their shoulders piled with ropes of different sizes. Aldous bears a tray of tools and Marwood has both hands full, stooping to drag a long wooden platform called a 'swinging plinth'. This contraption is rolled on six jangly red wheels, three on either side. Finally Marwood carries a peculiar kind of 'tightening rod' wrapped like a noose around his neck; it trails an ever thinning piece of hemp rose in its wake, black in colour and etched with curious white markings.

"Let the festivities begin!" Marwood cries and Aldous smiles, somewhat alarmed. The father places a wooden clock in its brass holder on the edge of the cordoned-off square of grass. "Now for the bodies!"

They return inside for the sacks of corn, two at a time, and Marwood rearranges them in order of weight smallest to largest along the swinging plinth. A period of maybe twenty minutes now passes. Marwood sits in a wicker chair under the shadow of a long brown fence; Aldous copies him by sitting in a homemade hammock between the apple trees. The hangman takes up some papers from a black surgical bag, the kind employed by doctors making house calls in the middle of the night. He drifts into sombre silence. The son rocks side to side in the hammock, creating an off-key hollow ripple on the tree trunks, while Marwood tips forward and back creaking the wicker chair. A peculiar dissonant harmony is achieved and Aldous grows sleepy. Overhead, the sun creeps into fullness and begins to disperse the clouds.

A head at the kitchen window, Ellen watches as a new experiment takes shape. She hears snippets of Marwood's voice as he tips Aldous from the hammock onto the grass, lifting the boy's chin with a second revelation. "You are a kestrel," Marwood is saying one moment, "so lengthen the rope from seven to eight feet to bring unconsciousness."

"Here, father?"

"Lower down."

"Oh."

Aldous marks the stops with white chalk, pauses and the cobbler makes the cut. Ellen taps on the crude window pane looking out just above waist height at the proceedings. She cannot see their faces, but wishes to remind Marwood to judge age and gender too, as a factor.

"Men are heavier than women," she cries. "I know it for a fact! And older people are lighter."

Marwood kneels down on the wet grass and turns his head sideways, so his face resembles a cylindrical drum used for collecting fruit from the fields, his nose for the handle. "You are a genius," he whispers. "So scientific!"

"I suggest you round up the figures for the men," she says, "and especially the men under forty, for a finishing touch. It's called 'impact force'."

"If you say so, my dear," Marwood's drum-face conveys approval, his feet staggering back. He presses his new measuring chart—a drop table—against the window, upside down. "This is the future of state execution," he says proudly. "No one had such a clean death until my hand!"

"You're a charmer," Ellen whispers to herself in the kitchen, then calls "Not in front of Aldous!"

"Yes, yes," Marwood replies. "Too late for that…"

Ellen squints at the placard in Marwood's hands through the dirty glass. "A system of weights and drops?"

"The markings made by a rigorous mind, dear, for the betterment of mankind—an ideal hanging 'drop', a wholly moral plan."

He is a good man, she tells herself, a good husband. But before he removes the placard from Ellen's view, the title 'weigh the clothed prisoner in pounds the day before execution' catches her eye, 'note 1 pound is 0.454 Kg, 1 foot is 30.5 cm and an inch is 2.5 cm' and finally 'the deceased shall hang for an hour after the execution, as is tradition'.

"Tradition," Ellen says to herself and knits her forehead, "what tradition?" But she dismisses the thought and takes up the rough sacks she is washing in the sink. "One day we will be guests at the town hall…"

Yet even as the thought enters her mind, a tiny image of a hanging body—Marwood's handiwork—leaps out from the calculations. The feeling is one of strange and fearful pride, but a faint disgust which she has to bury, a peculiarly social sense of rejection that she knows sticks to her clothes and her very skin, no matter how much washing she does, when she walks through the streets of Horncastle regarded by the women of the village. *There goes Ellen Marwood,* she hears, *the hangman's wife….talk about living off blood money. She probably even killed his first wife, and that's why he married her!*

At that moment, the table of drops is whisked away by the father-and-son team, but the image remains imprinted somewhere inside Ellen's conscience, hovering behind her conflicted face, proud and fearful at the same time. Above Ellen—giving the impression that she is underground—in the elevated garden displaying mostly his legs, Marwood is reading out the drop figures. Like another day at school, Aldous marks them with feather and ink on fresh parchment:

1892 table	
Weight of prisoner (in pounds)	Drop (in feet & inches)
105 & under	8' 0"
110	7' 10"
115	7' 3"
120	7' 0"
125	6' 9"
130	6' 5"
135	6' 2"
140	6' 0"
145	5' 9"
150	5' 7"
155	5' 5"
160	5' 3"
165	5' 1"
170	4' 11"
175	4' 9"
180	4' 8"
185	4' 7"
190	4' 5"
195	4' 4"
200 & over	4' 2"

So goes the theory—but Marwood's voice does not waver. Already the pulley is firing its first sack of corn over the brown fence, and vertically down to Foundry Lane. Immediately father and son peer over the fence from a corner of the garden—the highest vertical. Four feet below, the rough sack has burst in the dirt and corn is seeping from its wound. No one is around, though, since Foundry Lane is no more than a muddy track, a shortcut to Wesleyan Methodist Church. The hangman leans over the fence, his mind an intelligent spring recoiling itself, already aware of the adjustment needed.

"Too heavy," he says, and points at Aldous. "Raise the back of the plinth." The boy struggles with a wooden lever designed with a cog for lifting the corn higher, but the sack has already loaded and the whole operation is too heavy. Aldous stands wheezing in the pale sunshine, puzzled by his father's impositions. Wasting no time, Marwood skips over the fence and takes the weight, one arm holding the sack the other cranking the lever and balancing like a scarecrow, his legs stretching in a ridiculous posture. Aldous watches in half bafflement, half delight. "I forgot to round off the weight."

"Too late now!" Marwood cries. He positions the plinth at a diagonal angle and as he pulls a cord, the sack of corn slides down the plinth, catching slightly on the fence to simulate the static resistance of passing through the trapdoor. The rope rushes behind it, loose for about a second, flicks taut, and the experiment is suddenly over. From nowhere there's a scream, a woman seemingly in mortal terror, and Marwood peers down over the fence into the lane. An old woman, quite refined-looking in a purple bonnet—clearly on her way back from church—looks up in sunlight into Marwood's face. Again the sack has burst, but this time he can see why—the noose on the sack mouth is too tight—causing a shower of unexpected corn.

"You be more careful, young man," the old woman cries, "you could have killed somebody!"

"And scattering so much corn! I do apologise. Aldous, you know what to do!" The boy exits through a small trap-like door at the foot of the apple tree and appears in no time to help the old lady.

"Mrs Grimes," Aldous says.

"The same." She is batting herself down. "I'll thank you not to send explosions to catapult me into the next life. You Marwoods are all the same, always up to tricks!"

"We apologise, don't we, son?"

"Yes I…we do," Aldous says, flustered.

"I'll have the constable onto you."

"I know Inspector Mackay personally," Marwood says. "He is happy I conduct my drops here, out of harm's way."

Mrs Grimes stares incredulous and picks up her parasol, covered in mud after being frightened by Marwood's experiment. "Ruining people's belongings, just so you can ruin their lives." She looks up and down the street and then—Marwood is suspicious he knows what's coming—she spits quite magnificently at his feet. The saliva escapes her gums, lands harmlessly on the grass verge, and she shakes her scrawny fist. "We'd be better off without your kind," Mrs Grimes now adds, "to hell with you!"

"Thank you," Marwood replies, his wit momentarily lost.

Aldous lets go of her arm, and away Mrs Grimes stumbles in the direction of the High Street where people are passing, flattening her hat on her bird-like cranium as she goes. Pasted to her cheeks, grey hairs straddle her head with no suggestion of them meeting on her crown. He watches her go.

The excitement passes and man and boy resume their macabre experiments. Marwood begins chewing a pencil and after an hour or so, he takes to the hammock in unprovoked depression. "Please clear up the spilled corn, Aldous," he instructs, if only to occupy the boy and deflect some of his disappointment. And yet in watching Aldous move back and forth among the instruments, stepping from one apple tree to the next, resetting the handle crank on the plinth and being generally obedient, something remarkable happens. Marwood has a revelation.

"A man of fourteen stones," he is whispering, "given an eight feet drop, every half stone lighter would require another two-inch drop...."

"They seem so much heavier now," Aldous says.

"Yes," Marwood replies absently.

"Like they were made of lead. Just 'cos we fired 'em."

"So much heavier," Marwood repeats. "Yes, that's it." He gestures to a piece of parchment in his hand. "My *ready reckoner* is all wrong!"

"Father?"

"What did you say, Aldous? What did you say?"

"They are like lead."

"No, before that."

Marwood is all entangled in the hammock now, swinging uncontrollably. In surprise, Aldous cannot keep the sack of corn balanced on the firing drum—the same pulley system used on the third floor of a windmill just above the trapdoor—and away goes the corn sack flying through the air. Open-mouthed, Marwood staggers to his feet, expecting the sack to hit him and cause another revelation, but instead, it lands calmly at his feet and does not split.

"That's it!"

"Eureka," Aldous jokes. "At last!"

"The scale on my drop scale," Marwood continues, "shows the striking force of falling bodies *at different distances*, not different speeds. The machine is all wrong! We need the height to be different, not the speed of propulsion!"

"We need faster bags, father?"

"No, we need lighter bags, dropped from less height! Look at the weight—our bags are too heavy!"

Aldous turns to inspect the corn sacks, each about half the weight of a man but fired at twice the speed of gravity. Due to the swinging plinth, until now he believed speed was the answer—the faster the vertical projection, the greater the impact, the slower the fall the lesser the impact. But now he realises that speed is not necessary—it only knocks down the Mrs Grimeses of this world—since nature provides her own acceleration.

"I think I understand."

"We only need to remove the height of the condemned from the length of the rope," the executioner whispers. Marwood rushes over and crouches before his son, but resists taking the startled boy in his arms even at this split second of joyful epiphany. He remains a scientist-father.

"But...I don't understand."

Marwood scruffs up the boy's hair, scratches his chin. Next to Aldous's foot is an apple, pressed soft from lying in the shallow grass for several days. Marwood picks it up and taps it on Aldous's head, making the boy smile and frown. Then he drops it between their eyes, picks it up and drops it again.

"Gravity," he says. "Newton had the answer long ago. All we need is the machine, and gravity will do the rest." He raises his hands to the clouds, and mumbles a prayer.

For the rest of the day, Aldous is allowed to play outside since his father needs his quiet time. The boy goes out roaming the fields, his head full of pulleys, sacks of corn, disgruntled old ladies, and a magical force called gravity that apparently makes apples grow.

Back in the basement, Marwood abandons his machinery, the swinging plinth and pulley designed to imitate the rotation of a body and gruesomely inspired by the 'drawing' of the ancient punishment of being 'hanged, drawn and quartered'. As he already knows, the 'drawn' is more important than it seems, referring to the force necessary to swing the half-strangled victim to the anatomical table to suffer a torturous demise and pains beyond description. In layman's terms, without the 'drawn', there is no 'quartered'.

Now alone with his books and his reading of such 'crown

wickedness', Marwood pursues the idea of a moral hanging. Only partly discouraged by the failure of his corn sack device, he realises he must focus on the straight drop. History claims—aside from the 'jerk 'em up' technique from the young republic of America where felons are strangled upwards, raising their feet off the ground—the straight drop is the preferred English method. So with new inspiration Marwood drags his wicker chair inside, lights a thin Turkish cigarette, and with a glass of weak gin he resorts to reading the great minds of the past. A sane way to hang criminals cannot be far away!

By adapting his shoe-making skills to dismantling old clocks—a hobby he developed in his late forties—Marwood sits somewhat disconsolately for the next several hours, and is therefore surprised when the revelation returns. Almost unconsciously, he adapts the diagonal firing plinth into a vertical trapdoor. This change alone will create the straight drop as opposed to the skewed projection of his garden experiments. There is no stopping him. Next, as the light fades on this curious Valentine's Day, he combines a table of weights and drops into a new chart of more accurate figures—not particularly devastating in its appearance, but one many condemned men and women would be thankful to know. "Wouldn't you prefer the less painful method," he whispers to himself, "if you were tied at the end of a rope?"

Eventually he takes up Homer's *The Odyssey*, reminded of a passage in which Telemachus delivers a multiple hanging, Telemachus, son of Ulysses and 'the first hangman' of history. At that moment Marwood hears Ellen on the stairs, her gentle step intended to disturb without alarming him. Suddenly she is there, smiling, leaning on the wall. Her white blouse with its blue lining is lost in the darkness. In seeing her, Marwood remembers why he was attracted to her those five years ago when they met at a church fete, ironic by being one of the few days of the year when Catholic and Methodist churches agreed to share space on the Horncastle village green. Back then they were devout church-goers keenly loyal to their own denomination; Marwood has since slipped into his other more intellectual passions over the years, while Ellen has remained passionately Catholic—worse luck for Marwood—from pulpit to bedroom.

Seeing her cast in light, Marwood is pleased to have a caring wife, even though the desire of their first years has naturally waned.

Ellen enters the gloom of his basement work space, lifting a plank of wood aside, and balances on an armchair long abandoned from upstairs. Dust floats up, a collection of dead cells scattering to reveal her softly smiling face, a single tooth chipped at the corner of her mouth challenging her charm. Soon enough, murder and hanging are forgotten and the subject settles on the salvation of the mortal soul.

"Have you ever wondered," Ellen says, "why to reach the Catholic Church you must pass by Wesleyan Methodist? One is always first, whether you walk by Jubilee Way or Wharf Road to Church Lane—even around to Foundry."

"I don't know what you're suggesting. One thing I'll say is that both are better than Presbyterian—all that Calvinistic-style fate and pre-destination. Depression on the brain!"

"That's why we don't know any Presbyterians."

"True, true."

"At least you're a good solid Methodist who believes in free will, the ability of man to control and shape his own destiny."

Ellen smirks. "So that's why you can take a life?"

Marwood pauses and lays aside *The Odyssey*. "Quite a statement, Ellen. Free will is the essence of man, to kill or be executed, or be redeemed in the next life."

"That book,"—she taps her nails on Homer—"claims there is no afterlife, just an underworld."

"For the heathens," Marwood agrees and suspiciously removes the book.

"Catholics believe in free will too. Just a modified form of self-regulating free will."

"Yes, with strict boundaries, and God help you if you defy the doctrine...."

Ellen stands—the cue for their agreeing to disagree. "Just make sure Aldous is in before dark," she says, pointing at the back garden through a blackened grille, "in case the Bogeyman of Horncastle executes some free will."

"Aren't I the Bogeyman of Horncastle?"

Ellen smiles and taps on her chipped tooth. "You'll be the death of me, William Marwood." She rises along with the armchair dust and leaves her beloved hangman to his book; at the stairs, though, she turns in response to his reading the following out loud:

"Once some European travellers, the best in the land, suffered the unfortunate fate of being cast away on a desolate foreign shore. Finding human skeletons rotting in gibbets on the beach, rather than retreat fearfully into the waves, they rejoiced to the heavens. For now they knew they'd landed in a Christian country."

Marwood looks up, but Ellen is not amused.

"I will leave you to your games," she says. "Mind the boy."

"I will."

"We can't have him growing up like you."

"One more story," Marwood begs, "then you can go."

She is exasperated, but something about the entreaty in Marwood's voice and the strange scrutiny of his face delays her. The reading does not matter to her, and she does not listen much—more jokes about hanging and the plaintive twist of history.

"Once in the Welsh mountains…" Marwood begins, but the rest is a blur for her, except for his fixed determined look, the pleasure of his reading suspended by the horror of another tale.

Often Ellen recognises the same intensity in Aldous, this air of profound concentration, a quiet indifference to the world that paradoxically cares for its fellow man. She is reminded that Aldous is not her son by birth, but by inheritance; guiltily she thinks of Jessey Marwood. What kind of woman was she, what kind of wife? All Ellen knows is that Jessey was the daughter of a local policeman, and her gravestone is now completely overgrown in the Wesleyan Cemetery. This strange quality of disconnection, whether born of William or Jessey, survives in Aldous, the boy growing up in the house of the cobbler-hangman. For minutes Ellen's feeling persists, its explanation beyond the reach of the tangible world—that father and son somehow know that life's answers do not lie in human relations but in abstract fantasy worlds—Aldous with his adult toy soldiers, Marwood with his boyhood science tests played out with sacks of corn, ropes, pieces of old shoe straps.

At moments like these, Ellen feels that she does not belong, that she has no family at all, and that she is drifting through her own life simply waiting for the noose of ageing to tighten. Nevertheless she retreats to the stairs leading to the candlelit kitchen, but then changes her mind, and takes a seat beside her mysterious husband on the night he leaves for London.

The next hour passes with Marwood reading aloud details of Telemachus's shady profession. In a close translation of book twenty-two of *The Odyssey*, he tells how Penelope had a dozen impure handmaidens, all of whom her son decides to hang for their sin of no longer being virginal assistants to the queen, for daring to hint by proxy at Her Majesty's lack of faith. Telemachus's judgement is final. In a feat that is part magic, part brutal injustice, he suspends them all on a single rope circling the public dome.

Sickened by the story, Ellen shakes her head and demands Marwood to stop, so he resorts to a looser description of the scene. He takes up a recent monograph titled *On Hanging* (1866) by a respectable fellow of Trinity College Dublin, one Reverend Samuel Haughton, MD. At the author's spiritual sounding name, Ellen is consoled to hear the classical tale of the hanging—for better or worse. In a voice sad and meaningful, knowing the heart of Telemachus's scientific approach was moral if misguided, Marwood continues:

" 'The son of Ulysses was able to execute twelve women on a cable, its ends double secured...and although the science of neck-breaking was in its infancy, with a 'short drop' death *naturally* follows asphyxia caused by crushing of the windpipe, or apoplexy owing to pressure on the jugular'."

"What does that mean?"

"It means it's very painful, with convulsions lasting five to forty-five minutes."

"Why are you reading this to me?" Ellen suddenly bursts out. "It's terrible blasphemy! It'll send us all to hell."

Marwood catches the fire in her eyes. "But this is great poetry," he protests, "admittedly in translation, but by one of the finest classical poets!"

"No one even knows who Homer was or where he lived," Ellen cries back. "Explain to me why I have to listen to this sordid, inhuman nonsense!"

"Sordid maybe," Marwood replies, "but not inhuman. Never inhuman....I am reading the origins of hanging to help explain my discovery. How else to let the bags fall?"

"The bags?"

"The sandbags—they must fall, not swing!"

Ellen stares at him, incredulous. "I must find my son," she says, and pushes past Marwood for the back garden and Foundry Lane, all the time thinking of her predecessor's overgrown grave, how it could so easily be her. "Jessey's spirit is alive in the world," she mouths.

"What did you say?" Marwood asks. "Listen, it's all in Haughton's book, only he never put it into practice! **A 'long drop' death is a shock to the brain caused by snapping of the spinal column. Instantaneous and painless, no convulsions! A hangman must decide professionally: if he is stringent, there will be strangulation and long suffering, but if he is too subtle, the head may depart the body. A decapitation is swift and painless, but it loses its pleasantness and propriety....**

"Pleasantness and propriety! Decapitation!" Ellen cries, and she breaks open the door to Marwood's basement like she is opening the lid to a tomb or catacomb. "Time we had some air in this crypt. Aldous! Where are you?" She is gone.

"Thus Haughton's formula for a perfect hanging," Marwood whispers and reads on, not looking up. **Divide the weight of the patient in pounds into 2240, and the quotient will give the length of the long drop in feet. For example, a criminal weighing 160 pounds should be allowed a 14 feet drop.** He ruminates: "A tall client would need less rope than a short one, yes, to drop the same distance. At which point I cut the rope and make the noose..."

Later, as he supplements the rising moonlight with a tallow candle, Marwood reads a horrible story of man who was executed with a tracheotomy that they didn't know about. As Haughton describes, **the drop was too short, so the doctor had to put his finger over the aperture and so complete the clumsy work of the hangman.**

"So much for the Hippocratic oath," Marwood says grimly. "The aim of my enterprise is to reduce human suffering, including a criminal's last experience in retribution for his crimes. But how can I possibly reconcile the two?"

Such overtly moral recollections are difficult when Haughton reminds us that Telemachus hung the women **like bluebeard's wives, tit tat toe, all in a row!** Sometimes Marwood is not free from such thoughts himself, glancing down on the occasions he cannot resist to pictures of the murdered women—mid-execution—made to dance upon the air.

The moon is up.

"Made to dance upon the air...dance upon the air..." Marwood mumbles, half asleep. **From eight stone to sixteen stone, seven feet for heavy customers, twelve feet for the lightest and very long**

drops, probably with decapitations. Beautiful young women—innocent too—dancing upon the air…"

At nine o'clock Pierre Cruikshank arrives with the carriage and sounds the cow-bell he keeps in the front seat. At the same moment Ellen appears in the basement with Aldous, who was discovered arranging flowers on the gravestones of St David's Catholic Church.

"At least it was the Catholic Church," she says and as the bell grows impatient, Marwood follows them up. Here he says his goodbyes, taking Ellen close to his chest.

"Come back in one piece," she jokes.

"Never fear," Marwood says. "I go with God." Then he takes the black bag he has prepared for his weeklong visit to London—two days to reach the capital, three days to execute his professional duty, two days to return. "Let Aldous fix the February shoes in my absence. I've laid them out."

"Don't worry, William. Now you be careful."

A knock at the door reveals Pierre Cruikshank, a short powerful fellow with a tweed hat and sporting an ear of corn in his mouth, even after nightfall.

"Don't worry, Mrs M," he announces. "The killer's in safe hands with me! At least as far as Cambridge." And he rocks back his head and laughs. Ellen frowns, but Aldous doesn't seem to notice, his imagination caught by the ear of corn. Marwood notices, though, and plucks the stalk from Cruikshank's mouth and hands it to the boy.

"Quick hands," Cruikshank remarks.

Directly Marwood boards the carriage and Ellen and his son stand in the doorway to wave goodbye. For a few minutes Cruikshank struggles with two metal boxes containing Marwood's instruments and other new devices, miniature hanging constructions including a portable guillotine and some rope tools.

Meanwhile Marwood sits up front in the carriage, raised with peculiarly comedy high in the air. The moon cuts across his silhouetted figure, creating a strange mixture of a dapper undertaker and a skinny highwayman—men of life's borderlands. At that moment a dog comes rushing from under the house, a black Labrador with a white bushy mane, a mongrel recluse.

"Stay, Nero!" Marwood shouts from the carriage, and the dog is perplexed, head lolling. The moment is suspended, the dog uncertain of its master at so high an elevation, until Aldous steps forward and slips his fingers around Nero's invisible black collar; the gesture is minor but heartfelt, and Ellen places her hand on her son's head. Marwood looks away, almost betraying sadness but then corrects himself. Instead, he squints ahead past Church Lane into the open fields. A single scarecrow leans there, long since abandoned to the winter since last Hallow'en. Marwood can't remember if he has seen the scarecrow before, so he shifts his vision to the dirt track winding out of the village, another suffocating outpost far from the centre of life, and his eyes close with one more dream of London, his family quite forgotten.

Nero starts to bark. With a single whip of the carriage horse at the Marwood cottage gate, Cruikshank starts up the slow creaking of the large wooden water wheels—a 'Lincolnshire try' to imitate the hansom cabs of London—and they roll away. Not a word is shouted and Ellen resists raising her hand in case the message is one of approval for her husband's trip. Suspended in dim light, Marwood bounces up and down looking wholly incongruous, an undertaker on the way to the fair.

Aldous runs after the carriage, counting the spokes of the wheel as they triple over and over, blurring into one. Suddenly half way down the street Nero stops, and the effect is peculiar and painterly, the wife left at the house, the dog caught between the traveller and the home, puzzled—not knowing its new master, or its old—and the boy mesmerised by the scene, no more knowing this moment will change his life too. When will he see his father again? The thought does not enter his mind, pushed out by the marvellous speed of the carriage, a rare and expensive sight in Horncastle, and the sudden snort of cold air from the horse's nostrils, every indication that it came from the top of Marwood's head.

But at the end of Church Lane, as the carriage draws level with *The Portland Arms* about thirty yards from the Marwoods' cottage, it slows where two burly men are leaning predatorily on the pub wall. Aldous begins to feel quite different. Here he is, already in the village, and he can see the square and the clock tower lit, dimly, by the newly installed kerosene lamps long debated by the village council and secured in their Victorian lampposts. All is quiet. The carriage rocks an instant as though balanced on a precipice, the spokes slow to their individual eight, but Aldous does not count them. His eye is caught by the Tooley brothers and without knowing why, he is afraid. As the carriage turns and slides away through patches of darkness into the future, Aldous retreats, stepping gingerly over mud patches to where Ellen now stands in a distant doorway beckoning. He looks at his feet. A single piece of rope has fallen off the carriage, and he catches sight of it in the dim light, picks it up and turns it over in his fingers. He can tell it is Virginia hemp, the kind his father imports from America.

"A hanging rope," Aldous says and raises it high so the Tooleys can see. They point and smirk.

Then he turns to Church Lane again, just a boy caught between young life and Marwood's double professions. He follows Nero back home, the dog's tail despondently caught between its legs, the boy's rope on his shoulders, hanging lightly down his back.

Meanwhile a quite different mood has settled over the carriage as it cuts along the barren hedgerows and onto the Cambridge Road.

"The gibbet or the gallows cure?" Cruikshank is saying, steadying his lantern near the swishing horse's tail. "What's the difference?"

"No difference," Marwood says. He pulls his hat down to his cheeks for protection from the wind. "It's the old practice of a tumble and a kick. Both will cure you in the end."

"A tumble and a kick sounds like a good time, at least with some o' tha' girls I know."

Marwood refuses to take the bait. They discuss trapdoors for a while. It appears Marwood wants the prisoner encumbered by fewer steps to the scaffold. "The whole system needs overhauling in London for definite. Why make the prisoner suffer?"

Cruikshank coughs into his hand, wipes back his long hair. "The prisoner? What about the crowd? The ol' day out for the family?"

"Don't you mean the victim? What about their extended pain?" Marwood asks instead, closing his eyes as he feels the bumps in the road. "All's well 'cos the victim's suffering is over and done?"

"Right, guv'nor," Cruikshank retorts. "They're either dead or fled, so what's the difference matter to 'em."

"So what's justice all about?" Marwood asks. "Who is a hanging for?"

"Why, the people of course," Cruikshank says, pleased to have 'got one right', and eyes Marwood suspiciously. "Ask me a harder one! The state execution is 'right and just before God', end of story."

"And what about as a deterrence?"

"As a what?"

"Never mind."

The carriage lurches and Cruikshank again whips the horse, straightening her line on the road. "There's some apples ahead," he whispers in the animal's ear, only to receive an unpleasant snort. "The girl's too old, an' she'll probably end up killing us." He laughs a little too raucously but Marwood keeps a straight face.

A few minutes pass. "So I want no steps," the hangman says, "since it only weakens the knees, and makes the 'show'—as you'd say—harder to pass off smoothly. The last thing anyone wants is a delay, or a botched job. History is scattered with failed and half successful hangings, and they are not pretty. I want ramps and a pit below a trapdoor. No official hanging has yet to happen in this way, but—"

Here Marwood takes out a notebook and a pencil and begins to write, periodically adding phrases about drops and weights, height n' health of the 'deceased to be'—while Cruikshank is quiet, but finds himself shivering despite his sheepskin coat.

"Quite a grim business you got there, Mr Marwood. Hope you don't mind I ask—you ever get lonely?"

Marwood is momentarily caught off guard by the question and his face shows it. "No," he says, slowly, a touch defensively, "why would I?"

"Well, the people you work with are either putting people to death, or being put to death. Where's the life in that?"

Somehow this is the funniest thing Marwood has heard in a while, and the joke builds through his drawn-out face, not quite adding colour but a fascinated kind of passion so that his crows-feet all but disappear. His laugh is more of a cackle, halted in mid-cry because Marwood knows it is strange and bird-like, not at all suitable for public consumption. The end trails off in a wheezing sound, revealing the small pincer-like teeth he prefers to keep hidden. "I am a sober man," he says, "performing a sober trade. And the world needs more men like me."

"And fewer of the rest of us?"

"What are you suggesting?"

For a while they travel in silence. The carriage skips the potholes on the Cambridge Road, passing headstones marking 153 miles, 151 miles, and the occasional resting house. After a few hours they stop to water Ol' Betsy but Cruikshank resists giving her hay in case she becomes sleepy. So on she plods, and once again the men resume their hit-and-miss conversation.

"So I want an execution platform—a balcony opening to the street for the spectacle for the paying public—with the stage mounted on the same level as the condemned cell. In other words, no steps…"

"Indeed. You're a kind of artist, I suppose—eh?"

"Yes," replies Marwood. "'Yes—I call myself an artist—a fancy workman. Art improves nature'—as Ned Dennis the Hangman would say—'that's my motto'."

"Who's Dennis the Hangman?"

"Dickens," Marwood says, with a wide smile at odds with his long face. "One of my Sunday indulgences, you know, reading. Do you read, Mr Cruikshank?" He looks sideways at the driver, the reflection of the carriage in the moonlight casting silver shadows across Cruikshank's face, revealing a long scar. Marwood returns to his notebook, points out a few potholes in the road.

"Only the Bible," Cruikshank says. "The Book of Revelation—the Lord will return on a pale white horse, like Ol' Betsy 'ere, to judge the living and the dead. And then there'll be a big war between good n' evil—the Battle of Armageddon, right?"

"Exactly, Mr Cruikshank, the living and the dead. And the Lord will lead us into battle, and there shall be no more good and no more evil, just a holy battlefield."

Cruikshank's eyes widen at the prospect. "Should make things round here a touch more exciting."

"I imagine it will."

"So you have a steady hand, Mr Marwood?" He passes the reins across and the new driver's hands do not shake.

"The cool, calculating eye of an artist?"

"Like a Lincolnshire Turner."

"A what?"

"Our great painter, J. W. M. Turner."

"Oh 'im, yes."

"Sure, I practice art for art's sake. For the sake of my patrons." Marwood attempts to whip the horse, but remembers he only has the reins.

He hands them back.

Losing the thread of the conversation, Cruikshank goes quiet. But moments later, sensing Marwood's reading of *Barnaby Rudge* by lantern-light, he interrupts the hangman's quiet time to remark on his famous uncle—the illustrator George Cruikshank, who worked with Dickens until recently.

"I am not really a literary man, though," Marwood says, "but a man of science."

"So was Dickens, according to my uncle, so was Dickens."

"True enough," Marwood says, smiling as though searching for a confidante, a keen sparkle in his eyes suggesting Cruikshank may be harmless, so he continues with vocational purposefulness: "Too many cruel and dangerous men have sullied this profession, Mr Cruikshank. Scared men who couldn't sleep, drunks and wife-beaters, those who couldn't live with the consequences of their actions—you know the type. I want to dignify the profession, and get rid of these ghosts." Marwood pauses, conscious of the contradiction, reminded of how he once admired these men only to discover their failings. "The science of hanging has not changed in eight hundred years—not since the Anglo-Saxons brought the noose over in their Viking ships. True, we don't execute people by tying them in a sack with a monkey, a snake and a cockerel. We're no longer barbaric, Mr Cruikshank."

"Of course not, Mr Marwood."

"But the bungling old Calcrafts, all the Jack Ketch hangmen of the past must be forgotten—and make way for a new man, a strong man."

"A man like you?"

Cruikshank regards him shrewdly, and to his surprise Marwood reaches across and lays his hands on the reins. Instinctively Cruikshank lets go, and a curious thing happens. The horse stops. Her head rises and she sniffs the air, but the dead steady hand of the hangman, floating unseen in the night, is enough to calm her. Like drawing a last breath, a pure night calm settles over the whole carriage, the wheels stop, Marwood is still and there is no sound from the surrounding fields. All is quiet except for Cruikshank who can feel his heart beating under his rib-cage. Marwood leans in closer, his hat slipping a little from his cheeks, Cruikshank catching a whiff of his stale breath.

Again Marwood takes the reins. "By sectioning them off in my mind," he taps his head, "by reading about the victims, by knowing all the failed executions of the past in Lincolnshire and London, I know *what has to be done*. There will be another criminal—they're never too far behind the last hanging or the next holiday. Charles Peace has been caught, Mr Cruikshank, and I intend to hang him. In the meantime I aim to improve—to humanise—hanging. Do you understand?"

Cruikshank can barely move, and he feels a pulse touch his throat in a kind of panic.

"Hangmen are tricksters, Mr Cruikshank, and many of them were shoemakers or clockmakers, or worked in a belfry tower, or were keepers of the peace. Men who intimately knew engineering, ropes, or just common men raised to greatness because they grew a conscience, you see?" Marwood's finger grips the rope a little tighter, and Betsy obediently takes a step and pauses. She whinnies, caught in his magic hand, the gentle strength of the skilled hangman equal parts reassurance, equal parts authority. "These men had experience, like me, of the pinions and straps used to keep a murderer's arms down. You can't have a dying man's arms flailing about while you're trying to—"

This is too much for Cruikshank and without warning he jabs Marwood in the chest with his elbow, causing the hangman to tumble across the carriage, crashing low to the side door. It's a fast and unexpected move—the tension has been building—but like a coiled spring Marwood's body, instead of causing him to fly into the road, simply bends under the pressure. His head comes flinging at Cruikshank at such speed for a second it appears free of his body, ghost-like, his eyes blurred and ears twisted. The movement is unintentional and more of a lucky ricochet. But the driver ducks, not without some contact to his chin causing it to redden, while his straw hat flies up and is lost in darkness. Then it's all over.

"I apologise, Mr Marwood," he whispers breathlessly, clutching at his straggling hair. "But I was getting right scared by your speech—seems you enjoy your job, sir."

Before Marwood can react he notices the peculiar expression on the driver's face, a mixture of false fear and honest patronage. "It's too much, Mr Cruikshank. I will have to get down from this contraption."

"Truth be told, I wasn't too happy about picking you up."

Marwood presses his chest at the impact and rubs a circle. Meanwhile the driver touches his throat and his ear—he looks pale. Without another word Cruikshank retakes the reins, directing Betsey to halt under an overhanging oak—she does so. Across the adjoining frozen field, they witness the first glimpse of dawn, its silver haze softening the light of the two men's faces.

"I will take you to the station, anyways, Mr Marwood, as agreed."

"If you would be so kind," the hangman strains himself to reply.

The journey now continues in silence for several hours. Marwood drifts in and out of consciousness ruminating about his executioner predecessor, William Calcraft, not least because Calcraft was also a cobbler and desperate to escape a common occupation. "He hanged them; I execute them," he says in his dreams to the rocking of the carriage, and sensing—for the first time—what it must be like to swing on the end of the rope. Rarely does he dream of the executions, but the altercation with Cruikshank has set his nerves—usually so controlled—on knife edge. He sweats, and cries out, feeling the drop, the intake of breath, the snap, and the creak of the rope. It's only a dream, just a travelling nightmare. With a clatter of wheels pulling into the train terminal, Marwood is awake.

They have reached Cambridge Railway Station, the outskirts of its city's college doors and cobbled streets close enough to touch, but only a few spires give note of the university sleeping all around. The station's long classical *façade* and *porte-cochère* is before them, its famous solitary platform appearing through the arches as their carriage draws to a halt and Cruikshank leaps down. He immediately begins unloading Marwood's cases.

The hangman now ponderously lowers himself to the street, dusts his shirt down, and unfolds his long black coat to his ankles. He smiles at a nearby fruit-seller and buys an apple which he proceeds to throw up in the air with false jollity. Cruikshank presents his bags to the 'station boy' rushing over the rails dividing third- and first-class ends of the platform. A perk of his profession, Marwood will travel to London first-class. Pausing a moment, Cruikshank takes the horse's reins and waits for his tip, which Marwood begrudges him with a joke about the cost of modern travel.

"I would not see you go without, Mr Cruikshank, and then see you on the platform."

"You mean the hanging platform?"

"Of course, what other platform is there?"

Cruikshank shivers in the cold morning air, takes the tip of a half crown. He is tipped more by a common labourer for the same journey, but he's not in a complaining spirit. As they stand there a train rushes by, all the carriages blurred with marvellous speed—twenty miles per hour.

"An express," Marwood says, his voice echoing under the portico. "What an invention!"

"Just like your trapdoor idea," Cruikshank comments.

Marwood lets him have the last word, accustomed by now to the suspicion and fear he suffers at the hands of the public. He watches the carriage roll away in the dust, Cruikshank's new straw hat bobbing on top. Then he instructs the boy to lug his bags and boxes to the third-class end of the bay platform, a terminus for derelict engine parts and twisted metal, train doors all piled together but attached to nothing. He regards the doors with a frown.

At this hour, the newly appointed hangman for Sussex and London will travel cheaply—in third-class—and reclaim the first-class ticket on expenses. If he didn't receive a 'per rope' payment, he wonders, might he one day experience first-class travel? "I can only hope. Train is the greatest invention since the wheel—not including the rope, of course." The boy stares at the man talking to himself, only to be met by a calm expression.

Marwood regards the wooden board pinned to a brick wall announcing the day's trains in bright white chalk. The Varsity Line to Oxford, trains to the North and Leeds, 'The Flying Scotsman' to Edinburgh expected at four o'clock. The 'stopping train' to Hitchins runs on the City line: *Harston, Foxton, Shepreth, Meldreth, Royston, Ashwell and Morden, Baldock, Letchworth Garden City, Hitchin*. He's visited not a single place, and realizing this, Marwood feels an even greater urge to arrive at King's Cross. Fortunately, a wall map is hung by string to the City route's wooden board. Using this, he traces the Eastern Counties

Railway with the more permanent-looking Metropolitan route: *Stevenage, Knebworth, Welwyn Garden City, Hatfield, Welham Green, Brookmans Park, Potters Bar, Hadley Wood, New Barnet, Oakleigh Park, New Southgate Alexandra Palace, Hornsey, Harringay, Finsbury Park, London King's Cross*—a long line but a faster A2 train that can really clip along.

"The end of the line," Marwood whispers, and he rolls a brass ring deep in his pocket. It's not his marriage ring, not any jewellery, but the ring he will slip along the coiled rope under Charles Peace's neck. "Next stop, King's Cross, London town where I am king for a day...."

William Marwood, crown employee, methodical shoemaker, family man, at the same time is excited by the prospect of delivering a feat of mortal magic. He waits patiently. "The lady of the Old Bailey has decided. Charles Peace is guilty, and Newgate must have her day—so shall all the people of London!"

Quietly he reaches down and picks up his heavy black bag, rolling the ring through his fingers, pensively watching the morning mists weave up and down the Cambridge-London line. The weight feels right—just enough rope.

When Ellen goes to bed that Valentine's night the wind is picking up, cutting over the low-ploughed fields behind Foundry Lane. As she climbs the stairs from foyer to bedrooms, on the wall opposite is a picture of a hangman, one per double step. Here is Marwood's collection from Ketch to Calcraft—all the hangmen who came before—not their stories, but the expression in their eyes. Ellen once enjoyed these images early in their marriage when Marwood would make fun of the men—all dead and gone—describing them as comic grotesques and pulling faces to ridicule them.

Such unlikely buffoonery now. Reaching the top of the stairs she regards the last picture and is shocked even though she knows what to expect. It is Marwood himself—smiling from one corner of his mouth, long chin clear with intent, the purposeful reformation of society shining through his eyes.

"The man I love," Ellen whispers to herself, and she reaches to touch Marwood on the face, but her hand hovers, almost searching for the love-line on his cheek, a place unmarked by black hairs looping from wet hair slicked for the photographer—but she does not find it. Instead she lays her hand by her chest, smiles at her husband's joke of adding his head to the rogue's gallery, not without a shiver.

An hour later the house is silent, but not everyone is in bed. His father far away, Aldous goes downstairs to eat some bread and cheese, but doesn't go back upstairs. Instead he descends the cellar steps, curious to discover a secret or two, the disturbances of the evening fresh in his head. He lights a candle and secures it in the kerosene holder, takes the steps one at a time. Lining the basement wall are pictures of the French guillotines used in the Paris revolution, the faces of Robespierre and Lavoisier—he's has ignored them countless times. "Victims of The Mighty Widower!"

Carefully he steps down into the cool basement. Facing him is Marwood's work table. Here Aldous sits and touches the wood smoothed by the planning and stringing of a thousand shoes. Beside the vice, its edge folded under a chisel, he spies a piece of paper. Without thinking he unpeels it, the date showing first, and discovers a letter dated 1869, ten years' old.

Knowing little of his father's work away from the cobbler's room, Aldous reads the poorly written note, and only now, more than the guillotine pictures, black gallows humour, the ropes and buckles, or pieces of clothing and hair his father sells in the market on Sundays, the double life of William Marwood is brought to life:

Sir, in Replie to your Letter of this Day I will give you a Compleat Staitment for Executing a Prisoner.
1-Pinnion the Prisoner Round the Boadey and Arms Tight.
2-Place Bair The Neck.
3-Take The Prisoner to the Drop.
4-Place the Prisoner Beneath the Beam to stand Direct under the Rope from the Top of the Beam.
5-Strap the Prisoners Leggs Tight.
6-Putt on the Cap.
7-Putt on the Rope Round the Neck Thite. Let the Cap be Free from the Rope to hide the Face angin Down in Frunt.
8-Executioner to go Direct Quick to the Leaver Let Down the Trap Doors Quick. No—Greas be Putt on the Rope.

Aldous is surprised by the poor spelling of his father, but he is also in awe, the mundane and the macabre details striking his imagination. Little does he know that Marwood only spells poorly when dealing with authorities—to convince them he is a simpleton. Aldous reads the note again, trying to decipher what exactly is happening, just to make sure it isn't an animal being transported, or born, or put out of its misery—but it doesn't appear so.

He swallows and frowns. The fantastical, the violent, it seems, can be dull. He folds the letter over, replaces it at the corner of the table and vice. But the last words convince him—words sketched on the reverse side: "to improve the humanity of the operation, it should take the hangman four minutes from entering the cell, to calculate and perform the execution."

Aldous watches as the candle burns down, and the room takes on a deeper silence. For the next moments, it's like he's watching himself. The boy stands, arms on the table, and imagines the climb to his bedroom but then he spies his father's thinking chair—a large armchair just under the far window—and is drawn across the room. Sitting causes a flutter of dust, and a second piece of paper floats from the window ledge into his lap. At the top is written 'Re-shoeing. Mrs Purcell's clogs need planning, front to back, three inches. See stitching'.

As the candlelight mellows, Aldous reads on: If you tear the leather—judge the problem. If one stitch, create a fresh hole, checking the thread end to ensure it's not droopy. Cut neatly with scissors, or better still, a razor. Double-wax thread end every set of five-eight stitches. Measure out your thread three times the length of your seam, four for a beginner…. Nothing seems odd about the description. Aldous skips on to the end and realises—from the spelling alone—that these are his father's words, but his mother's writing.

The boy is growing tired. His eye strays to the bottom of the page. As the candle grows low, folding into its blue heart, he reads how the cobbling notes are only a prelude to 'hanging instructions'. Here all becomes strangely familiar, and yet perversely unreal. It sounds just like the shoes being mended all over again—except for one detail, clearly written by his father: Pleas this is to infom you I shall arive at the Prison on Thursday the 3rd day of April, well-timed, and brung all that is wanted for th' Execution. Sir, Pleas will you be so kind as to make some *improvment* in the *Pitt* in the *Length* of *the Drop.* Pleas will you take out three feet Squair in the *Senter* of the *Pitt* and 3 feet *Deep* of this be don it will make a great *improvment* in the *Execution* you may depend on me to arive on Thursday April the 3rd day.

The last thing Aldous sees, just as the candle goes out, is when he turns the page. Here is a new horror—a photograph of a male hanged head, eyes bulging, cheek sagging to one side and a rip in the neck where a body of flesh has come away. The technology is experimental. A water exposure using a *camera obscura* shows the hanged head is in colour: black, white and red, the eyes red, the blood black. A footnote says: All is anatomically correct—the rope and the pressure ring, the knot against the jugular.

But all Aldous sees in dreams—that night and for the next three nights—is the expression in the eyes, the slight comedic surprise, the overwhelming shock and disturbed pain. The head is complaining of injustice, yet seems complicit. Though calm-looking now, the victim did not understand and the sensitive boy relives his confusion after dark.

Waking each morning, Aldous feels the nameless man's contorted last seconds that freeze death in an expression of life. Here is an image, a photograph of the unknown, a human being in caricature alive for eternity, a waxwork doll of death. No longer does he look at the picture of his father on the wall. But with daylight comes relief, and he finds he can get through the day mending his father's orders in the same basement that terrified him by night.

Chapter 5
To London! Hansom Cabs and Southbound Trains
16th February 1879, Sunday

After reading the evening newspaper for a good while and watching darkness fall, Marwood notices the man opposite stirring. They are sharing a sleeper carriage on the train, though the journey should take no more than four hours from Cambridge to King's Cross.

"Time enough to kill," the man says conspiratorially.

"I beg your pardon."

"Oh, excuse me. Allow me to introduce myself. Sequin, Gil Sequin." He eyes the new addition to his usual sleeping booth and strokes his large moustache, curling it at the sides. "Detective Inspector Sequin, of Her Majesty's Scotland Yard."

"Oh," Marwood replies, sitting up. "I didn't mean…I'm William Marwood, Her Majesty's hangman, I mean, Gentleman Hangman for London and Middlesex."

"Gentleman, eh?"

Marwood says nothing and for a few seconds they sit in silence. Inspector Sequin adjusts his high Victorian collar, a red sash around his neck suggesting fastidiousness more than fashion; his features remain slow and immovable; his cheeks hang from his face like a depressed Doberman. Yet mysteriously encased in the flesh of his face, his eyes twinkle blue, sharp, unaffected by Marwood's visible discomfort in the presence of a man with greater social standing.

Inevitably their conversation turns to crime and not unsurprisingly, they are bound for London on similar business. Marwood is due to hang Charles Peace and Sequin is going to see him hanged.

"I did not work on the case directly, but my colleague Nimrod Jones did. I was only in Cambridge for the Mullins murder, the child case—"

"Awful, terrible," Marwood manages.

Sequin pauses, surprised by Marwood's need to stress his moral feeling. "Yes, and so for Jones's sake I will record the hanging details and he can remain in Cambridge for the duration."

"I see."

"And do you expect the hanging to be,"—he searches for *le mot juste*—"a success, my friend?"

Marwood nestles his coat tighter over his legs, tries to contain his feelings. "I have never yet failed."

A strange conspiracy of conversation now occurs. Having shared a joke—establishing trust between men above the law, who only make light of it among those similarly privileged—they chat for over an hour. But rather than talk personally, their banter remains professional, given they share a work-related appointment with Charles Peace in a couple of days.

"You know a man once recognised me on a train," Marwood says at one point, "and asked me whether we'd met before."

"And your reply?" Sequin encourages, wrapping his red sash over his shoulders, his lips not twitching at all for the punch line.

"I said, '*If so, it would not have been eight in the morning, for that's when I commit my hangings.*' He said very little after that, you see?"

"I do, Mr Marwood, I do."

After this story, Marwood conveys he once executed Percy Lefroy for a murder committed on the Brighton train during a robbery: "I had to be stern, Inspector. If I had not had him literally by the belt, he would have given me a run around the yard."

Sequin cracks a smile, but quickly the expression disappears in his cheeks. "Do you know of any men killed on trains? After all, we are discussing murder while enjoying the delights of modern travel." He gestures around the sleeper carriage which though third-class has curtains at the window, a little shared table and a maroon carpeted ceiling from which Sequin now removes his stubby finger.

"I can't say I do, Inspector."

"How convenient for me," the detective replies, "because I have just the tale. One I solved myself. You didn't happen to hang a Mr Franz Muller in 1864?"

Marwood affects an air of remembrance: "No, I'm sure I didn't."

"I already know you didn't," Sequin replies, displeasing Marwood somewhat. "I only tease because I solved this case myself, I know the outcome..."

"...and you're telling the story."

"Indeed." They regard each other closely. "Well, Mr Marwood of Charles Peace's demise, on which I compliment you..."— Marwood smiles—"let me take you back to Saturday 9th July 1864. Picture a suburban train on the North London line rolling into Hackney like any other morning on the late service, around ten fifteen. The guard notices a first-class compartment covered in blood, and a walking stick, bag and cloak in the carriage. According to the report, 'At ten fifteen, the body of a man was found on the cross-track between Bow Station and Hackney Wick.' He was still alive, but his skull was crushed and he died that day."

"You catch who did it?"

"Well, with Nimrod Jones's top-notch detective work, examining the walking stick, and realizing it belonged to the murderer and not the victim, we were able to trace down the very shop that sold the stick just off Carnaby Street. We got lucky, you could say. The shop clerk remembered a thick-accented German man, and found the name Franz Muller in his records."

"What happened?"

"Well, we were able to follow Muller as he attempted to flee to the United States on board the *Queen Victoria*. We made the arrest as her Majesty arrived in New York Harbor."

"Where the crowds wept for joy as they wept for the loss of Little Nell," Marwood says. Sequin flinches not an inch at his Dickensian reference.

"After four days' trial, Muller was found guilty and sentenced to death, and hanged on 14th November 1864."

"Hanged by whom?"

"I was hoping you could tell me that, Mr Marwood. You told me yourself, it wasn't you."

Clearly the tables have turned. But not one to resist a

challenge and seeing himself operating using the cool hand of an artist, Marwood sits pondering his next move.

"Why are men hanged at all?" he asks after a while.

"So that the rest of us may go free," Sequin says without hesitation, "to keep our souls empty and clean. As our national Police Procedural tells us," here the inspector winks, "the question is not one of softening a killer's heart or blessing the souls of murderers, but of saving the Queen's subjects from being murdered…"

"Correct, Inspector," Marwood says, softly nudging the 'mementos mori' in the black bag at his feet, the noose-twine from former hangings and scraps of clothing. Sequin frowns that anyone would carry such indecent souvenirs so openly. "Forgive me," Marwood continues, then removes a bloodied square of a shirt sleeve, holding it up into the light. "Hanging is a deterrent, a protection of property. Men are not hanged for stealing horses, but that horses may not be stolen…"

"And whose is that shirt?"

"Why, Mr Muller's of course," Marwood replies. "He was from Lincolnshire. They brought him back to Armley Gaol, and I hanged him myself."

Marwood smiles and watches the blood drain a little from Sequin's face, and sensing he has won the conversation, he can now counter the *façade* that they weren't jousting all along. "I still appreciate the story, Inspector Sequin. But let's not be in doubt as to who has the more *personal* job. As you know, Henry Wainwright shot Harriet Lane and buried her in chloride of lime, after he cut her up. Yes, you have to find the body and clean up the mess. But I have to put a rope around Wainwright's neck…take a breath…push a lever…listen to the air escape his throat and he drops through eternity…"

"And what does that sound like, Mr Marwood?" Sequin says, recovering his composure.

Marwood is shocked by the question, but he can't stop now. "It sounds like the breath of a small boy, when you squeeze him…."

"A pitiful sound…"

"Yes, like you are killing…a child…." The word hangs in the air. "You know, I keep a diary of my work, Inspector. Recent hangings, the crowd size, prayers, even the songs."

"A diary of remorse for the dying man?"

Marwood looks up, uncertain if Sequin is serious, but the blue eyes looking back are as clear as fresh water. "As much remorse as you feel, sir, for making the arrest."

"If you saw the scene of the crime, Mr Marwood, you'd feel no more remorse than I do on May Day—nothing to do and nothing to fear."

This angers Marwood and leaning forward in the carriage he begins coughing, only to find the train screeching to a halt. So intent on persuading Sequin of his inherent goodness, he realises that all he's accomplished is a series of confessions. "Your May Day is just hot air," he says, frowning, knowing he is digging a hole and should obey 'the rules of holes' and stop digging. "How would you like it if your job was hanging someone?"

"I would not—or perhaps I would."

"...and the moment you put the hood on, the condemned man gives you this beseeching look, like a calf licking the butcher's hand?"

Inspector Sequin stands and exist the carriage. "I would not, Mr Marwood," he half grins, "I would not like it at all."

Marwood is left to watch, aghast, as the self-assured detective casually squeezes through the carriage door, whips an umbrella from the walkway overhang and disappears whistling. All Marwood is left with is his black bag of professional trophies, a puzzled expression, and the noise of piston engines. What just happened? They've reached the end of the line—he detects burnt coal as he steps gingerly down onto the platform of King's Cross Station.

He looks both ways, but Sequin is already gone. "If that man were any less arrogant," he says to himself, "I'd be out of a job."

Two coffee bars later and a shot of gin on the Marylebone Road and the hangman reaches his London home, a two-storey flat at 29 Gloucester Place, Dorset Square, a government residence just off Baker Street. In the tradition of those before him, the most recent being the famous bungler William Calcraft, Marwood is bequeathed these rooms for all his formal hanging assignments, namely, the 'Queen's lodgings for a Gentleman Executioner'. The new tenant is uncertain what to expect—he pushes the door gently with his foot, unlocking it simultaneously with his hand.

As he does so there is a voice behind his ear. "Mr Marwood?" Immediately dropping all his belongings, to his alarm the miniature guillotine he showed Aldous rolls from his bag. "I'm so sorry, sir," the voice says, "but I was told I would find you here."

Marwood peers warily over his shoulder. Behind him the broad figure of a man is before him no more than twenty-five and resembling an overgrown greengrocer's delivery boy—owing to his apron.

"And who might you be?"

"Berry, James Berry. Policeman's assistant."

Time slows, while behind Berry the poplar trees lean in the wind over Dorset Square, darting around the circular iron railing, the triangular Victorian lampposts and newly installed red letterboxes. Marwood barely has time to adjust to the amusements of the capital before Bow Street's long arm surveillance is at his door.

"Not another!" Marwood cries, and swings his arm low for his coat. "And how can I help you?"

"I want to be your apprentice."

Marwood turns to the young man. "I don't need an apprentice. I work alone."

"But the Sheriff of Middlesex recommended me."

"Did he send you personally?"

"Well, no."

"Do you know him directly?"

"Well, not exactly,"

"Then listen to me, youngster, and listen good—there's the stigma of the hangman. My position is not a pleasant one. No, it is not a pleasant one." Above them a grey sky looks down dismissively—on two anonymous beings in the wide stretch of London streets.

"I understand, but…"

"No 'buts'. I have a job to do here. Now, if you'll excuse me."

"I need a job," the boy says as Marwood closes the door on him.

"There's only one hangman for London, Mr Berry. You will have to wait your turn!"

Marwood pauses just inside and hears the rain begin to fall. Then squinting through the letterbox, he is able to make out Berry pulling his apron over his head and slipping away in the shower.

Behind him the poplars sigh and the heavens resist opening, but down comes the familiar spitting advance drops of cold English rain. Marwood waits, Berry does not return. Rain begins bouncing off the stone porches all down Gloucester Place.

Marwood locks himself inside, finally, and rolls the iron bar onto a wooden lattice—he has a busy night ahead. The first sign of his den is now apparent, since hanging from the ceiling in the hall are some curious coils of rope. The previous tenant, the famously incompetent Calcraft, must have hung them there as souvenirs. Marwood hesitates, feels a trickle of recognition in Calcraft's desire to keep the trinkets of his profession for reward and out of strange personal affection. He reaches up to run one cord—the neck tightener—through his fingers. It feels like any other rope, dry and tough, with a few flecks of twine to grip the fingers. Even here though, Marwood can detect a clumsy slip-knot, no doubt as much a by-product of Calcraft's hanging days as a knot for securing the rope to the ceiling. He follows it down the hall into the house, looping several times above his head with the sensation of threatening to reach down and hook him under the neck.

Almost on tiptoe, like an intruder Marwood inspects the rest of the house: a front room with a bay window to the street; beyond the stairs is a kitchen with a fire grate, a cramped dark study, and some cold steps descending to a wine cellar. As he leans down into the gloom a musty smell rises to his nostrils, and his neck is jerked back instinctively. Turning he notices a portrait over his head dimly lit by a grate: Thomas Cheshire is grinning over him. A fat man and early hangman, 'Old Cheese' is known to Marwood from his reading of the *Newgate Calendar* as a sadistic drunk who enjoyed flogging his prisoners before hangings. The illustration, clearly a commissioned full-length portrait, decks Cheshire in broad snuff-coloured greatcoat, an Oriental cigar stabbing his lips with its drift of opium making his features wince.

"No wonder he was brutal to prisoners," Marwood whispers, "fogged up on dope all the long day." He remembers the songs how 'Old Cheese' would be chased by a stream of boys down the street like the Pied Piper of Hamelin, he was such an ostentatious and distracting sight—that is until, according to legend, Thomas Cheshire's wife threw two boys down to the cellar and broke their ankles. Marwood winces and peers closely in Cheshire's eyes, black slits with white centres like billiard cue balls stripped of all comedy. He cannot see any hint of empathy left.

The new hangman returns to the front room, where he rearranges papers from his bag on the main mahogany desk. After a ring at the door, a boy from the train deposits his delayed suitcase, then assists in carrying strays boxes down to the cellar. The boy bears a candle, but on reaching the bottom, he turns on his heel and races back upstairs. The front door slams.

Marwood turns the candle on this new underground room. All is dusty and dark. He removes some old books, a flat cap and decaying scarf, and piles the discarded clothes in a corner. He breaks though some cobwebs. Something winks in the darkness, and he shivers, wondering if a pigeon is trapped, or worse, a bat that could strike any moment, but he almost laughs at his own imagination. The wink is from a black glass bead, an eye, but quite unloving.

Pulling back a rafter that has sprung up at a sharp angle, Marwood spies a broken wooden rocking horse. A glint in the creature's eye suggests mischief, but could he fix the beast for Aldous, before the boy gets too old? Resisting his superstition for the horse's malevolence, more Rocinante than Pegasus, he touches its proud neck and folds its upright tail, only to be quite distracted. The beast is instantly forgotten, relegated to history and another tale.

For underneath, what does he encounter, but a trapdoor, a door in the floor, and the ideal practice tool. The coincidence is unlikely and yet he could easily never have found this door in the floor—a device he's been seeking for several years—in workable order since the premises were a private printer's, the trap used to pass metal plates efficiently between floors, and here it is, undamaged, in the hangman's house itself. Marwood raises the candle and looks underneath: he can already see how to adapt the iron hooks on either side for his newly formed 'long drop' technique. Not only does a 'sound hanging' consist of varying the rope length for the weight of each prisoner, he thinks, but the trapdoor can now be introduced—a trapdoor Old Cheshire Cheese lived with for years and never thought of using, seeing no advantage to its scientific application.

"But with attention to cold steel springs," Marwood whispers in the half gloom, "this trap could be a phenomenon." He flips the catch and watches the sudden fall of the disappearing floor. He imagines the decent of the cleanly wrapped body, its supple swing, the gentle jog of the feet, the silence. "It really could work….Closed when weightless like a sleeping beauty and then—the miracle!—freeing the weight of the prisoner!" In his excitement Marwood sets to work, opening the trapdoor and securing it. He clears the room of its random furniture and pushes old printing tables aside. The machinery he cannot move, he covers with a large red curtain so not to distract him, and he rather enjoys the effect of turning the room into a series of misshapen monsters.

"Bear witnesses to my experiments!" Retrieving his notebook and measuring the height from floor to ceiling, he begins to construct a 'table of possibilities', which he tests by dropping a sandbag of equal weight to the prisoner. As though caught on an imaginary hook, he scampers up and down the cellar steps. Sacks he discovers at the back of the kitchen, storage bags with 'flood watch' written on their grainy skins, dry as the day they were filled. Counting and recording, sliding a bag over the trapdoor, holding it steady, refilling the bag and sliding it again until the catch releases—and another innovation!

Here all is play, but once the lever is swung at the real hanging site, Marwood knows that the man will only fall if the rope length and the weight to trigger the trapdoor *are in unison*. There is no room for error before the man falls or he will not fall straight and true and the results could be unpredictable—and messy. Marwood ponders this potential embarrassment but decides the reward is worth the risk, given the success of his executions to date. Never again will a man choke to death in England over a painful hour. His neck will break, the crowd will cheer, and "Marwood Esq will become the executioner extraordinaire!"

Smiling as he works, the hangman ignores his heavy sweating. The snap and drop repeat over and over, the thump of the body bag on the underground stone floor silent to all but his beating heart. Up on the street not twenty feet away in Gloucester Place, the workers heading home pass by oblivious.

Towards midnight, after several hours of operating the trapdoor, Marwood has made his basic calculations and recorded them 'for posterity'. On this unlikely night, the very night of his arrival, he even realises that a greater drop is required if the knot is placed under the ear of the condemned and not under the chin. By catching one bag around the furry outer lip, its neck twisting sideways, a new idea is born, and by three o'clock in the morning he has realised that if the weight is greater by using the ear-knot, strangulation would be less likely.

How does he know this? "I know this because I am no longer standing on a burst sandbag." He gestures to the floor where the heaviest bag split on him with such force that no square inch three feet under the trapdoor is sand-free; yet just above Marwood's elbow is a final sandbag: it is the same weight, and yet because he tied it at the side of its rope-head, it has survived. "Dead, for sure," he says. "But not decapitated, or decollation—*capitis amputation*, as the Romans would say—just dead. My tip to the headsman!" and he pretends to doff an imaginary cap, sighing, and then all too real he collapses on the sawdust of his killing floor. "My tip to the headsman!"

When he wakes it is half-light, and a shocking sight brings back life. Sprawled under the trapdoor and swinging his body upwards, Marwood senses particles tumbling from his hair, magical grey matter mixed with his own drool, and he swallows in disgust. But more than the irritation of sand, directly above his head he is witness to a mural painting like an obscene reinvention of the Sistine Chapel. The amateur painter, his predecessor Calcraft, has somehow etched a giant mock-fresco to his own immortality on the ceiling, a macabre and foolish self-immolation of ego. There it sits, dripping in gory colour, the singular sweep of Calcraft among the clouds, the pompous patriot of the pulpit of death, or as Marwood prefers, "just a fat hangman decked out in purple livery for no one to see but the next man on the job."

The mural consists of Calcraft reclining on a bed of curling cirrus, high in the cosmos surrounded by moons and stars; the goddess Isis leans on his shoulder while being mortally slain by his brother Osiris, the god of darkness, signifying the end of another day. Moreover, painted on Calcraft's chest is the disturbing image of the raging face of Horus, son of Isis, who is thirsting to avenge his father's death and so bring about the light: the implication, of course, is that Calcraft—as executioner—brings a new dawn of justice to the land. At his feet sit a lion, griffin and the legendary unicorn, beasts at once real and fantastical, symbolizing all the valour and might of England.

Appropriate for this dramatic deception is the lack of Calcraft's usual clothing—his full grey beard, frock coat and gold chain, black bow tie or fob-chain. Instead he sports the white tunic of a Roman senator worshipping the Greek gods, incongruously overlaid with a red hunting jacket stolen from this eighteenth century, and a bizarre black dahlia in his buttonhole.

Within seconds of waking Marwood is horrified to witness this entire sight. He cannot believe he slept under the mural all night long, and much to his consternation there's no sign of Calcraft's dirty wide-awake hat, the common shooting waistcoat he liked to wear, or his extra twenty pounds of flesh. Even so, Marwood can hear the bungler's voice booming with the clarity of a church bell, that sonorous cry of arrogance up on the scaffold calling the sinful to confession and death, only now the voice is trapped inside Marwood's mind: "I must keep my clients in good spirits," Calcraft is saying. "You can trust me, ladies and gents, nothing like a merry morning drop!"

Finally, the mural is tastelessly surrounded by the emblems of Calcraft's earlier, failed careers: his time as a brewer is represented by mugs of ale under the lion's paws, as a butler by a top hat and tails in the claws of the unicorn. Even his passion for rabbit-breeding is represented by a border of those scampering creatures, whipped by the griffin's tail, in homage to his aborted teenage career as groundsman to the country seat of Lord Darlington of Dorset.

"A slow and painful killer!" Marwood whispers. "You are worse than your condemned; you choke your prisoners to death!"

The whole mural is a con, Marwood knows, since he knows Calcraft began his career in 1829, exactly fifty years ago, and has done nothing technical to improve his technique the whole time. Marwood can no longer look, and averts his eyes but Calcraft is there behind his eyelids, grinning like Old Cheshire Cheese.

Clambering to his feet, and dusting himself down, Marwood shakes his fist at the mural. But he receives little succour from the outburst—he feels more like a man rising from quicksand. "Like Lazarus....God knows how he felt."

Then he remembers his invention—how he almost perfected 'the long drop' last night. Without looking, he opens the trapdoor and floods the basement with light. A new day is born promising a future free of indulgence, the daily new chance, hope. "Death be not proud!"

The base of the trapdoor glints red in the sunlight, blood red, the colour of life, a brave new world no less, *that has such people in't!*

"You throttled them, but I honour and execute them," Marwood says to the empty basement and returns above ground.

For the rest of the day Marwood stays indoors, updating his scientific logs with his latest discovery. He listens to the rain, the winter wind whipping the house, no more aware of the coming darkness than the receding light.

Later he sits by the fire in the kitchen and examines a little collection of souvenirs from his hangings: photographs of Calcraft's clients that he pulls from his predecessor's folder: "my victims", as Calcraft calls them like a Victorian parlour game, faces clipped from newspapers, locks of hair—gifts, tokens and keepsakes 'snipped from the pit', quite literally, and sold off to Madame Tussaud's *Chamber of Horrors*. All told, the collection is gruesome: he knows that the clothes of the dead attract high buyers, quick fix cures for ailments, so too does a touch from the dead man's hand. But he's seen nothing like Calcraft's horde.

He lays the folder aside. Ropes chopped in pieces bring in more money—that he can understand—but whole waxworks constructed from a dead body? Surely the thirst to possess the dead in order to conquer death has gone too far? Guiltily reminded of his own Courvoisier death-mask, Marwood returns to his hanging notebooks. Here he lists the names, height, weight, age and sex of each hanging, the drop he gave, and the post-mortem findings. The page falls open at his next appointment even before he opens the book: Charles Peace, England's most wanted man, notorious Peace, criminal for the masses, talented anti-hero—musical, charming, with the nerve to kill and ask a policeman for directions, the guts to scorn his own execution.

"I will see Peace one morning soon," Marwood smiles. He taps the page and makes some more calculations based on second-hand information about Peace's height and weight. The figures do not seem accurate, at least from the reputation of Peace having a squat stocky build; the hangman will have to get a second opinion.

His first day on the job complete, Marwood grows drowsy

before the fire; his pencil and notebooks fall to the floor, the flames die harmlessly in the grate. Proud and ashamed of his profession, disappointed by its ugly past but confident of his own solitary struggle, his just reformation, his humanizing of hanging, he slips into the streams of Lethe. Down from Calcraft's clouds, he dreams of nothing if not weights and sandbags.

Chapter 6
An Accidental Meeting of Punch & Judy
17th February 1879, Monday

After a day searching the streets for old faces only to find them slipping into shadows, Kate finally arrives in Covent Garden as the sun is going down. She has an appointment. Somehow she sneaks up to the Piazza without realizing, her mind is so clouded, her nerves suspended. She heads through Maiden Lane and Shaftsbury Avenue, still shaking off the daze of her journey from the West End. Makeshift omnibuses smell of onions and paraffin as she ducks along High Street Kensington through its Vaseline odours from the perfumeries and pampering shops of the rich and idle, hiding her face to prevent being accosted and moved on. Eventually she reaches the antiseptic stench of Long Acre, Southampton Row, and finally Nelson's Column down to the Thames. Here the scent of London is momentarily sweetened by the smell of oranges loaded off the barges at sundown, a moment of ecstasy replaced by day-old herring carts heading to the alehouses. The whole city stinks of life, the earth itself wheezing with inflammation despite the cold, now that people are back on the streets looking for the night and each other, and somewhere to go.

Here Kate leans on a pillar under the swinging sign for *The Nell Gwynne*, the lady of the house laughing through the peeling paint. Kate pays the pub no attention but is curious about the swelling number of people entering the Piazza until it becomes clear that an

Italian Punch & Judy 'extravaganza' is about to begin, a prelude to the main act—titled 'The Road to Tyburn'. But Kate has no intention of watching. It only takes a few moments before her foil appears, shambling along the brickwork of *The Nell Gwynne*, counting the bricks as he goes and nervously stammering.

"Nathan Crane," she says, offering her best impression of a smile. "Well, I'll be damned!"

"Is that you?" Crane says, unfolding his fingers from their grey gloves. He is a pasty-faced man with a flat face and sandy hair, innocent-looking, like an overgrown schoolboy. Kate is contemptuous but does her best to smile.

"Of course it's me," she says, "now come here."

Nathan steps in close and they edge into the side alley. Kate opens her palm and reveals a few glinting stones of different colours.

"Take your pick."

"Garnets," Nathan says and peers up at Kate's darkening expression. "I'm not fooled."

"Well, I don't deny *that's* a garnet," Kate says, her fingernail stroking the other stones, "but that's an emerald chippin', still attached to gold. And that—nudging a larger stone—is a solitary ruby." Crane's lips narrow, then relax.

"I'm sorry, Kate, but I just don't have the skill to shift yer stones. Not today. I deal in bigger merchand-iiise," and he rolls the last syllable as though it has magical properties. "You know, nice furniture, household goods, handbags, that kind o' thing." His moustache is so close that Kate can detect his stale breath and black sprouting of chin stubble. "Body parts too…"

"What?"

"Let's not be coy, Kate, there's a big trade for organs n' all that. The hospital is cryin' out for that stuff, arms, legs, livers, 'earts. That's the real money—don' yer wanna be rich?"

Kate is stunned and waves him away contemptuously. "Furniture, you say? I can get you some a'that. I's a lodgin' with a family…less than secure, if you know what I mean?"

"Small securities, Kate," Crane says. "How you gonna get me the stuff, though? What your goon make, really, dealin' in the small stuff."

"What, like these?" she pursues and opens her hand again, but Crane sneers without looking down.

"Not that junk."

The conversation having taken this bad tact, soon they're talking at cross-purposes. For a moment there is a pitiful smile on Kate lips, as she sees the level to which her former friend Crane—her one-time lover—has now sunk, a criminal with no boundaries now selling all that humans own, inside and out. To her surprise Kate discovers she is repulsed by Crane who seems worse now than Jonathan Clatter but without the gentlemanly airs, just another street pusher.

Kate re-pockets her fake jewels. "Well, Nathan m'lad, that's all I have."

"Furniture and body parts," Crane says with a final breath and hands Kate a card with his address, *14 Gower Street just off Gilbert Place.* "Be in touch."

"I'll turn something up."

"You'd better, I won't meet you for paltry nothin'," Crane says and with a broken smile he slips into the shadows.

The creaking of *The Nell Gwynne* brings Kate back to the scene before her, where Covent Garden overflow is now bustling. Across from St Paul's Church a puppet show is beginning in the Italian style. Kate's thoughts are distracted, preoccupied by her boy Daniel and this being just the place where Jonathan Clatter will be testing out his new recruits, jabbing them on with a stick to steal more and more handkerchiefs, risking their necks. But something about a marionette in the puppet show catches her eye—not a glove-puppet but a full-size brass Mr Punch. She walks nearer and joins the crowd where a sign details how the show dates back to the sixteenth century *commedia dell'arte* and the original Punch Pulcinella. Kate smirks at the showmanship, but when the show starts, something about its family mayhem and fearful anticipation, makes her think back to her childhood in a little village called Killane in County Wexford, Ireland.

At first appearance, there is nothing to remind her of home. The Punch & Judy booth is a simple upright 'fit-up' with red and white stripes, while poking above the wide berth—to the crowd's familiar delight—are the baby, crocodile, string of sausages, the devil and Jack Ketch himself. The atmosphere is sufficient to trouble her for a moment, the noise, the shrieking of the wife; all that she remembers of home is present on the stage, the brutal rolling-pin wielding father, the authorities at the door, all except Jack Ketch the hangman whom she fortunately encountered in her childhood—the rest, inflated by surreal comedy for the pleasure of the London crowd, is all too real.

Today is a holiday and the winter solstice has been marked as a half day: many of the offices, the law courts, the doctor's surgeries and city administration have closed. The bodies on the streets are a mixture, the well-dressed professionals spilling into cold sunlight from doorways, the happy mob milling for the next easy opportunity, the cheap deal. Both kinds of people, surprisingly, are equally indulgent with their cravings. 'Too hot to eat' baked potatoes dance in their fingers, grease paper strews the ground, and meat pies hang from their faces like savoury birthday cakes. Children's hands grasp bottle of beers, Cornish cider, or the newly fashionable Turkish cigarettes and Havana cigars, many stolen from cellar smoking houses. As the crowd weaves together, the overhead vision of Covent Garden is like a basket woven of different strings, all competing for sustenance or distraction or both, and stitched together in a patchwork of human indulgence.

Kate is again distracted by the Punch & Judy show as it winds to an end, with Punch busy dispatching the Devil himself, exclaiming "Huzzah huzzah, I've killed the killer!" Kate smirks, thinking to herself how the show is really for overgrown children, for adults with low entertainment tastes, baby-brains with selfish indulgences intact. Just as she is thinking these deep thoughts, the man next to her says:

"Punch is a deformed, child-murdering, wife-beating psychopath who escapes scot-free—and is greatly enjoyed by small children."

"Excuse me?" Kate says, and stares at the man who is dressed in black. "Punch is a clown."

"He is the Devil and needs to be reformed," the man whispers. "Cigarette?"

Kate turns to face him, struck by his insistent chatter. "I think you've got the wrong person. You expectin' someone particula'? 'Cos I don't think I'm 'er." They are briefly interrupted by a group of newly minted policemen pushing through the crowd, patrolling the Piazza: the bobbies pass between them in black top hats and blue swallow-tail costs. "They're the real devils," Kate says with a wink for the stranger's benefit.

"Blue Devils or Real Blue Collarers, they're called, Miss…"

"I don't tell strange men my name, on account of propriety."

"Oh, well then let me tell you mine. I'm William Marwood of Horncastle, Lincolnshire."

"Nice to meet you," Kate says without feeling, and extends a faintly grubby hand. "And to what do I owe the pleasure?"

"Oh, just the pleasure of the day."

"And what do you do in Lincolnshire?"

"I am a cobbler…for the government."

"The Queen's cobbler, hey?"

They stare ahead, their words faltering a moment. Everything could easily have ended there, Kate rejoining the crowd, later disappearing to a drinking hole for the night, Marwood moping back to his room off Baker Street. But despite her worn appearance and slightly rough expression, something about the woman intrigues him. He notices her non-reaction to Punch & Judy's domestic horror, her lack of playing along with the crowd, her lack of laughter.

"They are called 'crushers, coppers' and 'peelers' after Robert Peel."

"Who?"

"The police," Marwood says, pointing at the last officer. "You know they used to wear red and were called the Bow Street Runners. A famous novelist called Henry Fielding created them as the first police force…."

"I didn't know that, Mr Marwood, that's interesting." Kate regards the puppeteer who has appeared with the marionettes on the Punch & Judy stage and is taking a bow. She is surprised the creator doesn't resemble any of his creatures, but is a man like any other and could be a greengrocer or newspaper vendor, or a cobbler.

"Yes, back then—oh, a hundred years ago—thief-takers were known as Robin Redbreasts or Raw Lobsters for their red vests. Then fifty years ago the New Police was founded—seventeen divisions of it." He looks up. "Very efficient aren't they?"

Kate follows the trail of Marwood's finger where the Bow Street Runners are lining the pubs of Henrietta Street. They look faux-elegant in their blue uniforms. But Kate sees nothing worth comment, so she peers back at her neighbour without hiding her suspicious face. However, she feels an odd sensation of warmth and fear under her skin. Marwood has one keen eye, and the other is cold-looking and lazy. He is handsome if a little sturdy and serious-looking and she is intrigued enough not to walk away. Perhaps there will be an opportunity here.

"Do you like cigarettes?" Marwood repeats, massaging the subject to ensure she does not grow bored. "I find them good company," meaning he is lonely after arriving in London and spending so long with his experiments.

"Sure."

"We have a vice in common, then," he says and hands her three cigarettes. "Take them. They are imported from Turkey—after the Crimean War." He watches her face change. "You can buy them from a shop on Queen Victoria Street or more expensive in Leicester Square. I usually smoke a pipe myself."

Uncertain how to react, Kate senses she could just flee and the crowd would part for her. But she finds herself—to her own rising consternation—removing a single cigarette and forcing a smile. Marwood sees the dubious state of her teeth and looks away, preferring to imagine an innocent smile. Instead, a wrinkle of 'crow's feet' ages her skin five years. To add two years to his estimate, he'd discover she is thirty years old. Little does he know, she celebrated her last birthday the previous November behind the steel bars of Liverpool's Walton Gaol.

A surge now pulls the crowd backward, as Kate finds herself placing two cigarettes back in Marwood's hand. Their fingers touch lightly—no comment is made but they sense a roughness to each other's skin. The Punch & Judy show is over.

"Are you staying for the festivities?" Kate asks.

"What is it?"

"A holiday execution in the old Tyburn style."

"That sounds a little squeamish for me."

"You'll enjoy it," she insists. "The rest of the crowd do."

"I fear I am not quite of the crowd, Miss…"

"Thomas," Kate says. "Miss Julia Thomas. You must forgive my clothing, I've been unwell."

"That's quite all right, Miss Thomas. Pleased to meet you," but he resists shaking her hand, frowning at himself. A match is now lit and he extends it for Kate who leans a little forward. She inhales the strict Oriental fumes with a sigh.

"Julia is my middle name. People usually call me Kate—my friends."

"Then Kate it is."

She makes no comment and Marwood resorts to fidgeting with his Toquilla straw hat.

"So what exactly is a 'Tyburn Reenactment'?"

"Well, I do have some knowledge of that," Marwood says but before he can continue, a wave of excitement disturbs the Piazza. There is a cry of 'hats off' and 'bring on the holiday execution!'

The word hangs in the air, hinting at pickpockets and prostitutes struggling to make a killing. All of a sudden, a kind of mania is felt, an atmosphere that only the French guillotine suggests with its beautiful silhouette and affectionate pseudonyms—*La Veuve*, the National Razor, the Avenger, the Patriotic Shortener, the topper and slicer. Marwood closes his eyes and sees *La Place de la Révolution* with its greatest fans in the front row, ready for the worship of the blade—the *tricoteuses*—those happy old crones who knitted all that Paris summer of 1789 at the foot of the scaffold, looping and stitching knots and sneering at the blood: they made new clothes while the people were derobed, the nation unknit.

"Even Robespierre was 'bound to the bascule' and sent under the knife."

"What's that?" Kate says forcing Marwood from his reverie. "Listen, if you're done talkin' to yerself, I got places to be. See?"

"Of course."

"That's right. I've got responsibilities." But when Marwood doesn't speak, something indefinable keeps Kate close to this dour, polite gentleman. "Do *you* have somewhere to go?"

"Stay for the show. It's not real, you know—there's nothing to be afraid of!" Marwood smiles faintly, and Kate again sees the discoloration in his sharp eye and the blankness of his lazy eye, each independent of the other. The effect is reassuring one moment, chilling the next.

"Who says I was afraid?"

For once Marwood looks at Kate directly: "You would be, if it were real."

He expects to deliver her a fright, but Kate's reaction is quite different. She is startled for a fraction of time, then a kind of gurgling builds in her chest almost like a wounded lioness. The result is a cackle—a vaguely sadistic sound. He steps back at her reaction, half comic, half menacing, and utterly strange: he has heard nothing like Kate's laugh. He should walk away but he does not, so different is this woman's behaviour from anyone he has met, including calm Ellen, the moodiness of his neighbours in Horncastle pubs or the compliments of women who proposition him in gin mills. Here—with Miss Kate Julia Thomas—the attraction is repulsion, the idiocy of the innocent moth drawn to the flame.

"You try to act so tough," Kate says. "It's funny."

"Doesn't it suit me?"

"Not really. Can I have another cigarette?"

As the light starts to fade, the atmosphere in Covent Garden grows more expectant and the stage comes into view. Kate witnesses a tall frame being erected—a triangular wooden beam.

A dwarfish man appears on the stage. "The Triple Tree!" He causes a cheer from the crowd, raising his hands. "Look on her and weep!"

"Our circus master!" Marwood says, but Kate is busy surveying her fellow Cockney audience. Balanced on market carts, over-excited and raucous, all are smoking, singing and drinking. Tavern-keepers and road-sweepers jostle for position with porters and brush-makers. From butcher's sons and warehouse-men to newspapers hawkers, London is everywhere beat-down, glorious and proud. The dirty poor with stolen fine clothes, the dirty rich with fob watches and purse-strings, in a single moment they surge forward for the entertainment. With the crowd distracted, the street-walkers, including the boys of Jonathan Clatter's school for pickpockets, select new clients.

"Everyone is here!" cries the circus master, "and I am your host, Sir Justice Denman. Today is Monday and one of our eight great hanging days—and it's my day off from the Old Bailey, so here I am!" A combination of boos and hurrahs is the response. "Bucks and swells, take your seats, lackies and aristocrats, rest your feet! And writers and artists do what you will, who cares what you write? A veritable theatre is about to begin. A real gala-day!"

The crowd has no qualms celebrating a holiday modelled on the hangings that once happened so near the Piazza.

"As you know," the Justice continues, "hanging is a brutal business that now takes place behind prison doors. Tyburn was long ago, so much so we changed the name to Marble Arch, the corner of Connaught Square, year of our Lord 1879. For the superstitious among you, there are thirteen steps to the top of the English gallows, then as now. Some of bodies are buried *in situ* but don't go digging them up unless you want to swing from the merry rope yourself—we can always bring back 'the invincible tree', hah ha ha!" Denman gestures to the wooden beams. "Room for as many as twenty on there!"

Kate looks up. "Who is being hanged?"

"None of this is real," Marwood says. "Some actor."

She grins, fascinated by the scene. To her left above the post office, an upper-class balcony is filling with spectators, wine bottles signalling an air of ugly festivity. Kate can't take her eyes off them. One family is enormously fat, setting up the afternoon to eat and drink, push each other's wigs back and laugh like all is well in the world. Nearby, a boy aristocrat begins squirting these dandies with whisky and soda from a nozzle at his hip, and gesturing to indicate his pelvis. Even these idiots are quiet, though, when the bell tolls, a sound they worship in mock solemnity. Below, a new silence overwhelms the normally rowdy square.

"Always the same," Marwood says, "I've read about this effect. It's complicity from the crowd, like they care for a moment, but really they show their awe for the powers staging the event, a quiet respect before the storm."

"Like a prayer for the dying."

"Exactly, Miss Thomas," and he looks at her curiously, "like a prayer for the killing." But it's a false alarm. Soon the crowd's natural barbarity is resumed, comfort is restored and any melancholy or introspection is washed away.

"Those balconies," Kate says, pointing, "how do you get up there?"

"You have to pay, like the stalls at a dog race. Mammy Douglas used to run them, the 'Tyburn pew-opener'. As Justice Denham said: 'For those who go to The Triple Tree—our three beams of beautiful truth—Tyburn is the land where they alight.' Listen, each beam can hang eight people, so that makes twenty-four."

"A lot for the crowd."

"A whole day's entertainment! You know, there was a house in Upper Bryanston Street that overlooked Tyburn and they made see-through iron balconies on the floor, so the gentry on the floor below could witness the execution through the feet of the sheriffs!"

Kate smiles sweetly, only half listening to Marwood, and

realises that here was a man with an intellectual disease—one she could profit by. All she has to do is get him alone, then a simple robbery, or maybe some real money could be made. He doesn't seem quite the lewd enough type. "I will have to play on his intellectual pretensions."

"Excuse me?"

Kate is shocked to find she's speaking out loud. Her hand automatically covers her mouth, and through her gums she begins coughing a white lie; finally she is saved by the voice of the condemned as he is forced to ascend the stage and act his own death. A thin man bows—in a dishevelled white coat resembling a wedding coat-and-tails—for the mock-comedy of the crowd, his legs shaking at the knee. This disconcerts a few people at the front who begin to boo, but a moment later the actor curls his toes over the stage and exaggerates his uncontrollable legs. A surge of glee and a kind of sadistic wonder sweeps over the front rows and infectiously passes backwards until Kate finds herself cheering too. In quiet contrast Marwood's only gesture is to tip his hat lower, not untouched by the notion of a death about to happen, but strangely, he appears more affected by the hammy acting sending up his own professional work.

For back here, he is just one of the crowd, a spectator permitted his release of feeling, neither on show on the stage, nor responsible. The temptation lingers in him to look up again, and cheer, but some confusion—a conflict between the hangman's role and the self-conscious spectator—prevents him.

Meanwhile the dying actor turns out to be a bit of a dandy and one with a story to tell. He is in no rush to die, and begins stripping off his jacket to reveal a purple waistcoat, which the crowd sighs over in mock offense—the religious colour quite blasphemous given the circumstances. The noise of shock-horror, good-natured jeering and abusive hectoring is all consuming. Marwood patiently places his fingers in his ears while Kate stares at this acting maestro, in awe as he takes the crowd high and low and around in feverish circles with the simple wave of his hand.

"Good afternoon," he cries, "and welcome to my death! Gracious people, in time-honoured tradition, this is my last speech. As you can see beside me, I am accompanied by the Sheriff of Holborn, Mr Stanley Faucet, and these gentleman"—pointing at two heavy-set men bearing ropes—"will assist me into the chains before loading me up"—indicating the horse and cart beside the stage. "But now for my story! I was a poor boy like you"—*boo!* "but I rose through the ranks of the handkerchief school, at the hands of a Mr Jonathan Clatter"—*cheer!* "who lives we know not where..."—*boo!*

Kate baulks at the mention of her associate, babysitter and schoolteacher, not to mention supplier of liquors for child services; she swallows, frowning and thinking of Daniel. A guilty feeling disturbs her insides, all the deeper for being declared on stage before so many, and she feels quite light-headed, leans a little closer to Marwood. He supports her arm briefly, believing her womanly sensibilities are being affected. Kate lets him, and a few seconds later she claims recovery, as the condemned finishes his tale of woe.

"...and rather than ship me to Australia with all the condemned, the theft of a single loaf of malt cake for my starving family—for my little sister—was surely just cause. What if the bread had been fruit-loaf? Would they have killed me in the baker's on Sloane Street? Before all the pretty wives and priceless dandies, can you imagine?" The mob cries its appreciation, but not enough to mask the victim's final words. "So here I am, for your delight and the equal pleasure of Her Majesty, the blessed Queen Victoria. I will die as an Englishman, long live the Queen!"

"Long live the Queen!" barks the crowd.

At that moment from the back of the stage there appears a caricature of Calcraft, hangman for the Crown—a fat man, drunk-looking, uncertain of his surroundings and twitching. The fear is immediately present in the victim's face as he turns back to the crowd, so without delay he begins to sing:

> The black, the fair, the red, the brown,
> That prance and dance it up and down,
> There's none like Nancy Dawson.
> Her easy mien, her shape so neat,
> She foots, she trips, she looks so sweet,
> Her very motion's so complete,
> I die for Nancy Dawson.

As with a real hanging, there is no explanation of Nancy Dawson's story—it is too late for that. Sir Justice Denman retreats to the scaffold steps, the two assistants step up, ready to manhandle the prisoner while the Calcraft impersonator does his best to tie ropes around the victim's hands and ankles. All these proceedings are mechanical and Marwood watches them carefully. The acting is poor—there is no real sense of the prisoner's struggle or resignation; he stands where instructed on the cart while the black hood is positioned around his neck, the noose looped over and tightened.

"Are they really going to hang him?"

"They'll whip the horse away," Marwood says, "and let him fall, then the assistants will kneel down with a black sheet before him, concealing a block of wood."

Kate frowns. "That will be obvious."

"You'd be surprised," Marwood replies. "By then he will be choking, with his hands to his neck, and the crowd will cheer his efforts. As long as he kicks his legs a few times, they'll be happy—it's his face they want to see."

"Most of them can't see nothin'."

"True," Marwood says. "That's why it's a show after all, a sham, a spectacle. No one up there is enacting history." With these words, the new hangman of London and Middlesex turns to Kate. "How do I know all this? Well, do you know who I am?"

She is surprised by the odd question. "No, what do you mean?"

Marwood hesitates. "Nothing," he says, "nothing. Listen, do you want to go get a drink?"

"I'd kill for a drink. But let's watch the end at least..."

"I know a private club near here, a place for a decent smoke."

"Fine with me," Kate says, grinning a little over her pinafore. Again, she apologises for her clothing, her red blouse and tartan belt making her the right side of presentable. "Don't miss the ending, though, Mr Marwood," and she points back at the stage.

At that moment Mr Justice Denman from the head of the cart cries out to the crowd, now baying for blood. In a single stroke he double-whips the dazed-looking horse and the beast rears its head in alarm and races away. The prisoner pivots for two seconds, aiming for suspension between life and death, secures his hidden feet on the assistants' block of wood, and manages to let out a scream. The crowd goes quiet and he holds his breath in short bursts, mimicking strangulation as his face turns crimson—he cannot simulate the ashen blue onset of *rigor mortis* for obvious reasons. Nevertheless, primed on hangings of the past and tales from the *Newgate Calendar,* the people of Covent Garden delight in this simulated death, no less disappointed because it is a fantasy. With a final gurgling, the man conveys he is dead, the assistants step aside, and like a magician, the hangman waves his hands over the audience, all children to his god.

"There, justice prevails, and once again, London is the greatest city on earth!"

The crowd is fooled in proportion to their alcoholic consumption. A last hurrah goes up: the executed actor dangles on the rope, mimicking death, his thumbs carefully clasped inside for an inch of breathing space. But already the centre of merriment has shifted. Somewhere in the Piazza a harpsichord player strikes up, and a woman can be seen on stilts making gestures to children, a brass tin for loose change on a string to her ankle in case of theft. At Kate's elbow a vendor calls out "toffee apples, hot-dipped toffee apples, good as Guy Fawkes tasted 'em before he got the stretch!"

The people remember they are on holiday, and that a hanging is merely something of the past, at least in public. Let the gin and the wines of life, the hedonism of the capital, resume!

Marwood turns to her and says: "I can show you a real execution."

She laughs of course. "How 'bout that drink first?"

"If you'll let me buy."

"Do I have to answer that? You look like a gentleman."

"A gentleman *extraordinaire,*" Marwood says, and smiles, revealing grey teeth, but teeth more appealing than his eyes. Kate finds few men frightening, anyway, so that is persuasion enough.

It is now dark. Marwood leads the way, suggesting they head for his tobacco club. "They do not like my secret profession anywhere else," he says cryptically, "too low-born for them!"

"How far is't?"

"Well, we must walk to Islington, not even an hour. Is that too far? It's where Sir Walter Raleigh first began to smoke. They allow women in the back parlour with the *aficionados*—away from the aristocrats up top. I can teach you to smoke a clay pipe." He offers his arm, and Kate takes it, shivering a little and affecting the need for warmth.

"I already know," she says. "You crush the herb into dry powder, use a spoon to press it to th'end of your pipe—and then put fire to it."

Marwood smiles. "Nothing finer than a woman who knows how to smoke," he says, thinking of his wife's distaste for the habit. "I think the Tobacco House will find you a delight!"

They do not make it to Islington, though, owing to Kate's lack of desire to head so far from the river and—without telling Marwood—from her son Daniel. Instead, exiting the Piazza and cutting through Cambridge Circus they enter Shaftsbury Avenue where Kate releases an impromptu cry, letting it ring in the darkness for an extra second. Marwood is startled but realises it's only someone carrying a lighted candle.

"Miss Thomas," Marwood says, reassuring her and taking her hand, "it's nothing, nobody." And he points at a real victim, the crumpled figure of an old man passing hunched and scraping along the wall, doing all he can to keep the flickering candle level so he does not have to return for a second one.

"Who is he?"

"Nobody," says Marwood, "a tramp—someone trying to evade the law that's all. It would be better if they chose activity over idleness."

Kate catches his tone, and ignores it, staring instead at the bony old man whose shawl has fallen off his shoulder revealing bare skin. She feels no pity, though, despite her closeness to his suffering.

"What did he do?"

"The penalty for insulting an alderman, probably. He must walk barefoot from Guildhall into Cheapside through Fleet Street carrying a three-pound candle in the hands. The people en route can treat him as they like!" Kate now laughs—ironically at real punishment after the false horror of the mock hanging—so reassuring her of the justice of both punishments, Marwood squeezes her hand.

They enter Dyott Street and are back under Victorian lights amid the people and hansom cabs rushing by, the upper crust heading to the theatres, the poor scrabbling to get home across the city.

"Did you know, Miss Thomas, that until 1790 women were hanged at Tyburn for killing their husbands?"

"Well, of course."

"But did you know women's corpses were publicly burned after hanging?"

"This is morbid, Mr Marwood. Can't we jabber about

something else? Will you be betting on the Grand National this year?"

"No, I will not. A dreadful vice!" and he shakes his head, disgruntled. "Those gamblers, they should be…"

"Hanged?"

"No…just…they should be charged. The state should make them pay."

"Just not with their lives."

"Let the punishment fit the crime," Marwood says. "Don't you agree?"

"What about 'turn the other cheek'?"

"It's not in the Bible. But 'an eye for an eye', that's in the Bible."

Kate smirks, and despite his dour personality, she finds her companion's dry humour appealing. She is even having second thoughts about robbing him. Even so, by complaining of her fright caused by 'the wandering candle' she persuades Marwood to change direction, closer to Piccadilly Circus and enter a nearby drinking den, *The Oxford & Cambridge Arms*. Despite its name, the place is packed with a boozy clientele neither physically nor spiritually washed, all looking for free drinks.

Kate leaves Marwood at the bar and disappears upstairs to a quiet nook where they won't be bothered. He finds her soon enough at a wooden table, a chipped mirror peering down on the scene.

"Tell me more about punishment," Kate says with a wink as he sets two pints of stout, a chaser of hot coffee, and begins knocking the ashes from his pipe. Something begins flickering in his left oddly-transparent eye but Kate does not notice; he soon steadies the skin on his forehead with his fingers, settling the eye.

"Well, you know the pillory? That's good entertainment."

"Tell me," she humours him. "You seem to be an expert."

"An expert *cobbler*," he corrects. "Manufacturing is behind all professions, except pen-pushing."

"Of course."

"So the public pillory was abolished in the summer of 1837. We should bring it back!"

"Hear hear!" Kate whispers.

"And humanise it."

"Human-what?"

"Make it safer, so it serves its purpose, and no one gets

severely injured, unintended, or gets stuck there for the night and murdered."

"Did that happen?"

"Yes, all the time. Still does."

Kate wonders how much Marwood is worth. If she gets him drunk, perhaps she can nestle him into a corner and rifle his coat—go through his pockets without throttling him. She is turning this over in her mind, sipping the coffee, when he starts to feel that Kate has a peculiar side to her demeanour—why is she gloating over the pillory, say, and not feeling repulsion? Aren't the details too graphic? At the same time he is gripped by the fact he has an audience, and a women too, for a dark and bloody conversation.

"So the pillory was essentially a 'just revenge' for fraud—humiliation really—and if you were guilty, Miss Thomas, you'd be drawn on a horse facing the tail and sporting a fool's cap. No expense spared because, as you know, the public must have its show. Then a band of pipers and trumpeters would lead you a merry dance around old London while people threw rotten fruit."

"Ug! Where was the pillory?"

"One was in Cheapside, one in Cornhill. Then the property you deceitfully sold, Miss Thomas, would be burned before your face! If you were a counterfeiter and dealt in false coins, those coins or dice were suspended on your neck." Kate's face droops at this litany but to play along she makes mock expressions of disgust. Nevertheless she is glad some of these punishments have slipped into the past. "If lying is your game, a whetstone was suspended from your neck, symbolizing a sharpened tongue."

Kate asks him for a cigarette then reaches for her drink—the whisky. She chases it down with the warm coffee and lets the glass phial cool in her palm. Marwood lights his pipe and hands it to her.

"Tell me about the hanging. The one at Tyburn."

"That's a tale and a half—you just witnessed it in the Piazza."

"You know as well as I," Kate whispers, "that was a fake."

Marwood leans back and draws deep on the pipe, blows through his hair to the dirty ceiling. He glances down the alley of booths, but no one is there, and then up to the stained-glass window overhead, displaying Christ the babe in its mother's arms, mother and child. He is uncomfortable, but slowly the fog of his pipe envelops him and the whisky begins to seep inside. Before he knows it he is talking, wondering why he is attracted to this ordinary girl: this Miss Thomas is certainly not pretty but she is younger than his wife, and she has an aloof quality, a kind of open vitality. Already he is caught in the web of her charm. The words tumble out of him and Kate affects deep concentration.

"Tyburn really begins," he whispers, "in Newgate Prison. About eleven in the morning the prisoners have their shackles removed, hands tied, and they are forced into the back of a horse-drawn cart." He takes a breath. "As the prison gate opens they see daylight. The two-mile journey could take up to three hours because of the crowds: by the 1750s, Miss Thomas, London was the biggest city on earth, its population almost three quarters of a million. Thousands attend the spectacle of a hanging—'tis theatre! The cart moves slowly down Broad onto St Giles and the Tyburn Road, now Oxford Street. Already the crowds are cheering their own survival, while the three-cornered gallows awaits!"

Marwood re-lights his pipe.

"A journey to Calvary."

"Exactly. Down from Newgate to Snow Bridge across Holborn Bridge and down Holborn Hill."

"I walk that way all the time."

"At the church of St Giles-in-the-Field, refreshments are served—jugs of ale."

"You make it sound like a gala-day."

"It was always a gala-day, Miss Thomas. The carts reach the foot of the Edgware Road, but not before stops at *The Bowl Inn* on St Giles where the prisoners could drink for half an hour, then *The Mighty George* in Holborn. For this is a slow procession, drowned in wine and ale but leading only one way—to the three tall posts of the Tyburn 'tree'."

"So what happened?"

"Well, imagine yourself in the crowd. You'd be hanging from a window for the best view, of course, and all around people'd be throwing rotten food. You know, girls would be blowing kisses, and the City Marshall'd keep the cart surrounded by armed guards on horseback—to prevent heroic escapes. Remember, this was the first time in weeks the prisoners tasted open air."

"Free, if not fresh," Kate giggles.

"Yes—and finally they reach the Mason's Arms, a pub in

Seymour Place. If you had the money, you could watch their last meal from a hollow wooden gallery overlooking a basement—a spectacle in a cage. You see, the City Marshall has to be supremely cautious here, but even so the prisoners were unlocked—for a last breath of freedom. Seymour Place still has the manacles on the walls. We can go there if you like?"

"No, thank you."

"Anyway, the cart would be reloaded, and it's probably about three o clock. Some wags would call—'I'll buy you a pint on the way back!'—and some of the prisoners would try to act all gallant. Some have a fantasy, you see, pumped up by the crowd, they're master of ceremonies, but really it's the City Marshall, priest, under-sheriff and guards. But the people are really in charge. The more bravado a man shows, the more admiration and glory he apparently gets by 'dying game'—turning up his thumb to the world."

Kate makes the gesture and Marwood smiles. "That's why the men dress in white wedding suits? To entertain the crowd?"

"Sure—but some prefer to insult the crowd, it all depends."

"On what?"

"Just personality. Who they decide to be, at the end. The last moment defines you, after all."

Kate ponders this a moment, takes another shot of whisky, then a coffee chaser.

"Sometimes, twenty thousand people heckled and mocked the men—it's hard to hear."

"You've been to these events?"

"Sure, when I was a boy. Well, not to Tyburn of course, as those public executions were banned in 1783. You know, over a thousand men and almost a hundred women were hanged at Tyburn last century, discounting the Smithfield and Tower Hill hangings. After 1783 Newgate hangings were easier to manage, and even then you could get a seat…"

Kate grows a little uneasy. "How do you know so much about this?"

"I like the history."

"You like it? Did you see 'justice prevail' recently?"

"The Anthony Klaus hanging," Marwood says. "I was…there."

"That was a long time ago."

"Wait. Yes, you're right. Ten years ago!"

"I would have been about nineteen."

"Well, that would have made me forty-nine, back then."

"Oh, okay. What happened to the Tyburn Tree?"

"It was cut down," Marwood smiles. "Turned into beer-butts for cask barrels in *The Carpenters' Arms*, a fitting end, wouldn't you say? People could drink to the unlucky souls for evermore. That was 1783. Then the New Drop came along—a two-beamed gallows at the Debtors' Door of Newgate Prison. You just stand under the gaol now and watch the execution, and that draws just as many people!"

"So, you didn't finish the Tyburn hanging. The details…"

"There's not much more to tell. The prisoners would be blindfolded and hooded, often with an amateur struggle. The crowd loved those who put up a fight, of course, even as they were swinging. The cart was pulled away and down they'd go. The priest hovered nearby, still preaching for their souls, as there could be as many as twenty on the 'fatal tree'…such slow death! Men could swing and gasp for air for up to three quarters of an hour."

"And then it was over?"

"Well, not quite. Like now, the crowd believed the dead could cure them of life. So they tried to steal the body, or at best touch the dead man's hand. A severed hand could bring ten guineas. Meanwhile the surgeons would wait for the guards to win the body for them, and beat down the crowd. But people would be grabbing the dead man's hand and placing it on their body,"—at this moment Marwood takes hold of Kate's hand, "if I may," and taps it on his collar bone, "I've seen ladies with their chest exposed just to get the touching cure of dead flesh."

Kate stares, open-mouthed.

"The worst was the anatomists' table—the Crown's stopped hanging, drawing and quartering in peace-time, of course. But people still feared their relatives being one of the chosen few, as only an intact body could lead to 'resurrection' after death. So dissection was a horrendous sacrilege, causing disputes between the anatomists and family. So the dead bodies were taken back to Newgate under 'surgeon security'. But the deals would begin earlier…"

"Deals?"

"Bartering for the dead. The relatives would pull on the legs of their family member to squeeze the life out quicker. Then they'd struggle with the City Marshall for possession of his body. In many cases this was a genuine claim, as they'd paid an 'Ordinary's Account' containing the relative's dying confessions and speeches, to make money from his loss. But deceit and corruption were rife among the authorities, you see. If the body looked healthy, the Surgeon's Hall at the Old Bailey took it away anyway. The bodies were prisoners even after death!"

Kate's eyes light up, completely lacking in fear, but she feigns disgust. A speck of water appears at the corner of her mouth.

"I'm sorry," Marwood says, realizing his intrusion. He sits back. "It won't happen again." Kate pretends to adjust her petticoat as though to straighten out his sin.

"No permanent damage," she says, trying to make her voice shaky like a lady's. "So what about the clothes?"

"People would try and get those too—the hangman William Calcraft was a terror. He'd sell the ropes to private collectors, people who like morbid curios, lucky charms. They want the gallows wood itself. Can you imagine?"

Kate pictures herself tearing down the Tyburn tree for the wood, a body still swinging there. Her expression remains a blank.

"For its miracle power?"

"Exactly, comparable to holy relics, like the spring at Bethesda. Ropes are good for the complexion, too, especially worn hanging ropes."

"What are you saying, Mr Marwood?"

"Nothing," he says, "nothing, I assure you."

There's another pause in the conversation before Kate begins her own tale, sensing the need for balance. She finishes the coffee and after Marwood hands her his pipe, she takes a contemplative toke or two, grinning softly, and causing him to smile in anticipation.

"I saw a man hanged once. He was a hangman himself. Funny that, isn't it?" She peers at Marwood and believes the skin on his forehead pulls back a little. "Yes, it was a long time ago, when I was a young girl—but I remember his name. Owing to the wall posters back then, y'see. Name o' John Price—'ad a price on his head—th'hangman who was hanged!"

"Where?"

"Hung in chains in Bunhill Fields—you know, the burial ground of the famed poets, those that don't make it to Poets' Corner in Westminster Abbey."

"Yes, William Blake's there…and Robert Browning."

"Anyway, close to that Bunhill place he attacked Elizabeth White, this apple seller, an' she dies four days later. Brutal crime, y'see. And the boy was young too."

"What's the moral of the story?"

"No moral," Kate says, and smiles. "Moral-less, in fact. He got what was comin' to 'im."

"Divine vengeance?"

"Human justice. The earth's justice. What's the difference, eh? They hanged him all the same—and he was guilty."

Marwood is quiet, then leans in. "I got one last story for you. Then I best be off."

"Me too—I got errands to run. Got a job an' all."

"Oh yes, where do you work, Miss Thomas?"

"South of the river, near Kew Gardens. Richmond-on-Thames."

"I know it—well, heard of it. Like a spa town."

"Something like that."

"Nice pubs," Kate adds and Marwood stares at her, a direct-speaking woman all puffed up and proper—he's long since guessed she's far from a London lady. He does not inquire about her job.

"The case of Ether Hilmer—it gives me nightmares," Marwood says, "since she was a woman, and the crime was so brutal. The worst of it was the hanging itself, while we're on the subject. It was that William Calcraft's debut killing—the bungler."

"But who was she?"

"Well, a murderer, an unpopular sadistic child-killer, probably insane. This is only recent too—took place in the age of the prison New Drop, inside the prison see, but open to the street for the crowds. That's how I know. I saw it live with my own eyes."

"Go on."

"She struggled with her guards, apparently dragged from her bed that morning and thrust in a straightjacket. She had to be held under the fatal beam, as the crowd hissed for her doom, and Calcraft, he cheered. Good old Calcraft, three cheers for the hangman, the bungler rewarded! Disgusting!"

"Mr Marwood…"

"No professional code of silence and quietness—just working

for the crowd."

"Are you a hangman?"

"…so Calcraft finally slips the noose over Ether's head and pulls the bolt on the New Drop and she drops through the floor. She was evil, though. This once time, the hangman was celebrated and the victim hated!"

"Is it envy?"

Marwood pauses, aware of Kate's questions. "You know, my wife is not interested in my job. I got the job in 1874. It's a private business."

"You're a police detective? A Bow Street man?"

"I'll tell you next time." He stands up and drains the whisky in his glass. "If you'd like to meet up for another drink?"

"Well, perhaps."

Marwood hands Kate his private business card—'Gentleman Executioner'.

Kate reads it. "I thought you were a cobbler?" she smirks, and in return she re-presents her name—Miss Thomas of Richmond. "I may be selling some furniture, if you're interested."

"I have a place—a government lodging," Marwood replies. "Goodbye, Miss Thomas. Write to me at the address on the reverse, if you'd like more company."

"I will, Mr Marwood," Kate says realizing she is losing her attempt at robbery. But learning the man she is talking to is a hangman—and the softening effect of the whisky—has distracted her. Marwood bows his long black coat, takes his hat and one last look at her, while balanced on his shoulder is the smiling cherub of the pub's stained-glass window.

Kate smirks awkwardly. "Goodbye," she says, as Marwood brushes past.

For a while she sinks down there, thinking—he can't be a real hangman. The short-term mugging having failed, Kate realises that the best method is the long con against this well-to-do man; for her, Marwood is not a cobbler but clearly a mysterious professional of some kind, a priest over-interested in death or a law clerk too keen on 'bringing hanging back' to a public arena.

What do I care, she muses, so long as he's got some money, even if his fancy clothes look like hanging garb. "For all I know," she says out loud, "he may be the Lord Mayor of London."

Kate Webster, alias Miss Thomas of genteel Richmond, tips the whisky back but remains in her seat, a little giddy.

Chapter 7
Inspector Gil Sequin and Deputy Nimrod Jones
18th February 1879, Tuesday

At that same moment, in a Bow Street window overlooking Covent Garden, Inspector Gil Sequin and Deputy Nimrod Jones are finishing their paperwork for the day.

"'Bout time we were back on the street, sir," says Nimrod, his throat dry.

"You're just thinking of booze," Sequin says, and folds his arms in disgust. "About time you went back on the wagon, you mean, the drink can't do your hunting brains good!"

"You do the hunting, sir, I do the catching."

"Well, true enough, Mr Jones, "true enough."

Ten minutes later they are standing in the Chandos pub near Trafalgar Square, the squat and stocky Nimrod Jones trying not to gulp his first pint of the day, Sequin leaning purposely on the bar to survey the room, a soda water in hand. As ever, he stares into the bubbles and waits for the music to begin.

"S'funny how you enjoy the grain," Sequin says, looking down on his assistant, "while my poison is the music, the Lethe bath I slip into while remaining alert and sober."

"I'm most alert and sober after a couple of these," Jones says and clinks his glass into Sequin's.

The inspector watches the bubbles fizz and swirls his glass to repeat the effect.

"Music to my ears…"

"…is drink to my stomach."

"Quite so, Mr Jones. Let's just hope I never have to drink again."

Jones stretches his calves as he stands on tiptoe to look Sequin in the eye, his boss a head taller at six-five to Jones's five-six. "You always threaten the doom of that day, sir. What actually happened?"

"Well, you know I was an army officer, disgraced."

"I do."

"Well, that's what happened—the disgraced part. I was doing a tour of Rajasthan with the Second Welsh Regiment, and I shouldn't have been in Agra, but my wife—God rest her soul—was left an inheritance by an uncle. He insisted she see the Taj Mahal, so I had to go along to make her happy!"

"I see."

"Well, it was so damn hot and humid, Jones, pardon your French. I had to drink gin with quinine for the mosquito bites and malaria, so there was every excuse. I was sozzled before breakfast most days. By the second weekend, it was honourable discharge and back to Blighty. My feet didn't touch the ground."

Jones giggles a little and Sequin stares at him quite sternly. "You've heard the story before. But basically, if you want to stay a Bow Street Runner, you keep me away from the head-blasting drinks or you won't have a boss to report to…"

"Agreed," Jones replies, and downs the rest of his pint. "So what's next on the roster?"

"This hangman fellow," Sequin says, pressing his monocle to his eye.

"I think I see him now."

Across the bar, Marwood has appeared in the doorway, poised uncertainly as his eye drifts over the room. For a brief second he is framed with Vice Admiral Lord Horatio Nelson's column over his shoulder, a heroic image that Jones points out.

Sequin steps forward. "Good morning. Mr Marwood, I presume? I am Inspector Gil Sequin of Scotland Yard, and this is Deputy Nimrod Jones."

"Pleased to meet you," Marwood says, extending a gloved hand, before he apologises and removes it. "Forgive the glove, I'm testing it for next week."

"Who is stepping off into eternity?"

"Charles Peace."

"Really?" Sequin says. "Of course, of course. I never thought it would really happen."

"It hasn't yet."

Marwood takes a moment and stares at his companions, the smaller one tilting the empty pint glass into his teeth searching for last beer drops in the foam, the other one taller than himself, precise-looking, a gentleman. The hangman is somehow affronted, certain to be exposed as a provincial type out of his depth in the capital.

"Inspector Sequin is very musical," Jones continues. "He loves the ballads of death!"

Sequin does not flinch, but Jones lets out a muffled guffaw at his own joke. Somehow it's the perfect icebreaker.

"I admit," Sequin begins, "I have a weakness for those Last Dying Speeches sold at hangings. A friend of mine used to sell them, and I got my hands on them cheap. He was known as a 'flying patterer'."

"Or 'death hunter'," Marwood adds, with a smile.

"Sold at the very moment of execution," Sequin says, his mind lost in the memory of childhood happiness, "halfpenny a sheet. We used to race down there on a Monday after school. So barbaric, I can't believe we did it now!" He tipples his soda water. Marwood can't tell if he's serious, given Sequin's manner of co-opting one's attitude while presenting an appearance of superior buttoned-up morals.

"I was a "pinner up" myself," Jones says, "sticking hundreds of those ballads on iron railings, on the 'dead wall' as they called it."

"It's still the dead wall," Marwood says, and the men stare at him.

"Sometimes they were bound in a scroll."

"Yes, a 'long song', " Sequin muses, "with many ballads together. But who could afford that?"

"Only you, sir." Jones smiles.

"My father was a barrowman in Covent Garden," Sequin says, puffing out his chest; his bearing is somehow enhanced by the inverted snobbery—again it remains impossible to tell if he's serious. "Don't pay too much attention to Jones," he continues, as though Marwood were more amazed by his deputy. "Nimrod is my witty foil, always making fun but secretly respecting me. You probably know the kind in your trade."

"I work alone. There's my son, but..." Marwood stops himself, not wanting to think of home.

"So down to business," Sequin says, downing the rest of his soda water with intent. "What time do you need the officers?"

Marwood is taken aback by the deference. "Well, the hanging is at eight."

"Naturally."

"But the walk from the condemned cell's about seven fifty. We don't want too much time on the platform, but it takes those minutes to attach the ropes, secure the prisoner, add the noose."

"Trigger the drop," Jones says.

Marwood looks at him squarely. "Yes, to release the drop."

"And the crowds start building at what time?"

"Well, normally the executions would be inside Newgate," Marwood says, "as usual. Gone are the days of ridiculous crowds— the Tyburn days—where we might have a wooden platform hanging over the street."

"True," says Sequin. "But Charles Peace is so famous, the mob will gather anyway." He produces a pencil from a hidden pocket, begins tapping its point against his cheek with a faintly ridiculous air. Jones stands quite still, his blue uniform catching the dull winter sun from a window.

"More drinks, gentleman?" inquires the Chandos barman and is waved quietly away by Sequin's hand, a gesture reminiscent of the Queen rolling down the Strand in her golden carriage.

"The point is," says Marwood, "that an exception is being made for Peace. He is famous, like you say, about as famous as Jesse James is in the United States—only we've caught Peace and Jesse James is still free."

"They'll string 'im up when they catch 'im," Jones says.

"Jerk 'em up," Marwood corrects. "They tie a rope to his neck, hoist the rope over a beam, and pull. The neck usually goes with the rope."

"What's the difference from the drop?"

"The direction," Marwood says, "or if you want to be technical, gravity." For the first time Sequin notices a speck of saliva at the corner of Marwood's mouth. He looks away with vague distaste but his eyes do not change.

"You know, murders are commissioned these days," Sequin says. "There's just too few executions!"

"It's true," from Jones. "It makes our job harder."

"Death's now a professional business. But we are serious detectives," says Sequin. "Take the streets in the south—the Waterloo district, out of our jurisdiction. They're the worst 'cos of the warehouses. From Ratcliffe Highway in Clerkenwell down to Hog Yard, Black Dog Alley, Money Bag Alley and Harebrain Court."

"All poison for coppers!"

"I've heard Water Lane off Fleet Street is bad," Marwood adds and Sequin raises his thin, meaningful eyebrows.

"Com-missi-oned," the inspector says. "Murder is a cold trading job like any other."

"There are still crimes of passion."

"Of course, but most is for profit. There's a place called *Blood Bowl House* where it costs six hundred guineas, less if you bargain, no questions asked. We shut it down last week."

Marwood turns to the barman and orders a pint. He is still not over his meeting with so-called Miss Thomas and this information about murder levels is quite startling. After travelling the country for six months in preparation for his London job, the hangings have become a way of life—but the extent of London's killing-for-hire is another story.

"This is not Horncastle," he whispers, and turns to sip his stout, before Jones follows his comparison like a pesky ferret.

"And these are not your ordinary police," Jones says.

"I'd take that as a compliment," Sequin says and nods. "But we didn't finalise plans for Monday. You say there'll be no platform."

"No, the opposite—the sheriff is making an exception for Charles Peace." Marwood frowns. "He knows the crowds'll be big, so it's better to put on a show. So the east wing entrance of Newgate will have the platform about thirty feet out, ten feet more than usual. I suggest your sheriffs are there from six-thirty, as the crowds build from then."

"But we don't have the manpower," Jones says, "for more than four dozen officers."

"If you have a hundred," Marwood says ignoring Jones's estimate, "that should calm things. They're expecting twenty thousand, but it could be anything from ten to forty."

"And you think twenty Bow Street Runners will serve any purpose?"

"Deterrent," Marwood says. "Just like the hanging itself."

"I thought it was a show," Jones says and grins. "Entertainment for the masses."

"No need to speak truth," Sequin says and tips his hat. "We all know it's entertainment more than a lesson."

"Point taken."

"Listen, Mr Marwood, we can have the men there from seven, don't you worry. All we need from you is a promise to see the end of Charlie Peace cleanly. I've seen enough of those Calcraft executions to last a lifetime."

"That is not something you need worry about," Marwood says. "Peace will pass away like a summer's eve."

Marwood smiles, showing his crooked teeth which he likes to keep secret. He looks along the bar at the dropouts and evening boozers, the occasional sailor, a girl hanging on a young banker's shoulder who looks like he needs to go home. For the first time since arriving in London, despite present Bow Street company, he begins to relax. Outside it is quite dark, and he pictures Miss Kate Thomas for a moment upstairs at *The Oxford & Cambridge Arms*, still sitting at that table—a strange mixture of refinement in a purple petticoat, he thinks, masked by obvious neglect and worry. Given they both have a son, he wonders, why didn't I ask her more about her boy? And where is the father?

"So tell me more about your love of hanging ballads?"

The question startles Sequin, who is exchanging a few words with Jones. "The songs, the music," he replies. "There's no mystery. I've heard them all my life. From 'Dinah' to 'Billy Barlow'. Do you know 'The Rat-Catcher's Daughter'?"

"I can't say I do."

"There's a boy plays it on Poland Street outside *The Mockingbird Tavern*. I confess it's quite beautiful, though Jones won't agree. But I drop him a penny, as he plays both the flute and a cracked guitar, and I always wonder how the guitar got damaged."

"Someone stepped on it," Jones says—clearly the stocky deputy is getting a little tired of the chit-chat. "I think we should go to another bar."

"Music is everywhere in London," Sequin says, holding up his hand. To outsiders he'd seem tipsy if it weren't for the soda water on the bar. "When I was a kid the streets were alive with barrel-organs, the bagpipes and the drums. Indian bands too, 'Abyssians' playing the violin, tambourine and castanets. It was all very exotic."

"Those people are still around—but paid to work the gin slings," Jones says. "Business again."

Marwood tries to join the revelry. "I know "Will You Meet Me at the Fountain?' 'Cos in Horncastle there was a deaf musician who played it on the violoncello with his feet, and a one-legged trombonist who drove him round in a bear-cart."

"A deaf musician?"

"That's how he advertised. A true Beethoven!" They laugh, and Marwood is pleased. Here he is, the new hangman of London and Middlesex with his friends, the detective inspector of Bow Street and his dog-like assistant. He continues with full-force, even jabbing Jones in the chest a little as he thinks he'll appreciate it; Jones clearly pretends to. "But, you know, I really don't have time to hear the street ballads—I must work on my experiments. I can't attend the cock-and-hen clubs or the 'free-and-easies' where you probably go, Mr Jones?"

"I certainly do," is the reply, "and please, sir, call me Nimrod, everyone does. What else is there to do after work than appeasing my boss for a few hours in the pub?"

"Go home," Sequin says, "and work on the case?"

"Well, I prefer the low ballads and pantomime humour of the devil's dens, while the inspector likes the street songs. Above ground is cleaner of course! So stick with me, Mr Marwood, if you want to be a porter-drinker and go slumming in the boozer kens of St Giles!"

"I appreciate the offer."

"Otherwise it's more dangerous above ground. You'll get caught by the 'sellers of false wares'. They'll show you a lurid picture with 'blood and flame mounted on a pole', London motifs, like the Tower and headless horsemen or some such nonsense to get your attention. Then they'll flog you a battery-powered hen."

"Don't worry," Marwood laughs, unworried his new associate Nimrod is losing the plot—clearly the pints are taking affect. "I've been around the block a time or two."

"But you like the Tyburn ballads?"

"Sure," Marwood says. "They're romantic."

It's Sequin's turn to laugh, and the uncommon sound escapes

his lips in a suppressed rush. "Ah, the flash songs as the poet says 'roaring in cadence rude'." For a man who does not drink when the abuse of alcohol is all around, the inspector reveals a peculiarly flamboyant side—the alternative singing career Sequin wishes he'd pursued. But he tries to keep it under wraps given the figure of fun he could become among the ordinary 'pavement pressers' at the Bow Street Runners. "The Tyburn ballads are full of rich feeling, don't you see? The highwayman romances are a slice of the past, the scaffold ballads mournful in slang and canting song!"

"Penny gaff melodramas," Jones says. "Too clean by half."

"Sure, they aim for the middle class of tradesmen, I can see that."

"Sung by dandies," Jones adds, appealing to Marwood. "It's worst on Sundays—all these gruff men dressed as babies and wet-nurses, wearing striped silk stockings and rollers in their cheeks."

"The Fox and Hounds Club," Sequin interjects. "Or the Temple of Flora!"

Without further ado the inspector breaks out into song, without moving an inch. He raises the 'penny dreadful' ballad just above the noise of the pub, and taps his fingers patiently on the bar. Below a curl of his black hair, his eyes are twinkling.

Up the ladder I did grope, that's no joke, that's no joke,
Up the ladder I did grope, that's no joke.
Up the ladder I did grope, and the hangman spread the rope,
O but never a word said I coming down, coming down,
O but never a word said I coming down.

When the verse ends, Sequin's expression turns to his normal, vaguely cynical opaque, layered on top of a smooth skin. He sips his soda water one more time, while Marwood stands quite stunned at the strange and somnambulant performance.

"You know, we were complimenting you just before you arrived," Jones says.

"Oh."

"Yes, the Lincolnshire cobbler, as I was saying, is the first to measure his job as a professional. You deliver a service—but I understand, so goes the rumour, that you only get paid at piece-rate?"

"How impertinent," Sequin says, and looks at Marwood for

the answer.

"Ever the detective," the hangman says. "It's true, sirs, I am only paid by the job. You should think of the unwanted fame the job attracts, though—or I should say, infamy. In the eyes of the sheriffs, I coin that attention. But the grandest of all is the free train journeys."

"Not to be sniffed at!"

"I'd cash in the fame, though—it's more of a stigma. Who wants to know the hangman? They'd rather I stayed away like the bogeyman."

"Well, we're happy to meet you," says Jones, over enthused, and slaps Marwood on the back. "To the cider den!"

"Really?"

"*The Cider Cellar* near the Adelphi theatre," Sequin explains. "For more penny gaffs by your best ballad-writers."

"Well," says Marwood, balancing his half empty glass, and thinking a moment of his rooms in Gloucester Place, the trapdoor experiments, the floor covered in sack corn. "Yes, you've trapped me—*The Cider Cellar* it is!"

Inspector Sequin lays his glass on the bar, and with a glance around the room, gestures for the door. Jones takes the lead and opens the cold air rising from the plinths of Trafalgar Square, as Sequin holds the heavy oak-n-brass door for Marwood.

From high in the darkening sky, Nelson holds guard over London, St Martin's-in-the-Fields church, the British Gallery and the four lions.

"I wonder who they'll put on the empty fourth plinth," Sequin asks.

"Why you, of course, Mr Marwood," Jones says. "When your time comes."

"I am not in my grave yet."

They edge through the crowd weaving deeper into the East End past the theatres of Drury Lane, the people parting slightly for the blue-uniformed Jones. From *The Bricklayer's Arms* to *The Black Bull* and *The Waterman's Arms* to *The Cat and Salutation*, Marwood keeps his own counsel while Jones leers enviously through the frosted glass, pointing to each dangling sign. The street lanterns have been lit, pooling pathetic light down Long Acre—the candles from inside the pubs are brighter. There goes *The Three Herrings, The Three Goats Heads, The Three Tuns* on Portman Mews and *The Three Compasses* in Rotherhithe Street until, appropriately enough, they turn at *The Finnegans Wake* into narrow Newcastle Place through 'murderer's alley' and back onto the far end of Regent's Street.

They drop lower to the river around the Inns of Court, Blackfriars Alley and the favourite haunt of the Chancery Lane lawyers, *The Black Friar* itself. This sign hangs unseemly low, the friar's black shawl rocking in the wind.

"Where the law goes to wash away its guilt," Marwood says. The other two men stare at him, smiling on the state of their own souls.

"We're all going down that river," Sequin says cryptically, "all gallows humour is temporary comfort."

Marwood regards the Thames, blanketed in evening mist. Across its mighty waters, the double-hearted artery of England, way east where Kate took her son to Jonathan Clatter's school, the warehouses of the South Bank poke dauntingly from the riverbank, a row of wooden shacks slipping down the bank all sixes and sevens. The men keep their eyes on the new lights of the east, some of the recent building of the northern shore where the City and St Paul's rise majestically in the night. Nearby is the greater law, the sentence and the judgement, the power and the glory everlasting. For here is Newgate Prison, the launch into eternal life, a place where time stands still until that horse and cart appears and the future rushes up on the prisoner—escaping for a moment, suspended in serious performance for the people—then is free from their imprisoning body.

Yet for all the grandeur of St Paul's dome rolling and disappearing behind the turrets and spikes of intervening buildings, the smell of the river is never absent. Supported by the shore mists hour after hour, in rolls the stench of baking meat, boiling glue, vinegar, tallow, horse-dung—the odour of shallow graveyards of Southwark and Shoreditch, of lives blighted by working all hours of the day, of children caught in the grind of factories, baling the sugar, honey, tar and a thousand other ingredients from the far-flung Empire into tight pots for the consumption of Kensington and Chelsea, from the King's Road to Buckingham Palace Road, for Westminster not three miles west. Marwood sees all, before the mist rolls back.

At last, under a low arch advertising 'delights scant available from Covent Garden to Mile End', the journey of these unlikely companions—the three good thieves—stops. Carefully they descend the stone steps, thankful to escape the Thames's glorious stench. Downstairs they can hear 'Jack Sheppard's last epistle' being played to the denizens of Drury Lane and St Giles, now transplanted to their current abode, the after-hours *Adelphi Cider Cellar*, just off Cannon Street.

A stocky Indian at the door grins and welcomes them, a rare sight for the coldest of winters, and clearly another exotic self-promotion.

"We are all the rage for low pantomime," he says and grins his gold-capped tooth. A peacock feather loops from his ear, and he awkwardly sweeps it aside to reveal the room—a collection of a dozen or so tables, the seated clientele a mixture of actresses after hours from their nights on stage, factory owners rolling in their seats with unprovoked laughter, gold fob watches dangling, and seedy-looking young men at scattered tables. Circular wall mirrors reflect the collective debauchery, the factory owners glancing at the actresses warily as though waiting to be caught by their wives. Serving drinks are teenage boys and dubious-looking women dressed as Egyptian pharaohs sliding among the guests. Marwood and the policemen take a table near the back and order drinks, an imperial stout for Jones, an ice water with lemon for Sequin, and a White Russian for Marwood.

"I like the mixture of burning milk," the hangman says, but no one is listening. A girl is on stage now, with little to accompany her clothing except a leopard-skin sash, a fake knife, and a Cobra encircling her shoulders. The effect is quite disconcerting given her choice of song: 'The Last Dying Ballad of Jack Sheppard'.

"Lovely snake," Jones says. "So who on earth was the rascal Jack Sheppard?"

"A popular daredevil," Marwood says. "Not to be confused with 'Sixteen-String' Jack Rann, a legendary highwayman hero who went to Tyburn in 1774."

Meanwhile Inspector Sequin is distracted by the performance, trying to look anywhere but at the stage. He resorts to sipping his ice water.

"Rann was a fancy man," Jones says. "I've read my *Newgate*

Calendar. He picked pockets on the Hounslow Road."

"The thing about Rann," Sequin interrupts, "is the buckles on his breeches were the balladeer's dream. At his death, they say he had sixteen strings of finest silk attached to his knees, and ladies were swooning!"

"And Sheppard?"

"I thought you'd know," Marwood says, "since he escaped prison a few times. Best of all, he employed a printer before his last arrest to prepare enough copies of his last speech!"

"And what was his crime?"

"Being a ridiculous dandy—he robbed a pawn-broker and bought a suit and silver sword to whip up the crowd. Then he hired a coach-and-four and rode right in front of Newgate. The printing presses couldn't print his name fast enough!"

"They don't entertain like that anymore."

"On Tyburn Road a penknife was confiscated from him or he would have escaped again, no doubt. The pamphlets he self-printed cried 'Woe to the Shopkeepers and Woe to the Dealers in Ware, for the roaring Lion is abroad.' Jack Sheppard, the one-man crime wave."

At this, Inspector Sequin goes quite red and leans forward. "Listen Mr Marwood there will be no more Jack Sheppards, Jack Ranns, Jack O'Lanterns or Jack-about-towns. I'll say this only once. We are the force to be reckoned with. The police force!"

"Understood, Mr Sequin."

"Inspector Sequin."

Nimrod Jones, glass in hand, glances back and forth wondering how the conversation has taken a direct turn.

"A refusal to be defeated, a compulsive cockiness, a vaunting celebration of cleverness and a disregard for conventional morality—that is not your average criminal."

"No criminal will walk under my nose," Sequin replies, frowning at his own words. "Whoever he may be."

"Understood, Inspector Sequin," Marwood says, a little fazed, but not beyond equanimity. "You forget, I am on your side."

Meanwhile the snake girl retreats to the wings; the atmosphere calms and Sequin leans back in his chair. Then quite suddenly, a chorus-line strikes up a familiar song off stage:

I sold candles short of weight, that's no joke, that's no joke,

I sold candles short of weight that's no joke;
I sold candles short of weight and they nap'd me by the sly,
All rogues must have their right so must I, so must I,
All rogues must have their right so must I…

"I forget myself, Mr Marwood," Sequin speaks over the song, disturbed by its jollity in the midst of his serious message. "I apologise."

"Think nothing of it."

Next a series of can-can girls appears, not exactly the show Marwood was expecting. After much stomping and 'yea-haw!' in the American West tradition, the stage clears and an old man walks on. A black jersey thrown over his shoulder, red-and-white socks pulled to the ankles and a ribbon on his buttonhole, he strikes up on his accordion. The contrast is bizarre and Marwood sits up in his seat. The tune is melancholy, suitably slow with a drowsy effect as though they had stumbled into a Turkish den thick with hookah smoke and music provided by an old English gentleman, a hangover from the Napoleonic wars:

O they told me in the jail where I lay, where I lay,
They told me in the jail where I lay,
They told me in the jail that I should drink no more brown ale,
But I swore I'd never fail 'till I die, 'till I die…

Now I must leave the cart toll the bell, toll the bell,
Now I must leave the cart toll the bell;
Now I must leave the cart sorrowful broken heart,
And the best of friends must part so farewell, so farewell,
And the best of friends must part so farewell.

"Very elegant," Sequin says, as the old man departs, tossing his *boutonnière*—a weary crocus—into the crowd. Marwood watches it fall on the floor, the boy-waiter accidentally stepping on it.

"Look, the petals are breathing," Jones says, giggles and then goes quiet. All three men impassively regard the crushed flower.

"When Lewis Aversham was hanged on Kennington Common in 1795," Marwood says, "he appeared entirely unconcerned with a flower in his mouth. He kept up a conversation with the other condemned in the cart, waving and nodding to acquaintances in the crowd. Afterwards he was hanged on Wimbledon Common in chains."

"The upper classes always hang well," Sequin replies, not wanting Marwood to claim all the tales of merry execution. "Lord Ferrers brought his own *landau*, if you remember? The sheriff's chariots followed empty behind, with a mourning coach-and-six, a hearse and the Queen's Horse Guards. Best of all, he swung in his white-and-silver wedding suit."

"His coachman was crying all the way," Jones says.

Wearying of the game but not wanting to be outdone, Marwood offers: "Dick Turpin hired five professional mourners to follow his cart!"

"You would hardly call Dick Turpin upper-class."

"My point, Inspector, is the frivolous fakery of these occasions. We mustn't forget they're public executions first and national holidays second—there is too much showmanship and self-aggrandisement all round. Half the criminals I hang are narcissists. Percy Lefroy committed a murder on the Brighton train during a robbery, *you* remember. Well, as I told you, I had to catch him by the belt before I hanged him by the neck. The ugly side of the business—what the public doesn't see."

"I hear you charge ten pounds per execution."

Marwood goes quite red, his anger piqued, but he manages to suppress it with a punning turn of phrase. "I perform a service to society," he whispers. "William Marwood, Public Executioner."

"And Dr George Lamson. Didn't he die like a gentleman?"

"On a Sunday afternoon."

"How do you feel afterwards?" Jones asks.

Marwood resents the question but given the company hides his displeasure. "I am neither happy to be rid of them nor depressed to have to resort to ingenuous technique to dispatch them. My satisfaction at a good job well done is theirs for a swift end, I imagine." The police are silent a while, struck by the candour of Marwood's speech. "I believe a bond connects the hangman and victim, between those two alone. In the end, I am dependent on him for co-operation, just as he relies on me for skill and speed."

"Quite intimate," Sequin says.

"Which we lack from the criminals, boss—I'm glad for it."

"It's a loss, though," Marwood says. "Sure, hanging is

intimate. Life and death are at stake, but I no more look at him as a killer, at the end, as he does me. We are helping each other." He turns to Jones and smiles. "They don't tell lies to the hangman."

"And I hear you are superstitious as well, Mr Marwood?"

"A man should never hang facing east. He faces west in order to enter the kingdom of God humbly—a gesture to the sun going down at the end of the day."

"A bit morbid."

"Hardly," Sequin says and looks over, a peculiar admiration in his expression. "Mr Marwood, I can catch them, but could never hang them."

"You leave that to the professionals," Jones quips, and raises his glass.

Together they toast *The Cider Cellar*—where no one has ordered cider—praising its music and musty air. Somehow the toast loosens Marwood even more about his technique. "I am also patient in quizzing the criminal about his crimes. I sleep better, in a way, if the prisoner confesses his guilt on the scaffold. Sometimes they struggle. Sometimes they go like lambs, and sometimes gentlemen." He leans in. "I have to suggest I could make their death uncomfortable to persuade them to co-operate."

"A little piece of nastiness," Jones says, "to make the medicine go down?"

Marwood looks him right in the eye. "I am their best friend at the end."

"But to get back to the point," Sequin says, pulling his chair in close. "You expect a large crowd in your experience for next week?"

"Twenty-five thousand—that's my professional guess for the demise of Mr Charles Peace. You judge how many streets to guard, of course."

"Don't worry about the details," Sequin smiles. "Bow Street will have the crowd sectioned off down Newgate Street. They'll see enough."

"They do expect a show though," Jones says. "Charles Peace lived a colourful life, and I doubt he'll want to sully his reputation at the end. A man who attends the trials of those accused in his place? Who asks a policeman for directions?"

"The showmen in life are not always the merriest to leave," Marwood says with such steady authority that Sequin peers at him carefully.

The hangman senses he is outliving his company and brushes down his Toquilla hat ready for departure. Not wanting to appear unprofessional, he grins for Jones's benefit and clinks glasses. "To the people—they'll have their theatre!"

The two policemen nod but keep a close eye on Marwood's last moments. The man from Lincolnshire appears a little drunk.

"All the criminals who keep us in jobs," Sequin replies.

"To the scum," Jones announces, with a smirk. "Where would we—the citizens—be without them?"

Marwood drains the last of his beer and stands. He feels faintly sick, the interview and discussion having outlasted its purpose. The stage is quiet, the music stopped, and as he leaves he staggers between the tables. A few chairs are knocked aside. With embarrassment he senses the eyes of Sequin and Jones on his back, watchful, judging. He keeps a rope-line for the exit, where he turns to witness Jones smiling faintly, Sequin squinting through the dark room and the can-can girls retaking the stage. Without knowing why he now makes a ridiculous salute as though hailing comrades across the Roman Senate, pulling his arm into a hanging position, twisting the knot. The reaction hardly matters—the police are busy watching the can-can girls. But sensing his own guilt, Marwood quickly turns on his heel and abandons *The Cider Cellar* to the pleasures of the law.

From upstairs comes the odour of drying matchboxes. The bells of St Paul's are tolling, a death knell to Marwood's ears as he stumbles away in search of a hansom. He knows he must head west, for further east are the pits of Bethnal Green and Stepney, the suffocating fodder yards where animals—pigs and goats—are chained. He does not want to wake to find himself at a Grange Hill market in the full fury of morning trade, the livestock picking at his ears and a hangover creeping through his blood. Being prodded awake by Cockney hawkers would be less than a perfect bookend to the evening—and if they discover they have the hangman of London on their territory, well, his life would not be worth living.

Marwood's fears are short-lived, though, as turning a corner to escape the chimes of Sir Christopher Wren, he finds himself somehow underneath his own future, one he does not know yet. Rising majestically with its cold stones into the night sky is the Old Bailey, and at her side like a prodigal sibling, a darker and more mysterious twin, is Newgate Prison herself. Tonight Marwood is tired, though, his encounter with the police and the planning of Charles Peace's execution exhausting him. Even so, intentional or absent-minded his fingers trail along the walls of Newgate like a whisper in the night, an echo of future sadness, the glory and defeat that await him. For a moment he imagines he hears a cry, a woman's voice, but he must be mistaken. For he does not know any women in Newgate, nor is he scheduled to hang one, the crimes of women being so much more palatable than their brothers. Fortunately he has never executed a woman, so *that* does not rest on his soul.

Despite Marwood's worries and struggle to negotiate the metropolis so far from tiny Horncastle, his mind is soon hollow as his feet shuffle through the streets of Westminster, north along Tottenham Court across Great Portland and onto the Marylebone Road. At last, Baker Street—the home of an infamous detective of whom Inspector Sequin is just a pale reflection—cuts across his path. The replacement building—the bank at 211b—looks down on Marwood imperiously, possessing none of the poetry of those fictional adventures, reminding him that Sherlock Holmes carries no reality when set against the cold stones of London. And yet, something about the doorway seems alive, his knowledge that he *cannot be certain* Holmes and Watson are not sitting up late, smoking and discussing crime detection, hieroglyphics and secret lost scrolls, skeleton keys, disappearing ink and deadly poisons.

Reminded again of Inspector Sequin's hubris, Marwood sneers as he unlocks his door on Gloucester Place and staggers into the hall, barely making the couch. He will sleep well tonight, but he will not dream. "The hangman's dreams are for the guilty."

Chapter 8
Tea for Two with Mrs Thomas
19th February 1879, Wednesday

That same evening Kate returns to Richmond after checking on Daniel at his 'school for pickpockets'. The boy is 'stealing well' she is told, and apparently eats like a racehorse. She does not trust Jonathan Clatter one inch and the gloomy pallor on Daniel's face is sign enough that she must rescue the boy. For now, she must hold her tongue given the useful enterprise of Clatter as part-caretaker and part-schoolmaster, Kate his silent accomplice. The boy does need some street skills, it is true, and she has no money. But hopefully that will change now.

Kate is back in Richmond for her five o'clock appointment with Mrs Thomas. She takes the Park Road with its odour of chocolate wafting up from Chrisp Street to Hammersmith Bridge—nicknamed 'Stinkhouse Bridge' for the sickly cocoa—while continually inhaling the sugary smell. For Kate, chocolate means polite society and a life of careless leisure. She pictures eiderdown sheets, a workday drinking and the ability to sleep all morning while Mrs Thomas attends church.

Avoiding the watchful public along Richmond High Street eventually Kate reaches the garden gate, adjusting her petticoat to renew her initial impression. For a split second she regards the copper plaque declaring 2 Mayfield Gardens, wondering if she could really earn enough from this tight-fisted widow. Then without conscious airs, she blatantly licks her lips and covets the pretty little cottage in a private fantasy. Made of grey stone, it is two-storey villa with a pink-tiled roof and lace curtains, a Hansel and Gretel House "complete with a nice old lady." She taps on the door.

Mrs Thomas appears, looking sprightly.

"Yes?"

"It is me," Kate says. "Catherine Lawler, as you requested."

"Lawler?"

"Catherine."

"Ah, yes—the maid." Mrs Thomas is wearing more jewellery, a sign of high spirits, Kate thinks. "Do come in. I was just getting ready for the evening."

Kate steps over the threshold, both warmed and piqued by Mrs Thomas's desire to be viewed as genteel. As she enters the house, through a window Kate notices a man look up from hoeing weeds along a side flowerbed. He straightens his back and rests his elbow on his pitchfork.

"Oh, don't mind him," Mrs Thomas says. "That's just Billy, he's harmless." And she closes the door. Once inside, Kate is led through the carpeted hall past the grandfather clock. "Mr Thomas passed away last year—the best of men, a devout Presbyterian—and Billy looks after the garden. He's no trouble, a bit slow-witted perhaps. You know?"

"Of course, I have..." Kate is about to say "a boy of my own," but stops herself. It's clear after witnessing Billy's eyes and Mrs Thomas's halting explanation, that Billy is her son, and a disappointment. "He lives at a half-way house in the village," she says. "He has trouble...relating to people." Kate wrinkles her mouth, surprised by Mrs Thomas's sudden confession.

"He's my husband's son, you see, and we agreed he should live in the village. My point, Catherine—" and the landlady rotates her head at the top of the stairs, her face serious and strikingly agile, while a plain wooden crucifix attached to the wall appears to wobble at her shoulder, "is that you'll be quite comfortable here." She smiles and they ascend another floor to the attic. "It's very quiet. We never have any trouble from outsiders. This will be your room." She nudges open the door.

Inside is what Kate has dreamed of—a real bed. Not since Liverpool, already three months ago and her first real governess position, has she lain down on a real feather pillow. Staring amazed on this plain yellow sheet, so cleanly smooth, tears threaten escape and she frowns them away.

"Thank you."

"What? Oh yes, it's not much, I know." Bony arms bare despite the cold, Mrs Thomas wrestles the window to let in a draft. Her chicken neck shaking a little, the tight bun of her grey hair is immobile like steel wire. Kate admires the sturdiness of the old woman, envying her and appreciating the room at the same time. "There," says Mrs Thomas, securing the window up. "Now, follow me to the parlour."

Down to the first floor, on the landing appear two other rooms but no bathroom. They pass down a narrow staircase, winding down the final three steps through the kitchen into a larder-like room.

"I sometimes sit here and do my knitting. You're permitted to be here when not in your room. It's too cold for my blood, though." The parlour is nothing but a space for cold meats, with a tiled floor and a dusty skylight casting frazzled light across the shelves. Kate regards the jars of pickles, a covered fruit basket, strange sauces preserved through the long winter. The invitation is a bit of an insult, given the most alarming inhabitant of the parlour is already present— a large half-plucked pheasant dangling from the ceiling at neck height, gently spinning in its strangled state as though still alive. The implication is clear, Kate realises: she is not wanted in the living room let alone the kitchen.

"I'll probably spend my time in my room."

"As you wish—what time you'll have—this is a house in need of much cleaning and attention. Billy can handle the outside, but I thought you looked quite strong, Miss Lawler, if you don't mind me saying so."

"Not at all."

"So I thought you could repair some of the drains, plus at least re-paint the back room." The landlady leads Kate into a second parlour room, adjacent to the kitchen. "I call this the coal-shed, though it's really a storage room for all kinds of materials. It's quite big, though, and you can sit here too, if you like."

This back room is marginally bigger than the parlour, but overall the temperature is even colder as three walls are open to the outside. It is actually a tin-lined garden shed that has been reattached to the house—the wooden seams are paper-thin, their joints overlapping only inches.

"Couldn't this detach in a gale?"

"Billy set this room up in the summer," Mrs Thomas says ignoring Kate's question, her voice a mixture of pride and sudden puzzlement. "He would use it for his drawings." She hovers on the threshold, clearly not wanting to spend time here: along the walls at different heights, some upside down and most lopsided, are the oeuvres of Billy's daytime nightmares. "I sometimes hear him working hard and making noises in the garden—not much you understand, just a little moan, especially if it starts to rain. Then he'll come here for the rest of the day." She runs her nail over the paintings—blazons of colours writ large, browns and greens for twigs and leaves, all bordered with splashes of black night.

"The edges he leaves white," Mrs Thomas says, "and he writes 'heaven' and 'tomorrow' as signatures, if you look closely. I can't understand them."

"Very...interesting...and alive," Kate says, and Mrs Thomas looks at her, taken aback.

"No one has ever called them that. But I suppose you're right, Miss Lawler. They are alive."

The women exchange a glance, nod. The tour of the house complete, Mrs Thomas's inner clock tells her to head to church. Back in the hallway, she turns square to Kate. "So I think six shillings a week, and a day off on Sunday as per my note, Catherine?"

"Yes," Kate says.

"And you already know your hours."

"Yes, six until three, and five until nine."

"Quite so." Mrs Thomas smiles—her face shrivelling to an hourglass-shape—but she is not handsome, more like a bird sucking on an egg. Somehow the effect is not comic. "I warn you once, Catherine, you will find me a stickler. Prim when the mood takes me, but more often tactless."

"I believe you," Kate whispers.

"Do so!—I have an ardour for cleanliness and method, as you will see. The only way to shape a maid is to shape her mind—just as I trained young Billy!"

Kate glances up at the window and is shocked to see a face there—a man's nose pressed purple against the glass, squashed a little, and Kate fears it is Billy come to reclaim his paintings and upbraid his mother. The moment passes as Mrs Thomas unhooks the latch.

"Mr Crabtree," she says, "we were just finishing up." In the doorway is a stout man in his late sixties dressed in a long beige suit with a white handkerchief in the pocket, his head polished like a Brussels sprout. He is clearly sweet on Mrs Thomas's elegant airs and steps into the hall frowning gently at Kate.

"The new maid," Mrs Thomas says, dismissing Kate with a wave of her fingers. Mr Crabtree—a gentleman churchgoer—bows to "mi-lady," and executing a cursory nod for "the new maid," he extends his arm. The next moment, the door gently clicks and Kate is alone in the house. Through the glass she sees Mrs Thomas cross the street, a noticeable spring in her step as several neighbours welcome her; the scene is fussy and clearly they are in no rush to actually arrive at St Barnabus Church. Along the curve of Mayfield Gardens where it meets Park Road, 'the new maid' spies the ol' *Hole in the Wall*—Mrs Hayhoe's famous pub—ideally the crutch to keep Kate away from her landlady's liquor cabinet.

Kate is dying for a drink. An hour later, she is fretting over exactly how much sherry she has drunk—how to get the correct consistently of colour back in the bottle? No matter how much brown toothpaste she adds or drops of vinegar, it is either too pale or too dark. Water only seems to discolour the decanter more. Naturally, in topping up the bottle Kate finds herself drinking even more sherry, despite the peculiar concoction she has created.

Around seven thirty she is awoken by a clattering downstairs. Sitting up, Kate is not lying on her own bed, as hoped, but full-length on Mrs Thomas's sheets. She cannot recall entering this forbidden room, but here she is, surrounded by countless floral patterns, daisies and dandelions beyond a sane person's enjoyment. The sheets are a soft purple colour, a quiet extravagance with what appears to be Cleopatra's 'barge of burnished gold' sewn into the fabric. All around Kate are cushions, pillows, curtains, bedspreads and blankets decorated—with excessive overkill—by myriad pastoral scenes of deer, rabbits and ducks. The moment is one of sheer horror, like waking in a taxidermist's front room only to discover the flora and fauna is double-stitched into the room itself. The curtains, duvet covers and furniture—the coffee table's *Bride* magazine and *European Monarchy*, the vanity mirror towering over the mahogany dresser—all are draped with imitation embroidered taffeta, silk and endless lace. A miniature but fake Turkish rug with three messages, 'Welcome', 'Love Thy Neighbour', and the macabre 'Rest in Peace' has fallen from the wall.

Kate screams, trips, and before she can catch a breath, she is crawling across the landing to her own room. Unfortunately Mrs Thomas has already seen her. The old woman's face—cornered at the top of the stairs—is already turning white. Her eyebrows are two thin slugs, arched over her nose and trapped in grooves of skin, feigning death in case they never get the chance to escape.

"What are you doing in my bedroom, Catherine?"

"Oh, Mrs Thomas, you surprised me. I was just tidying up."

They face each other. The landlady tries to restrain her temper. While they are the same height, Mrs Thomas possesses none of Kate's bulky power, but a scrawny torso that quivers and thick legs encased in church stockings. Kate assesses the situation in a single glance and decides to play nice.

"I thought I heard something, but it was just the creaky window, and when I went…"

"That window has never creaked."

"…inside, I decided I could do some dusting, tidy up."

Mrs Thomas brushes past her. "Don't do it in here," she calls over her shoulder. "The room is precious to me and…" She stops and stares at Kate. "It doesn't need to be clean."

"Yes, Mrs Thomas."

"I mean, please, go downstairs. There is some silver in the kitchen—the bottle and cloths are under the sink. I take it you know how to polish silver?"

"Of course," says Kate, aware she has never rubbed silver in her life.

They separate as night draws softly in—and the argument abates. The two women have to become friendly, given they are sharing the same roof, and Mrs Thomas clearly wants to feel comfortable on their first night together. An hour or so after her return, the landlady descends to inspect the silver.

"It turns out…you've done a good job." As though narrating a polishing contest, she breaks a particularly thin smile and lays a hand on the worker's shoulder. Kate nods in her direction, sensing Mrs Thomas's hand like a bird's claw but so light she can barely feel it.

"Thank you, they are pretty," Kate says.

"Yes, but don't you go getting any ideas." The moment lingers and Mrs Thomas realises she is making a hash of their relations again. So she heaves a sigh: "You know, Catherine, it would be nice if we went into London tomorrow. To get better acquainted, you see, and I've heard it's going to be a nice day. Maybe Green Park or Kensington Gardens. What do you say?"

Kate smiles, her teeth alarmingly big so that Mrs Thomas takes a step back.

"That would be wonderful."

"Lovely, my child, lovely—we won't need a post-and-four. But you can carry my umbrella."

"Of course—may I retire for the night, now, Mrs Thomas?"

"Yes, you may, dear."

The house now goes quiet. Kate ascends to her bedroom, half in the attic and cold, but not altogether unpleasant. She leans back, her mind spinning with housework, her strange location and the booze. A round skylight window lights her mattress bed where Mrs Thomas has prepared an extra blanket—without washing it—and a tray for moving her meals to her room. Kate glances around at the bare floorboards. A few inches from her bed a plank is torn and underneath she can spy the hallway—and is shocked to learn Mrs Thomas is visible. The old woman is sitting reading the newspaper. The moon rises to fill the skylight, offering a lucid view along the crack where Kate lowers her face, pressing her eye to the wood.

Below, Mrs Thomas is hobbling to bed bearing a tray with some pills, each one identifiable under the small candle she has lit. But more appealing is what she is also carrying—the silver candelabra Kate has spent the evening polishing, a behemoth with four different holders like half a menorah. She either needs a lot of light, Kate thinks, or she is going to pray very hard…"Or just hiding the silver."

"Catherine?" the voice sounds from below. But Kate does not move an inch from her mattress. She pulls the covers close, twists into the foetal position, and rolls over to hide the moon's watching eye.

The next morning Mrs Thomas is up just after dawn, the soft light illuminating her writing desk:

Dearest Richard,

All is well here, and I hope you and Charlotte are well at Gadby's House. How is the neighbourhood? Did they manage to remove the coal trucks from the end of Hammersmith Bridge? I hope so.

As you may have guessed, I am writing with a point. I have taken on a new maid, the third in as many months, I know. But I wanted to warn you that I am as yet uncertain of her behaviour. She seemed very enterprising and polite, but yesterday when I returned from St Barnabus, she was in my room, doing God knows what, pardon my blasphemy. But the situation calls for strong words, brother, since I am not yet comfortable. Please visit me anon, and pass my regards onto your wife.

For now, please note my maid's name is Catherine Lawler and I find her to be somewhat rugged and slapdash, though she was careful handling the silver after our discussion. She may well be clumsy by nature rather than wilful by custom, but that remains to be seen—I hope you like my double-entendre. No doubt it is the wild Celtic blood rising up in her. I will have to tame her, no doubt, as you would advise. She cleans and is fairly honest but nosy. This is not County Wexford, but Richmond and there is a difference!

Anyway, I am merely writing to settle my nerves, as you may have guessed. Please do write back by return or feel free to call at the weekend. I will be here all Sunday afternoon, as Billy will be around then also.

Your loving sister, Julia.

Mrs Thomas seals the envelope and tucks it inside her apron, feeling much better about the prospects for the day. Perhaps Catherine may even turn out to be a companion as well as maid, she muses. We will see!

Upstairs, Kate stirs within the hour and after being called to the landing, she descends to the kitchen to warm some muesli and milk for Mrs Thomas's sensitive digestion. Breakfast passes without a hitch and without mention of last night. Soon enough they are on the road, walking side by side from Mayfield Gardens up Park Road hill, past *The Tea Clipper* café where Kate once stopped for a drink. The day is sheet of London grey, the sun threatening to break through. Few people are up, though.

"I sympathise with girls of the unfortunate class," Mrs Thomas is saying, "because I used to be one! My father was broken—bless him—by the East India Company exams. He didn't have the education and they failed him on prejudice—a Scotch immigrant. So I was sent to one of the cheaper boarding school—Melling's, you wouldn't know the name..." Her babble continues as they board a hansom and begin the slow ride from Richmond through Kew, Barnes and Hammersmith, weaving into the West End. "It's good to get out, Catherine. The parks are the lungs of the city!"

Kate remains quiet for most of the day, enduring the company of her landlady for the sake of free board and room. There is no discussion over the itinerary—after some fumbling with a map, Mrs Thomas declares they walk from Victoria the four miles through Central London without leaving the royal parks.

"Not too far, I hope. As you're a girl with spirit, Catherine, horse-racing in Hyde Park it is!"

Kate smiles, not wishing to get too excited over the prospect of actual fun. "There's also boxing near Speaker's Corner?"

"Barbaric sport," Mrs Thomas snaps. "What can you be thinking? Gambling and all sorts of vice—we'll stay well away!"

Instead they weave between the manicured walkways of Green Park, over gravel paths and around stone fountains. Scattered wooden benches are laid out for admirers of the blue winter daffodils now coming into bloom; meanwhile the cold creeps around their necks as Green Park slopes into Hyde Park hill, descending to the Serpentine, its frosty waters less than welcoming.

"We should really head over to St Jim's Park, or Kenny Gardens."

Kate mock-grimaces at Mrs Thomas's attempt to re-name the royal parks with insider knowledge; in doing so, Kate senses a debilitating childish manner that makes the two women not dissimilar. Mrs Thomas takes her arm against the cold, which she endures, smiling at her employer.

"You know, ladies of doubtful morals walk under these trees," Mrs Thomas says with puritanical disgust, barely hiding her intrigue. "What creatures! Apparently they dangle gold watches from their necks as tokens of their trade. But where do they get the watches?"

Signalling her distance from the prostitutes but without realizing the irony, Mrs Thomas exposes her own gold watch. Kate eyes it silently, greedily.

"A quarter past two, and this is new quartz installed. It will last for a hundred years."

"Long after we're all…"

"Dead," says Mrs Thomas, "dead!" She laughs with peculiar insistence, and if Kate were not growing used to her strangeness, she would think her quite mad. On the contrary, Mrs Thomas is having a surprisingly good time.

"Yes—they come from Spa Fields in Clerkenwell where they learned their trade. Ever heard of it?"

"Only from the fliers."

"I hope you don't resent the question, dear. Many are fallen vaudeville actresses, or runaways from the circus. Fancy that, to run *away* from the circus! According to the Richmond News, they hang about the Grotto Gardens in Roso'man Street, boozing all day with song and music…"

"Sounds like fun."

Mrs Thomas stares at Kate then halts her speech. "Can't have you getting any ideas!" she laughs and releases Kate to the cold.

Soon they reach the water's edge of the Serpentine where, sails down, the pleasure-boats are moored.

"It looks cold," Mrs Thomas says. "Choppy. That'd be the end, if you fell in."

Kate says nothing. In the distance there is the faint sound of chatter. Curving the water they soon reach one of the famous green refreshment huts selling beer and punch, tobacco and snuff, sliced pork and whole chickens strung down a washing line. Nothing looks particularly appealing and the wise old trader, his eyeglass on tomorrow's newspaper as he snoozes, fails to see any reason to wake for their presence.

Instead the two sightseers arrive at Speakers' Corner where a 'running patterer' is crying lines from *The Beggar's Opera* to no one. Mrs Thomas pretends to recognise John Gay's famous words—

'The fly that sips treacle is lost in the sweets,
So he that tastes woman, woman, woman,
He that tastes woman, ruin meets'

—and mouths along with him. At the same moment a small boy is hawking newspapers: his similarity to Daniel catches in Kate's throat, especially when he offers a "pleasing fiction" sold as a catchpenny, and his voice is equally low and sad. Kate regards the empty soapboxes—mostly fruit crates—of Speakers' Corner and there is something woeful about its emptiness, the morning pedestals now abandoned. The only voice now is the small boy whispering "git yer *Evening Post!*" and "cos' yer less on a Sunday!" while the running patterer—a man in a tartan cummerbund and flat cap dressed—speaks over the top. Together boy and man sound like a discomforting bass and alto.

"Git yer *Evening Post!*"

"*Fill ev'ryglass, for wine inspires us, And fires us With courage, love and joy.*"

"Less on a Sunday!"

"*Women and wine should life employ. Is there ought else on earth desirous?*"

A pause, then:

"*From wine what sudden friendship springs!*" says Mrs Thomas, revealing her knowledge. A strange banter continues between the two adversaries.

"*And when a lady's in the case, you know all other things give place,*" says the patterer.

"*Lest men suspect your tale untrue, keep probability in view,*" Mrs Thomas says.

The man frowns, displeased by the suggestion, and attempts to ignore her. He raises his head back, grips his cummerbund, and regales the birch trees above as though addressing a hundred Londoners.

"That's from *The Painter Who Pleased Nobody and Everybody,*" Mrs Thomas concludes with a haughty smile and re-taking Kate's arms, marches her away. "How wise are the foolish."

It starts raining as they reach 49 Connaught Square where Hyde Park meets Rotten Row, the old parade round now a horse-track for rich clientele. But the Square's majesty is what attracts Kate the most—here is Aspley House, home of the Duke of Wellington and his descendants, framed in the misty rain, while nearby, Marble Arch gleams in its fixed position as the Brandenburg Gate of London.

Mrs Thomas lifts her arms, newly unimpressed by the splendour.

"What's there?"

"Why, Tyburn of course," Kate says. Walking forward, she crouches to the bare dirt and touches the ground. There is no record anymore of the famous hanging tree.

"But there's nothing here, dear."

Mrs Thomas stares about blankly. All that remains is a small brass plaque at where Connaught Square slides into the horse tracks, partly covered by a bush. Kate pushes back the leaves and Mrs Thomas reads in her best upper-class accent:

"'Ty Bourne' or Tyburn—meaning two brooks—was once in Middlesex County at this spot and named as a tributary of the River Thames. Here the famous triple tree, now deceased, was located for centuries and saw the demise of many an Englishman and Englishwoman. God rest their souls."

"Englishwomen too."

"We've taken a ride to Tyburn," Mrs Thomas says, trying to entertain, "but where's 'Lord of the Manor of Tyburn'?"

"You mean the hangman?"

"Of course I do, Catherine. Don't you know we're supposed to 'dance the Tyburn jig'?" Mrs Thomas waddles her arms like a chicken, and bizarrely reaches up to throttle her own neck. Kate cracks a smile, taken aback by Mrs Thomas's brief humour, and wonders if this job might work after all. She helps Mrs Thomas catch her breath and the older woman thanks her.

Avoiding the drizzle, they turn back to face Hyde Park's Rotten Row where the fruit-sellers, horse-carts and people ignore them. They pass on, but not without Kate spying a seller of Last Dying Speeches, a small girl with her wares gripped tight to her chest. Her curiosity aroused, Mrs Thomas slips Kate a halfpenny to buy one, and Kate obediently addresses the girl, makes the exchange, and is handed a dog-eared roll of paper.

"Who did you get?" Mrs Thomas asks eagerly. "They're all ripped from the *Newgate Calendar*, anyway."

"Jack Sheppard," Kate says, *"the thief and prison-breaker."*

"Oh, I've heard the name. Pass it here." And Mrs Thomas reads the inscription: *"Think back, gentle reader, to the 1720s in the year of our Lord, and be not frightened of the picture you see!* Rough-looking fellow," she says, and points at the outline of a scruffy man's image, a long straw flicking from his mouth, a smirk across his jaw line, and some kind of metal implement—a twist of copper wire—in his hand. *"A daring young fellow named Jack committed many a crime, but no prison could hold him, gentle reader. From Snow Hill and Giltspur Street he went to Bartholomew Fair, did ol' Jack Sheppard. There among the fair booths he was free before they caught him, then he escaped once more!"*

"What a rascal."

"There's a list of his crimes, but we can skip that…"

"Not important," Kate says with a wink.

"The ending is interesting, though. My, what a Devil! Disgusting, really. It says *during his last bout of freedom Sheppard swindled a pawn-broker, before claiming a silver sword and flamboyant suit. He wished to die the favourite of the crowd and he even visited a printer to prepare his own Last Dying Speech. Yes, Old Jack was tired o' this life and who can blame him!"*

"Did he hang?" Kate asks, and bites her tongue.

"Be patient girl," snaps Mrs Thomas. *"…here we are. Like an ambitious young genius he hired a coach n' four and rode through Newgate to announce his retirement from the game of life—too many successful robberies! But the Bow Street Runners were too quick this time. His appointment with the Triple Tree was set, where for all London he would perform his Final Escape!* That's it…."

"That's it?"

Mrs Thomas eyes the picture of rude Jack Sheppard, then Kate at her shoulder, her eyes feigning alarm. Meanwhile Kate is drinking in the wonder, trying not to be amused.

"On the road to Tyburn the victim-murderer concealed a penknife but it was discovered. Here, you read the last bit—words from the hanging itself, 172-."

Kate reads: *"Woe to the Shopkeepers and woe to the Dealers in Ware, for the roaring Lion is abroad."* She frowns. "What does it mean?"

"Very little," says Mrs Thomas. "For who is the Lion?"

"Jack?"

"No—the hanging authorities. They are the ones to show love but fear! They protect us all, but do not cross them—especially him."

"The King?"

"Yes, dear," Mrs Thomas says, a little exasperated. "The King is the Lion. Now let's go home, because there's work to be done!"

With these words, she takes the Last Dying Speech of Jack Sheppard and tears it down the middle. Kate is surprisingly shocked. Watching the old woman, a guttural sound reflexes in her throat, since she was feeling close to Jack Sheppard by thinking of her old past in Wexford and Liverpool surviving on her wits. For a brief moment she does not move, edging towards a tear, just as Mrs Thomas is ripping the Dying Speech into quarters. Kate's reaction is swift: she grabs the remaining paper.

"How dare you!"

A comic struggle now ensues with a frightening edge. Mrs Thomas lunges at Kate with the awkward swipe of an old hen clawing at the ground in a farmyard. A few stall-holders look on in angst, others with smiles. Kate steps aside as The Last Dying Speech is caught between them and the edges start tearing.

A brazen bald man at the street corner laughs: "You want me to throw rotten fruit at you ladies? Who's gonna win the paper-fight?"

"I am, dear," Mrs Thomas calls back perversely, although with a trace of fear. She is no match for Kate's sudden anger which buried deep inside now instinctively surges out, her blood curiously fired by the tale of the hanged man, a feeling that her own skin is peeling away with Jack's paper-life.

The fight is soon over.

"Give it me, stupid girl!" cries Mrs Thomas.

"I'll give it to you!"

"Over your…" and Mrs Thomas is suddenly paralysed by a pain in her neck.

"Over *my* dead body!" cries Kate, and pulls one more time.

Snatched away, the paper scatters from Kate's paw in a dozen pieces, little bits of funeral confetti tossed into the steel-blue morning across Connaught Square to Hyde Park, and over the one-time site of the Tyburn gallows. She sees it miraculously sweeping like snow through Marble Arch.

Mrs Thomas slumps down in the street, exhausted, and Kate looms over her, pressing palms to knees to catch her breath.

"Stupid girl—I thought you were a Christian!" Mrs Thomas screams.

Kate's sense of humour has evaporated too. "You believe in God," she replies. "I cannot afford to!"

"What's that supposed to mean?"

After a minute or so, Mrs Thomas regains her breath and composure. Brushing the dust from her shawl-coat, she clicks her fingers at Kate.

"Apologise!"

"Okay, one minute," is the maid's reply. They take a minute. Painfully, Kate capitulates and begs forgiveness for "the accident of caring too much about Jack Sheppard."

"A criminal," Mrs Thomas says. "Don't be sarcastic—he was a scoundrel, and we don't need his story. As for boxing, you can forget that shameless enterprise." She is pleased to have tamed her maid at last. "And clearly there is no horse-racing today—so you misled me about that as well!"

"I'm sorry."

"Humph—time to go home! And I am a Presbyterian, my dear. That's where your forgiveness will spring from—my belief in pre-destination. We are all determined to our end, good or bad! God would have wanted our little struggle here!"

Kate frowns, not discerning any care under God's will for her own skin.

"Death is unstoppable, dear, and so yours shall be. We must make the best of life while we have it!"

"I agree with that, Mrs Thomas."

"Then let us agree, dear."

For a street or two they walk in steely silence, before Mrs Thomas elects for a carriage to take them south of the river.

At last the weak winter sun finds its way outside the clouds and adds a few light-lines to the lonely masonry, the facades of opulent-white buildings they pass down the Strand, Charing Cross and eventually back to Victoria.

They cross the river in silence. Kate looks down to the water, but she cannot see her face's reflection.

Once back at 2 Mayfield Gardens the women separate for the rest of the day, Mrs Thomas putting on a show of concern for Kate at the door, and Kate acting as welcoming guest to Mrs Thomas by making her a cup of tea. They are alone together like two lodgers, but not before Kate has picked up a note—handwritten—from behind the front door.

It is addressed to Kate Webster, a name she fails to recognise for a moment, having been called Catherine and sometimes 'Rude Miss Lawler' all day. Once in her attic retreat, she tears back the seal with a tentative, dirty fingernail:

> Are you so kind as to accompane me to Batholemew Fair Friday afte'noon? If so, plesse honour me a replie 'by return' of William Marwood Esq, 29 Gloucester Place, nr. Baker Street.
> Regads, Wm.

Kate holds the card to her chest, her mind already working.

Meanwhile in her room, Mrs Thomas writes a second missive to her brother, Mr Hughes:

> Dear Richard,
> She has extreme eyes, dark, morose and peculiarly soulless—if that's possible—for I am unduly afraid. Only this afternoon, she snatched a newspaper from my hands and tore it venomously in my face. Is that the person to have for a maid, I ask you? I must look around for a replacement. But this will be the third maid in two months! Come see me on Sunday.
> Oh Richard, she has such slipshod, ramshackle clothing and a devilish habit of clunking the tea down so it spills on the saucer. And I can hear her snores from my room. It is too much! Not to mention her slowness after hearing the bells ring—what will become of me if I cannot get a decent cook general?
> Should I throw her out of the house?

Fortunately the exhaustion of the day sends both women to sleep. No doubt their dreams are more of Tyburn than the Serpentine, but in truth of mind, it is hard to tell. Let us imagine one dreams of the small boy in Speakers' Corner—perhaps named Daniel—and a little girl selling Last Dying Speeches, while the older dreams of the rich and idle's hansom cabs rolling through Piccadilly Circus.

Chapter 9
The Hanging of Charles Peace
20th February 1879, Thursday

Marwood is dreaming. He can hear the sound of rushing air and then a sudden crack, the unmistakable note of a breaking neck. In his mind's eye, the body falls, and he grabs the air, mouth half open in sudden regret and compassion for the hooded and bound man; and just as the body disappears from sight, the dream begins over—hearing the crack from the end of the rope snapping taut, and again he is tying the knots to the man's hands—the condemned alive again—and placing the hood over his head so close to his face he can feel the hot breath, the slight change in colour of the hood as it is gently sucked into the man's mouth, in and out, in and out, as he waits to die.

Marwood cries out in fear of his conscious life. Despite rolling to the edge of the bed, he cannot escape until the hard smack of the floor hits his head. He awakes in a roll of bedclothes to an echoing knock from his front door.

"I'm looking for Mr William," the man announces when Marwood throws open the casement, "Mr William Marwood."

"I'm Marwood," he calls, the top deck of an omnibus level with his head. "It's still dark. What can I do for you?"

Downstairs they sit before the fire, Marwood serving up a pot of tea in an old drum kettle, the visitor glancing warily at his host over his cup's brim.

"No tea pot?"

"Not yet," is the reply. "I just moved in, Mr Cottonwell, as you know."

"Quite."

They sip their tea. Mr Cottonwell sits quietly sinking into an old Edwardian armchair, the arms raised high, the back a luxurious arch; low on each shoulder is a tiny symbol of empire, a camel on the left hand, a tiger on the right. Mr Cottonwell does not notice either. He is more concerned with gauging his new employee.

"Who is Marwood in town to hang?" he asks cryptically. Again he sinks deeper, the cup raised higher as though he is saving it from drowning; a short man even when upright, he is clearly a city bureaucrat on an unwanted excursion to an undesirable abode, to meet an undesirable social outcast. He does not want to stay long, make small talk, or be seen entering or leaving the hangman's premises.

"Charles Peace, archetypal Victorian burglar and murderer."

"Indeed—whose very name strikes terror in the hearts of all the King's citizens."

"I thought William Calcraft took care of him?" Marwood smiles.

Mr Cottonwell refuses to take the bait; as under-commissioner for the previous hanging he is well aware of Calcraft's failure. "It's true, Peace was hanged at Armley Gaol, Leeds on 25th February 1879."

"Pray explain, what exactly went wrong?"

"As Sheriff of London and Middlesex, I can tell you, nothing exactly went wrong. Except Calcraft was drunk on the scaffold and decided to whip Mr Peace before hanging him. The whole time he was chanting the schoolboy song 'Whipping Maketh the Man'."

"Not one I know, Mr Cottonwell."

"Certainly, the Leeds drop was an embarrassment. So the execution has been moved to the capital and falls under my jurisdiction. As full sheriff, I intend a smooth operation."

"Hence bringing me down from the sticks?"

"Hence Mr Marwood, bringing you down *by train* from the provinces."

Marwood smiles and leans forward. "More tea, Mr Cottonwell?"

"Don't mind if I do."

"Are you sure there isn't a primary second reason, as it were, for the hanging to go public. Aren't the gaols the future of 'polite' capital punishment, as I'm led to believe in the enlightened age?"

"Well, I'd like to say so. But the Vice-Superintendent of Camden has an election coming up, and as you know, we need funds for counting both coffers and coffins, or we'll be out of a job. You included, see." Cottonwell returns a smile.

"I have no objection to the job," Marwood replies. "Just one demand, that it be done right with no interference. And modern techniques."

"That's two requests."

"Then two requests."

At this Mr Cottonwell places his tea on the back of the wooden camel, and leans forward on the tiger. His black circle of hair recedes as earnestness enters his eyes. "Do not be fooled, Mr Marwood, it will be done right. Armley Gaol may be known to the public as the last hanging of Charles Peace, but there is one yet! And we will not be made fools o' like some Yorkshire three-ring circus, I can assure you of that."

"Where is Peace now?"

"The man is very much alive. You can see him tomorrow morning from six-thirty, when he has his last meal. He will enter the holding cell at seven sharp along with the priest—those bars look on the parade ground. You can speak to him directly." Cottonwell again hunches forward, his fingers gripping inside the tiger's mouth. "I came here for one assurance, Mr Marwood, that you will not embarrass the Vice-Superintendent."

"You can sleep soundly on that one, Mr Sheriff. He already sent his dogs Sequin and Jones to check on me."

"Well, consider this a political visit too," Cottonwell adds, smiling.

"I shall," Marwood replies without wavering, and raises the rest of his cup, slurps his tea. Mr Cottonwell blinks and looks away.

"I have one more question, if you please," Cottonwell says. "Who follows this Peace? Will he attract the crowd we think he will?"

Marwood stands up by way of answer. "Let me read you a chapter of the revised edition of the American journal *Celebrity Killer*." He takes it from a shelf, turns to a bookmark, and reads with feeling:

"Charles Peace is as notorious in England as Jesse James is in America today. He lives a life of brazen theatrics—home break-ins and street muggings, eleventh-hour escapes, witnessing the trials of men accused of murders he in fact committed (according to this diary), a perverse love of fictionalizing his life story (and submitting it to newspapers), a wily way with the opposite sex, and a cheeky (if not downright dangerous) habit of asking directions from policemen.

But do not be fooled, good people. Like Jesse James, Charles Peace is a cold-hearted killer. He has a history of kidnapping (people of all ages), his gunmanship is fatal (once he murdered an officer trying to arrest him). His proudest aptitude, though, remains his trickery with a violin—in his own words, to 'make it weep'—as a means to seduce, corrupt, deceive and defraud. The sooner he hangs, dear England, the better!"

"He seems to have had one eye on posterity."

Marwood snaps the journal closed. "In other words, Mr Cottonwell, he is what the American newspapers now call a cop killer. I can guarantee the operation will be performed smoothly, on time, with accuracy to the satisfaction of all."

"Not too fast, of course, Mr Marwood. The crowd must have its money's worth."

"Neither fast nor slow but correct, Mr Cottonwell, is the only way. If his reputation is genuine, Mr Charles Peace shall provide the necessary theatrics. He was quite the entertainer as a criminal and fearless too—I doubt he'll change the performance of his death."

"Is that a problem?"

"Let's just say, he and I have not met, sir."

Mr Cottonwell looks solemnly at the hangman. Then he looks pleased, and stands to shake Marwood's hand limply. Then he heads for the door, turning on the threshold.

"One more question. Does it hurt?"

"The drop, you mean?"

"Hanging. Yes."

"Only for the guilty," Marwood replies and presses Mr

Cottonwell's shoulder, causing him to shiver. "Charles Peace lived wrongly, he will fall truly, and die humanely."

Cottonwell winces at this word too. "Humanely," he murmurs, and the hangman opens the door and closes it after the city bureaucrat all in one movement before Cottonwell can show his reaction.

For two hours Kate works hard in the house, and then she grows restless. The silver is re-polished, the carpets cleaned and her own insides mortally bored.

Richmond is a quiet suburban town, and before she begins her evening work there is little to do except walk the streets, over-tipple in the pubs, and watch the new mothers push their perambulators in Richmond Park. She needs some excitement, and on the way home she finds it, in a flier on the wall of Barnes Town Hall decrying *The Spectacular London Hanging of Charles Peace, Saturday 22nd February.*

So before she answers Marwood's request of a visit to Bartholomew Fair, Kate arrives at St Paul's Cathedral. It is just after dawn. Unlike the Tyburn re-enactment, the crowds are already swelling the streets. As the sunlight breaks over St Paul's spire, dozens of people are backed into side alleys to make room for horse-and-fours and the hansom carriages vying for the mud.

Kate takes up a position at the east wing entrance of Newgate, a lucky guess in fact because no one knows where the famous platform will emerge from the prison walls. Last used in 1868, it is more than a decade since a public hanging was permitted in the capital. All executions are now deemed unsuitable overstimulation of the public consciousness, and a harbinger of their ill morals, despite all evidence to the contrary that the public will is distracted from hunger and pestilence for a single day, even if by the spectacular death of one of their own. Even as she is standing there, the platform is revealed from behind a black cloak along the prison wall, a sheet masquerading as a repair blanket, and about thirty feet out, ten feet more than usual, the wooden stage is revealed.

Even at this early hour, a communal gasp is discernible from the crowd, more thrill than horror, and the bodies surge in the direction of its theatrical prop, the raised drop of immortality, the god-like moment of a mortal ending. There, in the cold winter sun, in the split second of life-in-death, the body will dangle as a demagogue above the heads of Londoners.

Kate grips onto the flier she took from Barnes, declaring *The Most Entertaining Criminal of the Day Meets the Cruellest Hangman* in *The Only Publik Hangin' of Newgate Since A.D. 1868.*

"Business first...Execution Day is always a public treat," she whispers to herself.

Before her, up rises Newgate Prison—a stone religion centuries old, grey and cold and implacable—with no indication of the surreal drama about to unfold. Uncovered now, the wooden platform creaks gently in the early morning wind. Kate pulls her shawl tighter. She listens for any sign of life from inside Newgate's walls, for inmates on the Master's Side with money for extra food and drink, for groans from the Common Side's debtors and felons.

But she has no idea of the prison geography or thickness of the walls, or that beyond the hanging 'Newgate Drop' platform there is only the quiet of the prison garden, the graveyard and last condemned cells, the press-yard for so-called 'prisoners of note' where men and women would be tied down with weights to extract confessions.

Instead, all is calm on the inside. Above the bustle and growing excitement of the public, Kate cannot hear a word of those suffering behind the walls of Newgate.

Six feet away from her, behind those walls, William Marwood is moving between cells. He peers into the gloom of each confined hole, a stout guard unlocking interlinked doorways until he reaches the condemned row—the last one. Now he is standing only yards from Kate, though neither will ever know.

Marwood looks at the man he is about to hang.

"Good morning, gentle sir," Charles Peace says, with a grin.

Marwood knows from his *Newgate Calendar* that in the past, prisoners often choose handsomely from the prison wardrobe. Many prefer to die dapper as bridegrooms rather than in a mourner's 'suits of solemn black'.

"I see you are dressed for the part," Marwood quips, surprising Peace a little. "I hope your sister knows what you're up to?"

The short man, revealing a long facial scar and scraggly hair, steps out of the shadows. His costume is unusual to say the least, and he stares malevolently back at Marwood.

"No need for comedy. It's my show, after all." Peace unfortunately resembles his mugshot from the Bow Street Runners 'Wanted' poster. Suffice to say, he is not blessed with an angelic face, but mimics the expression on an animal's face when run over by a carriage wheel—a stoat's face, but one crossed with the manic joy of a schoolboy just released for the summer holidays.

"Where did you get the costume?" Marwood pursues, knowing he must show no fear in order for the condemned to trust him: the worst thing he can do for Peace now is show lack of resolve. He is judge, jury and executioner—God himself—and the prisoner wishes to be taken firmly and unapologetically into God's arms.

"The warden sent it down special," Peace says, his bizarre expression of delight exposing his gums. Only a couple of teeth persist in a yellow backwater, his molars stranded like lepers by a mosquito lagoon. He does a twirl—for Peace's dying request is apparently to be a girl dressed in white, sporting a red silk scarf. In his left hand he holds a basket of daisies and oranges, the fruit of opulence: he plans to scatter these favours from his personal altar above the people. "I will bless them with my gifts," he says, holding up the basket, and then snatches it away as Marwood peers inside.

More shocking, somehow, is the white dress, such dazzling colour among the surrounding grime. As a final flourish, Peace's bonnet displays a white cockade for victory over the mortal world.

"I'm glad to see you suitably composed," Marwood says, his comment causing Peace to fall quiet for once, as though a caring hand were placed on his shoulder. Marwood risks no such contact, though, merely allowing the guard to push Peace deeper into the cell. Wearing his effeminate schoolboy look lightly, the prisoner approaches the bars.

"Make no mistake, Mr Marwood," he says, "I am ready to die."

"Good, because I am ready to hang you."

Little time now remains, and somewhere a clock chimes the

half hour. For air, Marwood walks with the guard along the condemned row, avoiding glancing in the remaining cells. He learns that many of the men are diseased, since no doctors will go in the dungeon. With its double iron windows, fortified steel rails, the seclusion and claustrophobia are beyond oppressive. If the outside world is remembered too often, the stench and gloom of this underworld snicker that death is the only release. To live here under Newgate is a hell of mind, body and soul that Dante might have conceived. And yet by the slow condensing of all three, the condemned grow accustomed to this inferno, their Chaos lacking comparison, and it becomes not only tolerable but even agreeable with men as impishly merry in their sufferings as they were in committing their crimes.

The guard now leads Marwood up a spiral staircase into his preparation room. Here he can hear the crowd through a sliver in the wall baying for entertainment—a busker's tune rises over cat-calls, market bartering and the occasional shriek of laughter. Marwood is introduced to Cottonwell, who stands back in the shadows, then the burly Sheriff of London, a moustached man named Constable. They shake hands.

"I trust you know what you're doing," the burly magistrate says.

"I've done this before. Now, gentlemen, I need your assistance. Please inform me of the door to the scaffold."

"The stage," says Constable, "is this one,"—and he points low to a partition of curved wood like the turret slits from the Tower of London. "First, the visitors will throw half-pennies at Peace in the press-yard. They are to be ignored. The stage is on the other side of the yard, via a similar door."

"Where do we perform the shackling and pinioning—in the public mêlée?"

"I'm afraid so, or he will be too difficult to walk across the yard."

Marwood frowns: "That is fine." Outside, St Paul's Cathedral chimes a quarter to eight.

"It is time," says Cottonwell, and steps forward with a rope. At that moment, the air seems to go out of the room. The guard steps back, as does the sheriff, and Marwood is handed the hanging rope. He is alone, bearing death between his fingers, and suddenly the men do not want to get close. Cottonwell retreats into the gloom, while at his shoulder, a silent Charles Peace is brought forward, a Catholic chaplain on one arm, a giant of a special protectorate provided by the City on the other. Across the room, Marwood peers through a spy-hole in the wall and counts St Paul's bells, echoing St Sepulchre's across Newgate.

"Tolling the knell of criminals since the days of Tyburn," the sheriff says.

They begin the walk. Each man in turn steps through the small door and into the prison yard. Marwood grimaces as he emerges, discovering a small rectangular scrubby yard running alongside the inner Newgate wall. The rectangle is bitten at one end into a triangle—the freedom of London, somewhere beyond the point, might as well be a million miles away. They approach like a chain-gang, only silent. Already he can hear the morning gala awakening just over the wall, a mixture of ribald devil-may-care voices and moments of hushed anticipation. The crowd is ready for the show. Marwood looks up, high where the weather-vane of a Newgate tower spins mournfully in the cold air, indicating nothing but grey skies—forlorn and comfortless—masking a light drizzle. The soft crunching of gravel underfoot should be a pleasant sound, but is more like a clock counting down to doomsday.

This prison break is a terrifying release for all. Witnesses, the condemned and executioner are all playing a role, courting Death's all-knowing indifference, coaxing His attention towards their inner world. No man here could know another man's fear.

The surroundings are absent, opaque, chilling in their barrenness. There are no windows yet the parallel outer wall boasts a makeshift wire fence, offset by heavy concrete boulders at uneven intervals. Each boulder is squared off at the top, where a dubious-looking prison guard stares down on all visitors, whom he lets in one at a time, seemingly by whim. These people file down a grassy slope running along the graveyard—wooden crucifixes jutting out of the freshly-turned soil—and disappear into the belly of Newgate, her blackened red stone wordlessly enclosing them into the Debtor's side of the prison.

Here, on the felons' side of hell, the procession continues unaffected. Their exit is barely noticed, the visitors are so keen to enter Newgate's walls. The sheriff leads the group, the bulldog offspring of Mr Pickwick, neck upright, fake golden sceptre in hand. Cottonwell follows closely, before a gap then the giant superintendent and Charles Peace, the malefactor cast in a straightjacket. Next is the Catholic Chaplain, Father McEnrey, carrying the 'dead warrant' signed by the powers of execution. Marwood is merely the gun for hire, the only signatures on paper being those of Constable, Cottonwell, and the Priest—politician, policeman and God's messenger. As is customary Marwood trails the procession, noting the expensive heels of the priest's shoes twisting on the press-yard gravel.

"I am the fall guy, as the Americans say," he mouths to himself. "Their hands on the paper, but mine on the neck."

The dead man's walk is over, and they step through the additional door and enter the stone-cold room. From a hole in the ceiling, light pierces all corners of this makeshift wooden room, casting the faces of all concerned into sudden revelation as though searching for their guilt, compassion, regret—all the emotions of their lives highlighted with no place to hide. Witnessing the death of another, even with the Queen's-anointed approval, exposes the finality of their faces, like dry candles on this cold Thursday morning. The 'stone-cold room', so termed after its namesake in the prison for solitary confinement, is the last refuge of the dead man. Fortunately there is no delay.

Charles Peace is positioned in the centre of the room. Although the pinioning and tying operation takes only three minutes, Marwood has plenty of time for reflection. Executing Peace is a story he can whisper to Ellen later tonight as a kind of perverse dark courtship, alone together in his workshop with hanging ropes and Courvoisier's head. But then he remembers Ellen's distaste for the whole subject. After the early years of their marriage he knows her preference is for shoes, created by him or not, over enlivening their bedroom with straps and pinions, though she never complains about the hanging salary. He has to tell someone—such is the nature of this bloody brutal business, as the *Horncastle Chronicle* likes to call it. Perhaps Aldous is old enough to care for the tale of Charles Peace's last breaths?

Either way, Marwood is determined to cast the next few minutes as a moral decision, one that improves life and will advance hanging techniques—ultimately to make hanging less painful to the condemned. That is the aim of his scientific experiments: why do criminals need to suffer for the state so long as they die anyway? Not that the criminal is not guilty—that is rarely in question. Take Charles Peace for example, who as the *South Bank Tribune* commented, *spoiled a career in petty crime by killing a policeman.*

Cottonwell steps forward: "Now do this right, Mr Marwood," he says. "Calcraft previously earned his living by flogging boys in Newgate—if this goes wrong, that'll be your new career."

"Are you aware of where we are?" Marwood says, and Cottonwell goes a little red, confused, and steps back.

The condemned man must have his delay, though, to the impatience of all but the hangman. So for ten minutes Peace does everything he can to delay the hanging—he finishes his prayers, he needs a drink, he stops for the chaplain's sermon, another drink, he says goodbye to friends he can nether see nor hear, finally he complains that the rope is too tight—before it is even fitted.

At last Marwood is ready. St Sepulchre chimes and the state will not permit more delay. Every dog has its day, and now the City must have hers.

"You know," Peace says equably, "I had had a persistent cough overnight. I wonder if Marwood could cure this cough of mine."

Marwood smiles gently and faces the dead man, who looks back with pale eyes. Peace's incredible appearance, his head like a squashed turnip, his face craggy and sallow with tiredness, lacks all appropriate respect for the event.

"A comedy of injustice…" he whispers. "I'd like to go home now."

From polite habit, Marwood greets his client. "Are you excited to see the crowd?"

"Overjoyed," Peace quips. Then suddenly, the fear washes over him, and he need assistance. A trickle of water appears at his feet. He looks down: "I wet myself." The prison guards and officials look away, and repeatedly, the priest makes the sign of the cross in the air, and then on Peace's chest.

"I hope you will not punish me, Ma-wood. I hope you will do your work quickly."

"You shall not suffer pain from my hand."

"God bless you."

They kneel and Father McEnrey asks God's blessing. Then all

three shake hands. The bells stop chiming and the door is flung open to reveal all Newgate Street. A cold wind cuts through the wall and one by one, they step out onto the floating wooden platform—the modern Newgate Drop. The scaffold wobbles a little as they spread out. They are twelve feet above the ground, all on the same level, and just twenty feet from their necks are the heads of hundreds of Londoners, ready for a jolly good show.

Immediately the prison officials feel better—all is in Marwood's hands now—and their trauma is lessened by breathing the open air. They will share Peace's end with the people more as spectators than authorities. Cottonwell is a little saddened at this loss—this being his first execution—but Sheriff Constable is relieved and lumbers out to greet his people. He swings the sceptre over their upturned chins, slicing as though cutting through their windpipes. The shriek of expectation is greeted by a general strain to view the killer, and even more infamously, the man in black commissioned to take his life.

Despite his good behaviour, Peace now begins a campaign to cause trouble right to the end. He has to be held in place, and due to this awkwardness, Marwood is forced to tie Peace's hands behind him instead of in front. This adapted technique frees a closer examination of the noose, since the shoulders are pulled back, and Marwood begins to realise that the hands should always remain firmly out of the way.

"Oh, it's too tight! It's too tight!"

"Keep still," Marwood says, attempting to quiet Peace, "I won't hurt you a bit."

Slowly the two men ascend the thirteen steps to the top of the drop. The others follow and assemble in pre-planned positions. No one speaks. Constable falls quiet. Somehow the crowd detects this solemnity, and fearing they will be robbed of their performance, they begin to jeer.

"Show us the murderer! We cannot see!"

Cottonwell has to intervene, and he makes Marwood know that Charles Peace must face his people for a last dying speech.

"I am well aware, sir," Marwood replies. "But once his speech is silent, we wish this to be over. I must therefore make the drop exact."

"Nonsense, man, the drop is set."

"If you interfere now, there could be a calamity," Marwood says.

But Cottonwell is determined to move proceedings at his own pace. He even bends down and realigns the rope, tossing it to Marwood. "Attach the damn thing. The prisoner has been weighed—you know the length of rope to use."

"I cannot drop him on their heads!"

"Just on his own..."

"The platform is thirty feet high," Marwood says, "the fall's no worry. He'll fly like an arrow." But he fears the platform has been moved: since the length of drop is determined by the prisoner's weight in his clothes, the result has been changed. The markings Marwood asked for on the rope are not present—a line should be painted on the noose end, marking the internal circumference.

"The 18 inch mark is missing," he says.

The sheriff notices the disturbance and steps forward. "We cannot stop now," he says. "There's the mark," and he points his sceptre at a scuff on the noose. "Tie and die, we must proceed."

Meanwhile Peace is allowed to hail the crowd. He steps forward ten feet to the edge, still fastened about the waist, legs pinioned. But somehow he conveys sprightliness and begins riding a surge of cat-calls from the crowd. There he is—the famous killer who got away for so long—one of us, one of the suffering people. He is their anti-hero and they will claim him to the end, so long as he entertains.

"Good people of London Town," Peace cries. "You know me, and I know you. Let us have a good time!"

Cheers!

"We 'ave come a long ways together, n' I dedicate my life to the good people of Newgate...You have friends behind these walls, they are your bruvvers n' sisters, your muvvers and fathers, and I will no forget them as I go...ta' life's last doorway!...I will drink the lees to th'end wi' you all, and make you merry. Let's git drunk on it!"

Hurrah! A fractional time delay ends his speech, but the sentiment about drinking is clear enough, and another roar goes up. Then Peace stumbles for words—so instead he does a little jig in his white schoolgirl dress. This naturally pleases the greatest range of execution-goers, and the laughter peels away to the top of St Paul's Cathedral. Peace almost forgets where he is, wobbling close the edge but the rope will not fail, being pinned to a boulder in the press-yard. "I always was a dashing man," he cries, "and I die game as your true servant." He does a bow, and the crowd laughs, but then Newgate market is strangely quiet and grows angry, knowing the initial performance is over.

"And now for my…last trick," Peace calls, "I will survive this hanging!" The laughter returns—he will give them his all! Then launched into the air from a scallywag's slingshot, what lands on the stage but a nosegay of 'one of the frail sisterhood'—the prostitutes sitting before the Church of the Holy Sepulchre. Peace squints to the scaffold floor, and scoops up the prize. He does his final jig with the nosegay in his mouth. Finally Sheriff Constable orders the guard to reel him back to the hanging spot.

Nearby, Marwood is fruitlessly explaining to Cottonwell the need for scientific accuracy. "The noose should lock the neck circumference to a matching distance from the spine, safely using an eyelet…or I cannot be responsible for the consequences."

"It is your first drop," Cottonwell says. "It is an experiment."

At these words, Charles Peace looks at Marwood with a pleading hang-dog expression, mixed with malevolence. "I won't go easy if it ain't pain-free, like wot you said."

"I'll make you a deal," Marwood says. "I don't want a *battle royal* from you, sir. You step here, and I'll see you don't suffer."

"Sir's right," Peace chuckles, and does as he's told. Constable steps back. The victim is in place, the chalk line hooped around his feet, front and back.

"Toe the line," says the sheriff.

"I ain't movin'," says Peace. "Not unless Mr Marwood says I do."

"Don't move," says Marwood.

The pause lasts three seconds before the hangman slips on the noose; he hears the condemned man inhale at the shock of the head covering, and shivers a little. Peace starts to sway.

"Did the reprieve letter arrive, Mr Marwood? On Her Majesty's Public Service?"

"No, Mr Peace, not yet." With these words, Marwood moves the knot on the slip rope to the side of the man's neck. He has read of the bone that will most likely sever the top vertebrae of the spine, resulting in immediate unconsciousness and an instant death—a preferable outcome to the slow strangulation that would occur with a front knot. Once this adjustment is in place he steps away from the dead man. For twenty seconds the chaplain says the Lord's Prayer.

"...deliver us from evil, from thine is the kingdom, the power and the glory..."

Before 'Amen' the sheriff gives the nod. Marwood does not hesitate and pushes the long black lever forward at his side. A cranking sound escapes the metal but Charles Peace does not make a sound...there is an awful ripping noise, and London is quiet.

Moments later, like a delayed trauma but on the scale of a city, a raucous riot begins trashing Newgate market. The uproar is instantaneous. The Bow Street Runners are far outnumbered and the men of criminal deterrent, even the mayor to the sheriff, have to retreat from the scaffold. But just as quickly, the crowd realises there is nothing more to be done....The show is over.

That evening, after the whole debacle is over, Marwood is known to have commented on the Peace hanging to the *London Illustrated News*: "I expected difficulties, because he was such a desperate man, but bless you, my dear sir, he passed away like a summer's eve." The caption shows a surprised Marwood outside his home at 29 Gloucester Place, one hand on his hat, the other testing the weather as though signalling a service well done for the public good.

That image of success, however, was not the real outcome of that bleak Thursday morning, high up alongside Newgate Prison. On the contrary, what happened next tells a very different story, while the black crows swirled above the Old Bailey and St Sepulchre's church bells were muffled by a shrill wind and the silence of the crowd.

At the crossed foot of the scaffold beam, Kate gently touches the wood as she arrives early for Peace's execution—she is superstitious. The death instrument itself is supposed to have healing powers, just as the fatal beam of the 'triple tree' at Tyburn was believed to cure desperate ailments, including those of the heart.

Kate has come here anonymously, this time dressed in one of Mrs Thomas's floral market dresses—the first time she has openly 'borrowed' one. She watches Marwood with new fascination. Before even approaching the scaffold she notices the hangman mounting the thirteen steps to the upper platform; and from her angle beside the pies sellers of Giltspur Street, she recognises him as the man she spent an afternoon drinking with at *The Oxford & Cambridge Arms* which he left so mysteriously. Today he is removed from the steady kindliness of the man she met, more focused, more deliberate, more determined. Kate attributes this to his professional courtesy for the condemned man—assuring the criminal that his 'just desserts' shall be eaten cold and that his guide shall not waver. The element of curiosity persists, however, between the Marwood who showed interest in her, admittedly as a fine lady of Richmond rather than her current down-at-hell existence, and the skilful conveyer of souls into eternity that he appears to be, in an all too earthly way, when she looks up at the scaffold.

Kate spends half an hour pushing through crowded bodies. Given her persistence and lack of concern for her safety, others let her through, grimacing but pleased she keeps moving forward. Eventually, from a position close up, she can hear the speech of Peace, his garbled assumption that the majority of the crowd have family members inside Newgate's walls. She listens to the delight of the crowd at his Punch & Judy jig, and the melancholy strangeness of hearing the Lord's Prayer read aloud while people below continue eating the pastries and soups of the street, filling their checks with toffee apples and hot potatoes, pausing only to hear the creak of the lever that separates the present from the unseen future, the living from the dead.

"Why does it have to take so long?" she asks her neighbour, an old man with a crooked back, hands resting on the wooden beam trying to encourage good health. Suddenly he turns a wart-filled face.

"You tell me, young lady."

A parcel of sky opens above them and the sun flashes through. But something else is visible too, the long suit of a man in a lady's white dress spinning like a toy thrown across the room by a spoiled child—but this fall is real. Charles Peace drops like a stone, slowed in motion, and surprises the squashed bodies under the scaffold who've never witnessed the rush of a human being falling into nothing. The execution is a disaster though—quite flawed—and due to the interference of Marwood's own ropes and lack of length marks, the final moments of Peace's life are all too quick and bloody, a painless ending, but not a clean one.

Peace's head is ripped from his torso in a single awkward jerk, more like the sluicing motion when a lock is opened and the water comes rushing the top and finally in a full torrent from the centre of breakage. The body kicks up and keeps swinging, almost mounting to the underside of the scaffold; while the head, wordlessly and without comedy flies away into the crowd, where it begins a macabre game of town-football thrown from one person to another in a disgusting horror show. A child covets it too long, another punches it on in frightening disgust, and no one is quite satisfied.

In fact, the men high on the scaffold are no more pleased, Marwood among them, with this devastating unplanned spectacle. And yet somehow the total grotesquery of Charles Peace's grinning, half-dead face contorting into shock as he is thrown mercilessly over the heads of his fellow Londoners, is an ending of sorts, and the beginning of a gala-day story with few peers. The broadsheets and tabloids will have a field day. The Last Dying Speech of Charles Peace will be overcome by the Last Singing Ballad of the criminal's decapitated head.

"Watch me, good people, I live for you, and you only!" a stranger cries. "I feel sleepy now, please put me back on my body!" Like string of Chinese whispers, comments and quips rival for the best joke.

Kate herself does not fare so luckily, though, distracted by coughing up her guts, since from the moment of the drop, the slice of the noose unleashes a torrent of blood on her head. At first it seems like rain, but a thick twine of gloop extends over her neighbours. A few people scream, some bawl with horror, while the even crazier—those huddled under the scaffold—see it as a prominent sign of good fortune, like Roman diviners pulling prosperous futures from the entrails of sacrificed animals. Such is the mess of the hanging crowd. Kate, on the other hand, just stands there in Mrs Thomas's bludgeoned floral dress, ruined beyond ruin, and within moments she fears for her job in Richmond—and thence her boy Daniel's upkeep.

"If I race home now," she thinks, "perhaps I can clean up!" Without looking down, she knows her dress is smeared like a bloodied new-born lamb. The smell of sticky human blood is enough to retch, but Kate has seen worse inside the prison of Killane and

Liverpool's dock holding cells. Nothing could prepare her to be so intimately involved with Charles Peace's demise, "but at least I have a story to tell William Marwood," she says, "if I ever see him again."

Carefully, broodingly, Kate makes her way through the Newgate crowd, the saner people parting for fear of soiling their own souls. A few call her a witch, except for the St Sepulchre whores, who merely stare in a vacuous daze of envy at the dramatic horror of her costume. Kate watches as Peace's coagulating blood flicks from the end of Mrs Thomas's boots. Drops are drying on the backs of people's legs, which scurry like crabs in all directions. The crowd is a rolling Red Sea retreating from one man's separated body, a few hawkers searching for his severed head, now lost.

Reaching the edge of the crowd, Kate disappears into King Street but fails to detect her proximity to certain individuals. If she had taken a slightly different route, she would have come face to face with a certain tall wiry frame unmistakable in soft black pumps, one Jonathan Clatter. Sipping on a makeshift spigot tied to a waistband of sling-gin, Clatter alternatively sucks on his preferred poison while through a monocle he spies on his string of opportunistic thieves. One by one the Artful Dodgers return to him, now with a pear or boiled egg, now a handkerchief, sometimes a bronze fob watch. Then he scuffs their hair and marks the success, for example, 'Little Jonty, extra apple' on his own wrist. What Kate does not see is Daniel, her own boy, return to Clatter empty-handed and receive a crack on the neck, hard enough to smart for the rest of the day.

Already Daniel is learning not to return without at least a morsel to eat. The consequences of being captured by a fruit-trader, though, are probably worse than by a commoner. Daniel knows each trader employs a 'running boy' who was no doubt at one time a veritable tea-leaf himself. Being caught robbing a business, and one that actually pays taxes, means bypassing the Bow Street Runners and straight to the magistrate for committal or transportation—jail or the horrendous Australian colony.

"I'd rather get hit by Clatter," Daniel says. He slinks through the crowd, avoiding a woman with blood on her shawl—he does not recognise his mother—and slips away into the brightness of darkening faces. Kate does not see him either. An encounter is unlikely, but now they are peddling the same streets—her with morbid fascination for Marwood, Daniel to avoid his rope altogether.

Moments later, Mr Clatter has transformed himself into a one-act salesman. He unpacks a folding table that also unhooks a poster advertising the rope from the hanging just witnessed—only moments after the dead man's drop. Any logical proprietor can see that the rope is a fake, the actual rope still hanging in the shadow of Newgate; while vanished amongst the crowd, Peace's own torso is being divided by the depraved minority for superstitious good luck and 'disease prevention'. That small group in-fights while the rest of the populace have pulled back to allow the Bow Street Runners to rescue Charles Peace's body.

While this is happening, Clatter has become a yeoman of the halter, offering 'amazing n' cheap' rope portions for sale. His poster shows a man grinning from the end of fine glowing rope, head and torso still intact, the resemblance to Peace uncanny.

"A shilling an inch," he cries. "I am a pub landlord and trustworthy as my sales. This rope is straight from inside Newgate—from the merciful hands of our new executioner!" Marwood of course is still up on the scaffold, but that does not stop the punters. "Get your morning dose of gin-and-bitters," Clatter calls while selling a common rope, the same he uses to train his army of pickpockets.

Finally, back at the foot of St Sepulchre's, the taller man admiring the whores lounging at the foot of the cathedral, the shorter marking in his notebook certain thoughts related to the petty crimes of his surroundings, are Inspector Sequin and Nimrod Jones. They came to see the initial performance of the hangman and in Sequin's own words, "we are displeased with the outcome." Marwood, they have already decided, will get one more chance to prove his talents.

"After that he'll find his head on a train back to Lincolnshire."

"Or in a noose."

"Either way," Sequin says, "set up a meeting. He may be useful in solving some old crimes—he can't be any worse as a detective."

"I don't think it was his fault, guv," Jones says, looking innocently at his superior's face.

"Of course it was his fault, Jones. He was the executioner, right?"

"Well, the man *was* hanged."

"Yes, all over the place. Look around you, Jones," he waits while his deputy does so, "is there really supposed to be so much blood?"

Chapter 10
A Wife's Promise or a Threat
20th February 1879, Thursday

My dear William, I trust your new premises at Gloucester Place are quite adequate for your work. I know you have only been gone a week, but I wanted to let you know about some strange occurrences with Aldous. It's not that he's stopped concentrating at school, but I think he's entered a kind of mania—brought on, I believe, by your absence. Last night I found him stooped over your cobbling tools in the basement, standing on your favourite chair, which was not to be tolerated. He has split the chair's spine with that thin mallet you use, and was wrapping the twine round and round his fingers in such a bizarre way. I can't imagine you've shown him anything like that—his imagination is beyond control! Anyway, I think you'll be pleased I have now locked the basement.

Then only last Thursday, Aldous was playing this strange game in the garden. He makes his friends re-enact the fleeing of Aeneas from Troy—acting the end of the Trojan War—since he's reading Virgil at school now. But all afternoon, he makes two other boys take the parts of Anchises and Ascanius, and Aldous insists on pushing one down the garden path as his son, and the *other as the old man on his back.*

William, what am I to make of all this? I think he is punishing himself for your departure. I beseech you let us know the dates of your return, so I can begin counting down the days with Aldous? I cannot lie to him, but he needs to be reassured, I think, that you have not left for good. Your son has stopped asking questions about you—a disturbing sign, don't you think?

In other news, Mrs Clapton had her baby—a four pound and eleven ounce killer! There is no sigh of her husband though since last Monday, and he was only supposed to leave for the weekend. Mrs Bottle and her old father Albert have taken her in, which means her house is empty. I fear it will be raided by the Fenians, who are making a local show of their bravado since you left, though no one has taken your name in vain, as far as I can tell. They still blame you for the Irish hangings, of course. But no one has accosted me in the street again.

I do not wish to jump subjects, but how is the work coming? Have you not carried out your commission? I trust it was successful?

Yours affectionately, Ellen

After two days:

My own Ellen, I have my doubts, but a strong desire to be moral. This hanging business requires perseverance if we are to ever have a just—and painless—execution. It is the least we can ask of our system of law, and reflects the English character of fair play, even to the undeserving. I do not wish to sound cryptic, but the hanging of Charles Peace was far from a success. Otherwise, I would sleep as soundly as a child.

Let me say I am greatly puzzled by George Dance's New Drop—the technique I employed at Newgate today. It is definitely an improvement over the old 'short drop' given its trapdoor and extended rope, but not enough to break the neck. The crowd has seen the body torn, and I am ashamed! Oh Ellen, such a sight is not worth repeating. Clearly we are in need of a 'long drop' by scientific means. I must be the one to perfect it.

But first, I do not think you need worry so badly about Aldous. He is growing into a young man, that is all, and naturally he wishes to play in my workshop while I am away—merely a consequence of my taking him there myself, perhaps a mistake on my part, but I do not think so. In a few short years he could help me with the shoe repairs and begin a minor apprenticeship, of benefit to us all. We would be able to book that caravan holiday in Suffolk long forgotten, or even that hotel in Scarborough. The fact that Aldous reenacts the fleeing of Aeneas does seem a peculiar sign, but making himself the young warrior is entirely appropriate. He does carry his father on his shoulders—that is true, my sweet—and he clearly carries a burden he associates with his own future son! It is perfectly natural, and shows a skilful theatricality that will no doubt be good in business. Just 'don't put your son on the stage, Mrs Marwood', at least not until I get back.

On that subject, I don't consider I'll be in London more than two weeks. I believe the sheriff—a man called Constable—has a second commission for me, perhaps two. It depends on the recent spate of 'felonies' and how many are being transported to Australia. I have to prove my salt as a new addition to the political-judicial machinery, as they term it. I feel far from Horncastle, and a little lost in London, but the police have taken a shine to me, and the occasional person strikes my interest. All men, you understand!

So, that is good news about Mrs Clapton's baby. You forgot to say—a boy or a girl? Bill will be back soon. Why not take Aldous to meet the child, so long as Mrs Bottle does not disapprove? I must work now, though—the hanging experiments call.

Yours only, William

By same-day return:

Dear William, I am coming to you. Last night the Fenians burned part of The Portland Arms, chanting your name. I had to take refuge in the basement, and double lock all the doors. I could hear them in the street, and see the lights from their burning torches. They were ready to set the house on fire!

I tried to restrain him but Aldous was not scared. He insisted on throwing stones from the underground window—the one blocked with tar. I do not know how he wedged the lower casement open, but the angle was a 'good egg', he said. One of his missiles bounced off a gravestone and that seemed to scare the Fenians and their lights receded. I realised they were only boys as they marched away, stamping on their burning torches. Clearly these weren't the ones who set the pub on fire. But I was terrified, William. I cannot stay here, so tomorrow—if I can get Mr and Mrs Clarkson to mind the house—I will leave on the last horse and cart. It will take a week, as Aldous will be with me too. I cannot say which day I will arrive, but please be home from 5-7 every day from next Monday, and I will be outside 29 Gloucester Place.

On the subject of a proposed long drop, my dear, I enclose your notes from Lord Aberdare's commission. Are they of any use? They read:

'Visit the hanging site the night before execution. Using a 17-18 inch 'paint-line' on the noose, knot a piece of thread at the calculated drop distance. Overhead is the beam and 'D-shaped' shackle. Attach the rope here. The prisoner's forehead should be able to touch the thread—a good measure of drop accuracy before proceeding....

Having prepared the apparatus as above, tie a sandbag (acting as the prisoner and roughly the same weight) to the noose, and leave your 'straw man' hanging overnight to remove stretch from the rope.

Visit early the next morning to remove the sandbag. Lock the lever before securing the trapdoors. Finally, steady the rope into a central position. You may then proceed at will....'

He goes on, but that's the gist of it. Do you need more? William, you've written after this paragraph—'I have only to test it!' Did you test it at Newgate today? If the rope length is what failed, is Lord Aberdare's technical report useful to you?

So, I am glad you sleep as soundly as a child—you always did. But everything worries me! We have survived an onslaught on our home—and I cannot stay here. Aldous needs his father. I am remaining calm, but I'm packing the bags as I write, though the candle is running low. I cannot write for a few days, but please send by return.

Your loving, Ellen

By overnight return:

Dear Ellen,

Thank you for your letter, and do rest assured I will be home from 5-7 every day, from Monday. I have plenty of room here. Did you inform the police about the Fenian attack? It will do no good, but they should be told. I will not be giving up my second great love, The Portland Arms, so easily. Yes, you should bring Aldous, of course. It will be his first great adventure to the metropolis—like father, like son.

I do not wish to be jocular, but we must get these events in proportion. All will be well—it always is. And Aldous's re-enactment of Aeneas is more than a good thing. It shows intelligence and imagination, and in many ways I wish to see his performance, though I suspect he'd need school friends to aid him. Are you aware that his fearlessness when the Fenians were outside came from this very classical consciousness—his knowledge of Virgil. I'd ask what was happening to Troy when Aeneas, the son of Venus, was fleeing? It was burning, of course, and yet the trilogy of fathers-and-sons managed to escape—Aeneas who founded Britain while his son Ascanius went onto found Rome. Arguably Romulus founded Rome too, but the Aeneid pre-dates that. My point? There could not be a more appropriate creation story for our son, a Briton of the future, and for whom I am trying to do my small bit by improving the country.

On that subject, I thank you for Aberdare's hanging description—dry reading but perfect for the apprentice executioner, as I see myself—though I am professional. The description relates to John Lee's hanging on the 23rd of February 1875, almost four years to the day. On that occasion the trap would not open, and Mr Lee—who killed his manservant over a shared lover—was reprieved after two more attempts to execute him. The problem was decapitation and precisely what I experienced firsthand this morning.

The irony does not escape me that had I only followed my initial instincts, Charles Peace would have retained his head, if not his life. But let me tell you, Ellen, the authorities do not seem to care either way. So long as the death is spectacular and monies can be raised for the City and Constable's re-election, life is good. Economics seems to be the only game in town. But I do not care, justice must be sought. As for the Mr Lee case, the Aberdare Committee transcribed extensive medical evidence for the public libraries and a central witness, Dr Marshall, described one hanging from 1878—only last year—as follows. So I tell you this because it helps me proceed in writing it down, but also so you know the importance of my work to the future of our nation. I have started to believe that I can truly make a difference—that a 'humane hanging' is now possible! But first the abominations of the past, so what we must avoid, must be understood. Here is Dr Marshall in his own words:

'I descended immediately into the pit where I found the pulse beating at the rate of 80 to the minute and the wretched man struggling desperately to get his hands and neck free. I came to this conclusion from the intense muscular action in the arms, forearms and hands, contractions not continuous but spasmodic, not repeated with any regularity but renewed in random directions and with desperation. From these signs I did not anticipate a placid expression on the face and I regret to say my fears were correct. On removing the white cap about 1 and 1/2 minutes after the fall, I found the eyes starting from the sockets and the tongue protruded, the face exhibiting unmistakable evidence of intense agony.'

Ellen, I do not desire to comment on this horrendous execution, only that I witnessed a similar debacle this morning at my own hand. It is substantive that early 'jerk 'em up' hangings in the USA had similar problems before the 'patient' and the 'doctor' were able to administer the process with 'due satisfaction to the state'. But we are not in America—here we must lead the world in all things, even humanizing the last moments of criminal life, and Dr Marshall's words must be testimony to us all!

My love, do not fret, but enjoy the journey to London. We shall reunite soon—journeys end when lovers meet, as the Bard famously wrote, shaking his spear. Curse those Fenians who move his bones.

Yours, and with loving resolve to the boy Aeneas,
William

Chapter 11
A Social Call to the Hangman's Home
20th February 1879, Thursday

After writing these words, and sending them down the wall-enclosed mailing chute for the street, Marwood sits at his desk on loan from the Cannongate Inns of Court. The whole of his lodging is government-owned: he is merely passing through, a ghost from the provinces, employed to create cadavers from the criminals of London's slums. Steadying his hands from the morning's work, he extinguishes the candle and sits in the dark.

For a few minutes his head lolls on its neck and Marwood is back in Horncastle in his basement chair, catching forty winks. The images flicker like rain under his eyelids. Within moments he is dreaming of a fairground show he saw as a boy, with a lion-tamer's head sitting inside the lion's mouth; he sees the twitch in the lion's eye, then the inevitable, unthinkable. Later he learned that the lion-tamer and lion spent sixteen years together before one day then lion bit down—and no one knew why. Not only that, the lion hardly seemed inconsolable, in fact his appetite for regular food got larger. The lion, one might say, felt a certain freedom.

But this is no horror comedy. In a loop of memory, Marwood now witnesses the crunch and the lion-tamer's low, muffled scream barely more than a shocked grunt. As though no time has passed, he sees the swinging lion's mane and calm puzzle on the beast's face—the shake of its neck in bursts, left and right, the kicking of the man's feet, the swish of the brute's tale and finally a surreal extended time with the tamed man kneeling—hunched inside the mouth—already dead, the lion almost cradling its old friend and master.

Then, like a pip from an orange the man's head spills out on the ground, while people are screaming and the boy Marwood is just sitting there pinned to his seat, watching the lion paw at the decapitated man, the smile torn from the body while the beast almost sadly, respectfully, walks around its now motionless keeper. Losing interest and uncertain how to react, the lion finally leaps back onto his place of performance—a red tun-sized barrel—as if nothing had happened, the old routine a comfort. The lion awaits and a moment later a whipcrack returns him to his prison-cage, signalling a new master's promotion from the ranks of apprentice tamers.

"The show must go on," says the sleeping boy-man. Marwood twists in his sleep and a new dream replaces the fable of mighty cat and lion-tamer—one of Punch. The boy is fascinated by the macabre madman, but fears him too, and his hope is for rebellious Mr Punch to fall silent at the hangman's command. But all that happens is Marwood's failed attempts to catch the slippery entertainer. Meanwhile, racing circles round the fairground stall, the two hand puppets claw over the red-white striped front, the operator below unseen, like within Maezel's famous chess-playing machine 'The Turk'. There is a trick unsolved but Marwood begins to sweat because he cannot detect any clues to the puppets' operation.

Long ago, Marwood saw this scene as a boy and was fascinated by Punch—and wanted to be Punch. But now he realises Punch's personality is fundamentally absent—is just not there—and so he becomes the dour hangman instead where he can be professional and control his world. But still he dreams of outlandish Mr Punch's freedom…"I don't want to have two sides," Marwood lectures his unconscious, still asleep. "I don't want to be the strict man of the daytime—planning a cruel fate for others—I just want their stepping into eternity to be painless!" Then like a bad devil, the other side of his personality argues back: "But who doesn't want to be Punch instead, in a world without boundaries? Why not be the man of your dreams, where cruelty is natural and suffering runs riot? Give in, you coward! It's when we no longer dream that life slides off the rails! Be brave!" "But I must return to the job at hand," Marwood cries, "or suffer the consequences of my derailed imaginings!"

At last the split in Marwood's head is too much, his dreams collapse in on themselves, and he is stung awake. Coughing and spluttering, he finds himself begging Mr Punch's to "give in to the hangman"!

He is awake, alive. There is a knock at the door—then another—loud enough to wake his drowsy mind. Marwood peers through the office gloom down the hallway. The letter box is open. A mouth is visible.

"Don't hoodwink me, Mr Marwood," a rough voice calls, "I know you're in there!"

Opening the oak door, Marwood is greeted by a dishevelled version of the refined young lady he remembers treating to a drink.

"Covent Garden."

"Miss Thomas?"

"Eh? Yes, of course. It's me," Kate says. "I need your help—I am desperate!" She gestures to the rain.

Confused a moment Marwood quickly recovers his manners and widens the door, allowing her over the threshold. She stands in the hallway shrewdly checking him up and down, before depositing Mrs Thomas's umbrella in a coat rack.

"Forgive me, Mr Marwood."

He does not know what to do but welcomes her into the front room, clears a space on the sofa—she sits back. Carefully he lights up a fire. The rain drips off Kate's tightened boots as she pulls the cheap, pink shawl she bought on Baker Street higher up her chest, quieting any looseness; the red stain of Charles Peace's blood is visible on her ankle socks, which she does her best to cover for propriety and good sense. *Not my blood*, she thinks, *ain't me killed him.*

Marwood stokes the fire aggressively, a show of forceful hospitality, and then sits adjacent to Miss Thomas smiling by way of strange comfort. The mismatched pair face a mock Elizabethan drinks cabinet displaying no drinks. Above the façade is a framed portrait of Gladstone, Disraeli and older less recognisable prime ministers, along with inexplicable pictures of dogs and cats clustering two walls. They look at the glowing embers of the fire, the crocodile rug behind the door keeping the heat circulating, the large bay window, the dust sprinkled on the crystal gems of a fake chandelier, the grandfather clock sleeping in the corner. A crazed orange rug is spread incongruously at their feet. Then they look back to each other.

First Marwood tries to get Kate to smoke filters—the new thing.

"The first odourless—the Cambridge cigarette."

"You think I'm a lady—who smokes." She reaches forward and takes one. "Too kind."

The match strikes and illuminates Kate's face and she hides it with her hand, as a lady would. But he has seen the pockmarks, and the lantern weight of her jaw. For a moment he fears she is a man dressed in costume, but he lets the thought—too strange for words—slip away.

"Well, I was at Newgate this morning. I saw the whole thing, quite upsetting really."

"You remembered my card," Marwood says.

"Yes, I hope you don't think me rude," Kate says. "I just...knew you wouldn't mind. I haven't made it back to Richmond yet—I don't think my sister would see me in this state. Some of the extra blood..."

"Blood?"

"From the victim..."

Marwood stares at her blankly. "You mean Mr Peace, the house-breaker and killer?"

"Yes."

On the walls, the dogs and cats grin down with human surprise. Disraeli and Gladstone exchange a tremulous flicker behind the eyes, nothing more, and the weight of any shock to their hearts remains hidden.

"A lady is caught by the bloody engine of the state," Marwood says, leans back and draw on his Cambridge filter. "A smooth smoke, don't you think?"

"Quite, Mr Marwood."

"Well, there is a bathroom at the end of the hall. Feel free, Miss Thomas, to get cleaned up. Then I'll be only too happy to show you the house." He dares an extra comment, mostly inspired by the heady flavour of smoke to his brain: "So you like executions, then?"

Kate takes the bait, and happily. "Yes, Mr Marwood. Perhaps you could teach me," and she leaves the room, the crocodile rug behind the door parting for her black shoes—borrowed from Julia Thomas. Seeing her ankle stockings, Marwood's nerves are tested. Isn't his wife Ellen far away? He has been in the metropolis for four days, quite alone, and he should enjoy some entertainment—even if only rescuing a woman from her genteel London suburb.

On her return, Kate reiterates her apologies. "I am interrupting your professional peace in your home."

"It's not my house—a rental."

"You must have a lot of paperwork to prepare...for next time."

"I don't know if there'll be a next time."

"Oh—I'm sorry to hear that."

"Politics."

Kate grins, and leans forward. "Would you perhaps show me the instruments of your trade?" she asks, quite bluntly.

Marwood stares at her, alternating his gaze between his sharp and lazy eyes, scrutinizing the widow's peak that meets—innocently but somehow frighteningly—in the middle of Kate's forehead.

"Your hair is awfully black."

"I know."

Remembering himself: "I apologise, I'd be happy to show you. I was about to have an afternoon dram, though. How do you feel? I'm not certain a girl—I mean lady—of your character would enjoy one after your morning shock?"

Almost choking on her words, Kate tries to sound polite in her thirst. "Er...I think I could handle a drink. On the contrary, Mr Marwood, that would be a fine delight."

"Good, good."

Attempting a bartender's flourish, he pours them both a large sherry from a glass cabinet. "Would you like to see some of the ropes?" he asks, courteously, as though offering a biscuit, or slice of Battenberg cake with her tea.

"That would be lovely. Perhaps a tale of two of hangings past—really—if that's not too much trouble? I'm sure you know several, and I'm in the mood."

"Well, I do have the *Newgate Calendar.*"

"So does Mrs Thomas.....I mean, so does my sister, Mrs Thomas. Lady Susan."

"A lady?"

"My sister. Not me—the thought of it!"

"Oh," Marwood nods, with no meaning, "I see." From a shelf above the fire he takes down a prize possession, *The Malefactor's*

Register of 1779 by George Borrow. "Just a slice of the *Calendar*," he says, bearing down a single leather-bound volume of six hundred pages. He demonstrates the fine copper engravings and Kate coos on cue.

"Here's one: The murder of Mrs Elizabeth Jeffries, 6 Trenchard Street, Bristol."

"Perfect." Kate sips her sherry, eyeing the distance from her hand to the bottle.

Marwood reads: "Known locally to be inordinately rich, Mrs Jeffries nevertheless housed only one maid, seemingly to protect the pleasure of her greed. She daily forced her maid to rise hours before dawn, often beating her and even denying her bed sheets and even food. Sarah Harriet Thomas joined this house as a sweet, trusting working-class girl and was soon discovered to be weeping desperately.

Elizabeth Jeffries was soon enduring an attack to head with a blunt instrument, according to police reports, causing her face 'to cave in'. Her new puppy was quite nastily strangled and rammed down the WC. Before long, Sarah was found shivering in her own residence's coal-cellar, with a week's food supply, a King James Bible, and covered in jewels. More than three thousand people signed a petition to save her,"—Kate's eyes widen—"but after famously stamping her feet in refusal, Sarah was carried to the scaffold by five or six assistants and executed by hangman William Calcraft, who later called her 'a sullen country lass and raw guttersnipe'. According to the executioner, Thomas's wickedness was inbred and perverse, alloyed to intelligence but pride too. She was deemed 'of the desert', disturbed by a savagery whose origin was remote, 'not human', and quite lacking in human feelings." Marwood closes the book. "She was addicted to drink too."

"Who in London is not?" Kate replies, aiming to amuse.

"Another?"

"Certainly." She gestures with her hand and Marwood does the decent thing: "'Mrs Bacon of Ordnance Terrace, Chatham, was hit on the head by a hatchet wielded by Elizabeth Laws, an ordinary childish girl of eighteen....' No, here's a better one, of foreign interest. 'The Case of Marguerite Dixblanc, a 'good-looking murderess'."

"That's the ticket," Kate says, hiccupping a little.

"'The scene of the crime was 13 Park Lane, London, where Miss Dixblanc killed her rich, French employer Mrs Riel at

11.30 AM in broad daylight. She hid the body in the garden coal-shed. When Mrs Riel came for more fuel, Dixblanc pretended there was no coal in the shed. Then Dixblanc swung open the cellar door and roping Riel's neck with a makeshift noose, she dragged her body upstairs to the larder. Again, a foreign murderess is the worst kind.' This is my favourite sentence," Marwood interrupts: " 'Dixblanc was later to suffer the ultimate penalty of the law, but she will be missed.'"

"You are an avid reader of these crimes, Mr Marwood."

"Ideally, a chronicler. One day, I'd like to write my own histories."

"Over your printer's dead body," Kate laughs and then stares seriously straight ahead, clearly tipsy by now.

For the only time that week Marwood lets go a laugh, a kind of strangulated gurgle from his throat, delayed in his mouth by a croak but quite forceful in its rumbling. Kate is taken aback and her laugh is equally surprising: for a hefty woman whose shoulders and jaw are robust, her laugh is quite soft and skittish.

"What a mellifluous laugh you have," Marwood says.

"I wish I could say the same for you."

They stare at each other, pause, and laugh again. Unnerved, Marwood pretends to dust invisible crumbs from his black cloak, still buttoned from the morning's work. "Come, *mi'lady*, let me take you on a tour of the premises."

"Delighted, William. I may call you William?"

He pauses, his first name sounding blasphemous on her lips, so straight-laced has his life been in Horncastle. He merely nods and opens the door—Kate swans through as though entering a new life.

"Little do you know, I only end lives."

"Mr Marwood!"

"Your cigarette is done," he says and relights Kate's Cambridge. The hall glows around them. "Let me show you my souvenirs first." He parts a velvet curtain, revealing a study-like room looking out over a narrow back garden: he gestures to the weeds growing under the casement. "The foliage makes me feel at home."

"Looks cosy," Kate says, remaining in the doorway.

"One of the hangman's perks is to keep the dead man's clothes." He gestures to a long casket-box in the corner. "There."

"What's that?"

"That, Miss Thomas, is Mr Charles Peace."

"Charles, in pieces."

Marwood stares at her, surprised. "No, the head and body are not there—of course not, but his clothes are. They're terribly bloody, so they were packed in ice. I get to keep them."

"Mementoes?"

"In a way. Hangman's credit—my calling card. The ropes used to dispose of them. They earn a tidy sum at a museum or I could exhibit them at a local fair, like Bartholomew. Depends on how famous the condemned was and if he 'died game'."

"'Died game'?"

"Merry. At peace…well, enough to entertain."

Kate takes a step into the room. "And the ropes?"

"The ropes are precious, Miss Thomas, since I am able to reuse them. I am a scientist, after all, and I need to practise and develop the art…"

"…of hanging?"

"Indeed. Well, it's more physics, a new branch of human science, more like humane with an 'e'. You sound sceptical?"

Kate tips her drink up and grins. "No, I believe yer, Mr Marwood. I mean, William. It's just a lot for a girl to take in." The hot sherry slips down her throat and she looks mournfully at the empty glass. Meanwhile her host reaches for a low-down cabinet and removes a half foot of tough hanging rope.

"Ropes, clothing, combs and jewellery, this room is a so-called 'black museum', Julia—you don't mind if I call you Julia?"

"Of course not, Julia or my first name Kate. Like the show at Madame Tussaud's or Scotland Yard with its ropes and hoods?"

"That's right. I get my ropes shipped from St. Louis made from Kentucky hemp—I have them stretched with irons to take the bounce out, and the fibres greased up with linseed oil so they slip easily. So effectively, after the drop, I only get my own ropes back…"

"To do over," Kate offers.

"Economical—for all concerned. I never hanged a man who came back to have the job done over."

Between them, from the open window, a few dust particles hang in the morning sunshine. They stand a few feet apart, the house very quiet now, with an eerie sense of proceeding too fast into a strange kind of intimacy.

Kate nods at Marwood's sincere intent. She cannot decide if

he is attractive in his black cloak, or dull in his desire to discuss his occupation. Part of her wonders why he is interested in her—her youth, or the fact she randomly witnessed the Tyburn re-enactment with him? She settles on his loneliness as a newcomer to the city; he just needs somehow to talk to, someone he can perform his brand of provincial genius at—an admirer.

"The hanging rope would sell for anything from a shilling to a guinea. Come with me," he says. "I want to show you something, nothing to be frightening of." Kate strategically picks up her glass so Marwood tilts the sherry bottle to top her up. He watches her eyes on the golden liquid, her murmur of "enough" after the polite moment when the glass is three quarters full.

They step out into the dim hallway, through a scrubby kitchen with some dangling pots and pans and into a narrow passage that leads to the pantry, the yard and cellar. Here Marwood strikes a match on the wall and lights a gas lamp. He hooks the lamp to the ceiling.

"Be careful where you stand." He gestures to the chalk on the floor and Kate stands well back. A black handle resembling the crook of a false hand is pulled into view—a Captain Hook-like lever. Immediately the floor falls away not five feet from Kate and she squeals with delight, half real, half for effect. The two folds of 'the door in the floor' open like a saloon entrance and balance at ninety degrees. A little chalk flies up.

"I am credited with introducing the split trapdoor."

"I like it."

"You do?" Marwood re-secures the trap. As he leans over Kate admires his gold watch-chain hanging down his waistcoat and her tongue licks her top lip. He is within the chalk boundary, manipulating the copper pin that holds the trap in place. Suddenly he steps aside and fires the trap.

"It's a stitch-up! It's a hanging!"

"I'll swing for you!" Marwood echoes and they laugh. Once more Kate drains her sherry and she leans a little on the wall, the gaslight illuminating her face.

"What's in the cellar?"

For once Marwood is uncomfortable. "That's private. A magician shouldn't reveal his secrets."

"To a London maid? What am I going to do—sell the story to the papers? Betrayal your secret to your rivals?"

"I don't have any rivals," Marwood says. "Just hacks."

"Dogs biting at your heels," Kate says, as Marwood catches her face in the lamplight; the cellar has a curved ceiling projecting their shadows as strange, elongated giants overhead. There is coldness in Kate's expression and despite the lamp, the sherry has drained the colour from her cheeks. He is unnerved.

"You look cold. Let's return to the lounge."

"Next time you can show me the sandbags—a true drop."

"Certainly," Marwood says and brushes past her. "You know that 1868 was the last public execution—not counting this morning! I cannot work more today, you see, but I'm happy to tell a tale or two."

"I'd be happy to listen."

"Okay—thank you."

Marwood leads the way back to the lounge. Kate follows, her eyes trailing the kitchen, its knives hanging from nails over the sink: here, she imagines, is the back of a Drury Lane theatre, the back of house—like the body that maintains the soul—versus the front for guests, the living rooms in contrast to this dead zone with its weeds caught in the window casement, the gaslight, and the copper pin separating the split trapdoor from a mysterious underground world.

"You have a secret, William," she says.

"Not many."

"Only the dead have no secrets."

"Very true." The strangeness continues as they re-enter the lounge, Kate choosing to stand by the bay window. Marwood does not seem to mind and answers her increasingly curious questions, the line of macabre inquiry long crossed.

"Well, the bodies are left for an hour after the drop—'the usual time' as the *London Illustrated* would say. Charles Peace did not really hang, as you saw, for other reasons. His headless fall, incidentally, was not my fault. There was great confusion on the scaffold—too many cooks."

"I understand. They were nervous?"

"The sheriff was, the chaplain less so. I always say 'we hang at eight, breakfast at nine', but they prefer to make a hash of the hanging. That's the usual way. You see, I'm a believer. I want to reform the system, make hanging 'humane'. But with amateurs a clean break is just not possible."

"The government, William. They have been the bane of my

life too, since Ireland. They accuse me of…things in my life…things I have not done….Sure, I did a little shoplifting in Liverpool…." Kate's hand covers her mouth—she has quite forgotten her disguise, her forged position in London life as a lady of Richmond.

But her words fall on deaf ears. Marwood is in a world apart, standing over the fire, eyes glowing with profound belief. "Society should be calm—and safe—and ordered. Even though they're new, the trains must run on time." He drums his fingers on the mantelpiece. "You see, I want to reform 'a tumble and a kick' into *Marwood's New Method*—that is my technique, until I dream up a better title. But I am a professional. So you know who invented hanging?"

"The Sheriff of Nottingham, for sure?"

"No Julia, it was the Irish, by way of the Greeks. Hanging crossed the Irish Sea just as you did, though it took a little longer. I've been reading a lot of Dr Haughton—he explains how Telemachus in Homer's *The Odyssey* strung up all the virgins on one line, the brute. But it took Haughton's account to explain the origins of this practice—as not Roman, as was long thought—but Greek, the so-called civilised race. Some say they inherited it from the Minoans. Think of it like chess—did the Persians really invent it? Or was it the Indians?"

Kate stares at him blankly.

"I want to write a book called *Prometheus of London Town*—you can guess why. The dead speak to us, rising from the flames to help us build a better society. You'd understand if you saw the rest of my cellar—I bring the criminals back to life. Freeing them of their sins…"

Kate moves to the door but Marwood steps back from the fire, causing her to pause. "Take a seat," he says, quite calmly. She feels a little trapped, yet exhilarated despite herself, the sherry and the peculiar intensity of Marwood's 'moral motivation' growing hypnotic. Her ankles feel bare as she sinks into the sofa. He shuts the door, sits with one space between them.

"Take Adam Smith's *Theory of Moral Sentiments*," Marwood says with fingers extended, as though lecturing to a room of undergraduates. "*A brave man is not rendered contemptible by being brought to the scaffold. The sympathy of the spectators supports him, and saves him from that shame…*"

"Dying shame," Kate says. "Go on."

"Yes—here lies the immortality of the executed. I can harness that strength and reuse their weights on my practice drops—even dress them in their own clothes. Science will benefit us in the end, you see. The deceased can *even assume the air, not only of perfect serenity, but of triumph and exultation!*"

"Well, William, I'm happy for your luck. Studyin' is something I could 'ave done, once."

"Julia, the great men of London support my claims. Even Dr Johnson laments the abolition of the Tyburn parade: 'The old method was most satisfactory to all parties; the publick was gratified by a procession; the criminal was supported by it. Why is all this to be swept away?' I couldn't say it better in a thousand years!"

"Well, one last story, Mr Marwood, since we are comfortable again."

"There's the demise of Thomas Neill Cream...or Sir Roger Casement. No, I'll tell you about the Trial of the Stauntons in 1877. What was the crime? Well, they faced accusations of the Penge Mystery, a conspiracy, at the Old Bailey before Sir Henry Hawkins. Four prisoners were on trial—Louis Staunton, her brother Patrick Staunton, Mrs Patrick Staunton, and Alice Rhodes, a sister of Mrs Patrick Staunton. All four were charged with murder of Mrs Louis Staunton by starvation, and sentenced to death. The public wanted blood, but there was really no evidence—apparently Mrs Louis Staunton was depressed and locked herself away for days on end. A miscarriage of justice no less! They were reprieved by the Home Secretary just one day before sentence." He pauses contemplatively.

"And?"

"Well, Alice Rhodes was released but the other Stauntons were sentenced to long terms of penal servitude. Some people believe they're now living in paradise off an Australian island....Clearly they are not."

"Perhaps Devil's Island."

"If not there, then Tasmania—for their manias."

Kate smiles politely. "So why are you mad on this stuff, William? Not just professional interest, is it?"

Marwood stands over Kate causing her to press her head backwards on the sofa, something that almost angers her, but she is simultaneously thrilled. The hangman is a gentleman and a bookish one at that, yet the trickle of certainly that he actually pulls the lever— her witnessing the end of Charles Peace—is something she cannot erase from memory.

"I really should be going, Mr Marwood."

"Well, next time I must show you my *Universal Dictionary of Hanging* with its buckish wit and pickpocket eloquence. We could act some of the roles—there's grand Jack Sheppard, or Mary de Winter who petitioned the government to execute her despite her committing no crime."

"Hardly a girl after my own heart," Kate quips. "Not quite my style."

"We could go to Bartholomew Fair instead. A merry outing, Julia, to the biggest gala-day of the metropolis. What do you say? The fair always refreshes."

"But there's no hanging?"

"No."

"Good," Kate says. "I was startin' to think we'd talk of nothing else."

At last Marwood opens the lounge door and releases Kate, who once she is free, hovers on the threshold. She cannot decide if her visit to Gloucester Place has been a vague form of indoctrination—her natural instincts abated by the drink and Marwood's intellectual insistence.

At the door Marwood presses something in her hand. "A lock of Charles Peace's hair," he says.

Kate feels a little drained, a victim of his words. As a recovery tonic, she turns in the street and blows him a kiss, round and suggestive in its fullness, a little over-indulgent.

Marwood is embarrassed, not having intended any sexual overtones for Julia's tour of the premises—but when she is gone he starts to dwell on the firm cut of her jaw, that a little powder could hide the blemishes of her face. A sparkle flickered behind her eyes, he thinks—a devilish hue he has never seen with Ellen—but he is uncertain how to react to his feelings. He closes the door and locks it.

Now alone, Marwood removes the copy of Courvoisier's death-mask from his pocket, an imitation of the original at Madame Tussaud's. The inscription reads: *Hanged before thirty thousand people. He will live forever.*

...I must save it for Julia and Bartholomew Fair, he muses. I'm sure she will be amused by Courvoisier's colourful extravagance, given she enjoys dressing in a lively way. He stole clothes after murdering his aristocratic master, of course....

"I have an aristocratic master," Marwood whispers. "We all do. Except Mrs Thomas—she is quite the lady."

She is late. Kate passes through the heart of London and Parliament Square, realizing she stayed too long at the hangman's house. The sherry has already worn off in the cold.

At Westminster Abbey she cuts through Shire Lane onto a half-street known as Rogues' Lane—no more than four feet in width. The alley's sign is half concealed in shadow, unreadable from the main street. There is a yelp and something surprises Kate. She is momentarily angered, but the hound is so hungry she can see its ribcage, assuming it's a solitary, domestic dog set loose. She doesn't need to be afraid of a roving pack. Carefully, Kate removes the silver candelabra—the one she polished so astutely—from inside her borrowed pinafore. Relieved after carrying it all day, she readjusts its base, curling it to her hips along the bone.

Rogues' Lane—a misnomer for a nothing street—opens into a wide courtyard. The square is deserted, although it usually acts as a gateway between legal and criminal worlds; a place daily and dishonestly staked out by crooks masquerading as 'pye men' and gingerbread 'hawkers'. Thieves, loose women or lost children: none are present in the dull winter light. And yet, as the sun abandons the grey rooftops to encroaching night, an eerie blessing appears in the shape of a few flakes of snow. They land on Kate's face softening her demeanour with their disarming touch. She steels her expression against them.

At last, unfollowed, she enters a lesser-known territory around St Clement Danes Church heading down to houses known as 'Cadgers' Hall and The Retreat. Here, crisscrosses of hazardous low wooden shacks are mounting each other. This is Smashers Alley—a thieves' bartering exchange, caught in ironic darkness within the shadow of Westminster Cathedral. Not present on a map, an underworld opens between the poor people's church and the cathedral of national pride. Kate slips into a doorway, chooses the third door down, and opens the alley into a blaze of light.

The smell of charcoal and burnt wood is overwhelming.

Inside, two lines of old men are melting down various metals in a furnace behind a makeshift trench. Behind a table is an enormous fat man, his spectacles buried in the folds of flesh that were once his baby face, now adult obesity, self-inflicted.

"Webster," he says. "You came back."

"I always do."

"No one followed you."

"On my life."

"What you got?"

"Triple-tongued candlestick." She peers at the smelting furnaces. "Working on alchemy?"

"Alchemy's a joke, and none of your business."

"I'm a good customer," Kate says.

The spectacles stare at her, the flesh shifting on the stool. "The jig's up on alchemy—we have to pay Bow Street a percentage so it's a dead duck. But if you 'ave gold and not silver next time, we could dance." He lays the silver candelabra on the table.

"Solid sterling," she pushes.

"Maybe half, if you ask me—and you're asking me."

"What happened to the counterfeitin' room?"

"Raided."

"Every room had its secret trap or panel. Why can't you build a new one?"

"Listen, Webster, I don't have all night. The entire coining could be bust open tonight. How'd you like to run a business off Parliament Square?"

"I'm dealing straight, and a good price," Kate says, a faint cackle at the end of her insult. "You make your cut from the politicians, risk-free—it's all over the papers."

"Don't believe everything you read," the fat man says. "You know, Mercury is the god of commerce. Well, he's also the god of swift flight. You know how the system works..."

"Yes, I do. Gold at the Bank of Ireland is turned into Mint guineas in the Tower of London—a short step from bank to gaol."

The fat man stares in a peculiar way. "Got yerself an education, di' ya?"

Kate says nothing.

"I'll give you twelve guineas."

"Twenty-five."

"Ten—last offer."

"Twenty."

The fat man looks back at the candelabra. Kate puts her hand on it. Behind them, one of the furnace men is leaning on his shovel. Resting on the shovel head is a hard round black pot, fire-burned and glowing with a speck of liquid gold.

"Last one, boss," he says.

The fat man grimaces. "Looks like your lucky night," he says to Kate. "Thirteen guineas."

"Fifteen."

"Fourteen."

"Deal."

They both spit and shake. Kate doesn't look back, but retraces her steps exactly from Smashers Alley to The Retreat, up from 'Cadgers' Hall and St Clement Dances Church to Rogues Lane, finally emerging into Parliament Square. The steeple of St Mary's Church glows white and sleet is gently lining the square. A grizzled stick of a man is asleep on a jugging flagstone, a sacrifice to central London, while two lovers are perched on a bench. Kate traverses two corners of the square and cuts down Parliament Street itself, then changes her mind and heads for the river.

She'd planned to visit 'the stockbroker' or goods' jobber in a Change Alley coffee house, but it's getting late—she's made a sufficient killing for one night. The fat man got a good deal. For business with the Custom House scriveners, the Excise Office in Old Broad Street, the Corn Exchange in Mark Lane and the Coal Exchange in Lower Thames Street, there's always another day. Commerce in London never sleeps—the honest deal in the morning, the shady business in the afternoon, and the downright criminal by night.

As she crosses Westminster Bridge, thankful to have the candelabra now free from her underwear, Kate glances up and down the Thames. So many bridges, she thinks, little knowing that Hammersmith Bridge, invisible from here and so far away, will figure prominently in her future. Tonight the city is her friend, taking her a little closer to home. South Sea House in Threadneedle Street and East India House in Leadenhall Street will have to wait a little longer for her wares—depending on Mrs Thomas's good will and how soon she notices the absence of her possessions.

What Kate does not realise, not tonight, is that Mrs Thomas needs no time at all. She is a sharp old lady, not at all the wizened and dotty old grandmother Kate believes of all women over seventy. Even now, Mrs Thomas has discovered the loss of her candelabra—so prominent was the ornament in the living room. The danger does not seem apparent to Kate because here, at night on the backstreets of Westminster, the danger must be worse. Richmond is peaceful, secluded, sleepy, and safe. Fifty miles from Central London—what could possibly happen? But what Kate overlooks is that the place is not the point in the incidence of crime—the person is the deciding factor. And so she makes her way south carefree, alone and suspicious on the bridge, and her step is not slow.

Now feeling on the run, she enjoys herself. "I will take my 'sanctuary rights' wherever I please," she whispers, meaning districts where the prisons fail to cast their shadows—physical and metaphorical—such as St Martin's le Grand, famous retreat of secular canons, or Whitefriars former home of the Carmelites. These places attract criminals, their associates and the hangers-on who feed on the vulnerable, only Kate is not sure in which category she belongs. Predator and prey, there is no space in the centre of established crime for a new personality. She must move on.

Hence her play is the counterfeit jewellery, the St Martin's beads she must now secure, or else the money will dry up. And when the money is gone, so is the drink. That will be the worst of all. Of course, Kate already has jewellery 'loaned' from Mrs Thomas she is looking to sell. But her landlady has noticed that too—missing pearls from her bedroom would never go unnoticed.

On either side of the river, the city and where Ireland and England meet, two classes of women are destined to clash heads. The master and servant relationship is not for Kate Webster's palate; the straight life is just too slow. South of the river, in a quiet suburb of Richmond, a perfect storm is brewing in an elegant lady's tea cup.

Chapter 12
The End of the Affair
21st February 1879, Friday

Kate arrives at 2 Mayfield Gardens past midnight, a little worse for wear from a bottle of gin she purloined at *The Pig & Whistle* on Richmond High Street before she was asked to leave, or face a lock-in. For once she recollects her landlady's address and ruminating confusedly on her evening with William Marwood, she lolls her way, hiccupping, along the leafy hedgerows.

Kate opens the front door, presses her face to the wood as she secures the lock, and almost collapses where she stands from drunken exhaustion. She is in for a shock. In the corner, under the curtains and next to the shelf of the missing candelabra, is what appears to be a life-sized mannequin of an old woman, wrapped up in blankets on the living room floor like the dead awakened. Kate peers into the gloom, and without thinking, she yanks the edge of the curtains sending a puddle of moonlight across the mannequin's face. It is Mrs Thomas herself, no less, eyes open, expression stony, her whole demeanour unimpressed by the maid she pays to keep her safe and comfortable.

"We need to have a talk," Mrs Thomas says and Kate hiccups a reply.

"I'm sure we do."

"Yes, we do. You can't continue here, Kate, I'm afraid. I couldn't wait until morning to tell you. This behaviour..."

"…is unacceptable."

"Yes."

Kate sways and half flops, half collapses in a seat facing the elder woman. "I'm sorry I'm"—hic!—"so late."

"It's not the hour, Kate, it's everything. Your whole attitude to service work is…not what I'm used to. It can't be tolerated." She gestures to the dusty sideboard.

"I see."

Mrs Thomas sits up and her blanket falls to reveal a thin white nightdress, a shawl covering her chest. "In any other circumstances, I would call the police. But I don't want to do that…given we must make new arrangements."

"We do?"

"Of course, Kate."

"But Mrs Thomas…I have nowhere else to go."

There's no reply. Despite the strange interview from this midnight ghost, the moonlight and her evening with the hangman, Kate is afraid—through her alcoholic haze and swivelling eyes she beings to absorb the reality of the scene.

"Go to bed, Kate, we can talk in the morning. I'd kindly ask you to carry me up there, now, though. I've sat here too long."

Kate stares at her employer. Inside an old feeling of rage—a familiar pulse—grips hold, even though she is softened by the gin. She knows she is being abused and feels burdened by the intense feeling of rejection. Since being a little girl in Killane, County Wexford, life has been uncertain for Kate. A string of disappointments and offenses, beginning with the death of her mother, and her father taking off with another woman, have damaged and skewed her vision of human relations. All is twinned extreme, healthy and unhealthy, either protective or predatory. Her father's new wife, with children of her own, was unloving to the new husband's previous family—especially teenage girls, who were essentially rivals for the one man.

So at sixteen Kate fled—still carrying around her illegible psychic wound. When attacked, she feels undermined in the same half-healed place, as though the people of Liverpool—and now London—know of her old emigrant's pain. "I am history itself, inside a wandering Irish soul," she'd say, if she could recognise her personality, the heated ice in her veins. But she does not, cannot.

All these feelings rush through Kate's consciousness, fed with the aggravated blood of her unsettled heart. The gin sits bright, cool and vicious behind her eyes, but she smiles to cover the vanity of her manipulations from this point forward. No longer are the jewellery and valuables of the house so important, since everything must be hers—the clothes, the furniture, the trinkets—the sense of possession. There remains the obstacle, of course, of an employer who chooses to attack her when she's vulnerable.

"Certainly, Mrs Thomas," Kate says. "I'd be happy to help you to bed."

With surprising tenderness she slips her hands under Mrs Thomas's knees and lifts. The old lady sighs softly, seeing nothing remiss in sacking her maid and being carried by her like a newborn.

"Sorry for your trouble," Kate says, but the old lady is frowning, even in her arms, as they approach the foot of the stairs.

"What's that on your blouse?"

Kate is careful to turn away from the moonlight. "Nothing, just beer from the pub."

"Oh, I think…are you sure you can climb the stairs? My son could assist me instead."

"That's quite all right." Kate now deliberates whether to tell Mrs Thomas about Charles Peace's blood, still visible on her blouse—to scare 'the old bat'. But she resists the confession due to mention of Mrs Thomas's son. Nevertheless, her anger is piqued and cannot be quelled.

They pause on the fifth step and lightheaded, Kate sways a little.

"What's wrong?"

"Nothing—Mrs Thomas, I trust you will pay me for my time?"

"Just put me down at the top."

Kate staggers and grips Mrs Thomas's chicken-legs tight, the old lady drawing her breath more rapidly. They make a strange sight, the bulky Kate, jaw fixed against the strain, eyes rolling from the morning excitement of Marwood's affection and her evening drinking, and the bossy older woman draped in her bourgeois night-gown, legs spindly while she tips picture frames to new angles, all illuminated by the glances of moonlight from the upstairs windows. Eventually they reach solid ground and Mrs Thomas is laid to rest.

Kate feels the opportunity strongly now as a flickering impulse of bile. Mrs Thomas abuses her generosity, or so she sees it,

and a cocktail of perceived insults and terminating her employment—
not to mention waiting up like a parent with a bone to pick—all
coalesce as Kate's very real jealousy. Hence Marwood's profession
and the decapitation of Charles Peace are long forgotten but the gin
and human emotions are not.

"There, there," Kate says. She feels her fingers twitch, and her
hand raised for a single blow, but the target of Mrs Thomas's neck is
unclear, both women being surprised by fear. The sweat trickles
between Kate's fingers—the moment suspended—and yet she does
not act, not yet. The old lady somehow defeats her with her foolish
belief in her superiority, her blasé attitude to having this slave-girl in
the house.

"You can go to bed now," Mrs Thomas says.

Kate smiles—there is spectacle in being abused by Mrs
Thomas, spectacle that can only stir her hunger, feed a tenuously
suppressed rage.

"I shall, since I am no longer at service here. But not until I
have said my piece! You are quite the dragon, Mrs Julia Thomas, to
use yer own words."

"Pardon, what…"

"I am not impressed, though yer neighbours may be. All I see
is a selfish ol' fool and I'm gonna bring you down to my level, if that's
all I can do." Kate grips her shoulder and squeezes. "'Cos what else
am I supposed to do? See?"

"I don't see, Miss Lawler! I ask you to desist, at once. You are
overstepping the lines of propriety."

"Propriety, ha!" Kate shouts, a snarl escaping her nostrils.
"Wha's you know 'bout pro-pri-ety! What do you knows about
good people?"

"I am a church-goer and I am not having this discussion now,
Miss Lawler." The old lady stares defiantly at Kate, who grins back
but then releases her hand too.

"We are not evenly matched," Kate says. "Not by a long chalk."

"No, I agree. You, young lady, are barely working class."

That is enough—the final straw. Kate grabs hold of Mrs
Thomas's collar, eyes rolling, and squeezes her on the throat. Four
thumbs press into the soft fleshy centre of Mrs Thomas's neck, two
pinning, two resisting. A gurgle begins, grows high-pitched. The
scuffle is short-lived, though, since a figure steps from the shadows,

struggles with Kate. It is the son, Billy, with his ridiculous mane of blond hair waving down the hallway. He slaps Kate's face on both cheeks, overpowering her, and all three people are left gasping for air. The situation now turns surreal, with Mrs Thomas in a bundle on the floor and Kate backed away against the wall. Since his body is twice the size of Kate, the son has no energy left. Rather than throw Kate out of the house, or down the stairs, Billy retreats to his room and sticks his head out of the window, ostensibly for air.

Through the door Kate can see him sit on the bed and begin rocking back and forth, and soon she realises he is not the genius artist Mrs Thomas makes out, but an overgrown child, a gifted *idiot savant*. So he's a self-absorbed painter, but she's seen enough of his paintings in the conservatory room hanging on the walls, a cry for help in a pristine house. For Kate, he's merely an intruder into her new world, a mentally retarded bully trying to school her while she's educating Mrs Thomas on manners—giving the old lady a lesson of her own. "But who wants to swallow their own medicine?"

The thought takes a fraction of a second. Kate picks Mrs Thomas under the arms, as though escorting her once again through the Royal Parks, and passes her son's room. He does not glance over. She enters Mrs Thomas's special room—with Cleopatra's barge and deer-hunting on the walls—and deposits her on the bed.

She then returns to the hallway, composes herself a little. Already Billy is lying on his bed himself in a state of shock, curled up and dreamy-looking but not afraid. Staring at this giant of a man with his innocent golden mane and meat-hook hands, dressed in the overalls of a common labourer in this genteel house, Kate is reassured he does not understand their fight, or its consequences. His face is turned towards hers and he smiles. Kate smiles back, and closes the door. Finally she retreats to her own room.

Once inside, she peels back the bedcovers and slips inside. Turning for the lamp, she discovers a letter lying on the bed, already opened by Mrs Thomas. At the top is scrawled:

Boys School of Enterprise.

Young Kate— o Richmond finery,
Bad news, Im fraid! I know where yer at, Immaculate
House, 2 Mayfield Gardens, Richmond. n I know yer left

some property at Smashers Alley yeserday. Word gets round, aint that tha Cockney truth. Dont call it blackmail— just that I know where the lumber came from, and yer could be in a new heap of trouble, and we aint talkin river water.

I have yers boy— hes mine now. As yer know hes learnin the arts of handkerchief dancin, only he aint very good at it, see. Not that he lacks smarts, mind. Boy is soft-hearted. Big problem, tender heart, in this game wes playin.

Lookee, heres the deal I giv ya. Yer want yers boy back, yer bring the lumber straight to me stead. I knows a man by name o Porter— Henry— who can get rid o it for us both. Good money too. Sounds good? Rest assured, yers Daniel might not be here long, if yer chooses not ta dice with my deal, see? He might go for a pleasur stroll off a short pier, and rivers only spittin distance. Dont take that as a threat. But lots of boys come unstuck— its a fast turnaround business— an lets be frank, the Bow Street Runners aint exactly worryin thur heads wot appens to this lil critters. Just nother devil off the streets.

Yers urchin is safe, but only if yer sweet n nice. Porter is a good family man. We deal with him straight, and nothin happens to the boy. Call on me.

What is it? Only a scruffy letter from Jonathan Clatter spilled with beer, lies and half-truths. "Why do some people never change? Why?—'cos they gets away wi' stuff, that's why!" Aware she is talking to herself, Kate presses the pillow to her face. Her cheek still stings where Mrs Thomas's son struck her. She grits her teeth and touches the soft, bruised flesh.

The day has been too much. She lies down in the heart of Mrs Thomas's special bed, closes her eyes in the light. Darkness fills her mind with a vision of Newgate and the prison scaffold, her brow lightly sweating under the elegant, fake mural of Cleopatra's barge.

Chapter 13
Alone with Everybody
21st February 1879, Friday

Back in his house, Marwood has retreated through his own trapdoor to the cellar he would not show his guest. He closes the trap overhead, preventing its doors creaking back and forth, and lowers the candle. The cellar is illuminated in its full width—about fifty yards—displaying numerous items of the hangman's trade. To the enclosed, windowless room he says "'Drop hanging' in England must be improved," as though encouraging his moral ego. At last, he is in his element.

The time spent with Kate—Miss Julia Thomas—now inspires his work, just as Marwood's work will inspire her. Carefully he clears a table of twine and lays down the books he has brought from the living room. Here is William Barrett's *Irrational Man* delving into existential philosophy, the problem of man presented in a radical new way. For the psychopathic criminal like Charles Peace, a new form of execution is necessary, one counterbalanced by the rationality of the state. Marwood fears these books in part because they explain the amorality at the heart of the criminal—the kind of mind that is controlled by a vastly inflated sense of superiority. Here, among bookish clues, Marwood draws up a seat closer to the dead wood-fire. He lights stray paper at the base, scrapes the embers, and slides an iron guard across its face. Soon he can feel its warmth.

From *Irrational Man* he learns neither science nor religion hold the truth for man, rather the fables of classical gods written centuries earlier by the Greeks. The half-man half-god Dionysus is the new vision of the lord of mankind, because he is both man and god, a creature of salvation, but far removed from Christianity. In Barrett's words certain individuals, in their souls without even knowing it, are sacred worshippers of Dionysus. The explanation is that the early Greeks developed cults to perform rituals in the god-man's honour. In an ode to this god of wine, they indulged in drunken orgies, seeking an ecstatic and mystical union.

Marwood scoffs a little, certain the men and women he has hanged—often uneducated and desperate—have never even heard of Dionysus, but he reads on.

Dionysus, according to Friedrich Nietzsche, was a supreme synthesis of the warring forces of culture and rabid instinct. He was

> humanity's saviour-god, freeing man to indulge both his rational and animalistic urges. Ecstasy was gained through Dionysus's self-destruction, a sacrifice serving up freedom for his followers. Yet fear was still paramount in the world. Neither glory for the god, nor pleasure for man, could release us from the burden of our mortal flesh, and darker thoughts. Free—only to suffer more!

Slowly, Marwood re-reads these words then writes in the margin his own disagreeing philosophy: 'Hence the need to control these human passions.... To *live dangerously* is to live callously, without humanity, and not only harm society itself, but harm the fabric of that society, namely individuals. To aspire in the soul to become a Dionysian god is a flawed philosophy, since there will be many victims; flawed, too, because it can be stopped by greater strengths—the guardians of power, the will of the state, the leaders, the people, the judge, jury and executioner.'

But despite himself, Marwood is drawn to Nietzsche's philosophy of strength—its universal support of might over morality. Surely the only difference between the killer and the hangman is the legal release of the trapdoor? Surely the roles are the same, changing only on different days—a life for a life, an eye for an eye. Marwood frowns at the contradiction, since the rule of law is a *will to power* too. Morality, in other words, is *naturally relative* and set by the highest power. Can this really be the case?

Glancing at his work table, no longer filled with the twine and heels of shoemaking but with hemp ropes and buckles, the slipknots and washers of the hanging trade, Marwood sighs at the mistakes of hangings past. He has watched many a drop in the style of old bungler Jack Ketch, the worst of all uncaring, inhumane hangmen, from whom the profession inherited such a dire reputation. For drunken Ketch, sometimes the rope snapped, or the cross-beam fell loose. 'Accidents happen', he would say, and how much can really go wrong at a hanging? But Marwood knows better. When two robbers were hanged by Ketch in Bury St Edmonds, the scaffold broke in two. One man hanged fine, but the other had to wait more than thirty minutes while workmen erected a temporary platform....

Partly angered, partly inspired by these memories and his philosophical reading, Marwood vows that his future executions must be perfect—or he will refuse and retire. Another incident like the Charles Peace debacle cannot be permitted or else his profession is doomed. Supposedly yesterday's condemnation in the *Chelsea & Kensington News* has not bothered him, any more than the surreptitious whistling of the Horncastle children. Seated at his desk with sincere intent, he reassures himself: "Charles Peace's headless flight was the government's fault! I never make a botch of my work."

Marwood knows he had a good idea by improving the straps to pinion arms *and* legs. First tested on Peace, the criminal could not move far on the platform despite his propensity to 'dance' before rope-dancing with a crowd-pleasing jig. Fixing shoes, too, has long encouraged Marwood's experiments with all manner of belts, loops and buckles, trying to secure the correct combination of strength and length. The main rope he still imports from Kentucky, though the American 'smooth and toughened' is now exported to the Empire and Commonwealth and secretly passed off as Her Majesty's finest. Furthermore, Marwood knows that Calcraft would use a rigid half-inch rope, and therein lay both his strangulation mania and worse, his propensity to decapitate; whereas Marwood has long discovered a soft, pliable five-ply Italian silk hemp with a three-quarter inch diameter. This rope was refused at the last minute for Charles Peace—never again.

Finally, Marwood's re-positioning of the noose's knot under the left ear, increasing the drop to between seven and eight feet, should ensure instantaneous unconsciousness. A magic final touch, a leather washer guaranteeing the rope will run smoothly, its metal ring replacing the unreliable slip-knot. "Knots are for sailors!"

Marwood returns to his reading, aware of all his improvements. But he is missing the final revelation to turn the Newgate Drop into the Long Drop—his famed invention that could transform hanging from suffering-and-death into just death.

For now, he reads the grim comedy of the tale of Robert Johnston's 1818 hanging for robbery in Edinburgh: **The drop was ill-prepared, so shallow the prisoner's feet touched the platform's side. He was desperately struggling, half-upright and half-dangling; so the hangman tried to chop at the noose to lengthen the drop, but the rope was twisted and only getting tighter. The crowd lost patience, seeing the man as one of their own, and began to hurl stones and mud in protest. In a fit of sympathy, someone leaped up and cut Johnston down, the catalyst before the crowd weighed in, ripped him free and carried him aloft.**

Johnston was unable to stand, but breathing still. The 'kidnappers' were chased by police, while others tore his coffin to firewood. A solemn public spectacle disintegrating further into the _mêlée_ of a reckless farce, the military was called in. Soldiers were ordered to assist in making arrests, clubbing the crowd with steel truncheons, thereby winning back the half-dead man. But in a scene ugly beyond imagination, the authorities had a surgeon refresh Johnston to 'steady his blood'. Then they hanged him again, semi-naked, without a hood. Regaining full consciousness in the noose's embrace, he tore at his bonds at the expense of his fingernails, further enraging the crowd. History repeating, the hangman yanked at Johnston's legs to speed the process. Someone, for shame or pity, threw a cloth over his face as he spluttered his last. The full execution, as reported in _The Scotsman_, endured near fifty minutes before the crowd tore the stage to pieces....

Immediately on reading this passage, all is clear—so lucid, in fact, that Marwood has to resist exclaiming 'Eureka' for fear of spoiling his discovery. He immediately realises that as a technique, the 'long drop' was created primarily for neck-breaking. He must calculate a planned fall, the distance as precise as possible, the consequence a 'snapping straight' of his Kentucky hemp. From his study of Newton, he knows the head flips backwards by propulsion, yet the body (in both senses) is still speeding to the ground under gravity's law. How else is the head caught by the noose? Death comes to us all, but rarely as a lightning-swift messenger of unconsciousness, unsensed, untroubled, unknown.

Soon enough, Marwood thinks, my brass eyelet innovation will engender the break sooner. With all force pressured to a single point, in slipping the eyelet down the rope to angle under the left jaw, nothing at all would be felt, death would be *inexperienced*. The cervical vertebrae would be decimated, cutting the spinal cord a touch below the brain stem—a practical, yet clinical, almost magical outcome. If the dream of a painless death is not too much of a strange delight (it is a social service after all), what dreams may come through science and practical application....

In other words, Marwood realises that strangulation and decapitation are not the only two shows in town—the neck can break, quite elegantly, rendering unconsciousness and death with *no feeling*. The condemned will not suffer needlessly, nor will a bloody headless spectacle occur, given the authorities finally accept decapitation's inhumanity. Marwood writes in the margin: 'Executioners can then move *inside* the prisons. Without entertainment, they are more privately felt, more professionally rewarded. Hmm.'

Later, long after the candle and fire are extinguished, he sits in the dark trying to remember how he discovered the seed of his idea. Like Newton he saw that the greater the fall, the greater the force when the object is arrested at the end of the rope. At the moment of creation, he knew exactly where the inspiration came from—it was something he witnessed on Church Lane, Horncastle next to the cemetery of Holy Trinity Church. As a boy of eleven he saw kestrels, hovering perfectly, soundlessly, and dropping crabs from the sky to break them. "The Long Drop challenge," he asks out loud. "How far must the condemned drop to guarantee the neck breaks but without decapitation?"

Laying the books aside, Marwood arranges his work tools on the desk—he stands, surveys the world below his fingers. He is godlike in his ambition now, not seeing that in his drive for humane revelation, he approaches the *will to power* and Dionysian spirit. He fails to see that the arc of relative morality means that the closer he perfects the execution tool, in a sense, the less humane it becomes. While the most efficient killer, the guillotine is waiting in the wings for the Paris uprising that very summer—the smiling Widow's wake. She offers a painless death but a carefree one, too, whose ease and scientific precision, whose speed is the apotheosis of what Marwood is pushing for in the smaller, more ancient world of rope hangings.

The hours pass and Marwood relinquishes food in his concentration. Having already developed 'the modern noose', by which a metal ring or brass 'eye' takes the place of the slipknot, he realises that a counterpoint is needed—a heavy metal plate—where the force of the slack delivers a strong blow to the patient's neck. All that remains are the drop ratios, the weight of each person calibrated to the length of the drop. Overall, the conclusion is undeniable—here is a theory of such magnitude and simplicity that science will surely bear out its truth in experimentation.

Marwood thinks back to the technique he used for the execution of Frederick Horry at Lincoln prison on 1st April 1872—something was missing. Earlier that morning saw the first woman he hanged, Frances Stewart, for the murder of her grandson—he remembers the half break, the brief strangulation. On both occasions he used the modern noose and yet a clean break did not result. What was missing? Nothing if not the Newtonian 'Long Drop'—the Dionysian fusion of man's design and godly control—the Nietzschean will employed for the first time for good. These thoughts all rush into Marwood's mind and he is high with the possibility of killing pain for the undeserving.

Using a dummy, he places the noose under the jaw on the left side, to stay secure, and to force the neck back for a clean break. All other positions for the brass eye run the noose dry and cause strangulation—but the proof will come with practice. In addition he wants a shorter climb to the scaffold, preferably ramps from the condemned cell, and the digging of a 'swing pit' below the trapdoor.

Marwood grabs his notebook. He must account for gender to a degree—women having less force of mass due to reduced muscle—and an added effect with age for men. He cannot calculate with limitless accuracy, but the main measured weight will be suitably precise. Tying the dummy with sandbags, Marwood repeats the drop again and again, as he would do with Aldous in his back garden in Horncastle. The experiments remind him of home, causing delay and tea breaks, but he pushes away the reminiscence and perseveres. Gradually a table of drops—the first ever—emerges in his notebook.

"The cool, steady hand, the calculating swift eye of an artist," he whispers to himself to maintain morale. "Working for peanuts, we hangmen practice art for art's sake!"

After each drop Marwood re-inspects his makeshift drop. He repeatedly climbs a dozen steps leading up the wall, where the exit through the brickwork is sealed. Here he watches the dummy fall from its makeshift scaffold—a wooden door on its side—and weighed down with sandbags. Then he retreats to the floor again, his desk, notebook and the fire. Each time he notes the marks on the dummy's neck, where the drop cuts the mannequin's soft leather made from leftover shoes. No experiment is as good as the real thing. But ultimately he ends up with a chart. He even makes a last innovation—it is not necessary to pinion the lower legs of the condemned.

"Giving someone enough rope—to hang themselves or so their neck will break? That is the question." He smiles, feeling erudite by ending the day with work, and his thoughts return to Ellen, Aldous, and finally Miss Thomas. Achievement is close, he can feel it. Here is the moment of quiet genius within Marwood's soul—the humility of the shoemaker, but the ambition of a man who sees the world by being prepared to transport souls humanely, in his own eyes, from life beyond death.

He writes in the notebook: **Inspired by an old Dublin gallows, the New Drop was designed to be portable by architect George Dance (the younger) in 1783. Set on wheels, it was positioned against a jail on an elevated platform high over the gawping crowd, with a double-swing trapdoor. The sides were sealed and opaque so the prisoners' approach was hidden. The drop was operated by a nifty pin-bolt, but unforeseen disasters were more common than comical, such as assistant hangmen losing their footing and disappearing through the trap. Twin beams could simultaneously dispose of twenty-two 'patients'—a la Telemachus's feat—before being replaced by a single beam, a nod to progress. Yet surely the New Drop remains quite barbaric, emphasising the non-science of strangulation?**

My design is a moral revelation, Marwood tells himself. The high stage is not necessary for the Long Drop—the Newgate Drop platform is just a trick to attract large crowds. My fall is shorter but relative to the weight of the condemned, so the name Long Drop is something of a misnomer except in the case of very heavy prisoners. Otherwise science dictates all. Whether light or heavy, the executioner will see the victim's head and shoulders, even to the waist, before he disappears from view.

"This is the burden of the hangman," he whispers. "I am the longest witness to my own act, both the hand clapping and the hand clapped. I am the prisoner's last friend, hope and reassurance, the taker of life…" But I am getting too philosophical, he thinks. So long as the drop is right, the state shall be happy, the prisoner dispatched without hue or cry, the end swift, the morning long, my family paid, and life will go on. "As I like to say, I sleep as soundly as a child—when my time comes, I too hope to pass away like a summer's eve."

In the street, the wind picks up but Marwood does not hear. No one sees his experiments, performed on the dummy hidden under Gloucester Place. The basement grows chilly as the night lengthens. Marwood is forced to retire to the upstairs world for supper, to the bed sheets bought by the City of London.

He climbs beneath them, and is soon dreaming of falling sandbags, pencils, notebooks, trapdoors and occasionally, the strangely animated face of Miss Julia Thomas—decapitated. He does not wake up, though, but rolls over, as though readjusting the rope and fixing the noose's angle could conquer his fear.

As future heir to Marwood's official hanging position—James Berry will one day write in his own notebook: Marwood was a good man of sorts, a precise, careful man who worried more about the prisoner's ease than dispatching the crook! Relieving pain was his métier—he really should have been a doctor. Yes, there was something unknowable in Marwood's soul. For all his scientific study and sympathy for the condemned, he was essentially mysterious.

He was England's honest man and his methods will assuredly make hanging live into the next century. With his scaffold experiments, and cost cutting making the government smile, he has certainly made my job secure.

Chapter 14
Murder on a Sunday Afternoon
23rd February 1879, Sunday

Kate wakes with her lifelong love of freedom and hatred of rules intact. Today is Sunday. Two days have gone by since her last argument with Mrs Thomas and all is looking well. She lies in bed thinking about her boy Daniel and the threats made by Jonathan Clatter. The time has come to act, and not be bossed around. "I have to prove I can look after my boy."

Kate is planning to leave for Norland Crescent, Notting Hill where she has already seen a new opportunity in the local rag, the *Hammersmith Guide*. Only yesterday she heard Mrs Thomas complaining to Mrs Ives, her neighbour from 3 Mayfield Gardens, about her fear of the dark since "the new maid—morose and savage-eyed"—moved in. The words repeat in Kate's mind until she forces herself out of bed: "Kate's slipshod, ramshackle clothing; Kate's devilish habit of clunking the tea on the tray; Kate's tardiness in reacting to the bells." It little helps that Kate has a hangover today. As late as nine o'clock, she rolls over and sips from a bottle of sherry beside the bed. The liquor of Mr Marwood's hospitality has given her a delicate new taste.

Meanwhile Mrs Thomas's concern has been less than exaggerated. More than once she has tried to get friends to stay over—all missed opportunities to no avail. She continues to write to her brother, Richard Hughes of Prestonville, Brighton and her solicitor Mr Batterbee, to manfully 'come and get rid of Kate'. In turn they reassure Julia 'the relationship will improve', viewing her complaints as being from a woman forced by age to share her house, albeit of her own volition.

When Kate stumbles into the hall from her attic room, she usually has a few minutes' respite. Yet now she finds Mrs Thomas already upset and dressed to go to church. Soon Mrs Thomas will tell her devout friends of Kate's wild sinister look, how the maid squared up to her in the narrow hallway.

"Kate, you look dishevelled. Are you not coming to church?"

"I'm a Catholic," Kate says, "not a Presbyterian, madam." A final scolding, here is the long-awaited spark for the powder keg. Peace is restored since Mrs Thomas is leaving the house, yet Mrs Thomas chooses this moment to deliver bad news.

"It's not working out, I'm afraid I'm going to ask you to seek new unemployment."

Kate laughs and Mrs Thomas stares. "You mean new *employment.*"

"I do, Kate. But Sunday is an unlucky travelling day for Irish Catholics, so I'm happy for you to stay three more days—Tuesday afternoon."

The maid's eyes narrow. "That's not even two days."

It could all so easily not have happened. Mrs Thomas takes out a pencil, standing in her dressing gown, and begins to make a note in her diary. Kate pounces towards her, snatches the diary and rips out dozens of pages with a bearswipe. She then marches to the bathroom and tosses the pieces like heavy confetti from the window. Mrs Thomas is speechless, open-mouthed, and in fright she scuttles downstairs and minces through the front door. However, she is in her nightgown and the embarrassment of transgressing Richmond's propriety, especially on a Sunday morning, overcomes her and she retreats back to the house.

Kate is nowhere to be seen, having returned to her attic room where she flops down on the bed. Meanwhile Mrs Thomas dresses, puts on her hat and leaves for church after all. Further up Richmond High Street she encounters her old servant, Moira Nicholls.

"You look pale and anxious."

But Mrs Thomas is too proud to confess her domestic worries, especially to a previous servant who wasn't up to par either.

"Thank you for your words, Moira," is all she manages. "Will see you at church."

With flushed face, overexcited and forgetful of herself to the extent she lets her bonnet slide, Mrs Thomas is thankful for the draughty peace of St Michael's. Soon she feels quite holy, even opting to kneel on the stone floor for all the prayers, not her common practice. She drinks in the sermon—about forgiveness—without a hint of irony.

In just under an hour, she returns to 2 Mayfield Gardens, despite being terrified and without asking a friend to accompany her. Something in her nature is wilfully embracing its own fate.

As Justice Denham later pronounces to the Old Bailey: "This can only be explained in that she was fascinated by Kate as a rabbit is fascinated by a snake—this is not to blame Julia Thomas for her demise, only it takes a rabbit to arouse a snake, and a vicious snake is what Mrs Thomas welcomed into her home."

Kate has lighted the gas in the hall, reasoning that if Mrs Thomas finds the place in darkness, she might be too intimidated to enter. Unfortunately for both women, this is not the case. But there is no direct verbal encounter, rather a pause unnerving the mind and sobering each party. As the Old Bailey court later verifies, at three o'clock Mrs Ives sees Mrs Thomas, trowel in hand, tending her rhododendrons in the front garden. At three forty as usual, Mrs Ives sees her again leaving for the Sunday sacrament at St Michael's Presbyterian Church in the Lecture Hall, Hill Street. At that point Mrs Ives enters her own cottage at 3 Mayfield Gardens, the two houses meeting on the corner. She lights the fire and begins her evening reading of George Eliot's *Middlemarch*—prepared to be undisturbed for the next few hours.

Trepidation and perverse excitement follows Mrs Thomas down the street as she passes Mrs Ives's house. On entering her home, another argument ensues about the maid's right to stay longer. Kate argues for a week, Mrs Thomas refuses. They stand together on the first floor hallway. The winter dusk gathers, the bathroom window only letting in minor light. All that lies ahead, far removed from the world of George Eliot, is a tense evening.

But calm does not arrive. Instead, Kate grabs Mrs Thomas by scrawny skin under her neck, causing her to squeal, and from the top of the stairs sends her like a rag doll bouncing off the wall and banisters down to the living room floor. Her left foot rests on the bottom step, twisted as though laying claim to something.

As Kate later explains in court questioned by her defence lawyer, Mr Warner Sleigh: "I knew she was seriously injured, see, and kind of lonely. I can't explain it. I became agitated at what 'appened, lost all control of myself, and to stop screaming n' getting in trouble, I went downstairs. I caught her by the throat, and in the struggle she was choked, n' I threw her on the floor again."

Then it was all over. What Kate does not say is the following, that like a crab she half creeps along the banister, containing her rage until she reaches the last step. Mrs Thomas opens her eyes, but Kate fails to see—she is so overpowered by a dark feeling of powerlessness. The wall between the two houses is thin, given Mrs Ives's living room borders 2 Mayfield Gardens, the houses being symmetrical reflections. The neighbour hears the cry, the thud, the commotion, and is pressing her ear as though acting in a Restoration Comedy tightly to the wall. Later in court, she would testify she head "a noise like the drop of a heavy chair," but she was not too agitated, believing that an accident with furniture could explain all, and moreover, she didn't want to leave her beloved Mr Casaubon of *Middlemarch*—despite his bookish boorishness—"for too long in the grip of deceitful Dorothea Brooke."

As Mrs Ives withdraws her ear from the wall, Kate rolls her broad fingers over Mrs Thomas's throat and chokes down her half-twitching neck and soft gurgling. She then picks up her landlady, with no more plan than expending the rest of her energy, and carries her downstairs to the basement. There Kate places her full-length on the old kitchen table, no longer used and a relic from when the house was fully operational with a full cast of servants. All this time Mrs Thomas is still alive, torpid and stupefied, perhaps, but still breathing.

For a moment, Kate collapses into a squashed maroon armchair in the half-dark. Sitting up, she patiently lights a candle, and the reality of her vigorous act begins to creep across her face. She expresses a feeling not so much horror as disappointment, a vague sense of entering strange new territory. And yet she feels no fear, certainly no remorse, but a kind of sadness as though defeating Mrs Thomas and becoming 'last woman standing' is a hollow kind of victory. She feels alone, and thinks of her boy Daniel.

From the corner of her eye she notices Mrs Thomas's chest is still rising and falling. However, the feeling of uncertainty passes quickly, especially as Kate spies a bottle of rum in a corner. Her arm swings out, tiptoes its fingers along the shelf, and pulls at the bottle with a lumbering scowl: she pulls the cork with her teeth, spits it free.

"Is it not true, Miss Lawler, or to employ your less deceitful name, Catherine Webster, that you pounced on your landlady in the long back bedroom where blood was found later, and struck her down with the meat-chopper before she could say a word?"

"Objection, Your Honour, Sir Denman is arguing."

"Not sustained. The court will hear the accused."

Kate takes a break, sipping the rum while Julia Thomas breathes her last. Despite claims to the contrary, she does not cut up Mrs Thomas *still alive*—though she has heard such tales.

"There is no barbarism in my actions," she says to the wall, pressing her eye to the rum bottle. "I just need to be taken seriously, but nobody cares!"

"Nobody cares," the bottle replies. Shocked, Kate holds it at arm's length but cannot bring herself to smash it. The murderess staggers to her feet, retreats upstairs where she waits in a state of frozen tension. Once more she wanders the house looking into Mrs Thomas's bedroom with its ostentatious designs, its narcissistic luxury. "False niceness," she mouths, "don't count for nothin' in this life." The last bedroom—at the end of the hall—she's never seen. The door is ajar and Kate has to push. It turns out to be a shrine to Mrs Thomas's husband, unchanged in twenty years. With a kind of pampered stillness, it offers a bitter contrast to her own room's discoloured curtains, her grotty ceiling cobwebbed with human dust. Kate sits gently on the bed and spies Mrs Thomas's diary, poking from under the pillow.

She turns the pages blankly. The life of the old woman means nothing—her opinions gone. Her barbs against her maid can no longer hurt. The landlady can no longer write her diary. She cannot sack Kate from employment. She cannot verbally abuse her, make her polish the silver, or force her to leave. "It's like the old woman ain't existed. She was never alive!"

Suddenly Kate feels a surge of euphoria. Deep inside there is a sense of controlling time, as though committing a murder no one knows about and pretending it didn't happen washes it away. However, the mind trick—of both desiring and embracing denial—

does not work. She cannot con herself. The guilt feels no heavier than the burden of continuing life. She did act and she must react, or the crime will be discovered.

She re-enters the kitchen basement with gaslight, candles, a can of peaches to mix with the rum, and new determination. She drags the body to the table. Working in a meticulous manner, she brings a large pot of water to the boil. Kate now prepares well. She ransacks the cupboards, laying out an assortment of sharp knives on the kitchen table, including a large meat cleaver. On a chair are two glass jars and a black leather bag. Beside the chair, on the floor, is a wooden box lined with cloth sacks and some brown paper.

Kate's mouth is drawn down while she is cutting up Mrs Thomas, but her heavy jaw does not waver, at least for the first hour. According to the judge, she takes "unmeasured pleasure from the lengthy, laborious and repulsive task." This is true for a while, since Kate has never cut a body open, and given the shock of a cadaver, and the fear it will reanimate under her hands, she is disgusted too.

"I was only able to maintain my task by the power of evil," Kate says in open court. "You'd only understand if you were there. The human heart has a depth of resources not used in daylight—and you'd not think yourself capable, but you are."

Silence from the court. Sir Justice Denman, prosecuting, takes up the thread:

"Fiend-like, truth be told, she cut the body up and tried to dispose of the limbs piecemeal. The smell alone must have been overwhelming. Yet there she sits, acting all innocent!"

Kate ignores the extended finger of the law, and sits upright in the dock. Her mind is back in the basement with the body of Mrs Thomas.

When coal deliverer Henry Wheatley knocks at the front door, Kate is relieved since she needs a break from mopping. The drains at 2 Mayfield Gardens, she has decided, cannot handle Mrs Thomas. Wearing an apron, she slides up the stairs to investigate, resting her chin on the third step to see. Outside, Wheatley is peering through the frosted glass, his face a puzzled blur. Meanwhile Kate is thinking of Mrs Thomas's gold bridgework that could probably garner six shillings or straight whisky at *The Hole in the Wall*. Time will tell. A few more knocks and Henry Wheatley goes away.

At this point, Kate remembers William Marwood's joke about

decapitation—that when William Makepeace Thackeray went to see the last of the Cato Street conspirators executed, the executioner dropped the last of the heads. He literally sliced it off with the axe and then dropped it. The crowd immediately cried "Butterfingers!" and the headsman was embarrassed and dismayed—what a way to upset the crowd!

Marwood had told her this story, of course, while empathising with the headsman's professional shame. He even embellished Thackeray's original with the awful pun that the executioner 'lost his head'. This evening, Kate remembers little beyond this punch line which at the end of a long day does not make her laugh *quite* so hard. She has a lot of work to do. Looking for an upside, though, she realises from Charles Peace's faded bloodstain on her blouse that "headless is clearly the way forward."

So she sets about the dire task with self-maddening zeal, first severing the dead woman's head with a razor, the blade slipping with horrible ease into the still loose, scrawny neck. Next she employs a meat saw to skewer off the limbs, arms before legs, biting her own gums to calm her nerves. Sometimes she squints through the fleshy horror, her haunches loping pink and bloodless, but she must focus so not to cause herself injury: that would be a horrible scene. Eventually she begins parboiling the torso in a copper pot on the stove, tidying the loose limbs to the skirting board like dismantled furniture ready for cellar storage. For a while she tries to disintegrate Mrs Thomas's intestines, the liver and some unrecognisable organs, by burning in a separate pot. But this proves a failure, the liver stinking under the flames far worse than the mound of disrupted flesh. At times Kate is disgusted—to the point of sickness—by the dark pools of blood edging away to the unsealed corners of the room. She knows hours of scrubbing lie ahead. Frequently she drinks directly from the bottle of rum, forgetting about the peaches, and even sings a little to keep her spirits up.

The blood becomes unreal. But after a few hours the smell is less distracting. Still taking no break, Kate methodically triple boils all of the body parts. She crams the remains—resembling more animal flesh than the human body—into a wooden box, except for one foot and the head itself. At some point she hits on the idea of selling the fatty tissue as dripping. But perhaps this is too risky, she thinks. "I am not a butcher after all."

In court, the neighbour will report the strange smell she remembers from next door. Mrs Ives explains her dismissal of the smell as some meats gone off, and masked the odour by cooking her own evening soup. Meanwhile, less than twelve feet away, Kate disposes of the spare foot in the drains but not before playfully peeling off the toenails for disguise. Finally she is left with the problem of the head, when she glances up and sees what Mrs Thomas uses to store the Christmas turkey—she decides to rope the old lady's skull inside a black bag.

Now she's ready for the pub. Leaving the torso on low boil, she can probably get three pints in the system to take her comfortably through the night, topped up by the last of the rum. Kate places the dangling head in the black bag, ties the noose, and pushes it under the table; then she changes her shawl, blouse, stockings and grabbing one of Mrs Thomas's coats from the kitchen door, she is away to *The Red Lion*, only half the chopping done. Behind her she drags a parcel containing a foot, the arms and stray flesh—the torso having been secured in the box and left behind.

At *The Red Lion* Kate enjoys herself less than expected. For once, she attracts little attention, being quiet and sinking her ales in the corner. She does not stay long, but wishes all "a good night" and then regrets the pleasantry. "They would swing for me, this lot, I can tell you!"

By dawn she has dismembered the body, boiled the bones and drained the thickest of the blood—surprisingly without staining the floor. The pot is sticky but the table can be washed clean with a bucket, leaving no presence of Mrs Thomas except her essence under Kate's skin, and a sense that she now inhabits every room in the house—as well as Kate's soul.

All morning a strong smell permeates the house and Kate opens all the windows to generate a free airflow, surprised by the cleansing effect of the winter breeze. By mid-morning she is more relaxed, listening to the sounds of Richmond market down the street, and her nerves loosen. With the relief and sense of danger lifted—not to mention the reality of Mrs Thomas in pieces not seeming quite so strange and twisted in daylight—Kate's attitude improves. In characteristic style, and true to her nature of emotional imbalance, she embraces these good feelings rather than suspect them. Trying to give the impression of normality, she hangs out some washing to dry close to the house. But standing in the garden, with no one watching, merely brings home her exhaustion from the heavy lifting, chopping, scraping and sweating of the night. She goes up to her own room, high into the attic, and is sleeping soundly within two minutes.

At seven in the evening she wakes to darkness, and at eight she leaves the house. The basement gives off a petulant reek of complaint as she passes the foot of the stairs, even with the door closed. No need to return there yet, she half smiles, Mrs Thomas 'will not wait up'. Still, there are plenty of body parts to take care of—only she will need some help. Despite her muscular frame, hidden under a new frock courtesy of her landlady, even Kate is not strong enough to drag the chest with the torso. As for the black bag with the head…first things first, Kate thinks, as she retrieves a few body parts accidentally discarded in the living room.

Much later, Mrs Thomas's right foot is found in a manure heap in allotment ground on Crop Hill, while the left foot is never found. On Kate's way back from ditching this appendage, Kate is a little more concerned—at this rate it will take her weeks to dispose of Mrs Thomas. Feeling a strange clarity, a kind of despair mixed with euphoria since Mrs Thomas's belongings are now essentially hers, Kate stops at *The Hole in the Wall* at the corner Byways Nook and Park Road. The publican Mrs Hayhoe later recalls at trial: "I little thought when Kate came in and I chatted with her that she had left her mistress boiling in a copper pot."

Another hour later, Kate is fortified with sufficient drink to return to the dark cellar. She focuses on cleaning the blood, and is surprised how efficiently she can soap the floor and walls, despite what she hears of bloodstains. The irony does not escape her—she is working harder than ever for Mrs Thomas.

'The dead truly do possess the living', she thinks, and even whistles powered by her drinking, but finds she cannot smile.

Chapter 15
Evening at Sunset
24th February 1879, Monday

Kate has taken a long walk to close the day. Emptying her mind, she meanders down Richmond High Street in the direction of London. The people of her past enter her memory—her long ago mother, the father who abandoned her—brothers and sisters she can barely remember—a scrub of land—bubbles rising through her brain before bursting with new surprise, if no longer pain, at the edge of her consciousness. Part of her no longer wishes to live. But every time she glances down at Mrs Thomas's frock, the surge of possibility revives her spirits: Am I finally beginning a new life?

Walking on, she is looking for a sign, not even the fulfilment of her hopes, but an indication that life is worth living. The anger she feels towards Mrs Thomas has receded, but nothing has replaced it. At the foot of the hill she pulls her landlady's shawl tight as two policemen pass her on the street. They are deep in conversation and pay her no mind. Slowly the river gleams with specks of coal-dust on it skin, and rises from the belly of curved land—a colourless snake in the glow of lamplights rather than actual water. It is pitch-smooth except for a single light that appears to move. Like a star guiding her, or so she believes, Kate follows the faint glow, tracing it arc as it appears and disappears behind the empty, broken windows of the warehouses.

As she reaches the riverbank, a horse and cart rushes by and yet the light remains. She takes hold of the railings and peers down the Thames to the St Albert Bridge, the quiet authority of Battersea Power Station and somewhere far distant, the ocean she has never seen—only the Irish Sea when she crossed to Liverpool as a teenager. The Thames is the closest Kate has come to comfort, and its constancy makes her think self-pityingly of her boy Daniel. But this sadness spikes her anger—not completely assuaged—at Daniel's treatment by Jonathan Clatter, a man who saved him from the Beadle's workhouse only by putting him on the streets, showing the false, self-serving compassion of the con artist.

"I should know what to do," Kate whispers. "I'm a mother...I should know. Why do I never get a sign?"

Tonight, though, she is not to be disappointed. The light re-emerges from the distant riverbank and cuts across Old Father Time. No other boats are present. She hears a bell, a call, a holler back. She witnesses a glorious moment for night Londoners, an exceptional fraction of time when a boatman 'shoots the river'—will fly under a bridge, blind to the current, against the tide and oncoming traffic. Without witnesses, without audience, except for the woman on the riverbank he never sees, the boatman risks all—Kate is privileged, and she admires his gumption. Cutting into the main flow of water, the boat surges forward—a gas-lamp dangles precariously from the prow, a dog barking at the stern, half in fear, half excitement. His wife is visible on the port side.

Kate strains forward on the railing, her voice caught in her throat. Suddenly the boat is rocking, the dog surprised and scared as he comically tries to stay steady. The whistle blows hard as the boat comes into view under the bridge lights—just an ordinary steam barge, long and thin. But for the people onboard, and for Kate, the barge is a *Flying Scotsman* splitting water, heroic and unmasked in the twinkling lights reflected under the bridge's arching stones.

Fearlessly, the captain navigates the rush of water through the middle arch, elevating both arms in his triumph, the man hallooing and the dog newly invigorated. The wife on the boat is silent with glee, as the spectator on the riverbank waves her shawl. The woman on the boat, an anonymous link between the imaginations of two women looking for excitement, seems to understand Kate for a heartbeat and waves back.... Afterwards the river is quiet again,

Battersea Power Station silhouetted in darkness, almost beautiful in its austere bulk, perhaps sleeping. Kate fathers her wits, exhilarated by the barge 'shooting the river', and begins the long walk home.

New life is beginning, Mrs Thomas, she tells herself. Tomorrow is a second chance.

Part Two
The Road to Tyburn

Sae rantingly, sae wantonly,
Sae dauntingly gaed he;
He play'd a spring, and danc'd it round,
Below the gallows-tree.

Robert Burns, *MacPherson's Farewell* (1788)

Chapter 16
A Walk on the Wild Side
25th February 1879, Tuesday

After getting Henry Porter's details from Jonathan Clatter, Kate meets his stooge, a man Clatter is blackmailing, on Lambeth High Street. Kate "cannot provide the candelabra already sold in Smashers Alley," but she is able "to provide a silver egg cup" she finds in Mrs Thomas's display cabinet, together with a 12-piece set of stainless steel cutlery.

They meet at the bar of *The Old Rover*, a beat-down Irish den that sells only liquor. For once Kate abstains. Porter is a burly man with a round arch of hair receding across the left side of his head in a friendly curve, like the slow cutting of a stream around a rock. In one glance she perceives his head is equally hard—in a dim rather than strong-minded sense—as he introduces himself as a family man "in need of sudden funds." Part of Kate instantly admires and is jealous of his mentioning a family.

"Yes, there's my son Robert, the wife, and Emma-Jane my daughter. My business—I'm a publican—has run into hard times 'cos we've fresh competition in Hammersmith." They repair to *The Old Rover*'s back room. "Hence, Mrs Thomas," Porter says openly, "I can make you a good deal."

"You ain't no professional?"

"I told you, I'm a publican."

"Well, the best deal I can offer is thirty guineas, for the lot."

Porter laughs, frowns. "I can't shift them at that price."

"Then I'll take my business elsewhere. I don't need every Tom, Dick n' Harry to barter wi' me—an' cheapen what I know is mine."

Porter presses her arm: "Okay, okay. Twenty-six?"

Kate smiles. "Twenty-seven will do just fine." She raises her finger to his objection. "So long as you perform a lil' task for me. Somethin' harmless."

"I pay just half today."

"Deal."

Henry Porter's son Robert meets Kate in Barnes not more than two hours later. The boy looks no older than fifteen but has the rangy, tough-looking body of eighteen. Kate has left the black bag behind, but the box is beside her in the street, transported by horse and cart to the river's edge.

Kate shakes the kid's hand, and looks at him with distaste. His intelligence looks even lower than his father's, but this seen through Kate's eyes—the street girl seeking wisdom in the publican's son but tricked by her own prejudice. Little does Kate know he spends his days reading Dostoevsky above the pub's main lounge. They have little to say to each other.

"What's the book you're reading?"

"A prison diary—*Notes from Underground*. Father's got one called *The Idiot* too."

"I'll bet. Autobiographical?"

"No, fiction. Next I'm gonna read *Crime and Punishment*."

Kate says nothing. Together they lug the box—a blanket over the lid giving off the air of a lady's belongings—past the railway station and a pawnbroker to the water's loading ramp.

"Heavy, ain't it?"

"Just keep walking."

They embark up Mt. Ararat Road. The handle is missing on one side of the box, so they swop as Robert's hands are grating. The steps up Richmond Bridge are not easy and Kate proclaims her weakness at this point.

"Did you bring rollers?"

Kate scowls. "No, I didn't."

They drag it a third of the way down the bridge, wobbling as Kate hands him an envelope. Richmond Bridge has five elliptical arches, and flanking either side of the middle arch is a cutaway seat. They set the box down in one of the seat's recesses.

Kate stands there. "I'll wait for the hansom here—it costs less."

Robert smiles innocently, and begins his walk to the steps where he accidentally drops the envelope, retrieving it quickly. For shame he turns to see if Kate has noticed, but she has not moved. Half way down the steps he hears a splash of something heavy hitting the water.

"The idiot," he whispers. "She's trouble, that one." He hurries off the bridge gripping the envelope, already thinking of his reading back home, head awash with Dostoevsky. But when he reaches the foot of the bridge, he realises his pockets are empty. His bus fare home is gone and must be fallen out on the journey. As he deliberates, someone is standing above him at the top of the stone steps.

"Nowhere to go?"

"I'll be fine," Robert says, but Kate catches up to him. "Where's the box?"

"I met my friend, and he took it."

"That right?"

"It is," Kate says. The boy shivers unintentionally and Kate sees her cue. "You're cold. Listen, I don't live far from here."

Robert is reluctant, but can't deny he's cold and hungry. He agrees to accompany Mrs Thomas safely to Hammersmith Station so he can catch the local home. They set off. But once arriving, the train is cancelled and Robert grows worried, changing his route to Richmond New Station, but they've spent so long dragging the box that the last train has gone.

Fortunately, the night carriage goes most of the way. So they head down Richmond Hill to the High Street, no box between them, and little conversation. Robert enters the dark house warily, before the supposed Mrs Thomas gives him some rum, and has a nip herself. He sits in the drawing room and is permitted to stoke the fire alive. Kate returns from the kitchen where she's noisily prepared the oven; she runs her fingers over the piano, acting Mrs Thomas again, and remarks "it has a very nice sound."

"Are you sure I cannot get a cab?" Robert inquires, fire poker in hand. "It's not too late?"

"No, it's not *too* late," Mrs Thomas says, "but I think you'd be more comfortable here."

"I really should get back. Father will…"

"…kill you?"

"Yes."

They smile, the new landlady more nervous than Robert. The boy's fair hair is almost white-transparent through the fire, Kate thinks, his colour so fresh and pale, like veal skin.

"A cab is six crowns to Hammersmith, I can give you the money if you like."

Robert looks back at the fire, the blue flames now curling into yellow tips. A breeze from inside the chimney blows a flake of ash cool onto his hand, a harbinger of new experience. A positive sign, he wonders?

"I must check on the turkey," Kate says, heading back to the kitchen. "I like playing hostess," she whispers to herself, with odd elation. "Such a lovely *tête-à-tête* for us!"

Kate pictures the scene and is half proud, half wary: the youth is only fifteen or so, perched in the drawing room surrounded by testimony, and yet clueless. All is real—the saws, the bloody knife, burnt human bones, boiling stains in the copper pot, the trunk box, the heavy black bag. The thrill of her achievement—the fact that no one suspects her—is strong in her blood tonight, if only because she is entertaining a boy, a minor, whose mind will be clouded—especially if she keeps feeding him the rum, as she intends to do. Despite her crimes, Kate is still a young woman at thirty, slipping downwards in her own eyes, but still passionate, chatty and amused, tempting herself to tell him *everything* while elaborately replenishing his glass with rum. Sexual play is a possibility, but caused by whom—would that help matters later on, if things came to a head? Would Robert give her away, or could he save her, becoming not just a lover but an ally?

Kate is aware of her own desperation and pushes these thoughts into deeper places, calling them ridiculous. The argument with Mrs Thomas now seems just a waking dream, and the instruments of death—the garden saws and meat-cleavers—just memories of a restless night.

"As for the black bag, am I keeping it as a souvenir?" Kate looks down on it. "Somehow I cannot burn it, so I must keep it until it frees me. Mrs Thomas's spirit will lead me now!" Kneeling, Kate tucks the black bag between a wooden log and the stove, causing pressure on the squashed head. "I'll move it soon enough."

Distracted by piano keys, Kate re-enters the drawing room with a fresh bottle of rum. She persuades Robert to sit with her on the sofa, which he does, he is so befuddled with attention and alcohol. He looks in this Mrs Thomas's eyes, faintly disgusted by her perfume, and is surprised that she appears quite a young woman for a widow. With the blunt innocence of youth, he stretches low on the sofa, his feet playing with the piano pedal. "When did your husband die?"

"Let's not discuss Mr Thomas," Kate says, frowning, and moves in close to the boy. She begins to twirl his black neck-tie. Robert is wearing half his school uniform, the waistcoat missing and his jacket abandoned to Mrs Thomas's coat stand. His hand reaches warily to scratch his chin, but by now Kate is already on top of him.

She kisses his forehead and abruptly dives for his mouth. Robert feels the struggle like a boy drowning, overcome by the surprise and struggling for a breath. The woman's haunches bear down on his boyish thighs, unable to take the pressure, and he lets go an uncontrollable whelp like a dog trapped in the corner of a room unprepared to be kicked by its master. But the scuffle does not last long—an embarrassing glance here and there—and all is forgiven.

Kate pours them both a glass of port as though any awkwardness captured in the fiery moment is long gone, believing the aggression of her sexuality too strong for the fifteen-year-old.

"Mr Thomas…" he pants.

"Two years ago—he died at Richmond Bridge, running away from an omnibus, fell in the river." She looks directly at Robert. "Drow-n-ed. That's why I don't like to go near the Thames."

"Oh." Robert sips his wine.

"He was gonna buy us the rental on a Kensington pub," Kate says, trying to speak the boy's language. "The capital fell through, you know. All he left was this dumpy place." Her eyes roll three-sixty round the room.

"It's a mighty lovely…"

"Sandown Park races, you bin there Robert? We use 'a go all the time, meet down at Hartley's and watch the clappers…I mean, the nags run like th'clappers."

"Mrs Thomas, are you a thief?"

"The expression's a tea-leaf, Robert."

"My Pa says you ain't Mrs Thomas at all, jus' a lowly relative, pokin' yer face in, see, pickin' up the stray jewels."

Kate grins, and taps his nose. "You little jester! Henry's quite the comedian."

"But, Mrs Thomas, I ain't sayin' you ain't who you sez you is. Just 'cos you say it in Cockney slang, don't mean you ain't one. My father says tea-leaves—I mean, thieves—are the worst scum of London. They should be hanged."

"So I should?"

"That's what my father says."

"Well, tell your Pappa to *toe the line*," Kate says, barely lifting her neck from her chest she's so tired. "I'll swing for him, that's what."

The conversation drifts, ending with some talk of Richmond market day, followed by the hanging of Charles Peace and Kate seeing the delights of Covent Garden.

"I ain't never bin."

"Too bad."

Robert leans down, head near her feet. Kate is confident he is too weary and intoxicated to snoop around the house, notice the black scuffs on the landing, the ghoulish marks on the wainscoting. He cannot see the bone fragments, splintered like pine needles and hardened to a rotting blouse in the kitchen grate—if only because Kate cannot see them herself. Comfortable in his tiredness, she feels vindicated; the purity of her action display their truth; the morality of deception will set her free—at least, not send her the way of Charles Peace.

But Robert has seen enough. He can see the discolouration on the walls in the living room, the hall, the drawing room too. Even the piano keys have bloodstains. The crime is transparent. And yet he is soon so happy-drunk, so teenage-comatose, it does not register. The blood means nothing. It is food colouring…it is decoration…it is a splash of colour on the black and white ivories. The night ends with Robert gurgling lines from Robbie Burns he's learning for school—

Sae rantingly, sae wantonly,
Sae dauntingly gaed he;
He play'd a spring, and danc'd it round...

"...Below the gallows tree," she whispers in his ear. Face ashen before the dying fire, Robert begins to snore. Is she tempted to tempt fate? Perhaps—he is a witness after all. But what purpose would it serve? He is only a boy, like her Daniel, just a child.

Kate leaves him, retiring to the finery of Mrs Thomas's bedroom. That might she sleeps calmly, in full belief she has committed the perfect landlady murder—"she's my second skin. Julia Thomas and Kate Lawler are one, and no one can splice us apart," she comments to the ceiling. "Not in this life..."

In the morning she cooks breakfast early and Robert wakes with a sore head. Before long a knock at the front door makes Kate hover nervously in the hall, but she is dressed the part, so opens up.

"I'm Charles Porter," the young man says, "lookin' for Robert." He leans into the house, so the new landlady invites him over the threshold. "Last night I almost got a ladder to get in upstairs through the window. We're not used to not 'avin Robert home, Mrs..."

"Thomas—Julia," Kate smiles, her teeth all angles. "He missed 'is train."

Charles, a bearded broader version of his brother, peers at Kate. "Well, come see us in Hammersmith, Mrs Thomas. Henry'll be expectin' yer. Good day." He yanks Robert up by the collar, and escorts him from the kitchen, barely noticing his surroundings.

"I've got some small rings n' postage stamps you might be interested in," Kate throws his way, as the brothers leave.

"Oh," Robert says. "Thank you, Mrs..."

"Silver watch and chain," Kate interrupts. "Good prices, n' the best dresses too."

Charles looks up and down the doorway. "Your place smells kind o' funny."

"Yes, we had turkey for dinner last night."

"It was good," Robert says as he's hauled up the drive. "Tasty."

At the north end of town, son held tightly in hand, Ellen Marwood steps off a train with her boy Aldous. Paid for by the City of Westminster, this journey is the first either has experienced by steam locomotive, everything from carriage curtains to hot-cross buns served by trolley. At faster-than-carriage speed, Ellen worries she might not be able to breathe—an old superstition—and stays busy massaging her neck from the moment they leave Horncastle. Inspired by his father, Aldous had no such trouble. Though sympathetic to his mother's fear, his first trip to the big city will not be damaged by farmers' rumours of train suffocation.

Approaching London, brand new St Pancras Station gleams with wrought iron brickwork above their heads. Stepping onto crowded Euston Road, with necks pulled back they squint at the architecture's gothic splendour, its steely turrets and redbrick towers, a hundred stained-glass windows like the church of an unimagined future. The screeching sound of a new train arriving, the human cries, the bright cold smell of steam, all disappear in that visual delight. Then the metropolis is back.

"London is big!" Aldous says. "How long before we get there?"

"A bus ride," Ellen says. "Straight west!" She points down the Euston Road towards the declining winter sun, a low cloudy haze. "He'll be expecting us before nightfall."

"Can we go to the fair?"

"You can ask your father, if he's not too busy. But wait until tomorrow." Ellen protects her neck from the wind, grips the boy underarm and together they negotiate the street—the Home Office has provided no money for a carriage. Slowly they cut across Regent's Park, escape the crowds and reach London Zoo.

A sign outside proclaims: '*Do not feed the animals—they do not respond well.*' Aldous frowns and remains puzzled by this turn of events—all the way to Marylebone to Baker Street, he puzzles this question.

"Do the animals eat each other?"

Ellen stares down at him, horrified. They reach the sheltered house facing Dorset Square, its basement quietly visible below the stoop.

"No, they do not. Now ring the bell for your father. He's probably downstairs." But Marwood is not home.

Chapter 17
A Splendid Date at Bartholomew Fair
25th February 1879, Tuesday

That same afternoon, Marwood is standing on top of Holborn Hill, eating a fresh egg from a market stall. At his side is Miss Julia Thomas, dressed in uncommon finery for the fair. She is wearing a pearl necklace over a purple gown tied elegantly at the hip. A winter's country hat of yellow lace is pinned under her chin. The day is surprisingly mellow, but Kate still receives as many wondering expressions regarding her high-born appearance as she does admiring looks. She is dressed to the nines with the skilful sophistication of a well-to-do grifter, a female con. Marwood is so smitten by her company at this point, he fails to notice the crowd's ambiguous stares.

The couple continues walking, north-west from King's Cross to the open fields, following the people. They talk of their respective boys, Daniel and Aldous—a new topic of conversation since *The Oxford & Cambridge Arms*. Kate explains that Daniel's father was a sailor who took off and left her, not on a ship, but with a mistress. Marwood sympathises while thinking of his wife, and conveys genuine feeling. Kate does not care one way or another; she still wonders why she hasn't robbed this man then remembers her indifference is because she enjoys his company.

At the boundary of Bartholomew Fair—a ditch—Marwood pays their entrance fee, a gallantry Kate politely ignores. They step along the cross-plank into a fantastical brave new world. Gone are the mocking insubordinations of the gallows crowd, the horror of the scaffold and the bloody basement, all gone, replaced by this merry-anarchic field of delights. Ubiquitous are the baked-potato stalls, smoking tents, cake shops hawking roly-poly and plum duff, the gambling dens with their colourful signs— 'Cards, Darts, Poker n' Bridge, we got the lot!'—any game to get the punters in the fairground spirit. In a second, London is a faraway dream.

"Welcome one, welcome all!" is cried behind their heads. Marwood and Kate turn to witness a man wobbling unconvincingly on stilts and fitted with soft shoes to prevent his sinking in the mud. "I am the Caller of Bartholomew Field, also known as your Mayor of London." The crowd parts, everyone blinking in the fresh sunlight, uncertain if he's speaking the truth.

"That really *is* the mayor," Marwood whispers. "And that man,"—he points at Mr Constance following the stilts with two gorilla-men—"is the sheriff."

"Oh."

"I've never seen the mayor in costume," Marwood says, "or in public. He's quite the performer." They watch as the legs wobble on, an awkward giant resembling a boy thrust up among the gods.

"He could fall."

"We all fall," Marwood says. They exchange a soft smile. "You know, you look lovely today, Miss Thomas. Your dress is a perfect fit."

"Thank you." She does a little curtsy. "Perhaps the Queen of England will invite me to dinner?"

"Perhaps," Marwood smiles, and fumbles to take her hand, but Kate has spun away distracted by the flowers in a straw-basket stall. He buys her a single blue tulip at her request, which Kate pins to her shoulder like a brooch. She does a twirl.

"You look…happy," says Marwood.

"A pleasure, kind sir!" Kate laughs, frowns comically and repeats her twirl.

"Jack Rann flirted with the crowd on his day of his execution, so I'm told."

"Why?"

"Well, the 'bright blades' his friends kitted him out in a nosegay—he had something to live up to. Jack quipped a 'flash ballad' before stepping into the air."

"He died game?" Kate asks and cocks her head in imitation of propriety.

"Exactly!"

"Talk about fancy clothes."

"Certainly," he says and squeezes her hand. "He stepped off at Bow Street, 1774 and impressed the crowd by knotting bright blue streamers to his leg irons. I watched it at Tyburn—Calcraft was sober for once—and it was a decent hanging. Sir John tied a bundle of flowers to his chest. He killed his auntie you know, for her inheritance. Before his arrest he strutted through the botanical gardens of Bagnigge Wells, bowing low to the ladies in a scarlet waistcoat and five-cornered hat."

"Very fancy."

"Yes—and before his trial, he even went to other unluckies' executions and claimed a front row seat out of 'professional interest'."

"Like yourself."

"Well, yes. I remember him so clearly. Every day *The Messenger* updated Jack Rann's lurid story—and wardrobe choices. For trial, he sported a costume of equal refinement and self-ridicule, his silver strings pinned to a lime-green suit, with a collarless shirt open at the nape. In the condemned cell at Newgate he dined with a coterie of well-wishing ladies, mixed with a few of the youthful street variety. When he 'toed the line', he looked almost debonair, a nosegay sprouting from his buttonhole!"

Kate smiles—more and more she is learning Marwood is fascinated by her because unlike his wife Ellen, she lacks social pretensions. She is different, or so he tells her. As for herself, Kate knows she is more different than ever.

"I enjoy the fair more than the scaffold," he says.

"I am pleased to hear it!"

Marwood looks at her mysteriously, his lazy and sharp eyes poised in unison conveying half serious, half zealous expression. "Who wouldn't want to be Lord Mayor?" He gestures after the stilts. "Look, he's changed his sword of state business to a sixpenny trumpet. See children, it's the *lord of misrule*, the carnival king of bacchanal!"

Kate lets go of his hand. "You must speak so I understand!" she says, immediately regretting the hint of confession. Yet as luck would have it, the next stall displays Punch & Judy ready for a fresh encounter. "Another Master of Mayhem!"

For a moment Marwood is worried, remembering his awful recent dreams of Punch's power—but he hardly wants to show Kate's his boyhood neurosis, so they settle close to the back of the show, standing.

"Welcome one, welcome all," declares a bearded man with jester's crown, "to our fairground spectacular, loved by grey-heads like me and boys n' girls alike! This is our Punch & Judy joust, with a little of the devil thrown in." The crowd—about ten rows of messy families—is sprawled on picnic rugs in the half-shade. A ripple of appreciative coos now escapes the white canvas tent: older children are hushed up, tiny ones mesmerised, and babies faced the correct way to learn about their heritage.

They watch the story unfolds. "It has its own Bloody Code," Marwood whispers, "called injustice. There's a subtext—that man Mr Punch needs the gibbet cure."

"And you're the one to give it to him."

"Sure," Marwood says, missing the joke.

The story of domestic abuse and insulting authority takes a different tack, however. Punch marches onstage wearing a jester's motley strapped to his shoulders and begins sliding around like Richard III. The children giggle without knowing why. "'A horse, a horse, a kingdom for my horse!'" His voice is a desperate squawk powered by the *swazzle* the puppeteer grits in his teeth. At the back of the crowd, Marwood is more unnerved by how Punch's hooked nose meets his jutting chin than his gleeful cackle: "That's the way to do it."

"There's your real Lord of Misrule," Kate says, "never a trickier figure alive!"

"You know before Judy, Punch had a first wife?" Marwood says. "But no one knows what happened to her. She was called Joan."

Kate stares at him.

"Whatever happened to Joan is whatever happened to Lilith, Adam's first wife. In the Bible."

"What did happen to her?"

Marwood points to the stage where the answer is performed—as follows. Punch beats Judy, she suffers; the police chase Punch, he eludes the police; the hangman chases Punch, Punch beats the hangman; the devil chases Punch, Punch hangs the devil.

Judy and the baby cry.

Chief Lord Justice: "You're a murderer, so you must come and be hanged."

Punch: "I'll be hanged if I do."

Curtain: *The End.*

The puppeteer ends the spectacle of abuse and violence with his own words 'sleep well tonight," breaking the spell of Mr Punch's energetic dominance of the children's faces. "So ladies and gents, although the crafty Mr Punch murders his wife and baby, he does outwit the hangman, Jack Ketch, and trick him into hanging himself!"

"Such a poor story," Marwood jokes, "not at all convincing!"

Kate grins and this time squeezes his hand back. "Lawmen and the devil himself, you're all the same."

"Thank you, Julia, but Mr Punch is real, you know. Sure, he's amorality made flesh and the bawdy soul of Rabelaisian wit. The crowd knows an anti-hero, and loves one—they don't miss a trick. Look at the sauciness of his crooked nose and high-pitched voice. He captures the same lust for life I see on the gallows!"

"The stupidity, you mean."

"No, by then it's too late for stupidity."

"It's never too late, William."

The Punch & Judy show ends with the puppeteer's invisible song, serenading the mismatched couple from the tent:

> "His money most free he spends;
> To laugh and grow fat he intends;
> With the girls he's a rogue and a rover;
> He lives while he can upon clover;
> When he dies—it's only all over;
> And there Punch's comedy ends."

As the song fades, Marwood pipes up in his resonant bass church voice with the next verse:

> "Who'd be plagued with a wife
> That could set himself free
> With a rope or a knife,
> Or a good stick like me?"

Kate, to Marwood's surprise, hollers back in her Irish brogue:

"I've done the trick!
Jack Ketch is dead—I'm free;
I do not care now, if Old Nick
Himself should come for me."

"He's a killer," Marwood says. "The man's a brute—a base criminal."

"He's no more brute than monkey," Kate says. "He just knows what he wants and demands it. To hell with authority!" She laughs and twirls free of Marwood's hands, glimpsing beyond the tents another kind of fairground spectacle—the mule race.

Marwood is shocked by these words from such a polite lady. "But he kills his wife, his own baby, he knocks down the Beadle, hangs Jack Ketch and tricks the Grand Seignor. Then he puts an end to the very devil himself!"

"And we're supposed to care about the devil?"

"Well, his genius is his victory over three social controls—wife, hangman, and devil, namely marriage, law and morality."

But Kate is no longer listening, pointing at she is in delight to a particular fat mule—a creature bored, stubborn-looking and with no discernible future.

"Let's bet on that one."

As she speaks, the 'mule-rush' is off and heading down-field. Eighteen mules to a heat, from a makeshift rope bursts a throng of vintage mules suffering all sorts of complexions, gaits, dispositions. Marwood remembers his reading of Mark Twain's diaries and paraphrases in his head: 'Some are handsome creatures, some not, some are sleek, some haven't had their fur brushed, some are incredibly gay and frisky, some are full of malice. Guessing from their looks, some of them think the matter is war, some think it a lark, the rest consider it a religious occasion. Each mule acts according to his convictions. For this picaresque occasion—a delightful fashion-freak—the riders are fully dressed in jockey costumes of bright-coloured silks, satins, and velvets. Moreover, each mule and rider has a distinct opinion how the race ought to be run—eighteen conflicting opinions—all whipped into fury by leather straps and the cat-calls of the crowd.'

However, the whole episode is more excitement than Kate can bear. A veritable Eliza Doolittle, she leaps in the air at every fall or surge, openly cheering for her favourite mule—a black beauty so sleek and arrogant it butts those to left and right and charges down the centre. Dust clouds hide the animals a few moments, before they return on the curve and grunting and dazed, the last few grind it out on the home straight.

Winning the race, Kate's mule sees no reason to lead the field, though, its personality needing an adversary. So it falls back within the pack and begins shoving and charging once again, swinging its bony head side to side and kicking viciously with its hooves. The whole race proceeds like a wave rolling and receding until eventually the animal's nemesis, a mule of white and flecked grey, breaks the tape at the closed circuit of five hundred yards. A few hats fly up in the air from the gambling winners, and there is a general sign of disgruntled relief from the others. The incoming mules blink in the sunshine, sweating indifferently.

"Oh no!"

"If Mark Twain is correct and we conduct our mule races like the Americans, one day there'll be a consolation race for beaten mules."

"It's only fair," Kate says straightening her blouse, trying to maintain her bruised dignity. "I really thought he'd win."

"He was more interested in killing the others."

"If he'd killed the others, he'd have won!" Kate says, winking her logic at Marwood and he notices the redness of her cheeks, lost summer cherries, he thinks, but says nothing for fear of embarrassment.

"Poor boy, he never stood a chance!"

"Next time," Marwood says, and escaping the mule-crowd through a turnstile they come face to face with a family-run game unfamiliar to Kate—the fairground guillotine.

Almost immediately, he persuades Kate to put her head in the block. Here's an opportunity to demonstrate his invention—the New Long Drop—to prove it's painless. But first Marwood sits coolly in the chair looking up at the arch of crossed wooden beams above his head. "Imagine the blade is a rope, but the angle different, that's all." The guillotine is so thin he cannot even see it. Besides, the device looks truncated by a magician's trick, a fairground fake probably not even sharp.

"One more buckle," Kate says.

"Ha, your turn." Marwood straps her in the seat as the operator appears at his elbow.

"Two bob a drop."

"I'll take one—for the lady."

"No, wait," Kate says, feigning fear, "is it safe? I don't want to go home a headless chicken." Despite her humour, a vision of the bloody-blue pockmarked features of Mrs Thomas appear behind her eyes, as though summoned from hell, isolated and hovering. But Kate closes her eyes and pushes them away—the nose, the mouth, the battered lips, a crack in her forehead blackened by the night in the kitchen, a night of long knives. Marwood watches Kate wriggle and cannot tell if she's comfortable or joking.

"Let me know if you want out."

Kate glares at him, then closes her eyes again. She concentrates, trying to sense a purging of her crime, as though seeking remorse or compassion for Mrs Thomas at the moment of double death. But Kate feels nothing, more like a heathen or unconscious psychopath, she cannot even conceive of a Bedlam case. What she does feel is infinitesimal, the pilot light of humanity in the basement, left on for no reason by an ancestor, a memory of tenderness from her childhood. No matter how she searches in the basement, she cannot recover the light and bring it to the surface. The glow of the flame is detectable, though, and she frowns with the pain of its existence. As for any purging contrition, acceptance, or guilt for 'striking' Mrs Thomas, they belong "in the land of make-believe."

"Julia?"

"Did I say something?"

"You said 'I see her head'. Whose head?"

Kate is silent. "Get me out of here! Please!" Marwood hurries, lifts her bodily, then pays the man.

"Are you okay?"

"I meant the mule's head—it was pretty scary." She looks back at the mock guillotine, where the operator is already loading a small boy into the seat. The boy leans back and the blade comes down. There is a scream, a giggle, and a boy's head sits up, unharmed.

"We didn't do it right," Kate says. "You have to trust the carny and he was shifty-looking."

"On the way back," Marwood says. "Perhaps."

Kate takes his arm. The next stall advertises 'Send a lock of your hair through the new Queen's Postal Service—for free!' With her nails, Kate twists off a greying lock and drops it in the glass pot.

"For Daniel," she says.

"Aren't you going to write the address?"

"He doesn't have an address—he's living with his uncle in Rotherhithe. They move around a lot."

"Oh," says Marwood. "I have a boy too. Aldous—he's eleven. Very bright."

"My boy is sharp-witted. Same thing! You'd like him—he knows how to tie knots. He's doing well in school. His teacher's a tough one but he's learning a lot."

"That's good, good. I teach Aldous at home. To mend shoes, you know, fold and wash the leather, arrange the buckles, laces, tie the pins. One day he could follow in my footsteps."

"To the scaffold?"

"Yes, you're probably right. It's a legacy I'm sure he doesn't need. Do you know what a body looks like after the drop?"

"No, no. Why would I?"

Marwood smiles. "The eyes popping, the tongue, the black skin, the cut neck."

"God forbid!"

"Sometimes the hangman has to pull on the victim's legs."

"Today?"

"In the old days, and especially at Tyburn with ten on the same rope—that's the cruelty of the Short Drop. The relatives of the prisoner would pay the hangman, though, to climb the scaffold and pull on the legs."

"To speed up the end?"

"Naturally." He looks at her. "But sometimes he still swings there, painfully, despite all their efforts. Or *she*, of course. Sometimes they lack the strength too. It makes no sense—the harder you pull, the more you feel weakened by killing someone you love."

"I can imagine."

The conversation quietens them for a while. To break the silence, Marwood tells a story to try and impress Kate. "So we have some Irish Republicans in Horncastle," he begins.

"Oh."

"I get harassed by them a bit—just because of the Phoenix Park murders. That's another story. Michael Bennett was a Fenian and the last publicly executed man in England. This is before they brought in the Newgate Drop, you understand, and hanging moved inside prisons, long before Charles Peace's ridiculous public hanging, one I am not responsible for, if I may say so. Anyway, for Bennett's drop—a Calcraft special—the old bungler pulled back the hood and Bennett's mouth was protruding and split like a snake's tongue, his features all black. They say he ratted on his friends."

"Did he?"

"Nobody knows, Julia. He faced the scaffold redheaded, with a red beard. But when they lowered him, they say all his hair was black, in redemption or fear, who can say...."

"Which city?"

"You just left it mile back. Newgate Prison, 1868, I was there. Two thousand people booed, jeered and sang Rule Britannia then 'Champagne Charlie' as his body dropped."

Suddenly Kate stops their walk. Up ahead she can see the boundary of Bartholomew Fair, a block stone wall. Stretching the distance are the dipping hills of Middlesex, a small hamlet and church steeple winking in the afternoon light. A trail of smoke rises from a farmhouse. As they approach the wall, Marwood puts his hand on the stone and a cow looks up in the next field, moans pointlessly, and lowers its neck again.

"They could chew for England."

"William, I was there at Newgate!" Kate says. "On that same day, I was nineteen years old."

"But...how?"

"We already spoke about this—at the Tyburn re-enactment. You don't remember?"

"I..."

"He was hung on 26th May 1868."

"That's right."

Marwood stares into her eyes, into what he believes are the delicate eyes of a refined Richmond lady: their watery grey gives nothing away. Somehow this shared event, albeit macabre and peculiar, bonds them in Marwood's mind. "I would remember!" he says. "That's why I brought it up, honestly. But why were you there, Julia? What was the attraction?" He looks out over the fields. "You know, I really know so little about you."

"Let's go for a drink," she says. "I'll tell you a few secrets. I wasn't always Miss Julia Thomas, you know."

"What do you mean?"

"Over a drink, William."

More planks have been laid over ditches to negotiate the boundary of the fair. Carefully they cross to dry ground avoiding the waterlogged grass. Smiling, they let the good people pass, then follow. "Look, there's the smoking and drinking tent."

"So it is," Kate says, and takes his hand. For the first time Marwood thinks of Ellen and her arrival in London, if not today, tomorrow she will be here, but he pushes the thought down.

They enter a white tent with staff pillars supporting its domed roof, like a circus big-top. Placards line the walls with table offerings of beer, wine, whisky and gin. Advertising slang for 'overindulging' is everywhere celebrated, painted on tarpaulin nailed to wooden beams: 'Let's get *crocked*, good fair-goers!' and 'Don't let the bishop know you're rat-arsed on a Sunday!' even 'The Queen knows you're 'up the Monument', 'half seas over' and three sheets to the wind—take a rest on Sunday!'

"I could do with a lil' tipple," Kate says.

"That makes two of us."

First they have to step over two young men sprawled in the entrance, both soldiers, redcoats covered in mud. But their commission is safe—their commanding officer is inside the tent. Two other officers, medals dangling from gold-tasselled shoulders, roll the drunkards into the fresh air, laughing.

A worse sight greets them at the next table—three desperately ill-looking men hawking 'jake/blue' methylated spirits in the open— and 'surge/white' better known as surgical spirit. With their pockmarked faces, bruises, cuts and a devilish stink evaporating from their clothes, the men are busy jabbering with no customers. Overhead, an ironic sign reads: "Don't get high on your own supply."

"They call those the death-drinkers," Marwood says, as though educating Kate on the city's underbelly of drug life. "Clearly the restrictions at the alcohol tent have sunk pretty low."

"I know. See, I do read the newspapers, William."

"Vagrants who drink crude alcohol neat. They don't even sell it at the fair. They must have brought their own."

"They're still human. One day we'll *all* be in the City Cemetery," Kate says and Marwood looks at her sideways.

"You mean Forest Gate?"

"I do," and his complete surprise, Kate breaks into a song:

> Of all the girls in our town,
> The black, the fair, the red, the brown,
> That prance and dance it up and down,
> There's none like Nancy Dawson.
> Her easy mien, her shape so neat,
> She foots, she trips, she looks so sweet,
> Her very motion's so complete,
> I die for Nancy Dawson.

She pauses to ruffle Marwood's hair, then flicks her neck sending black hair flying. Prancing round the room as though riding a deranged mule, Kate's second verse is louder:

> See how she comes to give surprise,
> With joy and pleasure in her eyes,
> To give delight she always tries,
> So means my Nancy Dawson;
> Was there no task t'obstruct the way
> No Shuter bold, nor House so gay,
> A Bet of fifty Pounds I'd lay,
> That I gain'd Nancy Dawson.

Marwood claps, hands held high, but the low rumble of noise in the tent means many people failed to notice. Kate takes a little bow, arms swivelling and heavy chest squashed together like Moll Flanders. Quickly she stands and readjusts her fraudulent and disguised clothing, but giving a convincing impression of a South London lady.

"They have beer-halls like this in Germany," Marwood says. "Three times the size, double-pint stein glasses. The latest Oktoberfest just opened in Munich, you know. You've reminded me of their brash frivolity."

"No, they have small beer and we have Bartholomew Fair!" She leads him to a fresh tumbler of cask ale, a new, translucent beer sweeping with metropolis known as London Pride. They each take a pint and pay the ale-man his shillings.

"To life's chances and death's certainties!"

"To drinking a long drop!"

They toast, taking large swigs and watching the other slyly over the glass rims. Thirty minutes later their faces are red, the English tongue mangled by jokes and their feet dangle freely under the table. On the fourth pint Kate keeps drinking even after Marwood breaks off, but she does not finish, caught up instead by her own rough-diamond laugh. Her glass goes cracking on the table, trembles in her palm, and the Maiden of Richmond coughs up beer and froth.

"So you want to know my story?" she shouts, with a hiccup. But before Marwood can answer, Kate is up on the table, takes a defensive stance, and reengages her song of Nancy Dawson. In normal circumstances Marwood would be offended but filled with beer and entertainment, surprise and emotional uncertainty, he leans back on the bench and drinks in the performance.

Kate twirls and mimics, boats and giggles the tale of Nancy the London dancer, famous in 1759 for swinging the hornpipe in the revival of John Gay's *The Beggar's Opera*. Kate does her best to imitate a hornpipe by puffing her cheeks suggestively and stamping her feet on the bench, on the table and back and forth. Fortunately there is no one to complain—the drinkers have all stood to watch, protecting their pints in their fists while the nightingale insists on a daytime tune:

> See how the Opera takes a run,
> Exceeding Hamlet, Lear, and Lun,
> Tho' in it there would be no fun,
> Was it not for Nancy Dawson:
> Though Beard and Brent charm every night
> And female Peachum's justly right,
> And Filch and Lockit please the sight
> 'Tis kept up by Nancy Dawson.

Kate jabs her feet playfully and winks at the strangers. The hangman watches, mouth open, as she does an impromptu jig.

> See little Davy strut and puff
> Pox on the Opera and such stuff
> My House is never full enough,
> A curse on Nancy Dawson:
> Though Garrick he has had his day

And for'd the Town his laws t'obey
And Johnny Rich is come in play
With the help of Nancy Dawson.

Again, Kate takes a bow.

"Does that make me Johnny Rich?" Marwood asks, as she skips back on her drinking-seat.

"If you like, William, if you like." She brings on her fifth pint.

For some reason, Kate's words bring Marwood to his senses a little. "We cannot drink in here all day."

"All night, then."

After a little struggle of words, she is persuaded to return to the fair, taking her pint too. They stumble between the benches, surprised to re-encounter daylight. The next booth is selling chap-books and broadside woodcuts of famous circus acts—mostly pictures of lions balanced on barrels, bears in chains, a lone elephant with feet tied on a concrete block and draped in the colours of the Union Jack.

Marwood complains to himself of the cruelty, yet he values the intricate designs, the sixpenny chap-books with a pull-out frontispiece. Meanwhile Kate is at the next stall, her fingers running over the lurid watercolours of faraway places, Venice, Rome, Istanbul, until the last one is Dublin, and the country fields of the southern provinces and she pulls away, not wanting to see images of home.

"Come on, I can hear the gamblers nearby."

"How many vices can we witness in one day?" calls Marwood. "You know I'm a real church-goer." Nevertheless he trails in her wake, the image of the patriotic elephant trapped in his head.

Nearby, a small brown tent is hanging onto the side of the beer big-top. Kate slips under the bouncer's arm, a meat hook of black hairs, and is caught by her wrist. She scowls and he loosens his grip, but Marwood pays the *tab* without eyeballing the 'door-monkey', who pats his cheek playfully, as they are sucked into the smoky room.

Strangely, there are no brutal faces inside, just the soft flesh of human desperation, more losers than winners. In a circle around a central pit, a man in a flash purple jacket, frowning, is taking bets at break-neck speed, passing out tickets and backhanding coins to a man in a bowler hat, who deposits them in a briefcase chained to a metal hoop on the floor.

"It's all for pleasure," Marwood says, "which makes it more frightening."

"I ain't... I mean, I'm not afraid."

Ten feet over the circular ring-floor and bound by a circular wooden beam like the top of a well, the men can barely see the damage they do to the animals on display. Better that way, Marwood knows from his own profession, it keeps the punters coming back.

The noise is suddenly hushed. The fighting cocks are brought in grain bags and pulled out blinking into cigar-laden air by two 'bottle-holders', men with affected sadness for their destruction—in reality enjoying every minute. The birds go quiet. They are soothed, handled like newborns, then jabbed and unleashed on each other. Soon enough both creatures are exhausted, bloodied and three-quarters blind. Yet they do not give up. As they take a last breath, an assistant blows cold water on them in a fine spray. They revive, and begin killing again. The weary eyes of the men widen, not cruelly but looking for the edge, the victor, the claw that will cut the other bird's neck to a final shred, but seeing only the spirit of competition. They have gambled in these pits so long they no longer realise the strange horror for outsiders, caught merely by the thrill of bloody, easy money. At these moments, the men's earnings and their livelihoods are on the line.

"I cannot watch," Marwood says, "this is not for me." He fails to notice Kate peering into the pit, since his eyes are closed tight. "I forgot how pointless this is."

"They're bred to fight."

"So much luck."

Once more the birds falter, yet both are still alive. The assistant draws them up and the two bottle-holders, two stocky boys, take the birds' heads in their mouths and hold them there, to warm back the perishing life. It is an ugly sight, Marwood thinks, offering life before death, but the scene is too much—he is sick on the canvas of the tent, his stomach contents mixing with sawdust and sticking to the side of the glistening white big-top. Immediately the bouncer steps in, smiling, and hurls Marwood outside before either bird is dead. Sitting in the mud, the hangman hears a cheer from the men and a groan. Kate has not even noticed his absence.

Soon she appears, elated, trying to hide it. "They tottered about," she says picking Marwood up, "dragged their wings and found each other. They struck a blind guess or two, then fall exhausted. But there's always a victor."

"And the other had to die."

"Had to!"

"No mercy?"

Kate looks at Marwood, puzzled. She helps him hobble away from the tents, past the toffee apple and candy floss stalls, to the children's side of the fair with its hoop games, shooting galleries, its baked potatoes, plum-duff and roly-poly.

"I'd like to go home," he says, but Kate is barely listening.

"Tell me—in witch burnings," she says, "the hangman sees that the victim strangled before the fire is burning. Isn't that right?"

"Hardly a sport, is it, witch burning?"

Kate laughs. "No, I suppose not."

They cross over the plank and re-enter the boundary of London, with a single leap.

"I want to go back home too, but..."

"You know, hanging can be cruel," Marwood whispers. "Especially the drawing and quartering. Even now, after a man is dropped, he is sensible and conscious he's hanging."

"That's a nice thought."

"Except with the Long Drop."

"But who knows how long those seconds last?"

Marwood looks at Kate in her fake jewellery and stolen dress, the murderess kitted out for the gala-day with her hangman. "Yes, who knows."

"It didn't work for Charlie Peace now, did it, that Long Drop of yours."

"No, it didn't."

They fall silent. Then, to break the awkwardness, Kate repeats her refrain once more:

> Her easy mien, her shape so neat,
> She foots, she trips, she looks so sweet,
> Her very motion's so complete,
> I die for Nancy Dawson.

She gets the final word on hanging tales, too, revealing one Marwood doesn't know:

"Wild man Jonathan?" she says, faking incredulity.

"I've heard of Jonathan Wild, if that's who you mean."

"Did you know he picked his chaplain's pocket while on the scaffold?"

"I did not. How do you know that?"

"*The Richmond News* prints all the best stories."

"Of course."

"And the best part is," Kate adds, "it caused a bit of embarrassment for the Reverend Thomas Purney."

"Why?"

"It was a corkscrew."

Marwood frowns, and then the penny drops. "They're all drinkers," he says. "They send people to their deaths with God's will on their consciences—I just do it for the state, and for greater humanity."

"Not for a single 'long' drop of pride?"

"Not a single one." And he means it.

Kate takes his hand, feeling safe if a little drunk, and they meander back where Bartholomew Fair re-enters the fantasy of Victorian London.

Chapter 18
Secrets of the River
26th February 1879, Wednesday

Inspector Sequin sits in *The Adelphi Cider Cellar*, ensconced in a maroon-cushioned booth, and opens the *Daily Telegraph*. Not quite front-page news—the headlines are reserved for more cotton mill strikes in Lancashire, of little concern for a London detective—his eye catches the local story of one Eleanor Ryan. Apparently on Monday morning she jolted her husband out of bed, throttled him, and began hacking his limbs off while he was still breathing. Imagining the man's horror, the inspector swallows, his Adam's apple turning in his throat. Then without more thought, he turns the page for the horseracing results. Jones appears with the drinks, two pints of afternoon porter.

"What's the world coming to, Mr Jones?"

"Search me, sir."

They both sip.

"A man here's been chopped up by his wife."

"Modern marriage," Jones replies with a downward glance. "District?"

"Chalk Farm, too far north."

"Franklin's territory. I wonder if the Middlesex boys'll catch her."

"They already have, by the sounds of it. Damn, 'African Explorer' was down in the fifth at Cheltenham. There goes my weekend."

Jones eyes his boss with an unsubtle glance. Sequin will be in no mood for police work now. "The Southwark case is a big story. Perhaps we should take the rest of the day off?"

"Not a chance," Sequin says, folding the newspaper. "Bow Street must know we're out patrolling...oh, what's this?" He notices the back page. "'Covent Garden boys must dust their brains. Charles Peace is not dead and buried and yet the killing continues...'"

"The Ryan case?"

"No, they're calling it 'The Barnes Mystery'. Seems a body's been found in a wooden trunk washed up near Barnes Bridge. Listen up:

The river speaks! A mysterious deal box was discovered at daybreak, Monday 24th February, by a coal man, one Henry Wheatley, a sixty-year-old native of Hammersmith. Mr Wheatley had a stomach-churning shock when he opened the trunk. He used his coal shovel to break the clasp, a simple padlock, then wished he'd never found the box. Inside were the human skin, flesh, and visible bones of a woman, age unknown. Inspector Harber of Barnes Police reported the investigation to Scotland Yard— though he's released a statement about being short-staffed due to the spate of so-called 'winter sickness'. Under Harber's supervision, the various body parts have been examined at the Royal College of Physicians who confirmed they were from an individual human female and added that the skin was so discoloured and blotchy white, it appears to have been boiled. Without the head, however, it is not possible to identify her....

"So much for Eleanor Ryan," Jones says. "This one's a solid hanging case, if we catch 'im."

Sequin peers at his deputy, a smile creeping across his face. "Sounds like Harber could use all the help he can get. Sign us up, Deputy Jones, sign us up."

"Where exactly?"

"Okay, well, let's just get the omnibus south of the river. That's a good enough start."

Sequin folds the *Daily Telegraph*, and they sit quietly as the pints slip down.

"So, it says these stories all follow a pattern, Mr Jones. Listen to this.

> *On 21st February two lads rowing upriver saw a large corded carpet bag resting on one of the abutments of Waterloo Bridge. Inside the carpet, rolled like a tobacco leaf, was the body of a garroted man. Apparently, under questioning, the toll-keeper remembered a short-stoutish man coming to the toll-house from the Strand side of the river the previous night with a carpet bag which he helped a mysterious lady carry over the iron plate of the stile. Clearly he didn't reach the other side of the bridge with her precious pedestrian cargo.*

"I'm sure whoever dropped this wooden trunk did more or less the same thing."

"Precisely, Jones. Only how heavy is a deal trunk?"

"No heavier than a carpet-bag."

"True, true," Sequin muses. "Well, we have to go south. Similar stories abound in the mud off Battersea Waterworks, and downriver at Greenwich and Rotherhithe. We deserve our share of the action!"

"We could visit this Monday morning."

"Nonsense, lad. We can solve this crime today, and get Marwood pressed into service tomorrow. This time next month, the London criminal world will be 'high swinging' or else half way to Australia."

Jones swigs his pint empty, a couple of gulps. "It'll be one or the other, Inspector," he says. "Now you know why I drink."

"I've been drinking my whole life," Sequin replies. "Now's time to solve a crime or two, make the Bow Street brethren sit up."

"You could make Captain."

"Not for a case outside our jurisdiction—they'll probably demote me for it."

"Then what's the attraction?"

"Nothing in particular. I just don't like women turning up dead in wooden boxes."

"You're sentimental."

"That could be it."

Sequin downs his pint, drops the *Daily Telegraph* and slides from their booth. A little wobbly from the three pints, he heads with

Jones back through the cider den with its German beer-hall smell, huddled bodies and semi-clad waitresses in black pinafores. They exit past the empty stage out into the evening lights of Covent Garden. The seedy people of the night are already abroad, smoking on street corners, curbs, lampposts, watching the policemen with suspicion. A dog cuts across their path, twists its neck, scampers away.

"Back to the drains, where the litter lives," Sequin says. He pulls his coat tight. Jones adjusts his hat, grips his baton.

The city is just coming alive.

Chapter 19
The Elixir of Life
26th February 1879, Wednesday

Kate wakes with a song in her head, not so much tormenting her as duping with a singy-song nursery rhyme effect, sending her back to sleep.

> Of all the crimes recorded,
> In history from the first,
> The horrid crime of murder,
> It is the very worst.

Somehow, though, an impulse of survival is alive in her blood. By instinct, and after her past exploits of petty theft and the advice of fellow convicts who've shared their stories, she knows there's a long way to go to cover her tracks.

After her day at Bartholomew Fair, a double mood of worry and elation surrounds Kate. Almost from the moment she wakes, she is compelled into a kind of mania. She continues to clean up the cottage, disposing of rags and as much evidence of boiling and cutting implements as she can. Little does she realise, she's used so many tools she cannot find them all; some are hiding in the hallway, under the sofa, others strewn about the floor, or hiding in kitchen drawers. For at least two hours Kate scrubs floors, cleans knives, rearranges furniture, and tries to hide all evidence of wrong-doing.

Since the day is warm, she 'borrows' one of Mrs Thomas's silk dresses, a winter shade of demure green. Just before setting out, she remembers something from the corner of the kitchen. There on the coat hook is a yellow ribbon sash, the finishing touch. The dead woman's clothes and jewellery are hers. From gold watch to shoes to perfume, Kate has finally become Mrs Thomas. But she knows the greater challenges lie ahead—she must talk and walk like a lady now, and remember her own name.

As Kate leaves the kitchen, though, she remembers. There, almost forgotten given its plant-pot shape, is something she thought she'd never overlook—it watches her from just inside the door. The object appears to have been left for the gardener—a supply of soil perhaps—no, it's a leathery black bag. Quickly she takes up the strings, not wanting to examine them too closely, cleans the base, and is surprised to find the bag heavy. She sprays it with her perfume, and dangling it from her arm on the cover strings like a handbag—new Mrs Thomas is ready.

Her first port of call is to dispose of the severed head—the former Mrs Thomas. But half way up Richmond High Street she notices the market in the beer garden of *The Hole in the Wall*, and spies Mrs Hayhoe, looking content behind a table piled high with leeks. Now is as good an opportunity as any, Kate thinks, and balanced on her new shoes, she negotiates the garden path. The operation is a risk, given her worry about resembling her employer, Kate being far bulkier in all directions. She can see Mrs Hayhoe sipping port, half a bottle deep, and besides, she has only met the lady twice. She approaches, uncaring, noticing the glances from the farmers in the open air, mistaking them for country gentlemen.

"Good afternoon," Kate says, causing Mrs Hayhoe to sit up at her table, coughing. "I've come to make a sale."

"Well, you've come to the right place, Mrs…"

"Thomas, Edith. Julia is my cousin."

"Oh, how lovely to meet you," Mrs Hayhoe replies, extending her fingers, the skin on her face tightening up like a prune, one eye narrowed.

"Yes, good strong dripping," says Kate. "I've come to sell."

"Dripping?"

"Two jars." Kate removes them somewhat daringly from her petticoat, raising Mrs Hayhoe's other eye.

"What sort of dripping?"

Mrs Thomas stares at her, but does not flinch. "The usual leftovers from Christmas, top quality." Kate regrets the word 'leftovers' right away, with its implication of lesser quality.

"Christmas is a while ago. How much?"

"A penny the pair."

"I'll give you a penny for one," Mrs Hayhoe says, and takes a sip of port. Kate looks at the bottle, her jaw falling open. She has completely sobered up from 'the good stuff—since her energetic night of the long knives.

"Twopenny," Kate insists, and stares. Meanwhile she has deposited the heavy black bag at the foot of the table. It sits on its neck.

"You have a lettuce in the bag too?"

"What?"

"In your bag? You have veggies to sell? Sweeten the deal."

Mrs Thomas adjusts her shawl in the breeze and lowers her lady's hat, a pheasant feather twirled around its rim. "No, thank you, not today. So do we have a deal?"

"Turkey dripping, you say?"

"Turkey with a secret, fresh flavouring. That's what the butcher told me." Somehow she hits on Mrs Hayhoe's favourite pastime—gossip.

"What could it be?" Mrs Hayhoe says, rattling in her seat, her face squeezed into a thousand volcano lines. Without another word, Kate twists the jars to face her client. "I left the labels blank—so you can resell them."

"Okay, two pence it is."

They shake, exchange, and Mrs Thomas is gone, her black bag carefully reattached to her arm. Mrs Hayhoe leans round her table and watches her go, smoke from the ovens of *The Hole in the Wall* kitchens obscuring her view. For a moment it appears Mrs Thomas stoops to carry her prize, the mysterious vegetable, and then Mrs Hayhoe remembers her port. She uncorks one of the jars of dripping and sniffs lightly at the surface, surprised at its fresh pique. "Turkey dripping—always the best!"

Within minutes, farmers' wives are inquiring about the jars, delighted by the idea of local produce that can be resold—the labels blank. But Mrs Hayhoe will not sell. She plans to use this dripping for her own cooking. It would be foolish to let go something so rare.

Meanwhile Mrs Thomas has begun the long walk to London. Keen to capitalise on her new energy, her brain is pumping blood as fast as her toes. At last, a business is hers! She can develop ideas for magical unguents and Leicester Square 'wonder cures'.

The rest of the day passes at break-neck speed. In the *Brixton Tea Ship* on Clapham High Street, Mrs Thomas goes to meet Emily Hoare. The plan is to sell jewels—at the least her landlady's silver watch—but the negotiations must be delayed. Emily Hoare does not have sufficient cash to satisfy Mrs Thomas, and apparently Mrs Thomas will not accept credit.

"What about half in cash now, and half credit later?"

"All cash, dearie," Mrs Thomas says. "I just can't afford delay, see, in these tough times."

"Well, you won't get a better price." Mrs Thomas deliberates like a cautious old lady, while inside, Kate tries to work out the cost of moving the furniture out of the house.

"These things are circular," says Emily Hoare, a learned lady, her skull reminding Kate of the head in the bag. Mrs Hoare continues: "When the South Sea Bubble burst in 1720, Jonathan Swift—the political satirist—described the speculators as being 'on Garraway's cliffs'. You're right to be cautious—they were 'a savage race by shipwrecks fed'."

"What...I mean, pardon?"

"My great-grandfather speculated in the Bubble. He lost it all in the crash—so I don't blame your hesitancy."

"Hesi-tan-cy? No—I thank you," says Mrs Thomas and turns on her heel. She fails to witness the twine of bile-blood stuck to black cotton dangling from her purse-bag; once free of its home, the smell is like a mixture of goat's cheese and turpentine. Emily Hoare, unconcerned by a lady's belongings, mops up the twine, and thinks nothing of it. Mrs Thomas is gone.

Outside, Kate is stung to find a sign in a window for the *Women's Temperance Society*. Once again she feels the pinch in her throat, a sensation like the pressure of the fob watch or swallowing the dripping herself. "Time for a dry-stall," she says, directing her own movements.

The day has cleared and shows slices of blue-red sky. Already Kate is feeling hot in Mrs Thomas's get-up. Central London is the only place to dispose of the watch. Not only that, she will pass the river en route, and the head can be rejoined to the body. Despite her discomfort, Kate finds this idea peculiarly satisfying, like a Brothers Grimm tale told to a child, only where the wicked witch is eaten, then magically restored for an adult thrill. After an hour she reaches Lambeth Bridge, its grey arc yawning over the bustling boats crisscrossing on the Thames below. Immediately her plan is scuppered. There are too many witnesses.

Even hurling the thinning bag mid-river, its fall would attract attention. Londoners would detect its grimace or grotty hair in the clear sunshine, its wink of desperation as it spins in the air. She is not even certain it would make the river, but might land on a steamboat, or worse, a shipping vessel with men on the deck. So Kate changes her plan—Mrs Thomas will begin her promenade north carrying her handbag.

Eventually Waterloo Station with its concrete arches, Embankment, and Charing Cross all fall from the horizon. Mrs Thomas keeps her direction firm. She passes a young man, an Italian immigrant washing his face in a pewter cup, but pays him no mind; in the classical music garden at Embankment, she discerns a girl-mother. Sporting a red jacket—the livery of the City of London—the youngster is splayed on a child's pram, blowing on a saucer of soup. At another crossing, a crossing-sweeper regards her pitifully while queuing at a portable baked-potato van, a Union Jack umbrella sprouting from its roof. All around, Londoners 'eat of their thumbs'—on the go—and Mrs Thomas, lady of the south, ignores all. She must reach her destination or else the jig is up. Night mustn't fall while she's lugging her heavy black bag, or else someone will make the unfortunate step of trying to steal it—and woebegone that thief. Kate smiles and looks to the sky: "Red-handed will be the least of it…"

Charing Cross is just a short walk across the Strand from Covent Garden. Kate, of course, has to resist a swift visit to *The Nell Gwynne*, but she knows the Bow Street Runners frequent this ancient pub, so she steers clear. Instead she pops into a ham-and-beef shop—you can bring your own meat, and all for a halfpenny have a waiter dress and sizzle it on a skillet. Here, Mrs Thomas will order directly from the menu—the smell of the bagged, severed head will be clouded amid the cooking odours. Of course, she hasn't brought here own meat, so has to leave.

But later, at a little wooden table in Cordon's Alley, a poor-woman's Parisian café for one, Kate eats hungrily of liver paste on toast. She forgets the table manners of refined Mrs Thomas, crossing her legs, licking her paws, eating like a voracious bear born too soon. The waiter even begins using her as an advertisement, stopping passers-by in their black clothes, bowler hats and Victorian end-of-day expressions. Dangling liverwurst on a fork, he gets few bites, and a few businessmen even bow to the lady.

After her break, Kate is filled with greater appetite to accomplish her two goals—to lose the burdensome head, the real goal of her expedition—and to meet the Porters again and 'bend them to her will'.

"Everybody needs an accomplice," Kate tells the street, "or who else can be found guilty? Why should I carry all the risk?" Frustrated, she draws the black bag to her chin. It's been a long time, she realises, since she looked inside. She watches people on The Strand, careful that no one has stopped walking. Then she turns sideways to face the darkness of Cordon's Alley. She pulls back the drawstring on the bag.

Inside is what appears to be a shrunken doll's head, oval-shaped with a bald spot in the middle. It looks miserable, a child's toy not played with for years then abandoned, lost. Strangely, the smell is of rough soap, a human smell, and the horror of living odour—such a surprise emanating from a bag of death—is what gets under Kate's skin. She closes the drawstring, promises never to look inside again.

For a split second, Kate leaves the bag and retrieves a newspaper from the pavement, the *London Illustrated News*. She uses the newspaper to tighten the bag's drawstring. Then she doesn't move, but lets her mind wander across the past few days, how the Porter boy, Robert, helped her, the unhelpfulness of Mrs Hayhoe and Emily Hoare. She remembers the strange man who took her to a pub, William of Horncastle, who she considered robbing and yet slipped away. Perhaps she could find him again? He seemed sweet on her and it would be a shame to let a mark go free. Mostly, though, she thinks of Daniel and his mistreatment by Clatter.

Kate picks up the paper. She almost falls off her seat at the headline: *Box Floats Up Near Barnes Bridge*. With Mrs Thomas's soul on her conscience, Kate's eyes stare, straining with effort and incomprehension:

Hallow'en comes early! Yesterday evening, Henry Wheatley, a coal porter working at the Old Merlin Inn, Kew, was driving his cart down the Thames south bank. On reaching Barnes' pedestrian Terrace, an object floating "half in an' half out of th' water" caches his "hawk's eye." Wheatley stops near Barnes Bridge for a better angle, but still mystified, he hooks *something* ashore. The treasure is a wooden box, constructed of plain deal, a metal lid and loose hinges. He cuts the cord with his cart-knife and gives the trophy a kick, whereupon it falls open, disclosing to his fervent disgust, "a coil of flesh."

His assistant, a man older than himself, says it's just "yard meat for horses," but Wheatley is suspicious. He goes to Barnes police station and reports his finding to Detective Johnson, the sergeant then on duty. A Dr Fleece is called and the flesh deemed "almost the entire body of a woman." From the papyrus-like look of the skin, and despite *rigor mortis* exacerbated by the freezing water, Dr Adams confirms it has been boiled.

N.B. 'An open verdict' is initially recorded in the inquest because the body cannot be fully identified.

Kate turns the page. To her horror there is a picture of the trunk—black and unsoiled by the river, only having spent a day underwater. The police have printed two questions underneath, 'How did it float so well?' and 'Why?' In even bigger letters, there is a standard reward: '*5 pounds for information leading to an arrest. 50 pounds for information leading to a conviction.*' Kate is a wanted criminal again—and she grins, but the reality of Mrs Thomas wipes the smile off her face. She stares gloomily at the grainy photograph.

Wedged on a sand bank Barnes Bridge in the background, the trunk's unreality is palpable. From 2 Mayfield Gardens's basement to its kitchen to the river, here it is, in black-and-white and yet fantastical. A sniffer dog is straining away from the contents, as though offended. The picture has a smear of black-stain—on the coffin-trunk itself—as pointed out by the cane of Inspector Harber. Here is visual proof already of her least respectable deed, yet she feels no remorse, not for Mrs Thomas, not for herself, only for Daniel.

Kate frowns, and for the first time, she is afraid. How will she survive, now? Who is on her side of the line? Her hands tremble for the first time. The black bag sits on the table, accusing her. She rolls up the *London Illustrated News*, gently taps on the bag's hidden head, and pulls her disguise tighter.

"I have to get through *this day.*"

Chapter 20
The Barnes Mystery
26th February 1879, Wednesday

Meanwhile, the Marwood family is waking up in Gloucester Place not far away. William rolls from the master bed and draws the curtains a crack, looks briefly out at Dorset Square and shivers from the cold. Dew has fallen in the night, washing the street and sprinkling the trees in the park with tiny iridescent icicles. An old man passes with a trolley, disappears up a side street. Marwood sits down on the bed, lays his arm on Ellen's shoulder. She murmurs but does not open her eyes.

In the next room, Aldous wakes in a strange bed and for a moment lies in the dark, sensing the strangeness. When he can bear it no longer he too slips to the window and peeks through the lattice. He watches the old man pushing his trolley—a shopping bag with a brown duffel—over cobblestones, his back arched like a question mark. From somewhere in the city, a crow is interrupted by a dog barking. "I wish I was still in Horn-cast-le." Soon enough, he can hear his parents talking.

They are sitting in the living room where the hangman and Mrs Thomas sat so recently, man and wife quietly drinking coffee. The new luxury item, roasted Spanish beans, are available on Baker Street, and Marwood has made a special trip to indulge Ellen. He is careful to spoon only a drop amount of milk. "Londoners like their coffee black. Like the weather."

"Whatever happened to a good cup of tea?" she jokes.

He smiles, nodding, and they drink. The grandfather clock ticks and chimes the hour, seven, answered by the bells of Marylebone Cathedral. Even with the familiarity of home, Marwood feels a tad uncomfortable. His family now joining the city of his hangings is a new challenge—a little close to home.

Ellen senses his uncertainty, tries to ease things with small talk of Horncastle, the early preparations for the horse-fair, Aldous's progress at school, gossip about sheep rustling, the new roof on the Presbyterian Church.

"Sounds like the old place."

"It is, and you're missed in *The Portland*."

"Ha, missed in the pub! As the best shoe-man in town?"

"William, no one thinks of you as the cobbler."

They are silent. On a whim, a suddenly enthused Marwood suggests a tour of the house, something he cannot perform without nostalgic thinking of his new acquaintance, Mrs Thomas, the lady of the south. Little does he know, Kate is selling the bones n' tallow dripping of Mrs Thomas this very morning outside the Houses of Parliament. Soon she'll be meeting Nathan Crane to negotiate a few extra sales, and Jonathan Clatter to retrieve her boy—for good. Meanwhile Marwood decides that fine art is preferable to his basement equipment—the ropes and hanging gear of his previous guest's delight. Though Ellen is not particularly artistic, she plays along.

"The Lord Mayor must believe all these paintings inspire you. What's this one?"

"A statue of Pitt the Younger," Marwood says. "Everything's for show—we're in government rented property, after all."

In the hall, pulling on a tiny drawstring to part a red curtain, he reveals 'The Eel Ships' by Wenceslaus Hollar. "Protect us from God's holy light!" The painting depicts the silver river—the mighty Thames—as a water god gripping an urn emitting a torrent of fish, the power of life. "Here you can see Mercury, squatting and pointing to the Latin inscription of L.O.N.D.O.N. *Emporium que toto orbe celeberrimum.*"

"What does it mean?"

"Not sure—fetch the boy."

Ellen calls up the stairs and Aldous appears in his pyjamas—a cotton one-piece tied with string. "Time for homework." She beckons him to the painting which he translates.

"The famous…"

"Most famous," Ellen corrects.

"Market…"

"…in the entire world," Marwood completes. "Literally 'of the whole world'. Ablative."

Aldous looks up at his father, tired eyes, blinking.

"It means the market-blood of this world is alive," Marwood says. "The abundance of fish…is the biggest market. Life is more important even than money."

"I don't have any money."

Ellen laughs. "No, or your father would take it away."

Marwood pretends to find this funny. "Buying and selling, Aldous, the harmonies of human life…are the economies of life itself. Look at the fish, see how they spring from the urn—the mighty life of the Thames."

"Yes, Daddy."

"We'll see the river later—first, get yourself ready."

The boy retreats up the stairs and Ellen turns to her husband. "Good teaching, I'm sure he'll remember your lesson."

"All my tricks are worth remembering."

Ellen looks backs at the picture. "You know, the river looks kind of grubby to me."

"You're kidding. You want to see a river from hell? Follow me."

As though leading her to the scaffold he shows her the rest of the Gloucester Place premises—under kitchen pans, past hall shrubs—gesturing to the basement. He secures the trapdoor to ensure its safety, then brings the painting up into the house.

"I can't believe they'd just hide a work of art underground. Hangmen have no taste!"

Marwood beckons her to the front door, where immediately below the arch appropriately hailed intermittently by blasts of cold air, he nails J. M. W. Turner's 'Old Blackfriars Bridge'.

"I know this one," Ellen says. "I mean, I know the bridge."

"An old city bridge, like you've never seen before. The river piers are still dark and wet, the atmosphere polluted. See that London Waterworks Company's water wheel—that's gone now." He points with his fingernail. "Tearing upstream, that's five thousand gallons a minute—you can even see the time, twenty-five to eleven, on the clock face of St Magnus the Martyr. Nothing beats a Turner, even a fake one!"

"Where's the bridge?"

"That's the point—it's too dark and murky."

Ellen gives him a sideways glance.

"If it's called Old Blackfriars Bridge, I want to see the bridge."

"It's all in the suggestion, dear, of a dark underbelly to the city. A crowded, awful place—you see the ruffled water a bit. Perhaps a casket floats up here into the Pool of London?"

"A coffin."

"Exactly."

They stare at the painting. Dark water is half the canvas, tapering into an unseen Lethe.

"Black with coal, blue with indigo, brown with tides," Marwood says. "Look closely, the river is also white with flour, purple with wine, and brown with tobacco."

"Time for some more coffee," Ellen says.

"All the colours of life."

"But no bridge."

"You imagine the bridge. The rigging and spars and planks blend together—it's a vision of endless turmoil. Look, there are barges, dark shapes shuffling rhythmically under the bridge's towering arches. As the poet says, 'masts to the horizon, masts like a bare forest in winter, finely branched'. We're all there, living this picture!"

"…under an invisible bridge," she quips.

"That's London."

"You're the artist."

"So what are you?"

Ellen smiles, pretends to wring her hands. "A mother—I don't have time."

Chapter 21
Home with the Porters
27th February 1879, Thursday

On her way back to Richmond and in no hurry to rediscover her crime scene, Kate decides to visit the Porter family at 10 Rose Gardens, Hammersmith. After more dealings in Smashers Alley by Westminster, this time selling Mrs Thomas's gold pin brooches—little crocodiles she covets but forces herself to flog—Kate becomes tired walking the north river. So she slips into a little grog-shop for a drop of inspiration, Dutch-courage style. The little bottle of gin slips nicely in her corset.

It is Robert Porter's birthday so next she buys him a present, a catapult 'of magnificent industrial power', so the label says, from a raggedly toy shop on Oxford Street. Uncertain how his parents will react, Kate deems the teenager's 'barman' lifestyle—living above the family pub—appropriate for such a toy-weapon. He already drinks for England and boys of his age regularly attend bear-baiting in Cockfosters so it's hardly a big deal.

"It's the thought that counts," Kate says, feeling merry now. Queen-like, though Victoria is rarely spied from any bridge, she waves to Big Ben's clock tower, its gold-panelled trunk glinting in sunshine as though offering hope. A final swig of gin takes Kate half way across to Belvedere Road.

She looks down at the water from Westminster Bridge, black and mysterious, and considers once more dropping Mrs Thomas's head. The loading drays have busied the morning river, although a lot of people are crossing on foot; the horse and carriages are crashing by too fast to notice, so perhaps it's worth the risk?

However, a thought now occurs to Kate. What if she attends the Porters with the head intact, as a kind of mythic totem, or mystery purchase and clue to her success? Would the thrill of Mrs Thomas's presence, and hence approval, not inspire Kate with greater persuasion? With the gin in her brain, her tiredness potentially alleviating and the prospect of energy from beyond the grave, draw telepathy from the little black bag? Kate decides it's a gem of an idea. She takes the 'blue ruin' gin from her pocket, empties the bottle, and watches it fall into the black water. What could possibly go wrong?

Two hours later, Mrs Porter opens the door of *The Rising Sun*, a side door where Kate had been instructed to call. She is ushered inside only to find herself in a sombre back room, walls unpainted. Through a dumb-waiter slit no wider than two feet, she can see the punters leaning on the bar from her hole in the wall, a spider of human arms circulating the lounge. Kate widens her view, vaguely envious of the daytime drinkers. Here is the 'ale life' the Porters have stoked up—free top-ups for pints short on liquid to keep 'em drinking—all revealed under a giant mirror. For a split second Kate catches her own reflected face, a ghostly shadow trapped in a corner of the mirror. She recoils, like the lady placing the last piece in the jigsaw who sees the murderer at the window—then smiles, listening for the sound of breaking glass. Her eyes rove on, but the windows are green and misty, purposely, as though drinking in the day is a crime. Two dozen are now hugging the bar, talking at medium volume, pints of 'free trade' Greene King in hand, cloth hats still attached to heads. But no one is leaving.

For a moment a premonition enters her head and she is back in Killane, Ireland, hearing a woman's voice calling 'tea'—her mother's perhaps, God rest her, or a lost aunt. As though projected on the wall from a *camera obscura*, the images fly across her brain— walls of the stone cottage, the draught, the smoke breathed out in whisper from the lip of the chimney, the absent father's heavy boots stamping on the grille, the fire going down by mid-morning, the mournful lowing of the single cow in the field.

Then all is gone without reason, just memories from a place deep inside, a hole in a child's heart, a message she cannot translate but is written in yesterday's ink on the brain, deep and bewildering. She is shaken back to the present, a decade of prison-street life intervening—to this West London working-woman's pub.

Mrs Porter reappears magically from a door adjacent to the dumb-waiter.

"Henry said you were coming."

"Yes, sorry I'm late."

"No bother—we are about to eat. If I could take your coat, thank you."

"I'm a little flustered."

"And your bag?"

"No," Kate says loudly, "I mean, no thank you, dear. I'll keep it."

The guest is led into the next room. For the final touch of her performance, Kate is wearing Mrs Thomas's gold watch chain and several of her rings. She notices Henry Porter spy them, but neither reacts. A pause ensues in which Kate surveys the full round table: the Porter parents, sprightly son Robert of box-carrying fame, fat daughter Emma-Jane, sixteen and posturing disinterest in life itself, and the boy Isaiah.

"You have another son."

Henry Porter stands. "Yes, Isaiah is just three, and a strapping lad he is too!" The toddler gurgles as though on cue, his chin precariously balanced on the table as though he wishes to comfortably view proceedings and rest his neck. "Have a seat, Mrs Thomas."

"Thank you."

"How long has it been?"

"Oh, I don't know," Kate says coyly. "I can't be sure." Taking her seat, she slips the head-bag under the table.

"Remind me, Clare?"

"Oh, about eight years," Mrs Porter says. "The last time was your brother's wedding, Julia, down in Richmond. I have to say, I don't think you've aged at all."

Kate lowers her eyelashes and touches the brim of her yellow silk hat, its pheasant feather angling low.

"No need for flattery," Mrs Porter adds, setting down Battenberg cakes on the table. She sits next to her husband, Isaiah behind her, while the teenagers flank Henry who now faces the guest.

"I hardly recognise you," he says, meaningfully, "but anyway, we have a little business. During the slow hours, there's always time for family affairs."

"Tea first," Mrs Porter says, and the discussion is delayed for this capital ritual. "First, the teapot is warmed, four teabags,"—she glances at Kate—"our Isaiah will abstain, though. No sugar or milk, just as the Chinese and Indians drink it. I do believe in a genuine cup of tea, don't you, Mrs Thomas?"

"I do."

"Better than pub cocoa," Emma-Jane says, "which tastes like mud."

"Or that new-fangled coffee," Kate says in similar spirit. "Ugh!"

"I agree," Henry says. "Anyway, it's Robert's birthday today—he's nineteen."

"Well, almost a man," Kate says inappropriately, and receives a circular glance. She smiles internally. "I thought I'd bring a present." She reaches under the table and brings up a bag—a relatively light one. Robert takes his gift and is told to open it later.

"Thank you, Mrs Thomas," Robert suspiciously, no more convinced than his father. But both are willing to play along.

"Nice doing business with you," the father says.

Kate pauses. "Of course. I want to thank you too, Robert, for your help the other morning—with the broken chairs legs."

"Chair legs?"

"The box."

"Nuthin' done—don't mention it."

"Robert, don't be rude!" Mother and son exchange a look.

"Now," Henry says, "I have no secrets from my family. Tell me a secret, I'll tell you fewer lies. Ged-dit? Point me in the right direction, Mrs Thomas."

"I'm here to sell. The rest of the furniture—good items, cheap."

"Good, good. How cheap?"

"Cheaper than a dream," Kate says, and folds her fingers into an imaginary house.

"Ha hah, perfect!" Henry and Kate eye one another as though playing the game of 'flinch'. Robert looks away first. A burly-faced man, his jowls hang low like a bull-dog of slightly stupid breed; he places his elbows on the table to indicate seriousness. Everyone else sipping tea, baby Isaiah gurgles and Mrs Porter turns to feed him—milk from a pint glass Kate wishes were in her tea. She watches the hairs on the bull-dog's jowls are sucked into his cheeks as he talks:

"So you're moving again?"

"Yes, I'm heading to Glasgow to see my sister. She's over from Dublin on the packet-boat."

"How lovely," says Mrs Porter. But something peculiar has occurred. Kate realises that in standing to hand Robert his birthday present, the black bag is no longer touching her feet. She holds her nerve.

"Yes, Margaret is my half-sister actually. We have different...mothers."

"Oh."

"My father was widowed, and then he married again—in England."

"I see."

Kate keeps digging her hole, feet shuffling under the table. After a few taps searching for Mrs Thomas, Robert looks at her, worried, and red in the face. Clearly he is still a little disturbed after spending the night at Kate's by this game of table 'footsie'—Kate feels cold on her neck. Did she just kick Mrs Thomas's head, or is she kicking Robert gently?

The confusion is frightening and yet amusing for Kate. She knows entertainment is the reason she has kept the liability of the head a secret, a souvenir-token of her achievement. In the same moment her horror resurfaces—the two emotions are inseparable. 'Am I going mad?' she wonders, laughs and covers her mouth.

The Porter stares. "Are you all right?"

"Pardon me, I don't feel well." Inside, Kate's confusion is mounting. She doubles up, clutches her stomach with pretend gusto and peers between her knees—there is the head, resting on Henry Porter's shoe!

"Oh, God." What remains is being caught, the cat being let out of the bag, her own neck stretching on the block or spliced on the guillotine, the lever pulled, the rope swinging, the crack, the broken neck, her headless body falling in the pit—it all seems so unreal, bizarre.

As she watches, Henry stands and flicks his toe unconsciously—Mrs Thomas's heavy black bag rolls gently back to

Kate. Her mouth open, she grabs it awkwardly, traps it between both ankles, and bangs her head sitting up.

"I'm okay."

The Porters are still staring, mouths open.

"Do you need to be sick?" Emma-Jane says.

"We have an outside latrine," adds Robert. "How do you feel?"

Kate waves her hand. "Quite recovered, thank you Robert." She squeezes her legs to check on Mrs Thomas's head and a squelching is audible. Isaiah giggles in his cot. The smell is now detectable in the mouth, a low odour of rotten eggs, like a chemical breeze from the river—but such is London. Kate relaxes her feet.

"Good, good. More tea?"

The meal proceeds in relative calm. A waitress appears, scrawny and dark much like Kate's undisguised shape, and serves a giant meal. The pub clientele can be heard from the next room, complaining but ignored while the Porters eat. Kate tells of her meagre breakfast and is rewarded with a veal cutlet soup and little steaks called 'devil's kidneys'.

"Too much."

"Just the starter, dear. We Londoners deserve our regular mutton or beef, fresh bread and strong beer. You came to a much-loved pub, you know."

"We're still a frugal business," Henry interjects, "relying on leftovers."

"Don't listen to him," Mrs Porter laughs, falsely. "It's all fresh as a country stream."

"Old as time, more like!" he quips. "Brandy and wine in this one—preservatives!"

Kate looks at her food. Vivid in colour, the meat glows while the carrots and onions look bright and hard, undercooked. "It's a feast for me. "I've been eatin' 'upon the stones' for the last two days."

"On the run?" Robert says.

"I mean," Kate corrects herself, "on the go. Running."

"Well, we're happy to give you a break," says Mrs Porter. "You'll have to forgive us—we're superstitious about our food. I'm not so picky but veal must be perfectly white for Henry, like the calves 'ave licked chalk."

"I agree with myself," Henry says. "The whiter the bread too, the more respect in the street you get."

"The best bakeries *are* in chalk farms," Mrs Thomas says and receives a general look of suspicion.

"They say bread is made 'under the counter' in parts of the city," Robert says, tapping his fork on his plate. "It's white 'cos it's made of alum and bone-ashes."

Mrs Porter tut-tuts. "Now don't tell *porkie pies*, Robert."

There's a general round of merriment at this food-related joke, but Kate still cannot believe her surroundings: this family actually seem to like each other.

"That's how it is in the wharf slums," Robert says. " 'Fish' down there's turkey and goose innards, and what they call 'cod-fish' is really just fins and tails."

"Even weirder is cow-heel and skin-o'-beef," Emma-Jane says. "And you wouldn't catch me eating Bermondsey patent beef!"

Mr Porter jabs his glass down, sending water across the table. He speaks solemnly. "That's enough now. Mrs Thomas and I have some business to discuss."

After ten minutes of relative quiet, the rest of the family exits the table, leaving Henry and Mrs Thomas alone. They face each other head on, divided by the leftover food; the waitress tries to remove the dishes and Henry waves her away.

"You love your food and ale?" Henry says to the guest, his two slugs of eyebrows tightening. "See, we're not finished yet."

Kate looks back at him nervously. "I think I've had enough."

"No, no, Mrs Thomas, we have some fine anchovy preserve for you to try—it can make you a little lazy and licentious, I speak for myself. Or perhaps some pickled tongue? A touch of cannibalism has a similar effect, I'm told, when served with clarified butter and refined *pâté de fois gras*."

Kate stares. "I don't understand what you're driving at."

"Well, let me put it this way. Robert, my son, tells me how he helped you carry a box over Richmond Bridge the other morning. How he left you on the bridge, and then heard a splash in the water." Henry leans forward, his eyebrows linking with controlled rage into an impressive unibrow. Kate looks to the door, contemplating making a run for it.

"I assure you nothing happened, with your son."

"Be that as it may, but what do you call this?" He tosses the

London Illustrated News on the table, the one Kate was reading that morning, replete with grainy picture of a wooden trunk. "Scotch mist?"

"I don't know what you mean." Kate scowls, ready to leap up.

"Well, let me be plainer. You're not Mrs Thomas, are you? Not the Mrs Thomas I remember. You look a little like her, but you're not fooling me."

Kate deliberates. "You're no fool, Mr Porter."

"I know."

They watch each other, and to hammer home his nonchalance Henry reaches out for a piece of toast, spreads some *pâté de fois gras* as threatened, and pops it in his mouth.

Kate takes a breath and sighs, pretending to be caught red-handed. "It's true. I am not Mrs Thomas, though don't tell your family, otherwise we can't do business together."

Henry stares at her. "Go on, I'm listening."

"Well, the truth is Julia doesn't own that house in Richmond. Never has. It belongs to me."

"How convenient."

Kate glares at him. "There's a second sister, Edie, Julia's sister. That's my mother from County Durham," Kate lies. "Edie left me the house in her will, only I didn't know 'til I came of age at eighteen, see."

"And now you want to dispose of it?"

"Contents and all," Kate says, a little eagerly. "Then I'll be returning to County Durham. I don't feel at home here. But the property stands empty, or full, rather. So what can an honest woman do?"

Henry Porter, not the subtlest of men, leans forward and interlaces his fingers. He bounces his fists up and down, giving the impression of deliberation. "I think it's a pack of lies. But let me put it this way. I'm a businessman as you say, and my family needs to eat. So it would be good for them. I can't say your story fills me with pity."

Kate eyes him narrowly. "It doesn't have to."

"Exactly—just you keep a low profile. I don't agree with all this...dress-up." He gestures with his fork at Kate's shawl and general demeanour. "You're not fooling anyone."

"I don't have to."

Henry smiles for the first time, his face softening. He reaches out and plucks an apple from the table. "You look kind of ridiculous."

Kate, surprised, nevertheless finds the words amusing. "I know—but it's for the entertainment. I look better at night."

"Don't we all."

Kate grins. They begin a deal and shake over the round table. "Will you be there in person?"

"Listen, I know a property broker, wheeler-dealer type, if you like. Mr Nathan Crane, an old buddy from the Crimea. We were gunnery sergeants together. You won't find a better man.

"Accomplice."

"Don't joke, Mrs Thomas. He can dispose of the furniture. You go with my boy Robert, and meet Nathan Crane in Richmond. I'll set up the meeting—you just be there tomorrow evening at six."

"Let's fix a price," Kate says, seeing her opportunity.

"Not without the inspection. First, Robert can carry the heavy stuff." A silence ensues. "Listen, you won't get rid of it any other way."

"Maybe I don't want your deal."

"You do—he'll take the jewellery and 'rich plate'. Who else deals in both?"

"Smashers Alley."

Henry seems surprised. "Oh, so you do know a few people? You're the most inconsistent person, young Mrs Thomas."

"Now you listen, Porter," Kate says, suddenly angry. "This is my deal, and no one's gonna corkscrew it out of me." She smiles and picks an apple from the table herself, takes a big bite. "We get to Hammersmith Bridge, your Nathan Crane will meet me first. We'll take a break in *The Oxford & Cambridge Arms*."

"You want to size him up first?"

"No, I just like to meet my clients," she emphasizes, "in a social setting before we do business."

"Just like today."

"Yes," Mrs Thomas says, looking around, "just like today."

They shake on it.

"Make it six," Henry says as they stand up. Kate nods, struggling to remove the black bag under the table. Somehow it's got stuck to the carpet.

"Of course," she says, her voice muffled. There's a little tear, the bag pops up, and is swung onto her shoulder. "My first takings," she says, then regrets the explanation.

"Oh, let me see—it looks pretty bulky. You have some books in there?"

"Not Bibles," she laughs hollowly. "I'd make you a good price, but they're already sold. The punter is waiting as we speak."

"What are they?"

"'Fool's gold' rings, and some old photographs of deceased relatives. I'm off to meet the in-laws. Anyway…"

"Yes, Kate, anyway," Henry says, suspiciously. "I only have one concern with you. Tomorrow. Robert will be there, with my eyes and ears. Don't let him stay long, the boy has work."

"The rings were heirlooms," Kate continues unnecessarily, her hands tightening on the bag. "I…it increases their respect to get them back."

"If you say so, Mrs Thomas. I'd be careful, though, if I were you."

Kate looks up in his judging eyes, and for a moment she believes he's a kindly man. "You're not me, though. I'll be careful. And if things go wrong?" She knows he's a former soldier, now publican and family man, but one who clearly dabbles in the ancient city ways—'underground trading'.

"You're on your own."

"We understand each other." They shake hands. "I know what furniture costs," Kate adds. "So don't think your man Crane can rip me off."

"What choice do you have?" Henry says and winks. She now notices a long, red wen-mark on his face—it appears only when he raises his unibrow. Being superstitious, she takes it for a hidden message, a bad omen. It's too late for memories, though, Kate knows.

Henry shows her the door, this time back through the open pub. The old men at the bar notice her bourgeois appearance, dismiss her as 'over fifty', and return to their pints. Kate walks into the street with her heavy black bag over her arm, a lady's handbag.

"I can't carry this woman forever," she says, and grimaces, hardly enjoying the moment.

Chapter 22
(Return to) the Scene of the Crime
28th February 1879, Friday

Kate wakes in Mrs Thomas's bed, early, and distracted by the fresh smell of the surrounding fields. She feels unusually rested. Hearing voices outside, she twitches back the curtain and sees a man leaning on the wooden fence—presumably the gardener—conversing with the neighbour Mrs Ives. She can only imagine what they're saying.

No sooner is she out of bed, but another knock at the door disturbs her. Kate is sitting in the kitchen with the black bag on the table—having hit on the idea of burying it in the garden—if only the gardener would leave. But she has to meet Nathan Crane at *Brook's Butcher's and Sons* at one o'clock.

"So much for the life of a genteel lady!" she says, staggering to her feet. Kate knows the Crane deal, as negotiated with Henry Porter, is worth fifty pounds at least, "so I can't miss that. Hang on, I'm coming," she calls to the stranger.

"Maman," the voice says. "You in 'dere?"

Kate pauses in the kitchen doorway and peers through the living room. A burly, dark-skinned man is visible in the frosty glass pane, his face scrambled like a detective photofit. He looks like a wanted man, Kate thinks, then looks down at her own dishevelled bed-appearance, her long hair, her knees showing—more Catherine Lawler than Mrs Landlady.

"Maman, I comes back fur de paintbrushes. I won't bother yer arter dat!"

He can barely speak English, Kate thinks, and contemplates opening the door—what the hell, she does so.

"You must be the painter."

"Where's maman?"

"She took off, kiddo—n' left it all to me." She checks him out—at least six feet three, ginger hair pulled back revealing a proud forehead, his bow furrowing. A scar cuts up his check all the way to his eye. "I'm Katrina, her sister-in-law."

The swarthy man stares. "No you's not. You's da maid. I sin's you befur."

Kate smiles, unconcerned she is placing herself at the scene of the crime; this kid's clearly demented: "Come in, young man, you want your paintings. Take 'em."

"I…"

"Who are you, sunshine?"

"I'm Mrs Thomas's son, Billy." He stretches out his hand, and Kate holds the door wider. "They're in the back."

Billy nods, smiles and takes a few lumbering paces past Kate. She spies him through the kitchen's mess of pots and pans, still strewn on the floor, heading back to the conservatory. For a minute she listens. He appears to be tearing a painting down, folding it up.

"Where's maman?"

"She went out for a while. She'll be back soon."

"She at church?" he says, now back in the kitchen where he looks up at the ceiling.

"Church, that's right. Now you've got all you needed? I've got lots of cleaning to do." She sees Billy look down at the black bag on the table. "You don't seem like Mrs Thomas's son."

"You don't know nothin'," he says. "I'm from Saint Croix where maman born. She brings me back in a basket like Moses in da' Bible."

"Listen," Kate says, taking his arm. "You know, if you come back later, I can make you a treat. You like pies? I can make you a pie."

Billy smiles, eyes and teeth lit up. "I likes dem pies, but I don't like you—not much. You'd the maid?"

"Well, yes, Billy. I'm the housekeeper and I look after your maman, so you should treat me good, see."

"Well, a-right. What tim'?"

"Tomorrow."

"You said later—dat today."

"Tomorrow, Billy. Lunch-time. Say one o'clock—and you can collect more of your paintings."

"Maman don't like me painting in da winter, she want house to hisself. Dunno why."

"Well, I'll cook Island Pie."

"Island Pie, wassat?"

"You'll see." Kate slams the door on the hulking intruder, breathes a sigh. "Easier not to be Mrs Thomas," she murmurs, "then no one asks who I am!"

She watches Billy walk away, his shadow fading into the glass. Then she goes upstairs and looks from the window—the gardener Mr Peels and the neighbour Mrs Ives are gone. Hardly risk averse, Kate decides now is a good time. She changes into one of Mrs Thomas's overcoats. Making sure to pull up her stockings, she sets her hair like her landlady and pulls on some yellow Wellington boots. They look conspicuous but Mrs Thomas would in them too.

Downstairs, Kate takes a trowel from the kitchen larder, drags a bucket into the garden and begins plucking at the weeds. She tosses a few experimentally in the bucket, feeling a strange melancholy—the exercise reminds her of being a girl back home, this garden in Richmond could be a hillside in Killane. But the loss is mixed with solace. "This is my house, my garden," she says, and the delusion is a pleasant one. "I can plant whatever I like."

With these words, Kate now brandishes the heavy black bag in one fist, almost like she has Mrs Thomas by the neck. Playfully, she swings it between her knees, surveying the garden for a good spot: the lawn in front of her is merely a ragged rectangle, divided in two, grass near the house and a vegetable patch at the back fence, with a little potting shed in a corner, looking lonely. Her curiosity leads her to investigate—so long as it's deep enough, the vegetable patch could be the best spot to plant her 'Isabella in a pot of basil'.

Just as Kate crosses the lawn, Mrs Ives's head pops up at the fence.

"Julia, what are you doing? Mr Peels just left—are you a better gardener?"

It's an odd quip insulting 'her green fingers', so without turning around Kate calls over her shoulder: "Mr Peels has done a poor job, so I'm just burying his head. I've got it in this bag."

Mrs Ives smiles in the cold sunshine. A little laughter is exchanged. Kate sets the bag on fresh soil under the brambles, then squints back at her neighbour. "You should be careful, or you'll be next."

Mrs Ives retreats from her fence with a "humpf!" then watches as Kate kneels over the bag, jamming her spade in the cold earth. Something is not right, she knows that much. Kate is muttering to herself—something about her boy Daniel.

"Have you got a cold?"

"In my soul," is Kate's strange answer. She knows pointless questions will follow. Growing tired of her spectator, she raises the spade above her head, lunges at the fence. "Shock can kill an old woman—the more the better!" Kate swings through. The spade cracks the wood fiercely, sending a ten-inch splinter the size of a tent peg into her neighbour's garden.

Mrs Ives screams—staggering up her lawn—and retreats inside, steadying herself at her kitchen sink. Still spying at a distance, she fails to recognise the crumpled ear bone of Mrs Thomas.

"She has clearly gone mad, burying one of her son's paintings. That must be it! It's one of Billy's strange, round sculptings, shaped like a human head. That's it."

Mrs Ives puts the kettle on, ignoring the clash of Kate's spade. Choosing not to dwell on the matter, she looks forward to a reassuring cup of tea. Meanwhile she calms down with a jot of whisky, pulling the curtains tight in the middle of the day. In her mind's eye, she can still see Kate's arm raised with muscular determination.

Chapter 23
Sleeping Policemen Awake
28th February 1879, Friday

Detective Gil Sequin leaves his residence, *The Ploughman's Arms* on Carnaby Street, and begins a hike to Trafalgar Square. Under his arm is the *Westminster News*, its central pages a black-and-grey photograph of the wooden box pulled from the Thames. Sequin quickens his pace, grits his teeth and scatters pigeons with a new cane. He is annoyed by the article's nerve suggesting that the box might have been a joke by medical students—'In need of cadavers, they could have deposited one in the river for a late-night prank. Such atrocities are not uncommon....'

"Nonsense!" Sequin fumes, whacking an unfortunate pigeon that got too close. According to the coroner, the limbs had been inexpertly chopped then sawn off.

"The conclusion?" London whispers in his ear, unnerving the inspector.

"Even Jones would have spotted that one. After twenty-three years in the business, I know a killing when I see one."

Sequin marches on, ignoring the ragged people and the smartly dressed Madame Tussaud lookalikes who stand and stare. Clerks, maids, housewives and businessmen with top hats are choking the pavements at lunchtime. Soon he is passing the beef-haunts of Paternoster Row, skipping in front of carriages, circumventing the cook-shops behind St Martin-in-the-Fields—affectionately Porridge

Island to locals. Here the inspector pauses, tests the air, frowning. Now the alleyways narrow, folding together in rickety wooden backdoors between pubs. Shady observers are smoking in doorways, cats look up from scratching each other—the air itself seems to grow suspicious as Sequin passes. Then he is lost, taking a wrong turn—for his sins.

Under an overhanging roof, a square-shouldered chef with a red apron offers him a cigarette. Clearly the man has been recognised, but Sequin knows the trick: the inspector politely refuses.

"I gave up. They'll kill you…"

"They keep me alive, guv." The chef grins, revealing no teeth.

"Pay your taxes." Sequin hurries on, still swinging the cane. All around the Queen's laws are being bent to snapping point quite openly: between these back doorways, from the cider dens to the cafés and vice versa, hard-gin and 'booster' ale are being carried under cover of pewter plates. It's an old jig—the pub provides the liquor, the restaurant the food, with neither paying taxes.

The contraband liquors are most popular, of course, as prized liquid bread and dripping, the *beef au jus* for the aristocrats and gin-and-ale for the working folk.

"Small fry," Sequin says, and steps over a dead rat into Mitre Lane. On the corner is *Dolly's Chop-House*. He enters and immediately meets young Nimrod Jones behind the door, who's already three sheets to the wind.

"Back room, siirrr…"

"Aye, aye, Captain."

"We got to catch this one," the inspector adds, and Jones sinks the rest of his pint, signalling intent.

The room turns out to be a private bar, secluded, and troubled by no one. Inspector Sequin hooks his cane on a stool and Deputy Jones sits at ninety degrees, expertly watching his boss. Down the wall is a giant mural of skiffs, fishing boats, barges and drays hawking barrels like gunpowder kegs—all teeming over the surface of the Thames, mostly in shadow. There, encased in wall paint across the mighty 'V' of Tower Bridge, high in the last sunset, floats a convict ship in ghostly golden grey. The hulk, jammed with prisoners freshly arrived from the provinces or freshly excommunicated to the colonies, is being forever towed by a blackened tug.

"It resembles *The Fighting Temeraire*, sir, only in cruder paint."

"Brasher colours. The wall's a fake," Sequin says. "A copy of a third-rate Turner knock-off."

"For sure," Jones nods, but offers a sad smile to London's recent past, his tipsy feeling contrasting with their artistic surroundings. In curtain-light ascending the bar, the sun appears to be climbing high on the British Empire, though in the painting's realm the sun is going down, setting slowly, the Thames at the apex of her hustle and flow. Trapped thus under a fictional Tower Bridge's faded glory, the two policemen converse:

"You read the papers?"

"I did—'The Barnes Mystery'."

Sequin unfolds the central pages. "We've got one, two days before this explodes in the sheriff's face, and the voting elite turn on him. We've got to get this fella—clearly a madman."

"There's an election coming up?"

"March," Sequin winces, "and it's March tomorrow."

"What was found in the box?" Jones asks, looking round for a waitress. "I'm hungry."

"No one'll serve us back here. I thought you read the *Illustrated?* A torso with the head missing, three or four ribs, a thigh, and a foot."

"Nasty—I recall now, a middle-aged woman."

"Which means," Sequin says, "the husband's on the run. Only we can't identify the body until we've a definite missing person."

"So it's a waiting game. I don't get it. So why the meeting?"

"You'll see."

With this mysterious comment, Sequin explains how they've received a few tips about a woman dressed up in costume, visiting Smashers Alley. They also have a number of false leads, so overall, they can't tell them apart. "Someone's broken into the Tower of London of all places, killing a guard. There's a racket running cross-river trips, too, offering a penny a shot then robbing any takers."

"An' an old man was found in the river at Shoreditch two days ago, except he was washed up on the sand, drowned."

"And he wasn't in a box?"

"No," Jones says, repressing a smile, Sequin seeming so serious today. "Why the change of interest?"

" 'Why?' " Sequin takes hold of Jones's collar, half joking. "Why, my little man, because we can't have respectable ladies being killed in our city, not while Bow Street is needed for 'theft crime' in the capital. Whatever next—eating babies?" He gives Jones a shake, trying to humble him. "Have some manners, son, and do the right thing—morality after church, not immorality before confession. We're a Protestant country, and I for one intend to keep it that way."

"But I'm a Catholic."

"Same thing, we're all in this together." Sequin rattles his cane on the stool, brushes loose hair from his forehead. His face has gone quite red, and in the paroxysm neither man has recognised the intruder standing before them. Stepping into the light, the guest extends his hand.

"Ah, yes, I do apologise," Sequin says. "We've been expecting you."

Gripping hands lightly, one by one, the hangman steps to the bar.

"How much of our conversation did you hear?"

"Very little," Marwood replies pursing his lips, "except the religious war."

"Oh, just two old friends," Sequin says. "Now listen, we've brought you here because…"

"Shouldn't we order first?" Jones says, and Sequin glares at him.

"Of course, my colleague is hungry, please excuse his manners. He does his thinking in the narrow window between a full belly and lying on the floor."

Marwood laughs politely. "Pray, may I ask why *Dolly's Chop-House?*"

"She's the finest publican and, as you know, Dolly is herself an 'outsider'. I'll let you into a secret Mr Marwood—Jones and myself, see, we're not from London. I'm from the Black Country and this one's from Cornwall somewhere."

"Truro," Jones smiles. "Though most crooks think I'm from Cardiff."

"With a name like *Jones?*" Sequin prompts.

"With a surname like Jones. And my first name—Nimrod—is classical Greek."

"The point is," Sequin says, "we can't get enough of this London food, see. The true 'Cockney' comes from 'coquina', the Latin for cookery. Hence we like sampling all the meats available, including goose and duck. Fowle is a lot cheaper here."

"Chicken and rabbit off the streets," Jones adds.

"What do you like, Mr Marwood?"

"I'm a vegetarian…. My doctor says it's healthier, a new import from the continent."

Sequin almost spits out his teeth. "Where are you from?"

"Lincolnshire, seat of good farming. I know, I know." Marwood looks at him with amused suspicion. "Just don't tell my family."

"So the only flesh you covet," Jones says, "is off the hangman's rope?" With a smirk he picks up Sequin's cane to protect himself, but Marwood doesn't take the bait.

"I used to eat meat. It's true, once you drop the trapdoor, that's enough for the day. Seriously, I can send a man to his death, but I don't need to kill an animal…."

The air hangs a moment.

"Crabs are cheap," Jones says, to stoke conversation, "as are flounder and mackerel."

"Not up north."

"Oysters twelve pence a *peck*, that's two gallons. We live on a mighty river, sir."

"Temporary for me—soon I'll be home. I just don't eat fish."

"Well, that's okay Mr Marwood 'cos something else has washed out of the Thames." The detective opens up the *Westminster News* to the picture of Julia Thomas's casket-coffin. "Still hungry? That's the remains—I can't believe they printed it." Barely covered by a blanket is the suggestion of a limb.

Marwood glances up. "Look, I just took the Queen's commission, you know that. How can I help you gentlemen?"

"We don't know who she is," Sequin says.

"And you want me to tell you?"

"We want to make you part of the investigation. You seem like a smart man to us. At least, we want to schedule the hanging now, to reassure the public."

"Before you have any clues?"

"We have clues."

Marwood leans in. "I already said, I take my commission from the Queen, via the Sheriff of London."

At this point, Sequin and Jones smile and turn to each other.

"Well, that's just where we come in," Jones says.

"Indeed," Sequin echoes and unrolls the sheriff's signature on a fresh sheet of paper, the accuser's name left a blank for the hanged party. The implication is that a name will go there, but the death penalty is assumed.

"I'm not signing that," Marwood says, "not before a trial."

"This one's a brutal killer," Sequin murmurs, taking Marwood's arm, the pen dangling in his other hand. "Whoever he is, he deserves to swing."

"That's for a court to decide." A momentary deadlock is reached but not before Marwood finishes his speech. "When you have a suspect, I'll reconsider with evidence. As for this pre-trial assassination, I won't do it. You think you can hang someone without a trial...?"

"We're the police," Jones says, at which Sequin rocks back with faux surprise and offence.

"Oh no, Mr Marwood, I hope you're not accusing us of sidelining a jury. The law will have due process."

"A legal term."

Marwood calms down. "Gentleman, I appreciate you inviting me to this greasy café for a discussion of the law and a little *pera-ale*. No one's served us—maybe we'll survive like crossing-sweepers by sniffing steam from the stalls."

"What's he talking about?"

"The smell of Smithfield is just a few yards away, where the cooked flesh of saints once also rose in smoke. Spleen, tripe, pig's head, veal hearts!"

"I've no idea, Jones."

"You can eat them all, gentleman, but until you know what it's like to hang a man, life's all horseplay to me. I've been to Bartholomew Fair. I know what a pointless day looks like—the aimless holiday of the horde, the vicious crowd, the mule race." Marwood raises his palms. "But the individual—the solitary human being, sir—has rights dating back to the *Magna Carta*. I'll protect those rights against the State, even while I work for the Queen!" To symbolise his commitment, he stands. "I bid you good day, gentlemen."

"No, no, you have this all wrong, Mr Marwood. No need to get in a huff."

"A huff," says Jones.

"We haven't even eaten," Sequin says. "Wait a second and you'll have country bread, yams and sweet potatoes from Virginia."

"*Dolly's* got rhubarb from China," says Jones.

"Have your lily-white vinegar, four pence a quart!" Sequin cries. "Preserve your heart, steady your nerves in formaldehyde, and prevent against disease!" He detains the hangman's arm. "But know this, I eat meat, and I intend to catch whoever committed this crime. You softened your nerves, Mr Marwood, but I tell you now—mine are on edge!"

"I can see that."

"Look at this picture, look at it!" He waves the *Westminster News* in Marwood's face. "No one should end up like this—chopped up and tossed in the river like a piece of meat!"

"I agree." The two men stare at each other, before the inspector cracks a smile and pats Marwood's shoulder. He squeezes.

"So what are you going to do about it?"

"I'll help with the investigation. The case is new to me, right, why would I have any information? I just won't subvert the law to appease the public." Marwood squeezes Sequin's shoulder, returning the favour. "The public will get their satisfaction soon enough, on hanging day."

"Indeed they will, whether it's inside the prison or the Newgate Drop."

"Or under my new Long Drop, sir."

"If it pleases you."

"A crime like this," Marwood says, gesturing to the mural of Tower Bridge, "I'm sure the sheriff wants all of London to witness. As you said, there's an election in the post."

Jones stands to support his boss. "Gotta give the Cockneys what they wants."

"Be that as it may," Marwood says, "the law-lords of the Old Bailey may see things differently." He tips his hat. "It's a horrific crime, and I'm sure you'll find the perpetrator. Thank you for lunch, gentleman, I can show myself out."

"We can still count on your support, Mr Marwood?" Sequin calls to his shadow, as Marwood turns in the curtain-guard to the main room.

"You can. I am the hangman of London and Middlesex, after

all." The curtain swishes, and he is gone. Marwood doesn't stop walking until he is outside, where all he can think of is Ellen and Aldous. "I left them to come meet these two clowns, again." He presses on.

Meanwhile a carriage clock ticks emptily behind the bar, long broken, its fake gold face twisting the dial. Sequin and Jones reseat themselves, a little dumbfounded by the visitor's passion, both believing Marwood was a cool, collected customer from their last meeting.

"Shows how hard they are to read, these hangmen. A funny bunch."

"Can we trust him?"

"No—so don't," Sequin says, picking up his cane. "Worse luck, he's in it for the money. Now how about some of those oysters and a little of that *pera-ale...*"

"What about the case?"

Sequin grimaces. "We'll get Mr Marwood his day in court, soon enough."

"And his day on the scaffold."

"Oh dear, yes, my Welsh friend," the inspector says, looking up at the wall mural's tugboat, at the dying light of the painted Thames. "The scaffold? That too, Mr Jones. We'll surprise them all, killer, lawyer and executioner. So long as that little black tug keeps towing her prison-ship—that too."

Chapter 24
Down The Rising Sun
1st March 1879, Saturday

The next morning Kate is up with renewed enthusiasm. Everything will be different in March with the coming of spring—fine flowers for Mrs Thomas's hats, great expectations for Daniel's future, a new plan for escaping London. The world is still possible. So after another hefty walk she meets Henry Porter at *The Dog and Biscuit*, Rose Gardens, Earl's Court. This time her tactic is different but no less dangerous. She will seduce him, brazenly, and get a good deal into the bargain. "I'll be rich by the end of the day."

Kate enters the pub, letting the door swing back like a Western saloon. An old barman is rubbing a glass and the regular barflies swivel on their stools and peer through the gloom, confused. Mrs Thomas does her best entrance: the lady is sporting a chic-blue dress, garnet necklace and emerald rings. No one gasps despite the theatrical need, and the disappointment lingers, given her heavy make-up and the strength of her perfume.

She sees her mark, Nathan Crane, and immediately strikes up a flirtatious relationship. After conducting the preliminaries of business and aided by two previous beers that morning, Kate lights up a Turkish cigarette, planning on several hours of drinking and smoking.

"Porter told me about you—'e said you was a wild one."

Mrs Thomas pouts, slips a hand on his knee. "Do I look wild to you?"

They're already in a booth, close together. Crane rolls his tongue along his lips. She tells him about the Richmond address, her poorly deceased husband, the need for a smaller residence, in brief, all the reasons for selling her furniture and jewellery. Crane doesn't believe her for a second.

"Now don't go getting me in trouble, Mrs Thomas. I'm a well-to-do tradesman."

She looks him over—sandy beard and moustache, flat forehead, small eyes and lank hair. His light tweed suit would be charming if it weren't for the deerstalker hat.

"What don't you tell me your story?" Kate asks, knowing the shortest route to his pocket-book.

"What's to tell?"

"Let's see—you look like a brave military man."

"Well, yes. I served during the Indian Mutiny, Bengal Regiment." His eyes close with nostalgia at the atrocity. "I signed up in Soho Square not far from here, 1857. The mutiny was that same year."

Kate covers her yawn, nods eagerly.

"Yes, then in 1860 I joined the 16th Hurrars and was discharged in 1866, when Porter still kept a public-house in Fulham. He never fought the Mutiny—supposedly he's got a bad heart."

"I'll say."

Crane smiles, pleased at her daring. "Yes, well, Porter bought *The Rising Sun* from a Mr Belcher for a hunn'ard quid, clean. Then I was coachman of Mr Allen of Pall Mall for two n' half years. More fool me. Business was the way forward, so I set up the *Brooker's Greengrocer* just after. I've been doing jobs for Porter ever since."

"Legal?"

"Mostly. Sometimes I don't ask where the stuff comes from."

"And your private life?"

"That would be tellin'."

"I told you mine."

"Well, since you ask, and we're gonna make a good deal."

"We certainly are." She touches his leg again.

"I'm a happily married man who likes a flutter on horses n' dogs." He squeezes her knee back. "But I wouldn't say no to a decent offer."

They kiss over the table, a mirror above their heads advertising the scene to the oblivious pub. The lunch hour is over and there aren't many onlookers now, just a bag-lady hunched over her belongings and knitting a skull-cap. The rest is sawdust, empty stools, a young lad wiping tables. The old barman seems to be polishing the same glass.

"Call that a kiss," Crane complains with a grin. Then he goes in for another, his moustache causing Kate distress. The bag-lady notices—under her frizz of crazy hair, a watery eye darts in their direction and she utters a few 'tut-tuts'. The sudden lovebirds ignore her and extend their face-lock, Crane wrestling for more angle, Mrs Thomas defeating him with a show of propriety, her mouth clamped shut.

He pulls away with puzzled excitement: "We could go somewhere more comfortable?"

"Like your greengrocer's?"

"Richmond," Crane says, taking the bait. "We have to go there anyway—to make the Porter deal."

"I thought you couldn't go today? Henry said you're busy."

"I can find time," Crane replies, then twirls his military lip, "for a good reason."

"For the right lady?" she encourages.

"For a bad girl."

The situation is ripe: Kate will get a good price now, and her imagination opens up. She begins to imagine a new life, if only to distract herself from Crane's hand reaching up her legs, his teeth hooking into her gums like fish-wire. But her words are steady: "I was hoping you'd say that."

While Crane takes advantage—a few neck caresses included—in her mind Kate is sitting in the lobby of the Queen's estate at Hampton Court Palace, a place she's never been but seen in newspapers. A fawning courtier is polishing her shoes, red leather slippers, with a bright golden rag then serves her champagne…before she's yanked back to reality by Nathan Crane fumbling at her bra strap in the pub booth.

"Clean your glass." The serving boy is standing over them. "Clean your glass, ma'am…"

"Get away, kid. Can't you see we're busy," and Crane bats at the boy's face, his head still dipped in Mrs Thomas's pinafore.

Suddenly the old barman is standing beside his son, and asking them to leave—when his pint glass, burnished to perfection, slips from his hand and smashes on the floor. Kate and Crane hurry from the pub, Crane laughing with excited anger, Kate giggling with frightened delight. Outside they jump in an omnibus—neither planning to pay—and make the hour's journey south to Richmond High Street and 2 Mayfield Gardens.

Kate is wary as they draw near, wondering if there'll be any police presence at the house. She knows Scotland Yard has found a body in the river, and fearing connection to the scene of the crime, however irrational, raises her temperature as they cross Richmond Bridge. But there is nothing, no guards, no Bow Street Runners, no ugly crowds straining necks for a glimpse of the house. They enter without incident.

"Do make yourself at home," Kate says, gesturing to the piano, the sofa, the front room in general, albeit in an unconvincing way. She's never had guests except the Porter boy.

Kate becomes quite professional, though, as she fishes a notebook from her pocket. She uncovers a bunch of keys—displaying ownership—a bank book, some papers, and then looks the part of someone with serious business to conduct.

First, though, she brings Crane a glass of wine, fresh from under the kitchen table where she carved up Mrs Thomas's body.

"Direct from the Dutch vineyards."

Crane, slumped on the living-room sofa, tastes the wine, frowns. "You're sure it's newly opened?"

"I drank some the other night."

"It'll do," he declares. "To you, Mrs Thomas, and your new home."

"New home, you say?"

"Yes, the place you're moving to—you never told me where."

"Oh, no," Kate stumbles, "I didn't. It's…ah…just around the corner, really. Vine Street. Number seven."

Crane peers over his glass. "Number seven, hey." His expression changes. "So why don't you come and sit next to me?"

"Well, let's get the business out o' the way." Kate fumbles with her notebook. "I'll have to show you the rooms, give you the tour. Everything must go, I mean, whatever you want. It's all for grabs, I mean, for sale." She giggles. "You'll have to forgive me. It's not long since Mr Thomas died," and in a masterful moment of theatrics, she pauses in front of the mantelpiece. Her hand moves lightly to a glass miniature, a fuzzy-looking portrait of a swarthy-skinned man in a business-suit, collar lifted as though by a breeze in the photographer's studio. "My husband, the late Mr Thomas."

Crane stands dramatically and strides over for the inspection. "Not much of man—he's a *darky* for one."

"No," Kate says. "He is from Saint Croix, that's all. A diplomat—we met on one of my visits to the country to release his daughter from jail. Jemima had to stay, but we came back. I have a son too..."

"Where's the daughter?"

"I said—she had to stay in Saint Croix."

"Where's that?"

"The Caribbean, for sure."

"What does she do?"

"Teaches—she teaches English—to the natives."

Crane squints, not believing a word of it again. Suddenly he grabs Kate and embraces her. "You won't need that picture today." He knocks it off the mantelpiece without concern, struggling with her in his arms.

Kate loses control and slaps Crane hard. He just stands there, surprised. She picks up the portrait and sets it back on the mantelpiece. "You needed a little cooling down."

"I don't deserve that—I'm loyal, and a good man!" Crane rubs his chin bristles, fakes a hang-dog expression. He seems affronted but a moment later the struggle is forgotten. The rejection is doubly sobering, somehow sealing a strange bond as though he can now take Kate seriously as a business partner. An afternoon's pleasure now seems remote; still, Kate cannot rule out any shenanigans at the end of their financial transaction—he might be welcome later.

"Follow me." She leads him around the house, itemizing furniture in her notebook. Crane offers a price each time, and Kate merely writes them down: two pounds for the carriage clock, twenty guineas for the side-table, four pounds for the glass cabinet. Upstairs she offloads a number of paintings, Crane offering more for the smaller ones—"they're easier to transport." When she has a total Kate doubles it, and negotiations follow. Crane is keen to wrestle the cost down to less than half, so the conversation becomes quite heated.

"What'll you do with it all, anyway?" he says, leaning nonchalantly on the wall. "I'll throw in the removal costs—that's at least hundred pounds."

"So your vans can damage them?"

"I use greengrocer vans, and we're all professional."

"Expert fruit sellers, you mean—not antiques."

The negotiations become circular, and before a final deal is struck, there's another knock at the door. Kate retreats downstairs more concerned about being discovered in Mrs Thomas's clothes now she's 'entertaining'.

"How can I help?"

"I hear-s the noise," Mrs Ives says, and knocks again. "Are you all right, Julia?"

"I'm fine, yes. What do you mean?"

"I don't know what's going on."

There's a pause, then another knock. "Please go away," Kate calls. "I'm busy today, and not feeling well."

"I can send Billy round if you like?"

"No, no need. I saw him yesterday, thank you! I'll call round later at yours…"

Mrs Ives's presses her cheeks on the glass, breathes on the pane. "I'm telling you, something strange is going on!"

"You always think that." The face pulls away and Kate hears Mrs Ives mumbling up the garden path, slamming the iron gate: "Stupid old crow!"

The footsteps are gone—Kate returns to her dealings. She even persuades Crane to bring the grocery carts that afternoon; with two labourers only half the furniture can be moved, but once Kate sees the carts—large country haywains—she grows excited at the possibility of success. They agree a final price, half to be moved before sundown, half by midday tomorrow.

Within an hour, Nathan Crane's apprentices begin the load-up using rope, blankets for the heavy furniture and trolley-boards on wheels. The paintings they wrap in three layers of mattress feathers, covered by brown paper tied with tough string. Kate watches the proceedings with a twinkle of admiration in her eye. She even opens a crate of beer for everyone including the teenage greengrocer boys, cousins of Crane by the names of Peter Smith and Michael Pliant. They toast the hoard.

"Where are you moving to, Mrs Thomas?" Peter Smith innocently asks, wedging the piano through the door.

"Up the road, not far—a smaller place."

Smith wipes sweat from his forehead, smiles. "What neighbourhood?"

"Now don't you go troubling Mrs Thomas," Crane says. "She's had a long day."

"Sir, n' ours ain't over yet!" Pliant says.

"So what? I'm paying you for a job well done, not to stand around gassing."

Both men receive a scowl from Crane, and the commotion causes Mrs Ives to revisit the scene. Completely taken aback by the proceedings she stands in her garden just over the fence, mouth open, hearing the piano's ivories rattling in the chilly winter air.

"Sorry, ma'am," Smith apologises. "I dinna mean for any musical accom-pinny-ment."

"What on earth's going on?" Mrs Ives cries, kitchen rag in hand, hair tied up in a big yellow net. A plump rather than stocky woman, Mrs Ives is about sixty—full five years younger than Mrs Thomas and so usually deferential. But her busybody state of nosiness has been stirred. Clearly she thinks her neighbour has gone quite mad, moving furniture in the middle of winter and at the close of day, without even telling her!

As though on perfect cue, they hear a distracting sound from the gloomy street. The movers pause, Mrs Ives turns her gape, and Kate and Crane, side by side, listen to the voice now growing stronger, a child's voice. The words "supposed murder" float on the wind, a shocking interruption to life. Then the paperboy goes by on his bicycle, a scrawny kid in shorts and grey knee socks, his full school-uniform: "Barnes Atrocity. Who dunnit? Get the latest *Illustrated London*. All the tales wot's fresh!" A huge wooden box wobbles on the front of his bike, so he's leaning backwards to counterbalance his ride. "Get yer *Illustrated!* Discovery of human remains found in box in Thames!" He looks sideways as he passes by, a ghost-boy in the fog.

"Here," Kate calls out instinctively, without thinking. She drains her beer glass and feigning amusement, calls out for her guests: "I expect that's a *catch penny*, but we might as well have a paper." She beckons the boy back, and buys one.

The thrill of flaunting her crime soon dissolves, though, when she is left with the newspaper in hand. The front page photograph glares up. Kate lowers herself carefully onto Mrs Thomas's front step. There's the box on the riverbank, there's the partial remains of the body under a nearby blanket—plus police officers Sequin and Jones, standing nearby, looking ominous. Suddenly it's all too real. He throat feels dry, constricted, and she covers her mouth and is coughing hoarsely. Meanwhile, Mrs Ives watches the furniture being loaded onto Crane's carts.

"I thought you'd leave me the piano," she says, but Kate is miles away. She's made blunders, she realises, invited too many people into her dealings. Now here they all are, in too quiet ol' Richmond, watching her. She wishes she'd slammed the door on Mrs Ives when she'd had chance—no, that would just result in another basement Mrs Thomas. She can't dress up as both of them!

Kate touches her head, feels a pain there, but Crane is asking her a question. There appear to be a few items missing.

"Are they part of the deal or aren't they?"

"What?"

"The dresses in the bedroom, your bedroom, Julia. Hanging on a peg."

"Eh?"

"I won't ask again."

"Yes, yes, go fetch them."

Crane pushes by her, and in one of the bedrooms he gathers the dresses: tattered cashmere, ball gowns, a white wedding dress, very creased. He lays a sheepskin coat on top, pads gingerly outside and rests them over the piano hood. Smith and Pliant begin tying the cart with ropes. Meanwhile, Crane seems to take pity on Kate's breakdown and removes a shiny dress. He lays it on her arms—black silk.

"We won't include that."

Kate smiles. "Okay, Nathan. I'll take it." She stands and re-enters the house, ignoring Mrs Ives's questions, and lays the dress on the living-room sofa. "My burial dress."

Suddenly Crane is behind her, and the agreement signed. She gets forty sovereigns up front, forty tomorrow with the rest of the house loot. In a week she gets fifteen more when the sales are final—and the piano proved a genuine Feurich.

Kate shuts the door, and collapses on the sofa next to the

dress, presses her face in its softness. "Money for the first time in my life, and I'm going to spend it." No more maid-slaving, she thinks, no more hustling in the streets. "Daniel can go to a proper school. I will go to the ball—wear all the pretty dresses—just like Cinderella." The fantasies of childhood fairy-tales, the dark edges smoothed over, fill her mind like living pictures.

She closes her eyes, if only to indulge a moment of lost girls' dreams. Little Red Riding Hood has made it through the wood, escaped the wicked old woman at the gingerbread cottage like Gretel, and still made it home. Sleeping Beauty has awoken, the dragon is slain, and Dick Whittington can claim the golden streets of London town! For half an hour Kate lies there amazed at the outcome of her crime. However, cabs and booze hold a double fascination for her and she can't lie there for long. What sort of celebration is that? "I'm not about to let the money go to waste."

Kate rushes upstairs and changes into the black dress, admiring herself in the mirror, and spends an hour setting her hair straight up to resemble a French demimonde of the seventeenth century Parisian court. Now all she needs is her Prince Charming, an aristocrat from Mayfair perhaps, or the Sheriff of London himself, so long as he can keep up! The night is alive, young and naïve with possibility, and she's go out to get drunk, richly and expensively.

First, she takes a cab in the direction of Hanging-Sword Alley, a salubrious upmarket meeting-place for blue bloods, despite its name. The aristocratic bourgeoisie—with both time and brains to kill—gather there nightly.

"Be careful," the cabbie says, grinning from his high chair, "they mix gin with fruit punch in these places, but the fruit ain't fresh."

"Ah, but the gin is," Kate says.

"Stick to the house classics n' the new Turkish coffee."

"I didn't wear this dress to drink coffee," Kate says, and the cabbie laughs.

"No, I don't suppose you did."

The hansom steers them towards the Thames, cutting a jagged line down the South Bank. Kate dangles her hand from the cab in the breeze, sensing the freedom and danger of London slipping through her fingers. The grim contrast with her elegant final destination could not be greater. "Such beautiful buildings," he offers as they pass the industries—mostly tobacco plants and breweries, all hugging the snaking water and draining narcotic-alcoholic waste from giant pipes just below the carriage's wheels. Broken-roofed houses pile on dead warehouses like termites building a grand home, chimneys trailing smoke into a dark sky. "That's a vinegar factory," the cabbie says, continuing the tour. "Everything is here, the dye-works, potteries, textile mills." He fails to mention the blacking factories, the lime kilns, bread stores, builders' yards, all the rest of the beating heart of the dirty south.

But Kate only has eyes for the river. She trains a melancholy glance at its brooding waters, the holder of so many secrets including her own. The box has been discovered but the image of it sliding from her grasp, tumbling from the bridge, and the mighty splash, remain—the moment she laid a woman to rest. Kate searches her heart for a feeling, guilt or remorse; she is almost testing herself during her current elation, to dwell a little deeper on the consequences of her actions. Yet there is nothing: in the same image of the box hitting the water, the dreadful second when she thought it might float, she holds the memory of Mrs Thomas's abuse of her, the idea that this woman could float to freedom in her box while Kate suffered her insults and must now take the blame—it is all too much. The overriding emotion for Kate, she knows, is the wounded pride of her mind, something she's had to protect since childhood, and the danger of the outside world causing her such trauma. After this depth of feeling, conserved for so long in her struggle between the streets, the cities, the prisons, there is little left for anyone else.

Her evening jaunt, though, is interrupted before the hansom even leaves Lambeth—the most arresting sight of Bethlem Hospital, known as Bedlam. Kate has heard about this establishment, half prison, half hospital. Its shadow follows in the wake of the carriage while the driver swings the wheels far from its gate—a giant monstrosity rising with iron fortitude into a foggy night. Curious, though, Kate peers from her seat. "The final resting place, they say, for the criminally insane," she whispers and in a moment of levity, she waves graciously twirling her hand like Queen Victoria as though greeting an old friend, or one she will see again.

Then before they exit the surrounding slum-alleys, Kate looks back as the streets of Lambeth retake Bedlam into their hungry heart. At the main thoroughfare they pass a crowd of working people, men with rough coats, heads down, moving through the night; Kate catches a glimpse of a woman on a corner, baby in a tight shawl in her arms. The mother—no more than a girl—holds the baby out, her expression blank as though offering the child up to the moving vehicle for better or worse. The cabbie cries "bloody hell!" followed by a crunching sound, and the hansom swerves. Then as though nothing had happened, the vehicle continues its journey to the fine nightspots of the northern bank.

There is no incident, no collision. Instead they pass *The Temple of Flora* and *The Dog and Duck Tavern*, awful pubs beneath prison gates, where St George's Fields meets the Lambeth Road. Next they reemerge along the river, more silent and darker now, close to Battersea Power Station. The building is creaking in the night, three funnels ploughing grey plumes into the sky, one mysteriously mute. "They call that the orphan chimney," the driver comments. "He's got a mind of his own." Kate grimaces at the aching funnels, barely wondering what is feeding them; the driver cuts a line north-west, now sensing Kate's impatience in the back seat. They cross St Albert Bridge, the passenger choosing not to look down at the water, but not because of vulnerability or fear. She is adjusting her hat, thinking about the fine people she will meet in the debonair districts, now they are getting close.

On the north bank they enter the Borough of Chelsea and Kensington—final destination, the West End. The curve of white houses in immediately inspiring, glowing with harmony and peacefulness; the streets have birch trees dipped quietly in square plots and the lamplights are all working. High up in windows, Kate can see people taking care of their lives, their children, some cutting out coloured paper for entertainment—she imagines—or reading three volume novels, writing journals, putting children to bed and then listening to Mozart on the gramophone.

The driver swings between Dorset Street and Magpie Alley, and there, captured like a beacon of civilisation in the darkness, are the lights of Hanging-Sword Alley.

"The weary traveller is home."

"I ain't never home," Kate says. "Jus' another notch on my journey."

She descends the hansom, tips the driver, and can already smell the booze and money mingling in her mouth. All down

Hanging-Sword Alley bars are twinkling their lights, two doormen to each private club, absently checking membership.

"Well, have a good night miss. I can pick you up later, if you like."

"No need, I can find my own way home."

"This place don't got the love of the south," he says, "the good-hearted people. I'd be careful."

Kate walks away: "I ain't good-hearted people," she says over her shoulder.

Chapter 25
Marwood Makes a Discovery
2nd March 1879, Sunday

The next day Kate goes to find the School for Pickpockets, to pick a bone. Once more it is a Sunday afternoon. She is feeling aggrieved—her night did not go according to plan. What really happened? She remembers, unevenly.... In dishevelled clothes with Mrs Thomas's hat lost, most of the evening was a blur. She did not make it back to Richmond, that she is sure of, and the gentleman whose favours she was courting vanished mid-morning, just as she'd hoped to follow him back to his place—and start a new romantic life or relive him of a few valuables. She never got the chance.

Instead, Hanging-Sword Alley did not prove to be the place for the upper-crust of London after all, but more a den of bourgeois middlemen, newspapers reporters—the last people she needs to fraternise with—and rich old men smoking cigars with little interest in women over the age of twenty-five.

So she spent her money, drifted from one strange smoking room to the next, peeling back curtains, smelling opium, hashish, all the drug-taking in the best possible taste—including mushrooms. If she could recount the splendour of the dresses, the paintings, the elegance of the glasses she would, but there was just as much mediocrity, overpriced liquor, poor music, and obnoxious people to convince Kate that the high life she's dreamed of only half exists among half the people, half the time, so what should have been a fairytale Cinderella evening is real only inside her mind.

Eventually Kate realises she has hoodwinked herself, by believing in something that wasn't there. Ever sentimental, she remains back there in memory—drunk on gin slings, but not enough to find refuge from Hanging-Sword Alley's upper-class chemical illusions. So she returns to the river, a half hour walk, St Albert Bridge, and stares up at Battersea Power Station, now quiet. A red moon rises over its insulting chimney fingers, their blackened jibes beckoning the future despite the past. For the first time, she senses what can only be described as an emotional epiphany. What matters in this world, she wonders? Not money, splendour, jewels, or alcohol. As for the freedom to go somewhere or be someone before it's too late, that too is a mirage, an image created from inside, in the belief that what externalises will bring inner calm, happiness, self-worth. Reputation does not matter either. For Kate, standing on the bridge, with London silent, and looking up with red eyes at the white moon, the only thing that matters is her flesh and blood, her energy, her movement for one place to the next, and her son—the future—the boy she lost.

"Give me a sign, anything. Just a bird flying at night, that kind of thing…" The moon stays red, and the power station silent. The city herself seems to be struggling, choking on the weight of human and mechanical burdens, on life itself. But not for long! As Kate is turning away, the small Battersea chimney begins to bellow smoke, thick black plumes detectable across the face of the moon. It is all Kate needs.

"I have to get Daniel back." She understands now—he is the future. "I must find my son!"

It is one o'clock before she arrives back at the wire fence where she last said goodbye to Daniel. She is expecting to see little activity, given the supposed 'day of rest' and the freezing temperature of the air.

By now the sun has risen to its full winter height—about two-thirds into the sky—revealing a swollen blue globe of the heavens, not a single cloud, just a sensation that snow is imminent. Kate tumbles down the earth bank she crawled up so ponderously before, lays her hands on the fence.

She looks around, astonished, squinting for Daniel. About a dozen boys are practicing their handkerchief-lifting skills on the washing line that Clatter has extended. One scrawny boy is balanced on a barrel, twitching the rope-line, while the 'mark' walks a plank over a sandpit. A third boy controls a higher cord, stretched parallel to the lower rope but overhead. Every now and then the victim reaches up to retrieve coloured handkerchiefs floating like pieces of Spanish bull-rag from the higher rope. But he is deceived by barrel-boys who distract the apprentice thief, raising the bar, and causing him to strain higher and harder for their pleasure—Clatter's thief-training technique at its best.

Then Kate sees Daniel—he is not in the crowd, nor on the plank straining. He is one of the boys on the barrel, provoking a new 'mark' trainee thief.

"Come a long way, your boy," Clatter says, appearing from the pub backroom, rolling a dirty dish rag. "He's got a fine wit."

"Easy to manage," Kate says. "To manipulate."

Clatter smiles and walks over. "And what can I do for you, Miss Lawler? I thought it'd be a month before I'd see you, if at all." The implication is clear, namely that leaving Daniel was an outright sale—but Kate doesn't rise to the bait.

They watch as Daniel hawks the handkerchief out of reach of the boy, who dangles, totters, and falls off.

"That Daniel's a natural."

"You think your rope really helps 'em pick old men's purses? They ain't reachin' that high."

"It's not a matter of height," Clatter says. "It's a matter of how hard they try—how much 'e wants the prize."

"And if they gets caught?"

"My method works, I can assure you, Miss Lawler. Dangle a carrot in front of a donkey. It still wants the carrot, even if it's not hungry." The schoolmaster opens the gate, allowing Kate entry, and smiles at his illustration. "Training is required." He flutters his palm side to side, dangling the imaginary carrot.

"My boy's no animal, if that's what yer saying."

"You look tired, come in to *The Cat and Salutation*. I'll fix you a drink—a hot one."

Kate looks at him warily, imagining a fire that doesn't exist:

"Fine."

She knows Clatter is trying to delay her speaking to Daniel, but Kate is too tired to argue. At the bar she sits in the same spot, her feet wet from the river's encroachment on the property. Beer barrels are still stacked on the bar, and presumably the basement is flooded. There is an audible creak Kate doesn't remember previously, like the building is groaning its complaints, liquid in its joints, water on the brain.

Clatter appears on the serving side, his remarkable height a weapon of false compassion. He hands Kate a tumbler.

"There you go. Drink it in one, like the boys do."

Kate drinks, but the smell of stagnant water offset by silt flavour is unappealing. But she can't remember the last pub she entered that *didn't* smell of people and booze.

"We're a veritable floating pub, a tide of our own," Clatter says proudly. "Soon we'll have to move the boys or we'll be washed away. We'll be the Atlantis of the pub world!"

Kate coughs up in her glass. "Move them where?"

"Wherever I go next, where else? Maybe I'll drown here n' sink to the bottom of the ocean. Miss Lawler, I jest! 'Tis certain your boy is safe here. I'm looking for cheap lodgings closer to the heart of Southwark. We gotta get out of Bell Wharf."

"Southwark's a worse dump."

Clatter smiles. "Only to some."

"What'd you feed the boys?" Kate says, changing the subject.

"I'm sorry, you know, I don't have all day for your questions. But just this once—I'm proud of my recipe, see. I feed 'em jus' what you's drinkin', Miss Lawler. Nothing but saloop!"

"Saloop?"

"Yes, saloop, saloop, saloop! Hot sweet sassafras wood, milk and sugar. Fixes you up rotten."

Kate squints down in her mug and wonders if she's been poisoned. "How much?"

"Three pence, half a bowl. Sometimes I mix in royal jelly honey, and of course, a lil' cheap sloe gin."

"For the boys?"

"Of course—when they've bin good. Magic hangover cure."

Kate tips up her mug, the molasses sliding out onto the bar-top. "You said they'd be no drinking—for Daniel."

"No, no, not 'im," Clatter says. "That one's still got a special privilege—the third room."

"Near you."

"They'd treat 'im rough otherwise…if I'd let 'em."

"If you let 'em?"

The schoolmaster smiles: "You ain't got nothin' t' worry 'bout, see."

"No?"

Clatter stretches his face thinner, his crown of wispy hair touching the wood rail of upside-down glasses. "I'm his protector."

"And you feed them this slop?"

"Sloo-oop—it's the drink of London, you know that. Sold in the street on wheely tables, you must 'a seen. Winter-times, they covers th'table with a tent screen o' vellum n' an old umbrella."

"I've seen 'em Mr Clatter."

"You get everyone round dem saloop stalls, whole o' London. Chimney-sweeps n' lawyers, ladies lik' yerself, and 'men 'bout town', clerks, teachers, crooks, the lot. All hangin' their heads over the steam to gratify their nasals."

"I've only seen the chimney-boys do that," Kate says, "to get the soot out they's eyes."

"Yes, well." A boy now appears in the doorway, but Clatter sends him away. "Ten more minutes," he calls, then turns back to Kate. "Now you listen here, my love, times is tough. I need all dese boys for the work, the hustle, see."

"What are you saying?"

"I'm sayin' this, Miss Lawler. You owe me money. You either pay now, or he's mine."

Clatter folds his arms. The atmosphere has changed and suddenly Kate feels cornered, trapped by a Bedlam boy or abusive ringmaster, a prefect feeding boys on beer and gin and forcing them to thieve for their food, clothes, shelter.

"Disgusting! Don't you ever clean up?" Kate surveys the mess—bottles, old pipe, stray glass and old clothes, rag blankets, dead flowers. Water is seeping into the soles of her shoes. Suddenly, the pub smells of rat-death and rotten food. Clatter's eye begins to twitch.

Kate steps back.

"The drink was nice n' hot, yes? Are you sure you aren't tryin' t'make a profit?"

"A profit?"

"Down in Hanging-Sword Alley. Rich men and loose girls makin' dynamite—boom!—busy work for the Devil."

"If you say so, Mr Clatter. I'll tell you one thing. The last thing I expected was to be left standing in the street, drunk, and wishing I could claw my way to *The Cat and Salutation*."

"And crying for your boy Daniel?"

Kate says nothing, detecting a new vicious undertone to his wit.

Downing his pint, Clatter leans over the bar. "Alone and filled with desperate self-pity? Listen, just because you dress like a lady, doesn't mean you's more than the filthy Irish tramp I see before me."

This is too much for Kate: as Clatter turns to allow his smug comment to linger, she takes a bottle from the bar, smashes it, and holds it to his neck as he inches forward in surprise at the noise. It goes into his throat, and Kate's anger rises, seeing his fear. The rest is impossible to see clearly. Clatter is punished in a frenzy of hot-blooded bottle blows, then lies gurgling on the floor. She jabs the bottle repeatedly into his chest, kneeling on his legs at forty-five degrees, Clatter's own hands at his throat.

The world turns, and is much the same afterwards. Kate is left stunned by her own action, her reaction, her shock. He is clearly dead, the blood no longer pumping from the gash in his neck, the sawdust on the floor pooling fast. Catching breaths, her face a bloody mask, Kate walks to the end of the bar, discovers a mop, and pulls it away from the wall. Behind it is a sign, long disused—*No Hanging Round The Bar*. She says nothing, the black humour lost on her empty mind. Instead, she swings the mop over the blood, smearing it, and creating new distributaries. They disappear under the bar, making a star-shape with Clatter's chest at the centre. The mop is useless, Kate decides, and in a strange act of trying to repair her damage, she replaces it neatly where she found it, once more glancing at the bar sign.

A bad omen? Like with Mrs Thomas—here is not murder, but provocation, antagonism, self-defence. *No Hanging Round The Bar.* Kate turns the sign around. For the first time she hears the rhythm, the sound of a manic child, her future unborn perhaps. She touches her belly, pained by the jingle-jangle sweetness of the voice:

When I grow rich,
Say the bells of Shoreditch.

When will that be?
Say the bells of Stepney

I do not know,
Says the great bell of Bow

Here comes a candle to light you to bed...

The song repeats in a loop, the melody intentionally forcing its justice—a kind of insanity—on Kate, faster and faster. "Here comes a chopper..."

She covers her ears, pressing hard until she feels dizzy, almost unconscious. When she removes her hands, the song is coming from the boys in the yard outside. The pickpockets, including her Daniel, are the ones singing:

Oranges and lemons,
Say the bells of St Clement's

You owe me five farthings,
Say the bells of St Martin's

When will you pay me?
Say the bells of Old Bailey.

Here comes a candle to light you to bed...

Here comes a chopper...

"To chop off your head," the boys shout in unison, rocking the plank at the same time. Kate is standing in the crumbling back door of *The Cat and Salutation*, her face smeared, stunned. In perverse blessing, it begins to rain at that moment. *Shanti, shanti, shanti.* The blood washes from her forehead and drains from her skin—the boy on the plank, now tumbling in the mud, is Daniel.

Still the boys do not stop their practice, trained by Clatter to work in all weathers. Another tiny kid—no more than six—is prodded with a stick off his barrel onto the plank: he begins the slow, wobbly walk twenty feet to the next barrel.

Kate simply walks over and picks Daniel up, her feet sinking in the mud. All the boys turn to her. "Clatter is gone," she says. "You are free to go..."

They stare at her blankly, and continue their game. But what if Clatter isn't gone? They know any act of defiance will result in a slap. Kate watches as pub grime drips from their arms in the rain, and they look at one another in confusion. She kneels next to Daniel in a rare act of tender submission.

"Come on, we're getting away."

"But my friends..."

"We can't take them, Daniel, they're too many."

One by one, the boys begin fleeing inside the pub to check on their teacher, the only father-figure they know. Kate knows time is short so hurries Daniel to the gate—they pass through and begin climbing the earth hill to Bankside Jetty. With two bottles of gin pressed inside her coat, she looks back at *The Cat and Salutation* leaning in the wind—a tragic painting of desperate reality—the boys clustered and conversing in the demented playground, the barrels and washing cord a strange game of playground torture, the whole scene threatening to collapse in the river.

"They'll leave," Kate says, "and become a gang."

Daniel looks up at her. "We *are* a gang."

"Not anymore," and she pulls him by the arm. "You forget that place now." In her last glance, she sees that the boy on the plank, the one Daniel was prodding with the stick, is still standing there regarding them mournfully. He raises his arms.

"I'd never leave without you," Kate says, and her arm slips around Daniel's neck and winds him north; meanwhile Daniel waves back at the boy, a lost boy of a tribe pushed into crime, less cared for than the genetically-modified beasts on the island of Dr. Moreau.

"Don't look back," Kate says, but Daniel is determined despite his exhaustion.

Soon they are back in the East End's brickworks and fish odours. As they pass close by, the timber wharfs of Holland Street tower overhead, casting shadows over their dishevelled shapes. The streets are empty, the rain and wind driving Londoners to shelter.

They pause under the aqueduct, take a breath, and Kate gives Daniel a hug squeezing him for her own life and safety, the pain she has been through.

"I didn't mean to leave you with Clatter," she says, injecting hope for the future. "It won't happen again."

"That's okay maman," the boy says with childish comfort. "I hoped you'd come back."

"You did, you did," she says, convincing herself. A tear sits in the corner of Kate's eye, a foreign feeling. But knowing Bleeding Heart Alley lies ahead, she presses her face dry, and crossing a bleak square strewn with weeds, she notices the men of the timber yard are all gone. It is past ten o' clock.

Behind Commercial Road, she halts Daniel and whistles into the dark. With no timbermen working the wharf, no labour-cooks are doling out the pea soup, no delivery carts anywhere. Only the Thames remains, dark as coal, visible by its absence in sudden cracks between ghost-buildings.

Tonight the snow is not falling: just dark rain drifting across the city. Kate finds the sign for *Sarah's Sweet Pies* slung sideways in the mud. She picks it up, props it upright. Then a fat woman trapped under a flatiron apron leers from an upstairs window.

"Who's there?"

"Kate Webster, I brought my boy." There's a pause. "Is that you, Mrs Crease?"

"Listen, why d'you bring him back? At this hour?" Coughing dramatically, Mrs Sarah Crease squints into the yard. "You in some kind of trouble?"

"No trouble. I just need you to keep him…mind him, I mean."

"Again?"

Kate winces, feeling the sting of abandoning her child, losing count of how many times she's had to pay for his well-being. "I brought you your medicine."

That word is all it takes—Mrs Crease is down the stairs so fast, Kate hears her clunking feet before she bursts through the crooked doorway, smiling wide and toothless for the boy.

"You're only young," Mrs Crease says. "How long you gonna keep this up?"

"This is the last time—a couple of days."

"Tuesday night then?" Her eyes linger on the bulge under Kate's cloak, 'the necessary' from Clatter's pub.

"Yes, same time, weather permitting," Kate says, and hands over the two bottles, which Mrs Crease's grabs by their necks. "I'll take good care of these," she says. "And your boy."

Kate steps forward. "You'd…better."

"Or what?"

"Or…"

Kate expects the soup-lady to 'twig' at this point, to recognise her ladylike disguise from 'The Barnes Mystery' in the newspapers. Kate's paranoia is temporary, though, and Mrs Crease is more likely to perform some deference, a curtsey perhaps. They are friendly together after all, yet the childminder's respect for Kate once more delivering up her child has diminished. Little does Kate know, Mrs Crease has already been drinking, a nice cocktail of soup-infused rum from the daily leftovers, so her need for 'medicine' is not so immediate.

"You should go by Newgate, see the people hanging rotting in the gibbets," Mrs Crease says, startling Kate. "Your boy should see it too."

"What?"

"'Cos that's where you'll end up."

Kate feels her teeth tightening, her jaw sticking out a little. An expression of smug enjoyment crosses Mrs Crease's face.

"What are you talking about?"

"I'll do it this time, Kate. But you and your boy are gonna get caught, if you don't start taking care o' him."

"There's nothing to fear," Kate says. "An' don't you threaten my boy with hanging, or whatever you're saying…"

"The gibbet."

"That's long gone—those bodies ain't real."

"What d'you think they do with d'prisoners after they hang 'em?"

"They bury them," Kate says, "in proper Christian fashion. Now you gonna take care o' my boy or what? If he gets hurt while you're cooking or drinking or one of those wharfmen come by, you'll have me to answer to." At this point, Kate opens Mrs Thomas's coat to reveal the bloodstains—smeared dark—from her time at Clatter's pub. She closes the coat.

"They ain't real," Mrs Crease says, "I can see pig's blood a mile away." But when she looks back in Kate's eyes, there's a reflected expression of concern, and all the ribald jockeying for position is gone. "Hand 'im over then."

Kate now looks weak, like she's played her last card. She pushes the boy by the shoulder—he is too tired to protest—and the two women regard each other, Mrs Crease in her doorway propping the entrance with an elbow, a bottle of gin in each hand, Kate in the rain, the wind blowing her hair up in swirls.

In a slow gesture, Daniel is turned back to his mother.

"She'll be back..."

"Will you?"

"Of course," Kate says softly, and seeing Daniel half asleep, she touches the top of his head. The boy murmurs.

Mrs Crease retreats. There is a glance of pained understanding between the two women, the smell of fear and white lies. Then the door is closed.

That night Kate begins the long trek north. After collapsing briefly in Bleeding Heart Alley, she escapes the shadow of the aqueduct, emerges into moonlight. After much self-accusation and some near-weeping, she resists throwing herself in the river. She does not escape the rain.

At the Mint buildings, tall and grey and gushing with drainwater, Kate imagines the money inside, all sweet-smelling and clean—dry. She considers taking refuge with the debtors visible right outside, clinging to the salvation of paper freedom only feet away: rows of quiet men, women and children slung against the stone walls of the City's economic master, the printer of money itself. Here, due to Olde English Law, the debtors can no longer be arrested and thrown in the Marshalsea debtors' prison.

"Unless they move," Kate says to joke with herself. "But I'll never become a beggar." So saying, she does not cease her plodding despite the dry wall and temptations of sleep.

Homeless for real now, she keeps heading north, dragging her feet to the point of exhaustion. Finally, with very little left in the tank she turns onto Marylebone Road and follows it, half blind in the drizzle, all the way to Baker Street—and her last hope.

Chapter 26
Inspection at 2 Mayfield Gardens
2nd March 1879, Sunday

The Bow Street Runners get a tip off: the neighbour Mrs Ives makes the journey herself to Covent Garden and leaves a report with a junior officer. Soon enough Sequin and Jones are informed.

According to Mrs Ives, something fishy is going on: "My neighbour and friend of fifteen years don't appear to be acting her normal self—she's turning very cold n' now she's moving furniture, without so much as a dickie bird. She's definitely that dead woman in the box I read about in the newspaper, if not worse, n' there's an imposter in her place. She don't even recognise her own son!"

It isn't much to go on. But when a letter turns up from a Mr Menhennick who tells them Henry Porter and Nathan Crane paid him a visit to offload furniture, they have enough to grow suspicious. Menhennick says he knows the real Mrs Thomas, and she would never consent to sell her belongings without being present. "She's a very cagey woman."

He reports this belief to Porter and Crane and—without knowing the mutual conversations in the background—the three men, together with Menhennick's solicitor, go to Richmond Police Station and file a criminal report. Scotland Yard is informed, and this information is passed to the leader detective on the case, one Gil Sequin. Moreover, the addresses match between the letter and the complaint Mrs Ives delivered the same day. It's sufficient coincidence to bring in Jones on a Sunday.

Sequin is at his desk when Jones appears, unfortunately drunk.

"We're heading south," Sequin says. "A search could solve this lead."

"So no point waiting 'til Monday?"

"Clearly."

Sequin eyes his assistant. "You're drunk."

"Of course I'm drunk, it's Sunday." Jones wobbles where he stands, then collapses in a chair. "But not enough to lose my..."

"Marbles?"

"My...job. Even on God's day of rest."

"Let's leave the big man out—this is detective work. You'll sober up in the hansom."

By the time they reach Richmond, it's started to spit down. People are leaving the market and the scaffolds are being buttoned up for the night. A weak sun is just touching *The Hole in the Wall*, but Mrs Hayhoe is no longer in her garden.

The policemen peer from the carriage's rain-canopy up the leafy street. They turn first into Victoria Lane, St Albert's Way and trundle by grand Georgian houses, all black-white wooden beams.

"Your retirement street, eh cap'n?" Jones hiccups.

"In my dreams."

"This plays like a dream!" Jones adds, pressing his stomach gingerly. "We need to stop."

"Buck up, we're almost there. You might have to tackle 'im too."

"A killer? Well, I couldn't arrest myself right now."

The houses get smaller but no less quaint, and turning a steep corner, the sign for Mayfield Gardens appears. It turns out to be a cul-de-sac, narrow front gardens widening into a close-knit arc of charming bungalows. On the corner of St Albert Street, the first house is number 2, adjacent to Park Road. The house looks normal, identical to its neighbours, delicate-looking lace curtains in the window.

The hansom rolls up, and the Bow Street Runners confer a moment.

"This shouldn't take long," Sequin says. As they climb down, Jones doubles over and is sick on the pavement. Sequin watches the display, standing back from the sudden spurt of retching with some spitting, and shakes his head. "You okay?" He decides not to approach Jones to offer a hand. They've only worked together a few months, and he's no idea about the reaction. "You could have waited 'til we got inside."

"No, better here…"

"Better out than in," says Henry Porter, stepping through a garden gate to shake Inspector Sequin's hand.

"Good afternoon, inspector. My name's Porter. I think I know the woman you're looking for."

"Woman?" Sequin says, Jones still retching in the background.

"Woman," Porter repeats, and they stare at each other, then up at the house. "Yes, she's called Mrs Thomas, Mrs Julia Thomas."

For half a minute, they look up at the house, the atmosphere growing surreal.

"You already think she's the one in the box?" Sequin asks.

"I do."

"Then my name's Inspector Gil Sequin, and this is my partner…" gesturing to the street, hopefully.

"I won't shake your hand," Jones says mischievously. "Deputy Jones—slave to the master, or whatever you prefer."

"Fine to meet you," Porter says. He is wearing a think overcoat giving an air of gentility, if it weren't for his woollen hat which looks like it's been round Covent Garden three times. The policemen can't see Porter's arch of receding hair, but they can imagine his bald pate from the strays dangling over his ears. Sequin hopes their guide is as ingenious as the oddity of his appearance, a raffish man with refined airs, one who retains the common touch.

"And where are you from, Mr Porter?"

"Ireland. I mean, I've lived here twenty years. I prefer Dublin pubs to London pubs, you know. I'm the landlord of *The Rising Sun* in Hammersmith."

"A publican," Jones says, helping him out.

"Yes, an ex-boozer too," Porter says, holding onto his hat. "I don't mind admitting, I had my fun." Courting being quizzed by Bow Street does not occur to him—he is far meeker now, in police company, than with Kate at his family table.

"So where's this Mr Crane?"

"Beats me—he's not even a regular. Just delivered the furniture. Doesn't change what I know about Mrs Thomas, though."

"Shall we go inside?" Sequin says, and leads the men through the garden gate up the gravel path. He tries the handle three times, not wishing to wait, and pushes the door back. "Hello," he calls, and there's no answer. He steps inside.

"Is he always this forward?"

Jones says nothing.

There's a strange smell inside, a combination of burnt tallow and rotting soup, indefinable, almost tangy. The three men sniff, sensing unpleasantness in the air, a kind of delayed effect.

"A horse's been here," Porter says, "dragged backwards."

Sequin gestures to the living room table. Jones and Porter sit in the bay window alcove, as he turns the piano stool round. "So, a few questions, please, Mr Porter. What's your involvement? We don't mind your presence while we search the house, no, but soon we'll ask you to wait in the hansom."

"Well, okay," Porter says. "Why did I come inside?"

"To tell us—your role, see," Jones smiles. He wipes the last ill-effects of lunch-pints from his mouth. "I play bad bobby, you play nice. And Detective Sequin just listens. Then won't have to arrest you, see."

Porter looks between the policemen: he gets only blank faces.

"Clearly something happened here," Sequins says.

"Can't you smell it?" the deputy adds. "That ain't horses or dead flowers, or rotten apples. An' we're only three feet inside the door." He looks at Sequin and smiles. "Someone's gonna swing for this one."

"Someone, sure."

Jones looks back at Porter, leans in, hunches his shoulders. "You're involved."

"No, that's not…the case."

"So what is the case? Tell us."

"Look, is this some kind of interrogation?"

"Not some kind," Jones says. "Listen, you go wait in the hansom, Mr Porter. We'll have plenty to talk about later."

Henry Porter stands, visibly shaken. "I…"

"You ain't got the words?"

"This has nothing to do with me."

Porter looks at Sequin, who turns and rattles a few keys on the piano: "Mr Porter, this is a police investigation, clearly. You're help is needed, appreciated..." He runs his finger up and down the keys, dabbles them ominously on the lower octaves. "Let's not get melodramatic. We'll search the house. You sit in the cab."

"We do trust you," Jones says, softening, and guides Mr Porter to the door, patting his shoulder. "But if you take off, the cabbie's gonna want the fare from Bow Street..."

"I'll wait," Porter says.

"That's a good idea."

Sequin and Jones watch as their helpful suspect meanders to the hansom. Porter crawls stumbling to the top seat and tips his bowler to the driver. He turns to the house; the door is already closed.

Jones leans back and sighs his relief.

"Are publicans always like this?"

"You tell me."

An hour later the police are done: they leave with an axe, razor and some charred bones, together with the missing handle from a trunk-box. Each item rests in a separate brown bag, carefully tied, and is brought out separately. Jones bears them up from his mid-riff like the crown jewels, in itemised bags.

"A stage of evidence," Sequin says, and closes the door to 2 Mayfield Gardens. "Victim, weapons, practically everything but the killer."

The policemen are wearing gloves, though Sequin's are mostly for show, while their expressions betray faux amusement dipped in barely concealed surprise. Knives and body parts take centre stage, neither man expecting a bloody hoard of human flesh—at least, the surprisingly large amount remains on the bone after boiling in a copper pot. Porter watches as they approach, mouth open, the driver busy with *The Times* crossword, cigarette dangling from his lip.

"All right, guv," he says, oblivious, as the *bobbies* take their seats.

"Bow Street, same way back. Take it slow."

"Aye, aye."

Thus on Monday morning, 3rd March, a full description of Kate Webster is circulated by the police in connection with the murder of Mrs Thomas and the theft of her effects. Her name and aliases are soon on many people's lips.

Then after Porter's interview, her movements are detected for the previous days. A wanted photofit is created from an artist's sketch—a modern composite in grey pencil showing Kate in mean scowling mood, red eyes staring and disjointed black hair pulled tight, teeth set like a coyote and just a twinge of sadistic delight at the corner of her mouth. Porter is shown the picture, finds it laughable, and remarks on its lack of accuracy. "You're looking for a monster?"

"A perfect image—the more theatrical the better. It's what we need so the public can act," Jones explains. "Or she'll be a hero by next week if not for the reward."

"For information?"

"Nice try, a reward for capture."

"I have a family," Porter says, his hands up almost in prayer. "I deserve something…"

"And you'll still have a family."

"All part of the Scotland Yard service."

"Finest in the British Isles," Sequin says, leans back and lets his bulldog-assistant do the work.

They've been in an underground interview room, the cask of the old chapel crypt adjoining Covent Garden chapel, for three hours now. The following names are now known in 'The Barnes Mystery': Mrs Ives, Mrs Thomas's son Billy, Mrs Hayhoe of Richmond—a local associate of Mrs Thomas—and Mr Nathan Crane, whom Porter indicates 'the prime suspect' often meets. Not forgetting Porter himself, his son Robert, or anyone else in London.

"All suspects, guilty under proven innocent," Jones says. "We have to work with a faster mentality than the courts. Or who'd get results?"

"The hangman?"

"Very good, very good," Sequin says. "Yes, we have an impressive hangman, name of Marwood. Very diligent, very thorough. But Henry Porter, you sir, you're the one here. You're in the hot seat so you get the questions. That's how this works."

Porter stays calm. No mention is made of Jonathan Clatter, since by living on the margins he does not even exist.

"We're underground, Mr Porter, and we have been a long time."

"Like a coffin."

"Or a grave."

"Or a game," Porter says. "Listen, gentleman, I've told you all I know. Mrs Thomas came to see me, and she was not herself. I suspected 'er being a man or maybe a woman dressed up to look like Mrs Thomas. But…"

"…but you still sent her looking for this Crane man…"

"Yes, Nathan Crane. I'm not…pointing fingers."

"But if you were, it would be at Nathan Crane…"

"No, Mr Jones, no. It's not like that. Honest to God."

Sequin smiles: "Oh yes, to God in all honesty, hey. You know how that sounds? So correct me if I'm wrong, Sir Porter," and he stands to circle the table—the only furniture in the room, "but your story is that you told a man-woman—someone dressed as a woman and claiming to be Mrs Thomas—that you know where to dispose of your friend Mrs Thomas's furniture—your friend, Mrs Thomas, who you *do* know?"

"Yes."

Sequin leans forward. "Be careful, Mr Porter, my friend Jones is short his daily tipple—he's dry from yesterday, look at the twitch in his hairline." Sequin points at Jones's face. "He's like a bear with a sore head, a dog lowered in a pit, but he's still on my chain. Do you follow me?"

"Yes."

"Do you understand?"

"Please. Yes, sir," Porter begins to sob. His hands slip down his cheeks and the policemen stare at the top of his bald head, faint sympathy behind their fake aggression.

"Just tell us the truth, Mr Porter, and you can go back to your family."

Porter looks up, wipes his face. "I've told you the truth."

"Perhaps."

An hour later the session ends and Porter is allowed to go; they can't charge him without the commissioner's approval, especially on a Sunday night. But something about his story sounds foolishly truthful too. After they usher him up the cold steps, Jones releases him into Covent Garden with a slap on the back. Sequin holds up the new criminal photofit, the bloated cartoon illustration of 'Mrs Thomas the Second', the same person who had dinner with Porter's family three nights ago.

"The Richmond Killer," Sequin says. "Tomorrow's news."

"We'll be seeing you again, Mr Porter." The abused man trundles away in the snow, thankful his freedom is crowned by the early fruit market. Starving, he buys a pear from the vendor—it's five in the morning—and staggers home.

When they're alone again, Sequin and Jones ditch the premises and head to the Chandos pub. They clink 'small scotches' at the bar.

"I trust him," Jones says, "somehow."

"Your gut never lies. I don't, but I know enough, that all roads lead to Nathan Crane. We find Crane, we'll find who did this crime."

Jones smiles over his whisky. "Crane sounds like a different character. We'll have to coax it out."

"We'll see, who knows. All I know is that Marwood took Charles Peace to task sooner than he bargained. He'll be ready."

"One more thing," Jones says, lifting a gold watch-n-chain from his waistcoat. "You know what this means?"

"You should have left that in Bow Street," Sequin says, "with the other items."

"It's not directly relevant to the crime. Anyway, you know I've got it."

"True, I do."

"Well, I figure we use it to catch the killer. Look at it this way, whoever's selling furniture ain't found this watch. And if they did…well…"

"Watch the house, you mean?"

"They'll be back."

Sequin considers. "Tomorrow the superintendent can get Terry down there, stake it out for three days. If this person shows, fine. If not, this case gets harder."

"So you'll delay the poster?"

"Tomorrow night we'll release the news to the public. The only way the murderer'll know, this way, is if Porter tells 'im."

Sequin takes the watch, taps the face. "Gold-plated," he says. "Looks thin, washed out."

"You can tell just by lookin'?"

"Right, I can tell just by lookin' Sequin lifts an item from his own pocket: the silver-polished handle of a trunk-box. "This is the other item we proceed with—away from the superintendent's eyes. If this is the handle on that trunk found off the Thames, we have the right house, the right body, and everythin' fits neater than an envelope."

"Than an envelope?" Jones says, mysterious to the ways of Sequin's detective skills. "I get it. The body is the letter?"

"This is real gold," Sequin says, and he tosses the handle to Jones who fumbles it in mid-air and it falls in his glass. Rather than dip his hand in, Jones downs the rest of his scotch.

"Better than getting conscripted in the navy," he says. He holds the scotch up to the light.

"Real gold," Sequin says. "Your round, I detect."

Chapter 27
The Witching Hour of Night
3rd March 1879, Monday

The boy wakes in a room he does not recognise and shakes his hair, aware he is half asleep but sensing consciousness. The images are still real in the room—the dream of the graveyard, the gravel of Church Lane, falling sandbags. He raises a hand and touches his nose. "Am I the hangman, already?" To banish the night—he is still afraid of the dark—the boy drops from bed, paces in bare feet to the window and peer over the street.

Aldous is chilly, alone in a room the size of his Horncastle bedroom, but twice as high; in the Lincolnshire cottage his parents' room is right next door. Here they are two floors down, and Aldous is pleased about that. He's been given the grand old attic room, dusty and unused but containing the relics of old wardrobes, chairs, antique curiosities. Already he's turned a brass Buddha to face the wall so it won't watch him and 'curse his soul'; now he finds the adjacent painting of a desert island equally disturbing with its fake palm tree, unreal sun. He is amused too, though—the Buddha is facing the island's shore where a black fin emerges from the ocean, twice the size of a raft of shipwrecked sailors, a comic threat that fails to disturb the Buddha's indefinable calm.

"Paradise or food," Aldous says, and passes his palm over his own face. "Slow death, fast death," lifting and dropping his hand. "Slow, fast…. When will the shark attack? What will the Buddha do?"

After this play-acting, he skips to the window to survey the real-life 'Curiosity Shop' over Dorset Square, the rain and wind bullying and bending weak trees to protect the inner circle of grass. He can discern the park benches, solid iron, even the boards of their wooden seats, but something about their stately and Crown-supplied elegance, their sturdy regularity chills him. He pads across the room and slips back under the covers.

Less than ten miles south, Daniel Webster is also awake, and staring into the night. Starting to lose his fear of the dark, though he has more to fear, his eyes look blankly at the marks on Mrs Crease's wall. A curtain separates Daniel from the mass of her sleeping flesh, rising and falling, her broken breaths void of dreams. He has been here before, but his preference would be Jonathan Clatter's polished 'special room', where he was protected from the gang's overcrowding. By contrast, Mrs Crease's dive is filthy and cluttered, a ground floor shack only inches from the outside world.

"No different from sleeping under a bridge…"

Daniel knows that feeling. Through a crack in the window, he can see the soup kettles outside, just paces from Bleeding Heart Alley and a minute more to the Thames. In an hour, the warehouse men will be arriving before daybreak, and their voices will wake Mrs Crease. She'll heat some old tea on the stove and pretend not to wake him—disturbing pots and pans on the wall—then feign surprise he's conscious. But he is not afraid; unlike Aldous further north on Gloucester Place, he has seen too much. Daniel waits for the sun's rays to softly light the room and dispel the gloomy shapes. Light will give definition to Mrs Crease's pea soup tins littering the floor mingled with her indecipherable clothing.

Then a single moment of happiness—the simple smell of recovery—the odour of freshly baking bread. Daniel pinches his nostrils, worried the pleasure will induce a panic! Where is the source, he wonders? He knows the bakers of London light their ovens just after midnight, adding more loafs in batches, but the bread's taste in the imagination is so overpowering they must have received a new load of charcoal for the furnaces. Demand must be high and as any Londoner can tell you, hunger begins with first light.

Daniel crawls from the bed in yesterday's clothes, caddish knickerbockers and a pea jacket, stolen by Mr Clatter and awarded in exchange for his first batch of filched handkerchiefs. He wears them proudly, though nothing suits him. The knickerbockers are baby girl's clothing, and the pea jacket is 'little rake of London town'. "I'm just a clown-boy clearing up wigs in the Big Top," except Daniel knows there's no one to entertain but Mrs Crease. "And this dump ain't much of a circus."

Further north, the smoke from separate ovens is oak smoke, the change from coal to wood wafting a rural breeze over Dorset Square. Aldous can smell the bread, and in the main bedroom two floors down, it wakes Marwood in the night. He turns to look at Ellen. She is sound asleep. Like his son, the hangman faces the ceiling, breathes in deep the fresh bread, settling his mind with memories of Horncastle and the surrounding countryside. He remembers his journey on the cart to the train station, how little he noticed the fields with his excitement to ride the rails. Any minor regret is now overpowered by the smell of cooking bread.

"I hope that's not the Sheriff of London," Marwood says, but believing it's a possibility, he slides from the room. He pauses to smell the fresh bread. Then he straightens up, groping the banister like a blind man. Suddenly there it is: the glory of day. Glinting through the hall window, the sun breaks it first ray across the wrought-iron benches of Dorset Square, beautifully cascading across the frozen pond beside the grass.

Upstairs the same light cuts into Aldous's room, and into Daniel Webster's face across town, onto Ellen's face as she rolls over in bed, and somewhere, it touches Kate Webster too, bringing her back into the hell of her own making, but filling her with the chance that like Eurydice trapped in the underworld, there may yet be a way out.

Downstairs, there is a repeating knock at the door.

Chapter 28
A Family Affair
3rd March 1879, Monday

At the third knock he peers through the peep-hole, ready to encounter his Bow Street friends Sequin and Jones for a late night call. Instead it is a woman, drenched to the bone.

"Mrs Thomas, what is happening? Are you..."

"Hurt? No, cold, yes. I'm terribly sorry to bother you, Mr Marwood. I can't believe..."

"I'd recognise you anywhere. Please, do come in, you must be freezing."

"Thank you—so much." Kate is genuinely distressed, her hands shaking, her hair matted to her neck. She takes Marwood's fingers over the threshold and he closes the door, leaving her in the hallway: she is quite the drowned rat, but still capable of a freakish kind of laugh, being saved by the hangman. "I could have drowned."

Marwood leads her into the kitchen, encouraging silence. He gestures to Turner's Old Blackfriars Bridge en route, but all Kate can think of is Richmond Bridge, Hammersmith Bridge and Barnes Bridge, throwing herself off them and forgetting about everything. But she is reminded of Daniel; she knows she cannot abandon him.

Marwood turns on a gaslight and the table hovers into view.

"How did you cut yourself?"

"A cat attacked me."

"A cat?"

"On Baker Street—a wild one."

Marwood peers at the red colour of her blouse. "Did you strangle it?"

Kate says nothing.

"Listen, Miss Thomas, I don't know what's going on. But I'm happy to help you—tonight."

"Thank you."

"It's late and we have lodgers upstairs. Please follow me."

He leads her to the basement via external steps, helping her over the sealed trapdoor. The scene would be quite comical—the hangman leading a twisty walk, Kate holding onto the back of his nightshirt—if she weren't so exhausted. Outside now, the gaslight leads them down stone steps to the basement.

"Take those blankets and spread them on the floor." She does as told. Marwood sets the lamp on a shelf and prepares a makeshift bed in the corner. "You can sleep here, it's the best we have." The bed is an old mattress, springs visible, the head torn off in some inexplicable incident.

"It belonged to the previous owner."

"More than enough," Kate says.

Marwood swings the lantern through shadows and illuminates the rest of the room—the sandbags, work table, bit of rope, metal noose rings, and two full-scale drops he's created: one is a long drop, the other a guillotine. He pulls the gaslight back.

"Tomorrow," he says. Kate looks up, face straining for tenderness. Only the anxieties of the day—the long walking, the sudden fighting, the daily hunger—remain behind her eyes. He nods. "I'll come see you in the morning, as soon as I can."

"Thank you." Kate listens as the hangman walks heavily up the stone steps, his shadow following. I can sleep now, she thinks, and collapses before he ascends like Orpheus through the trapdoor, without looking back.

Returning to bed, Marwood is worried Ellen is awake but she is lying in the same position, face to the door and placid. He does not check on Aldous but climbs into bed and stares at the ceiling. Once more he spiritually rejoins Aldous and Daniel, awake in the middle of the night, but no longer filled with a strange optimism.

In the morning Ellen decides to leave early for the Marylebone Market, and without uttering a word to Marwood, she decides to take Aldous along. After breakfast they're gone and immediately Marwood is back in the basement, checking on his guest, and is surprised to find Kate awake. She is sitting in the guillotine chair, a long bench, facing the wooden apparatus with a head-sized hole. She spins around.

"What is it?"

"Kind of like the stocks," he says, "only for the head."

Kate presses her head against the wood.

"No," Marwood says, crossing the room. "You lean back and the wood fits over your neck. You're trapped and the blade can easily…"

"The blade."

Kate bolts upright.

"Yes," Marwood says, "the blade." He points to the back of the guillotine where a hollow, rectangular shaft resembles the headboard of a four-poster bed. "She runs down there."

Kate giggles a little, surprising Marwood. "First I want to know how it works."

"Well, the French do things differently, including executions."

"I know that."

"This is a prototype, but the invention isn't new. 'With this machine I chop off your head in a twinkling, and you don't suffer.' So said Dr Joseph-Ignace Guillotin, the most humane of men. I take my calling from him."

"You use the guillotine?"

"No, but he was rational about executions—he saw no need for suffering. They should be painless affairs, you see, *humane*…"

The word lingers so Kate does her best impression of being interested. The device, of course, attracts her far more than the history, her eyelids paling a little as he continues:

"Joseph-Ignace Guillotin did not invent the machine, though it bears his name, nor did he succumb to its power. He was a politician—a democratic egalitarian in the best French sense—and he made executioners equable, fair for all."

"What do you mean?"

"Well, execution methods were divided by class."

"Once upon a time?"

"Yes, not too long ago. The sword was the most honourable and saved for military men, a straight beheading or else Japanese *harakiri*. Next is the axe and block for noblemen, and the ladder and rope—for the rest of us."

"And the blade?"

"*La guillotine*," Marwood says, "is for French aristocrats, the equivalent of our axe and headsman, except Joseph-Ignace saw things differently—and he had his way. The device is efficient, that's for sure, and fair in the political and physical senses, the body politic doubly satisfied." He now sits at his desk. "Miss Thomas, I'd like to do the same for hanging. Make it less painful for the common man, and eventually replace the aristocrats' axe."

Kate stares blankly. "I didn't know you're political?"

"I'm not—hence they'll never name my Long Drop after me. A politician will get the credit. Anyway, this Mr Guillotine declared the guillotine is good for all the French people, a 'democratic decollation'. We've been using the Halifax Gibbet for decades, and in Edinburgh they use the Scottish Maiden. For me it's just an experimental toy, but there's a certain glamour and elegance about the guillotine, don't you think?"

"Chop off my head," Kate says. "Go on. It'll be fun. My brain's never been much use to me."

"Why not your finger?" Marwood says. "I have a portable device, used for cigar chopping."

"No, no, the real thing."

Marwood obliges. The sun is streaming into the cold basement now, cutting the room in two and lighting on Kate's mattress and the stone steps; disused spaces behind the death machine are all in darkness. Kate swivels her legs either side of the guillotine bench and looks up at Marwood, expectantly. He can see she has changed her clothes to a frilly cotton shirt and a cashmere shawl, signs of a lady. There's no sign of Clatter's blood.

"You should remove your shawl," Marwood says, and laughs. He begins to fit the device together. "One name for this saviour is Saint Guillotine, protectress of patriots! You notice the French sense of humour and love of wordplay—history is littered with names for this machine, to mask what it really does!" He sticks his head through the guillotine. "Death is taboo after all."

Kate grins, enjoying winding up Marwood. It will be far easier to stay an extra night now, maybe even rob him as she first imagined during their first meeting in *The Oxford & Cambridge Arms*.

"Go on."

"Well, it was originally called 'louison' or 'louisette' after the real inventor Dr Antoine Louis, but that name didn't stick. Paris endorsed a flood of other names,"—he begins strapping leather supports and fastening bolts—"La Veuve or Widow, the National Razor, the Avenger, the topper, the slicer. My favourite is the Patriotic Shortener!"

"...with its beautiful silhouette."

"Exactly," Marwood says, and looks where Kate is pointing. On the wall opposite, in sunlight reflected off the white steps, is the black shadow of the guillotine, her wooden knife holder and slender neck. "All except the triangular blade, her missing teeth. They say she always grins at you before she falls, and her smile is beautiful."

"If you can call that beauty."

"I do," Marwood says. "The blade is not heavy enough, though. It needs to be fastened to a weighted 'ram' at the side to help it fall."

"Take your time," Kate says, and leans back.

Marwood pulls hard on the leather straps. "I'm almost ready."

"So what's the attraction? Why do all these devices interest you? It can't just be a job."

"No, you're right. When I think of executioners, see, I think of the French. We hear rumbles of a revolution, but Paris is very ordered, very controlled. I like that—plus they have all the trappings of worshipping the instrument, and dynasties of hereditary executioners."

"Aha, the men themselves—you're an admirer."

Marwood hesitates. "I must climb up to fit the blade."

"Go right ahead, Mr Marwood, do your worst."

He finds her enthusiasm a little unnerving, but he pulls up a chair. On tiptoes, he's level with the blade-holder. "You're right, Miss Thomas. To hold the office of Executioner of High Works would be a great honour. Unfortunately I'm an Englishman."

"Ha!"

"Yes, and the French will not allow it. Besides, I've only carried out British executions, well, and Irish." Kate goes quiet at the mention of actually hangings.

"Do you regret them? I heard about the Irish ones…"

"No, I don't. And I must beg for a little quiet now, Miss Thomas. I am testing the hook."

"Of course you are."

What Kate does not know is that Marwood is in fact fitting the blade, only upside down. The blunt end—a square edge capped with wood—faces the floor. "I have what you might call 'a love of the bourreaux', namely the family of French executioners where the profession is passed down from father to son. I am a Gentleman Executioner in that tradition."

"Only English?"

Marwood drops down from the chair. "Precisely. What I object to is that English hangmen are ostracised and feared. We are bogeymen, and when we operate as an arm of the State—like my trip to Ireland to hang the Fenians, we're hated even more. I don't make the laws, Miss Thomas, but I *can* improve them—a more perfect union—like the American states!"

"Well, they hang them in the streets in New York, I'm told."

"That's not true. You mean Virginia or way west in Texas. The streets in New York are too narrow. Either way, we're despised, Miss Thomas, a breed apart." He pulls down on the rope, tightens the upside-down blade. "Please close your eyes." With his free hand Marwood lowers four small wooden notches over Kate's head; invisible to her, these bolts will catch the blade. "Good, I'm now going to lift the stocks and you fit your head inside."

"For real?"

Marwood pauses. "Well, I thought you wanted to do this for real. I thought you didn't want your head?"

"I don't."

"Then please place it in the stocks."

"You mean the guillotine?"

"Yes, Miss Thomas. Where the majesty of the law is channelled into justice. But as I was saying, we are the unwanted doppelganger for everyman, we few hangmen, we unlucky few. The taboo of society, our own brand of *deus ex machina*. Outcasts? Perhaps. We serve the state, but the state cannot face its own image. So it creates a dark figure of us, something it can set outside society, exiled."

"Like this?"

"That's right." He turns a tiny screw to lock her in. "You can open your eyes."

Kate looks up, a little apprehensive, but grins. "I'll be there at the end," she says cryptically. "I'm both spectator and performer."

"How good is your acting?"

"How safe is your machine?"

"Aren't you leaving that question a little late?"

They smile at each other—mutual acts of reassurance.

"Are you ready? Where's your hood?"

"I need one more minute. As an arm of the law, I have to make sure you're secure, or the execution will fail."

"Don't lose your head…"

"Very good. One more thought as you die. Why am I hated? You see, the judge is honoured, the jury respected, the prosecuting counsel obeyed and the defence mitigated, even if wrong—and a criminal is on the stand. So why am I feared, stigmatised like a leper, and shunned in the street?"

"I have no idea, Mr Marwood. Could it be because you kill people for a living?"

"Perhaps. I have a natural self-confidence. I see myself as the benefactor of society. True, I go where no man may go, but I'm also forbidden their liberties. We are worlds apart, those men and I. They are connected to the whole. I inhabit a living taboo, our irrational side. I am an unpleasant stand-in for everyman, the common Jack Ketch carrying out the Bloody Code of Britain."

He looks down at Kate's head.

"And for what? To watch men suffer? True, they are guilty men. Take petty murder or 'petit' treason, as the French say, the killing of husbands by wives, wives by husbands. Those are the worst—the ones who kill those they love. They act guiltless too!"

"Wait…"

"Too late, Miss Thomas." He pulls the lever, there is a gentle creak stretched out to a second, and Kate begins to squirm in her head-clamp. He does not expect her scream but she does, utterly transformed by the surprise of the act. He has truly let the blade go. She can see it coming—eyes wide and frozen—then closed and terrified.

All is black. Then the light returns and Kate is looking up at the ceiling cut in two, and again screams. A few seconds and the room is steady: nothing is turning because her head is not tumbled in an imaginary basket. Marwood never even placed one to catch her in. The ceiling is split by the flat wood touching her nose—the base of the upside-down blade, extending from its holder eight feet high. Only then does she notice the blood.

"You cut me!" she cries, and wriggles her head. Her hair is trapped and again she cries out, until Marwood lays a hand on her forehead.

"Not you," he says, dipping his finger in the blood on her forehead. "Me. I cut myself lifting the blade the right way up."

"You flicked it when the blade fell!"

"I couldn't resist."

"Get me out of here," Kate says, her lips all twisted. "Or…"

"Or you'll kill me? It was you who elected to go under the knife. You're unharmed."

Kate glares at him. "Get me out of here."

"A joke's a joke," Marwood says. "I thought it would wake you up for breakfast. I'm not forgetting the dog-fight you wanted to see at Bartholomew Fair. You said you like extremes outside your own experience. Well, I can provide enough for your entertainment."

Kate says nothing as he realises the clasp. Then she sits upright, batting her arms in a show of togetherness. "You don't know who you're dealing with."

Marwood is quick to reassure her, though, searching for Kate's sense of humour. He rattles the blade in its wooden holder. "Look, it's has four stoppers, two on each side. I know the blade's weight—it'd need another four feet in height just to break the skin. You were quite safe."

"*You* were."

He holds out his finger. "A small cut, and that's from the wood. The blade's not sharp enough—she'd only take off half your head." He smiles, searching for the woman he remembers from their last meeting, but Kate no longer that woman. She is too tired and Daniel is disturbing her thoughts, not to mention

Jonathan Clatter.

"It was a mistake," she says. "I need to lie down again." She just stares at Marwood trying to decide, given her play execution, whether he's friend or foe. Without knowing how to handle her, Marwood begins talking again. Perhaps a story will soothe her, he thinks.

"You know, the original executioner of the guillotine," he begins, "cut off the head of Charles I."

"I suppose he's your hero?"

"Not Charles I, but the executioner, yes."

Kate looks up, interested despite herself. He waits for her to say "Why?"

"Well, young Richard Brandon, he worked for thirty years as a king's 'execution aide', then added 'esquire' after his name in pride. He executed Lord Stafford in May 1641 and Archbishop Laud on 10th January 1644..."

"So he's a prized killer?" Kate says, crossing to her mattress where she awkwardly folds Mrs Thomas's clothes.

"If you like—he had powerful friends after hanging the archbishop. Once he executed a nobleman, he could boast it up something rotten."

"So?"

"So, he was on the inside. The Garter King of Arms, Sir William Segar, was tricked into presenting a coat of arms to Brandon. So in 1616 he legally became a gentleman."

"And that's what you want for yourself?" Kate laughs, pointing at Marwood now sucking the finger he's cut.

"To continue my story, please. When the nobility rose up, Brandon refused to execute the king. He was rolled out of bed by a horse troop, the royal guard betraying him. Brandon faced a moral dilemma. Was he a rope for hire, or would he stand by his king? In the end, he was told to do his duty 'or else'."

"So he ran away?"

"No, he wasn't a moral soul. He received thirty pounds for the execution plus a pomander—that's a clove-studded orange—from the royal pocket. The king was summarily hanged on a very low scaffold outside Indigo Jones's Banqueting Hall in Whitehall."

Kate nods. "And the point of the story?"

"It's a tragedy, a true history lesson. Who doesn't want to be a gentleman? But who wants to hang the king? I want to get paid *and* be a part of the nobility—where else is one safer?"

"More in danger, you mean."

"Well, I don't want to be forced into an immoral hanging. The whole point, Miss Thomas," and here Marwood graces the arm of the guillotine, "is I am in favour of just executions, painless endings, total justice."

"You're quite sane?"

"Quite," says Marwood. "I believe that goodness is possible. We had the Short Drop yesterday, we have the Newgate Drop today. Now I've invented the Long Drop so never again will a criminal suffer a gratuitous hour on the rope!"

"So you'll get a tip from the victim—or family—for a swift and painless death?"

"I have *no* regard for the perks of the job," Marwood retorts. "I'm in it for the morality."

"Ha!" Kate cries. "That's rich. For the good of the people—you hang people!"

"Yes, for the good of the people, and I hang them for the good of the bad people too."

Kate touches her head. "You talk in riddles, Mr Marwood. I need to lie down."

"England is the next place for fair hangings," Marwood says, as Kate takes to her mattress. "Even a dog deserves a decent last minute." Kate says nothing.

Marwood sits on the guillotine bench and looks up at his hanging apparatus. The noose is swinging in the half-light, blown by a soft breeze from outside, his work table scattered with knots and stray shoelaces, metal clasps, a screwdriver, a hammer. He reaches down, takes a handful of grains from a sandbag and lets them run through his fingers.

"And the French call us immoral sometimes. You know, Miss Thomas, we used to cry 'behold the head of a traitor!' when an English enemy was hung, drawn and quartered. Nothing could be worse—even the French-style of four horses drawing you to the cardinal points of the compass. I ask you, who is more humane? The answer is clear—neither—just whoever adopts my Long Drop." He smiles wistfully. "See, the French standing gallows of Montfaucon outside Paris could carry fifty-eight clients at once. That puts

Telemachus to shame! They used a permanent beam dating back before Rabelais."

Kate looks over, amazed her host is still talking. "Are you okay, Mr Marwood?"

"The bodies were left swinging until their bones dropped into the charnel house. What is humane about that? The hangman wore his tricolour proud, as though the day were a festival or national holiday. But it's just a spectacle, a fear-monger for the people to know who's in charge, nothing God-like about it!"

"Except the hangman *plays* God."

Marwood stares at her. "I don't think of it like that."

"No, you wouldn't."

"If they adopt the Long Drop, I'll wear the Brandon coat of arms and a Union Jack intertwined!"

Kate scoffs so he leaves her to her nap, but he returns in an hour with some breakfast—bread, an apple, some milk. She's grateful and yet the confusion of their conversation still fails to disperse. Marwood adds how the French executioner was appointed by the king and not the local sheriff, assistants were 'valets', and the victim's hair was 'tailored' for execution since 'it was elegant and civilised to attend to their 'toilette'."

"So why don't you move to France?"

"I have a family," Marwood says. "But to quote *Sanson fils*, 'I am only the instrument—it is Justice that kills.' I'd be happy for my boy to continue in my footsteps."

"I wouldn't," Kate says.

"Your boy."

She looks at him. "You haven't even asked me about him? In all this time, where I was last night?"

"I…"

"I thought you cared."

Marwood looks at her blankly. "So that's my responsibility? I thought I was doing you a favour—by not asking."

"That's a lie. But now you're involved, and since you never asked, my boy is safe with a minder. But I don't trust her—you have to help me get her back."

"A minder?"

"A babysitter woman."

Marwood smiles. "So he's in mortal danger, somewhere with a

nice old lady."

"There are no nice old ladies," Kate says. "This woman's gettin' on a bit, but that doesn't make her nice. She ain't the smartest tool in the box, but I don't trust her with my boy neither."

"Listen," Marwood says. "Let's go upstairs for a while. It's far warmer. You can stay one more night."

"I can?"

"Yes, but we only have an hour. Come into the house, and we'll eat properly. Tomorrow you can fetch your boy."

Kate hides her grin, then looks Marwood full in the face, her gratitude undercut by humorous scheming. "Wouldn't it be easier to just marry me, William? I can still call you William, right. Well, we could go to Gretna Green, tonight, it's a village just over the Scottish border…"

"I know about Gretna—runaway couples get married by the local innkeeper."

"The blacksmith. I read it in the *London Illustrated*."

"Then it must be true. Yesterday's paper? We can check it upstairs."

"No, no," Kate says, backtracking, "that's not necessary. Just wouldn't it be nice, a jaunt up north, an escape to Scotland?"

"Escape—from what?—and it's hardly a 'jaunt' to the Scottish border. You are joking, Miss Thomas, right? You know I'm already married."

"Of course I'm joking, William," Kate smiles. "We both have children." She now affects a kind of hurt demeanour where she rolls one cheek into her neck like a cat. "I just thought…in another life we could…."

"In another life," Marwood says, and touches Kate's shoulder. She moves her hand—he lifts her to her feet. "Yes, in another life."

The moment lingers, and she looks up expecting a kiss, but Marwood is too reticent, not exactly shy but thinking of his family. Somehow he sees Ellen's face, the disapproval, an abrupt return to Horncastle leaving him in the London winter, and most of all, her figure heading back to St Pancras Station with Aldous trailing, yanked along a little, looking over his shoulder with childish fright. The image is painful, reminding Marwood how he felt sitting up on the cart that night leaving Lincolnshire, troubled, lonely—he cannot let this crazy woman get in his way, however needy she is.

"I'm sorry." He turns away.

But the next moment he hears footsteps on the cellar steps behind—Kate is not about to give up just yet.

Chapter 29
The Quiet Redeemer
4th March 1879, Tuesday

Meanwhile, Ellen is leading Aldous down Baker Street just as his father imagined, pulling his arm a little. Yet she is very conscious of traffic and lets the carriages go before making any turns, avoiding unsavoury-looking characters, walking with her wits about her. She passes *The Globe* pub at the corner of Marylebone Road and turns towards Dorset Square. In five minutes she'll be back in Gloucester Place. Under her arm she carries a half-read newspaper, today's *Morning Herald*.

Meanwhile at the house, Marwood and Kate are seated in the front room, sipping tea.

"Well, you must get back to your son. It's true what you told me, Miss Thomas, one cannot live without an heir."

"I know, and just because I was caught in a rainstorm and the roads were so bad. If I hadn't slipped on Great Portland Street…"

"It could've happened to anyone," he says, taking a seat opposite. "It's good to see you again, Julia."

"Thank you, you too, William."

"I'm not sure we can do this again, though. My family is here now. I'm settled in the city."

"You don't need any more fun?" she presses but Marwood does not answer. Kate lays her teacup aside, spilling into the saucer.

"If you don't need a single friend in London, I understand!"

"It's not that. It's only that, I cannot function if I am emotionally compromised."

"Emotionally what?"

"Confused."

"You mean you're in love with me? Maybe we should go to Gretna Green!"

Marwood stares. "No, I don't think this balancing act is for me. I can't endure the high-wire for long—I have too much to lose."

"We've all got something to lose," Kate says, standing. "I don't think I'll stay a second night."

"No, no," Marwood says, soothingly, and he rises to prevent her flight. He touches her shoulders, and Kate, a big woman with powerful arms buried under Mrs Thomas's shawl, openly relaxes. She hasn't quite finished her tea.

They sit. "Can I read you a poem?" Marwood says, surprising his guest.

"Well, of course, William."

As he lifts the book from the shelf, Kate lifts the tea-cup to her face, rolling her eyes. Will I ever get out of here, she wonders?

"Here it is, there's an introduction: 'Miss E. Clark was born in 1826 the sixth daughter of Mr Clark, a gentleman of Bristol. She fell from virtue through 'amorous glances', got pregnant, went to London as a maid, then prostitute. Soon she was discovered with a counterfeit five pound note.'"

"What are you trying to say?" Kate laughs, but her interest is sparked. "What happened to her?"

"It says 'Miss Clark was found guilty and dispatched to Australia for life after her Old Bailey Sessions; she was driven to 'a frenzy of despair' after the court ruled her baby must stay behind."

"Did she escape with him? Why are you telling me all this?"

"No, the boy had to remain in England. But 'Miss Clark addressed some poetry to her 'unborn boy' from the dock.'" Marwood holds up the book and with his best theatrical gesture imitates a woman's voice, only faintly comical:

And when the dark thought of my fate shall awaken
The deep blush of shame on thy innocent cheek;

When by all, but the God of the orphan forsaken,
A home, and a father, in vain thou shalt seek;
I know that the base world will seek to deceive thee,
With falsehood like that which thy mother beguild:
Deserted and helpless—to whom can I leave thee?
O! God of the fatherless—pity my child!

"That's what she said?"

"The very same—a footnote says, 'Miss Clark later gave birth to a girl in prison. Her whereabouts are unknown.'"

"She probably got remarried in Australia, and the kid probably became an English highwaywoman."

"Very true. A happy ending all round." Marwood sighs as he replaces the book. "Does it matter that mother and daughter will never see each other?"

"Maybe she should a' thought o' that before she went trawlin' London. If she keeps 'in the game' in Australia, she'll probably hang a free woman 'down under'!"

Marwood laughs. "I just thought a London tale might cheer you up a little—there are worse things in the world...."

"That not being with your child? I don't know many."

"Hang in there Miss Thomas,"—his mouth open realizing what he's said, "if you'll pardon my pun."

"I forgive you, William."

"You know, hanging is no job for a gentleman. Yet one can become a gentleman by hanging. A terrible irony."

"Only if yer think it's doing something bad."

"I think I'm doing something good," Marwood says innocently.

"I know you do, William, I know you do." They sip their tea.

"You know, there's a former hangman by the name of Gibbon Wakefield. He was the wisest, most humane neck-man and there's been some bad Jack Ketches along the way. Mr Wakefield said: All the world tremble at the thought of dying, and, therefore, behave as if they were born to live forever. Isn't that so?"

"Nice poetic justice."

"True, but there's been some nasty ones too. My predecessor, William Calcraft, by all accounts enjoyed a weekend angling in the New River. He was a devoted rabbit-hunter, a man of simple country habits. Yet he was a full-time sadistic hangman who saw his victims as less than human, more like the animals he'd trap on weekends."

"Well, I'm glad he lost his job."

"Yes," Marwood says. "Drunk in charge of the noose is no laughing matter. Many suffered at his hands."

Here Kate sits up. "But I thought you all had the power of healing, like doctors?"

"Well, you can believe that if you like."

"I do believe it."

"It helps me sell a few ropes on the side, scraps of the condemned man's clothes."

"You get to keep all that?"

"I do, I do. Superstition is what the hangman lives on—curing warts, welts and wens, tumours, cancers, heart palpitations, even love sickness on St Valentine's Day."

"And you believe that?"

"I believe what the public want me to…but I'm not about to cure their illusions."

Kate finishes her tea. "Well, that's all well and good, William, but I must go see my son. I can't cure Daniel's need for me, or mine for him."

"Of course," Marwood says. "The stories go on, though, Julia. Do you know in 1805 after the Battle of Trafalgar a woman exposed her breasts for the dead man's hands to be lain upon them. He was a traitorous sailor killed in action, and she the girl he left behind."

This stops Kate in her tracks. "No, and I don't wish to know that."

"Almost romantic, don't you think?"

"Are you trying to shock me, Mr Marwood?"

"Here's another: 'After Michael Holloway's execution in West Sussex in 1843, a teenage girl sat trembling with the dead man's fingers on her neck for ten minutes. She thought his hand could bring back her dead baby—the one her husband was being hanged for suffocating!'"

"The gallows are truly where miracles happen."

"The hangman is less important than you think," Marwood says, forgetting his guest's worry about her son—he is fresh from the excitement of the previous night. "The hanged man himself serves a greater social need—soothing the crowd."

"How so?"

"Well, consider this...." Marwood takes to his feet and begins strolling about the room. "The condemned man is a criminal god, who functions as the community's redeemer."

"He does?"

"As a quiet redeemer, since he suffers hidden by a hood and dies once. Otherwise he re-enacts the Prometheus myth, the man-God who rebelled against Zeus."

"You mean Christ?"

"Same physical form, different century. In the Greeks' ancient world, the gods were as real as men. Prometheus was a creative spirit, a god who fashioned man out of clay but created him imperfectly. You see Prometheus took pity on his creation, man—who lived in darkness—and so he stole fire from Mount Olympus."

"He was wrong."

"Exactly, for fighting the immortals! He became a criminal and Zeus punished him, like the state punishes,"—Marwood taps his chest—"the wrong-doer, the transgressor, the wayward son."

"So Zeus hanged him from a tree?"

"Worse. He makes Prometheus suffer eternally."

"Like I said—Christianity."

"Not exactly, but he died like the hanged man for us, for the eyes of the crowd. Prometheus was tied to a rock and an eagle devoured his heart every day, and every night it grew back so it could be re-eaten, over and over."

"How is that like the hanged man?"

"Well, it's like the condemned cell. Every night brings the promise of an end and every morning the prisoner wakes to fresh day. Hence Prometheus is the quiet redeemer, saving man because he is like man, weak and selfish, a criminal. On stage the prisoner becomes the hero of the crowd—he drinks and dances, makes a speech and spurns the power of the state."

"Before Zeus has his way."

"Yes, before our Queen has her way."

"So I don't wish to change the subject," Kate says, "but as a wayward mother, I must be getting back to my son. Call me Zeus, but I've got to find my little Prometheus."

"I thought you were staying one more night?"

"I was hoping so. But all this talk—I think I need to get back to Daniel."

"Daniel."

"Yes."

Marwood stops pacing, and calms down. "Yes, of course. Is there anything else I can do, Miss Thomas? You've had quite a shock from yesterday, with your fall."

"No, no," Kate begins, then an idea occurs. "Well, I am thinking of visiting relatives—in Ireland. I wonder if you could lend me some money, just for part of the way."

"Well…"

"I have to take Daniel back home."

"I can help a little," Marwood says. He digs in his pocket and excavates a few guineas. "This will get you to the boat. So you know where you're going?"

"Not really. Last time I went I was living in Liverpool, I took the ferry from Holyhead."

"Well, the direct route from London is best through Wales. Most go from Cardiff. So I didn't know you had relatives in Ireland?"

Kate sees her cue to leave, making sure she pockets the guineas first. "Thank you, William. I shan't be gone for long. It's my grandmother's family in County Cork—just a short visit."

"Oh, really. I visited Cork on my last trip. Which town?"

"I really have to be going, William." Kate's in the hallway now, but forgetting something. "I folded the blankets in the basement, but it's still a mess."

"Don't worry about that." He hands Kate her coat, and secures it around her shoulders. Kate takes her scarf, and in the lingering moment, she kisses him on the cheek.

Marwood is not expecting it, but he does not recoil. "It's good to know someone in London."

"Ireland," Kate says, then regrets the comment. "I'll be back soon."

"I've no doubt."

As he unlocks the front door, Ellen materialises, a ghost teetering on the stoop with Aldous, her hand extended with the key. The moment freezes for all the adults, while Aldous rushes inside and gives his father a hug.

"Miss Thomas," Kate says, "up from Richmond. I'm an acquaintance of your husband." She extends her arm, not in the least mortified and gauging Ellen's embarrassment.

"Oh, pleased to meet you."

"Miss Thomas suffered a fall last night," Marwood explains.

"Oh."

"I have to go," Kate says. "Thank you for the tea." Again the moment lingers.

"Hang on, I recognise you," Ellen says.

Kate smiles, then drifts across the street waving over both shoulders. A horse and carriage passes by, displacing her unseen into Dorset Square and she is gone. Uncertain what has happened, Marwood and Ellen are distracted by city clamour from the facing park, the prison-like railings showing ladies walking their pets, Scottish terriers and beagles, the businessmen on the corner of Gloucester Place and York Street. The world is suddenly absent Miss Julia Thomas, though no one misses Kate or is pining for her lost boy.

Once they are inside, Ellen opens the *Morning Herald* and shows Marwood the picture of 'Miss Thomas'.

"So explain how you know that woman?"

"A casual acquaintance—someone who knows London," Marwood says. "I met her in Covent Garden."

"Well, your new friend is wanted for the murder of Mrs Julia Thomas of Richmond, South London," Ellen says and jams the newspaper under his nose. Marwood stares at it blankly, disbelieving.

"I can't…"

"You can't or won't believe it. And you're supposed to be the hangman. The quiet redeemer, as you're always telling me!"

"No, that's the criminal. I'm just a rope for hire."

"Just keep her away from Aldous and me," Ellen says, "then do what you like!"

"Ellen, it's not like that."

"No, it never is! And she's a criminal—one of your new London friends. Unbelievable!"

Ellen stares him down. But Marwood is so shocked by the photofit—Kate's profile to a tee—he retreats to the basement to work on the shoes his wife has brought, the Horncastle orders. He cannot bring himself to look at the guillotine or the noose. He's still fixing shoes after sundown.

That evening the storm blows over, and Ellen brings him a

fresh cup of tea.

"You'll have to get back to the hanging sooner or later. She'd be a good one, if you ask me."

"I've met the police already," Marwood says without looking up. "They'll have to catch her first."

Chapter 30
The Unrepentant Tide
4th March 1879, Tuesday

The encounter with Ellen having thrown her off track, Kate decides to change her escape route. She picks her way to the river via Tottenham Court Road, mixing with the anonymous crowd, then cuts west to Cannon Street. Down the river, she glimpses the glue factories, their chimneys shooting up smoke at intervals, and is pleased to be escaping the metropolis. As she leaves the City for the north bank, the smells of raspberry jam, raw hides and tanning, the beer and leather shops create a blend of smells indescribable to an outsider—but all they remind Kate of Jonathan Clatter's *Cat and Salutation*, sinking down Bell Wharf, the boys all homeless—and Daniel hidden away in Bleeding Heart Alley. "I can't leave without him, or I've nothing left."

The detour is a mortal risk, but without her Daniel there is no future to lose. So despite her exhaustion of the last two days, the newspaper threats and sense of a noose closing about her neck, Kate once more makes the trip to Bleeding Heart Alley. There she finds Sarah Crease out 'on an errand', and Daniel just inside the room where she left him, playing a game of marbles alone. Kate is overjoyed, and after quickly packing his meagre belongings, they head back to Cannon Street.

"Where are we going?" he asks every few streets.

"To the City," Kate says, but juggles her story. "To St Paul's

Cathedral, except if it's closed, then the train to the countryside."

Daniel enjoys the trip, happy for now to be in his mother's company.

"You're not going to leave me again?"

Kate crouches as the modern new train, bellowing steam and whistles, slows into the platform at Cannon Street. She takes Daniel by the collar. "Never again. We're together now—until the end."

"The end of...?"

"Just the end—which is a long time."

"Okay," he says, genuinely convinced, and she takes him in her arms. Kate senses her tears, the memory of crying when she was a child, but they will not come. Looking over Daniel's shoulder, she has already changed her plan. She remembers that she told Marwood her destination—confided in the hangman of London! How could she have been so stupid?

"I just wanted someone to understand, explain why I am—the way I am." Kate pulls herself together. "He was hardly the one to ask. How could I?"

"Please, I don't understand."

"Neither do I, Danny." Crucial seconds drifting away, they pile onto the train heading for King's Cross.

Within an hour Kate and Daniel are en route to Liverpool, her first home in England. They don't have tickets but stow away near the toilets—Daniel is literally squashed on the luggage shelf. Once the guard has passed, Kate frees him and they sit on fold-down seats between carriages.

Kate watches as Daniel cuts his nails using a small nail file.

"Where did you get that?"

"The school-master gave it me." She does not reply.

In Crewe, they change for Holyhead before arriving in Liverpool. That afternoon, as the sun goes down, Kate books passage on an overnight coal boat for Dublin. At Holyhead they eat in the quiet *Three-Legged Mare*, a beat-down pub down the sea-front. Wordlessly she stares at the steely grey water, so distant down the beach it looks like mud. Daniel has fish and chips, Kate toad-in-the-hole, and for the first time they feel safe. By midnight they are on the boat.

Little do they know, Inspector Sequin and his worthy accomplice Nimrod Jones already have a tip-off. Ellen Marwood claims she was going to the butcher's that evening, but instead she reported her sighting of Catherine Lawler at the York Street police depot, informing the Bow Street Runners. Scotland Yard was quick to react, and as a result, Kate was followed by an officer to Cannon Street. Soon after, Ellen shows her husband the newspaper clippings.

"I never thought they would catch her," he tells himself before Kate's arrest, "or that Ellen would be so swift to report her."

That evening, as he works on his shoe-mending at Gloucester Place, the news spreads fast through the London constabularies. Before Marwood goes to bed, Kate is being followed on the pack-boat to Ireland.

After some rest on the boat, Kate and Daniel hitchhike their way south from Dublin. The day is long, but the weather fortunately mild and dry. Hay carts and water wagons and the occasional farmer's mower 'for a cut-price rate' bring them to County Wexford.

Cill Rathain, literally Church of the Fens, is half a mile between Rosslare Harbour and Wexford town. Another few miles and Kate is 'home from home'—back in Killane—population ninety-six. They are dropped at the bottom of a dirt road, and begin the last walk to the stone white house, gravel yard, and thatched cottage where Kate grew up.

There is little left, and what is left is overgrown. Yet the beauty is unchanged, the brook at the bottom of the garden still making the same peaceful sound Kate remembers from ten years ago; its soft voice reminds her of youth, and her youth lost, the reasons why she left—the poverty of her mother, the abuse at the hands of her uncle. But *that* at least is gone now. All she can hear is the soft, gentle flow of the water. She recollects those lost days in summer when she would sit on the wooden 'stepping point' over the brook, as they called it, and knit a daisy-chain, then take it home for her mother. Some days her mother would not be drinking, and would be delighted; other days only her uncle would be home.

"I was like you," Kate says, leading Daniel up the garden path. "I never really had a father. Who knows what happened to him—no one told me, and I never really found out. Anyway, this is the house I grew up in."

She knocks on the door. A long white gown, flustered-looking and strangely spiky red hair, answers the door. Kate knows only her great-aunt, Gillian Lawler, lives here now.

"Who is it?"

"Catherine, I came back, Aunt Gillian. I brought my boy."

"Boy?"

"Daniel."

The old woman—who must be close to ninety-five—peers at the two strangers, as Kate pushes Daniel, who is openly scared, into the doorway. The old woman ruffles his hair, smiles toothlessly. "Well, you bett'n come in, right n'all."

"Go on."

The boy tumbles inside. Soon, over dinner they learn that Uncle Lawler has long since passed on. Kate's mother is already lost to tuberculosis following her lifelong tobacco-pipe habit.

"She alla's enjoyed a smoke."

"This part of the country," Aunt Gillian says, serving them cabbage soup, the same Kate ate twenty years ago—"gets the most sunshine and least rain in Ireland."

"I remember."

The red hair turns to her. "Why did you leave, child?"

"I was in trouble with the law, you know. We weren't exactly rich."

"Don't be ashamed."

They look at Daniel, guzzling the soup, and decide to say no more. Neither has knowledge that two roving detectives from London, Terry Dowdell and George Macomb, are in County Wexford that night. They are blessed with one final night's sleep.

Kate is herself by the next afternoon, though, and leaving Daniel with his great-aunt, she seeks out a few drinks at *Help The Poor Struggler* in Cill Rathain. She decides staggering back after a skin-full will be the best welcome home.

But she doesn't get that far. She is stopped before midnight from 'helping her poor struggler' to an extra gin n' beer. Dowdell and Macomb enter the pub and with the help of the local constabulary—who watch suspiciously from the door—they produce a royal warrant for her arrest, something Inspector Sequin petitioned in London and signed by Prime Minister Disraeli himself. Dodwell marches over the

Kate where she is propping up the bar, six drinks deep.

"Catherine Lawler."

"Yes?"

"I am here on the Queen's business. I hereby arrest you for the murder of Mrs Julia Thomas of Richmond, South London. 'You have the right to remain silent, but anything you do say will be taken down and may be used in evidence against you.' Do you understand your legal rights?"

During this speech, Kate is regarding a sign behind the bar. By response, she reads:

> But valour the stronger grows,
> The stronger liquor we're drinking,
> And how can we feel our woes,
> When we've lost the trouble of thinking?

"I take that to mean you are in sound mind, Miss Lawler."

"What about my boy?"

"He'll be allowed to stay home. At least until your return."

Kate bows her head, then puts up a physical fight, legs flailing, and it takes both officers to restrain her. She is taken to Enniscorthy Gaol for an hour, and from there to Dublin where she is incarcerated in the Chancery Lane Station behind the Castle.

Eventually Sequin and Jones arrive to take over their charge, pleased to relieve Dodwell and Macomb of their coup, disappointed not to have made the arrest themselves. The first thought in Sequin's mind is that Kate is wearing Julia Thomas's clothing and jewellery.

She is transferred into Bow Street custody outside Chancery Lane near O'Connell Street. A few days pass with Kate alone in the cell. She is fed the same soup her Auntie Lawler is making Daniel but the strangeness of this knowledge fails to lessen the pain of leaving her son. Eventually she can be released for transfer once the parliamentary documents are approved: the British insignia is required in the Irish colony.

On a Friday morning, Kate silently awaits the packet-boat back to London. The guard releases her in handcuffs over to her new London jailors, and all three watch as the boat draws into Dublin Harbour. The inspector gestures to the Irish Sea, grey and flat like a sheet of iron and no sign of the Welsh mountains.

"Why did you do it, Kate?"

"You've got the wrong'un, see. Look for a Nathan Crane—he's the one. He'll tell you everything."

"We've already got Crane and he fingers you. It's your head on the block, Lawler."

"Webster."

Jones breathes in her face. "My first female killer! And guess who we're believin'? You're gonna swing for this one."

Kate stares at him malevolently. "Crane is his name. He's the one wot din'it." She fixes them with her Richmond grin, the same she gave to Mrs Hayhoe at *The Hole in the Wall* when coaxing her over two vats of prize dripping. "You have to charge me—where's the evidence?"

"Don't even bother," Sequin says. "This one's ripe for a confession. The priest'll work her...."

"Jus' 'cos we're in Ireland," Kate says, "don't mean I'm confessin' to nuthin'. You coppers is all the same—a little bark and no bite." She looks to the ocean. "Jus' take care o' my boy or it's your head, I can promise you that, cap'n."

"Well, just off the record, Miss Lawler, how is it Crane's doin' and not yours?"

"I'm tellin' yer, Crane is the one. He's a heavy drinker, first n' foremost. *That* don't help none. I only know 'im 'cos crazy Mrs Thomas does."

"Of course."

They climb aboard and all three shift closer to the rail of the pack-boat, watching the sun go down.

"I can't say much more."

"You'd better squeal and the sooner the better. Or we'll believe Crane's story, see."

"And frankly," Jones adds, "he's a lot more believable."

Kate's story is weak, but she knows it's better to talk. "Listen up, gentlemen! So I return one evening, a Sunday see, and the lights are down. I couldn't find my key, so I knocks...."

Sequin takes over. "Where was your key?"

"In my bag, I dun' like the lights out, see. But I mus' a' found it 'cos no one lets me in. Then I sees her straight away..." Kate widens her eyes in alarm and wonder. "Mrs Thomas is lying in the hall, struggling and groaning, n' there's blood...."

"A lot of blood, Miss Lawler."

"I know, hardening. And there's a card next to the body, thrown down for all to see, clear as day. So I picks it up, and it's Crane's card."

Sequin glances at Jones, folds his arm. "He left his calling card."

"I can think of nothing less convincing."

"It's true," Kate insists, "he wanted you to know. It don't say his name, jus' his address." She produces Nathan Crane's 'calling card' from her pocket, the one he gave her in *The Rising Sun*—with blood smeared on the back. She hands it to Sequin, and he hands it to Jones, who produces a small wooden box and drops it inside.

"First evidence of the case."

"If you discount the body," Sequin says, "and the trunk case, the house, the circumstantial evidence, and the witnesses."

"And the confession," Jones says.

Kate steadies herself against the rail as the packet-boat rocks. "I gave you what you need—a lead."

"We'll follow your lead," Sequin says, and then steps back. "If you think of anything else, Miss Lawler, just step inside. We'll be waiting. Don't stay in the weather all night." Sequin and Jones turn on their heel, Jones offering his best serious expression.

Kate keeps holds of the rail, smiling softly without malice, but she envies them their warm cabin. As a prisoner of the Crown, she will sleep on the lower deck with the night crew and just a few cushions. For now, no one is standing guard. She is free to throw herself in the ocean if she wishes.

"Nothing changes, wherever I go."

She looks over the sea-water, watching the waves roll together then separate, no centre to their movements. The sweep of the whole makes it unclear which is prey and which predator, since all appear to eat each other. The ocean's power under the boat is in charge, she decides, an elemental force ever present but declaring its nature to no one. The sea harbours her human secrets, both good and evil.

She looks up. The sun collapsing on the horizon is a blur of haze, neither blue nor red, somehow disturbing in its incestuous desire for ongoing, brutal life. Kate watches the dance of colour, puzzled but touched by an odd sense of the amorality of our universe, no more feeling herself as wrong-doer than feeling wronged; she remains incapable of seeing Mrs Thomas as a separate entity, only a piece of the whole: "I simply passed on the hurt that was done to me. Why am I the only villain?"

Eventually the sky goes black. When Kate wakes, she knows her life is controlled now, and she is no longer on the packet-boat.

The Irishwoman is back in England, only this time in the North. From Liverpool's Westy Row Station, her prison van rolls through the fields down to Shropshire, through hamlets and past old country pubs, a way of life she left in Wexford a long time ago. Next is West Midlands country, although her route does not enter Lincolnshire. Instead she is en route once more to the metropolis, and in Jones's friendly words "certain to be hanged."

Kate is silent while being ferried around. At last, she is taken to Richmond Police Station where she makes a statement on 5th March and is formally charged with the murder. The statement is read to her by a junior law clerk. Nathan Crane is also accused of 'being responsible' for Mrs Thomas's death and is arrested—discovered at home from the address on his trading card. He is viewed not as accomplice, but full participant. The same day, though, Crane argues for a strong alibi: he was at work in a timber yard all Sunday 23rd February and he is willing to assist police in the further implication of Kate, namely how she came to him on 1st March, acting suspiciously, and offered Mrs Thomas's furniture for sale—items he knew she could not possess by legal means.

At the committal hearing, the charges against Crane are dropped while Kate is remanded in custody. She is transferred to Newgate Prison to save the long journey by the horse-drawn prison van *Black Maria* across London each day for her trial.

The proceedings accelerate and Kate loses touch with distinct hours. Her mind is turbulent and she imagines the ocean rolling, the tides trapped between Ireland and England, forever shunted like an unwanted child. She thinks of Daniel missing her, overworked and enduring a sense of abandonment, ill or in danger, quietly fearing for his life and resenting her. She thinks of her great-aunt back in Killane, of the old house, the memories she does not want to confess.

During her last transfer she hears a snatch of song, whether from a chimney-sweep or child on the way home from school, she cannot tell. But Kate knows the lyrics well, and her humming, head down, turns into a comfort for the journey ahead. "Once I was a girl," she whispers, and the words come from deep inside:

> Two Sticks and Apple,
> Ring ye Bells at Whitechapple,
> Old Father Bald Pate,
> Ring ye Bells Aldgate,
> Maids in White Aprons,
> Ring ye Bells at St Catherines,
> Oranges and Lemmons,
> Ring ye bells at St Clemens,
> When will you pay me,
> Ring ye Bells at ye Old Bailey,
> When I am Rich,
> Ring ye Bells at Fleetditch,
> When will that be,
> Ring ye Bells at Stepney,
> When I am Old,
> Ring ye Bells at Pauls.

"Ring ye bells," Kate whispers alone in the van, and the bells of London will ring, whether St Paul's, St Sepulchre's or St Martin's in the Fields. They all ring for one purpose—for the downtrodden, the sinners—for the humble, the poor and dead-at-heart.

In just a few days, Kate's hair has grown long and tatty. She looks more menacing, like an abandoned pet tricked into a cage, or a dog lost in the fog. She knows they prefer it this way.

Again, the ocean enters her mind, its feeding frenzy, its peace, its sunset. Why did she not throw herself overboard? Then she remembers—but losing Daniel is the worst feeling she's known, doubly pained by her ignominious return to London. What will newspapers say now? What will her enemies, or the courts, tell her boy about his mother? She weeps for Daniel's future heartache and her lack of power to prevent it.

Not three miles away the Thames washes up its own secrets. Soon to be reported by the *Morning Star*, a foot is raised up at

Twickenham—a woman's foot. There is little left, no nails, the skin a hollow flap more like a glove more than human organ. A fisherman's boy plucks the foot from the water, and his father hands it to the nearest patrolling officer.

"Best catch of the day?" the bobby says, and the fisherman just stares. The boy watches all, sickened and yet fascinated by the severed foot.

Within the hour, the river's new evidence is declared to be match for Mrs Julia Thomas. Anger is stirred again at Scotland Yard, but by now, the suspect is in custody. The foot is a marker of the tide coming home.

Tomorrow is the first day of her trial, this chameleon of no fixed address but Newgate. At last, Catherine Lawler *aka* Kate Webster must 'toe the line' of colonial power. The Crown awaits— her past can no longer stay buried.

Part Three
Steady, Steady, This Won't Hurt a Bit

Be cheerful, sir.
Our revels now are ended. These our actors,
As I foretold you, were all spirits and
Are melted into air, into thin air:
And, like the baseless fabric of this vision,
The cloud-capp'd towers, the gorgeous palaces,
The solemn temples, the great globe itself,
Yea all which it inherit, shall dissolve
And, like this insubstantial pageant faded,
Leave not a rack behind. We are such stuff
As dreams are made on, and our little life
Is rounded with a sleep.

William Shakespeare, *The Tempest* (1611)

Chapter 31
The Virginia and Maryland Coffee House
7th March 1879, Friday

Marwood goes for a walk to escape the basement and Ellen is only too pleased to see him leave. She needs to arrange the house, and find Aldous a temporary tutor for their stay in London until school resumes in March.

All London is abroad, four o'clock closing on the weekend. The sun has already dipped out of sight. Baker Street is dark so Marwood decides to walk to Central London quickly, taking Great Portland down to Oxford Street.

On the corner of George Street he passes 'the game of cups'—a fraud with a history of a thousand years laid out on a small folding table, three paper cups and three peas. Londoners cannot stray too far from gambling, any street entertainment with a cocktail of humour and possible winnings. The odds are called to passers-by, all manipulated by a scrawny young woman, red hair flailing, white apron hinting at innocence. She plies her trade to punters like a rabbit teasing greyhounds, dapper businessmen and workmen in overalls, a few stray boys hankering like cats at the table edge. "Find the pea, choose yer favourite cup, double yer money. I only got slow 'ands... slow 'ands."

Immediately Marwood spies the 'stooge', the man in the crowd on the side of this angel whose job is to stoke the gamblers into an elevated sense of excitement, certainty, popularity—all on a

Friday afternoon. Marwood likes a game of ingenuity, but he is practised in their crafty illusions. The red-headed girl shuffles the cups and switches the centre twice, folds three together, separates them out. A laugh from the crowd calls out 'foolishness', but Marwood has his hand extended to the left cup.

"This one."

"You 'ave to place a bet sir—any time is good. Half a crown for yer choice."

"Can I change my cup?"

"Do it now."

"Then I bet a full crown on the middle cup. But I want to turn it over myself." There's a shuffle with a shove in the crowd and an odd-looking man is at Marwood's side, moustache up to his cheeks, bowler pulled low.

"You can't," the girl says. "You point out the cup, place your money on the top. I turn-s the cup, see."

"Okay, let's play another round."

She spins the cups, lifts them slow, flicks one over another with her little finger, getting a laugh. She separates them fast, places one big pea—the size of a small peach stone—under the right-side cup; she crouches and begins the slow circular movements and the crowd falls quiet, watching every move. The middle cup literally becomes the edge cup, vice versa, and the right-side cup appears to be in the middle, left, now back on the right. Someone even points.

"There," Marwood says, gesturing to the left cup. He places his little finger on its nose. She lifts the cup, and there is the pea.

"You win," the girl says, looking up with no feeling. She hands him the crown and his extra coin, pressing them in his palm. "Welcome to George Street—you're a regular customer now."

They play a second round and Marwood wins again using the same pattern, but the hangman is not encouraged to stay. As the third game begins he quits and slides into the crowd. The man in the bowler is watching him, arms folded; like a toffee apple on a string, drawing his 'evil eye' is followed by a military-fast approach and a jab in the ribs.

"You're not wanted here."

"Really? I could have told you that."

The boss-man points. "See that table, that girl, that corner. That's mine, okay. You know somethin' lad, cos she couldn't play da game, right." His nails grab part of Marwood's belly and twists. "You put a spell on 'er, so dun'yer come back now. London's a small place."

"And you'll find me."

"Yeah."

Marwood raises his hand as though to slap the man, who—a little surprised—lets go, and the hangman merely adjusts his black hat. "I appreciate the warning. If you want to find me, I'll be at Newgate Prison for the next few weeks."

The man looks puzzled. "You's a cage-bird?"

"No, sir. I'm the Queen's hangman." And he tips his hat. He turns on his heel then looks over his shoulder and sees his watcher still frowning. The pea-man flicks his fingers into a 'V' to encourage Marwood's departure, then folds him arms, restating proprietorship over his 'game of cups'.

"Good riddance, laddy!"

Marwood does not look back. Quietly he rolls the two crowns over his little fingers, smiles. And yet he does not know how he won.

"Perhaps I'm clairvoyant after all."

In the peculiar resonances of the mind, the day seems optimistic now. Soon he reaches 'club row' in Leicester Square, a placard on Panton Street announcing the street's hidden gems—for the pleasure of gentleman's minds. In four upstairs lounges above four pubs, you'll find the King's College Club, the Bar Bar for the Crown's barristers and A Common Married Man's Club for the Over 60s, an exclusive old den of London politicians, proud of their long-suffering marriages, their slogan being 'neither power at home nor abroad'.

Marwood observes the placard, a brass plate dug into the brick wall, for a description of all the other clubs. There's a Surly Club at a Smithfield **'sherry room'** for gentleman to pass the evening in **'colourful, ideally malicious swearing'**; a Liars' Club at the *Bell Tavern* in Westminster where **'no truth'** would be spoken; a Humdrum Club where men smoke pipes in silence until midnight, the only requirement being **'peaceable dispositions whether ball and chained, lifelong bachelors or otherwise'**; a Walking Wasters' Club where **'no water is tolerated on the premises'**; an Everlasting Club where three hundred and sixty-five members divide twenty-four hours to guarantee continual operation, each serving a full day a year and **'no person presuming to rise until he was relieved by his appointed** successor'; finally there's The Crunch Club in Crippelgate where gentleman of aristocratic heritage enjoy **'noisy crepitations to outfart one another for purpose of vigorous relaxation'.**

Marwood screws up his nose and traces his finger down a list of 'cutter clubs' for men-of-means, those with boats moored down the Thames from Deptford to Westminster. At last he finds the Law-Lord's Club that meets at *The Rainbow*, a coffee joint. After asking a stranger in Trafalgar Square, he winds his steps to this establishment—a new phenomenon in the city—off Fleet Street by the gate of the Inner Temple. He is greeted as soon as he steps through the door.

"William Marwood, I presume," and hands are shaken, "I'd recognise you anywhere. I just got in myself."

"Thank you, I mean, pleased…"

"Justice Denham, please call me David. Take a seat—I trust *all this* is relatively new to you." He gestures to two bar stools.

"Yes, London is new," Marwood says, clearing his voice. "The position is something I have experience with…"

"Hanging," Denham says. He is a tall man, with a bushel of blond hair arranged on his head like a swirl of ice-cream. His cheeks are glowing from the cold.

"That's right, but I'm not sure why I'm here. I had a telegram from Mr Cottonwell."

"Ah, Cottonwell," Denham says as though his meaning is perfectly clear. "There's a prize bureau-crat, if you see what I mean." A pasty expression hangs from the judge's freckles as though manipulated by marionette strings. "We'll see that one go far. Politics is a slippery slope I avoid, a dirty business." He laughs immediately, somehow giving the maxim a new truth.

"Yes, well, I am here about business," Marwood says. "I believe I'm due a commission. There are men in Newgate sentenced, all but executed. Not that I want to speed things up…"

"No no, heavens, of course not." He pats Marwood on the back. "I quite understand, I truly do. Now first things first…" Denham swivels his wiry frame to order their drinks; there's a comical obsequiousness about his desire to set his guest at ease, some unfathomable essence of personality.

Marwood looks at the bar expecting dark wood, but finds it hand-painted with rainbow colours. He can't quite trust his surroundings. Steel stein mugs—doubling at night for beer—hang upside down on a thin rail. The overwhelming odour of coffee is everywhere, a bitter richness floating like priceless dust. Denham rotates back to face him.

"Wonderful drink. Good for the heart and soul—and concentration, they say. I buy it for all my young clerks. They can't get enough."

"I've never tried it."

Denham spurts his first sip onto the bar. "Well sir, where have you been? We've seen a killer rush of coffee in the City. All from the naval islands and colonies—you must get in on the act!"

"Exporting?"

"No—drinking!" He slaps Marwood on his shoulder, agitating him given the assault from the pea-man on George Street. "All legal of course! I can't believe you've hardly tasted it."

"It doesn't really make it to Lincolnshire."

"Well, coffee's been in London since 1652—I'm a student of its divinity." He leans in. "Between you and me though, I can't stand the taste. You should try 'the Turkish drink' at St Michael's Alley, off Cornhill. That's the original home."

"That and the colonies," Marwood says, but gets no response from Denham. While the big man continues his diatribe on the rising fortunes of 'the Turkish drink', Marwood begins examining his surroundings, amazed by the culture of coffee he's so long avoided. The 'young agitator' is served in narrow wooden dishes with a candle in the hole at the end. Now and then a waiter pours the cooling drink in their glass steins, or you can drink it directly from the dish.

"Expensive stuff, though," Denham is saying. "You could try 'The Grecian' or 'The Cocoa-Tree'. Sometimes I smoke a pipe over at *The Amazonian*—and I don't mean tobacco."

"Sounds just a gentleman's club," Marwood says. "It's not enough to meet in public? We have to be cutting deals in dark rooms."

Denham regards him like a provincial out-of-towner, though not quite country bumpkin. "I'm sorry, Mr Marwood. But London is business. You're quite right—there's no time to waste in this city— and we all take our recreation with our business partners."

"Or you fall behind."

"Precisely. So if you prefer, we can adjourn to *The Jerusalem* in

Cornhill, haven of the West Indies sugar trade, if this place isn't sweet enough. You seem to have an international concern for London's imports."

"Not in the least, I just like to know where my meat comes from."

"And I too, Mr Marwood. Or where it was killed."

A pause lasts too long between them—overcome by Denham blowing on their coffee dish. The Justice serves Marwood the oily black liquid. "Seriously, we can go somewhere else more private. There's the *Old Slaughter Coffee House* in St Martin's Lane, generally for artists. Do you consider yourself a rope artist, Mr Marwood?"

"I'm a cobbler by trade. Not an artist."

"But I've heard you are the best...cobbler."

Again, they stare.

"I hold my own with the ropes."

"Or there's *The Roman* for lawyers is in Devereaux Court—solicitors, I mean—not my kind of practitioner. Of course, on the north side of Russell Street, Covent Garden, there's *Will's*, for city wits and authors. Dr Samuel Johnson of *Dictionary* fame's honoured on the wall there.... I feel, though, we may be outsmarted."

"That's a safe bet," Marwood says. He blows on the coffee then returns the favour by serving Denham. Neither man fails to notice the symbolism of their mutual servings.

"Now Justice Denham, I mean—David. Please can you tell me why Cottonwell requested we should meet?"

"Well, sir. Let me tell you—it's a matter of private legal business. That's why this coffee house is helpful." He waits as the waiter clears a table. "You see, we have a prisoner. We feel the event—the last hours—could be mighty popular. You see, it's an election year. So to put it crudely, we need a certain outcome."

"I don't follow you."

"A guilty verdict."

Marwood stops. "I believe that's for the Old Bailey to decide."

"And you believe right—the evidence is there, more than enough, but we need to know you're on board."

"Mr Denham, your meaning escapes me—are you asking me to be on a jury?"

Denham's whole frame swings back in alarm, his blond ice-cream swirling. "Good heavens, man, of course not. We're not involved in a conspiracy here, we just need a good old show." He nods at Marwood, adjusting his hair. "You're on our side, William."

"As opposed to whose?"

"Well, that is why Mr Cottonwell desires your company, along with the mayor."

"Of London…"

"Yes, they requested *The Virginia and Maryland Coffee House.* Sheriff Constable believes it has a certain quizzical charm—it's on the river. I don't suppose you know it, formerly *The Baltic* on Threadneedle Street."

"No, I don't. But tell me what you mean by a guilty verdict. There'll be a trial?"

"Of course there's a trial, dear boy—we must have a show. It's just that we need to plan the outcome, since the election's next month. The House of Lord goes to vote on the 14th and the Commons even earlier, on the 1st."

"Of April?"

Denham stares at his drink. "Rather comical date, I admit. Listen, Mr Marwood, you don't seem to be taking this to heart. Perhaps the coffee has gone to your head. You have a family, I see."

Marwood says nothing, then: "And whose business is that?"

"You have a boy. Eleven isn't he?"

"What are you saying?"

"So, if I were you, I'd take the trial *as read,*—well, you'll do the right thing."

With these words Justice Denham is up, his six foot four frame lolling to the door and crouching for the beams. His black coattails flap in the doorway, his freckled complexion and soft features at odds with his casually concealed abrupt manner. "I trust you for the bill."

Marwood sits in shock. He watches the door swing back, imagines Denham slipping back to the Inns of Court or perhaps one of the cocktail clubs in the West End, and sinks his elbows on the bar. In the distance Big Ben chimes the hour, already nine o'clock. A draught of cold air follows the barrister's departure, but the odour of coffee overpowers all—the feeling of memory being burned away by fire, reflecting the turmoil inside Marwood, not a baptismal or righteous fire, but an ordinary accident like the bread in a baker's shop.

He catches the eye of the barman and orders a gin, downs it in one.

"Two poisons for the day, sir."

"One poison, and one antidote," Marwood says. He orders one for the road and 'all the printing presses' of Fleet Street. He pays the tab and is soon grateful for London's dirty air, pleased to see the back of the strange, rainbow-coloured bar and her coffee delights.

Taking Charing Cross down to Embankment, he heads along the north bank of the Thames and soon approaches Threadneedle Street. What does Cottonwell mean by 'guilty verdict'? Do they really have such a high profile prisoner? Why involve him at all? The whole incident is a challenge to his usual steady balance.

"Perhaps there are no answers. Perhaps coffee and gin weren't the best idea." Looking out at the river, he thinks of his wife and boy back home in the lounge, Aldous writing his maths 'long division', Ellen knitting for St David's Catholic Church, the wind at the window a common comfort. Then he's distracted by the call of a sailor, a hand-wave from a timber barge approaching Practical Quay too fast, but it's not for him, but for a woman—the sailor's wife—on the jetty, tying the ropes with gusto, as though here comes Odysseus after a ten-year voyage and she has been faithful.

Behind her, the river is just smog, the fog of an overcrowded city, 'six million wasted lives'. Marwood smiles without understanding his feelings. He is troubled by Denham's words, by carrying the secrets of powerful men. "I am a tug," he thinks, glancing at the river, "looking for its anchor ship, lost somewhere on the riverbank."

Wind whistles over the water.

"Yes, I have a family. How could he even ask me those questions?"

"I know, I know," the wind calls.

Marwood almost laughs. Wrapping his coat tighter, he turns up an alley. On the corner, he politely accosts a man setting up a ladder to clean the upstairs windows of a pub, *The Cow n' Bell*, and learns he's passed *The Virginia and Maryland Coffee House*, the floating meeting-point. So he retraces his steps to the wharf past the metal hooks for hauling boats, all the while seeking the bitter coffee scent over the river's dirty water, odours he's fast becoming immune to. But there's no sign of the extravagant-sounding boat.

Only when he's hailed from under a street lantern does Marwood realise. "Mr Hangman, sir," someone calls, the note of self-amusement clear. "This way—I hope you don't mind if we got comfortable."

Marwood turns and passes Threadneedle Street once more, the Thames edging the pavement in a hidden miniature loop. There, tied in an inland jetty tight against the rubble of the street, is the face behind the voice.

"Mr Cottonwell."

"It is I."

Marwood steps down into the boat—a long twenty-foot barge painted in Union Jack stripes—and shakes his hand. A short man land-lubbing, Cottonwell on the Thames is shorter than ever, a giddy fish out of water as a city bureaucrat on a desirable excursion. "Welcome to my proud boast of an abode!"

"Forgive his theatrics, Mr Marwood," says a second man, appearing from under the hull. "You may remember me from the unfortunate business with Charles Peace."

"Yes, sir. We didn't have much time. William Marwood."

"Constable—Frederick. As you know, I'm up for re-election."

"I've heard that, sir."

"Nonsense, really—Cottonwell can tell you all about it." The Mayor of London grins like an old whale exposing yellow teeth, the same burly authority he was at the Newgate Drop. "Now, about this coffee business...."

"Coffee, sir?"

"Coffee. You like the stuff?"

"Not especially, sir. I just had my first brush with the brown oil."

"What?" Both city men stare at the hangman.

"I mean, I just met with Justice Denham and he introduced me to new roast coffee not half an hour ago."

"We know," Cottonwell says. "We set up the meeting. Suffice to say it went well?"

"Well, that's why I wanted to inquire..."

"Naturally—and that's why we brought you here." The mayor cups him round the shoulder. "Denham loves his African coffee. Let's go inside, Mr Marwood. We have a few deals to make. You like

London, I take it?"

Marwood endures the small talk as before, but is soon distracted by the floating house. He cannot decide if it's a bar, a restaurant, pub or coffee den—not to mention a working boat—so he settles on not deciding. The mayor gestures to an unseen landing point in the fog. "We used to be moored off the jetty by Somerset House, and called *The Magnificent Folley*, but that got too expensive. We're now *The Virginia and Maryland Coffee House*—'home away from home'."

"Another colonial theme," Marwood says.

"Excuse me?"

"I mean," Marwood says, "coffee is the bean of the New World, so very appropriate."

"Well, our American cousins are great believers in the future of coffee," the mayor says, "at home and aboard. So despite our little differences over the War of 1812, we named this boat as a symbol of future understanding."

"I thought Virginia was more a cotton state."

"It was once, but now its harbours all export coffee. Alexandria, Virginia—the old slave port—has a large processing plant, and ships refined beans back to the Old World. Cottonwell will give you the tour."

The mayor now hands his guest to his right-hand man, who delivers as a seasoned tour guide: "This boat—as you saw from the outside—is a bulky man-of-war, but one intended for pleasure—a 'coffee palace' if you will. It's divided into several rooms, for cocktails, coffee, tea. It's not all about the magic bean."

"That's good."

The guide frowns, clearly not in favour of comments. Marwood is led off the deck into a second room where two ladies and a sour-looking gentleman are playing backgammon, the coffee dish noticeably larger than at *The Rainbow*. From here Cottonwell beckons them down carpeted steps to a partitioned lower deck. Each room contains gambling pews with upright narrow seats, smoking lamps and air-restricted spluttering candles. The second room is the largest and triples as counting-house, auction room and navigation office.

"Very similar to *Garraway's*," the guide adds, waving his hands. "Coffee, alcohol and muffins served to encourage the bidding."

"What are these?" Marwood asks, pointing.

"Sleeping bunks, after the boat party."

"Naturally." Marwood peers through one of the port-holes, but the water is murky.

"We're almost done—this is the final space."

The stern of the boat opens into an oval-shaped room with polished mahogany tables, oil-lamps and in-folding French shutters with green curtains.

"Here we eat," Cottonwell continues. "Lamb chops and kidneys, bread and pickles."

On a giant table for London's finest political council—no doubt visited by the Prime Minister and the Queen herself—are plates of solid silver, iron forks, but no knives "for fear of customers murdering each other. You see, the ship has all the 'doubtful cake', scones and bread pudding anyone could eat." In a crystal decanter peering from wall-to-wall cabinets are countless bottles of Beaujolais.

"No knives," Marwood says.

"Safety."

"But there's a huge salt cellar, if guests want to clobber one another." Marwood picks up the weighty leaden object, taps it on the side of his head—but Cottonwell is not amused.

They ascend back to the upper desk where the beaming mayor has come to greet them. Together, the mayor and hangman look out over the fog-covered Thames, a glossy shine on the black waves reflected by low-floating clouds. The far side remains invisible.

"Kop's ale," the mayor says, and passes out three glasses.

"Not coffee?" Marwood jokes.

"The new drink is just for show. This is a real drink." All three men—Cottonwell included—raise their glasses. Lowering the toast, Marwood notices a sign on the wall: "Pocketing the sugar is not allowed." He wonders what the punishment would be, a few days in the galleys no doubt...

"So Mr Marwood, I've come to give you your commission. You are to oversee the hanging of Kate Webster, Catharine Lawler, also known as Julia Thomas." Marwood blurts his Kop's Ale over the side of the boat.

"I..."

"That's your job as hangman, isn't it? To do what we wish?" Sheriff Constable frowns. "I mean—to professionally execute your royal mandate."

Marwood looks at his hosts, his hands. Suddenly he pours the rest of his beer in the Thames, not quite believing what he's doing, but sensing his own conviction. "My job is to perform the orders of the highest criminal court in the country, the Old Bailey, no more and no less. I take my job quite seriously, and I am directed by the court, the judge and jury."

"But you're the final law—the executioner."

Marwood regards Cottonwell. "Yes, but the hangman is only the handle of justice, I mean, the hand, the unmoved mover. I carry out the sentence. Nothing more!"

"You are the rower in the boat, but not the coxswain," the mayor says, then glances at Cottonwell. "I used to row at Cambridge as a boy. I understand what Marwood is telling us. He's not a thinker—he's a doer, a man-of-action. Well if that case, Mr Marwood, we ask you to perform your duties to the utmost." He flicks his lounge coat over his shoulder. "Only do, Mr Marwood, only do not think. Honour this great city and we shall all get along famously."

"I will, sir. But are you sure you've caught the right woman?"

"Denham told you, didn't he? In any event, you may be invited to a party here afterwards. Meet the prime minter."

"Or the Queen. Bring the whole family."

"The point is, Mr Marwood, we need your help. You perform this one service for us—and we'll see your little Dublin problems with Cato Street go away. Disappear!"

Cottonwell fingers make an explosion in front of his face. "We hear you've been given some trouble back in Horncastle, from a couple of Irish roughnecks twins—the Tooley brothers."

"That so, Mr Marwood?"

"Nothing the Mayor of Horncastle can't handle."

The Mayor of London laughs. "Well, we can make that problem vanish—in an instant." He clicks his fingers, *clip*, and grins. "In the meantime, you're on board, and you'll behave yourself." He reaches into his waistband and hauls out an engraved *dieu et mon droit* gold medallion, symbolic of his governing powers. "Or else it's the Tower of London for you, my boy." The mayor rocks with merriment.

"I'd become a high-born criminal?"

"I'm joking, of course...." The mayor grins like a demented Cheshire cat, but the hangman looks quite serious, and begins questioning his present company.

"Anyone for more Kop's Ale?" Cottonwell says, gently topping up Marwood's empty glass.

Chapter 32
A Lady's Confession
8th March 1879, Saturday

Marwood makes it to Central London early the next day so he can avoid the beggars outside Newgate Prison. There are no visiting hours, so he just lines up with the mass of bodies—wives, children and men with unknown purpose—before the giant façade. For a brief moment, he lays his hand on the stone walls, thinking of the girl inside. It is still dark, the sun rising into the smog covering the Old Bailey. As the iron gate swings back, he glances up at the Central Criminal Court, craning his neck to the statuesque figurine of Lady Justice high on her golden spire. The iron gate opens, the portcullis lifts, the smog rolls back—transferring an indiscernible fear—and darkness envelops him.

Once inside Marwood passes through the press-yard, empty at this time of morning. A soft lining of dew has fallen in the night, giving the press-weights—used to extract confessions—an eerie misty glow despite lack of sunshine. Marwood walks the white line along with other 'outsiders' and is led towards a grand central hall, but not before passing the gibbets. He has seen gibbets before, swaying opposite Blackall and downriver at Bugsby's Hole or the Navy gallows, but never like this. Here is death-in-life, the Ancient Mariner left to rot before your eyes, doing penance for trading with the Devil.

"They restock every two weeks," a man says at his shoulder, "often enough to get a fresh stench."

Marwood looks up at a man and woman, side by side in separate cages, with a sign looped between them on a rope. Its red painted letters announce: 𝕯𝖎𝖓𝖌, 𝖉𝖔𝖓𝖌, 𝖙𝖍𝖊 𝖇𝖊𝖑𝖑𝖘 𝖆𝖗𝖊 𝖌𝖔𝖓𝖓𝖆 𝖈𝖍𝖎𝖒𝖊! 𝕿𝖍𝖊𝖞 𝖜𝖊𝖗𝖊 𝖒𝖆𝖗𝖗𝖎𝖊𝖉 𝖎𝖓 𝕹𝖊𝖜𝖌𝖆𝖙𝖊, 𝖓𝖔𝖜 𝖙𝖍𝖊𝖞'𝖗𝖊 𝖌𝖔𝖓𝖓𝖆 𝖉𝖎𝖓𝖊! Marwood sees all before clamping his eyes back on the walking white line. The man is naked and facing the wall, ribs jutting through his back like fish neck-bones, hands crossing his chest; the woman is still wearing her clothes, a single shawl, her arms eaten to the bone by crows, neck muscles twisted like copper wire, legs buckled as though she had only just collapsed. He remembers her face most, the eyes in the sockets half ashen, half black, with a faint supplicating plea of surprise and remorse, the broken teeth with a false expression of welcome. "Two weeks," the old man says. "They're due for the pit." Hanging from the gibbets are hand-painted signs. Her placard says: 𝕱𝖔𝖗 𝕭𝖔𝖉𝖎𝖑𝖞 𝕱𝖆𝖛𝖔𝖚𝖗𝖘 𝖔𝖓 𝖙𝖍𝖊 𝕲𝖗𝖔𝖚𝖓𝖉𝖘 𝖔𝖋 𝕳𝖆𝖒𝖕𝖙𝖔𝖓 𝕮𝖔𝖚𝖗𝖙 𝕻𝖆𝖑𝖆𝖈𝖊, 1878. 𝕿𝖗𝖎𝖈𝖐 𝖋𝖔𝖗 𝕳𝖊𝖗 𝕸𝖆𝖏𝖊𝖘𝖙𝖞. His replies: 𝕱𝖔𝖗 𝕯𝖊𝖆𝖑𝖎𝖓𝖌 𝕾𝖙𝖔𝖑𝖊𝖓 𝕲𝖔𝖔𝖉𝖘 𝖋𝖗𝖔𝖒 𝖙𝖍𝖊 𝕶𝖎𝖓𝖌'𝖘 𝕷𝖆𝖗𝖉𝖊𝖗, 1877. 𝕽𝖔𝖙 𝖎𝖓 𝕻𝖎𝖊𝖈𝖊𝖘.

Marwood shields the sight, cupping his nose. The visitors' line passes into the bowels of Newgate, arriving before a guide with a table. He signs his name on the visitors' chalkboard, making the swirl as unintelligible as possible, using his son's name. Above a hallway of cobblestones washed clean that morning, he hears clanking, the occasional wail, a plaintive muffled singing. The hallway narrows to a twisty passageway like in a castle, and then emerges into a grand holding cell. His fellow visitors disperse to the cages, counting the inmates, and Marwood is left standing there clueless.

A 'clink' approaches him, an alarmingly fat man with a pock-marked face. "Don't be fooled," he says, waving a wooden stick. "I got a knife too."

"Good to know."

"Who'd you want? We got horse-stealers, forgers, wiredrawers, brush-makers, printers, servants, porters, tailors, errand-boys."

Another guard, the pock-man's thin alter ego, appears at his elbow: "Or smiths, painters, sawyers, brass-founders, grooms, chair-carvers, drapers, whip-makers, steel-polishers, plasters, glass-cutters."

"You don't use numbers?" Marwood says.

"Names," the double act says, and waits. "You need the list again?"

"No, Webster is the name. Or Lawler, I'm not sure. You could try Julia Thomas."

"No, Thomas. We got a Webster-Catherine, though, holding cell four."

"Four."

"Four. Be careful, we've washed down the walls with toxic vinegar—to get the ventilation going. Don't touch the bars, neither."

"I won't."

Marwood begins his walk gingerly past the holding cells, glancing along dirty walls, and counting to four. The distance is only a matter of paces, each cell being only a dozen feet at the bars, but incredibly deep inside. There appears to be a pecking order, where the biggest men are at the bars, the smaller ones deeper in the dungeon. The second group cell appears to have older boys, the third old men, and the fourth women.

He stops. "Katherine Webster?" A short woman with a face like a round anvil is holding the bars, eyes narrow with suspicion.

"Who's askin'?"

"Her husband."

The woman laughs. "Lawless, your man's 'ere. Come giv' 'im a kiss." There's a giggle from inside, some pushing to get a view. "No one visits *me*, sweetie."

"Next time," Marwood says.

The fat guard appears at his shoulder. "You got fifteen minutes," and to Marwood's surprise he unlocks the cage after hitting the bars for the women—about thirty—to step back. "We only do this for number four."

Unconcerned, the women are scattered along low-slung seats hooked to the walls, some knitting, others picking nails, most just staring into space. The click is unconcerned, twists the key and opens two bars on a hinge. Breathing in, Kate squeezes her body through a space just wide enough for a child—she looks at Marwood.

"Thank you. No one else has come."

"I have news—believe it or not, from the mayor." He senses the women listening, so the guard gestures to the wooden table ten feet away. "Don't touch the wall," he warns. As they sit facing each other, female prisoners crowd the bars.

"I can't believe you're here, William." She takes his hand, but he pulls it away.

"I have to give you the news."

She frowns, and her expression borders on frightening. Clearly the trip to Ireland and the prison shock has taken its toll. Still, the incongruity of the real Mrs Thomas's clothes—no prison overalls—does not escape him.

"I need to know the truth, Miss Lawler."

"The truth?"

"From the beginning."

Kate shuffles around, already uncomfortable. "That would be *a deal!*" She laughs, placing her hand by accident on the wall; it burns with the disinfectant vinegar and she pulls it off, wraps it in Mrs Thomas's shawl. "Don't worry, I do it all the time." A shriek of merriment comes from the cage, and echoes before the inmates hush up to listen.

"You know, the men in here are 'rats', n' women are called 'mice'," she says, pointing. "But those women ain't no mice!"

"And neither are you."

"What do you mean?"

"I've seen the gibbets," Marwood says. "They put them up twenty at a time in Newgate Street. And if you avoid those, they save a 'married couple' box for you on the inside. What I'm saying is, Kate—you wouldn't be here without good reason…"

"I'm innocent."

"Of what? It's time you told me the truth. The story that put you here. Right or wrong, it's your only chance—I might be able to influence the council."

"The court?"

"I've met some people on the outside. Powerful people."

Kate is quiet, seems to consider. "I fear the gibbet the most, the exposure. Anything else, even your job, I can live with—I can die too, fair n' square. So let the people have what they want.…"

"What do you mean?"

She leans in. "With half a life, you chuck the rest away. I don't want to be displayed like a rat in a cage, chilled to the bone *after death!*—it's enough I have to live with a bunch of animals.…"

A jeer from the cage!

"I fear the gibbet more than dissection, or the public trial. William, you have to hear me, don't let them display my body."

Marwood shifts in his seat. "It won't come to that. Listen, you tell me your story, like you're already at trial—the truth. Then all will be fine. I can prevent the gibbet."

"But you don't know what they can do, William. Hanging's first, then you's tipped with tallow and fat, poked with a long branch, an' stuck with a tarred shirt that only peels away with your skin. You're fastened with iron bands...."

"I know, then hung in the gibbet to fall to dust. I've read the newspapers too, Kate. I've seen the iron cages. It's a spectacle not of measure, but of cruelty and excess. To give pause to the criminals. Don't even think about it...."

"I can't stop thinking about it!"

The women in the crowded cell start banging on the bars. "Put her in the gibbet!" one of them cries. "She's guilty as an old crow...."

Kate scowls at the bars, her expression reminding Marwood of his purpose. "Your story, Kate—I must have it."

After more humming and harring, Kate says: "I've had a hard life n' not always made the right decisions, but I'm not guilty of murder. I'll deny it 'til my dying day." Again the hysterical laugher, so she leans over the table and whispers, much to the annoyance of her *compadres*. "I was born in County Wexford, Ireland, in a hole in the ground. A throwaway little village called Killane. Very pretty when the sun goes down s' you'd forget about life."

"I need to know your crimes."

"This *is* my story. It was a poor wasted life, with nothing to recommend it. Like the old poem, William—

As. Soone. As. Wee. To. Bee. Begvnne:
We. Did. Beginne. To. Bee. Vndone.

Except mine's the truth. I was abused by my half-brother, and my father did nothing. Would you stay, I ask you? Killane is six miles from Enniscorthy—I had an uncle who was a farmer, and he'd make that six miles, and he'd hurt me too. Sometimes they did it together, all of them, when my mother was out."

"You can't tell that to a jury..."

"Why not? That's my past life—my first ex-communi-cation. Good Roman Catholics, we all got a story." Kate smiles. "That's when my mother died. So I got married—maybe I was fifteen—to a sea captain, so he claimed, name o' Webster. The British Merchant Navy said 'he was goin' up the fleet'. The world his oyster, said I was his pearl, but then I realised—I was t' keep the home fires burnin'…."

"Go on."

She looks at the table, then at Marwood. "I had four children, but all died before I was seventeen. Fortunately he 'bought it' too—that's Killane. And that's why I wanted out. I had a chance at last…"

"Kate, it's a bit of a yarn."

"It's true—all true! Yes, I got imprisoned in Ireland for petty theft. That's why I changed my name to Lawler. But I'm an honest Webster, you can check the Dublin 'family annals'."

"Kate, it's not your heritage that worries me, it's your crimes."

"I ain't got none!" She pouts her lip and folds her arms, much to the amusement of the women in the cage. "Nothing wot like they's accusing me of."

Marwood lays his palms up on the table, curls his fingers. "You have to play their game, Kate. If you don't give them something, they'll take it all, see, and you'll end up in the gibbet."

"Listen," she says, surprising Marwood. "As a child my half-brother—the oldest son, the one who abused me—he'd also read me stories. That's how he took advantage. One story I've never forgotten—the story of the Prague lady called Elizabeth Báthory. You heard o' her?"

"No, but Kate, please…"

"Listen. She was a courtier or countess or some-it, n' she used to kill all these young girls in the town, dozens of them. Not 'cos she was in fear o' her life, or these girls threatened 'er power, but ju' for the thrill o' it. She used to bathe in their blood, so the tale goes, 'cos she thought it good for her skin. Now, you don't think I'm like Báthory?"

"Of course not, Kate, and that's a just legend, a myth like Dracula of Transylvania." Marwood changes his tact. "Everything has a root in truth, though, you're right. So you must explain how you ended up here, or I'll refuse you further help." He crosses his arms.

Kate squints, knows he's serious. "Help me too much an' we'd be a matching pair, just like in the gibbet, ha hah. Okay, okay. I robbed lodging-houses in Liverpool—but not London, mind. I'm a clever actress too, yes, and a good liar. But those ain't capital crimes, is it?"

Marwood stares at her. "Were you ever sentenced in Liverpool?"

"No, not once. You see, William, you dun't *need* to be a criminal to end up in Newgate. They'll take anyone."

"So let's assume this is your first arrest."

"Let me tell the truth, at least."

"You just said you're a liar, Kate, if that's your real name."

"Not to you, William—and yes, that is my real name."

"So how did you get the boy?"

"The usual way," Kate smiles. "I met this man who was kind to me, like you. I knew his mother Sarah from Liverpool, n' you 'ave to remember I was only nineteen at the time."

"What was his name?"

"That don't matter now. Forrester Mitchell Crease. Or so he told me. What a name! He was twenty-three and that was a man, a world o' change. We come to London next, where the streets is paved with...fool's gold n' failure, ha! He was only 'second potman' at King's hotel, Twickenham." Kate's eyes grow a little misty, but she somehow holds back the tears. "We went to a little beerhouse known as *The New Inn*, but he spurned me a week later, see. But not without a little present."

"Daniel."

"Right. God know where Forrester is now. Sarah Crease won't even tell me. She's trapped my boy hostage, I tell you." At last the tears come, and they are real. "I left my boy with a woman who's own son abandoned me. Now I've lost Daniel too. What's gonna become o' *'im?* She told me Forrester would come back to help me. But they just wanna steal my boy away!"

Marwood tries to take all this in. Despite his efforts, he's been diverted from his purpose. "You're sure you've committed no other crimes?"

"What are you, my counsel? I ain't guilty! There's plenty o' religion in 'ere, if I want that treatment—a French Catholic priest." She glares at her visitor. "Don't it mean somethin' when I mention my boy? You have a son!"

"I do."

"And you know where he is?"

"Yes, I do."

"And what if you didn't? What if he was caught and put in a

school for pickpockets? What if…?"

Marwood leans in. "I'd get him out. Then I'd do everything I can to cooperate with those trying to help me."

"How? How'd you get him out?" But she's running out of time. The 'clink' appears over their table and taps on his set of brass keys.

"Time to go back to your family," he tells Kate but receives such a dirty look he passes onto the next cage—the middle cell where boys as young as nine are double-cramped at tables with seedy-looking 'controllers' like Jonathan Clatter. The 'clink' ignores them, begins circling back slowly.

"You know something, William. I arrived in London a whole year ago." She raises her finger as though to take the air. "And the first thing I saw was Holloway Prison—a rat-hole."

"Holloway is a fake-model prison," Marwood says. "I saw it too—it's only been open ten years—mainly for political prisoners. And thieves destined for Australia."

"A paradise. Anyway, I saw the entrance to Holloway. It had two stone griffins, emblems of the City, like messengers."

"A premonition of your future?"

Kate's eyes narrow and she runs a hand through her ragged black hair. "That's right, I was drawn up to them peaceful-like, and then I sees the prison behind. To see those griffins, such beauty standing guard over a prison. You've no idea, boy. I thought, 'if I ever go back to prison, it'll be dragged through golden gates like those…'"

"I thought you've never been in a prison."

Kate pulls a sad face that almost makes Marwood ashamed. "You know I've been in a prison before."

"I didn't—that's why I came here, Kate. You're not being helpful…."

"You're a learned man, William. The inscription below those griffins, you know what it said? I memorised 't: 'MAY GOD PRESERVE THE CITY OF LONDON, N' MAKE THIS PLACE A TERROR TO EVIL-DOERS.'"

"Perhaps you're in the best place," Marwood says. "In gaol you're safe from London—the big prison, at least. Gaol is where the dogs don't bite."

Kate beckons to the bars. "You don't think them dogs bite?" She stands and throws Mrs Thomas's shawl over her shoulder. The 'clink' is at her elbow and he leads her back to the cell.

"Hang on, Kate. I'll be at the trial."

"William," she says, twisting her neck, "I've never been to any place that I wanted to go back. *That's* my life story!"

The iron grille is opened and the stench rises, but the conversation is over.

Marwood is led to the door, back down the passageway past gibbets, and out to the portcullis and the iron door. The next moment he is out on the street. He does not want to go back to Newgate, but with his Queen's commission and his responsibility to Ellen, Daniel, Cottonwell, the mayor and Justice Denham, "what choice do I have?" He listens as though for Kate's reply, for more tales of Ireland, of prisons, of Daniel and the future…but her voice is gone.

This time, the hangman does not touch the prison wall. Silently he takes a cab back east to Gloucester Street, thankful to rejoin his family.

Chapter 33
Trial at the Old Bailey
18th March 1879, Tuesday

A s per the official historical records of *'The Proceedings'* at *London's Central Criminal Court*, dating back to 1674:

The Old Bailey is located about two hundred yards northwest of St Paul's Cathedral, just outside the former western wall of the City of London. It is named after the street on which it is located, which itself follows the line of the original fortified wall, or 'bailey' of the City. This ancient position of a courthouse close to Newgate Prison allows the accused to be conveniently brought to the courtroom for trial. So too, its position between the City of London and Westminster guarantees a suitable setting for trials involving people from all over the metropolis, north of the Thames into Middlesex, the provinces and beyond, stretching even to the colonies if the prisoner is sufficiently important, the trial newsworthy and the execution spectacular.

To control public access, a semi-circular brick wall circles the front of the courthouse, the bail dock.

This wall provides better security for the prisoners awaiting trial and prevents communication between prisoners and 'guests'. Any external public view of the courtroom windows is thereby obstructed. The narrow entrance also prevents an unwanted influx of spectators into the courtroom. In addition, all outside passageways between Newgate Prison and the Old Bailey are enclosed with brick walls, creating a fortress-like sense of secrecy.

The courthouse is a single room, one bearing luxurious facilities for court personnel — soft seats — as opposed to the jury's wooden bench and the legendary lack of a chair in the dock. Meanwhile, in an unseen separate room for witnesses — preventing their waiting in a nearby pub — the half dozen or so subpoenaed by the prosecution huddle around a draughty table, drinking hard but hardly speaking, as the tradition goes; the same witnesses are requested by the defence, though without the prosecution's Queen-appointed power to make them appear.

By Tuesday 18th March, the line-up is set. The Sessions for the Grand Jury having taken place earlier that week, the trial may begin in earnest. One by one they file out with legal pride: Sir Justice Denham, judge; Warner Sleigh, defence; Harry B. Poland, prosecutor; Sir Hardinge Gifford, K.C., consultant; Paddy Taplin, clerk of the court; Jean Baptiste Dupris, Catholic priest; witnesses for prosecution and defence; a jury of eight men and four women; a female foreman; William Marwood in the gods, and a public 'peanut gallery' capable of holding thirty or so onlookers. There is just one witness missing: Mr Jonathan Clatter, schoolmaster for Southwark.

When all are seated, Kate is led from below into the court. She is shackled at the ankles and bewildered but blinks to life once seated in the dock. The guard from Newgate stands at her side, whispers words of consolation. But Kate is already conformable. She surveys the new world that will pass sentence on her life.

She notices how the court is laid out to stress the opposition between a solitary accused and the prosecuting bench. The judge overlooks all from his triple-high seat. The bailiff now ushers Kate to stand at 'the bar', the dock directly facing the witness box where prosecution and defence witnesses will testify. Adjacent to the judge is a table with lawyers' clerks, notably a weary-looking scribe—resembling a young Charles Dickens the cub reporter for Parliament—taking shorthand notes for 'the Proceedings'.

The clock ticks: the room waits and shivers. Just as heads begin to nod, Sir Justice Denham enters the draughty room, wig firmly mounted. He tests the gavel, rolling it in his palm as if reassuring himself of its magical power, then seats himself. Next he ruffles some papers, coughs and finally looks out from his raised pulpit. The full courtroom is below; a consoling wisp of grey hair escapes his wig.

"For the initiated, for the lucky few," Denham begins in a voice removed from the casual tone of his pub chat with Marwood, "a trial is presently held at the Old Bailey eight times a year, for crimes committed within London and the county of Middlesex. Crimes tried in this court are high and petty treason, felony, forgery, larceny, burglary and murder. The Old Bailey ghost permitting,"—he arching an eyebrow at the ceiling dome—"this will be a fair and peaceable trial for the murder of one Mrs Julia Thomas of Richmond, South London, by one Catherine Lawler, alias Kate Webster. You may be seated."

There is a rush of chairs and murmurs, before the Justice waves his palms again, and points. "May the Lord have mercy on your soul, Miss Webster, and so I begin—ladies and gentlemen, the Old Bailey is, par excellence, the criminal court of the country. In it, all the truths and disadvantages of our criminal procedures are embodied to an extraordinary degree. Let us be aware of that flexibility!" He turns to the twelve jury members:

"The Old Bailey juries are at once more clear-sighted and more pig-headed than any country jury. Again, let us be aware of that curiosity! Nor am I infallible, though my wife disagrees. I pray the counsel to note that uncertainty too—let us begin!"

The Clerk of the Court now stands, a boy of no more than twenty: "Ladies and gentlemen, despite the newly fitted gas lighting, the old mirror—let us think of her as Themis, Goddess of Justice herself—will hang over the accused's head. This will reflect light from the windows onto the face of the accused—in order to see her guilt. Sir,"—gesturing to the bailiff's assistant—"please secure the sounding board. We shall also need to hear her voice."

The jurors are already present, grouped on a bench to the defendant's right—shoulder to shoulder so they can consult and arrive at verdicts without long delays. On the ceiling hang four brass chandeliers, and dominating the floor is a semi-circular mahogany table for Counsel pleas, reflecting the new role of lawyers. Since some prisoners are live-branded, set in the wall are two iron bars for confining convicts' hands while they're burned for identification. Liberally employed too—and the heat can be unbearable—is a large polished mirror, currently angled to reflect daylight onto the face of the accused. The legal notion is to prise out guilt from the eyes and skin—the mirror will be used on Kate soon enough. Above the jurors is a gallery for spectators, with a token entry fee. A wooden sign over the wall clock boasts 'all are welcome, so long as they are prompt'.

The boy-clerk continues from a Greek-style scroll: "In view of the seriousness of the crime, the Crown will be led by the Solicitor General, Sir Hardinge Gifford, assisted by Mr Harry B. Poland, and the defence by Mr Warner Sleigh."

Wig settled in place, Justice Denham turns his eye on Kate.

"Miss Webster, this is not the first time you are before us. The Grand Jury has assessed the indictments and decided sufficient evidence permits the case to go before a trial jury. 'Tis a *true bill*—we may proceed. Furthermore the so-called 'hope of London thieves' for an immediate pardon is not the will of the Old Bailey. The substantial evidence submitted by Inspector Gil Sequin has been delivered to the court from the Bow Street rotation offices, under the statute of Thomas De Veil, may he rest in peace. Miss Webster, are you or are you not a prisoner supplied by the keepers of Newgate Prison? You may answer 'I am, Your Honour', or 'I am not, Your Honour'."

Kate smiles. "I am, Your Honour." She is wearing an elaborate costume, her hair falling onto her shoulders from a fine thread net, or ladies' 'invisible'. Evidently she is trying to look attractive, but has chosen a complicated haircut bordering on mock-comedy, with the flat beaver-tail at the back, and a Piccadilly Fringe that sports a 'kiss-curl' or 'beau-catcher' at the front—what Hollywood would later term 'peek-a-boo', one eye peering out from a wisp of suspicious, yet seductive dark hair.

"As the accused, you will not take the sworn oath of testimony. But perjure this court at your own risk. You understand you will be permitted the aid of defence counsel, and you retain no right to a silent plea, or unworded defence. You may answer 'I understand, Your Honour.'"

"I *do* understand, Your Honour." Her voice is steady, but not loud.

"You may enter your plea. Henceforth, if you are found mute 'by visitation of God', whether by the Holy Spirit or immaculate conception, we retain the approval of Queen's questioning, namely *peine forte et dure*. You would be forced to lie down and have weights placed on you until you relent. Counsel, how will the accused plead?"

Mr Warner Sleigh stands from the bench, to the left of the high seat. "The accused pleads Not Guilty, Your Honour."

"Thank you, Counsel. Clerk, please record the plea of Not Guilty in the case of Miss Kate Webster, Trial 5949, 18th March, 1879." Denham turns his wig-head back to Kate. "Miss Webster, you are expected to disprove the evidence and establish your innocence. The truth is sought directly!" He turns to the bailiff. "Let London enter!"

At this juncture the upper galley is opened, funneling in a motley gathering of newspapermen, court recorders, general public and 'court tricotrices'. A small boy sits in the front row, quietly mesmerised Aldous Marwood. His mother Ellen sits beside him, gripping his hand for her own benefit.

"Opening salvos of justice. Mr Harry B. Poland, please to commence."

A scratchy-looking man with a Balaclava-beard climbs from the bench. He pauses for silence then begins marching up and down the room, gesturing wildly.

"Today she looks every drop the sweet cup of tea, but this court maintains—the jury will maintain—before you is a cruel and heartless woman. This woman killed her landlady, Mrs Julia Thomas of Richmond, in frozen-cold blood then stole the contents of her house. For pieces of silver and old furniture, she slit the lady's throat. She cut Mrs Thomas's head clean off! She boiled the bones in a pot; she sold the flesh as dripping to the pub next door. She is consumed by evil! She is ready to be hanged—for the good of society. For the sake of Mrs Thomas, do not be deceived!" He wipes his brow, stares directly at Kate. "On a Sunday afternoon—on a clean shirt day!" He raises his hands. "After church no less. But luckily for cruel Kate Webster, the next day was Monday—laundry day—so her crime was delayed its discovery. But I maintain she is wicked and guilty. She boiled water in a copper vat in the basement, then shamelessly wielded the chopper to brutalise her late employer. As our witnesses will contend, Mrs Thomas *did appear* to be cooking more than usual—and that was the truth! Mrs Thomas *was* doing a lot of cooking!" He jabs his finger at the dock, where Kate fails to flinch. "This animal defies all reason!"

"I object, Your Honour," Mr Sleigh appeals while seated. "Pointless insults!"

"Please to continue, Mr Poland. Miss Webster will prove she's not an animal in due course."

"Thank you, Your Honour." He bows with remarkable ostentation, not unappreciated by Denham's half-smile. "Let me explain, ladies and gentlemen of the jury. Mrs Thomas apparently went to visit her brother for a few nights, according to the so-called 'humane accused!' " He glances at Warner Sleigh to see home his palpable hit. "So, Miss Webster is left with the poor chore of stuffing and seasoning a goose, ostensibly for Easter week. Such trickery! This lurid little tale hides the absence of the mistress, and explains away the perpetual cooking odours in a single blow. If I may—when Mrs Thomas's flesh is squeezed into a thick tar, what does Kate do? She scrapes the fat off the copper rim, seals it in a jar and hurries next door to *The Hole in the Wall* public house. Here, ladies and gentlemen, she sells poor Mrs Thomas to the landlady, Mrs Hayhoe as 'Finest Turkey Dripping'."

There is a slow gasp from the crowd, and a creaking as the gallery spectators lean forward.

"For the next few days, turkey dripping sandwiches are considered 'delightful and tasty' by the regular pub clientele. Meanwhile Kate is hard at work trying to dissolve the grim collection of Mrs Thomas's bones in a boiling pot. Failing at this, her next plan is to scatter them around the streets of West London and drop the remainder in the Thames."

"Objection, Your Honour, unfounded."

"Overruled."

"Thank you, Your Honour," Mr Poland smiles. "So all Kate

Webster has left behind is the head. So she goes to Hammersmith to meet Mr Porter, publican at *The Rising Sun*. Her intention is to sell the Richmond furniture! Kate takes the decapitated head of Mrs Thomas in her basket and, without doubt, drops it into the river from Hammersmith Bridge. Hiding the evidence, ladies and gentlemen! Soon enough Sunday rolls around, and this Mr Porter turns up with a cart to empty Mrs Thomas's house. Voila the end of the line for our cunning killer Kate! What she hasn't realised is that 2 Mayfield Gardens was only *rented* to Mrs Thomas—fully furnished. The owner is Mrs Beryl Ives, who lives in the adjoining house! Naturally, Mrs Ives is a little surprised to witness her wares—a fine dressing table among them—being hauled up onto a wagon. What happens, you may well ask? Well, the dilemma is such a brazen 'scupper' to her plans, Kate Webster is entirely *lost for words*. So she takes to her heels!"

Picking up speed, Mr Poland now does a three-pointed spin encompassing the accused, the judge and jury, the tails of his gown looping his legs. "Her sole plan is to 'grift' the purloined furniture money in Smashers Alley and escape to new life, possibly in Italy or the United States. Yet without the furniture plunder, her only option is to retreat over the Irish Sea. A Bow Street investigation unearths her address in the village of Killane, County Wexford, and she is rightly arrested. That, sirs, is the truth!"

He takes a breath. "Ladies and gentlemen, I live in Richmond. I walk past *The Hole in the Wall* every day, as I did this morning. I am close to this repugnant crime, but not too close for sound judgement. And every morning I pass Mrs Hayhoe's pub, I think of the turkey dripping sandwiches being eaten there, I think of Miss Kate Webster and her brutal crime. Kate Webster has no tender bone in her body, less compassion in her little finger than I say she deserves in justice from this court. I seek the guilty verdict for this heinous crime, robbing a law-abiding and quiet Richmond of a dear, much-loved churchgoing lady. I thereby commit this animal to the mercy of the gallows, as the only sane commitment that this court has a duty to perform." He stomps his foot on the ground and takes his seat.

There is cheering from the gallows and two people—overcome by the scene—are pushed unceremoniously outside by the bailiff. They will be allowed to return in one hour, but for now, they listen with their ears to the wall to the defence's reply.

But first Justice Denham, a little worn out by Mr Poland's

invective, says: "Let the hangman in." No one understands, but after the judge snaps his fingers to the public gallery, the bailiff opens the door he has just shut. Mr Marwood is now permitted entry—perhaps, Denham is thinking, the rest of the trial will now be more clinical, given their political understanding through Mr Cottonwell, swift and painless and with a definite outcome, like Marwood's own performances. The hangman joins Ellen and Aldous on the front row, without a word. He pats his son on the head, grips the rail and Ellen's hand, and all three look down on the court with varied expressions of concern, his wife perplexed, his son excited, Marwood nurturing a peculiar fear he's never experienced before.

Below, Denham has barely paused for breath: "Mr Warner Sleigh, please to respond with opening salvo for the defence. Then we may call witnesses for the prosecution."

"Thank you, Your Honour." Mr Sleigh, court public-appointed defender, stands and squints through perfectly round glasses offering an air of country civility and sharp city tongue. "I am defending the accused, Miss Kate Webster, *in forma pauperis*. Clearly the sheriff and Mr Cottonwell and the mayor—while not in court—control the strings here. They need a big prosecution to show they are hard on crime!"

Mr Poland springs to his feet. "Outrage, Your Honour. Argument in the opening salvo, not to mention political treason."

Mr Justice Denham frowns and nods. "Sustained, Mr Poland. Kindly be seated—defence has only just begun. Please, Mr Sleigh."

"Thank you, Your Honour," the defence barrister says. He scowls at Mr Poland's jumpy impertinence, turns a soft eye on Kate where she is currently motionless in the dock, dolled up to the nines. "Look at the defendant, ladies and gentlemen," he swings his arm to the jury, "don't you find 'cruel Kate' deceiving? She is gentle as a lamb to her boy—yes, she has a son, Daniel."

He pauses while Kate starts to cry. Mr Sleigh and Kate have not met prior to the trial and this tactical sarcasm—appearing fake—is genuine.

"Look, she cries in open court at mention of Daniel's name. According to all accounts, she was inconsolable in prison when she could not see Daniel. And now, in the Old Bailey criminal dock, she weeps again, like Xerxes wept, ladies and gentlemen, because looking upon his army, he knew they'd all be dead in a hundred years."

"Objection, irrelevance."

"Overruled. Poetry is welcome, Mr Sleigh, with a point." He turns his gaze on the accused, back-lit from the Old Bailey's windows.

"There sits her boy." He points at Aldous Marwood in the peanut gallery.

Immediately Kate stops crying, shakes her head in denial. "Not *my* boy," she whispers. But the whole room follows Mr Sleigh's eyes.

"There is her boy, Daniel,"—still pointing at Aldous. "He is only ten years old. Have mercy, today, ladies and gentlemen of the jury. Whatever she did—and as we'll see, it was not unforgivable—she did it for her boy." Up on the galley Aldous goes white, and Ellen pulls him back from the handrail. Unmoving, his own face blank, Marwood stares down at the drama.

Waving away the mistaken identity, Mr Sleigh plows on. "Don't let this be a case of ugly words and greasy squalor, a cold, bleak-looking prison, an awful little iron door, three feet or so from the ground. Let this be a true trial by jury, a trial about how unfair landlady Mrs Julia Thomas really was, how provoking and nasty she could be—how deceitful her fellow creatures, her neighbours and relatives, in particular her next-door neighbour Mrs Beryl Ives, her brother Mr Richard, her son Billy, even her gardener."

He looks up as though to heaven itself.

"I say to you, this is a case of black caps, bullying counsel, prevaricating witnesses, and a miserable, trembling, damp prisoner in the dock. It is a railroading, as the American say, straight to hell. Did Kate Webster kill Mrs Thomas? No, I say! Was she provoked into leaving unjust employment? Certainly!"

"Please conclude your remarks, Mr Sleigh," Justice Denham interrupts. Sleigh has spoken for no longer than Harry Poland, but the judge knows his own interests, the deal he's made with the Mayor of London.

"Yes, Your Honour. In the case of a guilty verdict, the defence pleads for combination of Not Guilty but Insane. This is a verdict of the 1800 statute, following the passing of the 'Act for the Safe Custody of Insane Persons Charged with Offences.' We acknowledge the defendant's actions—as yet undefined—as a product of insanity, a *non compos mentis* verdict. Miss Webster is therefore a new class of criminal, if convicted, namely the criminally insane." He pauses. "Furthermore, if the accused be found guilty, we would petition a Guilty with Recommendation that the convict should be treated with mercy, since no violence was intended."

"Mr Sleigh, this is poor procedure. Now is not the time for recommendation. Your conclusion is confused—you wish to enter a Not Guilty but Insane plea, but in the event of guilt, a Guilty with Recommendation plea? There is only one plea, sir, and the defendant has already made it. She has pleaded Not Guilty. Let that statute stand."

"But Your Honour."

"I said stand. Now sit."

Mr Sleigh takes his seat. A general puzzled silence circulates the courtroom, a sense that the defendant's options are curtailed. To confirm, Justice Denham says: "Let it be known, the jury will strike from the record any thoughts regarding Not Guilty but Insane as pleas. As for Guilty with Recommendation, we will consider that option at the appropriate time—later."

"But Your Honour!"

"The verdict stands, Mr Sleigh, or you'll be in contempt. According to the 1800 Act, those defendants found Guilty but Insane are kept in custody 'until Her Majesty's Pleasure be known'. This is a hanging trial, Mr Sleigh, and the death penalty *will* be retained. Otherwise you'd create criminal lunatics of us all!"

"No, I mean yes, Your Honour. The plea of Not Guilty stands. I wish to vouch for defence with madness or provocation, despite the plea standing."

"Granted."

"Thank you. Under his breath, Mr Sleigh says: "A hanging trial with a hanging judge."

Kate is clearly growing weary on her feet, generally ignored. However, Mr Denham now offers the prosecution to present its witnesses, initiated with a 'conclusive rebuttal' to the defence's salvo.

Mr Poland leaps up at mention of his name. "My witnesses will corroborate the following, ladies and gentlemen. Let it please the court that from 19th to 22nd February, Mrs Thomas wrote several letters to her brother, Mr Richard Hughes. This period of notice was a fatal mistake for Mrs Thomas, and she became increasingly frightened of her employee Kate during its period, so much so that she asked friends from her church and relatives to stay in the house. Friday the

28th arrived and as Kate did not manage to find a new job or any accommodation, she pleaded with Mrs Thomas to be allowed to remain at 2 Mayfield Gardens over the weekend. Sadly, Mrs Thomas agreed to this—a decision that will soon cost *both* women their lives. I hereby call Mr Richard Hughes to the stand."

A tall man with wiry hair is ushered in and takes the witness box near to the bench, directly facing the accused. His face is ashen. On request, he points out Kate Webster, though he resists meeting her eye.

"Are you not, sir, the elder brother of Mrs Julia Thomas?"

"I am."

"How would you describe your relations?"

"Good terms."

"Very close, sir."

"Indeed."

"You cared for her welfare?"

"Very much, sir."

"Did you hear from your sister in the week of 17th February? Please describe how you communicated and the contents of the exchange...."

Richard Hughes grips the railing, looks at the jury. "I received three letters, each more agitated than the last. Julia was clearly unhappy with her new maid, who was scaring her."

"How scaring her?"

"Physically intimidating. She used the phrase 'unduly afraid'."

"Would you describe your sister as a frightening woman?"

"No, she was a gentle soul. Clearly you can see how this creature,"—he points at Kate—"could have overpowered her."

"I never!" Kate interjects. "She attacked me first, called me 'no basket of oranges', and I ain't no *blowen*, Your Honour! True, I gives 'er a bloody nose, but she deserves it!"

Mr Poland waves his hand furiously at the jury, as though accusing them all: "So let it be known," he cries. "She was assaulted. Here is the confession—in open court! She gave her a bloody nose— a vicious attack. We are half way to a conviction!"

"Objection!"

"Sustained. Mr Poland, pray keep your hopes to a minimum."

Relative calm is restored, including on the gallery—with no further expulsions from the public up in the gods.

"Apologies, Your Honour. I now tell you, members of the jury, on that Sunday morning 2nd of March, Mrs Thomas went to church as usual. Kate was allowed Sunday afternoons off, but had to be back in time for Mrs Thomas to go to the evening service. This Sunday afternoon Kate went to visit her son, who was in the care of Mrs Sarah Crease, timber yard cook—as usual. Kate then went to *The Hole in the Wall* on the way back, as witnessed by Mrs Hayhoe—the first of several visits—a visit verified in police records by Inspector Gil Sequin." He pauses, momentarily forgetting his way.

"Your point, sir?" Kate interjects, causing laughter in the court.

"Silence!" from Denham, and the finger of justice jabs in her direction.

"Thus," Mr Poland picks up the thread, "Kate returned late, upsetting Mrs Thomas who reproved her new employee again, before dashing off herself. The ushers at church sensed Mrs Thomas was unduly distracted; perhaps she feared Kate's good intentions, wondering, while she prayed, if her house was not being ransacked? Or did her worries spring from a naturally suspicious and proud, delicate temperament?"

"Objection!"

"Sustained."

"The root cause unknown, Mrs Thomas did leave the service and retreated home, but telling no one her concerns. She was therefore all alone from this point onwards, with the last person to see her alive—the defendant! I now call Mrs Beryl Ives."

A rapid procession of witnesses follows, only partially covered by Old Bailey records, and dismissed as fast as they are sworn in. First, Mrs Ives takes the stand and testifies to the strange sights, sounds and smells emanating from 2 Mayfield Gardens. "I awoke in the middle of Sunday night and I couldn't sleep for over an hour, it was so bad."

"And the next morning?" Poland prompts.

"I looks out the window, and sees a huge copper pot, but no clothes." Mrs Ives turns to the jury. "She ain't doin' no washin'."

Mr Henry Porter is asked to testify. "Yes, sir," he tells the court, "Miss Webster came for tea at *The Rising Sun*, maybe three o'clock, the Thursday."

"And what did she bring?"

"She brought Mrs Thomas's head in a heavy black bag."

"Objection Your Honour," Sleigh intervenes.

"Sustained!" and with a frown, Denham is forced to caution the prosecuting barrister, all for show. "Mr Poland, please refrain from feeding unsupportable evidence to your witness."

"Yes Your Honour, but respectfully, the head *is* Mr Porter's claim as to what the bag contained."

"Then make it sound like a claim—the bag has never been found."

"Then I move to question Mr Porter's son, Robert." Everyone now turns to where Mr Poland beckons the publican's fifteen-year-old, who steps gingerly into the witness box, clapped on the back by his father as he does.

"Tell us, in your own words, Robert," Poland begins, "what happened on Hammersmith Bridge?"

"Well, I was helping Miss Webster carry her belongings."

"And in particular?"

"Her wooden box, sir."

"Why, could she not carry it alone?"

Robert cocks his head to the side, realizing his is being fed lines, but seeing no alternative. "No, it was too heavy."

"So Miss Webster was left alone in the centre of the bridge, and you walked back?"

"Yes, sir."

"Then describe what you saw."

"Not much, sir."

"What did you hear?"

Robert looks to his father, who nods. "Well, I goes down the steps at the top of the bridge, near the street. Then I hears the splash. And when I looks up, there's Miss Webster, but no box."

Poland smiles. "Thank you, Robert. No further questions, Your Honour."

For the prosecution, two significant points of view remain. Nathan Crane tells of an attempted seduction of his person by Kate Webster in *The Rising Sun*. Perhaps the least damaging evidence, Crane's appearance goes a long way to discrediting a rumour that has been circulating, namely that Crane was an accomplice in the crimes. According to Kate's words to police on the packet-boat back from Ireland—now quoted by Nimrod Jones—"Crane was the instigator. 'e

was in it alone, n' I jus' watched. Crane was pullin' the strings."
However, on the witness stand, Crane's alibi comes into play, that he
was chair at a Slate Club meeting on the Sunday of the murder, and
this is verified by both the Club's ledger and further witnesses.

Mr Poland further supports Crane's words with a little
argumentative aside. "If Crane were guilty, he would not have had
portions of the murdered woman's property conveyed to his house.
Neither would he have tried to communicate with Mrs Ives, nor
sought out Mr Richard Hughes, or ascertained a crime had been
committed."

However, the judge—at Mr Sleigh's request—closes down the
prosecutor for 'prejudicial argument', not before the damage is done,
of course.

"He is throwing dust in the eyes of the jury," Sleigh cries. He
gestures wildly to the line of witnesses.

"Sustained. Mr Poland, you will desist from rhetorical speech-
making."

"Yes, sir." A glance is exchanged between the judge and
prosecutor.

Kate remains stoic through these testimonies and jostling
courtroom wordplay. Lacking a chair in the dock, she shifts her
weight from one foot to the next.

The most pathetically embarrassing witness, though, not least
because he appears such a bumbling specimen, is Richard Hughes.
Despite his initial testimony, he is recalled to comment on evidence.
The brother of Mrs Thomas has been emotionally tested, his voice
barely audible, his balding pate troubled by a wisp of hair that will not
sit down causing much unseasoned hilarity in the gallery, despite the
man's evident distress.

Mrs Thomas's anxious letters about her maid are produced.

"Did you take these letters seriously?" Poland inquires.

"Of course," Hughes replies, a little indignant.

"Speak up, man."

"Yes, I was considering a lawyer."

"A trial to remove the maid?"

The judge frowns, and interrupts the prosecutor. "I remind
you Mr Poland," with a smile, "this is a witness for the prosecution."

Poland gathers his bullying wits, and softens his approach.
"Of course. Mr Hughes, you wanted to help your sister."

"I did."

"And you feared this maid?"

"Not feared," Mr Hughes insists, "but Julia was afraid of her. I could not easily visit that week, but I should have." He trembles a little. "I should…"

"The question, Mr Hughes."

"It's all in the letters," he suddenly cries, the hair lifting from his skull. "She was terrified, and wanted me to remove this…woman." He points, and Kate looks away. "This killer!"

"Mr Hughes, you are clearly upset. But we have the handwriting expert to prove those letters were written by Mrs Julia Thomas."

"Of course they were! But yes, sir," and he looks directly at Judge Denham, "I paid a handwriting expert. And they were undoubtedly written by…"

"Mrs Thomas."

"Yes."

Richard Hughes is allowed to step down. As per procedure, the defence does not get the opportunity to examine the prosecution witnesses; rather Mr Warner Sleigh will produce his own witnesses, calling back the same people if necessary. He is permitted less time, however, such is the legal favouritism for the Crown. The assumption persists—supported by Acts of Parliament—that if Kate is not guilty, she would prove her case. Who needs extra time? Innocence will apparently shines through like God's own judgement.

The physical evidence is now produced, consisting primarily of two doctors disagreeing over remains in the box, Dr Bond stating Mrs Thomas to be in her mid-fifties, Dr Adams late sixties.

To cover this discrepancy, Inspector Gil Sequin is called for questioning by Mr Poland. "Are you not see, a bounty hunter, a gun for hire?"

"Yes, I'm a Bow Street Runner. I work with the Night Watchmen."

"Are you not paid?"

"I am, sir, as you are."

Someone laughs in the court—Nimrod Jones up in the gods—and Harry Poland looks up while asking the next question. "You are not an official policeman, though, sir."

"Your Honour, as you know, I am a 'thief-taker' on a pledged fee—we are the Bow Street Runners." He puffs out his chest. "When crimes are prevalent, the magistrates extend us powers of detection. Sir, all we do is keep the streets clean, and seize the criminals."

"And you, sir, are the Principal Officer of Bow Street?"

"I will be one day."

Nimrod Jones giggles now and is cautioned by the galley bailiff, whom he regards with an expression of contempt. Meanwhile, Sequin is asked his opinion of the accused, to which Sleigh objects but is overruled.

"As a man of upstanding policing, you may proceed, Mr Sequin."

"I believe, with all due respect, sirs," and Sequin glances round the entire Sessions, "she is a villain. Clearly the family and neighbours believe she did it. I've seen the copper pot, sirs, I've seen the wooden trunk. It all points in one direction, and her direction only."

"Thank you, inspector."

"You're welcome."

The turnaround has come, and there is no delay before the defence witnesses are called. As per tradition, Kate will primarily defend her own neck. But more and more, the Old Bailey allows a *coterie* of witnesses, the 'angels of innocence', although Judge Denham orders the jury "to take their testimony with a pinch of salt, defending as they are, an accused murderess."

"Accused being the key," Mr Sleigh says to Denham's frown. "In response, the defence calls Billy Thomas, the victim's only son."

There is a ripple of surprise from the court.

"Her duffer son," Kate is heard to say.

A burly, dark-skinned man now takes the stand, moving slow, his large frame dwarfing the small door. The bailiff remains in place to protect the judge, as though the witness will strike at any moment.

"Please state your name."

"Billy."

"And your family name?"

"Thomas." He looks at the court shyly, lacking in malevolence, a little confused.

"What was your relationship to Mrs Julia Thomas?"

"She looked after me."

"She was your mother."

"Yes."

"What kind of woman would you say your mother was?"

"Mother, yes."

Sleigh frowns, theatrically. "Was she a woman who sometimes beat you?"

"Sometimes."

"Objection Your Honour, the defence is leading the witness."

"Overruled. Proceed, Mr Sleigh."

"Thank you, Your Honour. Mr Hughes, did your mother often employ maids?"

"Yes, maids. Nice maids."

Sleigh raises his eyebrows. "And would you say Kate Webster was a nice girl?"

"Yes, nice girl. I paint pictures." The snickering comes down from the gallery.

"Okay Billy, I mean, Mr Thomas. Would your mother sometimes be mean to her maids, shout at them?" Here Mr Sleigh approaches the witness box and jabs his finger on the wooden banister. "Provoking your mother, perhaps?"

"Provoking."

"Objection, the witness is repeating."

"Sustained. Ask a question, please, Mr Sleigh."

"Did your mother beat the maid for her poor cleaning duties?"

Billy looks confused. "I have a greenhouse," he says. "I can hang my pictures in there. But they's not 'dere...not in 'dere now...not." The Court watches as Billy undergoes a brief breakdown, and to Mr Sleigh's great dismay, he can answer no further questions. The defence is forced to abandon the witness, but then a five-minute break in Sessions replaces the son with the neighbour.

"The defence calls Mrs Ives."

Working hard, Mr Sleigh attempts to discredit Beryl Ives's story of waking in the night.

"By what light did you witness the cooking in the pot?"

"By dawn."

"Half-light, then."

She peers narrowly. "I suppose."

"And you were awake for an hour in the night. So it would be fair to say you only had a few hours' sleep?"

"I went to bed early," she grins, and glances at Kate, who

glares back. "That's my house she was in—I wanted to know what was happening."

"Your police statement says you went to bed after midnight. I remind you, Mrs Ives, you are still under oath. So with only a few hours' sleep, we are expected to trust your hearing and sight—in half-light—from a frightened and elderly lady, with every intention to see and hear what she wants—what she fears—to witness."

"The question, Mr Sleigh," Judge Denham says.

"Did you see any blood?"

"No."

"Did you see Miss Webster with the body of Mrs Thomas?"

"Not exactly."

"You saw the clothes?"

"Yes."

"Some clothes."

"Yes."

"But you can't be certain they weren't Miss Webster's own clothes, and not Mrs Thomas's?"

"Well, they were nice clothes."

"But you can't be certain?"

"No, sir."

"And all you saw was clothes in the pot?"

"Yes, sir."

Mr Sleigh faces the duty and raises his hands. "It was washing day," he declares, "and the maid is washing the clothes. The witness may step down."

"Batty old spinster," Kate whispers under her breath. One after the other, more character witnesses take the witness-box in her defence. Sarah Crease is called, but is strangely absent from proceedings. For fifteen minutes, though, a former co-worker from Hammersmith, Elizabeth Loder, gives evidence of Kate's good nature. Then reaching for any low-level corruption, the defence counsel questions the motives of the prosecutor in bringing the case.

Mr Crane and Mr Porter, side by side, are called back, this time by the defence.

"Have you been paid by the court?"

"Yes, sir."

"You?"

"Yes, sir. Travel expenses." A ripple of laughter causes

Denham to bang the gavel. "Enough, gentleman. The defence rests its witness line-up. We are straying from the central issue! The trial proceeds to evidence."

One of the prosecution's problems is proving that the human remains the police found *are* Mrs Thomas. The sense of horror that a nice old lady is dead might be enough, but proof is the icing.

Knowing this, Mr Sleigh kicks off the direct argumentation. "Without the head, there is no means of positively identifying the body. Mrs Thomas could have died of natural causes, in view of her agitated state, shortly after she was seen leaving church on the Sunday afternoon."

"Nonsense," cries Denham. "On the contrary, as per the testimony of Dr Adams, the medical evidence shows that all the body parts belong to the same person and that they are from a woman in her mid-fifties."

Overall, the two doctors cancel each other out, and after the recent claims of 'standard legal bribery'—technically not illegal—the jury sees them as paid by whichever side they support.

The murmurs have grown, and the trial is taking far longer than the usual hour and a half. Justice Denham suddenly burps and everyone in the Old Bailey witnesses the indulgence. He bangs to gavel, silencing the crowd.

"Time for the accused to defend herself," he announces. "Now the truth will out! Bailiff!"

Up on the balcony, Marwood and his whole family lean forward. Kate is now removed from the dock, and taken to the stand for the performance of her life. Sleigh is allowed to lead the accused first, before the onslaught of Denham's 'reconfiguring of the truth'. Then as tradition, the Crown will have the last word.

Mr Sleigh clears his throat, pulls at his chin, and Kate copies his proud stance. He smiles and taps the dock's railing, seeking a theatrical vein of sympathy in the story of a poor immigrant woman fallen on hard times, struggling to eat. What's a girl supposed to do?

"Take us back to the beginning, Kate. You were born Catherine Lawler, so why are you called Webster?"

The question surprises Kate, especially from her own defence, but she sees to the root of the required response—she has led a hard life.

"Yes, I's born a Lawler, a good country family from Killane,

County Wexford. Good country captain, but I likes to live larger..."

"And the name, Kate?"

"Yea, so I marries a sea captain called Webster n' had four children—but the bloody devil took 'em all. 'Tis true, I stole brass for the ferry fare to Liverpool and with this n' that, I got a four-year stretch at the tender age o' eighteen. When I gets out, I cleans up me act, but cleans out mi'landlady in Liverpool. That's where I learned the trick, see."

"You're not on trial for stealing, Kate," smiles Sleigh, imitating friendliness for the court, "and you've paid your penalty. Tell us about your time after Liverpool."

"Well, I gets to London—it's summer '73—I takes a nice pad in Rose Gardens, Hammersmith area, with Henry n' Ann Porter. I gets on well with 'em, plus I got a cook job for this Captain Woolbest in Notting Hill, a rough sort, but drunk most o' the day. So I don't cook much! Working there I meets a man named Strong, who gets me pregnant again, n' me pride n' joy—the one I'm gonna keep!—was birthed on 19th April '74. Then I gets abandoned proper prompt by dandy Mr Strong. So I has to pick up me ol' ways. What choice does I 'ave?"

"We all must agree." Sleigh turns to the jury and up to the gallery. "This woman has been sorely used. She has tried to work, to take the good path, yet there has been no reward, no recompense, no mercy on the great road of life. You must feel her sorrows as hard as her sins, ladies and gentleman. Please go on, Kate."

"That's right, sir, I've always worked despite the brush with law-men. I get kicked free from Wandsworth in summer '77, two years since. So I gets domestic work—first the Mitchell family in Teddington, but they didn't have anything worth much."

"Kate!" Sleigh cries, but the words are out, and the Sessions—the Old Bailey's live audience—is greatly amused. Marwood tightens his coat, looks down with sad expression. Somehow Kate cannot resist the price of her entertainment and Mr Sleigh must stop her, but Kate remarkably saves herself.

"I 'as constantly on the move, usin' multi-good aliases includin' Webster, Price an' Lawler. I may be thirsty and sharp as a card, ladies n' gents, but I ain't no murderin' hussy, no sir. Crane agreed to *sell me* furniture from his own family for twenty shillin'," she points across to Nathan Crane's family, now seated, "but I didn't 'ave that kind o' money."

"Miss Webster, please," Sleigh interrupts.

" 'e tried to rip me off! An' Henry Porter there, 'e's a bad egg—'e's the father of m' unborn child!"

The shock is brief, given Kate's shouting diminishes her claim. Eventually Mr Sleigh gets Kate under control literally by rapping the handrail with his fingers, her expression of cornered animal turning on him, and he soothes her with a long, calming noise. Somehow this extraordinary ritual works—the lucid snake hypnotizing the belligerent prey—except under further questioning, Kate accuses Porter of the murder itself, confusing herself now, even transferring the date from the Sunday to the Monday.

At this point, Judge Denham intervenes and openly declares Henry Porter's acquittal of the capital crime, stating his position only as witness for the prosecution. "Mr Porter is simply not on trial, Miss Webster, so please to stop accusing him. You are on trial, and I caution you for perjury and slander, should you continue in this matter."

Kate cries "What have I got to lose—my honour?" causing great ribaldry throughout the room, the bailiff himself smiling. Knowing her true audience—the hanging crowd—is agitated in the peanut gallery, Kate goes a step further, claiming she was forced to fetch a cheap bottle of brandy from a street vendor during her meetings with Porter, re-accusing him of "licentious seduction." Her use of this legal phrase causes the room to fall about in greater merriment. Denham is positively thwacking the gavel on the block.

"You wanted to do the deed for money," Porter suddenly calls out, and is summarily removed from court.

Kate shouts from the dock, "that's false, you scoundrel. 'e was improper with me, I swear. I didn't even make a penny."

Mr Denham now stands and announces: "Silence. Anyone else will be in contempt of court, and serve thirty days in the debtors' wing of Newgate." The room goes quiet from the gallery to the witnesses to the jury. "Mr Sleigh, please proceed."

"Thank you, Your Honour. Kate, please be seated." Mr Sleigh turns to the jury and offers a contemplative face. "So, if the events of that Sunday evening were exactly as Mr Poland prefers, is it not strange that Mrs Ives did not hear the quarrel? Why were there bloodstains at the top of the stairs, if Mrs Thomas's injuries had occurred at the bottom?" He lets the jury ruminate. "The prosecution holds that Kate lay in wait for Mrs Thomas and hit her on the head with an axe causing her to fall down the stairs, whereupon she strangled her to prevent any further noise. I say to you, this is preposterous, outrageous! The evidence is only 'circumstantial' since *no one* can place Kate at the scene, and the body cannot be consistently identified. The prosecution's axe is a fantasy from *Crime and Punishment* more than anything from real, London life!" Kate is seen to smirk, in a jittery way.

Denham then looks to Poland who is allowed to intervene, and while the prosecutor is not quite ready, he takes his friend's cue and stands. "Ladies and gentleman, the truth is often preposterous. That is why it *is* the truth, for as humans we disregard the unlikely reality that surrounds us. We prefer fantasy. Yes, the truth is hard to find—but the truth is often right under our noses." He now produces a newspaper, with a golden image of the sun on its cover. "Welcome to the light of truth! This is a veritable news vendor, one of the earliest uses of colour on broadsheet. Look, the words shine with a truth undeniable!" The jury is heard to coo a little, while Mr Sleigh sinks his head in his hands. Kate looks puzzled.

The entire gallery leans forward. "According to the *Baltimore Sun*," Mr Poland continues, "delivered to the American Press direct from Inspector Sequin's police report, I quote, 'the servant stole upon her mistress after she came home, exhausted by prayer and devotion at her Presbyterian Chapel. As she was sitting before the fire, the maid tossed a long piece of cloth around her throat, threw her over backward to the floor, and choked her to death'. Poland pauses for effect and raises his voice. "An evil crime, ladies and gentleman, and I quote: 'Not content with murder, Kate is a vicious and dark killer, for she had to mutilate and dismember. She boiled bones until flesh came off. Then she put the flesh in the fire until it was ash.' In Kate's own words to Sequin and Jones, 'When I looked upon the dirty floor scene, blood around my feet, the horror and dread I felt was inconceivable. I never relished the sight of blood 'til now, though in many ways I'd bin careful...'"

"Fastidious?" Inspector Sequin offers.

"Yes," Poland says. "I will soon rest my case!"

"It's a lie," Kate now blurts out, so loud her throat hurts. "Bow Street's stitchin' me up! 'e'd put the noose round m' neck 'imself, if 'e could!"

Sequin looks directly back at Kate, wipes his mouth with his moustache, saying nothing. Meanwhile Deputy Nimrod Jones smiles first at Kate, then at Sequin, and leans back comfortable in his allegiance.

Mr Poland pursues his advantage: "Yes, Kate lay in wait for Mrs Thomas, and according to Dr Bond's medical report, she struck the elderly lady full-tilt on the head with an axe causing her to fall down the stairs, where she then strangled her. This scenario fits the crime of premeditated murder and is in line with the bloodstains. Whether Kate decided to kill Mrs Thomas in revenge for her earlier reprimand, or whether Kate saw an opportunity to steal from Mayfield Gardens, or both, is unclear. Certainly previously non-violent criminals are known to engage in murder. But what turned Kate to such appalling violence? Did she just snap or did she spend hours thinking about it? No, she was provoked and that means guilty!"

Sleigh demands: "By whom, Your Honour? Produce this mysterious witness!"

Poland is swift to respond. "The prosecution calls Jonathan Clatter, landlord of *The Cat and Salutation*, Southwark." There is a pause while Mr Poland regards the witness bench, but no one moves, and the condemning factor of Kate abandoning her child to a 'crooked school'—a testimony for which Clatter would be guaranteed immunity—evaporates on the spot.

In his place, a witness is surprised by an *ad hoc* subpoena to descend from the gallery—the hangman is called to give evidence. Kate is unnerved. The defence objects to having an official testify in court, but despite Sleigh's plea, the executioner is forced to leave Ellen and Aldous.

Mr Marwood takes his place in the witness box, a grey light cutting across his solemn face. He loosens his collar, does not look at Kate, nor she him, but both seem to bow their heads a little lower.

"Please state you name, sir."

"William Marwood, hangman for London and Middlesex." The crowd is quiet, and the wooden benches of the Sessions creaking; there is no other sound, only breathing. Marwood feels caught on all sides—between Denham, Kate, and his family. His sense of confinement is palpable, as though bred by the Old Bailey air.

"What is your connection to the accused?"

"I am a friend," Marwood says. Kate scrutinises the contours of his face: he can feel her eyes examining, not unkindly, but not without suspicion.

"How long have you known each other?"

"Before February…?"

"Before the date of the murder, yes."

"A week or so."

Poland smiles, nods, and begins a slow walk around the witness box. "And would you say she is of good character?"

"I don't understand the question."

"Good character, Mr Marwood," Poland pauses. "A moral, upright citizen. A good, kind person. Need I elaborate?"

"No, sir. I believe she is of sound mind."

"Not the same, Mr Marwood. Would you trust her with your children?"

"Objection, Your Honour."

"Overruled. Answer the question, Mr Marwood."

The hangman regards the hanging judge, grits his teeth a little, looks back at Poland. "I have a son, and he is old enough to look after himself."

"How convenient, sir. Now let me ask you this. Did you have close relations with Miss Webster? A little too friendly? Were you intimate? Were you lovers?" Poland raps on the handrail, and raises his hands. "Remember you are under oath, Mr Marwood."

"We did not," he replies, "although…"

Poland hesitates, "although…"

"Nothing. I remind you my wife and son are present in the courtroom."

"And I remind you, Mr Marwood," Poland cries, "that you are in the Sessions of the Old Bailey, before Queen and country, before God Almighty himself. Now answer the question!"

"Objection!"

"Overruled"

"No, sir," Marwood says quietly, "we did not. Although there were times when I wondered if we would. Miss Webster—Kate, I mean—she was well dressed, and showed a great deal of interest in my work."

"In your hanging?"

Marwood glances down sheepishly, but then looks up. "Yes,

in my hanging."

The Sessions takes another communal breath. Poland is making progress, and his chest expands with pompous 'barrister pride' only known to practitioners of legal performance, several of whom are present.

"But we *do* know," Poland says addressing the jury, "that you spent time at 2 Gloucester Place, a lot of time, for Inspector Sequin has observed your movements. We know you both went, for example, to Bartholomew Fair. Needless to say, you could be helping Miss Webster escape the noose."

"There is no such thought in my mind," Marwood says bluntly. "I wish for the long drop, should the sentence be guilty, and full exoneration in the press—including *The Times*—if she's found Not Guilty."

Kate interrupts laughing, and Marwood looks at her confused, for he is quite serious.

"I too pray, Mr Hangman, that you will do your job. But first you are compromised, manipulated by this woman. That much is clear! The jury will strike any character points you make from the record. For ladies and gentleman, here is the next victim, living and breathing, the hangman himself! You sir,"—turning back to Marwood and jabbing the air—"you are the foil, the appetite for her crimes, the catalyst for a happy ending you two would live out together in leafy Richmond. Picture the scene, members of the jury! Kate forever protected by the hangman, Marwood forever indebted to the mistress no one suspects—the moral man and the criminal, the bad girl with the state's favourite. A perfect match!"

"Preposterous," Marwood whispers, then raises his head. "Ridiculous, I am a married man! You think I would throw my life away, to live in sin in South London!"

"Now you sound like a snob, Mr Marwood," Poland replies. "Be careful what you say, for indeed your entire family watches. I have one more question for you, sir. Do you know of any reason why Kate Webster is not the killer of Mrs Julia Thomas?"

The question lingers, while Marwood feels the whole trial resting on his shoulders. His forehead is cold, the hair bristling. He stands there so long, drops of cold sweat appear on his neck.

"Please, Mr Marwood."

"I know of no evidence showing you've proved her guilty of

the crime."

"Step down, sir," Mr Poland says, and clicks his fingers. "An unreliable witness if ever there were one—the hangman himself, hardly to be trusted! True to his reputation, and that is why we employ only the best villains in London, for the dirtiest jobs."

Judge Denham sighs at his friend's theatrics, and waves away the hangman. "We are almost there—you may return to your job, Mr Marwood."

Leaving the witness box, Marwood cannot look at the defendant, feeling his defence of her is so weak. For some reason, though, he pauses by the dock.

Kate looks down on him and gently lays a hand on his shoulder.

"Thank you," she says. "I hope—I know—I will see you again." Marwood's mouth opens but no words come out. "Go back to your family…"

"I wanted to…I did my best." He lays his hand on hers, his body trembling like he might pass away. Up on the balcony, Aldous takes his mother's hand and soothes the resentment behind her eyes. Both moments are brief and rejoining his family, Marwood receives no welcome from Ellen, only an ambiguous smile from Aldous. Kate stands in the dock raising her hand for support, but the trio do not wave back.

Finally, the prosecution outlines a final character assassination of Kate—using her previous infractions. Nimrod Jones is called to the stand, and elaborates on her crimes against the Queen. "Her crimes in Ireland, beginning in Killane, County Wexford, are undeniable, and publicly documented. She robbed a lodging house for her boat-fare to the mainland. In 1867 she was sentenced in Liverpool to four years' penal servitude. She was let out on 'ticket-of-leave' after three years. Your Honour, a third arrest occurred on 4th May 1875, and a conviction at the Surrey Sessions on 36 charges of larceny. Further crimes were committed in and around Kingston, resulting in eighteen months in Wandsworth Prison. If I may present to the court, here is an artist's drawing of Miss Webster as a prisoner in Wandsworth." He holds up a sketch showing Kate in shackles looking through bars with moody eyes, her hair long and dishevelled.

"Are you done?" Sleigh interjects.

"Silence, defence counsellor," Denham says. "Proceed, Mr

Jones."

"Thank you, Your Honour. I am almost concluded. Most recently, on 6th February 1877, Kate Webster was charged with felony, and received a further twelve months in Wandsworth Prison. All told, she has served four prison terms ranging from two months to four years, all in the last ten years."

Kate lowers her head, and cannot bring herself to look at Marwood. "He knows the truth now," she whispers.

Next, with cross-examining permission, the defence attacks Mr Jones—who receives winks and nods from Inspector Sequin. Mr Sleigh's argument is that together the police duo will receive 'a reward' for her successful conviction, that essentially they are 'thief-takers'.

"Old news," Jones says.

"Similarly, was not Jonathan Clatter offered 'immunity from prosecution' for testifying against Miss Webster?"

"He was not, but where is he to assert to the fact?"

"*You* are here, Mr Jones," Sleigh says, "to assert to the fact. And it is a fact, yes or no?"

Jones looks at Sequin, who has no answer. "Yes, it is."

"So you'll be paid for a conviction?"

"Do not make me say so in open court, sir. I am a loyal servant of the Bow Street Runners."

"Say it."

"Yes, I take a salary for my work."

"And that salary is increased by commission, on conviction of apprehended criminals?"

"Yes."

"Yes, sir. No further questions, Your Honour."

Seizing his opportunity, Mr Poland now requests an additional witness, the star witness for the prosecution. Despite complaints from Mr Sleigh, a hatmaker named Mary Durden is admitted. She gives evidence telling the court that on the 25th of February, Kate divulged that she was going to Birmingham to take control of some property—mostly jewellery—that had been left her by a recently deceased aunt. This speech, the prosecution claims, is 'clear evidence of premeditation', since the conversation between Kate and Mary Durden occurred six days before the murder.

Denham raps his gavel on its sound block, effectively disallowing cross-examination 'due to time constraint'. He reaffirms how the defence 'need not examine every witness'.

"Ladies and gentlemen, the final witness is the accused herself, as we shall see." The judge peers at the jury and snaps his fingers for their attention. "The Old Bailey—or rather the Central Criminal Court—is, par excellence, the criminal court of the country. In its history, all the excellences and all the disadvantages of our criminal procedures are developed to an extraordinary degree. The Old Bailey juries are at once more clear-sighted and more pig-headed than any nation's jury. For your benefit, ladies and gentlemen, there is no future appeal option, but a pardon is possible by way the Queen. I therefore encourage you to be upright in your conviction of this crime. You have one hour. Recess!"

He stands and waddles off into the back lounge for tea—technically a grand jury room boasting eighteen leather armchairs, largely unused. Added in 1787, mooning down from the ceiling is a giant looking glass for appreciating one's own visage during extravagant dinners supported by 'winter warmer' cask ales and 'strong grape' from the wine cellar. Outside in the yard, a rain-protected colonnade hides a carriage for Justice Denham's swift departure, usually following an unpopular verdict.

Sir Hardinge follows close behind Denham, makes a beeline for the drinks cabinet. The sound of the Sessions grows muffled. The two men stand with elbows on the fireplace ledge, as though they had just finished a particularly strenuous game of fives or sat a schoolboy Latin exam.

"You know what I love about the Old Bailey," Denham says, pouring two glasses of sherry. "She's wonderfully compact. One can be judged, condemned, incarcerated and dutifully hanged, even buried here—without once escaping the premises, except trotting to the scaffold."

"This 'One' being a friend of yours in the criminal world?" Hardinge asks.

"All my friends at the top of the London power tree, you mean." Denham grins like a shark over his glass, eyes rolling over white.

"Same thing."

"Indeed, recent legislation has removed even burial exceptions, so now there's no occasion to go outside our four walls—'the thing' is carried out in the paved yard that separates the courthouse from the prison. It seems one can be tried in the drawing room, confined in the scullery, and hanged in the back garden."

"That would be your preference?" Hardinge says playing devil's advocate, but clearly enjoying Denham's self-indulgent glee.

"You know, Hardinge, not to change the subject, but there is something on my mind." He gestures to an upright chess table in the middle of the room, a carved miniature head looking over the pieces. "You see, I've not been sleeping on account of, well, that infernal game."

"Chess?"

"Precisely. Not so much the game, but a device you may have seen in *The Turk's Head Coffeehouse* in the Strand, deposited there from God knows where. Anyway, this one's a replica of a contraption called 'The Turk', which frequently watches me."

"Part man, part machine?" Denham laughs, but walks by to test his friend's hypothesis. The Turk—the turbaned torso of a mechanical man that plays chess as though by magic, remains motionless. As for its eyes, black beads set deep under a pale face, their central pupils seem to move.

"He's watching me."

"Yes," Denham says and sits upright. "Like that infernal Kate Webster in the court, watching me."

"Well, she *is* in the dock."

"I know, I know that, blast it. But the eyes, her eyes are demonic, truly."

"Nonsense."

"Don't, Hardinge, I ask you. The Turk's eyes are the same. A contraption—an automaton they call it—that can play chess. I never heard of anything so wonderful, or so frightening."

"A feat of mechanical engineering, dear boy, nothing more." Hardinge pats his friend's shoulder. "Come on, let's get you back in the Bailey. Mr Constable is expecting you to finish this one decently, or you won't be worth your salt."

"Don't you threaten me, Jack. I could spit out that mayor quicker than swallow him."

Hardinge says nothing, but lets Denham stand, then follows his purple-lined gown dragging on the plush carpet down to where the 'bailey' room changes to the cold stones of the court. They retake their seats. The entire room is already present.

Weary, but acting a passionate commitment, Justice Denham stands to sum up and effect sentencing. He faces the jury, adjusts his wig and raises his voice.

"Foreman, please stand. You had to choose between guilty, innocent, or partial verdict. If you choose a 'maiden session' where no one is condemned to death, the judge is presented with a pair of white gloves. My friend, do not look for those gloves, for you will not find them in this courtroom. I am not trying to sway you, but let your conscience be your guide. Have you come to a decision?"

"We have, Your Honour."

"Please to face the accused and pronounce the verdict."

The foreman—a woman of plain appearance and religious demeanour, hair parted at the centre like a Quaker—turns to Kate. She holds up her hand before God, and the parchment before the court. All is quiet. A cough is heard on the gallery.

"It'll all be over *Lloyd's Weekly* in the morning," someone says, then is silenced by the judge. The jury shift their feet, most not looking at Kate.

"On the count of the murder of Mrs Julia Thomas of Richmond, we the jury find the defendant guilty as charged. On the count of..."

Kate does not hear the rest, though she knows the counts are guilty too. Convicted on all charges—guilty—and yet she experiences an odd thought, that it is strange how the plea of Not Guilty contains the word guilty too, as though there is no alternative.

"Where is innocent?" she says. Then she raises her finger to Marwood in the gallery. "Where are you, hangman? All those tales you told me. Where's your innocent?"

"Miss Webster," Denham says, standing after hitting the gavel several times. "Order in the courtroom! Order!"

But the noise will not die down—and quickly becomes bedlam. Rumour is spreading into the street and through Newgate herself—Webster will hang. Denham brings down the gavel and to his surprise breaks its head, sending it toppling to the floor. He attempts to maintain decorum, gesturing for the bailiff to lift Kate where she has sunk like a ragdoll in the dock—mostly for lack of food—head lolling on her shoulders.

Denham reads out loud: "Miss Webster, you have shown your daring and desperation in your efforts to incriminate others, and you have been found guilty. You are not remorseful, but a creature of habit, weakness and wickedness untold. You are hereby worthy of Newgate's best, tried at the Old Bailey, and now you will be transferred to Wandsworth to suffer the extreme penalty of the law!"

"Your Honour, if I may."

Denham ignores a man now standing in the gallery. "Furthermore, you are primitive in your savageness, cunning like a tigress. You have unusual bodily strength, powerful limbs and a firmly knit frame, all used to overpower Mrs Thomas. You have extraordinary energy and determination, a capacity for great passion, but your personality is essentially mysterious, hollow, a person quite distinct from everyone else. If I may, your actions prove you subordinate from humanity. Miss Webster, you possess that amoral personality we call egomania—you live by no social rules. Now you've been tried by the highest court in the land, and you are found wanting."

William Marwood repeats his request for leniency, and the judge turns to him suspiciously.

"Denied," he announces.

Kate laughs at the word. "I'm innocent—of guilty charges. Why the need o' condemning me like this?" Again she laughs, her nerves breaking.

Denham waves what remains of the gavel, its loose stick handle. "I see the claim that people of innate homicidal feeling never enjoy a good laugh is plainly untrue. Fortunately, Miss Webster, the law is made for the protection of the weak against the strong."

Kate frowns at his eloquence, almost shrieks. But before she can, the man who came to her defence has appeared on the floor. "Your Honour, if I may." Marwood sways, the guard bracing himself for a throw-out, but the whole gallery pauses awaiting what the bogeyman of the noose, so rarely seen in public, will deliver.

Marwood looks up, regards Ellen's supportive face then Aldous', and finally turns to the court. His words are solid, not booming, and the Old Bailey echoes the poetry of his soliloquy:

> "Those lawyers see, with face of brass
> And wigs replete with learning;
> Whose far fetch'd apophthegms surpass
> Republicans' discerning.

For them to ancient forms be staunch,
To suit such worthy fellows;
Or, spare for them one legal branch,
I mean, reserve the gallows."

"Thank you, Mr Marwood, for such legal flattery," Denham says. "But we *will* be reserving the gallows for Miss Webster. Take her down. Case concluded!" From the gallery, people cheer and throw nuts down on the Old Bailey.

With Denham's nod, the Clerk of the Court stands. "Kate Webster, you stand convicted of lawful murder. Have you anything to say, why the Court should not pass judgement according to the law?"

"Yes," the accused says, shaking while seated. She clears her throat, the laughter gone. At the end there is a proud, if not regal side to Kate. "I am not bulky, nor dishevelled, but a thirty-year-old woman who had not been cared for in a long time. I am a child abandoned by parents, by country, by friends, colleagues, and now cut by the 'mercy' of the court." As she speaks there is unusual acuity in the arch of her lips, in her blank yet shrewd expression. "I am innocent because unloved. The crime is one between countries, between Ireland and Britain, and between the lawyers of this court." Kate stands, swaying. She grips the bar of the dock like she once gripped the bar of Jonathan Clatter's pub, moments before...

"I am not guilty, my lord, of the murder. I never done it, my lord. When I was taken into custody I was in a hurry, and I made a statement against Crane and Porter. That was wrong, and I want to clear their names! The man who is guilty of all this is not here at all, but why should I suffer for what other people have done? Who is he? Well, there was a child put in my hands in '74. I had to work for that child and go to prison for it, and he can be brought to you, that child, your lordship. He can. Anyone can tell it round Kingston or Richmond, too. Therefore the father of that child is the ruin of me since '73 up to this moment.... I have cherished him up to this minute, but I don't see why I should suffer for a scoundrel who left me, not after what he done!"

As Kate sits, Justice Denman stands. He adjusts his wig and nods to the jury. All are reseated and silent. The moment of Old Bailey judgement—and the only truth that counts—has arrived.

"Prisoner at the bar, after a long and painful enquiry, and a powerful advocacy on your behalf, you have been found guilty upon irrefutable testimony of the crime of wilful murder. Those you have accused of the same crime are exonerated and will not be sent to the scaffold upon the statement that you made against them. And so I no longer hesitate to pass the sentence of the law. Indeed, I have no option. My duty imperatively demands it, and I must perform it. Whether your statement is true or not, God only can tell. After many false statements you have made, in point of law, you have proved to be guilty of the crime of murder; indeed your desire to implicate others shows the justice of the verdict of the jury. I say no more. I do not wish to hurt your feelings by saying a single unnecessary word, but directly my duty is to pass upon you sentence of death." Here, he releases the convict to the Sheriff of Surrey for execution.

The Clerk of the Court reads: "Miss Webster is to be incarcerated in Newgate Prison at Her Majesty's pleasure. Thence, and without undue delay, Miss Webster is to be hung by the neck until dead."

Kate raises her hand, without even standing. "I condemn the court!"

"Miss Webster," Denham continues, "once those convicted of egregious crimes were hung in chains near the scene of their offence. That practice was supplemented in 1752 by delivery to the surgeons to be dissected and anatomised. You, Miss Webster, are fortunate these practices are now considered barbaric. I regret their loss!" He pauses. "In cases like yours, what could be more appropriate than dissection, the punishment to match the crime? But I digress, and I will digress no more. You remind me, Miss Webster, of Mrs Anne Turner a poisoner in the reign of James I, a woman of fashion who invented yellow starched collars. *Her* sentence, Miss Webster, was to be hanged in Tyburn 'in her tinny yellow ruff and cuff'." Denham smiles narrowly. "I too would see you hanged in your maid's costume, instead of clothes of your choice. I therefore forbid you to hang in Mrs Thomas's clothes, all stolen goods. Rather you will be hanged in the traditional manner. May the drop separate your neck and body, and that will be sufficient poetic justice for Mrs Thomas, God rest her soul, and the Crown, God Save the Queen. Case closed!" He hits the gavel.

"All stand," the bailiff orders and the Sessions does so.

"What's the point in standing?" Kate cries, "I'm only gonna

drop." There's a snigger in the room, its source uncertain.

Kate is hauled to her feet by a guard, led down from the dock. As she passes under the overhang she looks up for Marwood, for a sign, a moment of connection, but the gallery is too bright. She sees nothing but daylight streaming from Newgate Street where the market is packing up for the day.

Marwood, though, his hand on the rail knuckle-white, is looking down at her, Aldous by his side.

"Who is she, Papa?"

"Just someone I met in Covent Garden. Now sit back with your mama, there's a good boy."

Chapter 34
Basement of Delights
19th March 1879, Wednesday

The morning after the trial, Ellen has an odd request for her husband. She wants to see 'the basement of delights' mentioned by Kate in court.

"I don't understand," Marwood says, "you've never shown interest before."

"Well, it's time I did." From her voice Ellen is tired but earnest. "In Horncastle you were the cobbler, and hanging was a secret. But here, hanging is clearly the order of the day."

"I see. Well, I could show you now while Aldous is asleep." Marwood feels a slight thrill of excitement being asked by his own wife to show off the deadly accoutrements of his profession.

They take the outside steps, rather than the trapdoor. Marwood leads the way with a candle, turning on the gaslights that illuminate, in a musty corner, the two-handed beheading swords left by the previous occupant, William Calcraft. They are strapped to a rope between Marwood's sandbags, just adjacent to the guillotine where Kate recently sat.

"I want to sit there, in the cutter." Ellen says.

Marwood stares at her, uncertain why his wife is acting so strange. "You didn't before, and besides, you don't understand what it is."

"I know."

"You can of course, if you insist."

"I insist."

Ellen is wearing her nightgown. She is a small woman with a chiselled face, but this morning the corners of her mouth hint at excitement beyond Victorian virtue.

"I think London has gone to your head," Marwood says. Nevertheless he demonstrates the guillotine to his oddly calm wife, explaining that placing her head in the stocks is *enfourner*—to put in the oven.

Ellen nods: "So, do it. Put me in the oven."

"What? I don't have assistants…"

"That's not what we heard in court."

Already, Marwood is caught between uncertainty at the change in his wife and appreciation of her acting. With Ellen there is none of the trepidation he experienced with Kate, which reassures him, although he is puzzled by her sudden enthusiasm.

Ellen sits. He ties her legs with string, her arms with rope behind her back, fastens her to the see-saw and buckles her in place with leather straps. She breathes a little.

"When the head rolls," Marwood says, "it's as if the eyes are enraged."

"I prefer to keep my head."

"That's what you think."

"Now, don't joke, William. I just want to feel the rush."

"You know in Paris they have whole families to operate the device, the bourreaux. One family was the Sansons and each executioner was,"—he pauses—"a Monsieur de Paris."

"As though carrying out the will of the people."

"Always for the people."

Marwood lowers the bascule, positions Ellen's head in the lunette and ties the upper cowl directly above her nose. He prepares to cut her hair, but she declares herself satisfied: "Why cut the hair?"

"For a smooth drop. But really for the ritual of a clean cut."

"Very clean."

"I confess, Ellen, I'm fascinated by the trimming of the delicate hair on the back of the neck before an execution."

"Like Sweeney Todd demon barber of Fleet Street."

"Yes, like Sweeney Todd." He hesitates, knowing he could kill her. The blade is real though he has yet to raise it, or flick the safety catch—the double wooden pin.

Ellen's white blouse rises and falls with her breathing. She smiles coyly, neck twisting for her husband, but he is out of eyeshot. "Carry on, bring the blade down."

Marwood's face is blank. "You know what the French call decapitation. *Decollation*—say it."

"De-coll-at-i-on," Ellen whispers. "Pretty syllables."

"De-coll-ation because the neck is seen to disappear entirely. The victim is "de-necked, my dear." He pushes in the safety pin, raises the blade. This time the sharp end faces the floor, but he trusts his work since he used the guillotine so recently on Kate.

"Ready?"

"As I'll ever be."

Marwood looks up, sees the glint of the blade. "It's exactly the agony of hanging—the dog-like suffering—I want to replace."

"I can understand that."

"See, Ellen, the beauty and speed of the guillotine, the lack of pain." He releases the rope, causing the loose jiggle and swift drop that makes the splash of blood all the more surprising.

At that moment, a small boy's voice carries across the room. "Pa, why is she lying on the table?"

Marwood's hand shakes and growing more confused, he forgets he's already secured the safety pin. He panics as Aldous comes trotting down into the room wiping the sleep from his eyes. Quickly he unstraps his wife, and goes into a kind of shock. There is no blood—he imagined a spray—but he is disgusted by himself.

"I don't...I'm sorry." Ellen's head still lolls in the bascule. She is smiling faintly, with neither fear nor joy.

"Lift me up, William."

He does so, trailing into speech to control his mind. "Another aspect of the Bourreaux Dynasties...is they couldn't find wives outside their profession."

Ellen looks at him. "Something has changed," she says. Her face is pale, her shaking from excitement gone. "It's because we're married, William. Just remember this is all in jest, right?" But now she's noticeably scared of her husband. He tries to cover the discrepancy by demonstrating the safety pins on the guillotine, but she remains unimpressed. "You forgot to turn the blade over."

"Ellen, during a Roman crucifixion a slave who slept with a free woman could be crucified at home, without going to the courts."

"What are you talking about, William?"

"And vestal virgins who betrayed their chastity were entombed or buried alive!"

"Listen, you left the sharp end of the blade pointing down." She gestures to the floor where the blade has passed right through the guillotine, cutting open a bag of grain. The seeds are tumbling into a gentle mound. "That could have been my neck."

"Impossible," Marwood says, and tries to take her hand. "I told you this was a bad idea."

Meanwhile Ellen walks over to Aldous who has appeared on the threshold.

"Papa is working. Better not disturb his work." She ruffles Aldous's hair and turns him around. The boy now glimpses his father seated on the guillotine bench, still wondering why he did not turn the blade around.

"Hello Aldous."

"The boy has homework," Ellen says.

"He can spare five minutes." She releases Aldous and decides to abandon the basement herself, heading upstairs. The boy goes and sits next to his father, and together they look at the spilled grain.

"What did you do wrong, Papa?"

"Nothing, son. Come, let's sit over there, away from this...device."

They move deeper into the basement—Marwood carrying the gaslight—but they don't get far.

"What's this?" the boy asks, extending his finger.

"One day it'll be yours. It's mostly nuts and bolts, no nails, ingenious really." The whole contraption is painted red and designed for killing on the move.

"But what is it?"

"A miniature portable gallows," Marwood says, his brow creasing with nostalgia. He no longer uses this older travelling drop, now he has the position in London, and feels somewhat ashamed of its souvenir.

"Was Mama upset?"

"No, she doesn't like all the talk of death."

"You can tell me the stories!" Aldous says, causing his father to scrutinise his face, its innocent appeal containing the grain of intrigue he saw in Ellen's eyes before their failed experiment. "Please tell me."

"You're too young."

"But you said one day I'd be in charge."

Marwood laughs. "Yes, and one day you will be. Perhaps you'll be a London gentleman—with great expectations. You'll go to the Bar, or work in the City. The last thing you want to be is a…"

"Killer?"

"Hangman," Marwood says, not looking at his son. "We're not killers, we work for our Queen and country. For the good of the people, understand?"

"Yes, Papa. So can I hear a story now?"

They move to a long dusty sofa, and Marwood places the gaslight on the floor where it sends a warm glow to the ceiling. "They are all so grim," he says.

"I hear horror stories at school."

"You do?" He peers at the boy.

"Yes, every Friday afternoon. Edgar Allen Poe. *The Murders in the Rue Morgue.*"

"Really? Have you read *The Tell-Tale Heart?*"

Aldous looks up, thinking. "Not yet."

"Well, I've got one. Have you heard of *The Eastern Death of a Thousand Cuts?*"

"No." Aldous is quite still.

Marwood smiles sadly, knowing he has some thrilling tales, but confused as to why he tells the stories at all when they disgust his wife. But he cannot help himself—he is too far embroiled in the profession now. "Well, the Chinese have a basket of knives with each body part marked for a knife: a hand, leg, an ear." He notices a shoestring hanging over a rail, a silent critic of his storytelling.

"No!"

"It's true," Marwood smiles, and jabs Aldous gently in the ribs. "Sometimes the relatives would bribe the executioner to find the blade marked 'heart' quickly. But usually it takes a thousand cuts…" The boy grimaces, drinking in the fear.

"Tell me another one. What do people look like after they're hanged?"

"Like ghouls, like monsters."

"Ha!" Aldous says, and folds his arms. "Sounds like a story."

Marwood lightly touches his son's neck. "Okay, listen. Those who are hanged have bulbous eyes, stretched necks and strange terrible flowers edging from their mouths…"

"Flowers?"

"Their tongues—dangling from their lips, all blue, and stringy."

Aldous takes a moment to consider this, then pulls a face, but he is amused too. Marwood chooses the moment to go too far, though. Thinking back to his conversation with Ellen, trying to justify the elegance, the aristocratic value—the family values of the tradition—he says: "*Hara-kiri* was a communal affair too."

"Harry…"

"-kiri. Japanese suicide. One man cuts his own belly horizontally, then a second incision up as far as possible. But the *kaishaku* officials stood by to behead the man with a samurai sword if his courage failed—or failed to disembowel himself."

Aldous is stunned. "I don't understand."

"And in 'hung, drawn and quartered', the drawing just means being brought to the scaffold, not the disembowelling part. It's nothing to be frightened of."

Aldous says nothing.

"Here's a funny one. There's a true story of 'the dead man waiting'. He died just waiting for the rope, and fell into the executioner's arms. He had a broken heart because he'd just got married!"

"They didn't need to hang him?"

"No, he burned himself out, from the inside…"

Again, Aldous puzzles this possibility and shakes his head in half belief. "Tell me more."

"Okay, John Robert Radclive was a hangman who apprenticed with Calcraft, before my time. He was once in the Royal Navy, so he stitched up pirates in the China Seas."

"Tell me about America," Aldous says. "I like those stories best."

Marwood ponders this question. "You don't like pirates?"

"I prefer cowboys and Indians. We learned about the Great Lakes in Geography. There's Lake Superior, Lake Michigan, Lake *Eeerie*…"

"Why don't you tell me a story?"

Aldous smiles. "I don't know any."

"What about shootings? Or highwaymen. You told me about Dick Turpin last week."

The boy considers. "Okay, I have one. I know a firing squad has one man fire a blank, so no one knows who killed the prisoner."

"That's right. But did you know the riflemen say they can tell from the jolt—they know who fired the blank."

"I don't believe them."

Marwood smiles now. "Who knows? But that's not a real story—you need more details for a truthful tale. Here's a good one, if you'll listen."

"Yes…"

"Good. So twenty years ago in 1860, an incident took place in America, off Bedloe's Island on the East Coast. Almost twelve thousand people crossed from the mainland in rowing boats to witness the hanging of murderer Albert E. Hicks. After the counterweight was dropped, his body jerked up with alarming force for the crowd, but it took eleven minutes for 'Hicksie' to die. That's no way to go. He was executed under federal law, publicising the event as a 'sheriff's ball', a ticketed day. Very profitable for entrepreneurs too, including circus-man P. T. Barnum."

"I don't understand."

"Here's the point," Marwood says, gently. "No one should die like that. There's no need for all that suffering so everyone can have a good time."

"It doesn't make sense."

"That's right, it doesn't." He pauses. "So you want to hear what he did?"

"Yes."

"So 'Hicksie' was a secretive gangster wielding power in Manhattan, especially in gambling and loansharking, yet he was tried for 'piracy of the high seas'. He marshalled an oyster boat to Deep Creek, Virginia and apparently murdered the crew of three men before they docked. Innocent or guilty, 'piracy with aggravated treasonous intent in the Commonwealth of Virginia' was the charge. The Federal Marshall who executed Hicks was Captain Isaiah Rynders—I remember his vicious face. But they made a lot of money in the ol' American Way."

"The American Way?"

"It was a show. The name of the ship that took Hicksie to Bedloe's Island was called *The Red Jacket*—for the blood—and it cost the earth. There were other yachts, charters, skiffs, even steamships packed in sight of Hicksie's gallows." Marwood re-imagines the scene's congestion. "They say the authorities kept two-thirds of the space for themselves, all hungry to witness a death."

He pauses and Aldous is left on the edge of the sofa, literally.

"What happened, Papa? Did he escape?"

"I feel for the man, even now." Though he was never there, Marwood senses the whole spectacle; he speaks slowly, more in contrition than slowing the story for suspense. "The hangman cut the rope sending the man up. The jerk was supposed to be quick, but not this time—Hicks was drawn up slow, so all could see a real-life pirate die. It took a while, twenty minutes. He dangled there for the party while the refreshments were served. One more thing—the island became Liberty Island."

"The one for the stone lady?"

"Yes," Marwood says. "The one awaiting the statue of Lady Liberty. This summer at the Paris World Fair—the *Exposition Universelle*—they displayed her giant head. Her seven crown spikes or 'rays' of light show freedom cast over the seven seas and seven continents, little good she'll do Mr Hicks, though."

Aldous weighs the story, gauges his own fear, then asks "for another!"

"Rough Justice," Marwood says, then remembers his son. "I don't have any more. Come on, your mother said you have homework."

"But tell me why they had the party?"

Marwood stands up to lead the way, scooping up the gaslight.

"I don't know, really. People will go along with a crowd, Aldous. You should be careful about that. How to avoid these things? 'The Hand of an Artist' operates alone, I'd say. The rest is ugly."

"Papa?"

"You see, they even call the name for a post-hanging celebration 'splicing the rope. Like cutting a cake—a happy occasion."

"Papa, do you work alone?"

Marwood considers this carefully, knowing that other hangmen spring a trapdoor with help from three men all cutting strings to protect their guilt, like a firing squad. "Some don't. In Scotland, the hand tying the knot is never the same as the hand pulling the lever."

"But what about you?"

"I operate alone. Now time for homework—more Edgar Allen Poe and the Great Lakes."

They take a different route leaving the cellar, passing dangling leg straps and hoods, all indicating the last seconds of life. Aldous ducks under the clothes, unconcerned.

"…and the rustle of the condemned woman's gown troubled the ear of the old man."

"Papa?"

"Nothing, son." He is imagining Kate in a black dress under a white hood, and shivers. He has never executed a woman before. Now he must face the girl he met in Covent Garden and defended so bluntly in court. She will be his first….

As they reach the steps, Aldous's face goes white, not because of the story, but because of something he has seen. He extends his finger.

"I'll give her 'a quick twitch' on the end of an oiled rope," Marwood says. "It's just a saying—it means the unholy embrace of the rope."

"No, not that," the boy says, staggering backwards into his father's chest. He points again. There, on a table under the stone steps is a glowing object, caught in the false lamplight and giving off its own gleam. "What is it?"

"Oh, that's a fake! Nothing to fear…" He steps forward and lifts the skull into new light, turning it around. "Watch," he says, and placing it in front of his lips, he waggles the jaw. But the boy screams and is gone, suddenly running up the stairs. "I'm sorry," Marwood calls after him, "Aldous, I didn't mean to scare you." He lowers the skull of Charon—made from cow-bone—bony Charon the ferryman who conveys the dead across the River Styx. "We all have to pay the executioner. No hangman ever died rich."

"That's enough, William. Your playtime is over." He looks up the steps and sees Ellen glaring down at him, the boy in her aprons. She closes the door and turns on her heel, returning her husband into darkness.

He stands there, alone with his gadgets, bones and entrapments of a life spent killing for the state. Suddenly he feels cold, shut away from his family, a worn-out hollow but good heart, lit only by the fading gaslight and the man-made skull.

Chapter 35
Secrets of Newgate
19th March 1879, Wednesday

After her trial, Kate expects to be returned to the justice room at Bow Street Police Station, or perhaps the Extradition Court. Instead she is taken directly to Newgate via a passage under Holborn Viaduct. As she emerges inside the forbidding labyrinth, one side is a granite wall and the other is a long horizontal slit through which—like a false blessing—the dome of St Paul's Cathedral looms large against the sky.

Here the central courtyard divides into two exercise yards, divided by severe walls crowned with broken glass. The male prisoners' cells are visible diagonally, the females' cells hidden deeper in the bowels of the prison. At a small gate is 'the visiting box' where inmates are permitted conversation with 'outsiders' allowed only so far.

Kate is marched from the 'Master's Rooms' where prisoners could afford their own meals to the Common Side for average debtors, the press-yard for bribeworthy 'respectable inmates', and finally the women's wing. As 'fresh meat' she is led to the 'jack-office', a tiny room up a spiral staircase with barred windows ten feet from the Old Bailey itself. This den is upholstered like a cheap lawyer's office or East End counting-house, the typical trimmings—a green armchair, worn-down desk, window ledge and solitary shelf—overshadowed by a grandfather clock with prison bars for hands, and a lacquered map of Newgate spread over the floor, which Kate does her best to avoid.

The Women's Guard now arrives, a husky-looking man of about sixty in a straw hat and ragged beige suit. If not for his dirty trousers, he'd resemble a country undertaker more than a jailer. Without a word he points to the Old Bailey through a stone slit, then to the small, grated windows containing the unhappy creatures trapped in dismal cells while the busy scramble of London is only yards away. Following this dumb show, he asks Kate to sign a book for prisoners' autographs. It is then that she notices, on a shelf with some old writing-parchment, the head-cast of the notorious criminal Charles Peace, the very same man she saw executed. Peace is grinning as though he died the very same way he lived, amused by the absurdity of a world he manipulated.

The tour continues with the turnkey ascending a stone spiral staircase, Kate following, both entering a square room. He gestures to a heavy set of irons, those worn by the redoubtable Jack Sheppard.

"Who is Jack Sheppard?"

He glares at her with disgust. "You'll find out—and those'll be Dick Turpin's chains though I don't suppose you know 'im neither."

"The highwayman." She reaches down to touch his iron loops scarred with rust—but the turnkey pushes her to the door. Kate says nothing and succumbs, though her blood is up. She is prodded onwards, where a gate studded with nails opens onto a dank passage heading down a number of tortuous and intricate windings. Remarkably this route runs parallel with the Old Bailey so Kate can witness the very site of her trial in sudden pockets of promising light. Yet all cells are hemmed in by mesh iron grates, built to crush the idlest daydream of escape, and trap one in a labyrinth of confusion. The courthouse flits into view every few seconds—the witness box, the dock, the jury bench—but the trial seems so long ago. Wishing she were outside, if only to breathe living air, Kate peers down on the old College of Physicians, Newgate Street, and all the oblivious market-traders.

The turnkey exits into an inner courtyard, allowing one hour's exercise per day. He meanders as though getting his own exercise, until at last they enter the women's wing near the Sessions-house. Here Kate is met by her future cage-birds, some twenty women. Most stand and stare, while a few, aware of the presence of strangers, retreat to their cells. Kate glares back, careful to show no fear.

"Welcome to your new home," the turnkey announces. He waves for the women to ignore the new arrival; most are busy washing clothes over an open-air trough.

"What's that?" Kate says, pointing. One side of the women's yard is railed off into a kind of iron cage, four feet high and roofed at the top by iron bars.

"The communal Judas-hole for your visits," the turnkey says. "If you *have* any friends, that is. Quick, follow me." Kate is led to the inner ward, passing in an alcove a loping old woman under a bedraggled orange gown and Dutch sun hat. She is busy making frowning gestures with a skinny young boy—a visitor, just beyond touching distance—of about thirteen. With a stark recognition—deluded for a moment—Kate believes Daniel has come to see her. But it is not so. The boy is too poorly clad and too tall, a young teen shivering in the cold. The mother coughs up her latest scam and the boy nods with a weak smile, sensing failure but tightening his brow into a look of resolute desperation.

"You'll be joining the friendless group, then?" the turnkey says but Kate is silent. Worried about receiving a crack, she's heard enough about how Newgate jailors keep discipline.

Inside, the ward opens out. A fire is dying low in the grate, shadowing an oak table where a baker's dozen of women is huddled on a long, rickety bench. A loop of iron hooks is fixed to the wall, hoisting up the sleeping mats of the prisoners, their rugs underneath.

"This is a livin' room and for sleeping," the turnkey says. "You can use your *more private* cell if you like, but it's no matter. Just know the Good Book damn well, and you'll do fine." He points to the Bible passages pasted to the wall with an unknown gloopy substance.

The primary 'ward woman' steps forward, lays down her knitting. "I'm Molly Muggs," she says, "but you can call me Muggins." The other women laugh. "There's one bed 'ere, n' that's mind. No other rules."

"Oh," says Kate, eyeing boiled chicken in a cooking pot, black bread on the table.

The turnkey pushes Kate forward. "Come on, we'll be back soon enough. The grand tour ain't over yet!" Molly Muggs watches as the new inmate walks by.

"She'll be back," the turnkey reassures.

"No doubt," Molly Muggs smiles.

The next room brings a tear to Kate's eye, as it's where Daniel would be: the 'junior school', a learning hovel for boys under fifteen. Most have ripped blazers, school caps falling like dead rats over their foreheads. One boy has nothing except a pair of grey trousers chopped at the knee. A despairing schoolmaster—a prisoner himself—strokes his balding head in the corner, grimacing at the stony ground.

"In the words o' Dickens," says the turnkey, "there ain't nothing between 'em but a wink o' the gallows and the hulks."

Kate stares at these wasted children through the world's eyes. Here shame or contrition is entirely out of the question, and yet they are evidently gratified to be paraded. As per Charles Dickens's visit forty-six years earlier, the population seems not to have changed one whit. The boys' communal lark appears to be the excitable belief in the illusion of celebrity, a sense that ol' Newgate is a jolly affair. Hence every boy who 'falls in' actually seems pleased, as if he had done something delightful to arrive at Newgate's grand hotel. Kate simply ruffles a small boy's hair, causing much laughter to the schoolmaster's hopeless consternation.

The turnkey ignores all, and pushes through the school-yard to the men's quarters, returning in a loop to his office. Unlike the 'schoolboys', these men seem beat down, brutalised and listless, adrift from worlds of hope, energy and ambition. They pass a heavy-set ruffian in a smock-frock who glares at them murderously. He is chewing tobacco and busy berating a mute spaniel, the animal's head resting disconsolately on his hand.

The tour's spectacles have their desired effect on Kate. Her face grows sullen and placable. She won't cause no trouble, the turnkey tells himself.

"Dear Old Newgate!" he declares when they reach the office, "you *can* hate her. Some say her name is ugly and nothing but grease and squalor, a bleak-looking prison with an awful little iron door three feet from the ground. I say the opposite—this is home, sweet home, and you must grow to love her—if you're countin' on survivin'!"

"I've been in prison before," Kate says, holding her nerve.

"Not like this one you ain't."

Finally they repeat the beginning of the inner circle to the women's ward, but not before they enter the exercise yard. Here Kate spies the hole-in-the-wall where, without her knowing, William Marwood will stand thinking of her one night. She spies the open grate, its bars like a skull-and-crossbones, where an iron box sits for 'alms' ready to be pushed through the wall—to beg from all London. Later a chosen prisoner will cry "Remember Poor Newgate's Guests!" until midnight. For now the alms' box is empty and unmoving while the people of London pass by in daylight.

"It's banned and considered rude to ask for aid while the sun shines."

"Where is the kitchen?" Kate asks.

"Funny you should ask—through that door is a yard where the scaffold is erected. The kitchen's there."

"Near the gallows?"

"That's right. We prepare the meals at the New Drop just to remind the prisoners 'at chow' where it all ends." He guffaws into this collar. "A good ol' scaffold for us—none o' that execution shed business that's popular south of the river...."

Kate considers what he's saying, points through the door where she sees the small arc of a tomb. "And that's the graveyard?"

"You guessed it."

So I'll walk over the graves of the dead, Kate thinks, and be hung in the open air, no better than Charles Peace! "Can the inmates watch?"

"Of course they can—deterrent, innit, though too late for most." Again he chuckles. "We got all sorts in 'ere, house-breakers, perverts, coiners, murderers, washerwomen falsely accused of disturbing the peace, all bolted in stocks in a separate vaulted asylum. Our underground's known as 'Limbo', you know. Fittin', innit?"

"Quite," Kate says and shows her teeth, then showing a territorial disgust, she spits on the ground.

"Come on you, it's getting' dark."

Eventually he leaves her in the women's ward, where Kate is shown a communal cell. Molly Muggs gives her the blanket, and she is handed from turnkey to new boss—a fresh landlady. But no discussion of her crime takes place. The forewoman gives her a Bible.

"What's yer poison?"

"Gin," Kate says. "I'll drink anythin' though."

"We gots it all, missy. Listen 'ere, you treats us good n' sticks up for yer own, you can be someone. The moment you crosses us, though,"—she gestures to the other three women—"we'll cut you off. Then the men can 'ave yer."

"Gin," Kate says.

"Okay, Miss Web-star, you'll get yer cat-lick. Today we got sherry sack, lucky you. Wot I asks is politeness." Molly lifts the bottle, pours an amber-coloured liquid into a pewter cup. "If you like that, we got liquorish Ipocras. You earns that."

"With seditious preachings, an' holy prayers for the righteous blood," a second woman—knitting quietly—interjects. "If religion's yer true poison. Or is ya'a Satanist?"

"I am a True Believer," Kate says, "so don't try and test me."

"Don't talk to 'er like that," Molly Muggs says, and slaps Kate's hand, startling her. "So yer a Catholic, eh? Just know, you won't get away with *nowt* in 'ere. We's five and you's one, so you better kick off behavin'. Right?"

Kate considers five-to-one odds, her pride still smarting from the turnkey's patronising prison tour, but she relents.

"Listen, I jus' want the drink."

"Ask and ye shall receive—a lil' sufferin'." Molly Muggs passes her the sherry sack, third-full, and Kate downs it in one. "I got a walking tour fur yer too. You slip up and yer down in Limbo—the dungeon—unner-ground. I mean it."

"What's in Limbo?"

"Follow me." She walks off to the fire grate and opens a trapdoor—Kate at her elbow—and reveals a vertical stepladder reminiscent of Marwood's basement in Gloucester Road. One by one they descend, and another woman hands a wooden tray to Kate, two candles glued to its base.

The forewoman Molly then leads the way down a stone passageway. Already the reek of rotten flesh and hot air causes Kate to cover her mouth—nothing has so much reminded her of that slow night in the kitchen of 2 Mayfield Gardens with Mrs Thomas. She was far drunker then, too, and could resist the dreadful odours. Kate shakes her head to kill the memory.

In the first cell Molly reveals an inmate, a young girl no more than eighteen, forced to lie in a coffin for a bed. For the first time in a long time, Kate's eyes grow stark with pity. The girl is on her side, asleep, her shoulders protruding the skin at an awful angle to get comfortable, so she will awake sore and pained by the force of her own bones.

"What did she do?"

"Got in our way," Molly says. "These holding cells are just a stone bench with a mattress. She's a rebel, though, so we gave her the coffin bed."

"As a joke?"

Molly frowns, showing a mouth empty of teeth. "Yes, as our learnin' joke! We want to know will you ever betray us, Kate? We'll give you a chain-bed upstairs, but you *can* swop it for one down here." She smiles with her gums, showing little pits of nothing.

"I wouldn't change my chain for the Lord Mayor's neck chain."

"That's what we like to hear. Or you get this treatment." With a sweep of her arm, Molly reveals the rest of the prisoners' cells. As they come into view, their damp and darkness betrays scant life, but as her eyes adjust Kate sees the prisoners fettered and lock-bound. Each is trapped in a single Devil's Island, disciplined by the ladies above by having her feet strapped in irons. In addition, a wooden pole secures each leg brace into the stonework—jamming her into the very structure of Newgate.

"Now that's a prison! The keeper's house—that office you saw—is directly above. We can't go in the next room, though. It's for the hanging condemned." Molly turns to Kate with a sudden thought. "You ain't down to hang?"

"No," Kate says. "I just pushed my father under a hansom. He broke his leg so they give me fifteen years." The speech is a little rehearsed and Molly cocks her head, frowns, and sighs.

"If you say so, girl. Jus' don't think you can 'ide Bailey news. Now trust, you don't wanna see the condemned cell, even if I could show it. I ain't *that* trusted round here!" She is up close breathing into Kate's face. "A sub-terra-nean pit, see. A hellish place!"

"Why?"

"For one, it's ju' stone, no benches or need of irons. Just an open sewer running through the middle. You die of suffocation, if the rats don't get yer. Not a bad idea—they don't even 'ave to hang yer!"

"Enough, take me back upstairs."

"I say when enough, girlie. And okay—I says enough. I'll like you, Kate Webster, I can tell. Come upstairs n' meet the girls."

Within an hour Kate is more accepted, especially as the sherry sack flows. "My new favourite."

"One butt o' sherry a day," Molly jokes, all seated at the table now. "So long as we works—laundry, old clothes, mostly. A few dry matches. No crowd pickin' here."

"That's what my boy does," Kate says, then regrets it.

"You got a boy?"

"He's eleven," she says, gently hanging her head.

"Anyway," Molly takes up, not even noticing Kate's reaction, "as female prisoners we's allowed to make a profit on sales o' candles too. We jam 'em in these pyramid holders made of clay, see." She demonstrates one, accidentally breaking the end of the candle and all the women laugh, including Kate. Finally Molly joins in too.

"So you likes the gin, eh, Webster? A little fresh Kill-Grief, Meat-and-Drink or Washing-and-Lodging for you?"

"That's right."

"Well, go n' fill this!" She claps Kate on the shoulder with her pewter dish. Kate stands, as do other women as if by instinct, while Molly stays seated. "I told yer, Webster, do as we say."

Slowly Kate walks to the sherry butt, pauses and refills the table jugs, hiding her own jar of gin near the fire. She feels the lice under her feet as she returns from this makeshift tap-room, ready to serve the 'master' forewoman Molly Muggs.

"That's right, dear. Now you know your place. Welcome to Jack Ketch's living room!" She slaps Kate on the hips while all the women toast Jack Ketch—"the first and worst of hangmen!"

Quietly, Kate sips her gin, taking in her surroundings without comment. How can this hell be any better than the one below? At least there, she thinks, you are alone with the lunatics, while up here it's nothing but a 'nursery of crime', similar to Liverpool City Gaol. She must resist the poisons, she knows, or her decline will accelerate from stupid and senseless, to brutish and thoughtless, until she becomes a mere Newgate-bird, wicked, outrageous, 'dyed in the yard'.

For once, the thought is transformative.

"I could get married in here," Kate tells the table, feeling the effects of the gin. "If I met a nice man, n' he weren't hitched already. See, I've 'eard about jail knots, rites o' passion on the inside n' the like. I could be a prison wife."

One woman, a fat woman close to the fire, spits her drink out in amusement.

"Mock marriage is fine," Molly replies. "But we don't encourage it, 'cos the men get too close. We can't control 'em, see. But real marriage—well, every girl deserves wot's comin' to 'er. Secret an' unlawful an' performed by degraded clergymen for less than a guinea—if you're that way inclined—but you 'ave to leave Newgate for that."

"Where can I meet the clergymen?"

"Why, you got a fella in mind? There's a marrying house near St Paul's, *The Hand and Pen*, jus' an upstairs room in the tavern. But 'ow you gonna leave Newgate? It'll cost ya to git 'proper hitched' on the outside. Licence n' all."

"I'll find a way," Kate muses. "I'll find my Marwood."

"Ha, ha, ha," Molly says. "That you will, girl. Run over yer father, did yer? You *will* find yer Marwood! What is it they say, girls? If Pa killed Ma?"

"Who killed Pa?" the women cry in unison, all except Kate.

"Ma-wood! Listen, there's only one way outta here," Molly continues. "The Jack Sheppard way."

"Who's Jack Sheppard?" Kate asks, enduring another round of ridicule. "I've heard the name a lot."

"I bet you 'ave. Sheppard's not only the greatest robber n' prison-breaker of our time. Frieda, you tell it."

Here Molly slaps a dish-cloth on the table in the direction of Frida La Roche, a Frenchwoman who plays resident storyteller—a seventy-year-old ne'er-do-well locked up fifteen years ago for 'general vagrancy' who stayed—deciding she'd survive better on the inside. Without further complaint, Frida hitches up her stockings as though digging under her skin for the tale.

"Well, *madames*," she begins, dulling her accent for the guest, "when lil' Jacques first escaped it was to Bartholomew Fair, 1726, so says de' *Newgate Calendar*. But why, I hears you say, was he locked up? Robbery *oui*, tomfoolery *oui*, but for evadin' capture which policemen do not like, *non non non*, ladees." Frida chops her wrist at the air. "*Bien* 'e makes 'is escape good through crowds up Snow Hill and Giltspur Street, all the way t'Smithfield with those jolly souls of th'fair." Kate remains quiet about her memory of Bartholomew Fair, how Marwood said she would learn more of Sheppard soon enough. "This Jack, e' joins the crowd enjoying their full-hearted liberties—the smell of a London fields—among the booths and tacky shows of de fairground!"

But Kate can help it no longer. "Where was he born? Can't you tell it from the beginning?" Molly Muggs closes Kate down with another jab, this time to her ear. There's only so much Kate can take.

" 'e was born in White's Row, Spitalfields," Frida humours Kate with an evil-eye, "where the fields spit, so dey say. 'e was in a workhouse boy in Bishopsgate, then five years apprentice fur a Wych Street carpenter—but only four months to go, he goes fur a life o' crime! That is the beauty of his story—he didn't need to be a criminal, 'e could a bin you or me! Really, 'e's jus' a crazy Londoner!"

"Like you and me," Kate jokes.

"Like all of us now," Molly says.

"So 'e was first banged up in the St Giles Roundhouse," Frida says low, "but free inside a few hours. How'd 'e do that? Well, 'e prises off the roof n' swings issell down with a sheet, nothin' more. Then he takes up a quick career as a pickpocket in Leicester Fields, n' goes direct to the New Prison in Clerkenwell within twenty-four hours. 'e may be good at escapin' but 'e's not ver' bright at running!"

"So that's it?" Kate says. "He climbed out a window."

"Listen, girlie," Frida scowls, "you don't know Jack Sheppard, so listen up good. They pins 'im to the floor, links n' fetters style. So what 'e do? Only saws through the fetters n' breaks through a ten-inch oak door. How'd 'e get through? Well, with a metal shard hidden in 'is teeth,"—gesturing to her purple gums—"he gives it mute in Clerkenwell, when he sees the night watch comin'. Smart, see?"

"So far."

"Yes, well. That's why the governor Mr Faux-Jones keeps 'severed chairs' in his plush big office at the top o' Newgate. 'e likes the fact that Newgate makes 'istory, so the chairs was kept by the prison to 'preserve the Memory of this extraordinary Event and Villain'."

Kate nods, thinking of the governor admiring his own criminal wit. "So what happened to Sheppard?"

"Aha, so 'e goes to the Fair, and 'e's free just three months, right, before 'e gets captured by a bounty hunter. You 'eard o' Jonathan Wild? Big-time criminal turned thief-taker, like ol' Pat Garrett in America. So our boy Jackie gets reported by a cobbler in

Bishopsgate and this milkman in Islington. But 'e still catches 'im robbing a watch-maker's in Fleet Street. 'ow'd Jack do it? He tells the apprentice 'get in the back, lad, an' stick to yer tools n' don't use yer Master so bad'. Then he robs 'em blind."

Molly can bear it no longer, jumping to her feet. "Then he's in Newgate," she cries out, frightening a few at the table, "where they lock 'im to the floor with triple fetters. Listen up, 'e was chained upside down on the Stone Castle's top floor, legs and hands in irons." She raises her hands, crosses them at the wrist. "Did he get out? Adam n' Eve it, you bet he did!"

As she tells the tale, a larger crowd of women has gathered. They begin rattling their plates and cutlery. Suddenly, Molly is up on the table, making a mock speech before the Globe Theatre itself. "But 'e slipped a hand, n' with a tiny nail he relaxed the links on 'is leg-chains, then 'e's out—free like a contortionist at the Fair!"

"That's right," cries Frida, winning back the story. "But first 'e squeezed through the chimney with a piece o' broken chain, and climbed into the Red Room. With one nail he freed the bolt in under a minute n' entered the passage to the chapel. There 'e used a spike to force three more doors, all locked from the outside, n' after the last one, 'e found himself on the roof of the prison."

Molly swipes at Frida with her foot, and catches her good on the cheek. Everyone ignores the wounded woman who falls down, the crowd openly allied to the young forewoman Molly, the queen of entertainment, ruling the women's wing with her fists and feet. "That's right, girlie," Molly cries, not even looking at Frida, but staring at Kate. "But ol' Jack Sheppard forgets 'is blanket, so guess what? 'e lowered isself n' went back for it—fully down the chimney n' round, twice. Now's there's a classy prison-boy!"

Kate laughs with glee despite herself, and not thinking of the injured woman either. "What happened next? Did he get caught?"

Molly crouches to her ankles up on the table, and takes Kate by the chin. "Yes, my newbie girl, 'e did get caught. We all gets caught, don't we?"

"How then?"

The women turn to watch Kate's punishment for interruption, but Molly is too clever to hit her again. "Let me tell you, girlie, so you're right settled among us. You 'eard of last dying speeches? They make 'em on the day o' yer death. n' from what I hear, you'll be getting a speech o' yer own!" Kate says nothing but realises the allusion is to her own hanging. The room goes quiet. Frida climbs back from floor to table, ignored as she worries her chin with her hands.

Molly taps her finger to her nose: "Well, Sheppard knew 'bout speeches, of course, n' he wasn't gonna go down without a show, not our Jackie. So e' pays a lil' visit to a printer o' those end-o-the-line ballads, then everyone knows he's a free Cockney sparra—'cos he wrote the verses hisself!"

"He knew the game was up," Frida whispers, and is permitted to speak.

"To top all," Molly says, "'e robbed a rich man n' used the money to buy a top-notch suit n' a sparklin' silver sword. Then 'e hired a coach—a touch of genius, mind—n' rode through St Giles, blatant before th'coppers." She speaks low, silencing the room, her words directed at Kate. "Yes, Jackie gets arrested as 'e knows 'e would, but the pamphlets an' his costume are ready, so 'e'll ride to his death in style. The trial is swift n' Tyburn comes a-callin'!"

"Did he hang?"

"What do you think? Let's ju' say on his way to ol' Tyburn, Jonathan Wild finds a penknife on Jackie, disarms 'im. Wily ol' Wild is up to the task, see, but that dun't stop Jackie writin' his own last chance escape. He went to the gallows a brave man, a crowd-pleaser, dyin' game and proud, and *that's* the end we should all cleave to!"

The inmates murmur their support, with a veiled suspicion underneath.

Molly concludes: "Here is a lion, ladies, who escaped Newgate and guiltless and free, had the most soulful and glorious send-off of his life!"

"And death," Kate quips, which fortunately Molly does not hear. "Tell me, what's the point of escapin' and still gettin' caught?"

The table is silent. Kate is thinking of her boy Daniel, who one day *could* be a virtuous Jack Sheppard, but the thought is bitterly conceived. "*That* is no life," she says, and leaves the table, only to be hauled back by Molly Muggs. The story is over—there is only one woman in charge now—like the ghost of Mrs Thomas come to wreak divine vengeance. Molly spits on Kate, rubs the phlegm in her hair. For once, the rebellious killer does not react.

Alone, Kate wonders at herself, feeling weak, but calm too.

When all the women have eaten, she is finally allowed her sup of the chicken, then is left to clean up for everyone.

Chapter 36
Last Chance Saloon
20th March 1879, Thursday

The following morning after some deliberation, Marwood goes to see her in prison. He cannot leave Kate there to face her sentence and become a new member of a hardened clan with only a priest—whom Marwood doubts has visited her—to help her.

He enters the building alone, with the plan to give emotional sustenance to Kate in her hour of need, fresh from her sentencing. The irony does not escape him, although Kate probably does not yet know her hour of execution, or the role he will play. He can only focus on helping her in the present.

All thoughts evaporate once he enters Newgate's fortress. Once behind the walls, he passes the enclosed governor's house where all is quiet, and approaches the chapel. Here the Sunday service is often reserved for the quick, but not yet dead—the condemned forced to pray for their souls in advance of their own hangings. Trapped by the chapel's double oak doors, a desperate air persists: there is something otherworldly, yet uncanny in a hushed place of worship. The poverty of its furnishings is enough to make the soul shiver—the dead-eyed pulpit, its ragged curtains drained of maroon, the cracked too-small stone font, the over-large commandments chalked on a board for the congregation, the scattered cobwebs, the everlasting cold.

One sight in particular, though, demands Kate's already-anxious gut turn against her. For below the chalkboard is 'the condemned pew', a squat enclosure herding both men and women— those marked for death—to answer for their sins with self-abasement. Here they kneel with exhaustion before their fellow convicts, forced to hear prayers for their 'black souls', nod in acknowledgement of their crimes, and rapturously approve the vicar's speech to "learn God's justice by their fate!" Consider the emotions of those trapped in that terrible, narrow place, suspended as Charles Dickens reminds us, 'between the gallows and the knife'. Like all people, they would choose a pained life to no life at all, but they have no choice. Their last act is to be theatrically fed to their fellow suffering creatures, their fear of mortal death transformed into old doctrines of truth and moral certainty, while the prison leaders faithfully honour everlasting life.

Kate has come to the chapel to escape the women's ward, if only for an hour. She sits up in the women's galley as though watching her future self being read last rites. She has a fractured view over the audience's loping parapet—built to obscure the identities of her fellow prisoners 'up for the drop'—their crammed quarters adding separation to fear and blunting camaraderie. She is staring vertically at the pulpit when William Marwood enters. Instantly she covers her mouth, fearing an apparition: the hangman is dressed all in black, already mourning. She watches as he circles the chapel floor. He pauses at the preacher's pulpit and communion table near a box reserved for the Governor of the Gaol, then sits in the Chief Warder's seat beneath. Kate is more amused than offended, but the daring of Marwood's authority confuses her.

"And what gives you the right, sir?" she calls from above, causing Marwood to spring up and swivel on his heel for the source of the voice. "Up here, Mr Hangman, sir."

Laying his hand on the reading-desk, Marwood squints up through the dim light and spies a lone figure against the whitewashed walls of the chapel. Just at that moment, the harmonium begins the musical part of the service—the preacher's boy must be practicing— and they're both disturbed by the dissonance of the organ's foot-operated air-bellows striking the instrument invisibly into life. Kate covers her ears, but the sound ends just as abruptly with the appearance of Marwood next to her on the gallery.

"How are you, Kate?" He sits a few seats away, one row back.

"Bett'n can be expected. Why did you come 'ere, Mr

Hangman? Don't you 'ave a funeral to go?"

Marwood wonders, does she know I'm scheduled to perform her execution? "I shouldn't be here," he says, "on account of the governor. And please call me William."

"Ha! They call that frat-ern-i-sation. I know yer big words too, sir. I teach 'em to my boy, bless 'is soul. But don't think you can fool me now. No one is here to help me, not now." She looks up, half sheepish.

"But *I am*. I came here to help you."

"To make me 'toe the line', more like."

"Why'd you do it, Kate?" He pauses deliberately. "Was it worth it?"

"Is that what you came to ask me? What do *yer* know about my life?" She stands unexpectedly. "You comes with yer basement tricks an' jus' up n' helps me, then drops me like a stone at trial. And now you's back again. You keep bouncin' in n' out of my life, like you's got some divine right. Make yer mind up!"

"I know."

"What do you know of the heart of Catherine Lawler? You's jus' a country boy a' heart—I've lived in these cities since I 'as seventeen, that's hal' my life. What can *you* know of the big, bad world?"

"I know enough. I know people make it that way."

"Humph! The world is jus' confusion n' fightin'. 'Why'd I do it?' yer askin' me, point blank."

"And?"

"Ha! Why not? 'Cos I dun' get no respect, tha's why. Got nuthin' for my boy. Why should e' suffer? I had grand schemes for 'im. To get n'education an' all. To be somebody—a lawyer, and put other people away!" Kate laughs a little, seeing the comedy of her rebellion, but her face grows tired as long as she remembers her boy. "I have to go...."

"Yes?"

"My boy—Daniel? Will you take care of 'im?"

"Kate...I'm not sure. Where is he?"

"Bleedin' Heart Alley, 58. Southwark Way. Woman's called Sarah Crease, you saw her at the trial."

"I'll do what I can."

She turns her face, a grimace of genuine pleasure. "When is

that ever enough?"

Marwood stands and walks to the end of his pew, causing Kate to fear his departure. Instead he sits quietly in front of her, just ten feet away. He stares down at the condemned coffin in the chapel below, the anonymous last resting place of the next criminal to suffer 'Her Majesty's penalty'—perhaps Kate herself. The atmosphere is bizarre; coloured light from the towering stained glass windows dances across their legs. Marwood watches the coffin until all he can see is the darkness inside.

"You know, Kate—there are some terrible stories of people's lives. But you must have faith at the end. I trust that's why you're here?"

"It's just pointless."

"Well, I wanted to give you this." He opens his hand to reveal a twisted piece of metal, a hook at one end and razor blade at the other. Kate stares at the implement and pretends not to recognise it for a moment, but quickly changes her mind. She folds the metal over the razor blade, secures it in the hip of her robe. Then she touches Marwood's leg. He feels a strange shiver, part excitement at his contribution to her wayward life, half regret at some betrayal of himself.

"Thank you, William. I don't know what to say."

"That's all I can do," the hangman says, "but it is the least. I have some advice too."

"I'd prefer a story," Kate says, looking down at the empty chapel. "Something dark and dreary—those tales make me feel better."

"I only have tales of hangings, Kate, unless you want to hear about life in a cobbler's shop—how to mend a pair of shoes."

She smiles. "No, William. Tell me of the women who've died, and how they died. It's your specialty. Believe it or not, I want to know—what I'm facing."

"Perhaps it's better..." Marwood makes to leave now he's delivered his equivalent of a file in a cake. He's no idea how useful the implement will be, and underestimates the benefit stories will have on Kate's soul. She cannot change her personality, or her response to his tales, just because she's incarcerated.

"I'm at death's door," she jests, raising her hands to perform despair, lowering them with real sadness. "But I still have imagination—I can't help my taste for fairy tales."

"Well, okay, but some are dark, some less so."

"The darker the better," she grins.

Her expression is alarming: Kate will be Marwood's first woman and he is superstitious about executing her, even in the name of the Crown. He knows extended conversation will bring him nightmares but he reasons, staring at his shoes, it's the least he can do.

So he tells her of young Bathsheba Spooner, an American woman who in the American War of Independence pleaded her belly for killing her elderly husband. Marwood figures the story may inspire a new defence from Kate—the chance to 'plead her belly'.

"Miss Spooner was under fire because her family sided with the British—her father having been Chief Justice of Massachusetts. She was called 'the Tory Murderess' at her trial."

The name sparks Kate's interest. "So what does that make me?"

Marwood refuses to answer. "In 1778 she was condemned to death, so pleaded her belly. The first panel found she was not pregnant, and the second that she was with child, but they had no legal status."

"So was she strung up?"

"A violent thunderstorm caused another delay—but yes, she was hanged in Worcester, 2nd July 1778. Three other men—traitors to the Massachusetts rebels—were nailed in their coffins."

"Buried alive?"

"No, already dead." Here Marwood leans in. "But when Bathsheba was examined, they found inside her a perfectly developed male foetus, five or six months old."

"They took her to the anatomists?"

"Yes, but that's not the point, Kate. The point is they tricked her—they wanted her hanged. She pleaded her belly, but it was ignored. See?"

Kate nods, slowly. "Yes, I see. The point is, William, they hung her anyway."

Marwood pauses. "Okay, forget that one—I've comic tales too. You heard of Mary Young, also known as Jenny Diver? She'd dress up as a pregnant woman—as part of her thieving act."

"Acting the criminal," Kate smiles.

"Yes, but listen, she would hide a pair of artificial arms and hands beneath her dress. Then old Mary—"

"Jenny—"

"Right, this Miss Twice-Named would open theatregoers bags and purses with ease."

"She was a swiper."

"Yes."

Kate rocks back and laughs out loud, her voice carrying around the chapel, and echoing against the wood. She considers. "So all I have to do is plead mi' belly in the dock, maybe act a lil' desperate and put a blanket on my shoulders, pitiful-like."

"Maybe, Kate." He looks away from her. "Here's one more—the horrible story of Amy Channing who was burned at Maumbury Rings in 1702. Her being with child, milk actually sprouted from her when she was burned, from her chest, see. Thomas Hardy used to tell the story with great gaiety."

Kate looks at Marwood blankly, coughs a little, and then swipes him on the arm. Her latent anger rises a little. "Now that's disgusting!"

"Well, you said you wanted them dark!"

"But not foul."

"The point is—she was pregnant too."

Kate ponders this moral, then her mouth slides into a sideways slope. "Yes, she was, and she hanged too. So I don't get your point, hangman? I plead my belly then I swing. That seems to be your grand plan *pour la dame?*"

A strange thing now happens, though. The hangman is considering Kate's words when she seems to crack for a moment, and a sense of confession—something she thought she wasn't capable of—escapes her tongue. "I has feelings about what I's done, but…"

"Yes?"

"I constantly pushes 'em down because of life and in order to survive. I got a devil jabberin' in my ear, but I don't blame 'im, not really. I did wot I done, there's no denyin', an' out of a greedy search for easy pleasure."

"Not much penitence, is it?"

"No, but my better self is reserved for my boy, William, you gotta believe that…"

The words falter, but she wishes to tell her visitor that not only is Daniel everything, her last breath of tenderness, but that she sees him in Marwood's eyes, the same generosity and innocent enthusiasm of the child. The hangman tries to understand, nodding over and over, staring down at the condemned coffin on the chapel floor.

"But I know," Kate whispers. "Even my lighter—my good side for Daniel—is just the flip side of a rude protection of him. It makes me vicious for the world, jealous too. Does that make sense?" Her head hangs low and she runs out of words. "So I bully him, jabbing him, telling him how lucky he is…."

"It's okay, Kate, really. Everything will be okay. I'll go to Bleeding Heart Alley. I will."

"Please, William."

"Don't worry, Kate." He stands and takes her hand, squeezes it gently, watches as she forces a smile.

"I'm grateful." Suddenly she changes her tone, laughs. "I should teach you prison slang—that's my kind o' story. You don't know how 'eastenders' talk? You should learn."

"Cockney rhyming slang?"

"Sometimes, but mostly not. Take a footpad, he's an 'rdinary thief, see, a low Toby. A rampsman delivers a violent assault. I'm a 'rampswoman,' no more. Garrottin', that's an attack, but not *definitely* endin' in a dyin' garrotte. See, it's its own world."

"It certainly is. I know some ol' names," he says, patting Kate's hand and feeling sad inside, but he plays the game. "A house-breaker, that's a 'cracksman', an easy one. I know a 'bug hunter' picks the pockets of drunks, and a 'snoozer' books into a hotel before robbing the guests."

"What's an 'area Sneak'?"

"No idea."

"Someone who calls at kitchen doors hoping to find 'em open, then robs the food and plate. 'Cheating law' is false dice, 'versing law' is counterfeitin' coin, and the best one, 'tigging law' is cutting purses."

"Stealing."

"All forms. Got it from folks I us' to know in Liverpool." She grins. "They taught me flimpin' and smashin' a little. 'If I'm nailed, it's a lifer, guv!'"

Marwood looks at her puzzled, wondering what makes her tick, to switch so completely from one mood—a fully formed personality—to another.

"Speak the lingo," he says, "the local patter?"

"I'm jus' a villain n' a 'sharp', an' m' victim's a 'flat'. I 'ave to go, now, William—the ol' ward lackey Molly Muggs'll be wonderin' where I am."

They stand, and Kate leads the way down a creaky staircase to the chapel floor. No more words are exchanged: there's little to say. They close the doors of the chapel and proceed across an interior stone courtyard, emerging in the press-yard. Here, running parallel with Newgate market is a spindle-thin court. A cistern of water marks the end of the yard, its wide rectangle open to the elements and surrounded on three sides by severe walls crowned with *chevaux de frise*. At this hour no turnkeys are present but two men are loitering there, early jailbirds conversing quietly, their weary rags draped in cold morning sunlight. On a portable wooden table between them is a New Testament, the pages flapping back and forth in the breeze.

Watching these broken shadows, the two men watching them back, Kate and her hangman cross the long yard. Meanwhile Marwood relates one final story about a murderer, Michael Williams, who killed a whole family in New Gravel Lane off Ratcliffe highway.

"This is decades ago, but he's buried at the crossroads of Back Lane and Cannon Road, with the bloody hammer and chisel he used in killing, and a stake driven through his heart. That's how they used to treat the condemned."

"Is that supposed to make me feel better?"

"No, just that you'll get a Christian burial," and instantly he regrets the words, but Kate's pace does not slow, and she demands the rest of the story. "Well, since you ask, his skull was granted to the owner of the public house on the cross-roads. A souvenir—people seem to want them, and the grislier, the better! These bodies get dug up all the time, you know."

"A charmless story, William, unless you're tryin' to scare me?"

"I'm just trying to entertain—you ask me for these tales."

Kate smiles, and glances up at him. "Even when I'm in prison."

"I can't help that."

They are silent once more until Kate breaks the moment. "Tell me more about female killers—I know nothing of these women."

"Okay, I know just one and one only. She was called Catherine Hayes."

"Like me."

"Yes, a Catherine, like you. She was a proprietress of a tavern called *The Gentlemen in Trouble*, a long time ago, 1720s. She murdered her husband, no one really knows why. She severed his head, so the story goes, and tossed it into the Thames. Then she scattered the parts all over London."

Kate says nothing.

"What happened to her?"

"Aren't you interested in the husband?"

"Yes, well…"

"The head was recovered, and implicated her. But the authorities of the time had an odd sense of justice. They placed *his head*—the husband's—on a pole in the City Cemetery to scare people. And she was put on trial and became the last women to be burned at Tyburn."

"Tyburn…"

"Yes, you remember we saw the Tyburn re-enactment?"

"Of course…"

"Well, Catherine Hayes got that for real."

"In the neck," Kate says, but Marwood does not share her amusement.

"Anyway," he says, "those days are gone."

They've reached the door of the women's ward, where the turnkey 'guide' is silhouetted against a grey sky. He's wearing his straw hat, his collar turned up for the wind. With this same man who showed Kate her new home, as witness, Kate and Marwood face each other. They shake hands formally.

"The world is a prison, and London the busiest prison of all."

"The world is a stage," Kate replies, "you told me. Prison is nothin' but waiting in the wings."

Surprised by her eloquence, Marwood leans forward to kiss her cheek, but the turnkey prevents him, even raises his baton. They do not make a fuss.

"Next time."

"At my execution," she says, gritting her teeth, a spark in her eye, "I will wear a crepe mourning hood and hold my head up in the cart, lookin' like I'm painted."

"And the Tyburn crowd will applaud you. Everyone will be there, the newspapermen naturally and Mrs Dalton, the eccentric seller of gingerbread. Mother Douglas, the fat and drunken procuress. You'll be famous all over London."

Kate smiles weakly. "Give me more than enough rope."

"I'll do you no wrong, or shame, like Charles Peace. There'll be no pain—you've suffered enough."

"Thank you, William."

"God bless you."

The door opens and she disappears into darkness, the turnkey following. Marwood is left before the small iron door. He thinks of the Last Dying Speech of Catherine Hayes, a motto from Proverbs saying 'then they shall call upon God, but he will not answer'. For a few seconds he is sad, but then an unexpected mood—almost elation, nearer desperation—strikes him as he walks back across the press-yard. He's more than glad he came; he has done his best, surely. He can return to Horncastle a moral man, and face the Tooley brothers, once more bask in his family. He looks up—the sun is now bright, the globe itself unshielded by clouds, his shadow stretching his long frame on the ground before him.

Marwood re-passes the two Bible-felons, kneeling on the ground and paying him no mind. He remembers the words of Thomas More: "This littel Hole is as a little citty in a commonwealth," and just as quickly he recollects a tune celebrating his narrow freedom:

"In London and within a mile I weene
There are layles or Prisons full eighteene
And sixty Whipping-posts and Stocks and cages."

But the words sound hollow, as regrets more fitting to his feelings rise up. Kate Webster cannot be forgotten, and yet he tries to put her aside—to *not* personalise his experience. But more than ever, with visits like today, he knows he is sinking deeper.

When will it end…the recriminations…the sacrifices…the delays…the victims…the perpetrators…the murderers…the next generation!

Meanwhile Kate is following the turnkey, whispering words of her own—boasting—childish delight in the attentions of her recent visitor. Entering the women's ward she splays her arms as though receiving salvation, and to the suspicion of Molly and Frida, she calls out:

"He let me off the noose! Marwood's talking to the guv'nor right now. Orders from the Queen!"

"Can you believe it?" the two women cackle in unison reply, and somehow the joke is deflated.

Kate ignores them and retreats to her room. Now alone she removes the razor blade and metal hook from her hip, hides them with her own paper knife—a souvenir she purloined within ten minutes of entering Newgate from the turnkey's office. Later that night, she taps the knife on the window bars. Could this weapon be her way out? The irony of William supplying her is surreal and exciting. "At least someone believes I should be on the outside…."

In a slow-building frenzy, she continues singing the same two lines in her cell, in a kind of dizzy celebration, except more and more they sound like a limited consolation for all that's been, and preparation for what's to come:

> "We'll walk arme in arme
> As tho' we were leading one another…
>
> We'll walk arme in arme
> As tho' we were leading one another…
>
> We'll walk arme in arme
> As tho' we were leading one another…to Newgate."

Chapter 37
A Late Miracle
20th March 1879, Thursday

By late afternoon the court reconvenes due to the message Kate sends: 'I am unexpectedly with child', so mitigating circumstances must instigate a review. The Sessions is used to such actions, and while the jury is already dismissed, and witnesses released, the prosecutor and judge and various assistant lackeys will reconvene: the episode is considered a legal epilogue, after all, and will take no more than half an hour.

So Kate is allowed back into court to plead her belly. As Marwood once told her, prisoners could escape the trip from Holborn to the Deadly Never-Green at Tyburn by claiming 'benefit of clergy', reciting the 'neck verse' namely the first verse of Psalm LI, or by 'pleading the belly'. Since Kate is neither ordained nor versed in Latin, only one option remains. When she learns pregnant women cannot be transported or hanged, the injustice to her son Daniel becomes clear. Even Londoners are outraged, so she is told, by a scaffold-woman with a babe in her arms.

"I will have to get pregnant to delay proceedings." Not wishing for delay, Kate grows impatient and pleads the very next day.

Already she stands before Sir Warner Sleigh, gesturing to the swollen state of her belly. She is helped into the dock more carefully than the previous day, and her colour does seem to suggest illness, morning sickness, or the realisation that labour pains may be close at hand. The Old Bailey wavers in judgement: the legal men do not like these spectacles since at some point they must defer to the matrons of the court, who stand in the corner like bored harpies, ready with dubious medical advice.

The Sessions begins at midday. With the peanut gallery closed for 'state caution', voices echo through the sealed chamber with booming judgement. Lies already, Kate's words even sound falsely supplicating, weak and hollow. She begs the judges to escape the final humiliation of being 'anatomised and exposed', knowing that her body will not be sold—those days have passed—but requesting a guarantee it will remain within the jail. Kate grips her belly and grimaces, hoping that the refusal of her dissection plea will make the miracle of her prison child more believable.

Mr Sleigh immediately responds, his wig and robes flailing with impatience: "In reply to the Clerk of Arraigns, the prisoner pleads pregnancy for a stay of execution. Dr Bond, please examine her with the Head Matron in the new jury room."

Kate is ushered into the back room, and splayed out on a table. The Matron—a skinny woman with a dangling chicken neck—presses her elbows tight to the table. "Stand back," she says, pulling the straps over. Two assistants are instructed to "hold the patient down." Kate grits her teeth and is silent. The forceps are brought out and despite the horror, she cannot close her eyes. They are literally prodding for a baby—the master proof of buried presence being the level of pain. In ten minutes all is over; the Matron's fingers no longer spuriously rove Kate's belly.

The prisoner is returned to court supported by the assistants. A note is handed by the Matron to Mr Sleigh.

"The Sessions declares she is *by no definition* quick with child." The Matron agrees, and Mr Sleigh proceeds. "We hereby move to reinstate the recent judgement—of yesterday."

Judge Denham stands, a touch weary and bored. "The plea is heard. The case stands." He turns to face Kate in the dock. "The capital code is clear, madam, as is the *ancien régime*. The law must take its course despite the carnival humour and comic ineptitude of this case. You will be *sus. per col*—hanged by the neck until dead. Counsel, please note in the sentence ledger, *suspendatur per collum*."

"But the Murder Act of 1752," Kate says, remembering something Marwood told her.

Denham disregards her, stunned by the interruption. "We can move to immediate date of sentencing, Miss Webster, if you violate the court again."

"Violate?" Kate says under her breath, but heard by Denham.

"Vio-late!" he cries, causing the Matron to smirk, his voice booming. He smiles. "The Bailey's acoustics are still sound, I see. Miss Webster, the 1752 Murder Act—to add further terror to death—stipulates that bodies of the dead can be publicly dissected by surgeons and anatomists—a last indignity. I take it you do not wish for that sentence?"

"No, Your Honour."

"Then you will go about your sentence, as declared yesterday, and today:

> Blame not the law which dooms your son,
> Compar'd with you 'tis mild;
> 'Tis you have sentenc'd me to death,
> To hell have doom'd your child.

I wish you a good day. Sessions complete." He stands and hits the gavel, then strides pompously to his lounge regarding nobody, with Mr Sleigh trailing in his wake. "Warner, no hard feelings?" A tinkling sound of drinks is just audible, before the huge oak doors are closed by the turnkey.

In the dock, Kate is bewildered by the news. Never has it been so clearly conveyed that she will hang. The message seems all the clearer in the half empty court. The effect is to produce a surreal vision inside her mind, bred by the confusions of the trial and the trial of confusion that is her life. As per courtroom procedure, from a doorway her little boy is produced. He sits on the empty jury bench in a little powdered wig, Holland shirt and a nosegay, uncertain whether he is meant for comedy or not. The whole effect is to make light of Kate's demise. Daniel does not look afraid but his anxiety is visible under a stolid expression.

For Kate, seeing Daniel in the room merely adds to her perplexed feelings. Instead of racing to free him from the ordeal of watching his mother's last stance, all she can think of is Jonathan Clatter, the killing that her boy almost witnessed, how they escaped *The Cat and Salutation* and left that villain to sink in the mud of the

Thames, how mother and son scrambled back to London up a bank of earth, only for everything to culminate in nothing—in the Old Bailey—in court—in a sentence of condemnation—in death. But once he appears, Kate realises that Daniel is not truly in the Old Bailey. He is far away somewhere in Southwark still free and untroubled, she hopes, by the Bow Street Runners.

Kate screams. Almost immediately the Matron's assistants surround her, their meaty arms clamping over her wrists, while the chicken-woman gestures to the court's down-sloping exit. Kate is now taken away, for once struck dumb, but smouldering. She barks in the face of the Matron. Within minutes she is back in the women's ward, where a kind of mania sets in: she does not have her boy, she fears Molly's and Frida's iron rule, even the hangman has abandoned her. For the first time she feels the truth—the prisoner's blood knowledge—of being a 'lost soul'.

Loping over the fire, wringing her fingers, Kate considers her options. She could apply for a royal pardon—a long shot, but it's not too late. Death sentences, she knows, can be declared 'free pardons' as bureaucratic headaches, or else reduced in severity to 'conditional pardons' such as hard labor, branding or transportation to a penal colony. Pardons are proclaimed by the Queen or passed by Parliament:

"Fire, fire, on the wall, could this be my last way out?"

The response is clear and swift when Kate, alone that night, receives a small grey note. It reads: "This Justice Hall, the Sessions House, finds you guilty as charged. You shall serve your sentence before all of London and the gallows-man, for Her Majesty's pleasure."

The women of the ward stay clear of her, and she takes to the stone bed carved from the ground, and turns her face to the wall. And yet when the women are asleep, Kate wakes and has an epiphany in the dark. Like so many times before, in her childhood, her youth, in the bustling and brutal cities of Liverpool and London, she takes a settled breath of stale air. There is life in the old girl yet.

Slowly she crawls from her cell. All is quiet by the table and the fireplace has died low. A wisp of a girl-child is sleeping there, wrapped in a ragged blanket before the glowing embers. Stepping over this 'fresh meat', Kate tiptoes to the first door and removes the envelope knife she took from the turnkey's office. She tries the lock; it won't budge. She twists the knife left and right, twice—nothing. The blade is already worn, designed only for cutting paper. Behind her the girl at the fire groans, and Kate ducks deeper into the shadows. She tries the twisted piece of metal Marwood gave her in the chapel, a triple hook on the end, and curling it into the lock, the door clicks. Kate is amazed, but wastes no time, and eases the door open.

She is down the stone passage and out into the night. The press-yard is silent. Gingerly she steps out under the stars, each glinting with tiny light on the rough ground, the chill wind cutting away her breath. Kate pulls her shawl closer—one she retains from Mrs Thomas's house—and trembles where she stands, frightened for the first time. Capture would mean an accelerated hanging date, the certainty of no pardon.

Kate fixes her courage by holding the buttons on her coat. The brick wall is visible on the far side, too high to scale. Even if she made the parapet, the glass bottles broken on top would work their brutal magic; or the fall into the ditch-like moat would trap her, its double walls hold her—a guilty prize—until morning. So Kate stays close to the women's ward, reluctant to expose her desire to flee, and wishes she'd planned her escape route better, perhaps by trusting Molly Muggs and the other jailbirds.

But the image of Jack Sheppard is before her now, a ghostly figure leading the way. Wearing a mysterious black overcoat flapping in the press-yard, now vanishing and reappearing, Jack's heroic mirage in her mind—a beautiful boy with frazzled golden hair—leads the way. But at the corner he is gone forever, as Kate spies her route via the prison chapel. She remembers how Sheppard freed his chains' bolts in seven minutes before entering the prison's House of God.

Perhaps she can do the same. The chapel's door is locked—all prisoners being prevented access to the press-yard by night. But Kate remembers how the rectory has a low window for ventilation. Clambering the corner brickwork, using a drainpipe for foothold, the drop into the hall is only a dozen feet. A single wobble over the air pocket and Kate's not small frame takes her forward. Soon she is inside the cool atmosphere of the silent building, emerging a little dusty like a surprising female apparition from a dead priest's tomb. The outline of the pews leads up to the altar in a dim haze—row upon row of floating particles of light—between two plate-glass windows. Their splitting of heaven's own light carves coloured triangles along the stone floor.

Kate walks down the aisle, not untouched by a sudden fantasy of her own midnight wedding—but the illusion is broken by a cry. As she reaches the altar, the moon appears above the rear window, a depiction of Christ's crucifixion, half Roman Golgotha horror, half skylight to the heavens. Kate takes it as a sign and kneels. She looks up at the simple wooden cross, twice her size and hanging forward from the brickwork behind the pulpit. She lays her hand on the bare wooden step.

"Forgive me Father," she whispers, "for I have sinned." She pauses, but no tears will come. She does not understand why, and a kind of grimace, a disappointed strain, lowers her face. "Forgive me…" At the foot of the cross, she notices a weeping figure, and reaches out to touch the feet, believing it to be Mother Mary, but realizing too late it is Mary Magdalene, whose expression is both pale-innocent and guilt-red. Kate smiles, believing her evil is insurmountable and she will not be saved.

Again a scream echoes the prison, and Kate awakes from her reverie. She chastises herself and a weight of feeling collapses over her head, seemingly from above, flooding her consciousness with the truth of her solitude, her separation. Abandoning Mary Magdalene, she shuffles to the side door, finds it locked. Taking the twisted metal hook—Marwood's favoured tool—from between her teeth, she leans on the door and realises it's only stiff. With a gentle creak it reveals the rectory, all silent, a small room with wash-basin, hand-jug, and the priest's purple robes laid out.

Kate is amazed: how can he leave out such items at night? The cloak has a fake gold trim but the purple fascinates her more: she runs her fingers down the hem, the softness taking away her breath, the tender touch of fabric she's never felt. She smells it too, a little shamefully, and is reminded of honeysuckle far away in Wexford. Once more, though, she recollects herself and parting a velvet curtain, she is up on the priest's dresser—skidding on its white covering—and forcing a window open. The height is good but the gap is tiny.

Still, she must force herself, and with a little leap Kate is suddenly half in and half out of Newgate Prison, dangling in the chapel window, before the dome of St Paul's Cathedral and all London's night-watchmen if only they'd look up. She is fortunate: there is no gaslight at this corner of the prison. But there is a pit of rotten food beneath the window.

As her grip slackens, Kate muffles a scream and falls about twenty feet. Two-day old fruit cartons break her fall, her back bruising from a spike on a crate's handle. But she is out—Newgate Street is just a walk from the corner of the rubbish yard. Suddenly a gruff old man is facing her, beard swinging in the wind.

"'Ere, wot you doing?" He touches her with a cane.

"Hungry," she Kate, for want of ideas.

"I'm the night-guard. No Londoners allow'd. Git!" He prods her like moving a horse, so the last part of Kate's escape is being beaten to freedom. She tumbles out on all fours just as an aristocratic *barouche* passes by. Looking up, the lady peers from the window, curious, holding onto her hat, her expression puzzled and disgusted, then the carriage beats on into the night.

Kate stands, and looks back where the old man has retreated to his watching post, a cramped sentry-style cabinet. She sees his face glowing in the half-light from a candle on the floor, already reading his newspaper and smoking his pipe. Nothing could be less likely than an escaped jailbird this side of the prison—when does it ever happen? Kate presses her lips together to conceal her giggle, but only succeeds in bringing tears to her eyes. She raises her arms in the air and does a twirl. Only a black sky and St Paul's Cathedral look down, equally silent.

The prison chapel rises behind her, the glow from stained-glass reflecting the candle's colours, just a little brighter. Kate looks across to the Old Bailey, its grey brows peering down from its mock Greek-temple façade, and she does a little curtsey. "The long arm of the law ain't so long," she whispers, and crosses the street. Newgate is at her back, but she does not turn around. "Onwards and upwards." At last she has a single moment of beauty—not looking back—and feels away from her old life.

The night is old, but the moon is up and the outside air is warmer than the prison. Kate unbuttons her coat. "Now for my boy." She heads to Fleur-de-lis Court off Fleet Street, eyes forward, grinning down the dark streets, now and then raising an imaginary hat to the crossing-boys and chimney-sweeps already heading to work. They look back at her, puzzled, uncertain if they've seen the devil or the last lady of the night.

Chapter 38
The Quick and the Dead
21st March 1879, Friday

Within twenty-four hours word is out: the murderess Kate Webster has escaped immediately following her trial, an embarrassment to Judge Denham, the Sessions, the Bow Street Runners and the Mayor of London. Given their own failures, two ladies by the names of Molly Muggs and Frida La Roche have been sectioned into solitary confinement. The murderess will be caught.

Inspector Sequin is given a second chance. Marwood arrives early at the Chandos, where the inspector has asked to meet, both already knowing the news. Marwood settles in a corner booth. He drinks a porter for breakfast—a 'heavy wet' to settle his guts after the trial's trauma—a real hare-of-the-dog with no spices, no surprises. He peels the label on the bottle and finds the phrase *England drinks a porter for breakfast!* almost funny, but thinks better of it. For ten minutes he stews there in a daze, thinking of Ellen and Aldous, Horncastle and his local pub *The Portland Arms*—the Tooley brothers—the horse-fair, the Wesleyan Methodist Church. "Why has London got such a grip on me?"

He knows Kate was probably horrified by her crime, but in the midst of her trial, he imagined her cutting the body up, laughing at the theatre of it all, making parts of Mrs Thomas's body talk to other parts. Perhaps she cried out in confusion, a decapitated head in her hands, then laughed through her fear. He wonders, at any point does she weep or grow sick? In his heart, though, he fears the worst—that Mrs Thomas's body smelled strangely of life to her, the fullness of life, but that Kate's own body remained capable of sickness—in a way she had to extinguish—to feel good, to feel important, to feel socially graceful and rich, to feel wanted, loved. "Did she feel any of that compulsion, did she feel anything? Did she feel unique?"

Marwood's thoughts are interrupted by Nimrod Jones standing over the table. He crouches, resting his elbows, squaring his arms like a bulldog. "Good afternoon, Mr Hangman."

Marwood nods, and their expressions lock. "Where's Sequin?"

"He'll be along shortly. I hope you don't mind if it's just me, for now."

"Not at all, Mr Jones."

The bulldog slides into the booth, faces Marwood. "Tell me, where is your friend Kate Webster?"

"My friend?"

"Your friend." Jones lifts the salt, tips a few grains onto the triangle of skin between his thumb and index finger. He tosses them over his shoulder, but fails to elicit surprise.

"Feeling lucky? I've seen luckier movements on the scaffold."

"And you will again."

Marwood narrows his eyes. "What are you suggesting, Mr Jones, that I had something to do with her escape?"

"Your words, not mine."

"Listen, you may think I crawled into London from the sticks. But you'd be wrong to suspect I'm a bumpkin with no brains. I've hanged boys younger than you, son, and I'll hang Kate Webster when the time comes. If you can catch her."

Jones is quiet, but doesn't feel out of his league, having seen the bluster of many a suspect. "We know you know something, Mr Marwood, but we prefer your help."

"Yes, *we* would," Sequin answers, grinning over the *tête-à-tête*, then accompanies his partner. "It's not that Mr Jones is wrong to ask you, but he's wrong to be so direct. Mr Marwood, we know you've consorted with Kate Webster at Bartholomew Fair, that's apparent from the trial. We know you've also met her at Gloucester Place."

"How so?"

"You wife, Ellen."

Marwood frowns. "What…are you talking about? You've spoken to my wife?"

"And she's been very helpful concerning your friend, Miss Webster."

"I don't believe you. Ellen would never say anything."

"You know how we also know?"

"How?"

"Because you're telling us right now."

Marwood leans back on the soft upholstery. "I've told you nothing, except I met Kate once at Bartholomew Fair, just as I said in court."

At this point, Sequin smiles and tries to lighten the mood. Gesturing to the barman, he orders a pint of 'stingo', an ale spiced with pepper, as though making a statement of intent. "I prefer ale from the Huffe Cup brewery. You know, 'angel's food' and 'stride wide', little pick-me-ups, gems, don't you think, Mr Marwood?" The pint settles and he drinks a quarter in two large gulps.

"A little 'cutting' for me," Jones adds. "I prefer those fruit beers, especially with bay-berries and 'broom'. Good for the soul—makes the long drop last forever. Not that I'd know."

Marwood says nothing.

"A little story," Sequin continues, wiping his mouth. "You ever heard of 'the Sinister Cripple', Mr Marwood? I didn't think so—these are all London stories. Well, the sinister cripple was one Hugh Boone, a match-seller. I tell it to my son Billy to thrill and scare him to sleep all in one measure." Jones laughs politely, then shuts up quick. "Well, after begging all day and raking in the shillings—often ten pounds, by all accounts—poor ol' Boone would drag his paralysed body to Crosby Square. Thirty or forty seconds would tumble by, with as many passers-by. Then ol' Boone would up n' make his exit at another corner, miraculously transformed into a nimble young man. See?"

"Not quite, inspector."

"Call me Gil—please," he corrects. "The point is his real name was Cecil Brown Smith, and he lived in the genteel suburbs of Norbury. I arrested him last year on the grounds of 'thieving in the open air'. He's now in Newgate. Everyone thinks they can get away with it once."

"Once," echoes Jones.

"But I catch 'em just once." Here Sequin leans in, holding his collar as though it were Marwood's. "I always catch my man. And you're lookin' a bit shady, Mr Hangman, truth be told. A bit soft-gilled."

"No need for the insults," Marwood says, "Mr Sequin, sir." He grips his own collar, then stares from Sequin to the bulldog and back. "You may always catch your man, but Kate Webster is your first escaped woman, I take it?"

Neither policeman replies.

"I take it from your silence, gentlemen, that Miss Webster is your first. Well, she's my first too. She's the first person I've met who I have to hang, and that's no 'gift from the gods', I can tell you."

"Sorry for your troubles," Jones says.

"No, you're not," Marwood adds. "I know stories too, sirs, where I come from. You're probably never heard of Terence Price—Old Patch—before he moved to London. He pulled the old homeless trick in Lincolnshire, on foot and off the back of a cart, right. He was a compact little man of about forty. But he dressed like an old wastrel in an oversized camel coat, hiding a knife, if things got risky. A bit ridiculous, sure, he fastened a fisherman's cape under his chin, and wore famous green spectacles. He was the old man of stage comedy."

"And the point?"

"The point is, Gil, Nimrod, if that's your name—London ain't got the only art of the con, see. We breed them in the suburbs too. Now if you'll excuse me, I have a life—and a wife—to get back to."

"You won't help us find Kate Webster?"

"Not if you're accusing me of being her accomplice of some kind, and bothering my wife."

"Sit down, Mr Marwood," Sequin suddenly says, his voice authoritative beyond any Marwood has heard in London, mayor's henchman Mr Cottonwell included. "You think a little regional crime can impress us? We're the Bow Street Runners, boy. When I was a lad, you could still see impaled heads welcoming you to Westminster. You didn't see them when you arrived 'cos we live in civilised times. But when I was young, about ten,"—he smiles—"those heads were on London Bridge from Temple Bar to Blackfriars."

"I'm too young, but I heard of 'em," Jones adds. "Heads without the bodies, jus' like Kate Webster's treated us to—the old maid in the box." He taps Marwood's hand. "Down the river, people would rent spy-glasses at a half-penny a look."

"There was even a telescope in Leicester Fields. Spiking the heads has now ended—too barbarous apparently even for treason, though I disagree—but you can still see the spikes."

"They put false heads on 'em."

Marwood stands. "Gentlemen, I've heard enough. Clearly you've become as depraved as the city's guts. Don't call me boy, for starters. And second, I know more about heads—and decapitations—than you've smelled hot dinners. You may have noticed Charles Peace's head fly off his body, to my infinite regret, a few weeks ago. Well, perhaps you should try being the one pushing the lever, on a girl too. I bid you farewell."

Sequin raises his hands as though shocked at Marwood's incivility. "Just a little London history for you, sir. Nothing to get worked up about."

Marwood hesitates, grabs his hat from the table. "I'm the hangmen, you're the policemen. You do your job, and I'll do mine." He heads to the door, but naturally Jones has to call something in his wake.

"If that's how you want it, Mr Hangman. We'll find your girl. Then you'll have to tie the rope!"

Tripping a little on the exit, Marwood sees no comedy. He feels sick from his throat to his stomach. In the blaze of sudden sunlight, he meanders to the corner and looks down on Trafalgar Square. It can't be—it must be an illusion—but the alarming coincidence is real. He looks again, rubbing his eyes while turning over the scaffold words *toe the line, toe the line*. There, right after his conversation with Sequin and Jones, passing in front of Nelson's Column about fifty yards away, is the outline of girl he met at Covent Garden. He is close enough to recognise her face. Is it really her?

Quickly he hurries to the corner plinth before the British Library. He descends the stone steps, creating a new angle just as she is passing. The girl turns her face in his direction, but does not see him. Whether Kate or her double, she is gone—lost amid the dozens of faces passing disappearing down the Mall—in the direction of Buckingham Palace. But he can see her smile, laughing without restraint at the Punch & Judy show, sniggering in the Old Bailey under cross-examination, kneeling in blood and sweat as she saws off one of Mrs Thomas's limbs.

He covers his face, staggers on. But other visions grab his wounded psyche, colluding from memory and ripping into his present—Punch hanging the hangman from the scaffold, Kate pleading her belly in court, Ellen riding a horse and cart through Lincolnshire fields, their boy Aldous on her lap dreaming about his trip to the metropolis, the great world-circus of London town…

The images swirl and blur until Marwood lowers himself to the ground, bringing his knees to his chest. He taps his head on the corner plinth, closes his eyes in the sun. "When will it be all over?"

But the curtain will not come down, and the show must go on.

"I just need to go home…or I'll be too tired to do my job."

Chapter 39
Back to the Bleeding Heart
22nd March 1879, Saturday

Wooden houses insist on landlubbing for almost two miles along the south bank of the Thames from Paris Garden Stairs to the shady 'Beere Howse', just east of Tooley Street. Here we encounter Pickle Herring Stairs, where the Tabard Inn of Chaucer's *The Canterbury Tales* is a Southwark pub that points the way to the tanneries of Bermondsey, and here Kate is hotfooting as she leaves Trafalgar Square.

After sleeping rough near Charing Cross station, her plan is to see an old friend, a lady of the night called Emma Gosling, or 'Butter Bird' as her pimps-friends prefer. Kate wakes to the smell of baked potato and hurries through Kensington Gardens. Her destination is the south-east where Southwark leads to the Bankside brothels: here the house-madams wear velvet gowns and petticoats, and since the Middle Ages the young girls tease 'the johns' in striped garments. Though not strictly law, the wearing of such costumes is still an open sign of the profession, the preference of the gentleman's hour.

Kate heads to a house of ill fame on Cockspur Lane, where the famous pimp Gilbert le Strengmaker of Fleet Street began the earliest franchise in corporate history. His flashy women are straight-up whores—wagtails, blowzes, bunters, fallen birds, toffers, dirty puzzles, Mother Midnights, punchable nuns, ladybirds, jilts, window tappers, blonde-eyed bobtails and more often than not, wild-ey'd women of the night. They wear painted lips and eyebrows, false hair, and any man with a purse, a penny and a minute to spare could enjoy his choice 'in armour' for a threepenny upright. Then more than now, London is a modern Gomorrah, a dark and labyrinthine city of delight, excitement, forever mounting the illusion of eternity, seeking the betrayal of death.

Kate is upset, and the boy will have to wait—there's no point in rescuing Daniel without a penny to her name. Two lads of about fifteen are guarding the entrance, and Kate merely kicks them aside, the first 'toy wretch' falling into the second with surprise and dropping his knife. The second shakes his head as if arguing about something, choking to get the words out.

"Miller!" he cries, "you've got a live one!" The other boy merely coughs in the mud.

"Tell Miller to get Butter down," Kate says. "I want my money."

A giant of a man, over six-foot-four and two feet wide, appears on the stoop of the crumbling little house. He has a rope.

"Come o'er here," he says, "and I'll kill yer. We saw the back o' you a long time ago." Giggles escape the door behind.

Kate pauses, looks back to the teenage boys, their knives now visible.

"I came for my money. Emma Gosling owes me twenty shillings."

"What Butter earns stays in this house," the giant says. "Ain't that clear by now?"

Kate makes to advance—and by consequence, a round face in an explosion of ragged blond hair appears at the top window.

"Get lost, Kate Webster!" the hair cries. "You may 'a got out o' Newgate, but we knows yer's a killer. You won' get no sympathy 'ere."

"Ain't sympathy I'm lookin' for! You know I 'ave to come 'ere strong, or there'll be laughter."

Again, a few giggles come from inside but they appear more stage-managed. After a pause, the stand-off ends just as quickly as it began. Despite her pimp at the foot of the house—the enormous and elegantly named Mr Miller Charleston—Emma throws some money out. Kate literally falls in the mud to retrieve it, one of the boys instantly stepping his jack-boot on her back.

"Now git gone," the young pimp calls out, "n' don't come back. We don't want no Bow Street down 'ere on account o' yer. Or we'll be tellin' 'em about Bleeding Heart Alley."

"You wouldn't," Kate makes the mistakes of saying.

"We would," Emma calls from the top window. "You ran off, Kate Webster, thought yer could do better as a skivvy maid, hey. Well, look where that put yer!"

Kate produces the envelope knife she's been carrying since her prison break, and waves it at the boys. They don't retreat but come no closer. Moving in a slow arc, with Mr Charleston descending the steps, Kate is retreating in the street. Again she weighs up the house, its brown face threatening to collapse, the brickwork shoddy, the upstairs windows broken and the poor linen curtain flapping in the breeze, trying to escape.

"You should go to the Haymarket," Kate calls up to women she can't see, her old compatriots of a few weeks' 'protection'. "Get a lil' education. That's what I got girls, freedom!" She is thinking of a new statue of Eros at Piccadilly Circus. "It's made o' priceless aluminium. A lil' Cherub angel is clasping her hands t' her own bare breast. You ain't seen anything like it—nor will yer in this hole!"

"Get gone, girl," Mr Charleston says, and folds his arms. He motions the teenage boy-dogs back to the stoop. "The law will take care o' you. Get to Bleeding Heart Alley!"

Kate raises jeering fingers, turns them into a fist, but says nothing. She walks backwards, watching 'Butter' Emma's crazy hair flowing in the wind, other girls appearing at the dark windows. Then she remembers the money in her pocket and how Daniel will be waiting.

"That life is over now…" she tells herself.

Her heart slows its pounding, as a few stones fly by her retreat. Kate does not want to know who threw them. The images of the whorehouse—the bully Miller, the greedy Emma—begin to fade, street by street. "I'll endure any long walk…before going back."

Eventually she arrives in Lambeth, the riverside dumping-ground for steel yards, glass-blowers, soap and dye-makers, all attracting night thieves. An underclass survives here, on the waste of Babylon of the northern bank. Along Lambeth High Street people make a living, according to *The Weekly Dispatch*, by 'grave robbing, forging candles from the fat, extracting toxic alkalis from the bone marrow and, most profitably, selling the flesh as industrial pet food'. Here, Kate well remembers, she first learned of the trades that led her to make 'turkey dripping' of Mrs Thomas's body. All the court's accusations—the so-called preservation of Kate's landlady with a conscious effort for business—are indisputable—for she knew all about the human body's black market, and that sales could be made.

At this hour, though, with all that has happened, she wishes only to see her son—to rescue him outright. Her new plan is to flee to Australia, a self-imposed 'transportation' with a clever twist. "I'll work as an indentured woman assisting on the prison hulks," she tells herself. "Then I'll reveal my true identity, as a free woman of England, and they'll have to set me free." She trudges on through the empty, dark streets, the wind rising, the gaslights not yet lit. "I'll keep searching—for freedom—until my own bleeding heart is free!"

What Kate does not know, is that following Marwood's meeting with Sequin and Jones, police were dispatched to Southwark to answer a new clue. Just before midnight, a man claiming to be the cousin of Mr Jonty Clatterton entered the Bow Street office and declared Kate to be staying with one Sarah Crease, of 59 Bleeding Heart Alley, Southwark. Apparently Mrs Crease had told this mysterious man her whereabouts herself, most likely to split the Kate Webster reward, in exchange for the boy doing a day's timber work. There is no reason to disbelieve the man, one Albert Hue, and for precaution he is transferred to Scotland Yard for further questioning.

Soon after their failed attempt in the Chandos to teach Marwood about justice, Sequin and Jones get the news. They are on the 'beat' around Covent Garden that night, peering through the quiet market from a cider café, first light still hours away, and contemplating a midnight trip back to the Chandos for an after hours' game of poker. Around three, a boy is sent round from the Lord Mayor's office, and before they can entirely sober up they are in a hansom cab, cutting through the black and lonely streets south of Old Father Thames. Kate Webster has been spotted in Southwark on Cockspur Lane, the anonymous report from a man over six feet tall who runs a known house of ill repute, and describes himself as "an old friend."

Meanwhile Kate is meandering through the night, pining for her own alcohol fix. The gaslights are lit, illuminating her heavy feet as she leaps over oily puddles. But nowhere seems to be open: Southwark is one long string of warehouses and wharfs, buildings seemingly abandoned to host criminals and runaways. Before long Kate is beyond Bleeding Heart into a courtyard with pea soup vats, the home of Sarah Crease. All is silent, but she knows the tiny dilapidated frontage, and her mood is lighter now she's going to see her boy.

Kate raps on the window, waits. She glances down the alley where the Thames is murky, all its unseen water undisturbed except for tiny lights floating like stunned fireflies, the night fishing boats. Again she raps on the door.

A hand reaches through the dusty interior, unhooks the lock, opens it on the chain. A chin moves closer.

"Who's there?"

"Webster," Kate says, "I came for my boy."

"He's not here—he ran away." The news passes through Kate without register.

"Open up."

"Listen, it 'appened last night, dear. Boy said he got bett'n things to do. Was old enuf, trained good by Clatter-Man. Summut 'bout savin' *you* from the noose!"

The hand reaches for the chain, but Kate is too quick. She grabs the hand, and yanks it back with such ferocity that Mrs Crease's face squashes in the door crack, ripping a line from her nose to her cheek. Both women hang there, one bleeding on the other, both hunting for breaths.

"I ain't for the noose yet," Kate says. "I came 'ere for my boy, n' I'm not leavin' without 'im. Now you got yer money. So deliv'r the child, or I'll skin yer face right off yer head."

"He ain't 'ere!" Mrs Crease cries, and begins weeping.

"You know how a chicken looks when 'e's plucked," Kate says, then leans in to whisper. "'course you do—that's what you do down 'ere, right. You feed the men, so they won't clip your wings."

"You're the one locked up," Mrs Crease manages.

"Do I look like I'm locked up?" Again Kate twists the face in the lock, pushing Mrs Crease's hand lower to her knees, twisting her shoulder in the dark.

"Kate, give me breath!"

For a moment Kate struggles with her own fear, but somewhere inside the rage cannot be appeased and once more thinking of Daniel, the aggression overpowers her. The past is alive in the present. She is stirring the pot with Mrs Thomas's bones bobbing up from the hot juice; she is twisting the knife in Jonathan Clatter's chest. Didn't she escape in both cases? Wasn't justice served?

"Kate, please."

"Crimes of passion," she whispers. "Those kills are part of a holy trilogy, see, by which Daniel will be finally set free. You understand, Sarah? Tell me you understand. No one can tell me otherwise!"

"What—what are you talking about?" cries Mrs Crease. "Kate, we're friends. Let go, and I'll show you where the boy is."

Kate grabs Mrs Crease's nose with comic horror. "You said he ran away."

"I lied, he's right inside. I can show you!"

"It's too late, if he's inside I can find out for myself."

An awkward pause, and then Kate commits her first thoroughly conscious act, doing so by reliving her previous crimes. What she feels is desperation, a vague sense of power trapping Mrs Crease in the door, but mostly fear. One might think 'isn't she the carer, the babysitter for my boy?' protecting him from pickpocketing gangs. But no such notion intervenes. Kate cannot stomach Mrs Crease's lies—after the pressures of her trial, the humiliation of Newgate, the trauma and pride that constitutes her escape, she has reached the end of the line, the literal end of her rope.

"I take no pleasure," Kate says, but clearly on this occasion, the jury is out. Mrs Crease's gurgling begins; the door chain close to her neck starts to draw blood. Kate lifts her other hand and consciously pulls on the chain, for no other reason than to kill. It takes longer than she expects. But the angle is perfect, and within seconds Mrs Crease is collapsing, a mess of blood fanning her frock, the chain slippy in Kate's hands.

She wonders for the first time—why did she do it? It's the first time she's had, what, a twinge of guilt? Sarah Crease was her friend.... The act was a betrayal, a shameful excess, undoubtedly? Kate wrestles with a moment self-blame, of sudden responsibility. But the fear and anger is paramount—too strong and indentured in her personality; like Macbeth, too far waded in blood to turn back. Surely it is a sign of her love for Daniel? Love is the answer, mixed with feelings of righteous maternal aggression—yes, that's right—the certainty and acceptance of knowing she is a changed person since

Mrs Thomas and Clatter tried to challenge her moral authority. A moral revenge? Yes, that's right.

As thoughts rush her brain Kate begins relaxing the chain—fingers sodden—and Mrs Crease slumps to the floor, her hands dangling in pathetic, still twitching supplication at Kate's feet.

"I truly can bend the world to my will," she says to the body, mostly to gather her nerves. "I can escape from prison. I will and will save my boy. I will escape to Australia—because I can."

Kate soon realises, though, that she cannot open the door, each try merely tapping a little on her victim's skull as though politely requesting entry. Stunned, she hunts the soup yard for a hammer, cannot find one, but returns with an implement used for 'crowd control' during the workmen's meal-times, a wooden stake. She swings it repeatedly at the chain, and it breaks on the third try. The door opens without a creak, resting on Mrs Crease's pooling bloody chest—she is now still—revealing the surprise of her strangled face. Kate steps over, and enters the dark room.

One by one she searches both rooms, but Daniel is nowhere to be found. Very little remains, mostly Sarah Crease's clothes, cutouts of London buildings she appears to have pasted together, animal hairs and feline stench, but no sign of a cat. Kate literally holds her nose, the smell of food and the dank river is so strong, and mildew has dampened all walls from the inside; she grimaces away from the brown fungi-shaped octopus-like tentacles sprouting from the low wainscoting. Kate is superstitious, and retains the potential for disgust if something is alive but appears dead.

In the back room she sees a plaintive little bed. Crouching, she ruffles the single yellow sheet as though Daniel will materialise. The bed appears recently used—but there is no one to ask. Finally, she hunts around for some of Daniel's cast-off clothes, but can see nothing. Where is he?

Kate remains with Sarah Crease a few moments longer, regretting her actions. The remorse is palpable in the fetid air—the first act of betrayal of her helper and friend, of her only son Daniel and she believes, of herself. She feels a swirl of something, entirely unintelligible, but real in her gut—a morose pain, yet offset by her grandiose self-pity. Has she not betrayed herself? Is the Thames not there, now? Would that offer a modicum of glory? Perhaps there is nothing else to do, except like a Roman wife or Cleopatra herself, take her own life, or else seek redemption in the cup of Lethe—and Kate's preference has always been the latter.

"I must find a bottle," she says stepping back over Mrs Crease, without looking down. She tosses the wooden stake in the yard, sending it spinning in the moonlight, and her body drifts like a living shadow to Bleeding Heart Alley. She looks up at the stars, still piercing the night. "I must drown my soul."

As a devout follower of Silenus, Kate knows just where to go, even at the late hour. One o'clock is approaching but all is not lost. Just as Silenus, the drunken satyr she's never heard of, was tutor to Bacchus, the drink shall corrupt her accordingly and she will become a goddess—throwing off all the mortal agony of her day—the fear of Newgate, the failure to find Daniel—all through the excess of gin!

"I should have raided the cellar at 2 Mayfield Gardens," she tells herself, stumbling onto Lambeth High Street. "I knew the old bag had Rhineland wines down there!" Gascony, Burgundy and Madeira would have greeted her. "Perhaps they'll have them in Southwark," she jokes.

Soon enough, she has discovered her favourite place of old— known from the bouts of streetwalking she 'fell into' with Emma 'Butter' Gosling. She has not been there in nearly two years, but *The Mermaid Tavern* is still straddling the corner of Friday and Bread Street, built on the site of the famous *Mitre* ale-house after its consumption in the Great Fire. As she approaches, Kate can hear the games of dice she remembers, and pauses, wondering whether Mr Charleston will be present—one encounter is probably enough for the night. "But what do I care?"

The top-hatted bouncer on the door, a token gesture for the late hour, recognises her hunger; Kate does her best solicitous wink and the saloon-style door swings open. She already knows the place. The double-counter bar, a semi-circle, backs onto a public kitchen with eating benches, an oyster table, and a wine corner specialising in tawny ports, Canary sack and Syrah wines. Upstairs, maroon curtains separate the rooms, each embroidered with a suitable moniker: the Mischief, the Ne'er-Do-Well, the Archer's Heart and The Merry-Go-Round. The guest rooms do not need mentioning—Kate's days of accompanying a sailor upstairs, only for him to 'trick' her and mooch out the window without paying, are good and buried.

Even downstairs, though, the air is scented with popular

'angel-dust', and cuts a sharp contrast with Mrs Crease's dive. Without looking up, the too-sweet odour reminds Kate of the establishment's whoring promise of dove-white pillows, Egyptian cotton bed sheets, and armoires with false backs, their fronts stuffed with glass bowls masquerading as crystal. Affronted by memories but pushing them aside, Kate collapses on the first bar seat. She can see people in the kitchen, but so long as they don't aggravate her, she won't bother them.

Fortunately the night barman is new, a squat man who moves like a penguin. He lays his flippers on the bar and peers sleepily over the counter.

"What'll yer 'ave, luv?" He frowns at the specks of blood on her shawl, but pays them no mind.

"I could knock back a three pint o' white wine."

"No wine, dear. Jus' what you see."

Kate surveys the glass bottles, the labels clearly stuck on with glue.

"How can I trust yer wares?"

"They're all liquor," the penguin says, without apology.

Kate deliberates. "Maybe I should start with a beer."

"I've got a sweet beer, McCauley's. Or the new malt brown, fresh from the taxman." He gestures to a rail of bottles above the bar. This batch's got more hops, a real 'bitter beer', or there's 'half n' half', like Casanova drank."

Kate looks impressed, and wiggles her finger at the keg taps. 'And stout?"

"I've got brown stouts, *Irish Entire*, double stouts, three kinds o' 'heavy wets' n' *London Particular*."

"On second thoughts, I'll stick with the hard stuff. A triple gin, neat."

The barman stares at her, trying not to be ruffled by her rejecting his beer list, even at one in the morning. "The amount of alcohol flowing through the veins of London, I don't know! Are you celebrating something?"

"Yes, the last night of my life. I plan to drink myself to death." Kate hiccups, her gums loosened by liquor. "The end o' the night, the start o' a new day." She lifts her chin and downs the triple gin.

"Another."

"You know somethin', I run a hearse business. I can carry a body to any part of England."

"I may need your services." Kate tugs his shirt sleeve but he pulls away. "A woman is never happy in the present until she is drunk."

"Who said that?"

"I did," she says, grinning. "Gin is my closest friend."

With this comment, the penguin taps his moustache. "Your secret is safe." Behind him, the waiters in the kitchen are playing cards, indifferent to the last customer. The barman is appreciative of a little comfort, though, for once free of workmen and *Mermaid* girls. "Gin slings," he says, stroking his chin. "You know, you can get them in parliament too—a brew right at the top of the social ladder."

"And the bottom," Kate says. "Richmond too—you can get 'er anywhere."

"The hellish beauty of gin, the rush of angelic hell-fire, the tickle, the gurgle, the sweet aftertaste like champagne. It's a drink I've never tasted—perhaps you can enlighten me? I'm told the grip is the stomach, and then the slow gently burning feeling of relaxation."

"Sounds like you've no idea! You got it about right—the ol' demon of London."

"A liquid fire by which men drink hell before going there!"

Kate peers at him, then back at her empty glass. "Fill 'er up then, sir. I ain't goin' nowhere tonight."

"I see, and—?"

"Tomorrow, I'll be somewhere else." She kicks back the shot. "Where does gin come from anyway, other than hell?"

"Grain, sloe or juniper trees."

"Yes, the juniper drink!" She raises her glass, stares at the last grey drops. "They say juniper's harmless—good for the brain, for the memory."

"We should aspire to drink it like Kings and Queens, madam," he says, smiling softly. "Just like in magnificent gin palaces or elegant Geneva shops."

"We should, kind sir. Fill 'er up!" Kate raises her eyes to his imagination, to a transcendent world of clear-eyed drunkenness—but she is interrupted by a cry from the kitchen.

A fallen woman, stockings half peeled from her rear, tumbles into the bar on the shoulder of a local odd-job man. They disappear up the stairs, the girl giggling and twisting like a rag doll, the man tumbling on her neck, supported only by her weight. The penguin turns back to Kate as though nothing has happened. "As I was saying, gin palaces dazzling with a hundred plate-glass windows, gilded in red and gold. Retreat from the street into a happy fantasy world, my dear...."

"Delightful!" she cries, and lowers her chin to the bar.

"Had enough?"

"I think so."

"You owe me twelve shillings." He stands from his stool, strokes his moustache.

"That's a lot."

"You drank a lot." He twists his fingers with a twinkle of menace. "The Gin Act, dear, was in 1736. You drank a lot o' Sangree tonight, or Makeshift as they now says. No pub in London is a true freehouse, last time I looked."

"You didn't have to give me pricey tipples—that's a quick con."

"We're all in the same game," the barman replies. "Now pay me, if you don't want to mount the stairs and meet that sailor."

"You ain't in charge o' 'im—no one is."

The penguin hops from foot to foot, realizing he's caught a live one. But he keeps a steady expression. Kate sees her chance.

"Calm yerself, dear bottle man," she whispers. "I got the money." She takes out her last shilling, purloined surreptitiously from Mrs Crease. The penguin's eyes lower to where she clips it flat to the bar. "Now let me tell you a story—ever 'eard o' Judith Defour? See, I read about her in *The London Sun* yesterday. She took her year-old daughter from the workhouse, strangled 'er to strip 'er, sold the clothes and spent the money on gin."

"The Out and Out!"

"You got it—the 'No Mistake' and 'Good Fur Yer—she sank a pint n' half o' liquor, that's it, all for the blood of her kid." Kate leans over the bar. "Now what would you do, sir, if I told you I've killed three times for my boy. I'd do everythin' to protect 'im. But kill 'im myself? Never!"

The barman considers this story. "You don't sound so sure o' that."

"Never!" Kate barks back, "now pour me another!"

"How much did she get for the daughter's clothes?" He pours her shot, picks up the shilling.

"One shilling, four pence."

"Well, let me tell you a tale, missy. I didn't always work this beautiful mahogany bar, these casks of painted green and gold—and all these gin bottles." He tinkles his fingers over their glass lids at his shoulder. "No, I used to run a man's club, a tidy little joint for the after-work crowd, called *The Coal Hole*, Fountain Court. Strictly gentlemen, you understand. Gin did for me there—they smashed the whole ground floor, bottles n' all—so I had to step down."

"Down to usin' gas-jets to water down yer beer?" Kate points.

"Adding bubbles don't water down." He leans on the beer taps. "Listen, a man can be betrayed into mirth in the midst of great sorrow. Down here, there's more than enough sorrow."

"So you thought you'd bring a little mirth?"

The penguin laughs despite himself. "Yes, something like that. Now you should be gettin' home now, missy. I'll ask you kindly for the other coins."

"You can ask, kind barman."

The stand-off lingers a second time, Kate dancing on the last edge of sobriety and ready to breach new territory for the night. She is not ready for another killing though, her animosity quite dwindled past the point of self-defence or caring.

As though saved by the noose, at that moment, the salon door widens and the night enters, along with the wet muzzle of a large dog. The creature is motionless, aping Cerberus's heads in Kate's dizzy, imbibed state.

A whistle is heard, a kind of weeping rustle in the trees, and Kate believes she can hear the sound of the river—the swinging of the noose like a clock pendulum—the crying of her boy alone on a yellow sheet—the squeals of Mrs Thomas reeling from an axe-blow—the spluttering of Clatter on the ground—the gurgling of Mrs Crease as she asphyxiates with blood on her apron. What is happening? All these sounds invade, crushing together in a single point of collapse, her life before her eyes, her crimes of the past, her future narrowed to nothing. She looks up.

Inspector Sequin is standing in the door, Jones to his left off his leash, and a German Alsatian in Jones's fist, the lease wrapped twice to halt the attack.

"Dogs," says Kate, remembering Bartholomew Fair where she collapsed after seeing the dog-fight—all for her chaperone that day. "What are you doing here, officers? I was jus' havin' a quiet drink." To demonstrate, Kate raises the last shot of gin, winks through the glass. "One for the road?"

The prisoner is indicated to the dog, and the Bow Street Runners step forward, dog first. Kate does not move.

"We're here to take you to paradise," Jones says.

"Or failing that, Newgate Prison."

"Barman, stand back."

"We have reason to believe this is Kate Webster, wanted for murder. The night-watch directed us—and you should be closed too."

The penguin says nothing. The noise in the kitchen falls quiet, though the noises upstairs do not. Sequin is holding a long black truncheon, gently tapping his other palm. "We know a friend of yours—Mr Marwood, Esq. He wants to see you."

"He does?" Kate looks up, her eyes closing. "Oh, I get it. He wants to see me, on the scaffold with a hood."

"It's true," Sequin replies, "there's more than enough rope. I'd hang you near the spot where the crimes were committed, so you're lucky it's Marwood and not Calcraft. Maybe he'll take you to Richmond for a day out first."

"Ha!"

"Get back!"

The Alsatian begins to bark, its teeth spiked and drooling over its jaw. The bar-penguin does as he's told and retreats, raising his palms to show innocence but accidentally jangling the beer glasses. Kate cannot help but laugh, spinning round on her bar stool.

"I'm drunk—lay off wit' the beast. I won't make a fuss." To prove her statement she lays her cheek on the bar, linking her hands behind her back, as customary. "I won't make a big, fairy-tale show."

As Jones holds back the dog, Inspector Sequin walks the ten paces to Kate. She is half sitting, half collapsed.

"It's over," he says touching her shoulder, and she's ready to spit on his shoes, but he grabs her ear, twists. "That's not gonna help."

"I can't take it no more," Kate says. "I ain't no Jack Sheppard."

"There's only ever been one Sheppard."

"I know—he escaped like me."

"Yes," Jones says from behind, the dog growling support. "An' you know what happened next? He got hanged, good n' proper."

Chapter 40
Riding the Black Maria
23rd March 1879, Sunday

After a brief interrogation the next morning, Newgate is considered too public, too sociable, for Kate Webster, nursing her worst hangover of thirty years. The authorities, especially the mayor, cannot have her escape a second time. The criminal will be transported not to Australia but further south to Wandsworth Prison. Here the law will be upheld—she will promptly face the hangman.

The honour is served by the *Black Maria* prison truck. South they go to the river, two guards with the driver seated up top, just like a hansom. Sunday morning is quiet, just like the day of Mrs Thomas's murder; but no one in the truck comments on the occasion, all the men being hired without knowledge of the prisoner. The invention of the motor vehicle is only weeks old, so the prison truck is part motor-car, part adapted post-chaise with a hood. The guards sit silently, one either side of Kate, as the *Black Maria* rattles through the streets at break-neck engine-inspired speed, sometimes exceeding fifteen miles per hour. All the men grip the truck rails.

Kate leans forward and nurses her hangover. Perhaps she will never see London at dawn again, or wake up to the Thames in spring. But nor will she sleep rough now, slip into the mud, read of her horrid crimes in the newspaper or suffer the loss of her boy. Inside the *Black Maria* is so dark, Kate can only smell where she is. Outside, the city is changing. Tower Street now brings odours of wine and tea where once there was oil and cheese, the mixture of reality and memory creating cheesy wine and oily tea. Soon they are down in Shadwell stinking of sugar refineries, through Bermondsey beer distributaries, past the *tanyards* and pickle-storage plants where fruit is fomenting into jam. Each odour circulates inside the van, ignored by the guards, lurching Kate between bouts of sickness.

After a while she is outright sick, the floor scattering the watery dribble of no food, just a brown sludge of beer and gin, half digested. They stop the van, the guards simply kicking out the puke with their shoes, and the jolly ride continues, enjoying a worse London stench.

"Are we nearly there yet?" she says, and receives a truncheon jab in the ribs. Worse, with no food but only the *Marie*'s black awning, Kate she is left to the inside of her mind, its mercy now all but forgotten. She berates herself silently, rocking a little. Apparently dreaming of the gallows is a prophecy of great good fortune and so too, she has heard, is dreaming of beef. Or does hanging mean good fortune, like Death from a Tarot card, which never means death, and the beef is somehow bad—which way round is it? Kate presses her temples; right now it seems to matter.

She remembers once she had lodgings near the river, where Daniel played at low tide, long before they went to Hammersmith and stayed with the Porters. "Are we nearly at the river?" she asks, but receives no jab. Did she speak out loud?

The men begin making jibes, equally tired by the journey; up front they only see slivers of light affirming the prisoner is still there, weighed down in her ankle chains.

"Lookin' forward to bein' a gallows' bird?"

"She's gonna ride the three-legged mare!"

Kate looks up in the dark. "The parade to Tyburn Fair was long ago, gents."

"An' what d'yer know of it?"

She waits for the jab again, but it doesn't come. "The hangman told me so," Kate says. "I knew him personally."

"Whoever he is, he'll make yer piss when you couldn't whistle."

"n' take a leap in the dark."

"Weak," Kate says. "Is that the best you've got? What about I'm off t'ride a horse foaled by an acorn—that's the best Tyburn Tree one. But if you didn't know yet, they's hangin' us all. Hang 'em straight and high. Pull the lever, let em' fall, let 'em crawl, let me float 'til I croak." The two men start laughing, half shocked by Kate's hysteria. "The spectacle is all, gents! Roll up, roll up, one and all—come to the new modern drop, not even the Newgate Drop—this one's William Marwood's long drop! Safe inside prison walls!"

"She's 'gone west'." The second guard nudges the first.

"I ain't dead yet!" Kate cries, and stands in the van, her chains rattling. "Goin' west is just another sayin' fur the cart drive from Newgate to Tyburn. William taught me that!"

"She's gone bananas!" Each guard grabs her shoulder—the prison van swerving—and restrains Kate, but they can't stop her mouth:

"Win your Tyburn tippet! Cart me down Tyburn way! Send me to eternity!" Eventually Kate wears herself out, slipping into a corner to sulk and despair.

The world oblivious, the *Black Maria* rolls deeper south to Commercial Road. First they negotiate the cobbles of Mile's Lane, Duck's Foot Lane and Pickle-Herring Street, whose factories are skeletal and built from dust, old cranes and human voices dulled by newly invented machinery. The truck occupants, though, see nothing. Over Southwark Bridge at last, they escape the skeletal warehouses, entering a new region of bruised navy stores, sailors' hovels, rum dives and oyster dens. Shielded behind *Marie*'s black curtain, they pass the towering steam flour-mill of Ludgate.

The factory's wrath, sending black water-plumes high over road and river, seems to calm the prison guards, as though the brutal industry and endless work suggests all is well with humanity.

Inside the prison van, all is quiet. Soon enough, the rattle of the wheels changes, softens, as they reach a notorious stretch of muddy ground beside the river—the Isle of Dogs. The guards immediately exit the van and Kate can hear voices, a conference of shady, hushed business.

"I'd recognise that sound anywhere."

"Empty your load."

"You ain't got no precious cargo…"

Kate waits, forgetting her past in the fear she is about to become a victim. She lifts the corner of the black drape, sees halfpenny steamers lurching over the Thames—the ambitious holiday-makers seeking the spring—already heading to Greenwich, Gravesend, Ramsgate and Margate. Perhaps there is a slow boat back to Richmond—and she can unwind the clock, bring Mrs Thomas back to life, even get her old job back. Kate smiles, aware her brain is muddled, and shakes her head.

Through her own wiry dark hair, she spies her guards in a ring of men, shoulder to shoulder in a meeting of tricksters, confidence artists, all 'Abraham-men'. Some are even specialists recognised by Kate from their tools—ropes and picks on their shoulders—those clapper dodgers who fish for goods from open windows, and their counterparts, the 'priggers of prancers' gripping the bridles of their stolen horses. She leans back in the truck, catches her breath, digesting the amateur scene of petty crime.

Clearly my *Marie* is part of some act, she things, some racketeering swiz. Before she can contemplate escape, though, the two guards tumble back into the truck.

"Not paying those prices," one says, and the other encourages him to "shut it." Kate shifts on her haunches, tries to pretend nothing has happened. She knows they're trying to sell her as an indentured maid, or kept prostitute, but no one wants her. Worse, they could claim she fled on foot from the prison van, and still retain their jobs since they'd catch her the following morning, hauling the pimps into court for good measure. Kate knows she'd still go to jail. It's a common ruse, but never in a London minute did she consider herself a victim.

"Next time," the first guard says, turning to smile at Kate. "You got lucky."

The *Black Maria* rolls on, Kate's legs irons cutting into her ankles sideways, making them bruise and blister red. She itches the peeling skin and receives a yank on her foot chain. Finally she is quiet. Then for their own satisfaction, bored by the recent failure, the guards remove the truck's rear cover, allowing Kate to view the panoramic scene—the giant tobacco warehouse at Wapping, lurching for dominance over its sugar and alcohol neighbours, their chimneys a tangle of blackened vines gasping to escape an urban rainforest. Visible on the horizon, the Wapping tobacco monstrosity is publicised on a nearby wall mural as covering 'more ground under one roof than the pyramids of Egypt'. Kate smirks at this false claim. Soon the whole city will be addicted to cigarettes—'the heart of tobacco' dividing the limbs of the sugar and alcohol refineries, each spoon-feeding the other.

"A sugar mountain to sweeten the Inns of Court," the first guard says.

"Rum 'nuf to make half England drunk!"

Kate says nothing, lets them chatter as the truck swerves east. They hug the river for a long time as St Paul's veers out of view and the City's proud façade sinks down to grey. The dark rolling Thames is all—pressing Kate's with its brooding living weight. She thinks of something Marwood once told her, how *Tamasa* is the original name in Celtic for the Thames, meaning 'dark river'. She thinks of the wooden box rolling on the bottom of its sweeping bed, then remembers—Mrs Thomas cannot bother her now. The trunk has already been dug out, rolled ashore by a fisherman, confiscated by the Bow Street Runners and prised open for the photographer's eye.

"All in the past," she whispers, then covers her mouth. The jab does not come, though, as the guards are distracted by the view. Outside they have reached Execution Dock, a mobile unit north of Wapping, the truck slowly passing the empty gibbets, long abandoned but left hanging. Here, Navy deserters accused of crimes of the 'high seas' were dispatched into eternity. The human-sized cages are still there, swaying opposite Blackall, a dozen cells purposely arranged downriver to Bugsby's Hole, every gibbet-victim tormented by facing the freedom of the North Sea, which they never see.

Kate fears the gibbet, not wanting public display in that way, and is thankful the cages are empty. But the sight is awful and chills her skin, reminding her of the 'welcome gibbets' inside Newgate Prison, those macabre and comic traps, so witty and brutal in the English tradition, into whose arms she believes she is headed. Kate closes her eyes, presses on their lids. When will this journey be over? Now at a narrow stretch of the Thames, the *Black Maria* has to negotiate a hole in the road, coming so close to the dock, one guard reaches out and touches the metal cage.

"I can see bone," he says, and turns grinning to his companion.

"Sit down," the driver says.

Kate drops her head between her knees, but cannot be sick again. Even now, she fears the gibbet more than dissection, so is thankful—without being certain—that she won't be hung to rot. For hanging is only the first step, she knows. Afterwards the body is covered with goose fat and tallow, then pasted with a dirty shirt in iron bands and hung once more—to dissolve to dust.

The ordeal of the prison truck is only just beginning. From Rotherhithe via Tower Bridge they enter a new territory, showered with blue dust by collier yards, grey smoke peeling up from the wizened chimneys of ugly-fronted houses. Here at one time, a white moon illuminated the brightness of the buildings along its banks, but not now. Instead, the Isle of Dogs sinks lower in the mud, becoming the best kept secret and most squalid dump east of the City, wholly unknown to those outside. For here is Jacob's Island, a wasteland of marsh stretching from East India Dock's tidal sinking sands—three miles of treacherous mudflats—to where Commercial Road meets the western quay of Brunswick Dock.

They enter the island—so called because one route in means a separate route out to allow the sand to recover—at St Crispin's graveyard. Kate looks up just in time to see the forlorn-looking gravestones, edged in grassy dunes and jutting all angles from the solid-watery banks of the Thames. In between is a horrible sight of dozens of shack-homes, all sinking in the black ooze, their front gardens encroaching on the more permanent, borderless tombs.

Just as quickly she is distracted by a great mast-house of a hundred and twenty feet. This ominous building doubles as the police station, part lighthouse to guide lost ships down its Thames distributary, a narrow mud-channel and reminder of the law's long arm. Inside the police hideout, a notorious and feared *River-Book* details river suicides stretching back decades, a litany updated once a week and cross-referenced against bodies brought ashore. Here the *Black Maria* trundles to a stop.

A funny-looking man, all elbows and jutting neck, approaches the truck.

"Bow Street?"

"Prisoner for a quick sale," the first guard says.

"How'd I know you's legit?"

"You think we'd be 'ere if we weren't." The second guard takes Kate's wrist as though signalling his property.

"Well, my name's Mr Collector—good name for my job. I collect the ladies of the night, see, then I collect 'em when they fall in the river. Then I collect extra half from you if you don't pay, see."

"We know the drill," the second guard says. "Just do your inspection."

"I see, that's how it is." The man glares, reaches into the truck and lifts Kate's head up by the hair—for once she doesn't protest.

"She'll do."

"Same price?"

"Twelve silver, five pence."

"Done."

The guards haul Kate out, the cold wind catching her jaw, her chains sinking in the mud. She blinks around seeing only grey, the river darker than the land but no distinction otherwise. Two women pass by, giggle, and point at her, but she can't catch their words. Kate has never been to this place, but its economy is part of her psyche. At night these 'sailors' wives' trawl the mudflats fishing for men in their own delicate way—by flashing leg. Here fishnet stockings are born, here Jacob's Island spirals down to the primitive urges of city boys who take a late-night skiff across the Thames in desperation, long after the West End girls are asleep, to risk the Isle of Dogs.

Kate remembers—of all things—the Turner painting Marwood once showed her of Blackfriars Bridge, showing the water and the sandbars in perpetual embrace, the scattered debris of ships and bottles, cans, ash, bits of rope, pieces of ply all lapping up, which can be fished out too, if purpose can be forced from them. Discoloured copper, rotten wood, honeycombed stone, green dank deposits, black bile of the heart....

Here is an industrial wasteland feeding the swamp of the Isle of Dogs on human waste. Here is a place to drown and never be found. Who looks at this nothing-place, too, is looking at the future, the dregs of forgotten Victorian London awaiting a Docklands rebirth.

Here and now, though, the Dogs is the lowest of the low places, a London basin street. Here are stinking booze shops, indescribable in their grime and desperation. Here the business is one of 'dead houses'—a drop-off after the casket is fished up, and laid out to await the beadle or coroner. These are the people who live off what floats by, surviving on the rubbish of the rest of London, right under the eyes of a Bow Street outpost long-corrupted and 'on the take'. For each body found in the River-Book, two are never reported.

Meanwhile the toll-keepers take their cut too, letting the boats through, sometimes fishing a body out—lifeless, robbed n' stabbed—before selling the story with a sprinkling of dirty glamour—*he was only eighteen, he had a merry 'last' night*—to the newspapers. Here is a city of waste but no waste because everything turns into commerce to make money. Money is dirt—the bodies become saleable. Once the newspapers are sold, they too become paper for fish n' chips and ground into dust, mixed with cheese and sprinkled on baked potatoes. *And so, gentle readers, the people eat the waste that later rebuilds the city.* The cycle of life is muck-fresh....

The men exchange the money.

"What are those?" Kate asks, pointing.

"Dead houses," the man called Collector says. "You'll be working hard, girl, so get some rest."

"What d'yer mean dead houses?"

The buyer looks incredulous. "For the girls—don't tell me you've never seen a brothel-house, before. We've got so many sailors down 'ere, we don't need police protection—they jus' helps us now n' then. Now get yourself inside and meet the girls. Welcome home!"

But that's not what happens. Instead, the guards change their minds—one passes the money to the other—and they simply push Mr Collector down in the mud.

"Scum!"

"A waste of Cockney space," the first guard says. "We come to teach y'a lesson."

"Lesson taught." Mr Collector blinks up from the mud where it oozes around his body, covering his black jacket. He twists and turns, but can't get up.

"Stay down," the second guard says, and brandishes his truncheon. He waves to the *Black Maria*'s driver, who starts the motor up. The vehicle coughs into life, a wheezing dragon startling the women who just passed by—they make a run for it.

"You 'eard 'im." Together the guards bundle Kate back in the truck, and despite the mud, the wheels spin, and they're back on the road.

Kate is shocked by the turn of events, and confused whether to thank her handlers or not. Looking through her hair, she sees them counting the money, twelve shillings.

"We figured you're worth more n' our job."

"Thank you," she says.

"Shut up!" the first guard says. "Now you don't have to work, jus' toe the line. We dun' you a favour—but you're still outta this world quicker than a hop, skip n' a jump."

"Thank you," Kate repeats, and the two guards look at her incredulous. "I used to work in a—place like that," she adds. "I dun wanna never go back. I'd rather die."

The two guards say nothing. But later, they adjust her hands' chains and ride on in silence. Kate is not allowed to sit up front, but they remove the dividing leather screen. The atmosphere is different; all three look outside the *Black Maria* as a sliver of orange moon lowlights the Thames. The lighthouse of Jacob's Island recedes from view. They escape the Isle of Dogs and before long, the gravel of Commercial Road steadies the truck. Only the river remains, as always glistening with promise, the moon's hope-line cutting through the flow of darkness. Kate lowers her head and falls asleep.

"Toe the line, toe the line." She hears Marwood's voice in her dreams, the softer he speaks, the less horrified she feels. Not once does she wonder what will become of her or Daniel.... Sleep kills all, thank God, and Kate even smiles unconsciously.

Meanwhile the Thames is all, life and death in perpetual violent harmony. Everything in its path is created from above, then destroyed to new life below. In Kate's mind, like Marwood's far away, an imaginary future of energy and mass are wrestling against their separate yet mutual bonds, seeking each other in dreams, like water and land, innocence and guilt, tall tales and true lies. Can one ever escape the other's grip?

Kate wakes at last. One guard is asleep and the driver's eyelids heavy, but any thought of escape is muted. Her foot chains are too tight. Once more, she catches a glimpse of the river's broad expanse—the ghostly arc of its pallid face, silent with countless promises and dreams—all slinking away in the night to the East End. Who could ever tell its human secrets, its tributaries with their cycle of hopes, fears and sins?

Soon, they will head south to Vauxhall, Lambeth High Street and Wandsworth prison. But for now, all on the river is calm. Here emotion is dissolved into mud, life to water, swirling past and present incestuously into a grey, barren future.

Chapter 41
A Room of Her Own
24th March 1879, Monday

In 1851, the infamous Surrey House of Correction becomes Wandsworth Prison, a progressive fortress, an intellectual experiment. After Horsemonger Lane Gaol closes in 1878, it further expands, and in the last ten years it takes on the overflow of Surrey and those tried at the Sessions.

As a result, Wandsworth Prison becomes the pride of south London. Like Pentonville, the prison is built on the 'Panopticon' design to enable the 'system of separation', eight hundred prisoners in individual cells. Designed by D R Hill and constructed on thirty-two acres, its four wings radiate from a centre where a 'maestro' guard watches the cells day and night. The idea is that the inmates—not knowing if they are watched or not—will self-discipline, inducing their good behaviour out of fear, uncertainty and habit. It works on some prisoners. For others, being watched is meaningless and their behaviour gets worse, while for others still, the feeling of always being watched by an unknown power brings disintegration, even madness.

Despite this elaborate design and philosophy, though, Wandsworth is foremost a house of correction, so there is no historical precedent for the 'extreme penalty of the law'. This last difficulty is outweighed, however, by a new project—the construction of a private execution chamber or 'cold-meat' shed.

The starring role will be played by Catherine 'Lawless' as she is now nicknamed, if authorities have their way. She will be the first 'guinea pig' to be hanged away from the public eye—without the cheers of the crowd, the spectacle, the notoriety, the gala-day bravado, just the hangman, the noose and the long drop to salvation.

On arrival at Wandsworth, Kate is hauled from the *Black Maria* into the infirmary by two female 'reliefs', and inspected by a Sister of Compassion from the convent at St John's Wood. She is isolated from longstanding prisoners, and prodded along a stinking passage into an oval courtyard. The air is freezing. Facing her is a giant building with air-vents for windows and resolutely iron-barred: Here is the women's wing of Wandsworth, a dilapidated and grimacing hulk offering a three hundred-and-sixty degree cold shoulder to its new 'hotel guest'.

Inside, Kate is given her own 'holding cell', large enough for a dozen women, twenty by twenty, with a purposely low five-foot ceiling. Her water jug, night-basin and rug are half-buried in a cut in the stone flags. The requisite Bible, prayer book and mug are scattered randomly as though the last visitor left in a hurry. There is no stool. That night, on witnessing her barren compartment, Kate refuses to speak to her female minders. So the next morning, her 'guarding nun' fetches the chaplain, Rev Father Jean-Baptiste Dupris.

A tall man with flamboyant whiskers and kindly face, he stoops on entering her cell. Kate is sitting on her stool, doing nothing, the blanket over her shoulders.

They introduce themselves.

"Why am I here?" Kate asks, "and not in Newgate?"

"The law is fickle," Dupris says, crossing to the window without fear. "It's a better prison—you're lucky."

"Ha!"

"It's true, Kate, you should count your few blessings. Look at the space you have."

"If I'm a done deal, why not send me to the House of Correction at Millbank?"

"The mayor knows your case personally. You're a short-term convict because you're destined for the Almighty." She catches the twinkle in his eye, unsure whether to find it compassionate, rather than sarcastic. "Hence you're a visitor not to be released—you will remain within the walls of the prison."

Kate understands: "I'll be in the graveyard soon enough."

Dupris says nothing, but he cannot prevent Kate from grinning. "I don't know why I always find myself funny," she says, covering her mouth.

The priest hands her a Bible.

"I already have one—anyway, one glance is worth all the good books in the world."

"Ah, Jack Sheppard, I know his work intimately."

Kate stands, rubs her palms. "No offense, Father, but you seem crazy yourself."

"Perhaps, but a mad hope is alloyed to a good belief. Kate, you know sugar makes the medicine go down. We don't want to simply believe 'be good', we want to believe something bigger."

"Yes, the big lie over the small one. See, Father, I've already got prison fever...."

Dupris sighs, crouches then thinks better of it, and sits completely cross-legged on the cold floor. He is not wearing his dog collar, but a brown jacket worn at the elbows, as though today is Sunday and he is ready to read the newspapers after lunch. Kate pictures him with a pipe, a gentleman farmer or Dr Watson figure who's wandered into a freezing prison by mistake. Nothing about his demeanour scares her. Too bad, she thinks, knowing she might benefit from a little fire and brimstone.

"All our life," he says with a half-smile, "is but a going to the place of execution, of death. Kate, no one slept in the cart between Newgate and Tyburn—between prison and the place of execution. But why sleep, I ask, only to stall the grander, more precious sleep of death? Now I am no Shakespeare, but what is life but a prelude to a sleep? See, in life we are awake and yet 'we sleep all the way'. As John Donne tells us, 'from the womb to the grave we are never thoroughly awake'. Do you understand, my dear?"

Kate stares at him, her mouth almost wrinkling with amusement. "Father," she says, "you talk like a foreigner." She leans closer. "All I know is that if I'm guilty, my last day will be a fine day with a clear sky. But if I'm innocent a thunderstorm will come with thunder, lightning and rain."

"You're superstitious."

"I'm not even religious," Kate replies, and folds her arms.

"Now think back, Kate, when you were a baby. You must have had *some* faith."

"I lost it when my father put me out to work."

"Work is good—for the spirit."

"Just bad for the back. Listen, Father, I'm not sayin' I don't believe, I just don't see what there's to believe *in*. Not no more."

"Since when?"

"Since I come to this rotten egg o' England."

"So you once believed in Ireland? You brought up your boy to believe."

Kate nods, without looking up. "Yes, I brought 'im up to believe. I did good, Father."

"So what happened? Tell me child."

"I went to Liverpool."

"And?"

"I got attacked. Then I was pregnant. I was inside a short time fur nabbin' clothes now n' then. I jus' wasn't thinkin' o' my mortal soul, not on a daily basis!"

"I understand, Kate, I do."

She goes quiet.

"Are you ready to confess?"

"I think so."

"What happened in London—I hear you went to Hammersmith?"

"I was good there, met a man named Crane, through Porter. That's all. Both tried it on, rubbin' up to me, if yer know what I mean—so I ran away."

Dupris pauses, but doesn't challenge the story. "Tell me about Richmond. What happened there?"

Kate sighs, sensing the approach of her crime, so she tries a different tack. "I don't know, I forget."

"You must remember—the streets, the people."

"Well, it was a different world in Richmond, so polite. I knew nowt 'bout London proper. Once I seen this cuckold's sign," and she laughs at the memory, "this house with a flagpole up. You know a cuckold pole? Horns on the pole, and people doff their hats as they go. The funniest thing…" Her face softens into a kind of reminiscence, as though Richmond was home from home. "If only I'd played me cards true n'all. But I 'ad to do 't. She was harassing me."

"Now Kate, tell the truth."

"That's all—just that flagpole n' her weird bedroom fur 'r

husband, like a livin' shrine. Her son's paintings wur in the greenhouse downstairs too—they was a nutty bunch a' grapes, I did 'em all a favour."

"Remember your mortal soul, child."

Kate smiles. "I'm sorry, Father, it's been so long since I confessed." She lifts her fists in admonition, bringing the chains up too. "I've right forgot 'ow to do it!"

Realizing he's not being taken seriously, Dupris leaves Kate's new home. He pauses in the low door, strokes his cheeks meaningfully, and looks back at the prisoner on her stool.

"Please reconsider, Kate. You know where I am." He walks away.

"I do," she whispers, and she turns to the window bars. Wandsworth is not entirely real yet, but that changes when Kate is allowed to tour the inner courtyard. Here the sights are quite different from Newgate's living imprisonment: here death is more preciously sought. Removed from her cell for an hour, she is led in a half daze while the turnkey—a slouching man in a dirty canary-yellow suit—tells her stories of Wandsworth. First, there is the tale of one ancient prisoner, a devious thief who won his acquittal by bribing a judge.

"Treason did not deter the villain, and the judge himself was later hanged! Look, Miss Webster"—gesturing to a cell with no bars—"here's where we get our confessions. If only you'd arrived here before Newgate, we could have shown you personally."

"That's a shame."

"I know," he winks, flicking his coattails. They now enter the press-yard, where live punishments are being dispensed before Kate's eyes. One female prisoner is tied to an oversized pillory, her arms pinned through a vegetable pallet, legs stretched out in almost a straight line. A turnkey lingers close by, absently biting his fingernails, sometimes twisting her skin with a sharpened birch.

"That's the 'ordinary'," the turnkey says. "It's his business to break the spirit of the condemned, so he won't resist the hangman."

"How d'yer know she ain't lying?"

"You don't, until you put 'er in the stocks." He grins to express his feeling of 'justice being enacted'.

They pass on to a section of the press-yard overlooked by a ten-foot brick wall and isolated by a low wooden door. Instantly present are about six elderly female prisoners all under sentence of death, huddled around a single stove, awaiting the results of the recorder's report. Their communal future is unclear; for some, mitigating circumstances might yet ship them to Australia: though unlikely, they have hope. Others—one especially—can only expect the wheels of justice to run them over. Nothing can save them short of a miracle or divine intervention. "That rangy, crazy-looking creature," the turnkey whispers, "is a dead woman."

Kate grows weary of the grimy prison tour, bringing recollections of Newgate. When will Molly Muggs show up, she wonders? Why should I care for the men's ward—just to give the guards a little exercise? But she doesn't have to wait long to get her answer, and then regrets her impatience. Leaving the press-yard for a sliver of open grassland, they pass close to the execution shed, though the turnkey does not point to it, and Kate merely assumes the small, shell-like brick building is an outhouse, or a pen for transported animals.

"Nice day for it," the turnkey says, gesturing to the killing shed, but Kate adamantly faces away. They re-enter the prison via a dark, stale-smelling outhouse. Fastened—by their own belts—to its brick walls are two miserable men on their last ever morning, ready for 'carting to the scaffold'.

"Don't even ask," the turnkey says. "Your time will come."

For once, Kate does not want to know, but mostly she is distracted by the next sight of philanthropic visitors to the prison, the 'local ladies'. Bizarrely, Kate is now introduced to Elizabeth Fry, who famously makes the female wards at Wandsworth the scene of her pious labours, as well as Lady Pirie, apparently a constant visitor and 'etiquette teacher' for female inmates.

"We read, converse, and pray for our poor sisters," Lady Pirie says, while Elizabeth Fry curtsies like a child. Something about their demeanour, their rosy cheeks and white pinafore dresses, raises Kate's heckles. For once she sees the prison through the eyes of 'society', and despite the social shock the ladies receive—they rarely see the press-yard—Kate rocks her head back and laughs.

The turnkey apologises, then immediately drags Kate by an extension of her foot chains. Within minutes the condemned murderess is returned to her cell, being "not fit for human company." She sits on the stool, wraps the damp rug over her knees, and awaits a meal that never comes.

"You know something," the turnkey says. "I used to be a hangman myself—in the British Navy. I hanged four pirates in 1865, at the end of the American Civil War, that's right." He unlocks Kate's pinnacles from his own wrist. "They were bandits, pillaging Confederate ships but giving no 'tithe' to the Yankees—that's a crime of piracy, see. No taxes! They were Spanish or from one of those Caribbean islands, what does it matter now."

"Why are you tellin' me?"

He stares at her. "The point is 'justice will come', you know. We *always* find a way to hang yer. Your press-yard friend is lucky—those pirates got hanged from a ship's prow, too ill to stand. Now let's see you find that one funny."

Kate stares back malevolently, feeling hopeless now. Have I got the will to escape again, she wonders, the heart to tackle bullying guards? For the first time, she's not so sure. The turnkey rattles the bars as he strides away, a faceless man with heavy boots and an unseen expression of pride.

"That's what you get for not respectin' the correct social order," he calls out. "You fall from the grace of a lady. An' you did'n 'ave far to fall, girl."

Chapter 42
A Prayer for the Dying
24th March 1879, Monday

The chapel, as appropriate, is quiet and uncluttered. Below the gods, there are mezzanines for male and female prisoners, while the entire floor is empty save for the condemned's solitary chair. According to courtroom prophecy, here the Holy Ghost is honourably invited to deliver the Lord's righteous justice.

Like hundreds before her, Kate sits in a wooden pen of common black ash, facing her coffin. The 'sermon of the dead' is preached. For two hours, she remains in a mental state hovering between exhaustion, fear and contempt. No more than a dozen prisoners are there, in various states of prayer, ill-health, imbalance and desperation, many seeing 'Stigmata' visions with devotion to the spirit their saviour.

The very walls reek of fear. Kate suffers the uncanny madness of having the sentence 'hanged by the neck until dead' read out loud. She is not alone. While her death sentence is confirmed, the words are followed by a half-hearted 'The Lord's My Shepherd', the chorus boomed by a necklace forger to her left, a sheep-rustler to her right. With a smirk, she thinks of the condemned villains at Golgotha, feels a swift, hollow thrill of heresy. Yet she knows both her neighbours are reprieved, their sentences commuted and they will be out in five years, albeit with hard labour. Today is the last-ditch salvation for Kate alone.

Soon enough the service is over, and the forger even whistles as he leaves, glancing up with vindicated confusion to Christ on the cross. Kate follows his eyeline and concentrates as though expecting the holy wound to bleed in her defence. Then she bows her head, frustrated but not humbled, her own plight occupying all her feelings, her heart beating equal portions of contrition and self-pity.

Meanwhile a low, false hum of prisoners' voices unifies the room:

> "The Lord's my Shepherd, I'll not want;
> He makes me down to lie
> In pastures green; He leadeth me
> The quiet waters by."

The spectators, whether in sympathy or sadistic curiosity for their fellow accused, fall quiet. Already Kate has witnessed one of these scenes—in Liverpool long ago. She remembers the King in Council's 'final decision', the desire and dread, the torturous delay with prisoners' names being read out like prize-winners for the following week's execution. The pew would erupt in crazed joy and mute despair, side by side. In death as in life, the players were not separated. So envy, malice and rage played their parts, and altercations broke out in the chapel itself.

But here, all is silent. Only Kate is scheduled to hang, the first woman ever at Wandsworth Prison. At this same moment, peering over her coffin lid to the magnificently colourless stained glass windows, Kate catches sight of a small boy, his silhouette shimmering and lanky, spectre-like and yet real. For here is one of Newgate's chimney-sweeps, expertly straggling an outer wall. There he is now, clambering down from his temporary incarceration by a well-worn route, disregarding doorways and halls—proving that escape is always possible....

Kate stares, her mouth curling into glee, growing into a wheeze of amazement. Filled with 'the hope of the doomed', wobbling there in unrepentant sin before God, she discovers humour in the absurd work of this spider-boy. Elbows tight to the wall, the chimney-sweep is working hand over foot, avoiding loose-seeming masonry on his descent. He begins creeping along a ledge to neighbouring roofs, skipping over turrets, and enters a terrace—

almost frightening a child to death. The rest is easy: with the child crying, he drops anonymously into the street where, the day's work over, he disappears down Newgate Street.

Back inside, Kate is doubtful about copying the boy's manoeuvre. So what did she just witness? Perhaps her fellow inmates are correct and escape is impossible. No, the rumour is a lie—no one ever climbs up there except to smash bottles and tip glue—the old Newgate deterrents. In other words, Kate thinks, it *is* possible to climb that wall. We may all be prisoners inside Newgate, but only hemmed in by untested escape routes. As with the condemned pew, the fear is enough....

After the service, Kate is led to her solitary cell. There she is informed by Mr Cottonwell—patronizing her in person—that no reprieve is to be granted, given the lack of public agitation for commutation. She is to hang at eight o'clock tomorrow morning, as scheduled for the Queen's pleasure, and at the hand of Mr William Marwood.

"Prepare yourself," he says, puffing his chest as though advising a child how to best approach a difficult examination. "We're counting on Mr Marwood to do a good job, with your assistance...."

Kate is silent. The shock is a long time coming but she holds up well, until Cottonwell leaves. Then, on the eve of her hanging, she is quite ready to throw in the towel. Seeing nothing to live for, Kate contemplates how to hang herself prematurely. At least the last moments will be private. Despite the irony, she really knows too little of the art; she tries to remember what Marwood once showed her. The blanket is too soft and old, though, and tears even in her hands.

Dulled a little, despair is close now. Kate stands at the back of her cell, under the window, wishing for the end of suspense, the dread and anticipation that make the blood tormented. Repeatedly, like a wildcat, proud but humiliated and circling a cage with no way to relax, she paces, eternally seeking the blessing of exhaustion to overcome anxiety. But it does not. It is at this moment that her last 'spiritual comforter' arrives.

"Kate Webster, Father McEnrey," he says, his face filling the Judas-hole. "Your very own Catholic priest. Do you want to go to heaven, my girl? Why don't you ask the turnkey to peel away this door?"

Kate can tell from his accent he is south-east Irish. But given the turbulent feelings of comfort and loss that his brogue conjures, she keeps the door firmly shut.

"Let me in," he whispers. "I am the right one."

His words are so mysterious. Kate is tempted, but once more, she refuses.

"I am resigned to my fate. I would rather be executed than return to a life of misery and deception."

So quite simply, he opens the door himself: "I have my own key. I just wanted to see if you'd save yourself."

Standing before her is a man little resembling a serious-minded religious adviser, yet neither comical nor frivolous. On the contrary, Father McEnrey is over six feet three inches, barrel-chested, square-jawed, and walks with a grand step like he's entering the Houses of Parliament. Naturally he has to stoop a little to enter Kate's condemned cell, but that's nothing he hasn't faced before.

"Good evening," he says, and within seconds, Kate is at least ready to pry the camel's eye a little wider—she is not a rich woman, so perhaps it's not too late to get into heaven. "This is your last chance for the next life, Miss Webster."

"Yes, Father."

"I am here to help." He leans on the wall casually like he's about to strike a cigarette. "I could not survive *me own self* in one of dese rooms."

"Lucky for yer, you don't 'ave to stay."

"Neither do you," he fires back, and Kate is quiet. He presses his back on the stonework, folds his arms, and sizes her up—a brutish woman, as far as he can see, but not without feeling. Remorse might be another matter.

"Who is the true father of your child?"

Kate implicates Crane, claiming him as Daniel's father. But given McEnrey's knowledge of her arrest—obtained from Sequin and Jones—he knows the timeline is faulty.

"That's not possible. The boy is eleven. And you met Crane, according to his sworn testimony, only three months ago."

Kate literally twiddles her thumbs. She knows how confessions work; she hangs on to her story, but McEnrey won't let the subject go.

"I have until eternity, Kate. You do not. I suggest for your sanity you tell me." By opening her memory, he wears her down.

"Think of your Irish forefathers. You cannot go from here without shame, unless you speak."

"Fine, he's called Mr Marsh. He ran an oil shop in Holloway. I was induc'd to live with him on arriving in the city, and he seduced me. I was destitute. What choice did I have?"

"None at all, if that's the truth."

Kate finds his manner oddly beguiling. She knows McEnrey is protecting her mortal soul, or rather trying to redeem it at the last gate, and somehow she doesn't mind his efforts. His voice is soothing, cajoling, not without the odd curl of anger—a priest she doesn't fear. For the first time, she wants to tell.

"Don't make me beg you, Kate. Tell me the true story—tell me what really happened."

Kate squirms, crosses the room. "And what's in it for me? I don't want to sound greedy, see, but what do I get? Look at me, you have to help me."

"I don't have to do anything. You have to help yourself, Kate."

"Just get me out of here."

"All is not lost. You'll be out soon."

"Ha!"

They stare at one another. "The question is not what *could* you gain," McEnrey continues, "but what *will* you lose? It's Pythagoras's Wager. You may gain eternity so long as you confess genuinely, legitimately, in your soul. You will be free of here, at the foot of the Lord with all the angels and archangels. You will have done a good thing."

The last words resonate: "A good thing?"

"Think of Daniel."

"Don't play that card with me, sir. An' 'ow d'yer know my boy's name?"

McEnrey ignores the question. "Just tell me, Kate. You lose nothing. If you can tell me, I will bless you. Will you do that—deal?"

Kate sighs, almost losing her temper. But the phrase *a good thing* takes root, and in her weakened state, she feels the need to tell the story, as far as she remembers. "Okay, but the blunt truth, that's all. What I did, an' 'ow."

"Yes," McEnrey says. "Okay."

Turning away, Kate paces to the back of her cell. She touches the cold stone—as though communing with the past—and the image of Mrs Thomas presents itself, ghostly and yet sympathetic, as her employer appeared the day they met opening the door with a smile. "She was never a sweet lady..." But the memory of a living Mrs Thomas is enough to get Kate started. She covers ground quickly, oddly reminiscing over the first days of their shared existence in the Richmond house, as though everything could have been so different. Exaggerating her own maidly duties and courtesy, she realises there's no way of avoiding *what really did happen.*

Kate looks up through the bars at the sky, not facing her confessor. "So, we 'ad an argument which ripened into a quarrel. It's simple. In anger and rage, I threw 'er from the top of the stairs. It was a single push, I swear, but she had a heavy fall. I thought she was seriously injured and I became agitated, lost all control o' myself. To prevent her screamin' or gettin' me in trouble, I caught 'er by the throat and in the struggle, I must have choked 'er."

"Go on, my child. You know, at the trial, the prosecution painted a rather different picture. Mrs Thomas's neighbour, Mrs Ives, heard the noise of the fall, followed by silence. At first she thought no more of it."

"Well, Mrs Ives weren't there—I had the problem of what to do with the body. So instead of just leavin' it, I chopped it."

"Dismembered it?"

"Yes, dammit, if you like. Then I disposed o' the parts."

"How—tell me, now? What happened next?"

Reluctantly, Kate lowers her speech. "I chopped the head from the body usin' an open razor. Then I used the meat-saw and the carving knife to cut the body up. I prepared the copper pot to boil the bones to fuddle her identity, see." She whispers the rest. "But soon as I had succeeded in cutting 'er, she sank in the copper and boiled. I almost forgot I was cooking 'er." Kate looks at the ground, but she does not feel contrition.

"You used to argue with her, didn't you?"

"Yes, but I have to tell you. I opened the stomach with the carving knife, then burned up the parts, as many as I could."

Her speech over, Father McEnrey sighs and paces the room. "One of God's creatures is gone." Kate realises the interview is over. She stretches out her hand and he takes hold; it feels coarse, cold, but he detects her fingers aren't trembling. He blesses her three times, makes her say five Hail Marys.

"Have you seen your last cell?"

"I believe you're there."

"You'll be moved to another," he says. "Do not be alarmed, all is in God's hands."

"That's what…"

"God is merciful, Kate. You committed a crime but there is forgiveness. Never forget that. It doesn't seem right. How can one act betray you, after a good life?"

"Yes, I led a good life."

"I believe you, Kate. Sometimes this life does not make sense. You acted in a passion, a fit of fury, and only for a moment. Since then you have committed no more crimes. Correct?"

"Yes, Father. And you do consider the murder of Julia Thomas a crime, an awful impeachment of God's natural law?"

"Yes, unfortunately. Why, do you have something more to tell me?"

"No, Father." She is thinking of Sarah Crease, the only killing that causes her some pain, some wound to her psyche, a trace of guilt.

"Mrs Thomas was my landlady and I betrayed her."

"And she will forgive you in heaven," McEnrey replies. "I know the law considers you a murderess. And yet I know your heart is good and pure."

"Let me ask you, then, Father. How can the hangman do dozens?"

"Dozens?"

"The prisoners who've dropped at the end of his rope? Who's the bad person now? The hangman's got more blood on his 'ands than me! Or the mayor hangs 'undreds every year, how's 'e a moral man?"

McEnrey frowns, but he does not duck the questions and rises to his full height. "The mayor is not on trial, and neither is the hangman. He works for England, and the state works for God."

"But England is not God. What is good, Father, and what is evil?"

"I cannot answer that, child. The government and executioner are for the good of all. The hangman is not evil, any more than I, or the mayor who signs the death warrant."

"Then neither am I." Kate also rises and smiles at her

confessor, confusing him further. "I am at peace now, Father. I do thank you. But there is no right or wrong, I can assure you of that. My hangman is a good man, too, despite the crimes I throw at him. He will hang me good and true—he will make the drop painless—for the rope's my greatest fear."

"I've heard he's a man of science."

"A family man," Kate replies. "Now I must be alone." She indicates the door like he's leaving a dinner party, and he politely blesses her one last time. Placing her head in the Judas-hole, she watches his black figure fade into the gloom.

"We are all God's creatures," she says, and slides the peep-hole shut.

The wait is over; only the final hours remain of pulsing thoughts, feelings, breaths. "This is your last night," she tells herself, bearing the torturous privilege of a rare human knowledge. By knowing when and where she is to die, Kate is allowed a candle until ten o'clock. When the flame is extinguished, the prison noises start up—the scratching, begging for food, wailing.

Soon enough she begins to cry, soundlessly, in painful self-pity. Stored for a lifetime, the tears run into silence. For a moment she does not wipe them away.

"I must have been eighteen, the last time I cried." She waits for the moon to rise, and eventually, a thin glow is cast in ruffled, virgin half-light. "If I were a goddess," she toys with her mind, in an absurdly poetic last fantasy, "the moon would illuminate my soul." The rock in the sky offers no more solution than the sun in the day, just a smiling cold beneficence, the downside of the same desperate human coin, the tender of life.

Kate blows out the candle to emphasise the effect of solitude, a melancholy self-indulgence trying to suck the sourness entirely out of herself to see what the core would taste like: if not hollow happiness, then a zealous suicidal rush may inspire her to end everything at last, as quickly and cleanly as possible. But true to her own macabre selfishness, she remains too curious about the world, her last moments, the morning weather and crowd size, wishing still to experience her own death, even at the hands of others.

Taking her own life, Kate instinctively knows, would deny her infamy, any infamous legend for posterity, however delusional, certainly the reality of a Last Dying Speech. Cannot she mock-perform her own state justice, just as she enacted justice on others?

Bizarrely, these thoughts of revelling in condemnation soothe her fear of death, curtailing any physical tremors, the sick feeling under her skin. As for religion she won't deny its promise, as Pythagoras wagered. By midnight, if not absolutely redeemed, she feels curiously relaxed—if only due to McEnrey's kindness and the softening efforts of Jean-Baptiste Dupris before him.

Time passes quicker than she expects, now she's calmer. Her mind folds into the past. She thinks a little about Sarah Crease with evident regret, but retains no feeling for Julia Thomas, and certainly none for Jonathan Clatter. She cannot bear to imagine Daniel, she feels so empty about her mothering failure, so betraying of his innocent trust. To think of her son even for a moment, her heart would break.

As Father McEnrey warned, after midnight she is transported a few paces up the yard to the condemned cells. The opening is by a steep staircase descending to a dwarf-ceiling passageway, dank and rotten, resembling a human sewer pipe and casting the sinister afterglow of peat-driven stoves. These cells are built in the oldest alcoves of Wandsworth, cobwebbed port-holes letting in the thinnest stream of light. The world turns, while for Kate, this night is an imagined half-lived moment. The moon crosses the sky slowly, and yet the hours are gone. At seven the next morning, Kate feels her blood drying with the softening light, the sun rising somewhere over London—out there, over Westminster Abbey, over the Thames, over the field where Bartholomew Fair took place, over Covent Garden and its Punch & Judy Show.

Next she is removed to the 'dead man's cell', a holding ante-room. Here she will be dressed ready for the scaffold. The room is intensely cold, despite the clement weather outside, but Kate cannot tell her own body heat from the room temperature. The doors are five inches thick, the stone wall finished with plaster—a few scratches here and there mark the last hours of previous residents. One says MICHAEL WENT BRAVE. In the far corner, a deep groove in Latin spells out *fidelis per semper*, but she does not understand what it means. Another etching chalked over the door reads Every Dog Has Her Day.

Through a small grate, Kate can see more of the prison grounds than previously. On tiptoe, she watches a new arrival—a mousy woman, shivering yet somehow defiant—jabbed across the chapel yard to her first holding cell. Kate smiles faintly, as though with nostalgia for her first arrest long ago in Ireland, and then Liverpool. The girl looks very young.

Minute by minute, flesh and blood return to the earth—the prison comes back to life. Ashes to dust, dust to earth, then justice for all, on the morning of judgement. Am I guilty, Kate wonders for the first time? Will I be forsaken, like the son? She kneels in the middle of the cell, begins to pray.

"I am the resurrection, and I am the life. He...she who believes in me, though she dies, yet..."

She cannot finish. Her last night is over. When the warrant for a prisoner's execution arrives, Kate is lying on the floor fully conscious, wearing her final dress.

"I'm ready for the happy occasion. Let's not make the punters wait."

Chapter 43
The Last Station
25th March 1879, Tuesday

With the dawn, Kate is ushered to her very last room, the 'walking dead cell'. Here she will spend her last up to twenty-four hours. Tramping the damp passage to where two men were recently pinioned, she expects to see her fellow condemned for the first time at close-quarters, but the cells have been cleared, except for one.

This cell is a stone dungeon, eight feet long, seven wide and six high, a claustrophobic pit reeking of rat-droppings with a string mat for prayers, a horsehair rug for nightmares, a Bible and prayer book. An iron candlestick stands in a cosmetic arrowslit cut in the wall; a small high window admits as much air and light as could struggle between double-crossed iron bars. There is no table or chair.

Kate lights the candle, kneels on the string mat. She then witnesses a scroll of paper. The following words are nailed to the floor, left purposely in the cell by one of the philanthropic ladies, a Miss E. Clark:

> "And when the dark thought of my fate shall awaken
> The deep blush of shame on thy innocent cheek;
> When by all, but the God of the orphan forsaken,
> A home, and a father, in vain thou shalt seek;
> I know that the base world will seek to deceive thee,

With falsehood like that which thy mother beguild:
Deserted and helpless—to whom can I leave thee?
O! God of the fatherless—pity my child!"

Kate wishes she could send them her boy, the lines speak so eloquently to her feelings, but there is no possible means. At the same time, she is disgusted by the rawness of borrowed feelings—the last thing she needs to lose is her nerve.

Three hours remain before her hanging, an excruciating time. Of course, life goes on during Kate's preamble to execution, and there is always time for an official state inspection; the case is too public to risk another *faux pas* like her Newgate escape. Hence the Lord Mayor and sheriff wish to see the prisoner 'still walking'. They arrive accompanied by the House Secretary who will write a report for Parliament, Mr Cottonwell appearing from a side gate, an apparition of justice grinning from ear to ear. One by one they pass before Kate's cell, and look inside, convinced at last they have caught the notorious killer of Richmond. The Barnes Mystery is solved—Kate Webster and her 'heavy black bag' are destined for the *Newgate Calendar*—with a footnote that her hanging was privately reserved for Wandsworth's 'death-shed'.

What they see in the cell, though, is somewhat alarming. After being revived after her collapse, Kate has been allowed a nip of gin, and permitted to retain her own clothes, including a blouse that belonged to Mrs Thomas that was never confiscated. Remarkably, over the blouse, she is wearing a decadent full-length wedding dress, all frills, lace and tight bodice. Talking to herself, she seems to have a deluded idea of marrying Marwood, seemingly forgetting he is married already, amongst other obstacles to their happiness. The Mayor of London looks though the Judas-hole.

"He will divorce his wife and marry me," the prisoner sings. She is walking in a circle, imitating an animal in a cage. Every now and then she performs a little skip, cocks her ear to a hidden voice, and shakes her head as though persuaded. "Yes, he will divorce his wife and marry me! I will be known as the woman who murdered white satin!"

"What did she say?"

The mayor pulls his eye back from the Judas-hole in surprise. "It's not a wedding dress," he tells Cottonwell. "No one would be seen dead wearing that."

"Is that a joke? The law is clear," the House Secretary says, "the condemned can wear clothing of his or own choosing for the hanging."

Cottonwell peers at the Secretary closely. "Then the law will have to be changed. Besides, this is not a public execution."

"It can stand," the mayor interjects, and Cottonwell does not stop him. "It neither matters one way or the other. Let the Catholics have their fun."

The men pass on, Kate knowing nothing of their visit. A second visit, however, is unexpected. The hangman has been allowed access to the prison, taking his journey from Gloucester Road by train, as permitted by government expenses. His arrival has happened without Kate's knowledge, since she did not expect to see him again, at least not yet.

Marwood, like the other men, looks through the Judas-hole: His gift has arrived, though Kate does not know it came from his own pocket. Rather than the angelic little devil he imagined, fully clothed to save her shame, the effect is quite different. She is like a jailed princess trying to keep out the cold. He cannot mistake her wedding dress, though it now looks more like a party costume, or a clown from Bartholomew Fair—a muslin gown with a high 'empire' waist, tied with satin ribbon. The dress style is intended for her 'happy day', and yet one detail is stark by contrast—the dress is dyed deepest crimson, the colour of the Catholic martyr.

He presses his eye to the Judas-hole, a little in disbelief. No one else knows where she got the dress, but Kate has been wearing it since her criminal trial when he—against his family conscience yet knowing he must—delivered the dress personally to the Old Bailey. Why shouldn't she have a gift, he thought deludedly, given everything she'll have to face? Now the penny dropping in an instant: Marwood realises he might have made his job a little harder. "I thought she would appreciate it as a joke," he whispers—his past desire for Kate, even if subsumed, altered by present sympathies to do a good job— "has the joke really worn so thin?"

Seeing the dress now, Marwood feels a trembling flush of pride, despite its incongruous effect behind the bars, its strange dirty opulence. Since he trusted the Newgate turnkey, crossing his palm with a little silver, Kate has worn his gift, unknown to all including him, under her own now-discarded clothes—building for her the fantasy of a death-wedding. She will not die a faithful Catholic but the imagery is theatrically gaudy—her taste since childhood—so she will die looking like one. A matching white muslin cap shows her black hair, and a touch more colour is retained by high-laced maroon boots, frilly red cuffs on her wrists. As he watches her, Kate even slips primrose-coloured gloves over her forearms.

Marwood presses his fingers on the bars. "May I come in? It's William."

Recognizing his voice, Kate pauses in her dress-up, and examines his face sideways. "How can I let you in, d'yer think?"

"True, true, I have a key."

Carefully, he unlocks the heavy iron door, and reveals the cage-like room. He glances over the walls with a single roll of an eye, then focuses on Kate. From behind her back, she takes a bouquet of rue and other herbs and hurls them at Marwood, but they only scatter off his suit.

"So you've come to hang me?"

"I've come to see you." He steps forward. "Don't be alarmed, Kate. The morning is waning, but I was always going to visit."

"It's early," she replies, and does a little twirl. "And what can I do for you? Hold a little tea?"

Marwood gestures to the claustrophobic cell; there is only the string mat to sit on.

"Not exactly Gloucester Place, eh?" Kate says. "If I 'ad a table, I'd 'ave some use for that candlestick. I think they want me to hit myself over the 'ead." She laughs low, and curtsies for the guest.

"The mat is fine." He sits and crosses his legs, his black coattails billowing to the walls.

"I can entertain. Would you like some tea, or a slice of cake?" She indicates the candlestick as though it will magically produce food and drink.

"No, thank you. Kate, I've come to tell you what to expect. I don't usually do this, but I believe it is good to know about the procedure, and might make your day a little easier."

"My *hanging*, don't you mean?" For once, the old weariness has gone from her eyes. "We can meet for lunch if you like."

Her humour alarms him. Like a doctor paying her a house-call, he looks for a reaction but only sees an irrepressible grin, her comical and crooked teeth.

"Kate, they are making new plans—a delay until tomorrow. The Newgate drop has its equivalent here. A portable scaffold has been erected opposite the prison, and they expect a crowd—not a Newgate crowd, but hawkers, pickpockets, knitters."

"How many?"

"Hundreds, so I'm told."

Kate considers this news, and a kind of sadness creeps into her eyes. "Now I have another night but it's too long. I want the crowd, or who will see my costume? But I don't know what they think of me?"

"They came to support you."

"William, why did *you* come?"

"Kate, you know, the crowd is like the theatre, all the actors have their part, comic or tragic or in between, and you too. It's a moment to be proud...."

Kate tilts her head to the side, suspicious of his words, but Marwood sounds just as sincere as their long-ago meetings in his home. She is quiet, remembering their basement games with the hanging equipment, all the execution stories he told. What was the point of it all? To scare a stranger and practise his 'art'? Was it really all coincidence, or did she have a crazy death-wish to meet him again?

"Let me tell you, Kate, what a day it will be. You are famous, never forget that. I'm the stage manager, but you're the real master of ceremonies."

Kate plays along. "Tell me, William, tell me what it'll be like...."

"The day will be warm, and hats will come off in the crowd. Everyone will see you. The wind will blow like the murmur of an ocean shell, Kate, as you'll regally mount the scaffold."

"Don't mention the scaffold."

"Of course."

"So you'll be high above the world, a world calling out for hot pastry and beer, but no one buys."

"Because they're watching."

"Of course, yes. Windows will be packed 'round Wandsworth High Street. They'll come for miles by foot and horseback, ladies and their children in carriages. Newspapermen too."

"The she-assassin is here!" she cries. "I will smoke cigars."

"You'll be famous."

Kate pictures the scene, the drinking booths and food stalls, the indulgence of beer and brandy. "I wish I could be there myself."

"You will be," Marwood says, and regrets the comment. A frown crosses Kate's brow.

"What about Daniel, will he be there?"

Marwood pauses. "He'll be there. Daniel will—climb a tree, or something, to see...."

Kate frowns, but works hard to brush the thought away. "Tell me more of the crowd."

"They'll be a mixture, some bonneted and top-hatted, but mostly the merry mob."

"All to lift me up," she smirks, and Marwood pushes on:

"The energetic crowd, the fruit-seller, the broadside vendor, boys and dogs, the beggars and the bawds—just the way you'd like it."

"What does that mean? I want boys fighting and picking pockets?"

"It will be—elegant too. You'll see. It's different here in South London. Young girls will sell Hogarthian prints like *The idle 'prentice at Tyburn 1747*. A fair day, a festival."

"You make it sound like my wedding!"

"In a way..."

Kate pauses, realizing he is pushing his luck. "You know, William, I don't really believe you, but I appreciate the gesture. You can't fool me, though. My boy ain't coming. I know that."

"He might."

"How would he even find me?"

Without speaking, Marwood thinks of Thomas Hardy in Oxford, marvelling at the marble face of the dying woman on the rope in the glistening rain. She was Martha Brown, he remembers, 'hung between two trees', and in Hardy's mind what an elegant silhouette she showed against the white sky—the tightening black silk gown setting off her shape—until she twisted round, facing him.

"You know," Kate says, interrupting his vision, "I will not pull the cap down. I want people to see me."

Marwood cannot bring himself to explain that the hood will entirely cover her face.

"William, what if this long drop don't work?"

If the switch fails and the rope is too long, he thinks, the result will echo the fate of Charles Peace—a second professional humiliation for Marwood, and the end of his job. 'Justice will have been served', Cottonwell will no doubt say, since after Kate's head rolls so will Marwood's, and the life of the cobbler will beckon.

"The drop will work," he says. "My new tests were accurate." But if the drop is short, Kate's face, ears and lips will swell and her eyelids roll to the point of bursting. Her head will turn a bluish colour, eyes purple and protruding from their cavities while a bloody froth escapes her nostrils. The image is so grotesque that Marwood stands to take a breath and paces the tiny 'walking dead' cell.

"Will they make souvenirs of my clothes, William? I'm not sure I like that idea."

"Every 'occasion' has Irish basket-woman selling fruit," he says, avoiding the question, "drinking your damnation in a mixture of gin and brimstone."

"Ha! I'd be doing the same thing myself!"

"But yes, the *tricoteuses* will be there, knitting like last month's Paris guillotine—they're 'bound to the bascule', enjoying their countrymen sent under the knife. We just have our English ones, the typical tradespeople."

"They're like parasites," Kate says. "I've heard they sell potions and magical unguents, basically the blood of victims. Is it true, William?"

"No, no," he lies, "it's not true." For a moment, he pictures the scene of Kate being cut down, and feels the surprise of his sudden mourning. He will kiss her, even dead, but for half a crown he will give people her clothes. The rope he can sell for more in Covent Garden. "You will receive a good Christian burial."

The words stun Kate—it is the first time he's mentioned death. "William, I appreciate your visit—a visit from the hangman the night before—ha! But I think I need to be alone now." But she cannot resist her own questions. As he quietly prepares to leave, she grabs his hand.

"William, no. I cannot do it! You have to help me."

"Kate, please." He drags her a little. "I will send for the chaplain."

"I don't want to be forgotten," Kate says. "I can't have lived for *no reason*. No more priests, please. Just tell me a story, like you did in your basement those times. A hanging tale, if you like, but one that will help me! I need to understand, William, or I will go mad tonight."

Marwood pauses, then lifts Kate up to his own height. "I have to go, Kate," he says. "But there is one story. It's all I can do. Will you listen?"

A little bewildered, Kate frowns, but nods.

"Okay, listen—once there lived Ivetta de Balsham, a lady in the reign of Henry III, forgotten by history. Like any fairy-tale, hers is a tale of goodness. She was hanged overnight but survived and was given a pardon."

"But *today* the sentence is 'hanged 'til dead'."

"True," Marwood says, and thinks again. "Well, there is a better story I've never told you, Kate, as you resemble the only hangwoman there's ever been…"

"Hangwoman?"

"Yes, she was a Dublin girl, not dissimilar from you, and came to be known as Lady Betty."

"She was a lady."

"That's right, Lady Betty. She was harder on women than men, so you should be thankful for my being a man." Kate smiles—and Marwood touches her shoulder. "They used to say, *be quiet or Lady Betty will get you*. She was an impressive magistrate on the scaffold, and kind to her men. You can be kind to me tomorrow, too, Kate, and toe the line."

"I will."

"It will be best." He resists bringing her nearer, worried what might happen, a last embrace might be too much to resist—not that the authorities would care.

"Is it true what they say?"

"What's that?"

"'Only for an awful instant do you float free.'"

Marwood considers, just as he senses movement behind, a face appearing in the Judas-hole.

"Not at all," Marwood says, "if you float, it's an instant, but it floats you up to heaven."

Kate moves to hug Marwood for these words. But he steps back, allowing the mayor's assistant to enter, along with a man to weigh Kate. They proceed without words, allowing Kate to keep sporting her martyr's dress, given they can tie it just as easily.

Cottonwell stares at Marwood, the implication being it's time to leave. "We'll bring you the weight later, for your calculations."

"Yes, of course." The hangman glances back at Kate, where she is looking at him pleadingly. Yet she retains a remarkable mischief like she's not done yet. She is a girl dreading her first day of school, yet, at the same time, she is one who will bully her way to success—the lost anti-heroine who people rarely forget—and he cannot reconcile the two.

"I will be down the hall," he says in a soft business-like voice, as much to Kate as to Cottonwell.

That night Marwood prepares the drop. Alone, he consults the rope table. He takes his Kentucky hemp, makes sure the *Gutta Percha* covering the splice at each end is un-cracked. This does not take long. He is left to his thoughts, remembering how the long drop table began as an experiment with sandbags in the garden on Church Lane—how Aldous fell over the wall and into the street, surprising an old lady, his boy was so keen to help.

All of a sudden, something about this memory of Aldous's earnestness makes him pause, tightening the rope in his hand. He feels the emotion, part sadness, part fear, for all his family including himself, but he pushes the feeling down. Only thirty feet away, he knows Kate is sitting in her cell alone.

The noose measures twelve inches for the neck, calculated from the centre of the brass eye, marked by a piece of pack-thread. Along this line, he traces the exact drop required, to the nearest quarter inch, and marks again.

A knock at the door produces Cottonwell with the final weight of the prisoner. The timing could not be better. Marwood nods and readjusts the rope—the move is flexible. One last time, he pulls the knot tight.

"I'm ready," the mayor's man whispers.

"So am I."

They emerge into the passage, then silently into the night. The yard is quiet, the sun absent, and the prison is so dark the line between the sky and the wall is obscured. For a moment it seems like Wandsworth Prison is only a figment of their combined imagination—except Cottonwell is thinking of the mayor's election, Marwood of Kate's chances of escape.

Together they walk to the cold-meat shed, which Cottonwell unlocks and they enter. Inside, the mayor's man pays close attention to the hangman, as he pins the rope to a chain suspended from a roof beam. He adjusts the cut-mark so the drop is ready for the exact height of the condemned.

"Is all this really necessary?"

"We must avoid decapitation, right?"

Cottonwell says nothing. Feeling watched, Marwood puts the bag on the trap ensuring its sandy heart is equivalent to Kate's weight. He ties the noose round the bag's neck.

"Stand back."

Cottonwell does so, leaning on the wall, and grips the metal bar at chest height for extra safety. Marwood pulls the lever and the sandbag drops.

"That's it. The bag should be left hanging until three hours before the execution. Then I'll examine the copper wire to see if the rope has stretched. I'm not superstitious, incidentally. All this calibration readies the rope, so a sudden weight is no great surprise." He babbles on, as though silence would bring the final hour closer. "The rope can be adjusted, see, if the washer won't run smooth...but I doubt that. I don't think...anything will go wrong."

"I'm glad."

"Everything is ready."

"Good. Shall we?" He indicates the hangman to lead the way. Cottonwell tries to pursue conversation on the way back, but Marwood prefers the concealed torment of his own mind.

Chapter 44
Drink the Long Drop
26th March 1879, Wednesday

The morning brings Kate's birthday, although she tells no one. She is thirty-one years old. No one will know until long afterwards.

At 8:45 AM, the prison bell starts to toll and a few minutes before 9:00 AM the Under Sheriff, the prison governor, the prison doctor, two male warders and Marwood line up outside Kate's cell. Inside, the beadle and Father McEnrey—now acting as official prison chaplain—sit with the prisoner for the consolations of religion, while Jean-Baptiste Dupris declines to watch, declaring he has "greater concerns away from the Wandsworth parish."

Here is a reckoning for the living, unconsciously vicarious, and a solemn tribute of feeling for the victim. By candlelight in the dark cell, Kate is being ministered to by Father McEnrey. In her hand is a stiff tot of brandy. She sips it, nervous now at the end, neither wishing for the drink to end nor begin.

The governor enters her cell with the words "it's time," and she is led out between the two male warders and the priest into the yard.

"Why is there a separate building for the...?"

"Away from the prisoners," McEnrey says. He fails to explain that it's to spare the other prisoners from the sound of the trap falling, the messy removal of the body.

Marwood has taken a nip of whisky himself. "If you can't do it without whisky, don't do it," he tells himself, "and I can't do it without whisky."

In the prison yard, the day is clear. Only a few drops of rain have fallen in the night; remarkably, too, there is a fine silt-like covering, discernibly smudged to grey. It has snowed in the last few hours, the final blessing, the last cruelty of the earth giving up its coldness for the morning birth.

"A final reckoning for the criminal," the mayor whispers, looking at the open sky.

From the debtor's door, a human train emerges for the hanging. At their centre, the newly fearful woman drags her heels, since her limbs cannot quite support her. Kate grunts with each step. The men walk in single file, the governor in a longtailed suit as though his appointment is a black tie luncheon; next is the mayor, sporting a canary-yellow pocket handkerchief, seemingly ready to claim election victory at this hour, followed closely by Cottonwell in wiry black, the epitome of formality. At the rear ambles the beadle in mildewed clothes picked up cheap from his last execution. These men set the pace, light conversation sprinkling their brisk step, quite forgetting the prisoner lugging her chains.

"Tell me this, Cottonwell," the mayor says, "why is it more moral to put incarceration at the heart of our punishment politics and not the noose?"

"I agree, sir. A hanging saves space in the cells, and is less of a torment to the prisoners."

"Yes—all of them."

"Those that remain, sir."

A glance is exchanged between them, almost a smile. "Of course, of course," the mayor says. "Hanging is natural. The *ancien régime* is the capital code in the killing statutes."

"Even so, a civilised nation's depravity must be disguised," Cottonwell risks.

"I don't understand…"

"I mean, sir, now hanging's gone inside prisons, we can direct the masses better. No reason to pay for a big finale or gala-day. Multiple, same-day executions can be organised. Webster's only the second criminal to be hanged here."

The mayor twirls his moustache, only now hearing the idea.

"We can really clean up the street," he whispers. "More in-prison hangings, less crime. That's kind of ingenious, Cottonwell."

"Thank you, sir."

They look to their Queen's compadres struggling to keep up—the beadle dreaming of food, Father McEnrey with the silent prisoner between the two guards, and at the rear, the Crown's as yet unsuccessful hangman. Marwood is thinking of the legend of the Black Dog—an infamous ghost, a spirit of misfortune said to terrify London before an execution. But there are no streets here, just walls. Unlike at Newgate where the scaffold is erected before the Debtors' Door, this last act will take place inside, unwitnessed, unperformed.

Staring at Kate's maroon hood, her chains gently clinking together, Marwood wonders if she already knows. Does she remember his words of the night before? Will she blame him for his deception—the crowd scene he painted for her last moments? Today there is no elevated platform, no one waiting and no scores of Londoners to cheer and salute her brave end, no witty balladeer to pen hanging songs and merry rhymes, to create a lasting afterlife for Kate Webster. Nothing remains—except the rope, the knot, the drop and The End—all before the politicians' and jailors' breakfast time. All they want, Marwood thinks, is to make the Black Dog Walk, and tell Parliament the deed is done.

"I can see the dog," he whispers, "even if they cannot. The black dog is among us—I must help her mortal soul."

Father McEnrey turns to look back, hearing these words, and the hangman touches his mouth in gesture, makes the sign of the cross. McEnrey looks puzzled, but then understands and blesses Marwood in mid-air.

Meanwhile, Kate looks down underfoot. She is walking over open graves—covered with boards—back onto snow-covered ground. Normally prisoners are buried under quicklime within the prison's walls, but she does not expect to trample so freely on their last resting-places. It is an ugly feeling and makes her feel freshly sick. Father McEnrey says nothing: clearly they have constructed the hanging shed too close to the graveyard.

Fortunately there are no headstones, and Kate is able to convince herself that the planks are merely covering a dumping-ground or the secluded, better-kept graves for turnkeys' pets. But deep in her gut, she knows this is false. Perhaps her grave is dug.

"They won't have far to take me, Father."

"Courage," is his only word, but nothing can compete with Kate's sighting of the execution shed. As the path weaves close to the wall, she strains to see the platform over the street.

"Where's the Newgate drop?"

"This is different," one of the guards says. "The outside New Drop is old news, they tell me. You're being done in the tool shed."

"We're usin' the gallows from Horsemonger Lane Gaol," the other guard says. "They say it's looser, 'cos it's portable."

"Don't listen to them," Marwood says at Kate's elbow. "We'll be there soon."

But the hangman cannot hide the dominant sight of the shed. As they skirt the graveyard, the path turns to the coal yard and a skinny building seems to rise from the earth, overlooked by the women's wing. Kate has never seen it before, given her immediate isolation on entering the prison. Already, the square and serious faces of Kate's fellow females—most of whom she's never met—are pressed to their window bars.

"The Old Bailey claims that prison women are quieter than their male counterparts," Father McEnrey says.

"No comment," Cottonwell replies. "Good behaviour is relative in this part of the world."

A whoop goes up as the procession comes into view—perhaps Kate will have an audience after all. Scarves, rugs and bed sheets are merrily unfurled down the women's wing's filthy walls, dangling like flags of an underground nation. All are red, the hangman thinks, for anger, pity and celebration.

"They love a good show," Kate says, smiling for the first time. In Catholic countries, and here at Kate's request, the death hood has a hole cut out to allow the soul to escape and begin its journey heavenwards. To make sure, Kate's maroon hood has homemade eye-slits. But in sight of the women's banners, she pulls it from her head to give them a clear view, sending her dirty black hair down her neck. She raises both hands in greeting, hopeful supplication. Like a Roman amphitheatre, the crowd fills her with a surging feeling, a tear-inducing love that ebbs with pained-pleasure, embracing her regrets. But it is real, Kate knows—the support, the care, the attention.

"Put your hood back on," Father McEnrey advises and Kate frowns, but does as she's told. As they approach the shed everyone sees it has two stories, the platform beam on the first floor, and a gate on the ground floor for removal of the body.

One by one, they mount the steps, Kate's chains being removed so she can climb. At the long top step, she does not turn but feels the wind on her face, tips her head back theatrically and disappears into the gloom. Inside the shed is extremely neat, scrubbed to the point where the smell is only of lacquer. No shavings are present; no moss is creeping under the corrugated iron roof. Even the wooden floor is varnished.

Once inside, Kate receives an unwelcome surprise to counter her fear of dying alone. The shed opens partially to one flank, unseen from the women's wing, revealing a gallery for the reception of officers, attendants, the sheriff, javelin-men. In total, about twenty people are present, but only the mayor, priest, prisoner and hangman take centre stage. They are merry, and she becomes merry, but more a mania of sudden glitches, ticks, a delirium taking effect. Kate realises that no matter how much she is the focus of attention, she is not one of them. "I'm now the other side of a line...."

As Kate's eyes adjust to the semi-darkness, she sees the gallows with the rope dangling in front, already prepared. The noose lies on the trapdoor, ready to be coiled up chest level and the brass eyelet secured. Marwood is already there. He does not look in her eyes, but points to the chalk mark on the trapdoor.

"Toe the line, please."

Kate does so, still shaking. Instantly, he loops the leather body belt round her waist, double-fastens her wrists and pins her ankles. Ten seconds later, she is supported on the trap by two warders standing on planks, a precaution in case the prisoner faints.

The clock is ticking:

> Oranges and lemons,
> Say the bells of St Clement's.

Marwood is about to speak, but forces himself to continue. He removes her maroon hood, and places the white hood over her head—also with eye-slits—and hears the fearful in-take of breath. He ignores it and adjusts the noose, leaving the free rope running down her back like a braid of hair.

"Lord, have mercy upon me."

Marwood begins his preparations. He has inspected the shed, but never performed live in such close quarters with a cluster of uncertain witnesses only feet away. He feels like William Calcraft, ready to bungle the job. To remind everyone of his control, using the force of the lever, he slides iron bars into place, securing the trap on rollers. The noise is sleek, and the whispering of the audience stops. Father McEnrey even stops muttering a prayer, but crosses his black suit and bushy moustache with the sign of the cross.

<blockquote>
You owe me five farthings,
Say the bells of St Martin's.
</blockquote>

The beams loom a dozen inches above the trapdoor, which opens over an eight-foot brick-lined 'death-pit', dug with sheer walls. Long planks sit across the drop, and here the warders stand while Marwood holds the prisoner. Two other ropes hang down for the warders to protect themselves from the condemned's final movements. An iron handrail surrounds the room at waist height, which Father McEnrey and the London officials—including the mayor and Cottonwell—hold in one hand, mainly for psychological safety. Only Kate should be going through the trapdoor, but the trapdoor is wide at seven feet by five, and the entire area is only three times that size for seven bodies total. The wood creaks as some sway, but nobody moves.

<blockquote>
When will you pay me?
Say the bells of Old Bailey.
</blockquote>

Marwood now reaches up to chains hanging down, where the noose rope is already attached. But before he can go any further, Kate has another surprise, and before he can tie her hands, from her waist she produces a tiny 'catafalque', a high-plumed hat, its black feathers her only concession to the customary colour of mourning. The scene is ridiculous—she wishes to wear the catafalque over her white hanging hood, wishing to gauge the nerves of her only crowd, the jailors, politicians, men of the cloth and Marwood himself. But there is no laughter, no admiration of her secret possession—stolen from one of the prison's philanthropic visitors only yesterday, and more suitable for Royal Ascott than the Wandsworth 'long drop'.

"Please," Marwood says. "You are not allowed any time. The rules are different now." She has waited too long, and is disallowed from wearing the hat, deemed 'a distraction to guests'. Bizarrely, and not without mirth behind Kate's eye, Father McEnrey is asked to hold the hat.

"I won't get my opportunity to die game, but I'm glad I got to see that!"

"Silence, please," Cottonwell says but Kate will not listen. In her final hour she is not denied her wicked sense of humour, a belief scoured in her very bones that the ridiculous and the vicious are interwoven. "Go silence yerself!"

"I bid you be quiet."

"I bid you nothin'!"

"Sir, will you do the honours before this becomes a fiasco," the mayor intervenes.

"Yes please," the prisoner quips, "before *someone* gets out of hand!"

Marwood says nothing but winces a little, then just looks pale. He wants to tell her something, she can tell. So Kate leans in close but instead of soothing words, he merely repeats: "Just toe the line."

Kate is stunned, and senses she has been tricked all along. This man cares for her no more than the rest. Perhaps he could never save her, but not to utter a kind word?

"Please, William," she groans, "finish me tidily, for God's sake."

"I will."

He lifts the sandbag, pulls up the trapdoor by means of a chain and pulley blocks: the operating lever is set. Next he puts the three-quarter safety pin through the lever brackets, securing the washer with a ninety degree twist, preventing the noose from being accidentally moved. Next he coils the rope and ties it with pack-thread, leaving the noose suspended over Kate's chest.

When I grow rich,
Say the bells of Shoreditch.

Kate's head tips back, as though looking to heaven itself. Light from the skylight pierces her hood, and she looks for it, keeps her eyes open. A single cloud hovers in the sky. She wonders if her legs can stand the next few moments.

"Have mercy upon me, O God, according to thy loving-kindness…according unto the multitude of thy tender mercies, blot out my transgressions. O Lord…"

Marwood uses a leather washer on the rope, securing the brass ring on the noose. Finally, with a calf leather pinion strap he ties Kate's ankles, then her arms round her body tight. Kate whines a little. Her words are soft, but stark, and goes to Marwood's heart—distracting him.

"Betrayer," she whispers, "I will be praying for you in heaven tonight."

There's a chalk mark where the two halves of the trapdoor touch. "Toe the line," he says, nudging her toes back.

She moans one more time. The song in Kate's head, once silent, becomes audible as she approaches the final chorus:

> When will that be?
> Say the bells of Stepney.

Marwood looks up for better light, the shed more resembling a photographer's studio—suitable for holiday snaps on Margate sands—than any scaffold he's used. His fingers work the knots by heart. He opens a loose hole using an awl, rotating the tool in and out, just like cobbling a shoe. He holds the two braids in his palm and forces through the brass-eye washer—the implement that will break Kate's neck, all being well. Tehn he tightens both threads together.

While this is happening, Father McEnrey is reading John Donne's prayer, Meditation VXII:

"No man is an island, intire of it selfe; every man is a peece of the Continent, a part of the maine; if a Clod bee washed away by the Sea, Europe is the lesse, as well as if a Promontorie were, as well as if a Mannor of thy friends or of thine owne were; any mans death diminishes me, because I am involved in Mankinde; And therefore never send to know for whom the bell tolls; It tolls for thee."

"Don't fret," Marwood says. "There's nothing the matter." He moves to tie a handkerchief round her eyes, but she refuses.

"The pit's under the trap, three feet 'cross and three feet deep," Kate murmurs. "The pit's under the trap, three feet 'cross and…"

I do not know,
Says the great bell of Bow.

She turns her head here and there, blind and displaying surprise, and then remembers the rope. She looks about her with a wild, imploring look. Under the hood and unseen, her mouth contracts into a sort of pitiful grimace. The rope has not yet tightened.

Marwood now slips on his own hood, and to stop her wobbling, he stands before Kate, and looks through his eye-slits.

"It ain't nothing…but a tumble and a kick." He ties a dark red handkerchief over her eyes, and this time—giving herself to his touch—she does not stop him. "This life I mean…"

"Well, I can die but once," Kate says, her voice nearly inaudible.

Marwood, suddenly, is overcome with an incredible sadness. He feels choked himself, and has to touch his neck, but seeing Kate watching, he brushes it off and gets a hold of himself, so to speak.

"Murder is a fine art, Mr Marwood."

"So is hanging."

"I did it for you and my boy. In truth, I did it for no one but myself. And for nothing."

"Hush now."

She begins to sing, the song they shared once at Bartholomew Fair:

…There's none like Nancy Dawson.
Her easy mien, her shape so neat,
She foots, she trips, she looks so sweet,
Her very motion's so complete,
I die for Nancy Dawson…

As she stops, Marwood removes his hood, and can hear Cottonwell complaining. He touches Kate's cheek through her hood, and a tender moment passes between them. He sees Kate close her eyes.

To all spectators, the hangman is shaking a little. Was he ever man enough, he thinks, to see this through? Gripping one hand over the other, he knows he cannot stop. That would be the worst of all, and she would collapse from the sense of mixed fright, the danger of relief and reprieve, an agonising delay being the only result. The mayor wags his finger and Marwood summons a reserve of courage.

Kate takes a breath, tips her head back. "The Lord God take me. Pray for us sinners, now and at the hour..." She stops, and manages to scream, very loud, and completely unexpected for her subdued audience. She stops screaming.

The hangman of London and Middlesex steps to the side, the awful delay of a single second troubling his hand. A memory forces its way inside—he sees Kate next to him, prim and polite and stolen from a dream of their original meeting in Covent Garden—the working girl who could have slaked his heart, if she were never to have coveted Mrs Thomas's appearance. Was Kate ever so innocent? Could they have been closer in this life? Suddenly he feels somehow betrayed by his mind, a little humiliated to be nostalgic in Kate's presence at the very moment of her drop. But the memory persists. The image flickers behind his eyes, but professional to a fault, he blinks it away. He swallows, feeling a pain but cannot discover its centre. The execution shed creaks in the cold, and the audience sighs like a stuffy theatre crowd, impatient and expectant, or perhaps just concerned he will botch the job like Calcraft of old. They came to see a show after all, a demonstration of the new long drop in a private show, as though this were only a scientific experiment for the good of the prison system.

Marwood closes his eyes. Less than two feet from his hand, Kate is still praying, a softer voice than he remembers, tinged with fear and yet beseeching, as though if there is a God she may be forgiven after all. For this hangman, though, her offering of her soul is too little, much too late. Where was her gentleness before now?

His thoughts harden, his mind turning to Ellen and Aldous, his duty to his family. He firmly pulls the lever, hovering the body of Kate Webster for a second of earthbound grace, perhaps a moment of forgiveness, but the charm is a fraud and the reality a lie. Instead, her neck twists, her prayer ends and she plummets some seven feet downwards. A rush of air makes the spectators wobble, fists held to the walls, hearts held in their chests like precious, bloody clocks that have forgotten to tick....

The execution has taken about four minutes, but these seconds are far, far longer, and masked by a strange sense of liberation—a euphoria and the trembling certainty of their own survival in the presence of an absolute, the only absolute.

In the same moment of exultation, doubt is banished from their eyes. Like a baby's first witnessing of light, belief is born, however unconscious, for their own immortality. Could it be, they are different and will live forever? They feel it! Isn't the proof of their survival right before them? Why would this ever change? Their life is reaffirmed by the death of another! That is life! In the final reckoning, perhaps they will be the first to live through death? They cherish the notion as an unholy group, to live past death with a sense of glory, and all hearts beat as one except for Marwood's. His hand still on the level, he feels only distaste and a hollow eruption of nerves, like the bursting of his capillaries into an empty chamber around his organs, a feeling of sickening physicality which, though is all in the mind, he does his damnedest—his most professional—to conceal.

Meanwhile, Kate never expects to feel the rush of wind in her hair, but she does; the lightness on her face could be mistaken for an angel's whisper, just long enough to feel the devil's claw at her throat—it is only a lump, this rush of fear she is swallowing. Sometime in the next world, decades from now perhaps, she will crash into the brick-lined pit below, she tells herself, but no time soon. The two and a half seconds become life suspended...the feeling of being born and always being alone, the sad solitude of all human interactions...a horror of memories, a concentration of the eyes, a loss of breath.

Finally she feels the sweet resignation a tiny mammal must feel when it is lifted into the air, sensing its capture, and twitching in the eagle's jaw. Next she hears the vertical pull of the suddenly straight rope, a sound like the crack of a whip over a horse's back, but so close it could be Mars's whip on Pegasus's snow-white mane, teasing blood over its haunches. No such thoughts occur to Kate: her mind is blank, a single tight feeling of mad fear, her rage converted in the end to a swirl of primeval emotions. She is a shell of despair, a hollow nothing, no more, no less.

Like the long drop promises and the sandbags experiments have prepared, if all goes well her neck is now broken in six places, creating a near perfect circle. Marwood himself imagines as much. How could it be otherwise? Invisible to the spectators' eyes, though, the separation of the second and third vertebrae is incomplete. The men on the gallows know nothing of exact science, so in their eyes Marwood has effected—despite Charles Peace's bloody exit—the perfect hanging.

"Drink the long drop!" Cottonwell cries, and receives a scowl from the mayor as well as Father McEnrey.

"The leather washer makes the rope run smoothly?" the governor says, pointing to the taut rope.

"Right," Marwood says, motionless.

The final word is given by Cottonwell, relishing the bad taste: "She couldn't get to the end of her rhyme—

Here comes a candle to light you to bed.
And here comes a chopper to chop off your head."

He gets no reaction. The men emerge from the Cold Meat Shed into a guilty blessing, the bright morning sunshine.

After the fall, the rope is still. Under their feet, Kate's body is soundless and swings in the wind. Marwood swaggers, his knuckles white on the lever. He remains in shock, distant from his own professional hands. He presses them together, then apart, in disbelief. The long drop works and he is both thrilled by his invention, but disgusted by its power.

He senses part of the hanging went wrong. Didn't a knot, the weight, the brass eyelet fail in some infinitesimal way? His gut tells him she is still alive, but either way, she will be dead in two minutes. Already he knows he made the long drop too short. Kate may not be decapitated, but she may well be strangling without moving, dying the slow, invisible brain-death on the inside—which according to Dr Adams's court report, Mrs Julia Thomas never experienced.

"Justice..." Marwood says, weighting the word. He swallows, unnerved by his satisfaction that the hanging has been a textbook success, all he ever wanted.

Death is final, and that's all that matters, right? Convincing himself, he stifles any self-recrimination; he decides the science is irrefutable. She dropped clean, approximately seven feet, and while a break was never heard, the severe dislocation would surely have induced a swift end.

Meanwhile the men and women descend from the scaffold extension. Suddenly all are downstairs, guests included, admiring the body. They doff their hats in faux-humble gestures to where she hangs, as though saying goodbye to an old friend.

The time is 8:05 AM. Somewhere there is a tolling of a local church bell and the hoisting of a black flag over the prison. In response, two beggars in black coats are allowed into the press-yard and together with a blind fiddler, they sing the 104th Psalm. From the women's wing there is a hollow chant of false revelry, but the faintest note of hope is detectable. Still reliving the drop, the jailbird crowd cheers and wails at the same time, feeling the heroism and pain of the struggle, as if they were watching themselves debased and humiliated into the next life by the Crown. Many female prisoners missed 'the show', but their instinct tells them what happened. Fellow inmates always bear some hope for delay, for divine intervention, Marwood thinks. Isn't that the human impulse for watching?

However, on closer inspection, it appears that Kate's neck is unbroken. She still hangs, painfully, despite all his efforts. Marwood feels dizzy. Somehow all is a dream, surely, a waking dream. But looking down at his hands, the rope-marks bear witness. Even the creak of the tightened knot is still audible; she has no breath, no strength. But she is still alive, dying slowly the old-fashioned way in suffering spectacle for the state's glory, only with no one watching but the hangman.

Something inside Marwood fears her neck is half broken, and yet he cannot pull on her legs like the prisoner's relatives of old Tyburn drops. What can he do? The pit is constructed in a way that he cannot crawl inside; he might break his own legs. Nevertheless he rushes down the external scaffold steps—the only way in and out—and kneels under the shed to look down in the pit. He cannot save her but his heart and guilty conscience are reprieved. She does not suffer—her neck is broken clean. He can tell from the ashen silence of her face. Her eyes are open, purple now, but there is no sight, only contortion.

Soon enough, the prison doctor is brought to declare the prisoner dead, 'instantly dead', apparently. Marwood is not so sure, and yet he is now willing to believe in the success of his 'long drop'.

"She died game, too, quickly and retaining her head…" the

doctor says.

But Marwood says nothing. The execution party breaks up and he is free to go. Her body must hang for an hour. Soon enough, he is left there alone. The mayor chooses not to congratulate him, having been advised by Cottonwell. The strange occurrences of the Cold Meat Shed—the gentleness between executioner and prisoner—need not be investigated.

"The hangman is off the hook," the mayor says and walks away, Cottonwell scurrying at his heels. Father McEnrey optimistically retreats to the governor's office for a shot of whisky.

The time has come. Marwood slips his legs into the pit where Kate is hanging, her body revolving on the rope, her face hidden. He runs his fingers in the dirt, waiting for the tears. They do not come. He does not know why. Was he faking at the end? No, he thinks, but I too must toe the line. He knows Kate's body is left to hang for the usual hour before being cut down and prepared for burial. He hears sounds above, as he cradles Kate's foot to his shoulder, pulling the rope close. Is this macabre, he asks himself, should I be ashamed? Nothing feels strange or abnormal, but instead like a memory of the present, an old déjà vu, just another encounter with a creature he found fascinating, if evil.

Somewhere above, two newspaper reporters are now admitted, one from the *Daily Telegraph* and one from the *London Illustrated News*. They are polite to the turnkey, then when only the hangman remains, they begin chattering, a pair of magpies with a story for north of the river. They watch as Marwood emerges from his den, a hibernating animal resurfacing into sunlight. Their excitement is palpable, one making notes, the other beginning to sketch the hanging body. Wheeler-dealing raw reactions and by swopping copy and illustrations, they can run the same story in both newspapers—London is hungry for news of the poor Irish girl who killed her Richmond landlady 'for a few pieces of furniture'. The headline: *She Boiled Her Landlady's Bones in a Copper Pot—Webster's Bones Swing at Wandsworth!*

Overcome by feeling, Marwood takes a pile of earth and throws it at them, but it misses so badly, they do not even notice. He falls over in the act, coughing and dumbfounded by his behaviour. Staggering up, he turns away from Kate and the pup reporters, feeling doubly inadequate. For the first time in a while, he thinks about Ellen and Aldous. But the thought is more challenging than comforting. Why should *he* deserve a family? How can he return home after such a vicious event, another transforming experience on the scaffold? Charles Peace flew into the sky like an absurd May Day streamer, but Kate dropped low and grimy and scared.

Somehow this combination—of Peace's indignity and Kate's private shame—is worse for Marwood to bear than previous jobs, worse than the political assignment of hanging the Cato Street conspirators that so upset the Tooley brothers. In that instance, Marwood was emotionally removed, but now he knows what it feels like to be connected to the justice side of a crime. The scaffold assumes a lack of sadistic pleasure, but Marwood knows its calculation is a heavy weight to bear. For which is worse, he torments himself, the crime of passion or the certainty of deliberate justice? One is bloody and awful, the other supposedly blameless and yet looks a lot like a dish best served cold, the vengeance of the Crown designed to keep the mob's bloodlust in awe and reverence. Somewhere there is a drape for the dagger to piece, a mover to move this human machine, red in tooth and claw, power condensed, targeted and transformed into theatrical splendour.

"Just into entertainment..." Marwood says out loud. "Bloody bread just to distract us from the daily grind...and a little death to feed life's sodden, weary gut...."

His mind is spinning with this grand sense of betrayal, but Marwood's guilt is rooted to individuals. Charles and Kate died such different deaths, but only because they died at his hands. The bizarre, if morally questionable truth is that he knows, even now, that his feelings will blow over. As surely the next crime occurs and the next commissioned job looms, Marwood is still the hangman of London, and Horncastle feels a long time ago.

But when was the last time he took a woman's life? Somehow her gender matters—to this hangman—as a woman who killed another woman in a selfish, drunken tempter. He also knows Kate tried to capitalise on the crime, cover her tracks, and if not apprehended or punished, would undoubtedly murder again.... Marwood searches for the words, hoping to resist the same fixed morality of the state, but as certain as there is goodness in the world, kind feeling for others, everyday concern, a pat on the back for encouragement, there is a seething river of darkness, the pleasure of cutting and causing pain, the bile at the heart of London's greedy belly...

"Bile," he whispers. "I feel it now, for the first time." Then he does a strange thing—he goes directly back to Kate's final room, the 'walking dead' cell. He plans to drink for the afternoon 'on expenses' awaiting his train, return home to Gloucester Place a drunken mess. "A mindless action," he says, "will save me." Surely it's the least he can do for his soul—to forget body and heart. The decision is easier still, given the bottle of absinthe he brought with him—which he hoped not to need—has a brutally direct effect.

The cell is damp, spiritless, but he barely notices. Unable to hide from himself, Marwood falls under the green goblin's spell. He now realises something has been lost—in the movement of executions to private sheds inside prisons. Perhaps it was horrific before, with the public watching, but that was never his concern. His worry was only ever to let the prisoner die peacefully—with a lot less pain than the minutes of strangulation suffered by the victim every gala-day from Tyburn to today. In that, he has succeeded. But something has been lost.

Gone is the desperate spectacle, but mainly it is the prisoners' loss—their moment of fame, their victory being close to the people, of being known, of living on the lips of all who were there that day. Marwood takes a swig from the bottle. He remembers how he and Kate once attended an execution, separately, without knowing it. Mr Anthony Klaus was being dispatched by Calcraft, near the Liverpool Docks. She was neither the murderess nor he the hangman that day—they were there out of curiosity, his professional, hers merely the fascination of the hour. That shared moment is lost now too, a social bond, born of Mr Klaus's last minutes, but allowing the mingling of their untainted, morally good blood. Was that too a con, a swizz, another lively killing-day dressed up as moral rectitude?

Marwood does not see Kate's body cut down into the lime-pit. The smell is present even after an hour, when the two grave-diggers throw dirt at her body to dull the unmistakable human odour. *Rigor mortis* has not yet set in, but they jab her with a spade, swinging her limbs left and right, until the rope is cut.

A trunk-box coffin sits nearby, resembling one Kate once packed herself.

The same day, her body is buried in one of the exercise yards at Wandsworth Prison. The coroner writes a report that afternoon: she is inked in the published prison records as 'Irishwoman: Webster, Catherine, *returned to the earth* 26th March 1879, in an anonymous plot.' Since the tombs are odd-numbered on one side of the exercise yard and even on the other, she is buried in 'Hanged No. 3', not 2, though Kate is only the second prisoner—and first woman—to be executed inside the prison. From this moment onwards, her story is devalued, loses currency, and will sink in the annals of London crime— overwhelmed by that prototype serial killer, the eternally unknowable Jack the Ripper, and Fleet Street's bloody infamous barber, Sweeney Todd. History, that truest of liars, begins misconstruing her life early.

Following Kate's death, because she was executed at Wandsworth quietly and not before the Old Bailey on Newgate's scaffold, no 'Penny bloods' or hanging ballads are written. Reproduced within hours to coarsen the life story of a killer as cheaply as possible, these songs about the Irish maid would have served a nice platter for English appetites, selling with merry indecency to the London masses. Instead, Catherine Lawler is the girl without a face, a woman of many pseudonyms, personalities, identities, tempers and loves.

And yet, as though to mark a new era of private prison hangings and stress the prisoners' communal fate, a plaque is hung from the prison warden's 'Wall of Wandsworth', overlooking the street and advising:

𝔚elcome, but do not stay long.
𝔗hose who, within the precincts of the prison pay the extreme penalty of the law, are buried under the flagstones.

Quicklime is sealed in Kate's coffin that afternoon. On either side of her trunk-box—again mirroring Mrs Thomas's river-coffin— are two brass hanging eyelets, left by Marwood. He does not wish to sell them. They are the first two letters of Kate's true surname, so rather than W. E. for Webster, they read L. A. for Lawler, her birth and legal name. In death, she is the girl who was born in Killane,

County Wexford, once more.

However, William Marwood cannot leave Wandsworth just yet. He needs something chemical to numb the strange cocktail of regret, tenderness and foolishness he feels for knowing Kate Webster. As though seeking a sign, the promise of her lingering soul, he wanders her 'dead woman walking' steps—her final, chained shuffle—under the low roofs of her incarceration. He touches the cold stone in her condemned cell.

Drinking alone here, pretending he is destined to die in the morning, right here where Father McEnrey gave her a last blessing, Marwood wonders why he can't just be happy as a village shoemaker? What is this dark ambition that drives him? Nothing tells him to stop. No moral pressure inside or from beyond the prison, the city or the open sky ever insists that what he does is wrong...then why does it feel so wrong?

"What gives me the right to pass irreversible judgement on life and death?" The condemned cell creaks, echoes the prison's predatory and suffering sounds, other voices, other rooms. "Who am to reserve the right to make death swifter...to lessen the dancing body for the crowd?" He takes a swig from the bottle of absinthe. "I...what *do* I do? I make the end *less* painful for someone who probably deserves less. Who,"—a swig!—"what am I? Just another fool, that's what, a crazy man waiting for the Thames to ferry me to the Channel...." Another long mouthful of the green fairy! "And what's out there? What's it all *for*? Every day I just crawl on my belly to kiss the Queen's crown!"

Over ten minutes, Marwood drinks half the bottle, and begins hallucinating—grotesque neckless torsos, flesh on flesh mangled with bloody ropes, chains, and twisted red-and-white-dresses, a macabre Hallow'en of true evil and fear. The bottle rolls away and empties the rest of its contents, the odour rising like the genie of some forgotten fable, a cocktail of adventurous *A Thousand and One Nights* mixed with the squalid riverbank of Marwood's own great expectations of London, now brought to this...this sorry display, this self-abasement inseparable from grief.

His arms wave at the air, swatting invisible aggressors, his legs loose and his eyes wide with temporary insanity, as the demons and memories dance, before he screams and collapses on the floor, passing out. Fortunately, he will never know his own performance, as he is quite alone.

Eventually the torment recedes; shadows and the cold air of Wandsworth permeate his brain. He dreams of ropes and shoes, falling as though from an invisible heavenly scaffold, twisting their laces, brass eyelets and leather washers into an incestuous pit of confusion and self-torment. Naturally he fails to make it home. Whether penance, or guilt, he never knows. It's the hangman's last unconscious act, the least he can do, but a piece of his self-immolation pursued in memory of Kate.

Chapter 45
The Lady Killer
27th March 1879, Thursday

The next day, Marwood reads a mocking article in *Punch* magazine:

Wearing her 'mourning' best at Wandsworth Prison yesterday, Wednesday 26th March, the accused Miss Catherine 'Hatchet-Maid' Lawler, also known as Kate 'Killer' Webster, was carried off in lovely and accomplished style, her *Manteau à la Mannings* trimmed with *ruche en gibbets* and *têtes de mort bouffonées*. The neck was surmounted with a running cord, *à la Calcraft*, which finished in a satin *noeud coulant* under the left ear. For *chapeau*, she wore a *bonnet de pendue*, this sweet cap arranged to cover the whole face, and is likely to be thus worn during the approaching season. Despite the spectacular folly of Miss Webster, all agreed she wore her costume well, despite her two faces being covered by the hangman's hood. God rest her soul, and may the people of London prosper by her unfortunately thieving murderous absence. For the curious hungry, 'Webster tarts' are third price in Covent Garden all week.

Marwood is at home in the front room of Gloucester Place. The day is mild, and Ellen is taking a walk through Dorset Square with

Aldous—from the angle of the sofa he can see them under the trees. Ellen is showing Aldous a picture-book, probably one of the sea adventures of Jules Verne; she is turning the pages, staring back at the house. She may be looking, as curiously happens, at something entirely different, but Marwood feels the closeness of her judgement. Lowering his head, unseen in the dark room, he tries to concentrate to his own reading. The next article from the tabloid penny press tells of the respectable death that the villain mounted in her defence. She didn't kick up rough but was put away evenly, not least because of the surgical style of hangman William Marwood's technique.

"Surgical style?" He remembers the tasks he had to perform after the fact—his unhooking the choked body, the damp clothes, the twisted rope, pressing her shoulders down in the coffin. "But surgical? Was he giving life? Blessing her with a life-saving operation?"

Worse than the tabloid rags, though, are the broadsides of Upper Fleet Street. Since Mrs Thomas is a middle-class *lady of means,* the appetite for denigrating *the Irish vixen* is beyond the pale; the xenophobia is thinly veiled, the segue to *the Irish problem* advertised with *turn the page for the latest on Home Rule.* Repeatedly Kate is accused of other crimes in the city—coining, robbery, older murders. "Where is the evidence?" Marwood asks the newspaper—feeling ridiculous.

One article, though, tells of her persistence, her pertinacity as a clinger-on-to-life, only to conclude that her sheer love of life was both elementary and terrible. I ask you, dear readers, surely these murders were not her only crimes? The spirit of Kate Webster is still roaming the sunken streets!

Marwood takes up the *Penny Illustrated,* his final delving into the official reports, and reads:

> The extent of her trickery, as Catherine Lawler, alias Kate Webster, was unbounded. Her other pseudonyms included Webster, Gibbs, Porter, Lawler, and possibly your family name too! As a con artist, she employed 'the long firm swindle' as her *modus operandi*—win trust, then rob. The case of the Richmond Atrocity will not die soon! Look into the eyes of a killer!

There is a picture of Kate on the opposite half-verso, a back-street photograph found at 2 Mayfield Gardens—her strict mouth, absent eyes and bony jawline—which according to the *Penny Illustrated*, makes her a **frighteningly well-qualified effigy for the Chambers of Horrors.** She is dressed as Mrs Thomas, but Marwood neither sees the victim-landlady nor a killer in her skin. Instead, he dwells on Kate's veiled vulnerability, a certain rough beauty, a bold, defiant grace—for the *Penny Illustrated*, a **symmetry majestic in its hardness.**

"Enough," he tells himself, disgusted by himself and the reports. He retreats to haunt his cellar, to straighten out his thoughts. Carrying a gaslight, he pushes aside the hanging hoods and ropes, lays the lantern on the ground. He sits on the guillotine bench and reaches into a drawer, removes the dress—the crumple of Kate's red gown swims in his ear—telling of their first meeting in Covent Garden, their hurried drink in *The Oxford & Cambridge Arms*, how Kate witnessed the decapitation of Charles Peace, and how they went alone together to Bartholomew Fair. What was it all about? Why did she live to murder? Only to be killed and buried with the past?

"What was it all *for?*" Marwood says. He runs his fingers over the red dress, frilly cuffs, the white hood where the hangman's knot was slipped. After a hanging, he usually sells the body to surgeons. The burial-ground at Wandsworth Prison, though, was never part of the deal with the Mayor of London. Kate's body will achieve a final resting-place, safe from the usual nodding commerce between executioner and doctor.

I should be thankful, Marwood thinks. At least she got a secure plot in the ground.... And yet why does he still feel cheated? Why does his dutiful reward—his slightly elevated London fee—feel awfully minor on this occasion, and quite eclipsed by the cost? The perks of his trip from Lincolnshire were overstated, he now knows; even Peace's body was inaccessible, encased in formaldehyde in the Tower of London. If London is proving less lucrative than the promised pavings of gold, he's still tying necks with nooses, and making the drops happen, if not as scientifically perfect as he'd like, surely to the satisfaction of the authorities, not to mention the crowd.

"Is there any such thing as a perfect execution anyway? Who's complaining?" Then he realises, he is the one unnerved...by this last hanging of Kate? Or is it hanging in general? What about the science, the progress of humanity to moral enlightenment, greater civilisation? Just for a touch more civility? He has to pinch the thin skin of his wrist to ask himself, does he still believe? He does so. But the very idea of compassion now makes him feel hollow, a hack in the service of the government's employ, with the Crown's authority and prestige to mask the dirty human reality.

What is a hanging, if not a cleanup of undesirables from its fringes by the heart of England's power. The capital crime in the capital city itself—openly sanctioned and cheating those it claims to reward, all in the name of Queen and country. Marwood can hardly believe his own treasonous inklings. At the same time, he wonders, why did he feel none of this when hanging Charles Peace?

"Nothing will bring back Kate or Mrs Thomas. But I'm supposed to show Aldous how to hang more killers? While Ellen and I play happy family together?" Perhaps they were only the first to go, he thinks, sensing his own mortality, the first twinge of fear.

Even so, Marwood squeezes the dress, folding it over his wrists. It was a cheap hanging for the state, just a morning's work, no major compensation or body parts, not even the train ticket from Baker Street. "Worse things happen at sea...than the hangman being bought off cheap." He spares a thought for Kate and smiles, knowing she'd be amused now there's no physical body for him to lug round—she claims dominion over her body, if nothing else. "An unjust reward," he whispers, "given her postmortem treatment of Mrs..." He cannot bring himself to say Mrs Thomas's name.

And yet Marwood is somehow pleased for Kate, for this single victory. He glances up at the trunk—not dissimilar from the one fished out of the Thames—he would have used to transport her to the surgeons, Kate's body packed whole, of course, in ice. No need now.... Almost as swiftly, Marwood's momentary sadness is offset. Kate got her Christian burial in the end, despite being less than loyal in her religious attendance.

Puzzled by this sudden philosophical thought, Marwood realises has no conception of whether Kate believed in God or not. Would it matter? He then wonders if the thought itself is blasphemous, and laughs a little at the irony. Whether she rests in peace in the ground, in his memory, or lives on as a statistic of London's past, are entirely different matters. "Whatever Kate's legacy...her story is unfair, nasty, brutish and short; but isn't all life when viewed from the pulpit or the scaffold?" This last thought fails to produce a laugh from his conscience. "Enough talking to myself," he says with a half-smile. "Character is fate, and so..."

Marwood lays her dress aside, its maroon-coloured cuts and pleats still dazzling—a wedding dress apparently, for her special day. He got one souvenir, after all, the return of his gift to the dancing bride—the question is what to do with it? He cannot even bring himself to look at the only prize he brought away from the Wandsworth press-yard—Kate's martyring claim to future forgiveness, a return to her Catholic innocence. All he knows is that the dress was not officially approved, but made the fresh odours of burial a little softer, the turnkey a little richer for keeping his last gesture a secret. "My crime is small, by comparison," Marwood tells himself. "What's a crime, anyway, when doling out—or withholding—human feelings? When throwing the lever on someone you...?" Again he touches the red dress.

Now he is alone, in the vast metropolis, with a wife who cannot understand his work—and why would she? Ellen has moved south in England, but what is Marwood's South of England, other than a head in a noose?

Sitting there, on the guillotine, he fears the slow demise that a Yorkshireman called Tamahawl suffered at the hands of the law, a case he read about in the *Newgate Calendar*. He remembers Ellen particularly objected to the story, though Kate enjoyed its mix of gore and celebrity. After he was hanged by Calcraft, Tamahawl's body was roped and pulleyed backwards through Leeds to a medieval fort and dropped in its moat. He recalls how Thomas Raddall, a historian of Olde England punishment, claimed the bones became cemented in rock there, visible for over half a century. Nothing could be worse—even for a man like Tamahawl who killed his business partner—than being left alone in a ramshackle hut, never buried properly, left to rot only yards from where he spent his life.

"I took the souvenir," Marwood whispers, "so I'm responsible for my soul, and the soul of my family." He must find a way to dispose of her hanging dress. What would Kate do, he thinks?

But it's no good, he just cannot forget.

So he continues to drink—earlier and more often. Rather than ale, port or even gin from *The Globe* on the corner, he'll drain the inspired insanity of 'Baudelaire's tipple'. Perhaps the absinthe will open his mind, close his fears and guilt so he can understand why he came to London—for work, family, and to humanise the scaffold with his long drop? How, he amazes himself, did he become involved with a woman he was to execute? Why did he permit Kate to find him—accuse him, beg him for salvation?

Worse, why would he carry out the sentence, if only to protect his livelihood?

"Yes, just to keep my job. She swung for me...."

Still with the dress in his lap, Marwood reaches for the bottle under his folded guillotine, uncorks it, and drinks to the girl he hanged—his friend, acquaintance, the one who listened to his macabre tales, then met the same fate. Gritting his teeth, he takes a swig larger than half a pint, and wheezes with the effort. He waits for the wormwood to kick in—a herb that grows wild on the slopes of Val-de-Travers in the Swiss Alps, the key ingredient to counterbalance the mouth-numbing sweetness of the dominant flavour, *anise*. A relative of *tarragon* and *mugwort*, it gives a bitter edge—and here it comes—the aftertaste that screws up the eyes, leaving him wanting the sweetness of the initial hit of absinthe, so he goes for another. As Oscar Wilde said, 'After the first glass, you see things as you wish they were, after the second you see things as they are not; finally, you see things as they really are, and that is the most horrible thing in the world.'

Over the next hour, Marwood drains the bottle until it tumbles free, rolling across the room to gently rest on a sandbag. Reaching up, he holds one of the hanging chains, pulls too hard and its rope unravels, comes tumbling to the floor, the noose falling on his shoes. "I need to mend my own shoes," he moans, then frowns. "Am I a cobbler or a hangman? Ha! A hangman or a cobbler?"

His mind is doing a jig, yet his body is quite still. He wraps his toe in the noose, curves his wrist for grip, and pulls tight to his ankle. The noose captures his leg. "Now I just need someone to string me up." He stands, wobbles and little, and crosses to where the trapdoor swings low. "I need to get upstairs and carry out a hanging! *My* turn now, children! Watch and learn,"—and for some reason he pictures the contorted faces of the Old Bailey jury, listening close to his testimony, while Kate's guilt is laid out by the judge. "It's my fault," he whispers, burbling a little now, "it's all my fault."

Frighteningly, the *thujone* element to absinthe is keeping Marwood lucid while he gets drunk. So while the wormwood excites the nervous system, like a coachman whipping on a horse and soothing its speed at the same moment, Marwood's mind suddenly clears. His body is drunk yet his mind is logically soothed. Fortunately, hanging no longer seems like the solution, since his body has its own mindless brain. His limbs are like jelly and his irresponsible blood is up. In his meandering to the trapdoor, there are so many obstacles—all the accoutrements and paraphernalia of death—that ironically save his life. A harness for the guillotine becomes caught in the noose around his ankle, and he falls headlong, a sandbag saving his ear from smacking the stone floor. There he lies, his hand wrestling for sand and rustling the grains through his fingers, as he slips into unconsciousness.

The last words he senses make Marwood wish he'd stayed in the upstairs world, reading the newspapers and the *Newgate Calendar*, though both speak of death. The words belong to Gustave Flaubert, a comical self-portrait, and as an Englishman admiring a great French writer, Marwood keeps quiet. The line is ridiculous and sad but his true mirror: "Me and my books, in the same apartment, like a gherkin in its vinegar."

Marwood feels guilty, but lying on the floor, could this one sentence help him ward off despair? Is Flaubert serious in his comedy, or comforting in his exactitude? Have I wasted my life, the hangman thinks? Am I preserving myself for nothing, just surviving for decay? Living for an immortality that is no life? His eyes pale over white, heart beating in communion with all his London experiences, all stressful, strange, arresting and peculiar.

In the end, the hangman is like anyone else. He wants to live, though he fears this is the end.

Chapter 46
The Emerald Witch
2nd April 1879, Wednesday

Not only does Marwood not die, he recovers rather well, his earnest spirit of 'doing community good' reviving him, following a two-day hangover. The day after April Fools' Day, he plans to lecture in a worker's hall in Clapham about the 'lore of the rope'. The appointment is long arranged, but Marwood can no longer face the mob—he walks around Clapham Common instead, witnessing almost a hundred labouring men and women lining up outside the worker's hall, people he could and should help with a little god-fearing entertainment.

"But what can I teach these people?" He sits on a park bench, turning the pages of his speech. "I can't make light of my job." He considers altering his lecture's ending, but then crumples up the notebook—he is visibly moved, troubled after fearfully seeing Kate's face worn by a passer-by, hearing her last breath on the wind. "Why is this woman still haunting me?" He looks up, waving his arms, and demands of the sky: "What did I *do?*"

A decision is made. He will go to Southwark's Bleeding Heart Alley and in penance, kindliness, or despair at himself, he will try to find Daniel. The promise made to Kate is still fresh, meaningful, though he has no plans to take the boy with him—even if he finds the urchin. So he abandons his speech outright and heads to Clapham Common, aims to return to his basement for a lock of Kate's hair, her clothes, the ropes. "It has to be done."

First, though, he walks through the City and over Blackfriars Bridge in the direction of Bartholomew Fair. He is depressed and drinking, and just as wonderful sights of the burgeoning spring begin cleansing his body, he douses it with more booze—stopping in various pubs en route for his favourite pints of beer. Three sheets to the wind, he begins laughing at the iron figures hanging on the weathercock of St Paul's, nodding with mock apprehension while saluting the Old Bailey. Finally, by taking Regent's Park to Great Portland Street, he encounters—having forgotten in his 'distraction'—a majestic city festival for Her Royal Highness' Jubilee. Queen Victoria is fifty years in love with Prince Albert today!

Marwood is alarmed by the preparations for the day-long honour. Spread out on the grass is a huge wooden construction, a makeshift colosseum for an evening open-air performance of *A Midsummer Night's Dream*. Suddenly he is surrounded by stagehands carting metal scaffolding, carpenters and dress-makers setting up shop, and a baker's dozen of food and drink tables. Actors' masks, silver-and-gold, are strewn on the grass, while everyone trips over the Maypoles, reminding Marwood of the village green at Horncastle. Already he feels dizzy with the colour and excitement, almost sick from its glitz and city bustle.

"Over here!"

"Watch it, sonny!"

"Yer Bard's dead if you can't fix that stage!"

Collapsing, Marwood takes in the scene, catching sight of a boar in a cage, a zebra being set free, and a baboon leaping from elm to pine. Instead of London's famous 'portable zoo', a menagerie of animals has been unleashed inside Regent's Park, free to joyfully trample the flowers inside specially gated gardens. The hangman giggles, lifting his hands to these surreal images, claiming their reality as playful fantasy. A country boy at heart, he's never seen anything like it....

For the first time the rabble of London are invited, though sequestered—like the animals—to the outer garden rings and northern horse-paddocks. Signs advertise midnight rat duels and dog shows, performing monkeys, dancing bears dragged through the gardens on stiff ropes they'll use to fight with before bathing in the water fountains. A rabbit will skip upon an accordion, a circus-man 'perform with a fearsome mask of bees', a Belgian orphan girl demonstrate the words *Salve* and *Mea* on her eyelids. Fresh from 'famous Wardour Street', towards dusk, a lone donkey, haunches painted blood red, will pull a peep-show for theatregoers called *The Battle of Waterloo*—a feat of animal magic not to be missed!

For now, though, Regent's Park is quiet. Only the lads with advertising placards are strutting up and down, pitching the events to refined air-takers who live nearby in the white-colonnaded houses; these 'touts' ignore the regular beat-down Londoners. One sharp-eyed boy, languishing at a water fountain and acting a role of available debauchery with a foppish hat, suddenly cuts under an arbour of overhanging trees. He looks older, wind rustling through his hair. Marwood cannot avoid him and the urchin recognises him as a willing 'mark'.

"'Scuse me, sir, you knows the Jubilee's later? You can sign up now for our tent, if you like?"

"No, my son," Marwood says. "I'm in a hurry." He peers at the boy, wondering on a whim if Kate's boy is close by. "Do you know a Daniel Webster?"

"No, sir. But we got summut called 'The Blacksmith and the Performing Flea'. 'e's so skilled, the 'smith, 'e can tie a padlock, key *and* chain o'er the neck o' a performing flea."

"I'm sure he can."

"Don't forget the whipping of a blind bear. Or let me giv' ya a secret." He leans in. "This," pointing at the half-built theatre—"this here's da polite show, Victoria being Victoria, n'all. But after hours, come down Southwark. We's got bulls baited with peas in their ears, fireworks on their backs."

"I'm heading to Southwark now, boy."

"Well, stick 'round, sir. We got badger-baiting in Long Fields off the Tottenham Court Road. Or if you live round 'ere, dere's straight-up wrestling at *The Hockley-in-the-Hole*, two o'clock sharp."

"What's straight-up wrestling?"

"Men, sir, fighting."

"Of course." Marwood tips his hat. "Lad, you need to find a new profession. I've already been to Bartholomew Fair." He smiles and walks on, leaving the boy-salesman loping under the rustling trees.

"What 'bout the super dwarf?" he shouts, not letting his man escape scot free. "He's thirteen, n' only eighteen inches high. What a miracle, sir! Come *The Eagle n' Child* by Shoe Lane. Or there's 'The Mighty Turk'."

"What's that?"

"The magical automaton—a machine that plays chess. I can sell you n' extra ticket to play with the Queen."

"Now why would you 'ave a ticket like that?"

"Okay, I don't. But I can get you one o' those Tower Hill mechanical machines with 'Please to Encourage the Inventor'. You could go into business, chief, n' make a fortune...."

"I'm too old for alchemy," Marwood says and walks away. As he emerges from Regent's Park, he feels a flashback of the route further north to Bartholomew Fair. He remembers how Kate encouraged his telling of grisly *Brothers Grimm* real-life hanging tales, how they drank, watched the mule race, and Kate fell over in the beer tent. He remembers the people lining up, hungry for distraction from the daily grind—how all London wouldn't give a *doit* to relieve a lame beggar on the street, but would lay out ten to see a 'real dead Indian'.

Today, though, Marwood is reeling in drink, so as he winds his way deeper south, he leaves these memories one by one. They are replaced by the sounds of the working city, the cries of 'costards!' and 'diddle diddle dumplings ho!' As his shadow passes through street markets, the gamblers on Petticoat Lane cry out 'any card matches!' while the textile trade are busy pushing 'any wax or wafers, n' five pairs a shilling Holland socks!' Soon Marwood is down by the Thames's food stalls, where the punters are fished by the traders for 'five ropes a hard *on-yons*', the cheapest survival vegetable of the masses, and 'live mackerel, live mackerel for Jubilee's treat!' On and on the hangman stumbles, overwhelmed by the belly of London's hungry, muddy streets. All wares are chanted, screamed, or rhymed in Cockney—the market-sellers knowing life depends on it—while he inhales the streets like any other busy man of Victoria's famous reign.

Eventually the wanderer reaches the river and crosses St Albert Bridge into Battersea, taking a slow weaving arc into Lambeth and Southwark. Down the South Bank, the afternoon markets are more attuned to the wares of the sea. Whether the bell of the sow-gelder or the horn of the knife-grinder, both are sunken in sound by the occasional thundering clap of a pony-and-trap and the 'any-old-iron!' call of the rag-and-bone man. Here, amid the warehouses and towering edifices of the 'new' industries—glass, matchboxes, steel, French cigarettes—the fish markets of the Thames reign almighty. The call of the barrow man's 'shrimps and winkles all alive-o' is the North Sea's beating heart, matched only by the orchestral cacophony of the lavender-seller, the crab man with "'ere's yer sweet nipper', and the purveyor of dried hake, basket atop her head', screaming "'ake, 'ake, get yer fresh 'ake!' at the top of her lungs.

At one point Marwood notices that women from the outlying countryside are recognizable, even here, because of their straw hats and red shawls like Little Red Riding Hood. He wonders what Kate would have thought of these ladies of leisure, out-of-towners like herself: she would have laughed, not impressed, but amused—and pointed out that men from the countryside wear flowers in their hair. Perhaps that was Kate's aim all along, Marwood thinks, by murdering and impersonating Mrs Thomas, to become a 'lady who lunches'?

To escape these imaginary conversations with her ghost, Marwood picks up the pace. Soon enough he arrives on Stoney Street and passes, without this knowledge of her past, Kate's one-time home at Gilbert Le Strengmaker's *High-Hat Corinth*, its Fleet Street franchise. The bordello slopes lasciviously backwards, peaceful now, awaiting the red lights of trade permitted after midnight. Kate only lived there a few weeks, paying her way partly by cleaning and partly in the traditional manner, but could stand it no longer.

At the corner Marwood sees *The Mermaid Tavern*, another of Kate's landmark haunts, dominated by a timber factory seething smoke over its roof. Forced to retrace his steps down a side-alley, the hangman comes to a small door, the most direct route. To his surprise, there's no lock, but he gives a stern shove, holding his balance like a demented ballerina, and is surprised as the inner courtyard reveals itself. All he can think of is Dickens's poor Plornish family, struggling in the dark behind walls that protect and imprison. He steps over the threshold.

A decrepit old man is sitting on a stoop smoking a Turkish pipe, and Marwood leaps back, fearing a vision of his future.

"Welcome to Bleeding Heart," the man says, then continues his drawl, a withered sea-face crumpling, teeth long gone. "What can I fur ya do?"

"I'm looking for Sarah Crease."

"Dead as a doornail." The old man sucks in his gums along

with his pipe.

"How?"

"She got it in the neck, last week. In her own home." The old sea-dog burps. "Who's you, anyway? The taxman?"

"No," Marwood says, walking on. "I'm...the hangman of London and Middlesex."

"You don't say. You sound like you dun't believe yerself."

"I do. What number is it?"

"Thirty-seven."

"Can you show me?"

"Watch this," and the old man blows smoke rings from his eyes, then taps his feet and coughs. "Next alley, son. Do I get a tip?"

"Next time."

Marwood treads deeper into the yard. He skirts a box of wood chips, clambering on a makeshift walkway of spare pallets. He doesn't look back, feels nervous. What if this woman is just like Kate, he thinks? The warehouses have been abandoned for today, a rare holiday for Ash Wednesday. When he gets to Mrs Crease's, he finds the door unlocked, just a slight tap sends it open. The inside is gloomy, London's hazy sunset creeping in.

He steps softly calling out "Mrs Crease?" "Daniel?" and "a vis-i-tor!" but there's no reply. Just beyond the front room, he sees a bed, its legs splayed. Even at a distance the walls look discoloured, but this sight is delayed—overwhelmed—by the pungent smell. Clipping his nose in a pince-nez, elbows up high, Marwood steps over the rubbish and scattered clothes. He sees a fallen bookshelf with no books except the Bible, pages strewn, a few torn and lying crumpled on the floor. The cover—blank except for a silver cross—even bears a footprint, but whether Mrs Crease's or Daniel's, there's no way of knowing.

Marwood stands in the bedroom and surveys the room, but is quite shocked to see that what he thought was a body is only a mannequin, twisted and mangled. A few pins are stuck in its belly like a sacrifice, but the face is smooth and featureless, the skin a pasty brown. On the dummy's belly sits a litter of kittens, about four, burrowed deep in the hole in its wooden belly. The smell is overpowering, since most appear to be dead. At the foot of the bed, tail curled in her jaw, one eye damaged and bleeding, sits the mother cat. After a slow defensive purr, she is silent, which unnerves

Marwood even more. Otherwise, the room is empty—just empty wine bottles, and red underwear strewn tattily on the dress-doll, practice for Mrs Crease's profession as a handy-woman for the wives of the warehouse men. No Sarah, no Daniel, no bodies. "Time to go home."

Just as he emerges into sunlight, downcast by not finding Daniel, but relieved for at least acting on his promise to Kate, Marwood pauses and lights a cigar. He takes a long drag, closes the door a jar, leaving a crack for the dying kittens to escape; but he knows that if they could, they would have already—for one reason or another they are choosing to stay. Nothing else remains, no other animals or human noise. "Wherever Daniel may have fled," he tells himself, "the boy's long gone."

Marwood escapes the warehouse yards by retracing his steps, the old man now absent. One street from the Thames, next to *The White Sheep Tavern*, he stubs his cigar in the dirt. Next door is a three-story building, all hourglass figure and boarded-up windows, tottering over its one-story neighbour. The sign—in purple and black—says 'June Salmon's Waxworks'. The front door is painted yellow with a copper bell on a long chain, which he rings.

Third-time lucky, the door is not locked, so Marwood carefully nudges it open; he senses an attraction he does not understand. Close to criminal mischief or not, he tells himself to disturb nothing. On the ground floor is a toyshop, displaying crumpled dollhouses, snooker cues and cribbage boards, all covered in a thin layer of cobwebs. Any moment he expects Silas Wegg with his wooden leg to come hobbling into view.

For now, all is silent. Without knowing why, Marwood approaches the foot of a steep blockwood staircase, avoiding the dolls as he moves through the room. An old conceit from his own childhood, all the toys' eyes follow him, their crude beechy limbs dangling from ceiling hooks. "More like a torture chamber than a toyshop."

"Can I help you, sir?"

The voice comes from the foot of the stairs. A middle-aged woman hovers in a pink leotard, half princess half ballerina, her rotund figure spilling over a white leather belt. In her hand is a homemade wand, a red baton with a silver star on the end.

"Are you in business?"

"Always," she says, and waves the wand. "I'm Mrs Salmon, proprietress."

"I'm curious about your death-masks," Marwood offers as opening gambit.

His host peers through the gloom, front teeth protruding from her cheeks like hens' eggs. "Is that be fo' you, or a friend?"

"Neither—just what you have of past criminals."

"Sweetie, follow me." Mrs Salmon does a little skip, while her fright of orange hair—a toupee—bounces from her scalp. Like a schoolboy Marwood does as he's told, hiking up the staircase behind this colourful creature.

"Watch your step now, laddie. I've got precious works of art in here."

The upstairs is larger and gloomier, yet more crowded. Here is Miss Havisham's dressing-room after a few more years of neglect. Marwood literally tiptoes, and feels like holding his breath. There is barely space to move, even if he could see the objects he's avoiding.

"Where are we going?"

"Patience—to meet my family." Over in the far corner, Mrs Salmon yanks a heavy curtain and instantly, light glows over the dark floor. Marwood leaps back on the creaky floorboards—cries out—and almost does the splits. "Wait, wait!" He crouches, as though an army of oversized toy warriors were about to strike. For all around him are people, staring with life-sized eyes, and grinning with bloated red lips.

"Welcome to 'The Wax Workhouse'," Mrs Salmon says. "These are my good friends." She taps a couple of the uncanny figures on the back of the head, so they wobble back and forth, mounted on circular dials for easy movement. "We haven't had a show in years—but if you're buying, I'm selling."

"'Today's Dynamite Sale'," Marwood says, touching the ticket attached to the toe of one creature who's eyeballing him, a short man in a dapper cap.

"Yes, I assume that's why you's here? To buy."

"Ah...well." He avoids the dummy's eye, squints his confusion.

"Sorry for the sun. I can't open the curtain too far, but you can turn 'em into the light."

"Thank you, and yes, I'm always looking to buy."

Mrs Salmon is encouraged, and skips forward to demonstrate her wares. She is surprisingly nimble given her billowing weight. Marwood sees her as a relic of the winter's craze for theatrical opera, just another bubbly mincing woman dressed up in the fairy-fantasy clothing of a six-year-old, but he keeps these thoughts to himself.

First, she gestures to a lurid amber waxwork of Mother Shipton. "This one's special—mechanised, as they say. I release a lever n' she surprises passers-by with a kick." To prove her point, Mrs Salmon does just that, and Mother Shipton's blatant metal foot jerks up a little, her waxy expression unchanged, her black eye seemingly unamused.

"Chilling," says Marwood.

"Or I can offer you an effigy of the dead Queen Elizabeth, raised over her casket at her funeral...."

"Do you have any criminals?"

"The Queen not good enough for you, sir."

"It's not that, I..." He pauses. "Listen, I'm looking for an effigy of Charles Peace, the notorious criminal. Or Jack Sheppard."

Mrs Salmon peers at him, signalling by heavy lids that her customer is exasperating, bordering on 'always wrong'. Marwood wants to ask why The Wax Workhouse has so few clients: he holds his tongue, but she reads his mind. "I can sell to Madame Tussaud's now, so I don't need the street traffic." Rationalizing her trade, the effect is so disconcerting to Marwood that she seems part saleswoman, part devil; I have to get out of here soon, he thinks.

"I ain't got those particular ones, but I can have a look round for you." This she does by spinning a row of wax figures lining the wall, then skirting between them one by one, smiling as though greeting a church congregation. "Here, sir, this one's pretty fresh."

Marwood steps closer, wondering why he's even here. Doesn't he have enough hanging memories? Why take the physical doll to remember the body? Isn't it enough to have the ropes, a few clothes, a crop of hair? "No, that's not right. It looks like Courvoisier."

"'Cos it is. I made two copies an' Tussaud's got the better one." She touches the arm of the young swindler, killer of his own gentleman-master. "Look at his soft face. See those gentle lines! Who would ever suspect such a boy?"

"I've seen the real death-mask..."

"Oh yes? Know someone in Newgate do yer?"

"I did once."

Marwood examines Courvoisier's butler uniform, the cut of his cloak an imitation of the salt-and-pepper suit bought for him by his master.

"Looks a bit lonely, don't he?" Mrs Salmon says.

"Delicate," Marwood says. "His death-mask didn't convey the man in the flesh."

"In the wax."

"Oh yes." As he turns to follow her, Marwood is struck by a half-moulded outline. "Who's that?"

"Unfinished," Mrs Salmon says. "Gonna be Kate Webster, Richmond killer."

The surprise is drastic for Marwood, and his head lightens. For a moment he cannot understand the wax woman's words. "You mean, you're already modelling her?"

"She'll be famous, no doubt. Ain't a lot o' girl murderers, not this decade, see. The public hunger is there."

Marwood stares, legs unsteady, and places his hand on Courvoisier's shoulder. Meanwhile his guide kicks the base of the neighbouring dummy and Kate's torso spins into view. Her clothing is that of Mrs Thomas, the frock, the waistband, the blouse, the scarf—but nothing can prepare him for the face, a smoothly carved nothing, just a featureless blank.

"I ain't cut her nose yet."

"Or smile."

"Just the chin—they look odd with no face, hey?"

Marwood feels sick, but he has to recover quickly to take in the next shock.

"I've got a complete Kate here, spare—I made two full-size as Tussaud's was sweet business. Two weeks of solid work!" Pushing away a couple more dummies, the light is cast over another complete Kate Webster, same size, same weight, same age, solid wax. "She makes the blood run cold, even on me."

"How much?"

"Not for sale."

"I'll give you four pounds."

"Six an' you've a deal."

Marwood stares into the dummy's eyes, excited to have to opportunity to be near the person he half knew. Yet he feels cold—

the same rustle under his skin—just by being so close. Not fear, not exactly, just a mixture of apprehension, the proximity of a violent nature, the thrill of her passion for life, for vice and drink, all sequestered somewhere behind those beady-black doll's eyes.

"I can't afford that," Marwood says and reaches out and touches the bridge of Kate's nose, feels the toughness of the wax, the crude laughing sneer of her wide-set cheekbones, suggestive of snarling aggression. "She never really looked like that."

Mrs Salmon frowns. "What do you mean? I took her face from the newspaper."

"That's an artist's impression. She didn't really smile, and certainly not like that."

"I think she did once," Mrs Salmon replies, giving a little skip, and spinning the base of Kate's stand. "When she killed her landlady, see."

Marwood watches as Kate's eyes turns away in darkness, back to the collection of waxworks facing the wall. "I'm surprised you believe she's gonna to be remembered."

"She's a Tussaud waxwork," Mrs Salmon says, "she'll be remembered. But I'm guessing you want a male criminal for your…"

"Office," Marwood says, thinking of how 'private basement' might sound unusual. "I find company inspires good writing. I'm writing an autobiography of my life—as a shoemaker."

"Oh," Mrs Salmon says nonchalantly, "that'll be curious."

"Thank you." Marwood smiles softly. "But I'm afraid I should go now. I'm not sure I can afford your wares—if you'll forgive me, they're more for the commercial buyer."

"As I suspected."

"But I will take a Punchinello doll."

"Very good," the princess-ballerina says, and redraws the curtain near the staircase, making the upstairs den ever dimmer.

"It's funny," Marwood says, "I expected it to smell more of wax."

"I know, though I can't smell it anymore. Except on days when I'm carving. Once the wax is dry, they smell just like people, a little rotten and dusty, but that's all."

Marwood is shown downstairs, where in addition to the Punch doll, he takes one of Judy, the policeman Mr Plod, and the dog with the string of sausages, all for Aldous of course. He could return a few toys to Mrs Crease's, in case Daniel comes back, but he doesn't want to go back to Bleeding Heart Alley. For a brief instant, he catches his own reflection in a body-length mirror. "My promise to Kate is morally pure, right, if unsuccessful? I did try?" His doppelganger is silent.

"I'll throw in the hangman for free," Mrs Salmon says, giving Marwood a third shock. He's quite forgotten that the hangman is part of the Punch & Judy theatre. Fortunately the doll does not resemble him. The unexpected souvenir is a thin man in a black cape, black hood, carrying a giant noose, a cross between a Voodoo doll and a devil from Faust's damnation.

"Let me tell you," Marwood says, "I am actually William Marwood, hangman of London and Middlesex."

"I know you are," Mrs Salmon replies, and he does not question her.

"See, I think this doll has come to claim my soul, only in miniature."

"You'd be alarmed, though, if your doll had such a wide grin."

Marwood looks down at the generic likeness, the red mouth hooked from ear to ear. "It's perfect," he says. "Just like Jack Ketch of old."

"You definitely look like him."

"Perhaps if he's a cobbler part-time. I think he looks like a killer."

Mrs Salmon says nothing, takes the money, and closes up the ground floor once the strange man, whose face she knows from the newspaper, has gone. Later she considers making a waxwork of him too, but considering his forthright visit to her premises, she lets the thought go.

Upstairs now, she sits in the dark. Here she can feel the presence of all the wax people, her heart calmed by their hard exteriors, the hollowness of their absent souls.

"No," she whispers, "better to make a third Kate Webster. That's more likely to sell."

When Marwood gets home a letter, double-sealed and ink-stamped

Richmond, is waiting. Puzzled, he takes it to the front room, cuts it open with his envelope knife. He reads holding the knife, and is oddly affected:

Mr Marwood,
You don't know me, but I know you. I wish to thank you for the smooth execution of evil Webster last Wednesday—I read of the proceedings in the Barnes Express. To all intents and purposes, it appears you did a fine job.

My name is Richard Hughes. I remain the brother of Mrs Julia Thomas, widow of Lord Albert Thomas. Their son Billy would have been proud of your services. All I can say is thank you for seeing that bloody Kate Webster to her rightful place, hopefully one without rest! She was a villain—a weasel to me—who broke into my sister's home then carved her up in a brutal, devilishly unchristian way.

The copper pot, the body in the box, the severed head, we know the details are unmentionable. But I mention them to reinforce the justice of your act. Do not fret, or hesitate in your job, good sir. You have the makings of a master craftsman—you are indeed, the Queen's hangman, her very own protector, and I wanted to thank you, in the proverbial way, for 'a job well done'.

You keep my soul at rest. May the Lord grant you eternal peace.
Kind regards,
Richard Hughes,
Jason & Sons Barrister, 27 Rose Gardens,
Hammersmith

Marwood tears the letter into four neat pieces, lets them fall gently to the floor. He jabs the knife into his writing-table where it sticks upright, and he watches the handle waver, the blade shiver steady.

"I'm glad the death of someone can make someone else so happy," he says. "I despair of these people!"

Chapter 47
Flying the White Flag
6th August 1883, Monday

Execution could not be more popular for the next few years and yet the gentleman executioner returns to his cobbler's trade. After Kate's obituary is circulated as a pithy crime piece, his fame is soon secure, transforming his home business. Those in search of a new pair of heels go to the hangman. His shoe prices increase with demand, and there is a craze for buying bootlaces.

But he does not retire. Marwood plies his hanging trade through more winters until 1883, almost four years since the burial of Kate Webster. Somehow over time, his enthusiasm for official scientific exploration is gone. He begins to think more about the money, about security for his future and his family. The infamous hanging of Frances Stewart—who killed her grandson—maintains Marwood's pay around twenty pounds a year. The long drop 'rope fee' is extra, plus travel expenses and his disposal of the prisoner's clothes. In spring 1883, he takes up the smoking of Turkish 'Crimea' cigarettes, now he can afford them—they are elegant and refined, to match the image he wishes to project.

A hangman cannot work forever, though, and Marwood is getting old. After a Calcraft-like botch-up on a hot June day in York, he takes to the absinthe once more. *The Magistrates of York* pub allow four shots, two more than the London legal dose. Hence the hangman is tipsy. He ties the knots too loose, and prisoner Vincent Walker takes two minutes to depart. The crowd can only watch in fascinated horror. Already, William Marwood's reputation is on the slide. Such failures are publicised widely, and Marwood's good name is questioned in print. The old *London Illustrated* turns on him: once the 'humane hangman', he now fears he will be remembered as 'just another Calcraft', an unexpected prodigy of the greatest bungler of them all, and a mythical missionary has-been in the mould of arch-brutal hangman, Jack Ketch.

Marwood's last execution takes place in Durham on 6th August, 1883. He hangs a bigamist—James Burton who drowned his eighteen-year-old newlywed in the bath—as swiftly as humanly possible and faster, though he never knows it, than Burton used his own hands. Then the executioner hangs up his ropes—for retirement. Burton's vertebrae pull so cleanly, there's not even a sound: the rope straightens and the neck breaks simultaneously and immediately. Marwood collects his pay and takes the train back to Horncastle, claiming he will "sleep like a baby."

"Burton passed away like a summer's eve," he tells a man on the train, quoting himself from years earlier. But Marwood knows he has become a parody of himself. He also knows it was a woman who broke his executioner's nerve, despite her "clean, legal, most humane of deaths." She will forever be a lady killer, he thinks, and smiles softly, exposing his nostalgic memory through dirty teeth. An Irish maid with a sweet temperament, a little troubled perhaps, but suffering too, he thinks. Happy days. Just thirty-one years old for eternity....

Was she different from the rest of us? Disregarding her failings, Marwood entertains this question nightly, failing to see any irony clouding his strange desire.

The future closes in, stretching to a single colourless point—where the future's confusion meets the past's clarity—namely, the regret of an ageing man for a guilty young woman. He remains morally blind. For Marwood, the story worth telling is Kate's, but the unaccountable, too human reality is that she got under his skin. Somehow the romance of Covert Garden and *The Oxford & Cambridge Arms* are impossible pasts he can never relinquish. She sweetens his blood, while poisoning his mind.

Chapter 48
Queen's Jubilee
19th June 1887, Sunday

Eight years go by. Marwood is older, the years sitting heavy, but he is embracing these last, calmer days of this life. All the events of London are unforgotten, but eventually belong to another world altogether.

Long back in Horncastle, Marwood is asleep in his garden chair drifting in and out of consciousness, dozing on a Sunday afternoon. Summer has come to Lincolnshire at last; the mornings of London hangings, day-long drinking and strange fairgrounds seem long departed. Faraway encounters with Sequin and Jones of Bow Street are all but forgotten. William Calcraft 'the bungling butler' is no longer a painful hereditary shadow, now that Marwood's retirement is well under way. Even the name of Kate Webster has relaxed in his memory, transferred to a place where acute personal feelings, curiosity and fear for his own safety and Ellen's, are all overwhelmed by the finality and reality of her awful crimes. Marwood remains the moral guardian of history, she its victim, but neither prisoner to the other. Kate is free in death, her own executioner free in the slow pleasures of retirement.

Instead, Marwood reminisces over his boy, Aldous, gone to sea now on *The Marchioness* to explore the South Sea Islands, a perilous trip. A cabin boy when he left, Aldous has graduated—so his letters say—to Cook's Mate, a look-out who climbs into the crow's nest. The hangman likes to believe that Aldous's home training with ropes and sand weights inspired him to become a good climber. In his last letter, Aldous described the view from the ship's mast—'the ocean all around like a giant mouth without a body, waiting to swallow its prey.' For days, his father cannot empty the image from his mind—the prospect of the son being swallowed alive by the waves, like Zeus's children being swallowed—by the king of the Olympians himself—to prevent their rise to rebellious power.

The hangman shifts in his chair. He remembers his last visit to London, where they booed him. Times are changing. In eight short years, hanging has lost a lot of popularity. He remembers driving past Barclay's Brewery in Park Street, Southwark, only last year, and witnessing the goliath of the coming modern age of machinery—he was horrified and astounded at the same time—how can they build such monstrous buildings? Even so, every few years he goes back to London, sometimes just to witness a hanging, sometimes for no reason other than to torment his memory. Every time he takes a cheap ride beside this brewery in Southwark, past the London Docks and Execution Dock, but never to Bleeding Heart Alley. On these visits, he witnesses steam engines powering the pipes, daily filling a dozen thousand caskets. He sees overloaded carts, lanky and groaning like abused camels, pulling beer exports on sleighs down to courtyards where the buyers congregate. He sees dwarfish huddled men heaving the special deliveries on rude drays. He sees upper-class West Enders in *phaetons* pointing and giggling, while the butchers' boys laugh and swear back, hawking horse-cuts outside the brewery and mixing gallons of beer with streetmeats.

Far from Marwood's consciousness, Daniel Webster is now one of these butchers' boys, sporting a blue apron typical of his trade. His daily task is lifting up a tin jug and soaking the booze on the sausages, creating a liquid diet of cheapmeats and ale. From a boy picking up street tobacco butts and selling them at 6d 10d per pound—his scrabbling life after a police arrest and learning that pickpocketing will only go one way—Daniel is press-ganged into this butchering trade. But Marwood thinks of him infrequently now, just another London mite surviving on the appetite of the masses, the boy who never had a chance, the son of 'Kate the killer' who is better off without her. Yet Daniel has not gone far, working the same streets his mother worked, sleeping not far from the old dive of Sarah Crease, even close to the drowned pub of Jonathan Clatter. "Another of the six million lost souls..." For the city's poor, Marwood considers from his rural comfort, what change could come too soon? That is why he only goes back to London to stir his mind, to remind himself why he came away.

Today is the Jubilee fiftieth anniversary of Queen Victoria's ascension to the throne. But this time Marwood has decided to stay home; instead, Ellen has gone to London to pay her respects to Her Majesty. The ageing hangman, now close to seventy, is hence left alone with his doubts, hopes for respect, and dubious memories. What Marwood does not—cannot—remember is Jonathan Clatter's demise. Today, though, the memory of that event is included in the newspaper, for the anniversary bizarrely occurs the same day. He learns that Clatter's body is never discovered by Sequin or Jones, once his pub was claimed by the Thames. Instead, the landlord of *The Cat and Salutation* was led the way of all rivers, to the wider ocean, and without endorsement by Bow Street or the Old Bailey, his bones deposited without legal judgement. *The Times* is brief, too, because of the Golden Jubilee. Unlike Fagin's pickpockets' infamy, the brand of educational cruelty that Jonathan Clatter imparted to his charges will remain unknown.

"Cheer up, William," a voice calls from his shoulder so *The Times* shakes in Marwood's hands. "It ain't so bad, she'll be back the day after tomorrow."

"Eh?"

"Ellen, your Ellen. She'll be back anon, soon enough."

Marwood swivels on the seat, strains upright. "I was just thinking of the past."

The man nods, offers a broad confident smile. "That's another world—better just focus on this one."

"Not very Christian of you, James..."

"Who said anything about belief?"

"Not I, for sure," Marwood says, and digs his wrists into the armrests. He cannot quite stand, until his former apprentice helps.

James Berry pats down the old man's shoulders. Berry is the hangman of Shropshire and Hertfordshire, a former apprentice, and who better to learn from than the scientific master? Marwood is not fully retired, and their exchanges are more like the awkward transition of power from father to surrogate son; the relationship is murky to both of them, so they focus on the work mostly, and making jokes.

"You're the escaped criminal, William, always dodging your own noose."

"I ain't swung yet."

"Half true," the young man quips.

"True enough," Marwood fires back. "Let's go to the basement. That's where I do my thinking."

The younger man allows Marwood to take the lead, eyeing him carefully. James Berry is thirty-one, a retired Bow Street Runner, and part-time gravedigger. He knew Sequin and Jones at arm's length, and was put in touch with 'the master' through their old records. "Two rats make a pack," is all Marwood would say, and he repeats it now. "No offense to Bow Street, you understand, but they hounded me to bring the case, then simply moved on once the girl was hanged."

"But that was their job—still is."

"Cold," Marwood says. "It's just a profession for them."

"And for you?"

The elder hangman raises an eyebrow and touches his thinning black hair. "I thought so too, back then."

Berry searches Marwood's face, uncertain how to interpret this comment, but the old man provides no further clue.

"You did?"

"Hadn't I hanged plenty of others? She was a bad girl, sure. But James, she didn't deserve what she got."

"Not at the end?"

Marwood turns when he sees the trapdoor. "No, she was right to hang. She just didn't get a good chance in life—from the start."

"You know her whole story, then? You could tell me properly."

"James, I know enough."

They head to the basement, down cold steps which remind him of under Gloucester Place where he once took Kate. He does not think of her now as he enters this private sanctuary. Rather he instructs Berry to lock him into the guillotine.

"Tight."

The apprentice stares at his teacher, uncertain if he's being tested, when Marwood seems to experience an epiphany. For a few seconds the seventy-year-old is so lively, he unabashedly breaks into a jig. "No, young sir, I've changed my mind. Follow me!" and they hurry back upstairs. "Bring the noose and sandbags." He waits while Berry makes three trips lowering equipment from the ground floor.

"William, are you sure?"

"At least Ellen won't be coming home." So saying, Marwood changes from the guillotine 'National Razor'—unconsciously left sleeping ready for her Paris début across *la Manche*—to his old, trusted hanging noose. "The perfection of my own invention," he grins.

"But the drop is too short."

"You miscalculate. I am light."

Berry stares again, uncertain. "You're joking. This is just an experiment, right?"

"Just a trial run."

Next Marwood clarifies how his famous 'long drop' is usually between four and ten feet, depending on the weight—and strength—of the prisoner.

"As an old man, I won't struggle long. This drop, James, offers a 'striking' force of twelve hundred pounds, whoever you hang. Plus I don't weigh what I used to, though that's not a crime! Anyway, combining this force with the noose under my ear,"—Marwood presses the brass eyelet to his cheek—"causes a fracture by dislocating the neck, usually between second and third vertebrae, or fourth and fifth."

"Understood, boss." Berry looks worried and then nods, showing—for a young man only recently delivered from Bow Street—his gravedigger's teeth.

"I call this the classic 'hangman's fracture'. The length of the drop is worked out by dividing 1,260 foot pounds by the body weight of the prisoner in pounds, and this equals the drop in feet."

"Okay."

"Any more questions?"

Berry scratches his head. "When should I bring up the sandbags?"

"No need," Marwood says. "Not this time." He folds the trapdoor shutters back in place, bolts the iron clip, and prods the surface with his foot. Berry looks vacant, not catching his meaning. To make his point clear, he steps on the trap's double doors. Fortunately, nothing happens.

"Good, they shouldn't open until you remove the pin."

Marwood gestures to the iron clip. "I don't have a lever unfortunately—this amateur will have to do. It'll work just the same."

Berry does not move. "I don't understand."

"You will in time," Marwood says. "You do want my job, don't you?"

"Well, yes. But not like this!"

"All in good time, dear boy." Marwood taps his foot. See now, I made it pretty secure after all," and he smiles, looking with his watery eyes at Berry. "Who'd have thought!"

"It's not natural."

"What is?" the old man says. Marwood then becomes quite philosophical. "My position is not a pleasant one! No, it is *not* a pleasant one. I would prefer if you hurried, young man."

Frowning, Berry moves gently into position, takes up the leg straps, pinions, and then the noose. He adjusts the rope to the hook Marwood has hung from the ceiling.

"That's right, now the hood. I won't say any more."

"No, you should be quiet."

Surprisingly, Marwood does as he's told, and Berry takes the hood and secures it over the hangman's face. He tightens it around the neck. Next he surveys the pulley system, checks the sandbags at the base; clearly Marwood has measured his own weight, length of fall and thickness of rope.

"I should double-check the drop. It's part of the job, after all."

Marwood sways on the trapdoor. "I must say, I don't want to speak, but I think you need a little help, a gentle push. I've checked the drop, you needn't worry. You know, once in Glasgow…"

"Only the noose to go," Berry interrupts.

"A man gets a last speech, I believe."

"Of course."

"As I was saying, once in Glasgow a telegram arrived concerning the prisoner I was half way through hanging, a boy of seventeen called Jennings. He'd killed his girlfriend. The governor snapped his fingers for me to stop—a last-minute reprieve? No such luck. So, I ask you, young man, what do you think I did?"

"I don't know. Abandon ship?"

Marwood's expression is almost vulgar through the hood, the blood in his face. "No, James, I gave no flicker of hesitancy to the young man in my noose that anything peculiar was afoot. You see, it's important to take care of a prisoner—to the last. I've always said it, and I'll say it again. They must drop away like a summer's eve. See?"

Berry looks at the old man, the noose in his hand. "Yes, I think so." He steps forward.

"I shall tell you one last secret, then you can do your job." Marwood's voice begins to waver. "I'll never forget the time I hung Kate Webster, the Barnes killer. You remember, she killed her landlady."

"I was young," Berry says, "but I remember the newspaper reports."

"You see, Kate trembled on the scaffold only a little, and her face didn't move. She betrayed no fear, no weakness, just an open malice. And yet I pitied her.... I sensed her breath through her hood."

"I'm ready," Berry says. He grips the iron pin, secures it between index finger and thumb.

"Not yet," the prisoner replies, "I must be allowed to finish my story."

"You'll finish it in the next life, William. Are we still joking here? I came all this way...."

"Patience."

"Is this the lesson?"

"No, *she* gave the last lesson—everyone loves a good hanging. I remember the newspapers saying 'As Kate heard the trapdoor open, she thought of hell.' How would they know? All that happened was she moaned a little. Okay, she was thinking of a devil inside her. She was frowning..." He frowns too. "She was puzzled but no doubt appreciating a good, crude joke."

"A good joke?" Berry echoes.

"Yes," Marwood says. "Now pull the lever. And be brave in your choice!"

The hangman pulls the pin, the trapdoor gapes wide an instant, revealing the darkness of the basement like the mouth of Hades if not for the gaslight they've left below. Inside the hood, Marwood feels the light pierce behind his eyes, and for a second—elongated, since he does not fall—he thinks it is the light of heaven.

"Wait!"

The next moment, he is sliding through the open trapdoor which flaps back against his legs, causing him to rotate a little. The rope pulls him back, begins unravelling, though not snapping yet.

"Bon voyage," Berry calls from above, their mutual joke maintained to the last, despite the strange behaviour of Marwood believing they are taking it all seriously. The rush of air is felt on the prisoner's cheeks and Marwood unconsciously draws a breath—as he imagines Kate tried to—only to feel the clip of the rope, the swing and collapse as the quiver occurs. He has tied a snapping chain—a device to break to rope above Berry's head—so he feels the snap cue a release. His timing is perfect, the noose locks around his neck, but not tight enough, and he gargles a little as it takes his breath away.

"Jam...es..."

"William, what's happening?"

For a second Marwood is almost excited by the rush of blood to his head, the lightheaded feeling of being a victim that combines with the fear he sensed in Kate's tiny moan. Then it is all over. The rope is released, runs up over his chin, and even rips his hood off.

Marwood is left on his knees on the basement floor, the rest of the rope piling on top of his head, the snapping device falling nearby. He takes a breath.

"Are you all right, boss?"

The old hangman—now the prisoner—begins to cry, still trapped in his memory of that day in the Cold Meat Shed. It is the fifth time he has performed the experiment, four times with his son Aldous, and now with Berry his apprentice. Charles Peace and Kate Webster died the same way, but each occasion had its hanging strengths and weaknesses. Surely not enough to cry for years later?

"But the slightly short drop suffered by Kate was the worst."

"I'm sorry, what did you say, William?"

"I'm good," Marwood lies, pressing his face and lips to the cold stone, his mind light, his heart beating fast. He wipes away the tears. "Not for the faint-hearted..."

"Perhaps you shouldn't play this game anymore."

"There are other things in life?" Marwood looks down. He feels barren, sick, a touch disgusted by his excitement. "I'm fine."

Chapter 49
Rest for the Wicked
26th June 1890, Thursday

After the fake execution, Marwood tries to return to normal life but struggles. His trade as a cobbler no longer satisfies his interest or waning moods, and he feels his personality is changing. Even with his dignified scientific approach, hanging becomes not so humane after all—especially now he is ageing. Perhaps the 'levelling noose' does not liberate society but rather brings a dark secret, delivering evil into the world. Perhaps shoemaking is a tame excuse for the mortal sin of ambition. One profession is too innocent, the other too guilty, and he is torn between them. He spends days reading and dreaming of the past. Soon, even his family is no longer sufficient consolation, now that Aldous has left.

Marwood is not useful, adventurous or loving enough for Ellen either. She sleeps most of the day alone with a locket containing the hair of Aldous. She cruelly misses her boy and the oft-visiting James Berry, at age thirty-one, cannot replace him. "A house bereft of a family is not a home," she murmurs on a loop, like a Catholic prayer, but words cannot bring Aldous home. Like two lost ghosts, Marwood and Ellen move independently around the house greeting one another, then drift back into separate worlds.

While Ellen suffers with memories of her boy—Aldous writes home infrequently—Marwood develops a new vice, escaping to

London. Appearing every inch the washed-up old man, he passes Whitechapel 'peep-shows' telling strangers the story of the Ripper murders. After making these journeys, he re-imagines them back in Horncastle while lying in bed or sometimes sleepwalking. He is increasingly drawn to the dark side of life—all his experiences have taken their toll, somehow shaping a weary dual personality. He is an anonymous shoemaker no one cares about, and an infamous hangman no one remembers, let alone cares about.

Now, at the end, Marwood realises that he has 'used darkness', wielded it like a lantern to a moth: he appealed to Kate's bourgeois interest in parading the city, a gentleman to her fantasy of rich lady, but also to her true nature of expressing great, long-suppressed rage. He created her, as much as she created his last true moment on the scaffold—the one that broke his will to hang.

When alone in the metropolis, he begins to lose his centre of mental gravity. "I knew that in swinging her safely to the Lord, I could stay good, and just, and human. For what did I have left?" Walking the East End, he raises a finger, eyes blind to the peep-shows. "She charmed me with her dark side—but this also repulsed me. Is that it? Tell me, Kate, from beyond the grave!" He addresses a brick wall now, befuddled a moment, then laughs at nothing and continues. "Tricked by her, I embraced the devil, and after I hanged her, she hanged me. Is this what happened?" Once more he plays another scenario in his mind.

More and more, Marwood breaks out of his fossilised existence, and makes trips to London. But these episodes take on the delights of vice and perversion, more than any moral recovery or understanding of the past. He returns to tell his Horncastle neighbours—and church-goers—of an alternative world, the notorious sights of the capital: lunatics at Bedlam, the whipping of half-naked women at Bridewell, the stoning to death of pilloried men and women, and the hangings at Tyburn. The good people of Horncastle are aware that these 'trips' are memories extracts from his reading, his imagination. They know, with the innate wit of country folk, that while Bedlam is a real place, the inmates are never paraded for the hilarity and inspection of uncommonly cruel Londoners. All is make believe, and so Marwood too becomes a figure of fun, a local liar, an immoral man to match their suspicions of the city's dark doings. Soon, no one remembers his humane innovation of the 'long drop' in the shadow of his new ravings.

And why should they? Here is a man who frequents the rage for knockabout pantomimes, who goes to see plays solely because they promise an 'olde' re-enactment of gibbeting, or burials at cross-roads of suicides with stakes through their hearts, hanged bodies sent to unconsecrated and quicklimed graves. When he returns to Horncastle, the Sundowner on the porch cannot render such black hobbies holy or nostalgic. For his mind is filled with the images of London shock-theatricals, the meat and potatoes of rough pantomime, the street parades in Covent Garden that have become even coarser than the Tyburn re-enactments he once witnessed there with Kate Webster.

Instead of rising with the dawn's enthusiasm, he is far closer to a last sunset. In Milton's Garden of Eden, the first man once thought the oncoming night would prove eternal: now Marwood sees that the night will prove eternal and Adam was right. The romantic past, the sleepy sunken world of a Horncastle horse-show, with its grasses and toffee apples on a summer's day, the melons buried in straw in the farmers' wagons, even the gentler delights of Bartholomew Fair, the candy floss and tombola games, the donkey rides, the rare passionate smile on Kate's lips, all are gone, not only dulled by memory, but coarsened by the brutish flavour of more modern entertainments—the ones Marwood cannot help seeking in London. Together they will taint his blood, rot his skin, and peel away the last protections of his soul. All the rat-sparring, dog-bouts, cock-fights and bear-baiting have been pushed to the fringes of city life, only to reappear on the stage. And so to the West End's Theatreland Mr Marwood must go, in a never-fixed cycle of trying to understand his past, his present, and his chosen profession as Crown's Officer.

All this changes, however, with a single door tap in Church Lane. Staggering a little, Marwood unlocks the divide and reveals a young man—younger than Berry—hovering in the doorway.

"My boy!" Marwood cries overcome with emotion; he almost calls to Ellen before realising his mistake. "Aldous, you came back?"

"Excuse me, sir, but I'm looking for Mr Marwood."

"And you've found him, Aldous! Come on in," Marwood says, pushing his disappointment with the boy's face—this is not his son—down in his psyche. He will deny all, and everything will be fine.

"No, no," the boy insists, "My name's not Aldous."

Marwood stares, while finding the portable cigar chopper in his pocket—the tiny guillotine Aldous used to play with—and he produces it now, smiling.

"A portable scaffold, a gift..."

The boy takes the present, nervously, and holds it. "That is why I am here. I met a Mr James Berry in Southwark last week. He told me he had business with the matchstick merchants down there, but I work there too, in the timber yard."

"You do?"

"Yes, sir."

They regard each other curiously.

"Yes, my name is Webster, Daniel. I know you hanged my mother, Catherine Lawler, at least the court documents say so."

Marwood staggers backwards, retreating to his seat, where he bends himself, and eventually collapses. He grips his eyes to the boy.

"So now you've come to kill me?"

Daniel takes a step into the room, his black coattails flapping. He lifts his leather cap. "Mr Marwood, I've come for a job."

"A...job?"

"I want to be a minister of justice," and he smiles. "I don't like the timber work. I just fell into a warehouse job, and no one likes to work with me, like I'm under some spell. Or I'm cursed." He fidgets with his cap, and looks down. "I mean, I'm a good worker, but they don't understand me."

Marwood is pressing his head against the back of his chair. "Go on, son," he says, for want of better words. "Do come in."

"Thank you, sir. I just know the hangman is not liked, pardon me saying, but it's no great loss to me. That's what I mean." Once more he smiles, nervously, sideways. "I ain't no street urchin, not no more, those times is gone. I've worked three years in the timber trade—I learn fast too."

"We just don't need any help," Marwood says bluntly, struggling from his seat. But by then Daniel is standing near him, looking down.

"I'd work hard, and be no trouble."

Marwood looks up, worried. "Well, Mr Berry is the hangman, now."

"...for my mother," the boy says.

The words cut through Marwood. Despite his efforts to push

down the past, a new hope touches his mind. Here is his chance at redemption. No Catholic priest will give him penance, he knows, but the boy has come to his very door. Perhaps, after all that's happened, they can help each other.

"I no longer hang. But if you prove good enough, you can be Berry's apprentice."

Immediately the boy is on his knees, shaking Marwood's ankle a little vigorously. "Oh thank you, Mr Marwood, thank you."

The old hangman is overcome with guilt, but he stretches his hand out and touches the top of the boy's head. For a moment Marwood thinks of Aldous, his feeling disturbed only by a sound from the doorway. It is not Berry, but Ellen, poised with puzzlement, her hand to her heart.

"Ma'am, Daniel Webster," the boy says, leaping up to shake her free hand. "I'm here for a job."

Ellen looks to Marwood, who nods, and in that moment husband and wife make the first step to reunited recognition. They see a chance to share in the boy. "Never as a replacement," as Ellen would say to her last day, but "enough to ease the pain."

Within the first hour of meeting, Marwood makes it clear that he does not intend to talk of "your mother," and Daniel is happy to agree. The boy is resourceful, though, for all his fifteen years, and before he even meets Berry, he explains to the old 'long drop' master how he's practiced on textile drums near the timber yard's mills.

"We could even go to the local fairs," he says, "and reproduce the drop to sell it. We're entering the 'capitalist age', Mr Marwood, and there's no going back, so why be a labourer? Instead, we take our real hangings on the road, doubling a show. We have magic lanterns prepared for the process of pinioning and the hanging ritual, plus a *camera obscura* print—a photograph, sir—of you standing hooded, noosed, and ready to tumble into the gallows pit."

"As though I'm the prisoner?"

"And I the executioner," the boy says. "All for show, of course."

"I can't," Marwood says, visibly upset—his mind back in Covent Garden and Bartholomew Fair. "I simply cannot."

That is where the conversation ends: Daniel tries to persuade Marwood, but the best he can achieve is a temporary apprenticeship under James Berry, and a lodging on Church Lane at their own house.

He will be given the laundry room next to Aldous's L-shaped room, the latter preserved for the prodigal son's return. Daniel is happy with the arrangement, sleeping for the first time ever on a real bed.

Rather than tour with 'the Marwood show', though, Daniel is able to frequent music halls and advertise himself as expert in phrenology as well as 'neck breaking'. He talks about death-cell repentance, which he witnessed at Armley Gaol, Leeds—the site of Marwood's early hangings—and even 'last second confessions' made to fire-and-brimstone priests. Half of these tales are made up, the other half drawn from scattered conversations with Marwood.

Meanwhile the old man stays home, visiting *The Portland Arms* now and then, reading and drifting through the village graveyards. Time slips by, mysterious as ever. He dreams deeper into the past. He knows that Jack the Ripper, a true tale not yet cold on the lips of Londoners, especially the poor, will wipe out any legend of wicked Kate Webster. Inciting the greatest fear, the Ripper will become the fable of London's underbelly.

"Perhaps Kate was convincing as a performer," he ruminates, talking to himself. "She conned that Mrs Thomas through trickery, but what for? 'Cos part of her wanted to be middle-class? Respectability was her downfall." He daily fusses over her legacy. "Her lies and her trial, her violence and her past keep coming back, but always overshadowed by Jack!"

Marwood does not write any of these thoughts down. Instead, most afternoons after a little shoe work, he sits down with the *Newgate Calendar* and reads one last time of Jack Sheppard, how the thief secured his fame. The trickster and escape artist, a defeater of Newgate—just like Kate Webster years later—visited ballad printer-shops to dramatise the adventure of his last journey to the rope, to let all London know he was free. Marwood examines the story and despite his misgivings, his ambiguous reaction to this unapologetic criminal, he is still enthused by Sheppard's tale. Repeatedly he reads of Sheppard's bravado how, tasting freedom, Jack first robbed a pawn-broker in Drury Lane, using the money to buy a silver sword and a dashing suit. Then he hired a royal coach and rides right under the Old Bailey, taunting Lady Justice with the sword. But his run cannot last. Time has run out—so he bids farewell dancing a jig on the fatal tree—while all day long the death pamphlets cry: *Woe to the Shopkeepers, and woe to the Dealers in Ware, for the roaring Lion is abroad.*

"Such genius!" Marwood cannot help but admire Sheppard's gumption, his *nouce*, his bravery, and he smiles thinking of Kate as the natural inheritor of Jack's crown. He knows, of course, that Kate never robbed or tricked anyone for fame, to boost posterity's accounts of her life, only for her boy, always for Daniel.

Marwood smiles faintly, remembering these larger-than-life criminals of old. He pinioned Charles Peace the same way, albeit felt nothing while executing him—no heart-skip nor nerve-jump. But then Marwood recalls the outcome of that Newgate festival, how the hemp rope stretched and how Peace lost his head. The blood that flew and hit Kate Webster—did that influence her murderous spree?

The hangman shakes his head, safe from the horror of that one-time professional failure, and turns the *Newgate Calendar* page. On the surface, he no longer entertains any sentimental thoughts about his victims. "I sleep as soundly as a child," he often tells his wife. However, according to James Berry, on occasion Marwood 'jabbers' to himself—a symptom Berry attributes to his strange, surrogate stepfather—which Marwood has become—feeling the open disgust with which his office is regarded.

Reading about Sheppard's gaiety, Marwood is saddened. His entire life, he has tried to make the profession if not acceptable then dignified, but it persists as notorious. Death cannot be changed in the public's mind—the black fear, the pit, the lake of fire, the pain and eternity—all are imaginatively irrefutable. The myths are too powerful. And yet even now, something catches his eye: there is a song on the Jack Sheppard *Calendar* page, which he knows by heart, since Kate Webster—the one who almost got away—would often sing it:

> I sold candles short of weight, that's no joke, that's no joke,
> I sold candles short of weight that's no joke;
> I sold candles short of weight and they nap'd me by the sly,
> All rogues must have their right so must I, so must I,
> All rogues must have their right so must I...

The music is jaunty in his mind. Marwood frowns, pained without understanding his feelings. Why do these lyrics, he thinks, a simple acceptance and celebration of sin move me so much? *All rogues must have their right so must I, so must I.* Marwood is a believer, but only when the rogue who knows he's a rogue confesses. And yet what happens to truth, to beauty, to morality, when a fraudster has such an elegant pride in his self-knowledge? "The criminal singer knows more of the human soul than…the rest of us…" Marwood remains confused, pleased and disturbed by a sad song.

So now and then, when Berry is away on a job and Daniel is busy with his 'hanging show' at a local fair, Marwood retreats to his basement—with his store of ropes, pinions, the guillotine and sandbags, all transported back from Gloucester Place.

Sometimes he takes out the black dress that 'vicious Mrs Manning' wore when he hanged her, a long time ago. She wore black satin, making the material unpopular for years—she was hanged in Cheltenham, his first woman on the scaffold. He smiles, remembering how sales of the black dress never recovered. He goes to the basement now, and runs his fingers down Kate's dress, its smooth edges and hem, communing with the dead in a way an outsider might find suspect. But for Marwood, the memory is all, the comforting claustrophobia of keeping the clothes, objects and trinkets he cannot throw away. They are a part of him now, and freeing them or freeing himself from them, he fears would end his life, another pale Don Quixote facing the reality that his dreams are just broken lies, a handful of dust slipping through his armour.

At times like this, at moments of his greatest despair, the dress does not succour his regret, since Mrs Manning meant too little. Her dress cannot bring him to commune with the past, or foster the life-affirming sense of survival over inhuman objects that he sometimes needs. At these times, Marwood turns to the body of the latest woman he hanged, once more. Having learned a trick or two from Mrs Salmon regarding the preservation of wax, namely the need for a cool, well-shaded environment, he moves beyond temptation and purchases a waxwork dummy—a body in the correct shape. An excursion to her emporium is unavoidable; it seems nothing is free from buying and selling.

As expected, Mrs Salmon has made one sale to Madame Tussaud's already, but the *doppelgänger* of Kate—her copy of the 'original' waxwork taken from Wandsworth Prison days before the end—remains in her attic of dolls. "Everyone deserves a piece of the pie," she tells Marwood, when he visits to pick up the life-size body of his own private Kate Webster. "And you too it seems…for whatever reason, I won't ask." She grins, but he ignores her flippant words as

James Berry is waiting in the cart outside.

Safely on the road, Marwood uncovers the sheet protecting the reconstructed body of Kate. She is dressed in the same red dress—her costume still resembling a surreal wedding gown—from the very hour she dropped through the floor of Wandsworth's execution shed.

"To this day, I've kept my promise to you," Marwood whispers, pressing close to her. He runs his fingertips along the neckline, much the same way he did with Mrs Manning's silk dress—that one on a clothes-dummy, this one on a shapely dummy of wax—but the feeling is different. The sense is not so much excitement, as a kind of suspended eroticism, all his hopes and regrets for the girl he met so long ago, brought to life under his shaking, ageing hands. "I would never fob you off to a bunch of surgeons."

When he uncovers the head, however, here we see how far Marwood has descended into a perversion of the past. For here is Mrs Thomas's head mounted on Kate's body—but a waxy head resembling Kate's masquerade to look like Mrs Thomas—the skin stretched, the insides of glue and plaster, the body clearly Kate's and bearing no resemblance to her employer's small frame. The upright, grinning mannequin is even wearing Mrs Thomas's clothes.

At last Marwood—without trying—has made Kate's hope of survival a reality. Here, in a toxic concoction that would repulse the murderess herself, is Kate-as-Mrs Thomas. Two women in one, and yet neither of them whole.

Who says, he thinks, that the innocent do not get enough attention? That justice does not prevail? For here 'she' is, the face more resembling Mrs Thomas, once more alive and preserved in a glass head case, on top of Kate Webster's body. Surely a just and delicate balance respectful to both parties, the punishing landlady and the punished killer...

Marwood speaks a few more silent words to his Kate-Julia, reminiscing on how they first met, just by accident, and the first words they spoke. He remembers offering her a cigarette, when she was only Kate, in Covent Garden.

"Cigarette?"

"I think you've got the wrong person. You expectin' someone particula'? 'Cos I don't think I'm 'er."

James Berry does not have the hangman's London job for long after Marwood. Soon the national position, re-advertised in the provinces, passes to Bartholomew Binns, and Daniel Webster becomes his assistant too. During his last days, though, Berry makes a name for himself. Nicknamed 'the reluctant executioner', he writes verses to read to his victims, coaxing rather than demanding repentance. He uses Marwood's table of height-weight drop ratios from the start, but then leaves the profession altogether to become a poet.

Meanwhile Daniel Webster returns to London to assist Bartholomew Binns in the extreme penalty of the law. His first assignment is to assist in a hanging at Pentonville Prison, which he does with professional coldness on the outside, but a slight thrill of re-possessing his soul on the inside. Every day he works as a hangman, Daniel feels he is exacting legal, moral and social revenge for his mother. Through the skylights of every Cold Meat Shed he works in, he knows Kate is looking down on him.

Ultimately Daniel Webster will become local hangman for Balham, assistant to the under-sheriff of London, one Lord Cottonwell. He is never asked to perform a hanging at Wandsworth Prison—though he performs dozens at Newgate where a 'prison shed' has been constructed for executions, far from the public eye. Webster serves the scaffold without ever forgetting his family history, purposeful and yet conflicted, given his own childhood life of crime. But should he feel guilty? As his mother's son, he does not. Kate would have been proud.

The end of his career is far away, for the practice of state execution has changed forever—but far from abolished. In the markets around the Old Bailey, St Paul's Cathedral and Newgate Street, no one knows these executions are taking place. With secret executions happening inside prisons, why the need for public knowledge? For the first time, the law is carried out for justice and not spectacle, for the victim and not the Crown, for the country and not the hangman. The role remains notorious, still prestigious if more conspiratorial, as suits the approaching twentieth century.

Whatever the politics, the perks are what people enjoy, and Kate's son is no different. Daniel Webster is paid part of his salary in first-class train travel like Bartholomew Binns, James Berry, William Marwood and William Calcraft before him.

The truth about Marwood, too, is that he lives—outwardly—as a professional hangman to the end. His last execution passes off smoothly, dispatching bigamist James Burton who murdered his second 'wife'. Only four weeks later, Marwood himself dies, propped up in his cobbling seat, mending a shoe, and not even thinking of hanging in any way—a rare return to the comforts and homely frustrations of his original trade.

> O they told me in the jail where I lay, where I lay,
> They told me in the jail where I lay,
> They told me in the jail that I should drink no more brown ale,
> But I swore I'd never fail 'till I die, 'till I die…

The newspapers say Marwood dies of drink, but really he dies of lung disease aged sixty-three, having given up the booze, but never the refined Turkish cigarettes. He is a victim of inflammation of the lungs, complicated by jaundice after suffering much pain, but at the end, passing on with relative ease.

What he feels inside is another matter, of little regard to the newspapers or the whisperers at *The Portland Arms*, friends or enemies. Sadly, Ellen too is beyond discovering the secret of his overburdened soul—that Kate Webster lives inside his memory, in guilt and desire—for he knows that harming her now would be the end for both of them. Instead, Marwood takes his silence and all the turmoil of knowing Kate Webster, to the grave.

On 4th September 1883, he is buried at Holy Trinity Church on Church Lane, Horncastle, in an unmarked grave. The local people guard the grave that night, to prevent boys from other villages scouring chips off the headstone. The congregation's prayers go out to St Crispian, patron saint of cobblers and shoemakers.

The idle rumour remains that he is poisoned by Irish sympathisers whilst taking a few drinks in neighbouring Sleaford's *The Ring O' Bells*—revenge for executing the Phoenix Park murderers.

Another account suggests that Marwood's demise was precipitated, that James Burton's death was another rare example of a botched job, with the rope uncharacteristically slipping and the condemned man having to be hauled and 'dropped' a second time—and that this disaster was the end of Marwood.

The obituary in *The Morning Herald* carries a new photograph of the hangman's door plaque:

William Marwood, Esq
Crown Officer & Public Executioner
Church Lane, Horncastle, Lincolnshire
For hire, for the public good

The Crown Office 'quietly recognises' his official government work, the obituary reads. The fine print adds: 'Most weekends, industrious Mr Marwood would repair boots, shoes and cobble harnesses, and offer tips on tying strong knots. He will be equally missed in the horse-rearing communities of Lincolnshire.'

Ellen Marwood, a closet drinker and billed in the same article as 'having a taste for the good stuff', outlasts her husband by only a few weeks. She manages to sell his cravats and favourite hanging shoes to Madame Tussaud's for their *History of Hanging* archive, and the ropes to a lucky Tommy Duffy of Shoe Lane, Goulceby. Mr Duffy's descendants, Lincolnshire horse-traders, inherit the Kentucky hemp rope that hanged Kate Webster. The rest of the hangman's clothes are sold cheaply at Madame Tussaud's inaugural waxwork 'salon'. Ellen even buries the family dog, Nero, who dies of unnatural causes of a political nature—a public kicking by the Tooley brothers. Since Aldous Marwood cannot be traced, the remaining possessions are unlawfully auctioned—including the portable guillotine.

After a lifetime of frugal struggle, one surprise is that Marwood's private business has been a success. The local press reports his 'collection of Norfolk thatched cottages'—though none are confirmed or ever found. According to the *Herald*, 'the executioner is all around, ironically not present to reap the benefits.' However, in his will, one Billy Thomas—son of Mrs Julia Thomas and a painter now living in Italy—is said to have left one Aldous Marwood, only surviving son of the Marwood lineage, a huge collection of Victorian art, hidden and preserved inside a mountain outside Palermo. Perhaps claiming this marvellous treasure, perhaps deluded by a fantasy, Aldous Marwood heads south to rescue his birthright, and is never heard from again.

Meanwhile to this day, curio-seekers are seen in Horncastle chipping away at William Marwood's tomb for fragments, souvenirs, connection to this strange, clinical, but—so the locals say—quietly compassionate man. The grave survives for several decades until there is nothing left, at which point the tombstone is mysteriously restored in full, and the process restarts. Some say Daniel Webster is responsible for these repairs, but whoever is Marwood's graveyard guardian angel, people tear down the grave once more.

Like all the London poor before her, wherever they come from or go, Kate Webster is buried in an unmarked grave, a standard six feet under the cold-meat shed of Wandsworth Prison. Every now and then, they say, her spirit roams free, north to the Thames via Bleeding Heart Alley, or over to Covent Garden, where she likes to sit by night listening to soft music and laughing voices drifting from the theatres, the markets, the pubs. Sometimes she eats a hot potato from a Drury Lane stall, before she feels lost and lonely, sad but no longer angry, and goes searching through the night for her boy Daniel.

Chapter 50
The Memory Chamber
31st December 1899, Sunday

Daniel Webster, a grown man, brings in the turn of the century witnessing the bright lights of London. The gaslights have been double-lit all down the South Bank from Tower Bridge to Westminster Bridge, easing Daniel's nerves into a contemplative mood. An unwashed human river rushes downstream, chasing itself, crying out, the head challenging the tail and provoking hijinks—the tossing of balloons, buttons, streamers. In this atmosphere, the Bow Street Runners are relaxed, but ever the eagle-eyed child, Daniel witnesses the small pickpockets—huddled boys with hands deep in their treasure-trove pockets—moving silently through the crowd. The past is present for a moment.

All is jolly, though, and well in the world. So when Daniel passes a door wedged open on a trapdoor string and hears music, he is obliged to enter. He pays the entry tab, descends into *The Adelphi Cider Cellar*. Here the London hangman who pulled the lever on his mother's drop once met wily Inspector Sequin and his bulldog Nimrod Jones, though Daniel has no way of knowing this. The drinking den is near full—all eyes blinkered by the Can-Can girls just taking the stage—but Daniel has no trouble finding a seat at the back.

Half amused, he watches a live scene unfold, evidently not part of the usual show, whereby someone grabs the foot of one of the girls and the newly employed bouncers grab the drunken spectator and drag him by the neck to the door. The music is briefly interrupted, but some of the girls refuse to go on, the scene breaks up, and the curtain falls, throwing the Can-Can line into chaos to the hilarity of the crowd. The drinks will flow freely now. The next entertainment is a New Year's version of 'The Irish Rover', sung at a miniature upright organ by a middle-aged man resembling a schoolmaster, clearly a deviation to kill time. The song is ignored by most of the crowd but Daniel is strangely moved. Watching the schoolmaster's evident pleasure at the abandonment of the Irish Rover's life, Daniel is lulled by the performance. Note after note, he is drawn by a faint hereditary memory, the music of an unknown past.

The spell is broken. A choral quartet of white-suited men takes to the stage for the next song, which turns out to be a favourite hanging ballad. Each man sings a line, all four chiming on 'deceitful Emma Hay':

> I'd sooner be by a Serpent stung,
> Or hugg'd by a grizzly Bear,
> Or crush'd by one of Pickford's Vans,
> Or blown into the Air;
> I'd sooner be by Marwood hung -
> Or slowly fade away,
> Than have the least connection
> With deceitful Emma Hay.

The experience is too much for Daniel. He leaves before ordering a drink, just as the waitress is appearing. The bouncer scowls at him on the way out, but does nothing. Back on the street, he takes a gulp of London's fog-air, cold enough to quell his anxiety. "I'd sooner be by Marwood hung…" he whispers. "I'd sooner be…"

Naturally the past cannot stay buried for long: the new hangman's family will guarantee the mind will turn back on itself. Daniel has two children now—a boy and girl—six-year-old twins. Terence and Mary came along shortly after 'the drop', born to his live-in maid, a sprightly Welsh girl called Melissa, after a hurried wedding. All these people will populate his world, his working hours, his waking life, and yet the undertow of his childhood is close to the surface, even now. Melissa is a good wife, but she has no patience for the troubles of a child-man; meanwhile Terence and Mary know nothing of their father's past—even if they could understand—and he intends to maintain their innocence. But that does not stop their questions. "Where have you been Daddy?" and "Can you take us with you?"

Tonight, Daniel heads home, north to Baker Street, from where it remains a short step to the hangman's lodgings, once again at Gloucester Place. He puts the sound of New Year's Eve to rest, catching *Auld Lang Syne* as he cuts across the part of Dorset Square where Ellen Marwood once sat with her boy Aldous long ago, wishing they were back in Horncastle and away from William and London. Long, long ago…

Tonight, Daniel Webster's family will already be asleep. He stands there, looking up, wondering at the past, dwelling on the unwritten future. He touches the bricks—like Marwood did at Newgate Prison long ago. Immediately Daniel's energy is drained and he feels faint. He must get away.

The next morning—New Year's Day, 1900—he is much recovered, even sprightly. On a whim, after their pleading, he takes the children to the new attraction, an early prototype of the Chamber of Horrors called 'The Basement of Doom'. Supporting their marriage, Melissa is busy cleaning a nearby house on Marylebone Street. As they stand in the street, the children in awe of the horror show to come, Daniel is unworried, convinced of the attraction's lack of danger from its name alone. He holds up his hands, entrusts Mary and Terence his coattails.

"The Basement of Doom will never catch on," he says, leading his charges down to 'the necropolis'. A shock of poor judgement awaits him, for here is a barbaric world of torture laid out for his children—who rush on ahead. Daniel pays the three halfpence for 'family entry' and follows placidly into twilight, through the Renaissance flaying, past 'The Iron Maiden', to an incongruous punishment of Ancient Rome called 'the parricide's doom'. This latter captures the children's attention the most: a stout leather bag is suspended from the ceiling, prized open to reveal its imprisoned contents, namely a waxen old woman, playing victim by silently screaming, together with a snake, a monkey and a cockerel. The death-bag hovers on a pulley, ready to be tossed into a river of blue paper. An instructive sign nearby—a wooden stake in the riverbank— has 'The Old Tiber' crossed out, replacing it with 'The New Thames' as though in wish-fulfilment.

"What has she done, Daddy?" Terence asks, staring at the old woman as though waiting for her to flinch, but she is only plaster, hair and old clothes. "Is she playing with the animals?" Equally transfixed, Mary says nothing, as though she knows what is happening.

Daniel is stunned by the graphic depictions. Why did he bring them here? The worst of all is a heretic man boiled in a copper pot, his face melting to reveal a blooding eyeball, at which Daniel decides they have to leave. He calls for Mary and Terence, but there's no response. Pacing into the next room, he finds them chanting:

Mary:
"If Pa killed Ma, who'd kill Pa?"

Terence:
"Mar-wood."

After the third time, they swop roles then Terence asks the question, prodding Mary in the side for her reply:
"If Ma killed Pa, who'd kill Ma?"

"Pa-wood," the girl says, and giggles. She does a little skip as they repeat the macabre game, even gripping each other's necks to imitate choking. Daniel is horrified and amused too, but he resists grabbing them by the hands and leading them into sunlight. Instead, the children ask about the 'strange woman' before them.

Daniel looks up—at his own mother—at the black-eyed stare, the solid jaw, and he cannot deny his recognition. A memory flickers into life of his mother's back fading away up the riverbank, over and over, as he is passed like a prize to Jonathan Clatter 'useful employment', namely pickpocket lessons at *The Cat and Salutation*; he searches for the pain of this memory, that day she left him there, an apprentice thief, but there is nothing—only Kate's blank expression. She has no answers. And yet Daniel is surprised by his own lack of feeling, just hollowness and a little fear too; but he does not want anything from her. "Death is a little too late," he murmurs. Here she is, reunited with him at last, despite all the years in between. Why didn't he know this moment was possible? But what kind of reunion is this, an accident brought about by randomness—a day out for *his* children—and nothing to do with *her* efforts.

"She's nobody," he says, and distracts the children. But despite his efforts, they are drawn to her effigy, her body, her wooden-hearted double.

They point at the sign at Kate's feet:

```
Wanted, for stealing plate &c. and supposed
murder of mistress, aged near thirty-one, five
feet four inches, complexion sallow, slightly
freckled, teeth rather good and prominent.
```

"It says she's 'Wanted'," Terence says.

"Wanted for what?" Mary says. "Ain't she a good girl, Papa?"

Daniel stares, squints for the name plaque. "I don't know…. It says she was a famous criminal. 'A bad woman', but good things are sometimes born of bad women." Still, he will not tell them. Something inside Daniel refuses to nod to the figure or make any sign of greeting. She is uncannily small, just a tiny woman really, now her son is over six feet, and part of him just wishes to push over the model. But he doesn't. "The face is not accurate."

They look at him, puzzled, and he frowns in a pained way before disappearing up the stone steps. The boy and girl peer back through iron bars at the waxen face of Kate Webster. Her father departing, the girl is suddenly chilled, uncertain and cautious, yet sees something sad in the eyes. The boy is transfixed by Kate, but he does not shiver, he only stares and stares. Together they stand there, a tableau of the next generation, looking into the motivations of the past, excited by the silence of their own unknown history.

Meanwhile, half way up the steps, Daniel encounters a second waxwork a few feet from Kate in a dark corner, noose raised high. For here is 'William Marwood, Esq—Gentleman Executioner' according to his sign—inexpertly grinning—his expression far removed from the true flesh and blood. Close to Marwood's foot reads a third sign, announcing 'execution on loan from Madame Tussaud's for the re-naming of The Basement of Doom'.

Half a level below, the children are still linger, comfortable with the falseness of Kate's dummy.

"Webster," that's our name," Mary says, but the boy keeps on staring at Kate, ignoring his sister.

"I know," Terence replies. "She told me."

"What are you talking about?"

"She told me it was her name...."

"You're crazy," Mary says and leaves her brother in the chamber.

Terence remains, a sliver of sunlight reassuring him that London is close by, awaiting his return. All goes silent as he looks back at Catherine Lawler, 'the Richmond Killer'.

"'Bye," he says, and nods, eyes level, as though not trusting her from springing into life. Kate seems to him strange, more real than his sister, the fake dungeon, or the next waxwork of the hangman with a noose. He has no idea she is his grandmother.

Suddenly the voice of their father is calling from upstairs, telling them of the sunshine, and the beautiful day, and reluctantly their Chamber of Horrors is over for the day. They turn instinctively at the bottom of the stairs, look back for one extended second at Kate's blank face, as though she might move yet and speak to them. Ignoring each other, hiding their own private expressions, they are a little disappointed when she remains silent. Then they are gone.

Neither of them sees William Marwood on the way up.

Daniel will write the story of his mother Kate as a play. He aims for a dramatic piece with a small but colourful cast—titled 'Mrs Thomas's Head', or 'The Lady Killer'—and plans to tell it from Marwood's point of view. One evening he puts pen to paper in his Clapham lodging house and begins writing, alarmed at how fast the dialogue flows. He even acknowledges the ambiguity of the title: reclaiming his mother as a lady. Mrs Thomas, meanwhile, will be a character so proud and zealous in her bossiness over her maid that—in Daniel's own words—'she had it comin' to 'er'.

However, the young scribe is frequently disturbed by his neighbours' cries and dogs barking on nearby Clapham Common, the general hustle and bustle of pubs and gin-shops surrounding the park. He already needs a new location—somewhere more conducive to inspiration, less raucous. Even now below his window, the mercury-women are selling the "London gazette" and crying out 'Pa-a-per!" to women pushing perambulators down Pavement Street.

Hence, within a week, *The Chapter One Coffee House* on

Paternoster Row, opposite Ivy Lane, soon becomes Daniel's location for writing the play. With its oak beamed ceilings and arrow-slit walls, the coffee house invites an air of twilight even at midday, perfect for concentration, while allowing London's new hangman to keep a regular schedule. His foray last year as a butcher's boy, oft en being nocturnal, cutting up cow's hides in the middle of the night, was an experience he does not want to repeat.

The Chapter One, by welcome contrast, is a haunt for booksellers and aspiring writers, affectionately called the 'Wet Paper Club'. Coffee is expensive at four pence, while four ham sandwiches with a glass of sherry are a moderate three pence. The serving-man is always immaculately spruced in black breeches, silk trousers and a trim white bowtie. He expects a tip that Daniel cannot give, to the point where a joke surrounds the young writer, suggesting 'he is confused—*The Blue Boar* was doubtless on Warwick Lane.' Daniel merely smiles though he makes sure to order a coffee—the expensive option—at least once a day. The waiter's cheeky humour fails to ruffle him, as Daniel flees his home for this second home. He knows *The Blue Boar* is a house for 'hacks' and 'pen-drivers', and fuelled by the new London craze for coffee, *The Chapter One* will be his saving grace, a café pub that segues coffee into alcohol over a long seamless afternoon, often using the same cup.

Daniel sits there now, writing his masterpiece. Upstairs from his corner, he can see a shrunken St Paul's Cathedral through an arrow slit, its Gothic spires, ephemeral and ghostly, stirring old memories. Every now and then a maid appears to stoke a large pot of cheap saloop heated over the charcoal fire, smiling as she exits, each time sending his mind reeling back to Kate, his mother the hanged criminal, herself once a maid. Just as quickly she morphs into the physical shape of Jonathan Clatter his one-time mentor, and Sarah Crease his alternative non-mother. He pauses and ladles some inspiration from the coffee stalls, takes a hard-boiled egg, his Woodbine cigarette, and settles back at his writing table.

Daniel's dreams of gentleman status are almost faded now—at one point he wanted to become a great man, a doctor, combining Marwood's scientific skills with Kate's ability to dissect. Instead, he has his own story to tell, their stories too. He will no longer become a doctor—he will become the latest hangman of London and Middlesex, dissolving the memory of Marwood entirely. His mother deserves no less. Nevertheless, ironically, in order to tear down Marwood's memory and reputation, even his legacy, Daniel will begin his play with his predecessor's so-called achievement, the invention of the 'long drop' technique for a less painful hanging. Why not capitalise on recent history?

Still, blackening his teacher's name is only part of the game. Marwood Esq, Daniel knows, had his weakness for romance, for sympathy, for imagining a better world. Hence, the playwright will begin the story with Marwood standing outside Newgate Prison, while in one of the condemned cells is the woman he will hang, Kathy Lawton, who will never know how Marwood came to see her that night. If he can ever publish this story, Daniel thinks, now peeling his hard-boiled egg while glancing through the rain at the distant, golden funnel of Big Ben's clock tower, he will notify the 1900 Home Office report committee; he will recommend a table of calculated drops, standardised ropes and scaffold structures in honour of his predecessor. The official stamp of approval: William would have liked it that way.

Marwood shall not be forgotten. Hanging must live on, but live on in the spirit in which justice is included, with truth, courtesy, good science, and a firm hand. Through the artistry of the stage—and the name of Webster—the satisfaction of safer hanging will be achieved. Humanity will be far kinder to its fellow man in the new century. He will be loved by police, criminals and theatregoers alike!

"Toe the line," Daniel whispers, and begins to write…

In real life, of course, Kate never reveals what she does with the head of Julia Thomas. Apparently it was thrown in the river along with her body, so the secret remains long buried. But sooner or later, Daniel must encounter this fact in his theatrical retelling and deal with the artistic obstacle.…

So eventually Kate's son—the *pera-ale* show-man—goes to the basement of 29 Gloucester Place, embarking on an official clean-up of the house, now Marwood is dead. These will be his lodgings now—the home Kate could never find. On a quiet Sunday afternoon, a brother to that murderous afternoon so many years ago, Daniel heads downstairs, lowering himself on a rope through the trapdoor. Who else is going to empty the basement, he thinks, other than the new tenant? The Mayor of London?

The shock is indescribable. There, neither shop dummy nor chamber of horrors waxwork, the old woman's head is revealed—in the centre of the room—preserved in formaldehyde. Time collapses in the darkness, and expands to fill the room. His head is throbbing.

Daniel tells himself it is Mrs Thomas's head, but it is really Kate's—his mother's head—that Marwood kept after the execution. Without thinking, he breaks the glass case and is shocked by how fast it disintegrates, the formaldehyde flooding out. Finally, he takes Kate's head upstairs and rests it in the bath, lights a candle for a last, torrid communion. Melissa will receive quite a shock. Then he leaves the house.

Outside he takes some bread from a cart, and with the smog rising over London he walks down to the West End. With a wild, imploring look, he pauses on the banks of the Thames. A prison ship, a hulking obelisk, is being towed by a coughing baby tug boat. Daniel is reminded of *The Fighting Temeraire*, one of the painting copies in Marwood's old hanging house—now his—only here the ghostly ship is a black against the sun, every golden glimmer absorbed. He watches the prison ship snaking downriver for ten minutes, disappearing under Tower Bridge. He imagines it floating out to greater waves, tossed on storms and becalmed, far beyond the Thames estuary, free of London.

Daniel looks back at the wake of water as it passes. He steps backwards and into the future, marked by the ghosts inside him—his own past, his childhood with Clatter, Crease, and briefly Webster, the absent mother. He is a product of their messy lives, a father now himself, married, confident to the point of unselfconscious, a professional hangman too—the irony does not escape him. He will write a great play, see it performed nightly and then retire to the countryside on his riches. "Lincolnshire perhaps, I've heard it's a nice part of England...unspectacular...a place for hard-pressed Londoners to retire...."

Somewhere above or below, Kate wishes this for her boy too. Daniel is still her greatest concern after life's end, perhaps trapped in purgatory—he will always be her loving sympathetic concern, after herself of course.

As for Daniel, he cannot conceive of Kate quietly residing in hell. We are all fallen angles, even thrown on a lake of fire. Hell or high water, life goes on: hence he has the power to decide her dramatic afterlife on the stage. So why would he give her anything other than a positive ending? It is the natural, human thing to do. "All these players to create a scene…and only so much coffee and alcohol…"

For now, the morning rays are swinging low, burning the mist off the river. Like the Thames, life itself rolls on, ephemeral, all the eternal day.

Chapter 51
The Untouched River
1900 onwards

Rivers rush, interweave, die, and are resurrected from the oceans and clouds to new life. From the landing-stages and jetties of London's warehouse industries, the River Thames reigns supreme, as a transporter, messenger, a silent witness not judging but welcoming all, never giving up her truth. Lightly she carries her past knowledge, and future blessings, yet she sings loud as the grave. She is the colour of silver, of the alchemist, the sweet-singing girl, the silver-footed Thames. So too she is old Father Thames, a life split in two, genderless with a panorama of oars and sails, three thousand ships a day on the water, frigates, yawls, cutters and tea clippers. From *The Three Goats Heads* to *The Stiliard*, *The Cole Harbour* to *The Old Swan*, the Thames ferries us with her, and away from her, by morning and night, the handmaiden and servant to the sun itself.

While the Thames rules all above-ground, a quite different mistress rules below. Looking down through 'The Pool of London', from London Bridge close to where Mrs Thomas's trunk was fished out, there is another world, a dark world of influences, a Looking-Glass down into Hades. Here is a second life that communicates with our own, a giant membrane of oceanic forces connected to our daily lives. For the River Tyburn is a lost river, an emblem of what is missing and lost and yet still there. The River Tyburn, like an underground well, but one continually changing and altered by the rivers of the surface, is our communal memory, unseen, untapped, yet brutally alive, bursting forth with the 'id' of a killer, the soft touch of a child. Two rivers—but one heart....

The Tyburn is the unconquered past, the future's undiscovered country—immortal death unseen under the feet of the living. Like all the missing rivers of London, the Stamford Brook, the Falcon, the Fleet, the Neckinger, the Earl's Sluice, the mythical Tyburn lives, running today through a giant steel pipe under the platform of Vauxhall's underground 'Tube' station. The Tyburn— repository of all our dreams, childish fantasies and ancestor's struggles—is then carried in great pipes 'hidden in open view' below Baker Street and Victoria's own station. We live surrounded by yesterday's nameless graves and watery fountains of rebirth: crime committed over water, reborn in the blood.

Rivers circulate everything: all our histories, all our stories, the material of our bones themselves. We are old Julia Thomas and William Marwood, Esq; we are the hanging dead and buried alive. Whether we like it or not, we are Kate Webster alias Lawler too; we are her boy Daniel, and Ellen and Aldous Marwood, lost at sea but with a love-child he never knew. We are Liverpool, County Wexford, and Horncastle, Lincolnshire. We are the London exported to the world, yet flowing deep in the heart of its City through West and East End, in the silt and human bones deposits of the Thames estuary, in the memory of Tyburn, both river and noose, forgotten underground.

Epilogue
A New Dawn
6th September 1900, Thursday

So Daniel has become the next hangman for all London, rekindling and giving new life to the bourreaux tradition of hanging family dynasties. Death is always a good living—his mother once told him so—and James Berry showed the way. The fact that he works in the same profession as his mother's killer is just an irony he savours with the ebb and flow of living. Revenge and murder do not appeal—he is strictly a man of the state, the final days of Victoria, and as such, he could almost be William's own son.

Daniel now lives in the age of modern prisons, a new time of social theory—more democratic in word if not deed—heralding 'live and let live' rehabilitation. One by one the old prisons close, replaced by gleaming glass monstrosities that will 'humanise' incarceration cell by cell. From the penitential jail of the Knights Templar to the debtors' prison in Whitecross Street, to the Clink in Deadman's Place, Bankside, to the Compter in Giltspur Street, the years are closed in darkness, fresh rubble, and the lives of prisoners forgotten. Several old debtors are set free under the new 'bail' system, a lucky minority given a last boon, bewildered men in their seventies and eighties literally waving goodbye on a Thursday morning—to an ancient system of justice. The Old Bailey too, mother and father to hundreds, closes its door under new Victorian laws. Even the Queen's rule is coming to an end, though she does not know it.

In the early twentieth century, the foundations are laid for Wormwood Scrubs in East Acton. Drugs are the new prison trade and absinthe is available more freely. In the 'new model prison' at Pentonville, inmates are obliged to wear face masks in a curious experiment of social anonymity, while the 'new prison' at Millbank is a panopticon of devilish design—the central tower is not even manned by a guard, but by a light-detection device that can tell if a prisoner is present or not. A crude wall of light is projected through each cell, and if unbroken for nine hours straight—the most a prisoner is permitted to sleep—a water weight activates the alarm. In theory, no criminal will have more than nine hours advantage over the guards.

It works too—no one escapes from Millbank.

Once upon a time the gallows was known as 'the cheat', conning life from its victims, but never tricking death. In the next stage of criminal justice, the New Drop replaced Tyburn, swinging 'the walking dead' from the very walls that imprisoned them. Hanging was then privatised, moving from the public domain inside prisons, and the cold-meat shed was born. William Marwood was a cog-piece of that 'human economy', Kate Webster the tricky grease, and through their separate descendants the machinery still turns....

An age of open cruelty is passing. But as the sun sets on the execution as spectacle, a new dawn of secret punishment begins, closed-door deals, back-room interrogation, off-shore cells, camps, 'black sites', all in the righteous name of public good. For health, for reason, for sanity, civility, for citizenship of the world, for all the bad scenes 'we fight'.

The killer no longer gets a day on the scaffold, but neither do any surviving victims of the criminal's handiwork. The public thirst for blood is dampened, and yet not everyone is happy.

'The age is running mad after innovation', Samuel Johnson told the world in 1783. His words are alive today: 'Sir, executions are intended to draw spectators. If they don't draw spectators, they don't answer their purpose. The old method was most satisfactory to all parties: the public was gratified by a procession: the criminal was supported by it. Why is all this to be swept away?'

Dr Johnson mourns an old English tradition, the ability to clean up a mess, to set things in order, to carve a pattern from chaos. We are the children of Dr Johnson's wit, savvy and determined intellect; so too, we are the inheritors of Kate Webster's blood and William Marwood's brain. We sometimes lose our heads like Charles Peace, but let's not bury our heads like Julia Thomas. Let us stand up and seek justice, but never vengeance dressed as justice, a false forgiveness. Let us make a hanging table of drops, and follow it. Let us do our homework, go to bed after nightfall, and sleep well tonight. Tomorrow we will wake as better human beings. For what alternative do we have? Our future consciences are scarred, yet free. We inherit sins in our spines, but while we chase the glory of our ancestors, we seek the blessing of our children.

So we continue to toe the line, for our appetites remain the same as Kate's and William's, as aspiring as Aldous's hope for the future, as imaginative as Daniel's desire to rewrite the past. We are as proud, greedy, tender and absurd as always: 'Like beer and tea, sprouts and plum duff, hanging suited England.'

Sing us a song of sixpence, the hangman sins in our ear. For I'll tell you no lies, sings the prisoner inside us all:

> Now I must leave the cart toll the bell, toll the bell,
> Now I must leave the cart toll the bell;
> Now I must leave the cart sorrowful broken heart,
> And the best of friends must part so farewell, so farewell,
> And the best of friends must part so farewell.

Credit: Phil Marwood

Marwood family coat of arms

Acknowledgements

I owe these people and sources many thanks for their knowledge of the underbelly of English criminal life: Peter Ackroyd and his book *London: The Biography* (2001); Richard Clark and his website www.capitalpunishmentuk.org; Charles Dickens's *A Visit to Newgate* (1836); Howard Engel and his book *Lord High Executioner: An Unabashed Look at Hangmen, Headsmen, and Their Kind* (1998); V. A. C. Gatrell and his book *The Hanging Tree: Execution and the English People 1770-1868* (1996); Bill Greenwell's 'Lost Lives' Project at www.billgreenwell.com; HRI Online Publications' *The Proceedings of the Old Bailey, London's Central Criminal Court, 1674-1913* at www.oldbaileyonline.org; David M. Kiely and his book *Bloody Women, Ireland's Female Killers* (1999); Henry Mayhew's *London Characters and the Humorous Side of London Life* (1871); a little-known volume, now out of print, called *The Trial of Kate Webster* (1925) edited by E. O'Donnell; and Ingrid Pitt's 'A Grisly Murder and Pork Dripping' at www.denofgeek.com. Finally, I owe credit to Elizabeth Jones aka Maestra Damiana Illaria d'Onde for her helpfully detailed 'A Beginner's Addendum to Making Shoes'.

Many thanks to Sir David Attenborough for his kind letter about the discovery of Julia Thomas's skull; Alicia Wenman and Emma Lloyd of *Beyond Productions* (Sydney, Australia) and the *Deadly Women* TV programme; Paul Bentley of the *Daily Mail*; Eddie Nestor at BBC Radio London 94.9; Stewart Evans for the signed photograph of William Marwood; and everyone at U.S. writing residencies *I-Park* in Old Saybrook, Connecticut and the *Vermont Studio Center* in Johnson, Vermont. My final thanks to Katharine Willers, Jennifer Fullerty and Charlie Greenhill, for all your careful reading.

R.I.P. Julia Thomas.

WM. MARWOOD,

EXECUTIONER,

CHURCH LANE,

HORNCASTLE,

LINCOLNSHIRE, ENGLAND.

William Marwood official business card

Hangman for the Crown, December 1874–September 1883

Also by Parkgate Press (F Street Books)

www.parkgatepress.com
www.fstreetbooks.com

Katharine E. Willers

WHAT TOOK ME OUT TO THE BALL GAME

The Determinants of Attendance of
Major League Baseball Games from 1989–1999
and the Implications of the 1994 Labor Strike

Matt Fullerty, Ph.D.

THE PROFESSORROMANE

The British and American Academic Novel 1945–2012
Lost in the Academy
The Comic Campus, The Tragic Self

Also by Parkgate Press (Dionysus Books)

Tom Robertson

NAPOLEON Vs. THE TURK

A play based on the chess match of Napoleon Bonaparte
and 'The Turk', the famous 18th century chess automaton.
Who will triumph, the master tactician or the technology?
First performed at the Toronto Fringe Festival.

Engin Inel Holmstrom

LOVESWEPT

A Cross-Cultural Romance of 1950s Turkey.
Neri falls in love and marries young, but which of three
men will win her heart?

About the Author

www.mattfullerty.com

Matt Fullerty has been writing fiction and imagining nineteenth century London since his schooldays. On a visit to Madame Tussaud's Chamber of Horrors, he was struck by the waxworks of notorious but forgotten killer Kate Webster and the man who executed her, London's royally appointed hangman, William Marwood. Matt has taught British and American literature at George Washington University in Washington, D.C. and recently taught Creative Writing (fiction) at the University of London, Royal Holloway. He is currently Assistant Professor of English and Creative Writing at Chowan University in North Carolina.

Matt is the author of novels *The Knight of New Orleans* and the forthcoming *American Con Artist*. A graduate of Oxford University, the University of East Anglia and with a PhD in English from GW, he has published reviews, articles and interviews for *The Daily Mail*, *The St. Ann's Review*, BBC Radio London and the Discovery Channel's *Deadly Women* TV series. In 2011 he attended the *Vermont Studio Center* on an Artist's Grant.

Matt Fullerty lives in Falls Church, Virginia and Murfreesboro, North Carolina.

This title is also available in hardback from Parkgate Originals and as an ebook from Parkgate Digital.

www.ingramcontent.com/pod-product-compliance
Lightning Source LLC
Chambersburg PA
CBHW070732180626
46818CB00007B/2811